MAN'S BOOK

A HOT
AND COPPER SKY

Jon Burmeister

*

THE DOMINATOR

Andrew York

*

THE BLACK CAMELS
OF QASHRAN

Ronald Johnston

ODHAMS BOOKS
LONDON

MADE AND PRINTED IN GREAT BRITAIN
BY ODHAMS (WATFORD) LTD.
SBN.600778851
1.71.

CONTENTS

A HOT
AND COPPER SKY

Jon Burmeister

'A Hot and Copper Sky' is published
by Michael Joseph Ltd.

The Author

Jon Burmeister is a solicitor by profession. Thirty-eight, he was born in South Africa and was educated at an English-style public school at Grahamstown. Married with two children, he lives in East London. Being an outdoor person he spends as much time as he can close to the sea pursuing his hobbies of fishing, surfing and sand ski-ing. He says he has also dabbled in rough shooting, body-building, photography and collecting old guns.

For DENYS HANSEN *and*
PHILLIP PENN—*who did so much*

The author wishes to acknowledge with gratitude the assistance given to him during the preparation of this novel by Mr. D. G. Malan, the then Managing Director of South African Marine Corporation Limited. Thanks are also due to Captain George Clarke, Master of the *S.A. Trader* for his co-operation.

All in a hot and copper sky
The Bloody sun at noon;
Right above the mast did stand
No bigger than the moon.

THE ANCIENT MARINER
Samuel Taylor Coleridge

CHAPTER ONE

THE JET FIGHTER-BOMBER came very low across the harbour,
bringing with it an immensity of sound like the rushing of a great
wind. It was an angular Corsair with part of its undercarriage
shot loose, so that a fractured wheel-stay protruded from its belly
like a broken bone from a wound. It slewed in the air, fishtailing
wildly, and as it neared the cargo ship moored on the left bank
it dropped its ugly snout as though it were homing for a strike.

But the pilot was a twenty-three-year-old boy from New Jersey,
and he was trying very hard to stay alive. The snout lifted and
the jet screamed overhead so low that the officers on the bridge
wing flung themselves on the deck as a reflex action.

The pilot saw the shaking, blurred image of the ship with the
red duster drooped at the stern. His mother had come from England as a war bride. He recognized the flag. And he had time to
say in a shocked, shaking voice, 'Jesus, you Goddam Limeys!'
before the ship was gone and he was thundering up over Haiphong with the Corsair clawing for air as the lazy ack-ack came
awake and reached up to try and find it.

The ship was called the *Florence Hurst*. The men on her bridge
got up: Grove, the Captain, then Proctor and Lucas, the Second
and Third Officers, then Stephen Lincott, the Medical Officer.

'Bloody fool!' Grove was trembling from the sudden fright.
But his eyes were fastened on the jet.

All of them watched it. 'That Yank's in trouble.' Peter Proctor
nudged Lucas. 'See its wheels, Max? There's something—'

'Undercarriage,' Lucas said. 'In aeronautical parlance you
never refer to the wheels. It's like calling the bows of a ship the
sharp end.'

Grove flung an arm up, ramrod straight, quivering. 'Look!
Look! There's a . . . oh, God!'

The ground-to-air missile seemed to float quite lazily out of

a cluster of buildings on the far side of the City. It had a bluntly
conical head and a pencil-thin body. It accelerated rapidly,
propelled by an orange-coloured glow under the shark-like tail
fin. It angled its flight with a vicious and frightening precision.
It was a mechanical hound and the tiny spiralling jet was its
mechanical hare. It slavered rocket-fuel and bayed with the howling noise of its thrust.

The jet pilot sensed his danger. He sent the Corsair around in a
wild, erratic turn. Then he flung it over on its back and cork-
screwed off at a new angle. But the hound was snapping at his
heels now. Within another second the kill was made. The missile
appeared to leap the last few feet. It merged with the jet and
became part of it. There was a millionth of a second when nothing happened. Then the sky spawned a miraculous blossom of
smoke-ringed flame. On top of it came the thick belting punch
of the explosion.

There was a long and terrible silence. The smoke ring
broadened, like a giant wreath.

Grove turned away from the rail, sickened and trembling.
Below him on the dockside he heard the stevedores erupt suddenly
into shrill jubilation. Grove shook his head blindly. What a hell
of a thing, to cheer when you saw a man die, murdered by remote
control. But he was too sick to be angry. It was still very early in
the morning. Only an hour ago he had clawed his way out of a
wild, heavy sleep into the grey, bitter reality of a crippling hangover. For a moment he thought he was going to vomit. He rushed
across the bridge wing into the wheelhouse and slammed the door,
grabbing the telegraph and hugging it, grinding his teeth
together, forcing his head down while he fought the spasms of
nausea in his empty, inflamed stomach.

Proctor and Lucas heard the noise of the door shutting. But
they paid no attention. They were staring, fascinated, at the sky
where the flame-blossom was dying. Long, withered pointers of
smoke tears drooped down towards the city.

Proctor's lips hardly moved. 'You poor bloody Yank. Why
didn't you burn your draft card?'

'Or slip across into Canada.' Lucas lowered his gaze from the
sky. 'What a dope.'

Proctor shrugged. '*Sic transit gloria.* No more pizza pie.'

'No more turkey and cranberry at Thanksgiving.'

'No more fornicating in Saigon.'

'That will larn them for being so nasty to the Red Indians.'

They both laughed. Proctor glanced around at the wheelhouse.
'The Old Man is having a puke. Or trying. He probably thought
it was a pink elephant that got torpedoed.'

'Never. It was a bottle with wings.'

They laughed again. Lincott moved forward from where he had been standing next to the top of the companion. There were two bright spots of shock-colour in his cheeks. He trembled in helpless fury. 'I don't suppose it's any good pointing out to you that you have just seen a man die?'

'Look,' Lucas said, 'it's not our war. If the Yanks want to get clobbered by the Vietnamese it's their business. The French tried and you know what happened to them.'

Lincott knew it was hopeless. But restrained his anger and tried once more. 'That's not the point at all. Can't you understand that—'

'Oh, cork it!' Proctor raised his voice above the noise of the dockers which had settled into a cadence, like a chant. 'Don't dig, so deep, pill-roller. You're too bloody intense for everybody's good.' He grinned to take the sting out of his words. He was long and lean and debonair in his snowy tropicals. 'Just leave me out of your crusading, huh? It makes me hyperventilate.'

Lucas laughed. He was bull necked, with bristly flaxen hair and blue eyes. Nature had played an ethnological trick on him. He belonged twenty-five years in the past, in the turret of a Tiger tank. 'That's one for the book. Know what it means, Doc?'

Lincott flushed. He looked from one to the other. They were grinning at him. Then he turned and went into the wheelhouse, leaving the door open.

Grove was straightening. He stared at Lincott out of his swollen, bloodshot eyes. 'What the hell do you want?'

Lincott ignored the rudeness. 'I wondered if I could do anything for you.'

'Anything you can do for me,' Grove said, 'you can do when I come to you feet first on a stretcher. Got it?'

'I already knew it.' Lincott began to turn away. 'But if I were you I would get some Vitamin B into my system.' He reached the door.

'Doctor Lincott,' Grove said sharply. 'I am still talking to you.'

Lincott turned back woodenly and Grove grinned, enjoying the moment while he found a cigarette and lit it. He gagged over the first draw, then coughed furiously. Straightening, he wiped his streaming eyes. 'What the hell is that noise out there?'

'It's the dockers,' Lincott said. 'They're chanting something.'

Grove shouldered him rudely out of the way and walked out on to the bridge wing.

Proctor grinned at him. 'You all right, Wal?'

'Of course I'm bloody-well all right,' Grove growled. He went to the rail and looked down while Proctor and Lucas exchanged winks behind his back.

The dock had been cordoned off with rope into a square of nearly a hundred yards, of which the *Florence Hurst* made one side. Within the square were stacked the coffins she was loading, tier upon tier of them, about three hundred all told, waiting to go into number three hold to join the two thousand seven hundred loaded yesterday.

The dockers were People's Militia, specially brought in for the work. They wore rumpled blue uniforms and their rifles were stacked nearby. They had lined up now in front of the coffins, grinning, looking up at the bridge. When they saw Grove appear one of them stepped forward. He was small, with a mop of dense, blue-black hair.

'Hey, you Eenglishman, you Captain?'

Grove's face flushed darkly. From behind him Proctor said diplomatically, 'Let's not annoy the locals.'

Grove nodded silent affirmation at the Vietnamese.

The Vietnamese grinned. 'You glad American fascist dead, yes?'

Grove went an even deeper red. Fury boiled up in him visibly. But he was hamstrung by his responsibilities. He shook his head. 'It's no concern of mine.'

The spokesman scowled. 'Oh yes. American son-of-a-bitch is white. You white. He talk Eenglish. You talk Eenglish. He your cousin, hey?' He laughed and said something to the men behind him. They laughed shrilly.

Grove remained silent. It was an impasse.

The Vietnamese became suddenly furious. 'Fascist dead!' he screamed. He turned to the men behind him and made an angry, commanding sign.

'Fascist dead! Fascist dead! Fascist dead!' they chorused. It went on and on, an idiotic two-word litany.

Grove's control snapped. 'Shut up! Shut up, you bloody swine!'

The Vietnamese laughed. Then they went on with their chant again.

Grove turned away, trembling. He looked at Proctor. He had to shout above the racket from the dock. 'Peter, go down there and do something before I get a three-oh-three from the armoury and drill one of those bastards!'

Proctor was appalled. He moved uneasily away from the rail and headed for the companion-way. This is not for me, he thought, I'm a delicate sort of chap. I don't go around barking orders and pushing in people's faces. The only commands he normally gave were to women, and they were delighted to obey.

Where the blazes, he wondered, was Gilbert Quinan, the Chief Officer? He was equipped to handle this sort of problem. He had the size and total lack of imagination necessary.

Proctor was starting to go down the companion-way when an iron voice rang out from the foredeck. He stopped. Relief flooded over him like a tide. That was Quinan. Good old Gil! He should have known Quinan would be there in a pinch. He turned and went back the few steps up the companion-way, crossed the bridge-wing and looked down with the others at the foredeck.

He was in time to see a square figure in white tropicals stride menacingly down the gangway.

'Oh, no!' Lucas couldn't take his eyes off the Chief Officer but his appeal was addressed to Grove. 'He's going ashore. And he's going to give somebody a thick ear. Then they'll all storm up here and we'll be massacred.'

'I don't think so,' Lincott said quietly. 'Quinan can handle this sort of thing.' Surprisingly, Grove nodded his agreement. He remained silent, fascinatedly watching as his Chief Officer reached the dock.

Quinan stopped there. The dockers were twenty paces away, suddenly silent, studying him uneasily. There was no hesitation in Quinan's momentary stillness. It was a cold-blooded pause while his eyes sought out the spokesman and held his glance. Then he began to walk again, slowly, his long arms at his sides, his brown fingers flexing, his eyes never leaving the man.

As the distance narrowed, the Vietnamese dropped his eyes. He fidgeted. Quinan's voice rang out again, implacable, speaking a language Proctor didn't understand.

Suddenly the dockers peeled away. They trotted over to the nearest tier of coffins and stood there waiting, sullen but obedient.

Quinan turned, looking up at the foredeck. The officers on the bridge saw the grin break out on his face. Then he signalled briefly with one hand. The winch rattled, the derrick loomed overhead and the sling fell next to the coffins with a soft whooshing of rope mesh. The dockers began to fill it.

Quinan trotted back up the gangplank. There was sweat running in rivulets down his cheeks and his white ducks had streaks of grime on them. He turned aft down the port working alleyway and was going inside, heading for the bridge, when someone touched him from behind. He turned around and saw the American girl they had taken on board at Hong Kong.

He smiled. 'I'm a little busy,' he said gently.

'I know.' She had a soft, hurried, nervous way of talking. She was very pretty and under the shorts and top she wore, her body had clean, rounded lines. But the blonde came out of a bottle because there was an inch of dark hair-root showing and her eyes had an uncertain, lost look. Her clothes had marks on them and her hair needed brushing. She reminded Quinan of a cat that had stopped licking its fur.

'I saw you out there on the quay,' she said. 'What did you say to those guys?'

Quinan smiled. He took his hands off the rails. He was not in all that much of a hurry.

'I swore at them in bad Malay. Some of them understood. That spokesman, he's been around. I told them this was a Government job, if they cheated it was Ho Chi himself who would be down on their necks.' He shrugged. 'You can imagine the effect. The one thing these boys really understand is fear. On top of which I'm the first one to have gone ashore and I think that helped a bit.'

'I'll say.' She had an ingenuous smile, like a boy. 'You're so big!' Then she looked down and plucked at her blouse. 'Say, what I wanted to ask you—was that an American plane came over?'

Quinan nodded. She said, 'I was—below, I think you say?' Again the smile. Then her face went still. 'Was the pilot—did he bail out?'

'No.' Quinan looked at the down-turned head. She must have somebody who flies one of those things, he thought.

He was watching her when she looked up. 'But he could have ejected, couldn't he? I mean, he must have seen the missile coming?'

'I suppose so. Yes, I should think he could have.'

Her eyes met his and held them. 'He must have been a pretty brave guy not to eject, when he could have.' She waved a hand. 'These jet pilots, they're so young.' The hand jerked as she brought it back to her side.

Quinan wondered about her. 'It was a very brave thing to do. Especially because he'd been shot up, you know. His under-carriage was hanging loose. I think he was off course, too.'

'Thanks,' she said. The half-blonde head went down again, the long slender fingers played with loose ends on the blouse. There was a moment of silence. When she looked up the impact of her eyes was startling.

'Hearing a thing like that, it kind of restores your faith in humanity, doesn't it?'

'Do you mean because he was brave?'

'Yes.'

'Then it does, if you need it.'

There was a moment of silence. Then she said: 'You're one of the officers, aren't you?' It was more of a statement than a question. When he nodded she went on, 'Gee, I'm sorry, but I can't remember your name.'

'I'm Quinan,' he smiled. 'The Chief Officer.'

'Irish?'

'A long time ago.'

'I'm from Chicago.' There was the smallest pause. 'At least I used to be.'

'Did you like it there?' She had come aboard in Hong Kong, which was a hell of a long way from Chicago. It had been raining, and she had looked small and shabby in a cheap green raincoat. The overhead light in the Purser's office had accentuated the dark smudges of fatigue or illness under her eyes.

'Oh, it was okay.' She waved her hands. 'You know—big city, lots of noise. Nobody really knows you.'

'I know.'

You must have been lonely, he thought.

She looked away again, down on to the dock where the coffins were stacked. She shivered. 'All those dead people. Why are you taking them on board?'

Quinan shrugged. 'They're French war dead. From the Indo-China campaign.' When she looked puzzled he explained, 'Fourteen years ago, even more than that, the French tried to do what you Yanks are trying to do now. This place was all a French colony then, and the French wanted to hang on to it. If they'd had a bit of help they might have succeeded. But it all ended, really, at a place called Dien Bien Phu. The Reds moved in and the French moved out. The bodies we're taking on board have been exhumed. The French Government wants them home and Hanoi has agreed. Most of these chaps were killed in nineteen-fifty-four, some at Dien Bien Phu, some around the Delta, places like that.' He smiled at her again. 'We're just doing the transporting.'

She was still looking down at the coffins. They were made of plain, untreated deal and some of the boards had tried to warp under the firm clamp of the new, bright screws. The name, rank and serial number of each dead soldier was stencilled in furry black paint on the top and sides.

'I hope they're happier over there in France, those young fellows,' she said.

It was a strange thing to say. She turned to him and became suddenly fraught with quick guilt. 'Look, I'm keeping you. I'm sorry. I plain forgot. It's been nice talking to you, Mister Quinan.' She turned to go and then stopped. 'By the way, my name is Mary Jane Fannin.'

Quinan smiled. 'It's on the passenger list.'

'Oh, sure,' she said. 'I'm just silly, I guess.' She turned again and began to walk rapidly along the alleyway.

Quinan shook his head, staring after her for a moment. Then he turned inside abruptly and went up the long companion-way to the bridge.

Grove was waiting on the bridge wing. 'Well done, Gil! Christ, you had me worried there for a moment. I thought you were going to hit one of those slit-eyed sods.'

He grinned and slapped Quinan on the back. 'But you handled it perfectly. You know how careful we've got to be. That lot don't even know we've got Americans on board. If they did!'—he rolled his eyes, then gestured with a flick of his head. 'Here. Come into the wheelhouse. I want to talk to you.'

Quinan went in and Grove shut the door, immediately turning to him. He put out both his hands and dug steely fingers into Quinan's arms. 'Gil, did you see that poor kid in the jet? Did you see what happened?'

'It wasn't nice,' Quinan said. He studied Grove, knowing that he'd wrapped himself around a bottle of gin last night. Grove looked old and lined. He was bone-thin, with a face that had been good-looking before the liquor had stamped a tracery of blue veins across the cheeks and blurred the outlines of his nose.

'Wasn't nice! God, but you're a master of under-statement. When I picture what happened to that poor kid! He was probably thinking of his home, his mother, and then—' Grove broke off. His eyes had become wet with tears. 'It's bloody wrong, Gil!'

Quinan was moved only by irritation. For God's sake, he thought, get your feet back on the ground.

'Come off it, Wally.' His voice was urgent. 'You had a heavy night. You're still all fuddled. We've got a ship to sail. The Yanks have lost something like seven hundred planes in Vietnam. One more or less doesn't make any difference. That boy knew what he was going into. Think of all the Vietnamese kids we've seen with burned faces and—'

'Okay, okay!' Grove said nastily. He dropped his hands and stood staring at Quinan. There was a lot of perception in him. He grinned suddenly. 'Pouring cold water over me, eh? All right, Mister, I'll function. I'll go and get some Vitamin B just now. And no more grog for a while. I promise.' He gave Quinan a sudden, deeply sincere smile. 'I know I've been overdoing it, Gil. It's nice to know I've got such a competent nursemaid at hand.' He became briskly efficient. 'Now, how's the cargo going?'

Quinan's relief showed in his smile. 'Now that the Militia have started working again, it shouldn't take long. About an hour and we'll be buttoned up.'

'Fine. Fine.' Grove led the way to the door and they went out on to the bridge wing, joining Proctor, Lucas and Lincott who were smoking and looking down on the foredeck, where Number Three hold gaped open. In its shadowed interior the stumbling, sweating forms of the crew could be seen, stripped to the waist, streaming sweat while they stacked the coffins.

'That lot must be unhappy,' Grove observed.

'They're full of moans,' Quinan agreed. 'No shore leave and having to work cargo. You know what Hawes, Ludd and company are like.'

'What the hell do they expect?' Grove had become snappy. 'Dammit, Mister, this is a Communist port. I had my instructions. Nobody goes ashore and only the pilot comes aboard. There was no other way of doing it.'

Proctor joined them. 'The biggest complaint from our deli-cately-minded crew,' the Second Officer said mildly, 'is the—ah—nature of the cargo.'

Grove flushed angrily. 'So they don't like carrying dead men, eh? God, I've had them on board before, and I slept as soundly as ever.'

He turned to face his officers. 'In your dealings with the crew—and as far as you gentlemen yourselves are concerned—get one thing straight. This ship carries cargo as a business. That's what pays our salaries. We were damned lucky to get this cargo and the price is good. Very good. We just happened to be Johnny-on-the-spot, but if there'd been a French ship handy we wouldn't have smelt it. So the *Florence Hurst* is carrying three thousand corpses and that's the way it's going to stay until we dump them ashore in Marseilles.' He glared at them. 'Any comments?'

'Heaven help us,' Proctor said. 'I don't care whether we carry chamber-pots or chastity belts. It's just that the crew . . .'

'To hell with the crew!' Grove barked. 'They're a rotten shower of bastards, and for a lot of them it's their last voyage with me!'

He looked at them half-angrily, half-plaintively. 'God dammit, what more? As it is we're shorthanded. Our full complement is fifty-one and as you know we number less than forty. We're short in deckhands, we're short in the engine-room, even the bloody cook has a long face because he's trying to make do without enough helpers!' He waved a hand. 'I want no more bloody grousing, let me make that clear right now.'

Quinan studied him. I will never get used to you, he thought. That didn't bother you last night when you were getting yourself quietly smashed. And now, you jump from woman-like emotion to fierce authority. When Grove was good he was very good. And nobody would deny that he was a hell of a fine seaman. But when he was bad . . .

Proctor was gazing down at the foredeck. 'Here comes our itinerant Evangelist, *et uxor.*'

The others looked down. A man and a woman had come into view on the foredeck from the starboard working alley-way. The man was tall, bulky, and on the wrong side of fifty. He wore a Panama hat and an old-fashioned drill suit that was black with sweat under the armpits. The woman was more than twenty years his junior. She was voluptuously slender. Her body was ripe with womanhood, full in the hips, narrow in the waist, taut and firm at the breasts. She wore her dark hair short in a bob and it accentuated the pale beauty of her face.

Their names were Carlton and Mercy Attwell, and they were husband and wife. They had come on board at Hong Kong, in the rain, only half an hour before the ship had sailed.

Quinan, seeing them standing in the Purser's office, had remembered them instantly. The Albert Hall, eight years ago. Two hours of brilliant revivalism, polished, slick, perfectly stage-managed. Attwell had been a big name then, second only to Billy Graham. He had published two books and his records were on sale everywhere. But for Quinan everything had been a little too perfect. Attwell had been too much Bible Belt, over-playing the simple rustic to an extent where one had expected corn shucks to fall from his hair. He had hammed the thing, part showman and part Puritan, badgering his audience with their neglect of God. It was only when Mercy Attwell had taken the stage for a brief fifteen minutes to talk on 'What a woman thinks of God', that he had felt uplifted. She had been barely twenty-one, then, but in the quiet voice with its mid-western accent there had been a pure dedication that had touched Quinan immediately with its total sincerity.

He had often wondered, since, what had happened to them. Seeing them on the *Florence Hurst,* seeing the small pile of battered suitcases and their worn clothes, hearing Attwell's over-ready, nervous laugh and noticing the silent, expressionless, withdrawn way his wife studied him, he had drawn his own conclusions.

The derrick swung over and hovered above the hold. Grove tapped Quinan on the arm, bringing him out of his reverie.

'Get that clot off the foredeck before he gets a coffin on his head.'

Quinan smiled and passed the buck. 'You, Mister Proctor. You're our diplomat. Remove Mister Attwell and his wife.'

Proctor was not sure whether he detected sarcasm in the words.

One never knew with Quinan. He frowned and shrugged, then leaned over the rail and called down.

'Mister Attwell, Sir. Good morning to you.'

The Attwells looked up. Mercy Attwell's eyes met Proctor's and then glanced away.

Attwell smiled. He had a big, square American face, healthily pink as though it had just been massaged.

'Well, hello there. Good morning, Captain, gentlemen.'

'I'm afraid you're off limits, Sir.' Proctor was watching Mercy Attwell.

Attwell stood his ground. He obviously wanted to say something. Proctor gestured impatiently at the winch operator, who stood back. The men working the cargo appeared in the open hatch and a silence fell over the foredeck.

Attwell addressed himself to Grove. His voice was magic. It had the impulse of electricity. It crackled with timbre. It had the harmonic resonance of a deep organ.

'Captain, there was a boy killed up there just now.' His glance rose briefly to the sky and came back to them. 'He was an American boy. These men down here'—one big hand gestured briefly to the hold—'were French. But they all died one way, that American and these French lads. In violence, at the hands of their fellow-men. They died frightened, angry, bewildered. They died believing, they died disbelieving. They died pure and they died sinning. They were flowers that rose up, and were cut down again, cut down when the bud had only just become a blossom, before it could seed.'

He looked around slowly, letting the silence run. Then he spoke softly. The organ note slackened to a hum. 'God took them. You need have no doubt, they are with Him.' Without warning the organ crashed out suddenly, fortissimo, startling them. 'Oh yes! They are safe in the arms of Jesus, and for that I give thanks to Him!' He flung his arms up, gesturing to heaven. The last thundering echo of his voice died.

Slowly he lowered his arms. Meekly, pianissimo, in a voice that was just a crisp whisper, he added, 'For that I am glad. For that I can give thanks. I am going to say a little prayer, now, because my heart is so full of joy. Join me, if you would like to.'

He flung himself on his knees on the iron deck, back straight, clasped hands thrust out and up. It was a masterfully-posed attitude of supplication. The organ notes of his voice rang out into the heated air, rolling straight up to heaven. He began to pray: 'Almighty God, with whom do live the spirits of them that depart hence in the Lord . . .'

Mercy Attwell prayed, Oh, sweet Jesus, she prayed, don't let anyone laugh. Let them pray with him for my sake. Let them go through this ridiculous parody of worship, I beg of you.

She opened her eyes. Some of the crew had their heads bowed. Others were looking at Carl. None watched her. She raised her glance to the bridge. She could just see the heads of the officers. Grove and Quinan had theirs bowed, woodenly. What are they thinking, she wondered.

Lincott was looking at her. She held his eyes for a moment only, then looked away, uneasy. Ever since they had come on board he had been watching her like this, and there had been too much to read on his face, as though by mere looking alone he could absorb her into himself. It did not frighten her, because she had learned long ago to detect evil and there was none in him.

But she didn't want goodness now, either. I have lived with goodness too long, she reflected bitterly. I don't want goodness or sincerity, I don't want soulfulness or love because love is a rotten word without meaning. I just want to live. I know enough about you, God. All my life I have lived with you. Now I want to be a woman.

She turned her eyes to Proctor and Lucas. They were studying her openly and Proctor was grinning at her. They were young and sublimely sure of themselves. They didn't have to stop to think. They want me and they are going to try and have me, she thought. She wondered what it would be like to be with them, to mingle her body with theirs. An exciting, electric spasm of sudden delicious physical want contracted the flat muscles of her stomach. Her clasped hands whitened as she squeezed them desperately together. Oh God, she thought, what is happening to me? But it was not a prayer this time.

Carl Attwell's magnetic voice stopped. He lifted his head and smiled. 'Thank you. And now, I think a little breakfast would not be a bad idea.'

Some of the crew laughed. The winch started up again and the cargo net was eased into the hold.

On the bridge, Proctor let out a sigh of relief. 'What a ham. I thought the old goat would never stop. He studied the involuntary swing of Mercy Attwell's hips as she followed her husband out of sight. 'But his wife, now. That's a different story. She could preach to me all day.' He winked. 'I would like to tiptoe barefoot through a naked acre of those lovely tits.'

'You're not the only one,' Lucas grinned. 'I would like to have Mercy on me.'

Everybody laughed except Lincott, who flushed angrily. He looked at Proctor and Lucas with real hatred.

Proctor saw it in his eyes. He sniggered and dug Lucas in the ribs. 'You're defaming the pill-roller's girl friend. Lay off.'

'Ah, yes, I'd forgotten. Forgive me.' Lucas pretended to be humble, but his eyes were full of malice. 'Lewd Lincott, the dirty Doctor. King of the sad eyes and heavy sigh routine.' He rounded on Lincott and slapped him jovially. 'Women go for that line Doc. Just as long as you take it a bit further. Pills are not just for rolling. But I'm on your side. I've got a fiver that says the good Lincott will lose his virginity before we reach Manila. Any takers?'

'Never.' Proctor shook his head solemnly. 'It's a sure thing.'

Quinan tore his eyes from Lincott's humiliated face. 'That's enough, you two. Cut it out.'

'Nonsense.' Grove was laughing. 'Lincott is too touchy. Come on, Doctor, snap out of it. It's only good-natured leg-pulling.' He grabbed Proctor and Lucas around the shoulders and hugged them, looking at each of them in turn with real affection. 'If it wasn't for these two twits I'd never laugh.'

Quinan caught Lincott's eye and shrugged. He turned away, suddenly very angry with Grove.

There was a hail from the dock. The Vietnamese were departing, filing off in orderly lines with their rifles at the trail. And walking carelessly through their midst, disrupting their ranks and ignoring their shrill protests, marched a spare, elderly figure, grinning up at the group on the bridge.

'It's General de Gaulle,' Proctor said.

Grove went to the port side. 'Good morning, Monsieur,' he called. 'I was beginning to think we'd have to sail without you.'

The man on the dock was now alone. He raised a hand and threw a kiss at Grove. 'Good morning, delightful Captain. Without dwelling on the charming quaintness of your pronunciation I think perhaps it would be better if you employed the English equivalent.'

Grove laughed. 'Okay, *Mister* Puget. Come up.'

He turned to the others. 'What a hell of a man to put in charge of bodies.'

Puget leapt lightly up the companion. He was in his sixties, Quinan guessed, but his breathing was even and undisturbed after the climb.

'I have been for a constitutional. The morning was lovely, but it is now getting damnably hot.' He half-bowed to the other officers. 'Good morning, Mister Puget. Are you well this morning, Mister Puget? Did you dream well, Mister Puget? Is it not for youth to greet age first?'

The officers laughed and chorused an ironic greeting.

Puget beamed. 'I dreamt well, but, alas, all of the past. Such strength I had then!' He raised some fingers. 'Two, three, maybe even four times in one night. I was a veritable bull.' He turned to Grove. 'How goes it? Have you loaded all my lovely bodies?' The last sling was going aboard. 'Just about,' Grove said.

'Fine, fine.' Puget turned to survey Haiphong. 'It is a pity you could not go ashore, you people. There is much of France still over there. It was sad, in a way. But there is also much that is new.' He pointed to a grey, utilitarian structure rising near the harbour. 'Like that building. It is a new radio station. For propaganda broadcasts. so my spies tell me.'

'Tommy Tucker's hide-out, probably,' Proctor suggested.

The remark seemed to annoy Lucas, who saw things largely in black and white. 'Bloody Quisling bastard.'

Puget looked at them. 'Who is this?'

Proctor shrugged. 'An American Lord Haw Haw. He broadcasts sedition to the Yank forces. Sparks picked him up on the radio just outside Hong Kong. He's called Tommy Tucker. He sings for his supper, get it?'

'More or less.' Puget looked across at the building. 'But whatever he sings he cannot do so at the moment. The station is closed temporarily, so they say.'

The Radio Officer came out of his cabin behind the chartroom, slamming the door. His name was Bertram Osgood but he was known universally as Sparks. He was a small, flabby, filthy and unbearably untidy man. He was also a chronic alcoholic. Passing Lincott, he gave him a weak, frightened smile, remembering the agony of the Antabus which Lincott had used a few months ago to try and cure him.

He reached Grove. 'Radio okay.'

Grove scowled at him, nodded, and dismissed him with a flip of the hand. He did not like to be reminded about Osgood, who had, strictly speaking, already been fired. He would leave the *Florence Hurst* when she got home.

Sparks looked sideways at Lincott again. Then he shifted his eyes, remaining mute, staring momentarily into space. After a moment he shuffled off the bridge, his hands shaking like the fluttering wings of a butterfly.

Six seamen clustered on the starboard side of the mast table on the foredeck, hidden from the officers on the bridge. Five of them were deckhands and the sixth was Willy Hookins, one of the stewards. The five made a semicircle around Hookins, who had his back to the iron bulk of the table.

'Okay, give it to me again.' Feller Hawes was built like a keg, balding, black-browed, with small gold rings set in the lobes of his ears. 'Where did you last see it?'

Hookins's voice was low and frantic. His eyes darted from one man to the next, then back to Hawes. 'I tell you, I had it that night. It was fastened to my belt. You know that it's always fastened to my belt. But it's not there any more. You can see where the link snapped. Here—here, I'll show you.'

His hands were shaking as he grabbed savagely at the belt that supported his jeans and pulled it away from the cloth, holding it with his fingers hooked under the leather so that they could see the brass clip and an inch of slender brass chain that dangled loosely.

'Then she's got it. She must have it.' Dike Ludd looked at the others. He was a middle-sized man in his forties with a beaky nose above a strange, old-fashioned cavalry-type moustache. His face was disfigured by a tremendous diagonal scar running from his right temple, where even the bone was indented, to his left cheek The left eye was a bloodshot, opaque disc. It had all originated in a savage fight in a weapon-pit in the Apennines, twenty-five years before.

Hawes sneered. 'She didn't like you, Willy. She kept clawing at your belt while she was screaming. Remember?' Hawes leapt forward and grabbed a handful of Hookins's shirt and pulled him up savagely against him. 'Do you remember, you stupid bastard?'

Kiddy Kyle giggled. He was slender and girlish, with black hair hanging down to his shoulders. 'And she kept saying "Oh dear God, Oh dear God," all the time, like that.'

'Ease up, Feller, let him go a little.' Ludd moved in. 'We've got to get the truth out of the sod.'

Hawes threw Hookins back against the iron wall of the table. Hookins was shaking like a leaf. He suddenly put his hands to his face and began to sob, his body heaving with the paroxysms.

'Wants his old Mum,' Rummy Knowles suggested. He was a little drunken man of indeterminate age. He dug Draper in the ribs. 'Huh, Flesh? Wants his old Mum.' He laughed in a cackling treble.

'Stuff you,' Draper said. He was a bodybuilder, gigantically wide across the shoulders, with a huge, smooth, pink face. To Hookins he said: 'When did you miss it?'

The steward took his hands from his face. Tears glistened on his cheeks. 'Next morning.'

Hawes butted in, 'And you waited till now to tell us?'

Hookins's hands fluttered without purpose. 'I thought I'd find it. I kept thinking I'd find it—in the heads or somewhere.'

Ludd swore. It was a verbal excrescence. 'You've sunk us, you sod, you realize that? She must have had it in her hand when the bloody rozzers found her.'

Hookins said desperately and unconvincingly, 'Well, we're miles from Hong Kong. Who the hell is to know it's my . . .'

Hawes shook his head. 'Oh, Christ, but you're stupid. That Goddam charm of yours is known in half the pubs there. Every man on this ship knows it.' He became heavily sarcastic. 'I suppose every other bloke you meet has got a winged silver dollar dangling from his belt.'

'With the initials W.H. engraved on the coin,' Kiddy Kyle added. He giggled again.

Hookins stared at each one of them in turn. His face was working. 'Can't we just go to the Old Man and tell him we . . . we found her like that? We could just say we were walking along and there she was—there they were—lying there next to the car and . . .'

His words were cut off in the flat smack of Hawes's open hand across his cheek. Hookins cried out and cringed back, his eyes like those of a frightened rabbit. They darted about, never settling. The marks of Hawes's fingers came up in a stinging red weal.

'Don't crack, Willy-boy,' Hawes said softly. 'We wouldn't like to think you're going to crack. Would we, blokes?'

'It makes us nervous, just to think about it,' Draper said.

They closed in on Hookins. Ludd's fist took him in the belly. Hookins gagged and doubled up.

'Up, Willy, up,' Hawes said gently. 'We want to give you a little lesson. Don't crack, Willy-boy.' He took a handful of the steward's hair and yanked him upright, looking into the terrified eyes. 'Give him some more, Dike. Give the sod a couple low down, where it hurts.'

Lucas, the Third Officer, came suddenly around the corner of the mast table, his shoulders stretching the white cotton of his shirt, his blue eyes hard and alert.

'What the hell is going on here?'

They cordoned Hookins, making a rough line between him and the officer. 'Young 'Ookins 'ad a fall, Sir,' Kiddy Kyle said. He giggled. 'We was 'elpin' him up.'

'Like hell.' Lucas looked at the steward. 'Want to say anything?'

The steward stared at Lucas. His lips trembled. Then he shook his head.

Lucas turned his eyes on Hawes. He walked two paces forward until his chest was touching Hawes. It was a deliberate, provocative movement.

'You're the boss, Feller. What happened?'

Hawes's eyes were riveted on Lucas. 'It's like Kiddy says, Sir.'
He licked his lips. One of these days, he thought. One of these
days, you blond bastard. One of these days in a back alley. You'll
wish to God you'd never been born.

Lucas moved back slowly. 'Shake a leg, you lot. We want to
get out of here. And leave Hookins alone.' He turned and walked
away.

The *Florence Hurst* left port half an hour later, destination
Singapore.

CHAPTER TWO

IT WAS FOUR BELLS: two o'clock. The Attwells had lunched and
retired to their cabin for Carl's afternoon rest. Haiphong was an
early-morning memory and the *Florence Hurst* was making good
headway through the duckpond calm of the Gulf of Tongkin.

Carl was seated on the edge of his bed. He grunted as he bent
to unlace a shoe. This rest had become a ritual with him over
the last two years. To Mercy it was as much a part of him as his
food fads, the dentures he removed every evening, his slow
fumbling stiffness in the morning and the choking, alarming,
old man's sounds he made in his sleep.

Carl flung himself back on the bed. Sweat had made teardrops
on the hollows under his eyes and beaded his upper lip.

'This Goddam heat.' His irritability, too, was something which
had increased over the years. 'Living in a tin can doesn't make
it any easier.'

Mercy Attwell slipped off her dress and draped it over the
only chair. 'The *Florence Hurst* is not the *Queen Mary*, Carl.
She is a twenty-year-old cargo boat licensed to carry eight
passengers. And you shouldn't swear like that. One of these days
it is going to happen in public.'

He had found a cigarette and lit it. His eyes were on the smoke
trailing up to the ceiling. 'I'll Goddam swear if I want.'

His tone was petulant. He was only trying to assert himself,
and after what had happened in Vietnam it was understandable,
she knew. Vietnam had done Carl a lot of harm. It had been a
crushing blow to his ego.

Mercy sighed. 'It's hot enough without the temperament.' She
stooped, removed her half-slip and stood lithely before the mirror
in her panties and bra. Then on an impulse she took off the bra
as well. I wonder if he will notice, she thought. It had been such
a long time since he'd touched her. She sat down at the dresser
and began to fiddle with her hair.

Carl blew smoke at the ceiling. It hung in a cloud over him. There was no moving air in the cabin.

'I guess we'll have to write the Far East tour off to experience.'

Mercy nearly laughed. But bitterness rose up into her throat and choked it off. Experience! Oh, dear God!

Tears flooded her eyes so quickly and unexpectedly that she had to blink to hold them back. So that, she thought, is the extent of my humiliation. My eyes weep spontaneously. And they can distinguish between humility and humiliation. She was used to humility. As a good servant of the Lord humility was a right and proper thing. It was a way of life. But humiliation was an agony.

Even my eyes remember, she thought, they remember South Vietnam in the rainy season, the rallies held under low sombre clouds that poured a steady slanting drizzle, the marquee flapping under the buffeting of the wind, the rows of empty wet benches that glistened in the overhead lights and the audiences—ten, twenty men lost amongst the emptiness, always the same slickered tobacco-chewing rustics who came for the hand-clapping and the brimstone prayers and the jazzy, countrified hymns.

At intermission Carl had always plugged his record albums. A stack of them were displayed on the edge of the stage. The price was special to servicemen, Carl maintained. He'd got a bite here, a bite there, but never without a deal, never without a hot bargaining session from these furiously Puritanical customers of his who had been horse-trading all their young lives.

One night, as the tour progressed, Carl had suddenly given away the whole stack. He hadn't spoken to her until the next day.

Back home, music stores hadn't stocked the albums in four years.

These things, she thought, my eyes remember. She studied Carl in the mirror. He looked old, lying there with his neck muscles slack, his chin lost in jowls. But I can't blame his age, she thought. Age was inevitable. Some people grew older and stronger. Carl had not. Age had brought blindness, a stubborn refusal to quit while he was ahead. Now, in a way, it was too late to quit. Carl still lived in a world of managers and press agents, public relations men and literary agents. They were all long gone, but he could not accept the fact. He could not realize that he was through. He could not even understand that within himself he had retrogressed, that he had lost all his subtlety and had reverted to his barn-storming days in the sticks when God had of necessity to be hellfire and utter damnation.

'Far East tour.' She repeated the words silently within herself, but it was a mute, jeering reproduction. They conjured up such stirring visions of a mass religious response, an eruption of desire, amongst Americans particularly, to return to God out here. That was the way Carl had pictured it, together with full coverage by *Life* and *Time* and interviews on television. But it hadn't worked out that way. 'Far East tour' instead, had meant a lonely husband-and-wife team dismally failing within the strictures of a threadbare bank account.

They had become an embarrassment in a Vietnam which was already critically embarrassed, and a bad example to the locals. So they had been talked out of the country by a young-old Colonel, a rear-echelon Colonel with a paunch who had suddenly been caught up in the fighting and had been too tired to realize that he had got his lines crossed. He had spoken about how everybody wanted to 'entertain' the servicemen, but that there was only room for so many 'shows'. As an afterthought he'd thrown in the news that Saigon had been mortared the night before.

Carl, puffy-eyed and suddenly defeated, hadn't even bothered to put him straight. He had passively allowed the remainder of his itinerary to be deleted from the official schedules.

Hong Kong had simply added to the nightmare. It had been intended purely as a port of call on the way home. But Carl had become interested in the Colony. They had left their ship on his sudden whim, and, with a lot of dollar-juggling, taken cheap lodgings in the City. Carl had organized one agonizing meeting on a night that had coincided with the Communist riots. A British police officer had come to close them down under emergency regulations that had prohibited any sort of gathering. He had been, to Mercy, a strange American-looking man in an un-American uniform, speaking a clinical kind of English that had resounded with the purity of its enunciation. He had looked out at the audience of a few scattered Chinese and six misplaced Highlanders, dourly drunk and in full dress uniform. And although he had kept his thoughts to himself they were there for her to see in the clarity of his very blue eyes. Mercy had had to suppress an hysterical desire to sob on one shoulder of his immaculately-pressed uniform.

Carl twisted on the bed and came up on one elbow. 'Turn that damned ventilator on, will you?' He scrubbed a forearm nervously across his forehead. 'I saw a guy once in a sweat-box, in Georgia. Chain gang. Now I know what it was like.'

Mercy got up. 'The ventilator is just about full on.' She crossed the cabin to the bulkhead and slid the lipped cover another half-inch to its maximum. His eyes had been on her as she walked, watching the strong jounce of her breasts. They were a girl's

breasts, fresh and effervescent, full creamy-white below the pale
biscuit tan of her neck and shoulders. I can be proud of them,
she thought. I can be proud of them the way a man is proud of
his shoulders, or the girth of his arms. There is no sin in it.

'Do you always strip for a lie-down these days?'

Mercy stopped in the middle of the cabin. 'It's hot, Carl. Have
I done something wrong, to take my clothes off?'

' "Give not yourself unto vanity." ' But he was smiling at
her.

'Psalm Sixty-two.' She sat on the edge of her bed. He still had
this surprising insight. It made her uneasy, sometimes.

His eyes were sharp and shrewd, searching. 'Something's eating
you, honey.'

She shook her head, the short dark curls bouncing against her
cheeks. 'Don't be silly.'

He slumped back against the pillow. 'You never did that
before.' His eyes were on the ceiling again.

'Walked across a room with my bra off?' She said it sharply to
underline the absurdity of his remark.

He twisted his neck to look at her. 'I didn't mean just that.
You know I didn't mean just that. It was a . . . a . . . gesture.'

'Cut it out, Carl. I'm as hot as you are.' She sank down on the
bed and swung her legs up. I would like, she thought, to be on
the lower boat deck, playing darts with the Second Officer. I
don't need an old man's rest. It was an angry, rebel thought, but
she let it stay with her. Vietnam did that to me, she thought,
Vietnam and the rain and the Hill-Billies chanting against Carl's
desperate, slogging, bull-like descant. Vietnam and Hong Kong
and the drunken Highlanders waving their bristly sporrans at her.

Carl changed the subject. 'What's the state of our finances?'

Well, now, she thought sourly, he is being magnanimous. He
had finally figured out that there wasn't much original sin in his
wife walking around the room without her bra.

'Parlous.'

'I guessed as much.' The heat had made him restless. And that
damned, accursed enthusiasm was coming back. When she turned
her head she could see it in his eyes. Holy Jesus, she thought, what
is it this time? And a quick apology for the Lord. I am not
blaspheming, Lord. I am just desperate.

He brought himself up on one elbow again. 'You wait until
we get to France, honey. Just you wait. You saw it today, out
there on the foredeck. You saw the crew. It's that old magic.' He
put out a massive hand, the fingers curled, rigid. 'I had them right
there. Right in that little old hand.'

Her voice came out flat and cold in the stuffy heat of the cabin.

'You speak French? You are going to convert a lot of Frenchmen in Kansas American?'

The silence was absolute and complete for a long moment. When he spoke his voice was fumbling and confused. 'I know it's been a long time, honey. It's been so hot. The food is different. I've been under strain. I promise . . .'

She turned to him quickly, the firm breasts falling evenly together with a dark, warm, smooth line between them as she lay on her side. 'There's no need to promise anything, Carl.'

'I feel bad about it.' He reached across and took one of her breasts gently in his hand. She twisted over on her back, letting him fondle her. A sudden warm, lazy sexuality flooded her. You difficult, brilliant, lovable old bastard, she thought. Here I go, swearing like him. But it didn't matter.

'So much is possible, still,' she said.

The hand stopped its caressing. She lay a moment.

'Carl?'

When there was no answer she came upright, wide-eyed, staring at him.

He was asleep.

Her stomach muscles were cold, and ridged like blue marble. There was a sweet agony in her now that nothing could quench. The twentieth time, she thought. No, the twenty-first. If I cry now, my tears will steam on my cheeks.

She laughed suddenly and sharply. Sweet Jesus, she prayed, is it wrong for me to want to be back on the lower boat deck with Proctor and his cold-eyed blond friend Lucas, because they are so young and the fire in their loins singes me and cries out to me?

She lay back, trembling, knowing that sleep was impossible.

Quinan stood on the foredeck near Number Three hatch. He was leaning on the port rail looking down at the water rushing past the side of the *Florence Hurst*. There was a mesmerizing effect in doing this, he knew. The theory was that you unknowingly leaned further and further out until your point of balance changed and you went overboard. But as long as you were aware of the danger it was all right and there was something analgesic in the experience. You became insensible, you lapsed into an agreeable dullness.

He had been very busy until now. His day had started early, finalizing the loading of the coffins so that they could depart Haiphong on schedule. And it had been complicated by the destruction of the jet, the behaviour of the People's Militia who had done the stevedoring and the deliberate slowness of the *Florence Hurst*'s unwilling crew.

It was now just after four bells in the afternoon watch, and for the first time he was really free. The passengers had retired to their cabins and a sort of post-prandial dullness had settled over the ship. But the morning had left him tired and a little depressed, which was something that had happened to him recently when he had nothing immediate on his hands.

He could sense the coffins beneath his feet. I don't like it, he thought. I am a damned silly superstitious sailor but I don't like it and to hell with what Grove says.

Three thousand men fourteen years violently dead. Three thousand restless souls. What was left behind in those crude wooden boxes? A handful of mould, probably. It would depend upon what the ants had done. He must ask Lincott what was likely.

He shook himself irritably. He had enough worries without foolishly adding to them.

For a start, Grove was drinking too much. Years of heavy intemperance had slid quickly and without fuss into regular drunkenness. It had started suddenly like the slamming of a door, and it had taken Quinan a while to realize it. Then he suddenly grasped that what had been a cheerful nightly alcoholic fog had become a regular procedure in which Grove with graph-like precision climbed a short peak to a height of loose-tongued charm and then plunged like a toboggan down a long slope of progressive deterioration into a valley that was glassy-eyed stupor and a urine-sodden bed and the agony of the next morning.

There was no immediate explanation for the metamorphosis, but its effects were very apparent. Apart from looking like hell, the effect of the booze was bringing to the surface the immaturity, always there but latent, together with too much liquored-up emotion, over-compassion and a conflicting and unpredictable hellishness.

That was the first of the worries. He had Grove on his mind much of the time, rather like a time-bomb of uncertain mechanism. He was not prepared to be dramatic about it. He had no fear of immediate disaster. But lately he had found himself studying Grove's decisions, checking his calculations, scrutinizing his log entries. On top of which a great deal of additional work had fallen on his own shoulders. He was becoming increasingly disenchanted.

He found and lit a cigarette and let the match disappear in its long angled flight to the tumbled water. His eyes lost it as it fell.

Generally, he thought, a pervading slackness had begun to manifest itself. There was too much Christian-naming and back-slapping on the bridge. And those two clowns, Proctor and Lucas, had guzzled the whole hand of the extended finger. Osgood, the Radio Officer, was going over the hill. He was a bumbling drunk who was going to do something idiotic one day. His condition was ignored by everybody except Lincott, but between the Doctor and the Captain any entente that might once have existed was long gone, so Lincott's entreaties and warnings about Osgood fell on a stubbornly deaf ear.

Quinan stared down at the racing water. Finally, of course, there was the matter of Hookins. Lucas had reported what had happened behind the mast table.

They're running a racket, those boys, Quinan thought, and Hookins is crossing them or fouling them up somewhere. He wondered what it was. The usual thing was liquor or cigarettes, but this was undoubtedly more serious. Drugs? Or was there altogether some other cause? He stared out across the calm sea, more bothered than he would have been prepared to admit.

He was stirring to go further forward when a hand touched him lightly on the back. He turned and found himself looking at Mary Fannin.

'Hello, there.' The greeting was solemn, with only a hint of a smile in the eyes. She still hurried her words and he wondered whether, early this morning, he had read fear into this mannerism. Because fear there was not. Only a sort of purposelessness. She had lost her confidence somewhere, somehow. It had made her small in her own mind and so she talked quickly in case the audience did not stay to listen. But Quinan had heard her out this morning and so she had rather adopted him, anxious for company and afraid to try anywhere else. Quinan had felt like that once, two years ago, and because he thought he understood her, he warmed to her.

She sensed it. She smiled this time, when she said, 'A penny for them?'

Quinan shook his head. 'Uh-uh. You wouldn't like them at all.' She had brushed her hair, he noticed. 'You weren't at lunch,' he said accusingly.

'I didn't feel too good.' She tried to make light of it. 'I guess hitting the open sea did things to my tummy.'

Quinan studied her. Her face, apart from lipstick, was devoid of make-up. There was a tiny scar above her left eyebrow. Her features were very good but the skin was pale and dull. The eyes worried him. They had shadows in them as well as under them. This girl could be really beautiful if she wanted to. But she did not want to.

He asked her suddenly, 'What were you doing in Hong Kong?'

She looked at him gravely. 'Singing. Singing in a night club.' There was no need to tell him that it had been a joint, and that her neckline had been split down to her navel.

Quinan knew Hong Kong well. He wanted to ask her which night club, but he sensed her reluctance. 'What did you sing? I'm not sure of my terminology.'

'Oldies, "Body and Soul". "Smoke Gets In Your Eyes." "Blue Moon." Strictly mood. I came on late, when the guys wanted to cry into their booze.' She hesitated a moment and then went on as though she were trying to improve his mental image of her. 'I play the guitar quite well. I like Spanish music—flamencos, *conte jondos*. I prefer that. But it didn't quite seem to fit the tone of the place.'

'Did you like what you were doing?'

'No.' She was going to leave it at that. But then she saw that he thought he'd offended her. 'It was a way to eat. I was out of a job.'

Just like that, Quinan thought. She couldn't be more than twenty-three, but the spirit had died in her. She was going through the motions, bumping along like a twig in a stream, wherever the current took her.

'Here,' he said, 'come and have a good look at the Nan Hai. That's another name for the South China Sea. It's quite a notorious place. Pirates. Typhoons. Ever read Joseph Conrad?'

She shook her head, turned her face up to look at him. Her hands on the teak rail were slender, with long, scarlet-painted nails. They were the hands of a guitar player, but the gaudy nails were out of place in the hot sunlight.

'I never had the chance to read much. I guess I was an early drop-out. I haven't had much education, Mister Quinan.'

There was a definite challenge in the words. She was studying him, waiting for a reaction.

He smiled. 'I have a copy of *Typhoon*, by Conrad, in my cabin. Would you like to try it?'

Whatever she saw in his face seemed to satisfy her. 'That would be nice.'

There was a silence while they both looked out over the water. Then she raised a hand and pointed. 'There's a small boat way out there. It seems awful low in the water.'

'Where?' Quinan narrowed his eyes against the sunglare.

She took his hand and pointed it for him. Her grip was strong and firm, her hands cool. 'Over there.'

Quinan found it. 'Oh. That's a sampan. She's a long way out for such a small craft.' He stiffened slightly, concentrating on the boat. It was more than half a mile away on the port bow, but even without the aid of binoculars he could see that it was down by the bows.

He swung about quickly. 'She's in trouble.' On an impulse he took her arm. 'Come with me.'

She resisted at first. Mild alarm showed in her face. 'Why? Where're we going?'

'To the bridge. Come on, you can come with me.'

When he smiled at her she relaxed suddenly and let him tow her at a trot along the deck. She moved very lightly, without awkwardness.

They climbed the companion and found Proctor on the bridge-wing, his glasses slung around his neck. He raised his eyebrows when he saw Mary Fannin.

'What's up?'

Quinan pointed. 'Sampan. Port bow, about half a mile. Have a look.'

Proctor put his glasses to his eyes. There was a second of silence while he concentrated. Then he let them fall and stared at Quinan. 'She's sinking. Heavily down by the bows. Won't last much longer, I shouldn't think. There's a fellow in the stern jumping about and waving everything except his what-not.' He bowed at Mary Fannin. 'Forgive me, honey-chile.'

Grove came out of the wheelhouse. His hangover, assisted by Vitamin B tablets and the passage of time, had moved on and was lying in wait for him, next time around. He was calm now, even stimulated by the thought of tonight's drinking.

He trained his own glasses a moment. 'She's going down soon, Gil. Lookout must have had his eyes up his arse. We'll head over there and pick that bloke up. Feel like handling it?'

Quinan shrugged. He did most things that could have been delegated, but it didn't matter. 'Okay.'

'Fine. And you'd better have Lincott with you.' Grove turned and snapped his fingers at the stand-by man in the wheelhouse, a young seaman called Usher. 'Get the Doctor. Tell him to come right away.' The man clattered down the companion-way and Grove went back into the wheelhouse to give orders to the helmsman.

The *Florence Hurst* altered course. A six-man boat crew mustered and the port lifeboat was swung out on its Whelin-McClachlan davits and lowered to embarkation level. The boat's crew, led by the Boatswain, Woods, got on board, with Usher standing by the davit brake.

The *Florence Hurst* swooped down upon the sampan. The bridge telegraph clanged and down in the hot hell of the engine room the engines were put over. The *Florence Hurst* hove to.

Quinan got aboard the lifeboat. From there he called to Proctor, on the bridge wing: 'Where the heck is Lincott?'

There was a momentary delay. Proctor disappeared and then came back. For a moment Mary Fannin stood alone, a rather forlorn figure. Quinan lifted a hand to her and saw her quick smile. Then Proctor was back, clattering down the short companion-way and trotting up to the falls.

He was grinning. 'We can't find him. He's probably in the heads. He does a lot of his reading there.'

Quinan laughed. 'For God's sake! Tell him to meet me in the hospital when we get back.' He nodded to Usher on the brake. 'Okay. Lower away.'

The boat went slowly down until it struck the water with a solid thump. Woods, in the bow, pushed off.

Quinan nodded to the crew, who were eyeing him expectantly. 'All together, now. Let's try not to look like a lopsided water beetle.'

The men grinned and heaved at the oars. Quinan took the tiller and aimed the lifeboat's blunt prow at the sampan where it wallowed in the slight swell fifty yards away. It was an ancient and battered craft, with a small tattered rag of sail. Looking at it with amazement, Quinan wondered how it had managed to stay afloat this long.

There was a man on the stern of the sampan. He capered about feebly, waving his arms. They could hear his voice: 'Over here! Over here!'

Woods looked at Quinan. 'That's a white man we're going to fetch.'

Gauldie, a redheaded Scot on the bow oar, pulled a face. 'He thinks we're going past him to the wreck of the *Hesperus*, nae doubt.'

'Stow it. Save your breath for rowing.' Quinan stood up as the lifeboat closed with the sampan, watching the man on its stern.

He was a big man, and young still, wearing the bottom half of a pair of plum-coloured Vietnamese pyjamas. His hair was long and shaggy and he had a stubble of beard. He kept moving his arms and legs as though he were doing some kind of ridiculous dance. And the words streamed through his caked lips: 'I got me a big red boat to come and save me. Hallelujah! And an Admiral in charge. You, Sir. Thank you kindly, Sir, for your trouble. That's it, boys, easy now. Easy. You get old Bunny off and turn that great big lifeboat around and take Bunny back to the ship before this Goddam floating Panama hat takes a dip.' He babbled on as the lifeboat rubbed alongside the sampan.

'A Yank,' said Gauldie.

'A loon, too,' Gindle, the next oar, chipped in.

The survivor extended his arms, palms facing outward in a halting gesture as Quinan put his foot up on the gunwale of the sampan. 'There's no need to come aboard, buddy. The others are dead.' He had light coloured eyes. 'Look, Sir, I'm mighty grateful to you. But in a moment we're going to be swimming in awful deep water. Can't we just drive back to the ship, huh?'

Quinan didn't like to be hurried. He shook his head. 'She won't sink for a while yet. You say there are dead men on board? Can I have a look at them?'

The American gave a despairing laugh. 'Look, buddy, I don't quite know how to get through to you. I'm sure they're dead, if that's what you mean. They stink. You read me? So all I'm suggesting, old buddy-boy, is that . . .'

'My name is Quinan. Chief Officer of the *Florence Hurst*.' Quinan was getting tired of the flood of words, the nonsensical familiarity. His face showed it.

The American stared at him. 'Whoah. Whoooaah. Keep a civil tongue in your head, O'Connor, the man's getting mad.' He half bowed. 'Hail, great white man. Salud, oh breaker of Atlantic records. Forgive thy servant for his disrespect. The dead men are that way. But go alone, Sire. I'm for this here boat.' He turned and jumped across, was caught by Woods and deposited on a thwart.

Quinan splashed his way forward through ankle-deep water to a crude matting cabin. The doorless opening was an oblong of gloom. As he put his head inside the putrid stench of rotting flesh caught him in the throat. It was like slamming into a wall, it was so strong. He retreated, gagging. He would willingly have given up, there and then, but he was conscious of the interested silence from the bobbing lifeboat. The men were watching him. It was now or never. He took a deep breath of clean air, ducked his head and went in.

Three white men lay on the deck. They were sprawled in the loose attitudes of death. Two wore the same plum-coloured pyjamas as the survivor, the other was dressed in the tattered remnants of a uniform. The hair of the corpses was long, matted with filth. They were bearded. All were thin to the point of emaciation except for their bellies, which were distended with the pressure of internal gases, giving them a pregnant and un-natural grossness.

Quinan gritted his teeth, clenching his jaws against the sudden sharp spasm of nausea that shook him. With eyes that had grown used to the gloom he looked around quickly. Apart from the bodies there was only a splintered and smashed table and a broken earthenware bowl.

He backed out of the cabin and shudderingly sucked air into his lungs. The sky was blue and the sea danced about him. It was suddenly a better world. He turned his back on the cabin and got aboard the bobbing lifeboat.

The survivor was seated in the sternsheets, out of the way of the oars. Quinan joined him while the port oarsmen pushed away and the lifeboat headed back for the ship.

The American was grinning. 'Get their dog-tags?'

Quinan shook his head. The horror in the sampan's cabin was still with him and he was unable immediately to speak.

'Rough, huh?' The American was staring at him. 'Don't say I didn't warn you.' He jingled his pocket. 'I was only kidding you, anyway. I've got the dog-tags. Their names were Jones, Graham and Niemack. A Major and two Lieutenants. I'm O'Connor, Lieutenant, United States Navy. Jet Pilot. People call me Bunny.'

They shook hands. 'Sure as hell, I'm grateful to you guys.' O'Connor had a big, meaty nose, full lips. He was inclined to a petulant heaviness around the chin.

'You were a prisoner of the Viet-Minh?' Quinan had recovered at last. 'A P.O.W.?'

'That's right.' The American swallowed nervously. His face twitched. For the first time he was manifesting visible physical signs of ordeal. 'Say, you got a cigarette?'

Quinan found one and lit it for him. 'How long have you been at sea?'

'I dunno.' He drew on his cigarette and coughed. 'I'm not used to these things. Three, four days, I guess. Nearly got spotted a couple of times by coastal craft. Those other guys, they died yesterday. No, wait a minute.' He closed his eyes. 'Jonesy died yesterday, Graham and Mack the day before.'

'How do you feel?'

'Lousy. Dry as a cork. Guess I need some water. If you guys have got a swimming pool on board, I'll drink that.' He laughed again.

The boat reached the *Florence Hurst*'s side and was hooked on. The electric engine at the davits started up and the boat began its tortoise-like upward crawl. O'Connor fell silent, puffing nervously at his cigarette.

Lincott was waiting for them when they came on board. His eyes flicked quickly over O'Connor as he was handed out. He nodded when Quinan gave him O'Connor's name and rank. 'I'm the doctor. Can you manage? The hospital is that way.' He nodded his head aft.

'Show me the way, healer,' O'Connor grinned. He turned to
Quinan and ostentatiously tugged at his forelock. 'Thank you,
Excellency, for saving my life. And I'm sorry you got your feet
wet. Salutations!' He saluted and turned away with the Doctor.

Lincott had unlocked the hospital. He and the American
walked in together. It was a middle-sized room containing six
iron bedsteads painted white, a small table and two chairs. A glass
drug cabinet filled with rows of bottles and ampoules and stainless steel instruments lined one bulkhead.

O'Connor looked around. 'This is Goddam depressing. You're
not putting me in one of those, are you?' He pointed to the
beds.

'We'll see.' Lincott indicated one of the chairs. 'Sit down.'

'I feel a bit weak,' O'Connor said. 'Otherwise okay.'

'It's understandable.' Lincott studied him. Sunburnt on the
cheeks, nose and forehead. That was always misleading. Thin,
but with a reserve of flesh on the stomach and rather flabby
pectorals. Eyes blood-injected. That could be the sun or lack of
Vitamin A or a combination of both. His skin was slightly rough.
That was a deficiency sign, too. Vitamin B lack. A quick check
showed that his gums were all right.

'Do you mind standing up?' He popped a thermometer into
O'Connor's mouth and let him stand there mumbling while he
pulled the loose-fitting pyjama pants down and examined his
privates.

The thermometer came out. 'Jesus, Doc!' The American
hauled at his pants. 'You think that's suffering from thirst, too?'

Lincott was studying the thermometer. One hundred degrees.
Again, probably the sun. Time would tell, but there was nothing
much wrong with the man. Debilitated, certainly. He had
probably been on a limited and starchy diet for some time. As a
matter of pure routine Lincott checked his heart, chest and pulse,
and found nothing out of the ordinary.

'You are going to live, Lieutenant.' Lincott smiled at the big
face with its heavy chin.

The American laughed and shook his head. 'Say, I just love
this Leftenant business. You Limeys! You're sure I'm okay?'

Lincott looked at him sharply. 'Of course I'm sure.'

The American bowed his head. 'Apologies, Effendi.' He looked
up in alarm. 'Say, what in hell are you doing?'

Lincott was filling a hypodermic. 'I'm going to give you a
booster shot. Vitamins, that's all. You're run down and have a
mild temperature. Then I think you should lie down this afternoon. If you feel all right later on you can join us for dinner.'

Sweat beaded O'Connor's forehead. 'I don't like the needle.'

'Why?'

'It's—I—well, in this prison camp they gave us shots, every now and again. Goddam blunt needles.'

'This needle has never been used before.' Lincott tried to be patient above his rising dislike of the man.

O'Connor studied him. 'Just vitamins, huh? Well, okay.'

Lincott gave him the injection and two aspirins for his temperature. Then the American had a long drink of water which Lincott made him take in small sips.

'Come on.' Lincott waved a hand. 'I agree, this is a pretty grim place. Our Radio Officer uses the spare cabin nearby for a complicated tape recorder and stereo set-up he plays with. But the cabin has beds. You can lie up there for the rest of the afternoon. Try and sleep, if you can. Feel like some food? You can't have much, you know.'

They were standing at the hospital door. O'Connor considered. 'Guess I could do with a steak and trimmings. And do you think you could dig up a beer?'

Lincott nodded. 'That's in order. About half-an-hour, probably. I'll show you the cabin.'

They started to go out of the door. At that moment a blaring, magnified and weirdly distorted voice shattered the heat-laden silence. It was a man's voice, American, intensely nasal, and there was a note of slobbering, vicious hatred in it that set Lincott's nerves on end. It bayed like a mad dog. Lincott caught only a few short phrases: 'Your sister is out whoring, soldier, because you're not there nights to keep her in check. You married? Know what your wife is doing? You, Colonel, you know what your kids are doing? Are you happy? Are you dedicatedly fighting a war nobody wants except the warmongering capitalists who are counting the gains on their steel shares? You think the little guy wants this war? You think John Dough wants it? You want to hear? Well, just in case you don't believe me, I've got a few interviews lined up that will . . .'

The voice cut off. There was an incredible silence.

'What in the name of Christ! What in the name of Christ!' O'Connor's face had turned a dirty grey colour. He cringed in the doorway, his body vibrating with a rough ague.

Lincott stared at him. His own stomach was still fluttering with reaction, but O'Connor had obviously had an ugly fright.

'Here, are you all right? It's nothing to be upset about.' Lincott put a reassuring hand on the man's shoulder. 'Sparks has recorded a chap called Tommy Tucker who broadcasts from North Vietnam to your field forces. He's a Yank. A traitor. We picked up the broadcast just outside Hong Kong.'

He tugged gently on the arm. 'Come on, now. Pull yourself together.'

O'Connor straightened slowly. He swiped a forearm at his wet forehead.

'You got any more nuts on this boat?' He stared at Lincott. 'In this camp I was in they had a tannoy blaring at us all the time. Propaganda, instructions, brainwashing. Do this, do that. They used to wake us up at night with it. It got so you never thought of anything else at all. You just waited for it. I thought this was it.'

Suddenly, horrifyingly, Lincott realized that O'Connor was going to weep. He had put his face against the cool bulkhead. Tears cascaded down his cheeks. His bulky shoulders shook with uncontrollable sobs.

Lincott went back into the hospital and fetched two tranquillizers and a glass of water. 'Here. Take these.'

The American gulped them down. His glistening eyes regarded Lincott with a sort of wild despair. 'It's a shitting Goddam world!'

'I know.' Lincott patted his shoulder. 'You've been through a hell of a rough time. That broadcast was most unfortunate. Come along. I'll show you the cabin.'

He led O'Connor a few yards down the alleyway, stopped at a door, knocked perfunctorily and entered.

Sparks was crouched at a big tape recorder in the middle of the cabin. He looked up, his sheep's eyes red with blood, his hair rumpled, his shirt hanging out.

Lincott regarded him dispassionately. He was about three-parts gone, but still functional. Tchaikovsky's *Pathétique* rebounded from the steel walls, deafeningly loud.

'In here,' Lincott said. He shouted at Sparks, 'Stop that bloody noise!'

Tchaikovsky was cut off in mid-bar. Sparks came groggily erect. Whisky fumes filled the cabin.

'Out!' Lincott jerked a thumb at the door. 'Out, or I'll inject you with anti-booze in your sleep!'

Sparks trotted out obediently. Lincott was curt with O'Connor, too. He could not help it. 'Lie down, now. Your food will be along. And the beer.'

He shut the door. Sparks was leaning against the alleyway bulkhead, solemnly regarding him.

'You bloody fool,' Lincott said cuttingly. 'You and that stupid Tommy Tucker recording. That bloke has just come out of a Vietcong prison camp. You nearly gave him a heart condition!'

Sparks collected himself. He picked words he could handle.

'Sorry about that. I thought I had the *Pathétique* on one hundred and forty but it must have been on one sixty or so.'

Lincott shook his head. 'You're supposed to be on duty. This is the last time I let you off. Now go back to your set. I'm coming there just now, and if I find a bottle you go straight to the Old Man.'

Sparks tittered. 'I can think of worse fates. Toodle-doo.' He turned around and stumbled off, one shoulder banging against the bulkhead as he went.

Lincott watched him go. Then he looked at the closed door of the cabin. Finally he shrugged and walked away to report. He was surprised at his own reactions. The incident had upset him more than it should. I could do with a beer, he thought. Which was also surprising, because he was not a drinking man, and it was only just after three in the afternoon.

CHAPTER THREE

IT WAS LATE AFTERNOON. Grove sat in his quarters directly below the bridge. He was reading a letter from his daughter:

'. . . and then after prayers Miss Frenton made a scene and said she was disgusted with our behaviour and she couldn't understand how big girls could behave in such an incredibly childish manner. Big girls! There are only big girls and little girls to Miss Frenton. Mummy says I am being terribly unfair, but I am positive that Miss Frenton is psychotic. She is a spinster, don't forget, and I think that she subconsciously resents our emergent womanhood. This has played upon her mind over the years to such an extent . . .'

Grove put the letter down and laughed. Holy Moses! When you were sixteen the world was a fine, fiery place, full of struggles and problems. There was a fresh, free smell to everything, like the earth after a rain. Everything about you was virgin: your palate, your nose, your ears, your eyes. All your senses were awakening. They were reaching out to touch. The brain was unfettered by habit, or dogma. It was an aromatic time when you were sixteen. The world was charged with pungency. The mind kicked out with a restless urgency, the way the body kicked in the womb.

He put the letter away and got up. He felt suddenly flat. I am forty-six, he thought. All I've got is the memory of those times. But they were strong. The nutty taste of a cigarette. The sweet, heady smell of a woman's groin. An overpowering sense of strength.

He shook his head. Thirty years later there wasn't much left. Now the cigarettes had a bitter taste like the harsh smell of fire-wood. The last woman he had been with had been his own wife, three months ago, and that had degenerated into the inevitable bitter whisperings in the dark.

He was caught up in a sudden, overwhelming mood of depression, and it was not just post-alcoholic. There was a way, he thought, a special magic formula for keeping the mind pristine. He had met a few people who had it. But mostly the mind got bruised and buffeted, gnarled along the way. You attained success but the by-products of a wrong turning some-where rubbed off. You were strung with tension and you drank too much.

Like me, he thought. And the Chief Officer knows it and is worried about it. And the Doctor knows it and looks down on me for it, through those damn supercilious eyes of his.

He went to the drink cabinet and poured himself a gin and tonic. Hookins had brought the ice twenty minutes ago, while he was in the shower, and already half of it had melted. Then he took the drink over to the window. He stood looking down on the *Florence Hurst*, stretching out ahead of him to the spear-pointed bows.

The tonic was sharp on his tongue, bitter with its hint of quinine. My ship, he thought. My iron mistress. He smiled. His four-hundred-and-ninety-foot lover. A wave of sentiment swept over him. The *Florence Hurst* was so undemanding, so willingly servient. If only his wife were like that. But he had lost her to her endless social work, so that whenever he returned home she looked at him vaguely, as though he were a stranger, a stranger who disrupted her busy schedules and demanded her body for his incontinent loving. His daughter, too, was not really his. He would lose her ultimately, to maturity and marriage. But the *Florence Hurst* was his. He was a damned fine seaman and the Company knew it and his officers knew it. Nobody would take the *Florence Hurst* away from him. Not while he still had his senses.

It was just a pity that she had to carry dead men.

The thought took him unawares. It irritated him violently, but the anger was mostly at himself for allowing the thought to intrude. He had been subconsciously warding it off all day.

Why the hell couldn't the French carry their own blasted dead? What was the matter with the Company? He was as superstitious as any other sailor and he had lied to his officers when he had told them that he had carried dead men before. It was true that cargo was cargo, and broadly speaking he would carry almost anything almost anywhere on the Far East run. But there were limits.

He had finished the drink. He went and poured another. Then he sat down at his desk and began to fiddle through some papers. But his mind was not on the work. After a minute he pushed them away and lit a cigarette, sitting quite still and staring across the cabin.

This leg of the voyage had had the most peculiar beginnings. First there had been the tense, claustrophobic atmosphere of Communist Haiphong. Then sixteen miles of tortuous navigation down the silted bends of the Cua Cam. That had set his nerves on edge. Then they had picked the strange American off the sampan at midday. And over everything, hovering like a shadow on his mind, had been the thought of the three thousand corpses in Number Three hold. It would be very dark in there. Would there be any sound above the ship's noises? Could you expect three thousand bodies to lie quite quietly?

He swore suddenly, out loud, and shook himself. He felt shut in. The heat was oppressive. He got up and checked the barometer but it was normal. There was that feeling in him that a storm was brooding over the horizon. It was a sense almost of fore-boding. There was an electrical impulse to the air. It worried him and made him uneasy.

He went back to his desk, took his half-empty glass and drained it. His wristwatch ticked the time at him. Six-thirty. Thank God. He had asked the passengers for drinks at seven, in the lounge. He could start changing.

He put the empty glass down and went into his cabin. He began to dress. But when he was only half-finished he stopped and con-sulted his watch. He made small estimates. Then he went to the cabinet again. There was time for one more drink.

Mary Fannin sat at her dresser. She was naked, and droplets of water from the shower still clung to her smooth skin. She had not bothered to dry herself. The aching heat was doing that.

The small travelling clock in front of her showed six-thirty. It was time to get dressed for the Captain's party. She shrugged, opened a drawer and began to fiddle reluctantly amongst its contents. I have so little, she thought, in every sense of the word, in possessions and in spirit.

She made an inventory in her mind: three dresses, three pairs of shoes, two pairs of nylons, a green plastic raincoat, some underthings, an old guitar in a canvas case. And the diamond pendant Glen Erley had given her.

She took the pendant out and held it up by the ends of the spider-web chain. It was small and expensive and glittered even in the cabin's dull light. She put it on and leant forward, looking at herself in the mirror, studying the diamonds as they hung clustered, pendulate, between her full breasts. Her mouth curved in a tiny smile. That is the way Glen would have liked me to dress, she thought. Just the pendant, a-glitter against the white skin. It would have made a great picture. One to show the boys.

The thought made her angry. She had excluded him for so long. It was not as though he mattered any more. There was no anger any more, no hurt, no churn of the stomach, no feeling as though the world had just begun or just ended or that rocks could sprout roots and the wind blow downward, the way it had once been. I am like a tree, she thought, blasted by lightning, but with none of the dark scars showing, but the tree is hollow, beneath.

She moved away from the mirror. It was wrong sitting there naked wearing just the pendant. There was something suggestive about it. The pendant and her nudity combined to give an impression of erotic expectancy when there was none.

She got up, went to the wardrobe, and took out a dress. She was very tired. She was always tired. She had seen a doctor about it in Hong Kong but physically there was nothing wrong with her. I guess, she thought, that I am plain worn out. When you gave so much of yourself it could reach a stage where there was nothing left, no reserve.

It took her fifteen minutes to dress and apply her make-up. Then she went back to the mirror and studied herself quite critically. Not bad, she thought. At least the Chief Officer, who looks at me with those sharp, appraising, probing eyes, will see that I can be clean. He was a nice guy, that Mister Quinan. And he probably had a plain wife and six brats. All the nice ones were married. She thought of Glen Erley, then shook her head, reversing her phraseology. No, not all the married ones were nice.

She let herself out of the cabin. The alleyway stretched out ahead of her like the inside of a rectangular telescope. It was sparsely lit by dim bulbs in the ceiling. She began to walk along it towards the door at the far end, listening to the tap of her heels, her body moving through alternate bars of light and shadow.

The cork came out with an explosive, ringing pop. Champagne frothed volcanically out of the mouth of the bottle and ran down its domed, jade-coloured sides on to Hookins's white-gloved hands.

He swore, flicked his fingers, then picked up the bottle and filled the six glasses on his tray, trying to control the trembling of his hand.

He had a bruise on his ribs where Dike Ludd's fist had landed, and his chest hurt when he breathed. His legs ached from the way he had walked, scouring the ship to find the missing charm. All the time, the eyes of Hawes and Ludd and the others had been on him. Every time he turned a corner, every time he went down an alleyway, they were there. But he hadn't found it. He felt emasculated without it: weak and gutless. And there was the growing terror of what would happen to him now.

The woman has it, he thought. She ripped it off my belt when I was . . . He closed his eyes for a moment, forcibly preventing his mind from going any further with the picture. God forgive me, he prayed. God forgive me for my madness.

He picked up the tray and took it to the group standing near the port bulkhead.

'Champagne, Sir?'

Attwell turned. 'No thanks, son. But dig out a tomato juice for me, will you?'

Hookins nodded and moved to Mercy Attwell.

'Champagne, Madam?'

She looked across the circle of people and smiled at Mary Fannin. 'What are you going to have, Miss Fannin?'

She looks, Mary thought, as fine-drawn as a terribly tightly strung wire. She was very beautiful, though. Her pale face was devoid of any make-up except for a dusting of powder over the cheeks. Her dark bobbed hair clung to her cheeks and her huge haunting eyes moved restlessly, hovering, soaring, darting like a dragonfly amongst the group.

Mary smiled back. 'Champagne makes me giggle. I guess it will do for a start.'

'That sounds good.' Mercy Attwell took a glass off the tray. 'A giggle now and then won't do any of us any harm.'

Carl Attwell turned towards her. His hand lightly warded the drink away from her lips. 'Darling, you . . .'

'Darling,' she interrupted, mimicking his tone, 'they don't serve sarsaparilla on British boats. I will have the champagne, please.'

It was a difficult moment for Attwell. The 'please' had been pure habit, and he knew it. He tried his best. 'I wonder if you should, honey? You're not all that used to it and . . .'

Mercy Attwell's eyes had flicked around the room and come back. They were like stones. 'Just you try and stop me,' she said softly.

Blood rose into Attwell's face and neck while a struggle went on within him. Then he smiled: 'Sure, honey. If that's what you want.'

There were six of them in the group, including Stephen Lincott, McBlain the Chief Engineer, a small sad-faced, worried-looking man, and Lucien Puget.

Puget broke the awkward pause. He turned to Attwell. 'What is this terrible affair I hear about in Hong Kong? A murder, I believe, and worse.' He grinned unrepentantly. 'You must understand, I do not wish to gossip, but it became a little tiresome, cooped up with a bunch of Maoists while my work was proceeding. I am eager for news.'

Attwell smiled and then grew serious. 'It wasn't very nice, Sir. It happened the night before we sailed. A British Army major and his wife were murdered outside the city. He must have been killed first, because she'd been raped five, maybe six times before she—she met her end.' He managed, despite the sickening euphemism, not to sound unctuous.

'Communists, I suppose? There was that trouble in Hong Kong, about that time.'

Attwell shook his head. 'Apparently not. The police were sure it was Caucasians. It could have been . . .'

There was a resounding, tinny crash as Hookins dropped his tray. White-faced, he bent and began to mop up the mess.

Quinan came in at that moment. Mary Fannin gave him a brief, fluttering wave of her hand, surprised at her own pleasure in seeing him. It is his strength, she thought. He is a strong person. He radiates it.

He came over to her, smiling. He had thinning brown hair and his face was mahogany dark against his white uniform.

'Hi,' she said solemnly.

His eyes took in the dress, the neat hair, the carefully-applied make-up. 'The South China Sea is good for girls, I notice.'

She laughed and fingered her hair. 'Oh, say! I don't look that good.'

'You do, you know. After the show, maybe we can have dinner somewhere.'

She smiled at him. 'I might just take you up on that when we get to Marseilles.'

He winked. 'I know a place.'

Hookins came past and Quinan stopped him. The steward stood trembling, waiting for the order.

Quinan said softly, 'You all right, Willy?'

Hookins' eyes avoided Quinan's. 'Yes, Sir.'

'Sure? If you like, Sloan can relieve you for a while. I'll fix it with the Purser.'

Hookins had moist brown eyes like a puppy. 'I'm all right, Sir, thank you.'

Quinan nodded. 'Okay.' He turned to Mary. 'Would you like something, Miss Fannin?'

She held up her empty glass. 'Guess I'm due for a refill. But I can't stay with the champagne. I'll have whatever you have.'

Quinan ordered two whiskies with water and ice and Hookins went away.

Proctor, just arrived, drifted up, elegant in his glinting white tropicals, very lean, tanned and debonair.

He raised his eyebrows when he saw Mary Fannin. 'Well, well. If it isn't honeychile. Where have you been hiding all the glam?' Then he moved on and gently touched Mercy Attwell on the shoulder.

She looked about. Her face registered quick, delighted surprise. She became suddenly alive. They began to talk animatedly while Lincott, withdrawn, watched them over his drink. Hormones, thought Mary Fannin wryly, were amazing things. Lincott was wearing his heart red, rampant and firmly fixed to his sleeve. But her money was on Proctor, who was doing a very fine job in his stock Don Juan role, his insincerity radiating, to a keen eye, as patently as Lincott's dedication. And it was all rather silly when one remembered that Mercy Attwell was a deeply religious woman, and that her husband was on board.

The open door clattered as somebody collided with it on his way in. Grove had arrived. There was an exaggerated, loose-jointed freedom to his movements and Quinan, detecting the signs, felt a moment of intense disappointment. But it was coloured with anger. Damn it, Wally, he thought, you promised me this morning. I thought you meant it.

Grove had reached a stage of cheerful eloquence. 'Sorry I'm late. Captain's privilege. I was ready to leave when the Purser called with a whole lot of confounded items I had to go through. Most annoying.'

He looked around the group. 'Mister and Mrs. Attwell, Miss Mannin, Mister Puget. Welcome aboard. I know that three out of four of you have been with us since Hong Kong, but the weather hasn't been too good and we haven't seen much of you. Then on top of that we had to get bottled up in Haiphong for twenty-four hours. So this seemed the first real opportunity for a good old British get-together.'

'*L'Angleterre est une nation de boutiquiers.*' Puget quoted solemnly the phrase attributed to Napoleon. 'The truth of the matter is that the Captain has been delaying giving you a drink to increase his Company's profit.'

They all laughed, even the Americans who didn't understand the French but caught the meaning. Smiling, Grove half-bowed to him. 'Touché, Monsieur.' He ignored Puget's stage wince at his pronunciation. 'Mister Puget joined us in Haiphong, of course. He represents the War Graves people.'

'What he means,' Puget said, 'but is too delicate to say, is that I am in charge of all those bodies in Number Three.' He rolled his eyes at Mercy Attwell. 'You are not afraid of ghosts, I hope, Madame.'

She reacted with a spontaneous, schoolgirl giggle. Merriment took her and her shoulders shook. Her eyes watered and she put her hand on Proctor's arm. She had finished her champagne and was sharing his drink with him. She looks, Mary Fannin thought, as though she has never, ever, been really gay. She is exploding with it.

A voice came suddenly from the door: 'Well now, isn't that nice. They're giving me a party.'

Everyone turned. O'Connor sauntered slowly into the room, grinning. He looked refreshed. He was shaven and his hair was combed. He was wearing a pair of pale denim slacks, a light-weight linen jacket and an open-neck shirt.

'The pants are Mister Proctor's.' He inclined his head at the officer. 'And the jacket, I believe, belongs to Admiral Quinan, who brought his old red lifeboat over and hooked me off that basketwork shoe-rack this morning.' His eyes found Quinan's. 'Once more my thanks and felicitations, O Lord and Master.'

'Welcome aboard, Lieutenant.' Grove had managed to get a drink from Hookins and finish it in less than five minutes. Briefly, he introduced O'Connor to those who hadn't met him. Then he turned to the American, as sincere and open-hearted as six drinks could make him. 'I am very glad indeed that we managed to turn up when we did. I am just sorry that we were too late to save the other poor fellows.'

O'Connor's full lips went down at the corners. 'Listen, Captain. There was nothing you or anybody else could have done for those guys. They were finished. They'd been in the camp longer than me. They were dying when they got on the boat.' He looked around at them. 'There is nothing you can do to stop a guy dying when he's got the wings of the Angel of Death beating against his face.' He made a brutal, chopping motion with the edge of one big hand. 'Finito, buddy.'

Hookins brought him a drink. O'Connor took it and raised it, looking at Grove. 'To you, Captain, and all your men. I want to say a big American thank you. It was rough out there. Very rough. I'm mighty grateful to be here.' His eyes went to the

Attwells, then Mary Fannin. 'And it's great to see free American faces again. Here's to the good old Stars and Stripes.'

It was over-simplified. Over-corned. They drank in an acute silence, the Americans in embarrassment. Then Proctor cleared his throat. 'How many of you Americans were there in your camp, Lieutenant O'Connor?'

O'Connor shook his head, grinning. 'Jeez, I love this Leftenant crap. You guys trying to brainwash me, or something?' Then he looked at Proctor. 'Must have been going on two hundred. But it wasn't just Americans. There were two Aussies as well. Crazy guys. Their names were Cockett and Smith. They didn't like the Viets. They wouldn't stay in line. They got beaten every day.'

This thought seemed to take him away from them. His voice trailed off and he stared fixedly over their heads as the seconds ticked by. The group moved awkwardly. Then suddenly he was back with them. His voice had become loud. 'They were mad, those guys. It was farting against thunder, what they did. And then the Americans got hardnose too. Day in and day out, guys got beaten. They seemed to like it. They would scream at the guards, "Piss off, you Goddam Commie!" There were short rations and forced marches and beatings and wakings in the middle of the night, but it didn't help. All the time the guys were shouting, "Piss off, Commie!" It echoed over the compound like a crazy battle-cry.'

In the intense silence O'Connor glared around at them, his body trembling. 'You got to stay in line, you want to live!' he shouted. He looked wildly at them. Then he swore and drank all his whisky in one tumultuous convulsion of his throat.

There was a long, awkward pause. Then Lincott said in his clear accents, 'Here, Lieutenant, have this drink.' He passed across his own, untouched. His tones were as cold as if he had been prescribing a sedative. They seemed to restore the American to normality.

He smiled weakly. 'Thanks, healer. Guess I got a little upset, back there.'

They went in to dinner.

The cook had done his best. But he had made the mistake of serving, in the best British tradition: soup, an entrée, roast beef and Yorkshire pudding, and plum duff. In the tropics it was a nightmare meal and by the time they were finished sweat was running in rivulets down the cheeks of the diners.

Wine had been served with each course, including sherry with the sweet. Grove was finally showing the pace. He had eaten hardly anything, but he had stayed with the wine. A cigar clamped between his teeth, he unsteadily led the way back into the lounge for coffee.

They had been discussing the command of a ship.

'It's not easy,' he said loudly. 'You're alone, when you're Captain. All alone.' Even now, he was not slurring his words. 'You've got to bear all that responsibility, by yourself. It's not easy.' He took the cigar from his mouth and clumsily tapped thick ash on to the carpet. 'For example, take . . .' he trailed away, frowned, and then laughed thickly. 'Now where the hell was I?'

There was an awkward silence, broken by Proctor. He moved to Attwell's side. 'Sir, your wife would very much like to see the bridge. Would you mind if I showed her around?' He turned to Grove. 'If you don't mind, of course, Sir.'

Grove nodded drunkenly. He knew that his articulation was about to fail so he shoved the cigar back into his mouth and mumbled through it. 'Show her where the hell you like, Peter. Huh, Attwell?' He grunted with laughter. 'Harmless boy, this. Good fellow.' He flicked his head at Quinan. 'Come here, Gil. Wanna discuss something with you. Ship's business. C'mere.'

Quinan had been standing with Mary Fannin and Lincott. He excused himself and walked over.

Grove took him into a corner of the lounge, on the port side where the library filled the bulkhead from deck to ceiling. When they were alone Grove cocked a bloodshot eye at his Chief Officer. He said softly: 'I'm blind, Gil old boy. Take me to bed.'

Attwell was saying to Proctor, 'Why, sure, son. Show her the bridge. There's somebody up there?'

'Oh, yes.' Candour shone from Proctor's eyes. 'Mister Lucas, the Third. The helmsman. The standby man. It's all perfectly okay, Sir.'

Attwell smiled. 'Oh, I'm sure. It's just that she's all I've got and she's kind of precious.' He looked at Mercy. 'I will be in my cabin in half an hour,' he said firmly.

The *Florence Hurst* ploughed quietly through the velvet night. Mercy Attwell was panting from her climb up the vertical ladder that led on to the flying bridge. Below her feet, in the lighted wheelhouse, Lucas was winking at the helmsman.

'Oh, it's beautiful up here.' Mercy Attwell looked at the heavens. 'See the stars, like a tapestry.' She pointed a slim arm and then padded over to the helm. Proctor had made her remove her high-heeled shoes for the climb. 'Why is there another wheel, here?'

'This is the flying bridge,' Proctor said. 'We also call it the

monkey island. You can work from up here, if necessary. Apart
from the masts, this is the highest part of the ship.'

It is wonderful, Mercy thought, to be a girl again. No, not
'again'. I have never been one.

When Proctor put his arm around her she went still. She
had known that it was going to happen but she trembled with
excitement nevertheless. The heavens sang to her and the air
was thick with the scent of roses.

She went hard up against him, her cheek on his chest. 'Peter,'
she said, 'I am married. I am . . .'

He kissed her. Suddenly any doubts, any reservations that
might have been there were gone. She responded eagerly, clinging
to him, thrusting her body rampantly against his.

Proctor put his hand over her breast. Mercy broke away,
gasping. 'No. No, Peter. I . . .'

'Yes,' he said.

Her breath was roaring in her own ears. When he kissed her
again she let him leave his hand there while they strained
together. Her body raged and ached with agonizing want. Her
breasts were hard with it. When he let her go she stood
drooped before him. 'Oh, Peter. Oh, dear God, leave me.'

He said fiercely, 'I must see you tomorrow night. It's useless
now. Will you? Can you fix it somehow?'

Her hair was wild. The dress was in disarray about her breasts.
'No! I can't! You must understand. I'm not an ordinary woman,
Peter. It's not just because I'm married that I am saying this.
Carl and I have a way of life together. If we want people to believe
Carl, to understand him and the importance of what he says,
then we have to live our own lives properly, without moral
blemish. I . . .'

'To hell with Carl. To hell with your way of life.' He took her
hand and held it tightly, as though he wanted to crush it with
the intensity of his conviction. 'You're young. You've never had
a chance, never known what life can be like. Forget all the
bloody ifs and buts.'

She pulled her hand away. She dropped her arms and stood
looking at him, her beautiful face congested, creased with the
captive, explosive exaltation within her. 'Oh hell, Peter.' She
smiled weakly. 'I'm not even supposed to swear, and I'm doing
just that. What must I do? What must I say?'

'Say that you'll come.' He came against her and held her
around the waist, looking down into her upturned face. 'Promise.'

She shook her head, smiling. 'I can't promise. Anything can
happen. But I'll try. Surely that's good enough. Your cabin,
about nine o'clock?'

'You're a doll,' he said, and kissed her again.

O'Connor was sitting on the edge of his bed, taking his shoes off. There was a tap at the door and Sparks came in.

O'Connor grinned. 'Well, if it isn't Mister Osgood himself. Say, where were you when the bugles blew? We missed you at dinner, old buddy.'

Sparks's eyes, weak and sheep-like, heavily bloodshot, fixed slowly on the American. He needed a shave and his rumpled shirt was dirty. There was black grime under his finger nails. He was beaded with sweat.

He lifted one hand and twiddled the fingers. It was his standard greeting. 'Hallo. I've been busy. I want to fix a few things here, if you don't mind.'

'Be my guest.' O'Connor lit a cigarette and watched him.

Sparks hovered over the tape recorder. It was a big Japanese model with four tracks and stereo speakers. He wound the tape back a way, his eyes on the footage counter. After a moment he pressed playback and the sobbing violins of the *Pathétique* once more filled the room.

A slow, contented grin spread over his round face. 'I had to hear that before I went to bed.' He became serious. 'Tchaikovsky was a homosexual, you know.' His eyes strayed over the recorder as though he were wishing it were a piano, and that his blunt fingers were stroking the delicate keys. 'But his mind was beautiful.'

The suffused eyes turned to O'Connor. 'That's all that matters, isn't it? I mean, the beauty of the spirit supersedes the carnality of the body. The ugly things of the flesh.'

O'Connor shook his head and laughed. 'You're way above me, buddy. I piloted a jet. Music was never my strong point.' He delved under the bed suddenly. 'Listen, buster, what about a hooker? I fast-talked my way into a bottle after the Captain got canned and the party broke up.'

Sparks studied O'Connor thoughtfully. 'Grove is hitting the bottle. He's going to go over the hill if he doesn't watch out.' It sounded queerly pathetic, coming from him. 'Did you know that he is going to have me fired when we get home? Three years I've been with this ship.' He looked at the bottle O'Connor was holding and sighed, his lips bulging with the force of the expelled breath. 'I've been in some heavy weather, today. I've had a few.' A look of earnestness came into his expression. 'What people don't understand is that I become emotionally involved in my music. It drains me.' He smiled again. 'I suppose I could have a . . . hooker, as you call it. A nightcap.'

'That's great.' O'Connor unscrewed the cap. 'Sorry, no glasses, old buddy-boy. Have a pull.'

Osgood took the bottle and upended it. 'Phew! Brandy, isn't it?'

'No, Bourbon. They had a bottle, believe it or not. Great, isn't it?'

'It's not bad.' Sparks gave the bottle back.

O'Connor laughed. 'You Britishers are crazy. You'll have me talking like a Limey soon. "It's not bad." That means you like it, huh?' He took a quick swig at the bottle. 'Ouch. This stuff hits you right on the peptic ulcer.' He fiddled with the cap a moment, tossing it up and down in his palm. 'Say. You've got this recording of this crazy guy called Tommy Tucker, haven't you? You know, the fellow who gives the American servicemen the old Tokyo-Rose spiel?'

'Yes.' Sparks pressed a button on the machine and the reels whirred backward. 'I'll let you hear some. It's too ghastly for words. Listen to . . .'

'Can it!' O'Connor flung up a hand. 'I don't want to hear him. He would make any decent American puke. But speaking as an American citizen, as a guy who would do his own share of killing if I ever got my hands on the bastard's throat, wouldn't you do me a little favour, old buddy-boy, considering that you nearly gave me a heart-attack when I heard him, and erase the thing, huh? It's all too close still—the camp, the guards, you know? If I hear that voice again I'll flip.'

Sparks considered him for a moment. 'May I have another drink?'

'Sure.' O'Connor passed the bottle.

Osgood swigged and gave it back. 'You want me to erase this recording of Tommy Tucker?'

O'Connor threw his hands apart, palms outward. 'Suit yourself. It's just that I'm going to have nightmares while I know I might hear it.'

Sparks looked at him. 'I hope you don't think I'm being rude, but I'll leave it for a while. It interests me. You don't mind?'

O'Connor extinguished the cigarette. 'How could I? It's yours, buddy.' He took out the bottle again. 'One for the road?'

Sparks shook his head. He put the cover over the tape recorder and locked it. 'I've had it. I'm going to get some shut-eye.' He got up, teetered. He was now very drunk. 'Toodle-doo.'

O'Connor laughed. 'Toodle-doo.'

Grove's body was thin and hot under Quinan's encircling arm.

The smell of sour perspiration and stale alcohol hung over him like an aura. It made Quinan's stomach turn.

He opened the door to Grove's quarters. 'Okay. Come on.'

'I'm all right. Lemme go.' Unsteadily, Grove walked in. He homed inevitably to the drink cabinet. 'We gotta have another drink, you and me. One for the road. Old pals, you and me, huh, Gil ol' boy?' He nodded his head loosely as he splashed whisky into two glasses. 'Ol' pals.'

Quinan took his glass. 'Good luck.' The whisky was without water or ice. It burned a raw passage down his throat.

Grove looked solemn. ' "Good luck", he says.' He cackled suddenly with morbid humour. 'We're going to need all the luck there is.' He looked at Quinan through dull eyes that were struggling to focus. 'You believe in omens?'

'No.'

Grove swayed suddenly and corrected. 'Well, I do. It was a bad omen, seeing that boy killed this morning in his jet. It gave me a pre . . . premonition of death.'

Quinan sipped at his drink, wanting to get away. 'Don't talk nonsense, Wally. Why don't you go to bed? We've all had enough.'

' 'Cause I don' wanna. And it's not nonsense.' This last drink was hitting him very hard. He flung out a hand and nearly lost his balance. Whisky slopped on to his white jacket. 'To see that, when you're carrying a cargo of death!'

His vision was now definitely blurring. He was looking only in Quinan's general direction. And he had lost track of what he was saying, standing there swaying like a tree in a high wind, drunkenly mumbling to himself.

Quinan took him by the arm. 'Come on, go to bed.'

This time Grove allowed himself to be led. He seemed suddenly to find the thread of his monologue as he staggered through with Quinan into his cabin.

'I'm a superstitious old bastard, Gil. We're gonna have trouble. I feel it in my bones.' He collapsed on to the bed. 'Oh Christ. Bloody room's going round.'

Quinan went to the foot of the bed and pulled Grove's shoes off. 'You better let me help you out of your clothes.'

'Nah.' Grove was staring up at the ceiling. His voice had become thick and drowsy. 'I'll piss in my pants if I want to. Not the first time. Not the first time, huh, Gil?'

No, Quinan thought. Nor the last, by the looks of things. He leaned over the bed and unfastened the two top buttons of Grove's tunic. 'I'll be off now.'

'Not so fast, not so fast.' Grove's eyes swivelled suddenly and met Quinan's. For one moment he looked surprisingly sober. 'You're in a hell of a hurry.' He giggled and winked. 'Betcha I know where you're going. Going to the Fannin bird's cabin, eh?' He came up on one elbow. 'I've seen the way you watch her.' He lowered his voice. 'She any good? Got an experimental look about her. She any good, Mister Quinan?'

Quinan remembered that strange, lost look in Mary Fannin's eyes. I doubt, he thought reluctantly, that she's any good. But he didn't want to think about her in that way. He looked down at Grove's eyes, so red they looked contused, and experienced a sudden feeling of revulsion. 'I've never asked her.'

'You lie, you bastard.' Grove fell back on the pillows. 'I'll bet you're filling your boots. I envy you. That old bag I married, you've got to go down on your knees and pray for it. But the Fannin girl . . .' He stopped suddenly and came bolt upright. 'I think I'm going to puke.' He put his hands to his head, trying to control its whirling. 'Oh, Jesus.'

'Good night,' Quinan said. He turned slowly and walked through to the door. When he had his hands on it he heard the sudden strained, frantic vomiting from the cabin. He hesitated a moment, torn between sympathy and anger. No, he thought, not sympathy, pity. He'd been talking to the shell of the Walter Grove of twelve months ago. But the feeling of pity passed. Let him sleep in his own puke, he thought. Perhaps that would make him lay off for a while. Abruptly, he opened the door and went out, shutting off the sounds of Grove's retching. He stood still, staring at the door. Then he sighed deeply and wearily. What he wanted now, more than anything, was to be cool and clean. A cold shower, crisp clothes that weren't sweat-limp, a green garden a thousand miles from here. He shook his head. Thinking like that was simply emulating Grove, but in another way. It was a weakening, as much a form of escapism as his drinking. What a hell of a day and night this has been, he thought, and went down the companion-way.

Outside the passenger accommodation he nearly bumped into Hookins. 'You're around late, Hookins.'

'Yes, Sir.' Hookins wouldn't look at him. 'I've been to the American, Lieutenant O'Connor, Sir, to find out whether he has early morning tea or coffee.'

There was a bulge under Hookins's crisp white jacket. The Yank, thought Quinan wearily, has bummed liquor and passed some of it on to this kid. Oh hell. It didn't matter. With the trouble Hookins was in, whatever it was, a few shots before he went to bed would do him more good than harm.

'Still don't want to talk, Willy?'

Hookins looked at him with large, exhausted eyes. 'About what, Sir?'

'You know. Mister Lucas told me what happened today.'

'There's nothing to say, Sir.'

Quinan shrugged. 'It's up to you, boy.'

'Yes, Sir.' Hookins bent over in the typical steward's crouch and hurried off. He had not gone very far when Quinan hailed him.

'Oh, Hookins!'

'Yes, Sir.' Hookins stopped. There was still the wire-thin tremble to his body.

'What's happened to that charm you always wear?' Quinan pointed to the naked belt and its loose, dangling brass chain under Hookins's gaping jacket. 'I've never seen you without it before.'

Hookins went a chalky colour. He cringed against the bulkhead and stared at Quinan with his frightened-rabbit eyes. There was a long silence while Quinan looked at him in amazement.

'I've lost it, Sir.' It was a far-away whisper, almost unheard in the long, gleaming length of the alleyway.

There was another silence while they stared at each other. Then Hookins quivered with a sudden, involuntary tremor and was gone, disappearing with a thump of the door at the far end.

Quinan headed for his quarters. An earlier thought returned to him, but he shortened it. What a hell of a night. His footsteps rang along the alleyway, echoing in the early-silent ship.

CHAPTER FOUR

STEPHEN LINCOTT sat alone in his cabin. He was wearing only his underpants, because a naked body gave an illusion of coolness.

His diary lay open before him, already headed 'Tuesday'. He was a keen and dedicated diarist. Now he picked up his pen, the silver one his father had given him for his thirtieth birthday, and began to write:

9.30 p.m. Or perhaps I should have put 21.30 hours. I am still fooled by the twenty-four-hour clock and have to do silly calculations to find the time.

I am sleepy, probably because I have done nothing much all day. The weather is quite perfect, if you discount the insufferable heat. The water is like a duck pond. We sighted a big Yank carrier early this morning, very far away. Made a monstrous blip on the radar. Otherwise, nothing, which is strange. The South China Sea is normally a busy place, especially now with all the material the Americans are pumping into Vietnam. It is almost as though other ships are avoiding us, as though they sense what we carry. On second thoughts that was rather a foolish thing to say. I am a doctor, and bodies are bodies. In fact, who knows how honest the Viets have been? The coffins might be empty. But it looks as though I have become something of a sailor as well as a medico. I cannot deny a slight feeling of unease, probably because I detect the same symptoms in a person as sensible and level-headed as Gil Quinan. I know he doesn't like the idea. He will be relieved to see this particular section of our cargo dumped on the quay at Marseilles. Render unto de Gaulle the things that are de Gaulle's. Thank God I don't believe in ghosts.

I have been consulted only twice since leaving Hong Kong. The Fannin girl asked for tranquillizers. She has something very unhappy in her past which she was not prepared to tell me. Physically she is strong. I am no psychiatrist, but I think I detect plenty of mental strength too, more than she realizes. It's a pity she won't tell me what it's all about.

Then I had to treat Max Lucas this morning for a very badly bruised instep. It was a strange injury, looked very much like the imprint of a woman's heel. No comment, but cheers for Miss Fannin.

Our American P.O.W. is an odd sort of duck. Other than a vitamin deficiency there was never much wrong with him. I think he was badly treated in the prison camp. I am sorry for him, but I can't say that I am drawn to him.

I am worried about Grove. Our relationship, for one reason and another, has never been very good, but he is still my concern. He is hitting the bottle very hard and got thoroughly motherless (Peter Proctor's phrase) again tonight. That makes it three nights in a row.

Osgood is going downhill mentally. He is manifesting very strong signs of the alcoholic psychosis. I have spoken to Grove, but all he will admit is that Sparks is incompetent. Perhaps this is fellow-feeling. He says Osgood will be paid off when we get home, but my own opinion is that the problem is more pressing. I think Sparks is due to fold very soon. His liver is packing up. He hardly eats at all. He won't let me come near him since we tried the Antabus. I hope to God he lasts until we reach Singapore where I can get a second opinion and perhaps convince Grove. Sparks should be removed as soon as possible, and a new man flown in.

Lincott stopped writing and sucked the pen thoughtfully. His thoughts had moved on. And with this next entry he was strangely reluctant, even in the privacy of his diary, to reveal himself fully. He wasted two lines while he thought, drawing a series of neat, interlocking cubes. Then, finally, he wrote:

Mercy Attwell is a most beautiful woman, probably the loveliest person I have ever known. I sincerely hope that she does not become involved with Proctor and his song-and-dance-act partner, Max Lucas. I do not like them.

He closed the diary abruptly and put his pen down. There were other things he had wanted to say, but his thoughts had suddenly soured.

He got on to his bed, lying on top of the sheets, and picked up the book on the locker. It was an old copy of *Martin Rattler* that he had bought in Hong Kong. He began to read, knowing now that sleep would not come easily.

CHAPTER FIVE

IT WAS FIVE O'CLOCK on Wednesday afternoon. The dappled Nan Hai parted beneath the *Florence Hurst*'s sharp bows, giving way in an explosion of foam, of sundered water. But it swept in again astern in the form of a strong, relentless, following swell. The sun, canted over in the west, still lacked the crimson suffusion of evening. It hung on the starboard quarter, throwing the foredeck into early gloom. On the bridge it highlighted Lucas's flaxen hair and made pockets of shadow in the hollows of his face.

He limped as he crossed the port bridge wing to where Peter Proctor stood. It was Quinan's watch, but the two of them often talked up there. He favoured his right foot. Every time he put it down a pulse of pain shot through it. That Yank bitch Fannin had done it on Monday night. If ever I've been wrong, he thought. But he was still puzzled. She had those been-around eyes. The knowledge in them was plain to see, whether she was talking about the weather or asking where her luggage had to be stowed. A woman couldn't conceal a thing like that, especially with a body as ripe as hers. He had read all the signals and made his plans accordingly, confident of an interesting voyage.

Until he'd got his instep tramped on.

He was still shaking his head like a young grizzly bear, a wounded grizzly bear, when he reached Proctor. It had been a painful incident in more ways than one. His loins were throbbing with unreleased want. Every time he moved, his crutch ached. It served to goad his memory. He wasn't going to forget it. Oh hell, no, he told himself bitterly.

Proctor had his chin resting on his folded hands while he studied the empty foredeck. He did not move when Lucas arrived.

Lucas stood next to him. There was no sense of lack when he was with Proctor, unlike when he was with Quinan. Quinan had that bloody funny way of looking at you that made you feel inadequate, even when he was smiling, and you weren't sure whether it was because of your inadequacy.

He nudged Proctor in the ribs. 'I see you made it, last night. It's written all over your haggard countenance. Come on, spill the beans!'

Proctor stirred and passed a hand over his face. He was still hungover. Whenever he broke a wind he tasted gin. But he felt beatific, even if it was rather difficult to sort out what had happened. He felt as though he had been passed through a hammer-mill.

He looked at Lucas and grinned weakly. '*Da mihi castitatem et continentiam, sed noli modo*. That, old chap, means "Give me chastity and continency, but do not give it yet".'

'Shove the Latin.' Lucas trembled vicariously, prodded by his own explosive frustration. 'What happened?'

Proctor felt a twinge of unease. They had always done this, he and Lucas. They had always held post mortems the next day, up here on the bridge wing. But this time he was strangely reluctant. Want stored up ten years had no limits. The fire had been a raging conflagration that had consumed both him and Mercy Attwell, as though the heat in the cabin had imparted itself into their bodies. It caught him by the throat even now to remember his bare body streaming sweat in great waves, the juniper-scented gin and his head a great vague balloon, his cotton-spittled mouth in which the frantic words dried out and his body straining beyond pleasure in an eternal frenetic romp that had no limits upon the sweat-sodden bed.

Ah God ah God ah God ah God. The gin rushing crystal out of the bottle, the warm water, the sticky cork of his mouth. Tangled, vastly-crumpled sheets. Those long, strong, clamping legs with the hollow athletic flanks. And the crazy poem that kept running through his mind about the girl who was nine-teenly firm-flanked, flat-bellied, and slim-shanked, russetly-nippled the colour of shells. But by God he'd never had a twenty-nine-year-old near-virgin on his hands, the clot who'd written that. And all the time the Ah God ah God ah God ah God, on and on, a sort of sobbing paean of praise. Peter, Peter. Peter, you're good. My God, I'm good, I know I'm good. More gin, clear like a rushing stream, treacherously sweet upon his tongue. The harsh carpet under his feet. The ravished bed. The sweat beaded upon her belly like tears. Ah God ah God ah God ah God . . .

Proctor passed a hand across his face. Lucas was staring at him. To hell with you, he thought, suddenly angry. This memory was like a barred light, it was brightness and shadow, it was kaleidoscopic with explosive patterns of movement that had left him blinded and vague from their intensity. It could not be put into words. It would become tame with the telling. And shabby.

Proctor looked at Lucas. He did not want to offend him. He opened his mouth to say something innocuous, to gloss over what had developed into a stubborn refusal to tell him anything. But the words never came.

The *Florence Hurst*'s stern lifted, as though she were tucking up her skirts to accommodate the swell that heaved under her. In that moment they heard the frantic scream of the engines howling up from the bowels of the ship through the fanlight on the boat deck. Then sudden silence as the governor cut in, the engine was shut down, and the telegraph, rung from below, jangled on the bridge. Almost instantly came the flat, smacking sound of Quinan's palm on the bridge telegraph handle, slamming the lever over to 'stop'.

The *Florence Hurst* seemed to wallow a moment over the swell. Lucas clutched the bridge rail and Proctor, not as quick, slammed into it. Then silence.

'What the hell?' Lucas had gone white around the mouth. His heart was drumming with quick fright. He and Proctor stared at each other for the moment that it took them to adjust. Then they turned in unison and ran for the wheelhouse.

The door was open against the heat. They crowded through it and found Quinan there, his hand still on the telegraph. Proctor had a sudden thought that Quinan was carved out of teak. He was the colour of it, against the white of his uniform. But the life in his eyes showed that there was no wood in him.

'In God's name, Gil. What the blazes has happened?' Proctor was nearly stuttering.

'We've dropped our screw.' Quinan took his hand from the telegraph. His movements were steady and sure. 'I've sent for the Old Man. He'll be along in a moment.' He looked at them while he fiddled for a cigarette, found one and lit it. 'Ever happened to you?'

God, Proctor thought. We've lost our propeller in the middle of the South China Sea. The bloody thing has fallen off and is probably still gurgling its way down to the bottom. There's the spare, God knows how many tons of it, clamped to the fore-end bulkhead of the poop deck house. Fitting it at sea was out of the question, although he'd heard stories about it being done. But it was either that or radio for a tow. And this calm bastard, he thought, is acting as though he's lost one of the rings for deck-quoits.

'No,' he said. 'It's never happened to me.'

'Or me.' Quinan drew on his cigarette. 'But I was wondering when it would. Everything is subject to corrosion, even propellers and their fittings.'

Proctor stared at him. The *Florence Hurst* ploughed on through the calm sea, her loss of momentum hardly noticeable. The momentum of her great steel body would force her on for more than a mile before she lost way. But she had died. The tremor of life that was always there in the faint quiver of her decks, the vibration that was the pulse-beat of her engines, had gone.

Proctor cleared his throat. 'So what do we do?' He looked beyond Quinan to Usher at the wheel. Usher's eyes were on the First Officer. He is not afraid, Proctor thought, because Quinan is not afraid. He draws his strength from Quinan. Quinan gave out strength like a pump, like a transfusion. He felt a quick resentment. That's all very well, he thought. You're built like a tree and you have this way of convincing and reassuring people, but your wife divorced you and you couldn't stop that.

'What would you do?' Quinan smiled and flicked ash.

Proctor considered. Quinan is too polite, he thought, to suggest that I should know. But he is implying that I should know. I should have given him the alternatives. He became confused between his clear resentment of Quinan on the one hand and his realization of Quinan's patently decent attitude on the other. The situation was too intricate for him, but before he could evolve an answer there was a clatter on the companion-way and Grove burst in through the chartroom door.

He stopped just inside the wheelhouse. He had been sleeping and his face was still indented with the red pattern of the pillow-creases. His eyes were hooded and bloodshot and his disarranged, greying hair, thin upon the scalp, was dark with sweat.

Grove's eyes swept across the three officers and stopped on Quinan. 'That was a hell of a thing to do, Gil. I was fast asleep. It's not really gone, is it?'

His voice was still thick with sleep.

Quinan nodded. 'I'm afraid so.'

Grove didn't want to believe it. But he felt the dead deck under his feet. And he knew his Chief Officer.

'Did we hit anything?'

'No.'

'So it just fell off. It just undid the lock-nut and slid away?' Grove's lips twisted.

Nobody answered him. He was filled with a wild anger and had to fight against his unreasoning impulse to grab Quinan and shake him out of his imperturbability. A tumult of half-thoughts tumbled through his confused mind. To be woken out of a dead sleep to hear this, he thought. But he was coming fully awake now and the main import of what had happened began to make itself known: days crippled; the staggering cost of a tow; a money loss that could escalate frighteningly as you worked out the endless snowballing permutations of lost profit; the owners' nagging, landlubberly incredulity. God!

Grove put shaking hands to his collar and fiddled with the buttons. 'Get McBlain up here.'

'He's on his way, Sir.'

Grove looked at Quinan. Yes, he thought, trust you. You would think of everything, including the fact that I am going to blame my Chief Engineer. But it's not your broad shoulders that have to carry the can, it is my narrow ones.

Frustration and anger boiled inside him. His stomach had become rock-hard with tension and there was the sour taste of acidity in his throat. His head manifested physically the mental dullness he was experiencing. It felt as though it were stuffed full of cotton. He had a dull headache. Part of the anger was directed at himself for what he felt was his fumbling inability to adjust. It was a bad thing, this. He should be crisply authoritative, competently and efficiently assessing the situation and giving the necessary orders; or, at the worst, humorously fatalistic. Whatever he did, anything would be better than standing here in an agonized silence, his officers in tableau behind him, waiting for McBlain.

Bitterness welled in him. Words tumbled out on his tongue before he could stop them. And he said them to nobody in particular, as he stood staring out of the bridge window.

'This is bloody marvellous. Really marvellous.' The anger and self-pity were suddenly too strong to control. He could not stop himself. 'The oldest ship in the Company. The worst Chief Engineer. What bleeding bloody luck. I'm star-crossed.' He turned suddenly to look at Quinan. 'It's incredible, isn't it, First, the luck I have? I'm star-crossed, eh?'

Quinan looked away. He met Usher's suddenly troubled eyes. He wanted to tell the man to go, but that was impossible. Instead he looked out at the deserted starboard bridge wing, hearing the scrape of a match as Grove lit a cigarette.

Lucas cleared his throat. 'We could fit the spare prop, surely, Sir? It's been done before. I . . .'

'Shut up!' Grove whirled on him and Lucas went still. Grove's eyes were unnaturally wide, the whites yellowed and roughly ridged with veins. 'Don't you come your footling bloody ideas on me, you stupid fool!'

Lucas went white around the mouth. His shocked eyes protested. His lips quivered. 'Sir, I . . .'

The words dried up as Grove swung back to face the window, ignoring him. There was a long, acutely brittle silence. Then McBlain came in, small, puckish, still shocked from the hellishing noise of the engines before they'd been cut off.

'You wanted me.'

Grove flung his hands into the air so suddenly that Proctor, who was nearest, recoiled. ' "You wanted me." Oh, Good Lord above! Yes, Chief, I wanted you. I thought we might do a Morris dance on the bridge. Or we could rig a Maypole, and you could be Queen of the May.' He looked as though he were going to have a fit. His face had gone plum-coloured with fury. He swung violently about to look at the others including Usher. 'Have you heard anything like it? Have you ever in all your born days heard anything like it? We've lost our prop and he says, "You wanted me".'

Savagely, he turned on McBlain. 'For the love of God, man, pull yourself together! Why the bloody hell have we lost our screw? You're going to have some answering to do, McBlain, I warn you. I'm not going to be the scapegoat for you and your mucky engineers. And I'm not prepared to condone your criminal neglect. Now what are you going to do about the fix we're in?'

McBlain had gone chalky white. He began to tremble, so that he shook with a steady spasm over which he had no control.

'Ye'll not talk to me like that. I'm the Chief Engineer of this ship.' He fumbled a surprisingly clean white handkerchief out of his dungaree pocket and mopped his grimy face, his hand jerking. 'Ye know yourself, Captain, it can happen on any ship. It is wear and tear, corrosion. This ship is old, her engines are old. I . . .'

'And her Chief Engineer is a bloody old fool!' Grove shouted.

McBlain looked at him as though he could not believe his eyes. 'I warn ye, Grove, I will . . .'

'You warn me? You dare to warn me? Why, you bastard, I'll have you in irons!'

McBlain began to shout. And he became thickly Scottish. 'Grove, ye canna talk like this. Ye're out of your mind, man. Ye're daft. Dinna think I will stand for one more word of this!' He stood staring at Grove, his chest heaving, his face again shiny with new sweat.

Grove hovered over him, bent like a steel pin. He reached out a ramrod finger and stabbed McBlain on the chest. 'I am the Master of this ship. I will speak as I wish. You are responsible for a major disaster and I want to know . . .'

'I am not responsible!' McBlain looked away, shaking his head violently, unbelievingly. 'You will not speak to me in this manner.' His eye caught Usher's. 'You there! Get Mister Norton. I want him tae witness this. I want this logged. I'll log it myself if I have to.'

Usher began to move uncertainly, but Grove shot out an arm and stopped him. 'Get back, man.'

McBlain began to shout again. 'D'ye think you can talk to me like a cabin boy in front of your officers and men? I want a . . .'

'Shut up!' Grove screamed.

He is mad, Quinan thought. He has gone stark, staring, raving bloody mad. He moved forward quickly, using his weight to separate the two men. 'Stop it! Stop it! For God's sake!' He looked at them in turn. 'Name-calling isn't going to get us anywhere. Can't we rather try and figure out what we're going to do next?'

McBlain mopped his face again, panting. 'There speaks the voice of reason. That's all I've been appealing for, reason. Just reason. That's all.'

For one long moment Quinan thought that Grove was going to strike him. He stood square and strong, looking into Grove's wild eyes. Then Grove saw the strength there, and the resolution, and suddenly relaxed.

He smiled. It was sudden and unexpected, quite out of keeping with his mood. And it was a tender, woman-like smile, radiating his regard for Quinan.

'Old strong and silent. You bastard, you're good for me.' He reached out steely fingers and took Quinan by the biceps and gripped him hard. 'We're in a proper fix, Gil, aren't we?' His voice was newly calm, as reflective as though nothing had happened. He was now in the mood he should have been in when he arrived on the bridge. He knew it himself. He began to relax, feeling the iron grooves of tension in his stomach give way to a warm looseness.

Quinan gently disengaged his arm. He smiled faintly. 'We are. But it could be worse. We could be on fire, or sinking. The only thing that's worrying me is the cost of the tow.'

Grove shook his head. 'Don't even say it. It's too bloody horrifying to think about. It would put this ship in the red for the rest of her life.' He shook his head again, more certain. 'No, that's out, Gil. Forget it. The Company would crucify me.' He stared out of the window for a moment, seeing nothing. Then he met Quinan's eyes again. 'There's an alternative, of course.' He studied Quinan, wanting to see how he'd react.

Quinan pursed his lips. 'You mean, fit the spare propeller.' His face showed his doubt. 'Wal, that's a hell of an undertaking. Let's not rush into things. You realize all the factors involved?'

McBlain was looking more than just doubtful. He was looking alarmed. 'Aye. I wouldna say it straight out like that, Captain. It's a hell of a task. First of all, ye'll . . .'

Grove interrupted rudely, looking nettled. 'I'm not a complete bloody fool. Of course I realize all the factors.' He began to think out loud. 'We're lightly laden, thank God, very lightly laden. That's terribly fortunate. It won't take much to lift the Florry's arse out of the water to expose the shaft.' He looked sharply at Quinan. 'What have we got in Number Five? Paint?'

Quinan nodded. 'Paint in the dirty hatch. In drums.'

Grove began to look pleased. 'That's easily handled. We can get it out of Number Five, transfer it forward. There's room in One and Two, isn't there?'

Quinan nodded reluctantly. God, he thought, he talks about it like a picnic, but it will take days of back-breaking work.

'If you're serious about this, we could also pump out the after peak fresh water tank, and fill the fore peak with ballast. Except then we'd have a water shortage on board.'

Grove studied him for a moment. 'Damn good idea. But I will probably see how we go with the cargo transferring first.' He flicked his head. 'Come into the chartroom.'

They went through. Grove cast brooding eyes on the chart. 'We're here.' He stabbed his finger on it and read off the sounding. 'Just over 600 fathoms. Let's check.' He turned and switched on the echo sounder. They both watched the circling stylus for a moment, but nothing appeared on the sensitized paper. 'Well, that bears that out,' he growled. His eyes flicked across the chartroom momentarily. 'Barometer on the rise, if anything.' He looked at the chart again. 'We're in a warm, north-east current. Not very strong. Joins the Kuro Shio further on, of course. Prevailing winds are the exact opposite. We'll drift very slowly. It's too deep to drop a hook, but I wouldn't be keen on anchoring, anyway.'

He looked up. 'Got any idea of the weather, Gil?'

Quinan was still reluctant. 'It's going to be very good. Hardly any wind. Calm. Even this swell should die down.' God, he thought, even the weather is playing into Grove's hands.

Grove was looking more and more pleased with himself. 'Let's summarize, Gil.' His forefinger moved across the chart, slowly.

'That's the line of our drift. Open water. Good weather conditions. A lightly laden ship.' His eyes flicked up to Quinan's. 'The South China Sea is about eight-hundred-and-ninety-five-thousand square miles in area. That's not a hell of a lot less than the Med. The water's deep and it gets deeper on the line of our drift. Maximum depth is as much as sixteen thousand feet. There are islands and reefs scattered about, but we should be all right in that respect for quite a few days. The only minor disadvantage is that we'll drift out of the regular shipping lanes. And then again, is it such a disadvantage? Drifting not under command, I'd a damn-side sooner have plenty of sea-room and no other traffic to worry about.' He appeared to come to an abrupt decision. 'Let's go through.'

They went back into the wheelhouse where Proctor, Lucas and McBlain awaited them. None of them seemed to have moved.

Grove looked around at them, rubbing his hands together. 'By God, we'll do it!' He ignored the wooden looks of Quinan and McBlain. Instead he gazed out through the bridge window at the steadily gathering dark. Night was not far away. He made up his mind, finally.

'There is nothing we can do tonight. I must examine this entire problem most carefully. Work will start at first light, and from tomorrow night we'll work through darkness, under clusters.' He looked around. 'Mister Proctor, get the Not-Under-Command lights up, at once. Any questions, gentlemen?' When there were none, he nodded abruptly. Some of the bitterness returned. And it finally began to dawn on him that he had set himself and his crew a task of forbidding magnitude. His enthusiasm ebbed. 'God, what a shambles. What a bleeding, bloody shambles.'

He turned to Usher. 'Looks as though she's lost way altogether. Does she answer?'

Usher played with the wheel to show him. 'No, Sir. She's not taking any helm, Sir.'

'All right. Get Mister Osgood in here, then. Look sharp, there!'

Usher abandoned the wheel and ran out. McBlain fiddled a moment and then said, 'Still need me?' Grove shook his head and the Chief Engineer left.

Grove looked at Quinan, hearing the clatter of McBlain's feet on the companion-way 'What's the matter with him, Gil? There's something eating the man.'

Quinan studied Grove. 'It's his wife. She's worse than ever.' And, he added to himself, you've browbeaten him. He would have given you a beautiful go, two years ago.

Grove made an automatic, apologetic sound with his lips. 'Ah, yes. I heard she wasn't well. What's the trouble?'

'Cancer.'

Grove jutted his chin at Quinan. 'I can see you're sorry for him, First. But you mustn't let that sort of thing cloud your outlook. The man is still a prick, no matter what has happened to his wife, isn't he?'

He laughed in a precautionary manner, his eyes quickly jumping to Proctor and Lucas. 'I mean, naturally, between the four of us, gentlemen. This is a bridge confidence, of course.'

Proctor and Lucas looked at Quinan, who looked away. There was a silence broken by Usher coming back.

'Mister Osgood's coming, Sir.' He went and stood, uselessly, by the wheel.

'Well, he's taking his own sweet time.'

Grove paced a bit, wanting to talk, handicapped by having Usher back. Two minutes went by. Finally Sparks came shambling into the wheelhouse.

'Yes, Sir?'

Grove let his eyes travel over the man. Osgood was indescribably untidy. His soiled, crumped white shirt hung over the top of his dark trousers. He smelt of sweat and whisky. His eyes had a boiled, swollen, unfocused look. His hand shook as he put it to his mouth, waiting for Grove to speak.

'Where the hell have you been?' Grove's voice was snappy, quick irritation returning.

Sparks fiddled with his bottom lip. His eyes looked beyond Grove's left shoulder. He said nothing.

'Osgood!' Grove shouted. He reached out a violent hand and pushed the man so that he staggered back one pace. The abused eyes finally fixed on Grove.

'I . . . I'm not well, Sir.'

'My God, I'll say you're not!' Grove lashed him with contempt. 'You haven't bathed in a week. You're an apology for an officer. You're a disgrace to this ship.' He crowded in on the man, impaling him with his furious glare. 'Now listen to me, Osgood. Listen carefully, or you're going to be in more trouble than you can handle. We're in a fix. We've lost our screw. Mister Quinan is going to draft two messages for you. The first one is to our agents in Singapore, and to the owners, direct. It will state our predicament, give our position and say what we propose to do. It will stress that we do not require assistance and that further reports will follow. The second message will be to all shipping, giving the same details and warning that we are drifting NUC.' His eyes went to Quinan. 'I think that would be advisable in the circumstances.'

Quinan nodded. 'I'll draft them now.'

Grove was looking at Osgood again. 'I want those messages to go immediately, you understand?'

The Radio Officer nodded miserably.

Grove stood back. 'All right, then. Go into the chartroom with Mister Quinan.' He turned to the Chief Officer. 'Write them down for him clearly, Gil, or he'll muck up the whole bloody business.' He swung back on Osgood. 'And when you've sent the messages, get yourself a bath. I want you at dinner, and I want you clean!'

Sparks stood for a moment, staring at Grove. His breathing had quickened. There was a long silence. For God's sake, Quinan thought, what had got into Grove? This was the second officer in half an hour to be torn to pieces in front of Usher.

Deliberately, he broke the tableau by crossing to the chartroom door, opening it, and signalling Sparks to come through. Then he shut the door, sealing the two of them off from the wheelhouse.

Quinan sat down at the table and Sparks stood over him. His breathing was rank and rotten in the close stifling atmosphere, heavy with overtones of whisky.

'Sod him. Sod him. Who does he think he is?' He stared at Quinan. 'How can he talk to me like that? I'm not a schoolboy. And I'm tired. I've been feeling rotten all day. I'm not in a state to be spoken to like that.' He went silent suddenly and put a hand to his forehead. He shut his eyes.

Quinan was mildly alarmed. He got up. 'You been drinking, Sparks?'

Osgood opened his eyes. 'No! I swear I haven't. I . . . I . . . I've been too damn sick to drink.'

'I can smell it on you.'

Sparks dropped his eyes. 'Well, just one or two. But it hasn't affected me.'

No, Quinan thought sadly, it takes a whole bottle to do that, these days.

'Here.' He printed the messages on a piece of paper. 'Get those off. Then go and see Lincott. He'll give you something.'

Sparks took the paper in a trembling hand. 'You shouldn't have let him talk to me like that. I thought you were a friend of mine.'

Quinan felt suddenly guilty. He thought of McBlain. The Chief was also a friend. He slapped Sparks on the shoulder. 'Forget it. The Old Man's had a hell of a shock. Get those messages off, now.'

Sparks went through into his cabin. He shut the door, sagged against it. The room revolved once and was still again. He crossed unsteadily to his set and sat down. The set blurred and he blinked his eyes, trying to clear them. When he looked again the set was still blurred. Its outlines were fuzzy. It's not me, he thought, it's the set. It looked as though it was encased in fur. A hairy radio. He laughed suddenly and sharply. He reached down beneath his chair and brought out a bottle of whisky, uncorked it and gulped three, four times. Then he wrenched the bottle from his lips, coughing and choking. Spit ran down his chin but he ignored it.

He felt strange. Anger was building up in him but he had difficulty in remembering why. He felt suddenly wildly restless. He got up and prowled about the cabin, picking things up and putting them down again. He stopped at the cupboard next to his desk and knocked, sharply, on its wooden top. For a moment, he was back in a place called *The Sailorman*, a favourite haunt of his in Singapore, and he was shouting to get attention amidst the din and the howling music.

'You there!' His voice was sharp, authoritative. 'Two whiskies. One for me. One for the Old Man. I'll take mine with water, but you can piss in his.' He laughed again. The sod! The sod! How he'd love to spring a trick like that on the bastard.

He walked around the cabin again. Passing the door, he rammed the bolt home. Then he went back to the set. His mind had become startlingly clear, and empty except for the raging tiger of anger that prowled it alone. He sat down at the set, staring at the main console. Then he began to laugh. To hell with the Old Man and his pricking message. He stood up again, shaking and laughing.

'I'll be home soon, Mum,' he said. 'I'm finished here. I've been fired. I won't be needing the radio any longer.' He stared at it, remembering how long he had controlled it. Then he looked around the room, his eyes stopping when they reached a corner. A hand-axe lay there, together with some other old tools. They'd been there for months and he couldn't remember who had brought them, or for what purpose. But the hand-axe would do fine. He went and fetched it, then came back to the set. He lifted the axe and held it up, behind his right shoulder. He began to shake and laugh. Then with a sudden vicious violence he swung the axe, scythe-like, into the metal panel of the main console.

There was a crash of metal. Broken glass tinkled. Something exploded with a pop, and a smell of burning hung in the heavy air.

Osgood shouted. He felt filled with a sense of elemental power. He raised the axe and swung it again, saw it bite cleanly into the metal, wrenched it out and swung it again and again. Then, turning, he let the blade sink into the radio telephone fastened to the bulkhead behind him. One blow was enough. On a course of complete destruction, now, he stooped and hammered the axe into the lifeboat set that stood open on the floor in its orange-painted metal housing. It was toughly constructed, meant to take the knocks that could be expected if the ship were abandoned, but its innards were as weak as the rest. Again, one blow was enough.

There was a thundering at the door, the noise of voices shouting. Osgood paused a moment, panting, sweat running in rivulets down his cheeks, down his forehead, dripping off his nose. His shirt was soaked with it. Then he snarled and renewed his attack on the main bank, reducing it to a scarred metal corpse, its skin slashed open, its lacerated intestines falling out.

The door burst open suddenly, the bolt bending and then springing out of its socket. Men poured into the room: Quinan, Proctor, Lucas, Feller Hawes and Dike Ludd, with Grove hovering in the background.

Osgood lifted the axe threateningly. He made an uncontrolled, animal sound.

They hesitated for a moment. Then Hawes came angling in towards him with Ludd, while Proctor and Lucas circled around, keeping as close to the bulkhead as they could. Osgood struck out at Lucas. Lucas jumped back, cursing, scared by the bright blade. But Hawes and Ludd came in from their side and grappled with him. He struggled with unbelievable fury, but the axe was wrenched out of his grasp and his arms pinioned behind him by the sweating, panting men.

He went suddenly still, his eyes wild and wary. His shirt had torn and was hanging in ribbons about his waist. There was something pathetic about the plump, flabby white chest with its big, woman-like nipples.

Lincott was there suddenly, thrusting through the men. He held a hypodermic in one hand. There was a bead of liquid at the tip of the needle.

'Hold him very tight. I'm going to inject him in the arm.'

Osgood screamed when he saw the needle coming. It plunged into the thick flesh of his bicep and there was a silent, quivering struggle to keep him still for the five seconds it took to empty the hypodermic. Then Lincott withdrew the needle and stood back. 'Get him down to the hospital. This will take about ten minutes to work, so be careful. Hold on to him.'

Proctor passed a shaking hand over his face, wiping away the sweat. 'What did you give him?'

'Paraldehyde. It will knock him out for about two hours.'

Usher came in. Sparks had given up, suddenly. He was quite conscious but his body was slack, his eyes dull and vacant. Usher and Hawes took his arms and Ludd his legs. They carried him out to the bridge companion-way where Gindle and Kyle helped get him down the ladder. Lincott brought up the rear.

Grove stood alone with Quinan in the wreckage of the radio cabin. He looked all around, slowly, not quite able to believe what had happened but knowing that it was true. His eyes rested on each piece of apparatus in turn, as though he were trying to will it back into working order. But even somebody knowing nothing at all about radio would have been able to tell that the sets had been ravaged beyond repair. The *Florence Hurst* had become voiceless.

'This has rather torn it, Gil.' Grove's voice was surprisingly soft, but Quinan detected the tremor of shock, of disbelief. 'God, if ever I needed a drink, I need one now.' He rubbed a wrist hard across his forehead as though to smooth away some sort of pain. 'When I think of that mad bastard. He looked like a fat, helpless schoolboy. It's impossible to believe he did all this.' He waved a hand at the wreckage. Then his eyes met Quinan's. There was momentary honesty in them. For a moment, at least, he was facing up to the facts. 'Well, it's too late, now, to yell for help. We'll have to fit that spare propeller—or else.'

Quinan spoke quickly. Grove was in the mood where he might listen. 'We could put up the distress signals right now, Wal. There's every chance we'd be seen in a very short time. Let's stop kidding ourselves about the spare propeller.'

'No. No.' Grove shook his head. 'I'm satisfied it can be done. You people must lose your . . . your defeatist outlook.'

He seemed to lose interest and Quinan knew that it was hopeless pressing the point. Already Grove's eyes had left him, they were roaming the cabin while his fingers fidgeted with the buttons of his uniform. He spoke apologetically. 'Sparks usually had a bottle up here. We all turned a blind eye to it. What do you say we have a drink, Gil? I'm so ruddy shaken, if I don't have one I'll collapse.' He stood looking at Quinan with an expression of vulnerability on his face.

Quinan struggled with a sense of disbelief and finally pushed it aside. He said nothing, knowing that Grove was watching him. Instead he moved around the cabin peering into cupboards and looking behind things. He missed the half-empty bottle on the floor at the foot of the radio table but found another, quite full, behind a row of books on the desk, together with a finger-smudged tumbler. He held them up for Grove to see.

'Wonderful!' Grove took them, put the glass down and splashed whisky into it. Just the sight of the liquor had made him perversely cheerful. 'This is not normally my sort of poison. But after today I'll drink anything.' He held the glass up, his eyes suddenly sparkling, oblivious of the fact that Quinan had not joined him. 'Cheers, Mate. Here's to success!'

Quinan hated him suddenly. For a moment he did not even want to look at Grove. It was as though a clattering, upflung shutter had all at once revealed a consciously hidden, very private section of his mind. It is you, he thought with angry vehemence, it is you who are disenchanting me. I'm losing interest in the sea, and it is you who are responsible, you unpredictable, unreliable, mercurial bastard.

Looking away, he said gruffly, 'What about getting McBlain and Lincott back? There are two very important entries to be made in the log.'

Entry in the log of the *Florence Hurst*:

1745 hours. Bertram Osgood, Radio Officer, went berserk while on duty. He destroyed the radio before he could be overpowered. The *Florence Hurst* is now without communication. Mister Osgood is suffering from acute alcoholism, resulting in temporary derangement. He has been placed under sedation.

| W. L. Grove | G. J. Quinan | S. C. Lincott |
| Master. | Chief Officer. | Medical Officer. |

CHAPTER SIX

A HOT DARKNESS mantled the *Florence Hurst*. Encompassed by night, she hung over a green world thirteen thousand feet deep. She had a closed, still, stationary look, like a toy ship floating on a pond. The life-beat of her engines was gone. The rumble, the quiver, the nerve-ends of vibration had stopped. There was no torn water at her bow. No froth at the stern. Idle, oil-slicked water moved gently in tiny currents around the stump of shaft that jutted from her skin under the surface like an amputation. She was a shop with the shutters up, a broken-down pantechnicon on a lonely road. The double red glare of the Not-Under-Command lights showed her condition. They burned bloodily from the masthead and were visible all round except behind the bulk of the poop-deck, at the stern. It was half-dark here. The after white light was also cut off, but it broke the blackness into shadow in which the five men were visible.

They were bare-bodied. Hawes, Ludd, Knowles and Kyle wore only their jeans and were barefooted against the heat. Draper loomed like a pinkly peeled prawn, gigantically muscular in a pair of nylon underpants. He had been working out with his weights and the animal smell of his sweat lay strongly on the heavy air.

'Third is prowling.' There was the swish of Kyle's black, filthy hair against his neck. And then the inevitable nervous giggle. 'He's got his eye on you, Feller. You're his meat.'

'Ah, Christ.' Hawes looked down at his hands, clenching and unclenching them. You and me, Max Lucas, he thought. In that alley where I'm going to find you one day. There're no officers in an alley. Just cats squalling and the clang of garbage bins and the noise of the nearest bar to drown out the uglier sounds. We'll see how you go then, you cocky bastard, with your tight muscular arse and straight back and thick neck and that cannonball head with its bristle of platinum hair.

A wave of weakness passed over him. It was like waking up in the morning, when you couldn't close your hands properly. That's not weakness, he thought. That's how much I want him. He made a fist out of his right hand and slammed it against the open palm of his left. The impact made an ugly, shocking noise in the silence.

'He's gone by.' They had all been talking softly. Hawes's voice, even in a near-whisper, rumbled in deep bass. He rubbed at a long tear of sweat that trickled down one cheek. 'He won't be back. He's gone to Mister Proctor's cabin. They're waiting for the Yank woman. The dark one. The Evangelist's wife.'

Draper moved spasmodically in the darkness. He grabbed at the thin cloth of his underpants. 'She's hot, that one. Married to an old man. Never gets it. That's very bad, that.'

'The blonde one is all right, too.' Ludd's thick North Country accents broke in. 'Mister Quinan is filling his socks with her.'

'Don't talk like that.' Knowles sounded agitated. 'Mister Quinan knows what goes on. I was RN, remember? We had men like that in the Navy. They had eyes in the backs of their heads.' He looked around fearfully, as though expecting Quinan to materialize out of the darkness.

'Shut up, you old boozer. It's no wonder the Navy threw you out.' Hawes made a disgusted sound. He let his cigarette go. It plummeted like a tiny falling star, struck the water and was consumed. 'Where the flippin' hell is the steward?'

'Here he comes.' There was a moving white blur in the darkness that was Hookins's white tunic. He joined them like a wraith. His fear of them showed in the tremble of his voice.

'I'll get it in the neck if I'm caught up here. We'll all be in trouble.'

A beam of light caught the milky disc of Ludd's disfigured eye, making it glitter a moment. 'He talks of trouble, this fool. As if we aren't in trouble enough already.' His anger brought a spasm of violence. It had to manifest itself physically. He swung back his open right hand and hit Hookins with the flat of it, on the stomach. Hookins, taken unawares, lost his wind. He buckled and retched.

'Stop spouting crap, man. The ship is out of kilter. The Old Man kicked all the officers off the bridge and is up there by himself, dithering. The rest are below. Now let's have some sense out of you.'

A match popped, flared, smoked. Hawes sent it arcing out into the darkness and drew on his new cigarette.

'You haven't found the charm, have you, Willy?'

Hookins stayed silent, still bent, fighting air into his lungs. From behind Draper put two fiercely impatient hands on his shoulders and a bent knee into his backside and dragged him erect. 'Answer the man, Willy.'

'He doesn't need to.' Hawes waved a cigarette. 'We all know he hasn't found it. That's right, eh, Willy-me-boy?' When the steward didn't answer he went on. 'See? Two days we've given him to search. So now we know. The woman pulled it off his belt. He was the last on, remember? She had it in her dead hand when we left her and now the flatfeet have got it. It won't take them long to figure out it was sailors done it. Remember the Army sergeant and the Johnny Gurkhas on the back of the truck? They didn't like us, those boys. They'll talk.'

He stopped. There was silence for a moment. Then Kyle said quickly, ' 'Course they'll talk. The cops will show that charm in the pubs. They'll ask questions in Victoria 'arbour. Maybe some of the barmen will recognize it. If they do, we're sunk. And even if they don't, the cops will find out what's been there and what's sailed. They'll radio Manila and Singapore and other places, telling them to check all the new arrivals. They'll give 'em a description of the charm.'

'The Mate knows,' Draper broke in. 'Monday night, he asked Willy what had happened to his charm. All friendly-like. "What's happened to your charm, Willy?" he says. Willy panics. When he got back to his quarters he could hardly talk. But he told me.'

Hawes's bull voice brushed away the others. 'And then you got soused, Tuesday morning, Willy. Hell of a time to get drunk, wasn't it? Sloan had to serve breakfast, you were so bad. Musta lain awake all night, eh, Willy? And then you turned to the bottle. No tit to suck on. Poor Willy. So you used the Yank's booze instead.'

Tears glinted in Hookins's eyes. 'I wasn't the only one. I know . . .'

'Shut up, Willy.' Hawes was almost gentle. 'We don't want to hear you. We want you to listen to us. We're scared you're going to talk, Willy-boy. On Monday, you said we should tell the Old Man. Now we don't want to do that. We think that would be very bad. Bad for us. We're in trouble enough.'

Hookins began to shiver. 'I've changed me mind. I'm not going to say anything. Honest I'm not. I never was, really. It was only an idea.'

'It was a bad idea. Forget it.' He raised his voice. 'Now get below, and keep your lips buttoned.' He brought back a hand and gave Hookins a sudden shove. The steward reeled backward and was caught by Draper, who enfolded him in his massive arms. He held Hookins like a frail, crippled bird and began to crush him. Hookins's arms beat like pinioned wings. His feet drummed uselessly on the deck. Draper grinned.

'Here, let him go,' Hawes said roughly. 'It's no good hurting him, you bloody fool.'

Draper let Hookins go suddenly. The steward fell on all fours on the deck, his long hair cascading over his face, struggling once more to get air into his tortured lungs.

'Get up, damn you.' Ludd put out a bare foot and kicked Hookins in the face. The blow made a meaty noise in the darkness. Hookins's head flipped up and down from the impact.

'Cut it out!' Hawes turned violently on Ludd. 'What's the matter with you? If you've marked him the Mate will be asking a lot of questions.' He pushed the others aside and dragged Hookins to his feet. The steward stared at them with dull, pain-racked eyes. A trickle of blood ran down his chin.

'Get below.' Hawes gave him a rough shove. 'Wipe your mug and go back on duty. And God help you if you say one word of what's happened.'

The five men stood in silence while Hookins lurched away. Then Kyle said, 'We're in a proper 'ole, we are. We'll 'ang if they catch us. It'll be the rope for us.'

'Shut up!' Draper thrust up to Kyle. 'What d'you have to talk like that for, you stupid sod?' His voice suddenly shaking with real fear, he turned to Hawes. 'I don't want to hang, by Jesus, Feller!'

'It was a mad thing we did,' Knowles burst in, 'a crazy mad thing. I wanted no part in it, do you remember? I told you to leave the woman alone. I said . . .'

'You!' Ludd pointed a shaking, threatening hand in his face. 'You lie in your teeth, you rotten, stinking . . .'

'Cut it out!' Raging, Hawes pushed them aside violently, shoving them out of reach of each other. He stood wide-legged, his thick body half-cocked with ready violence. He looked at each of them in turn. 'By God, I'll smash the next man to talk this kind of rubbish. It's no good panicking, you stupid sons of bitches! And stop blaming each other. We're all as guilty as hell, and you know it. Fighting amongst ourselves isn't going to help.'

There was a silence while they considered this. Then Draper said, 'It's no good blinding yourself to the facts, Feller. We haven't got a chance. We're stuck on this crippled scow. What can we do?'

'Plenty,' Hawes said positively. 'First of all, it's good that we're disabled. Nobody knows where the hell we are. If the skipper doesn't get that spare prop on, we'll be derelict, drifting until we can drop a hook somewhere, or until they find us. That suits us. We need time.'

He pointed a thick arm for'ard. 'Tomorrow we'll have to lighten Number Five, like as not, to get the stern out of the water. Well, you know what to do. Work slow. Get fagged out. Take your time. And when we rig the tackles to sling the spare prop, accidents can happen. They've happened before.' He made one big, gnarled hand into a fist. 'Just remember. We're in no hurry to get anywhere.'

Ludd looked at him sullenly. 'And then what? What if we drift for a week We'll be found sooner or later. This muckin' sea isn't all that big.'

'It's the time we need, you thick-head. I've got an idea. A good one.' Hawes tapped his forehead. 'I use my loaf, see? And I've never let you down yet, have I?'

They looked at him silently, half-convinced. Hawes could see the doubt in them. Immediately he recognized the need to break up the discussion before they could pin him down for the details he did not possess.

He looked at his watch. 'You lot had better get below. We shouldn't be seen together too much. Come on now, push off.'

They mooched away slowly, dissatisfied and low-spirited. Ludd was the last to go. He stood looking at Hawes for a moment. Then he said, 'We'll talk again tomorrow, Feller,' and walked away.

Hawes swore at him under his breath. Ludd was the toughest and the shrewdest. And he didn't like being told what to do. He had always wanted to be at the top, but now that they were in a jam he would bide his time. Ludd would bear watching. Of the rest, only Kyle had any brains. Draper and Knowles would be the first to crack. Draper, for all his bulk, was chicken-hearted, and Knowles was half-cracked.

He lit another cigarette, turned and leaned over the rail. He stayed there a long time, smoking and staring out over the water. Then he straightened slowly. He spoke aloud, but he was looking within himself with bitterness.

'A man's a fool all his life,' he said.

The torchlight made a conical yellow stripe against the total darkness. It painted it without penetrating it. A million dust-motes rose in hordes and choked the beam. They filtered through it in silver multitudes, making the darkness look as though it were filled with sand.

The dust made Puget cough. It irritated his nose and for a moment he thought he was going to sneeze, but he put his finger under his nostrils and held it back.

He walked slowly down the lane between the stacked coffins, stumbling over the rough dunnage floor. The coffins were in tiers on either side of him, held firm by thin wooden uprights to stop them shifting in a rough sea.

I am walking, thought Puget, in a great temporary cemetery. There is the stillness of death, everywhere. He stopped and shone the torch on a coffin. The damned dust was so thick he had to keep checking. There was stencilling on the side of the coffin as well as the top. It read: *'Rene C. J. Cpl. No. 7956734. Decede le 19 Fevrier 1954. Dien Bien Phu.'*

Puget swore mildly and went on a few paces, shone the torch again. This time the coffin read: *Poisson L. S./Chef. No. 8997049. Decede le 3 Mars 1954. Dien Bien Phu.'*

'Here,' Puget said aloud. He was excited. 'It is this pile.' With the torch in one hand he began to scramble clumsily up the coffins, finding toeholds in their uneven stacking. Breathing heavily, crouching, he reached the top of the tier. Standing precariously, he shone the torch downwards, read the stencilling, then moved the beam forward to the next coffin.

'Ah!' Stiffly, he got on his knees. He held the torch over the coffin like a lamp. The furry stencilling on the pale wood read: *'Puget P. L. Lt. No. 3976621. Decede le 11 Mai 1954. Dien Bien Phu.'*

Puget put the torch down. 'Hello, my son.' His voice seemed to come from far away. It rings, he thought, my old voice rings like a carillon of bells. It has been such a long time. I turned my back when they put you in this coffin. I saw all the other bodies but I could not look at you. My strong, young, blond son, fourteen years dead.

'It is good, Pierre, to be with you again,' he said chokily. He tried to fight back the hot tears of love but he could not, and for a moment he wept silently. Then he brushed at his cheeks with a forefinger, smiled, and began to fumble through the bulging pockets of his linen jacket. He took out a bottle of wine, a half-round of cheese, and put them down next to him.

His voice came back to him. 'Forgive me, my boy. But it is fifteen years since we were last alone together. Your father is a silly old fool.'

He found a small stainless steel pocket-knife and cut a sliver of cheese, munched it, then pulled the half-drawn cork from the bottle and swigged some wine. 'The cheese is not too bad. No body, though. It is colourless, like so much that is English. The wine is a fair Beaujolais, although not one of the good years. We drank some better stuff the day you landed at Marignane, Pierre, remember?'

He took another sip of the wine. That was the last time he had seen Pierre, that furlough of only ten days when he had come grinning out of the aircraft, tough in his pale khakis and red beret, a boy-man, already blooded in Indo-China. They had greeted each other with unusual restraint, probably because of the tremendous emotion pent-up in both of them. But on the run back to Marseilles they had turned off at Suasset-les-Pins with its humming summer pinewoods. They had ordered Beaujolais at a café, and in the middle of his first glass Pierre had suddenly turned to his father and embraced him and said in a choked voice, *'Ah, Papa, il y a si longtemps que tu me manques,'* and his strong, man's fingers about Lucien Puget's neck had been the little chubby, grubby ones that had hugged him twenty years before.

After that, the ten days had had a magic quality for them. They were father and son but they were men, too, the old and the young, the wise and the strong, alike in their delight of each other and in their love of their home. They had treated that time as a time to explore, to rediscover the Marseilles they had loved before Pierre had gone to St. Cyr, which had been the beginning of their endless partings. They had prowled the Old Port, and from there taken the Corniche to Borely Park because Pierre, who had an interest in archaeology, wanted to see again the Roquerpertuse Portico with its strange statues and the collection of amphora which had always fascinated him. Then back to Marseilles through the avenues of the Prado.

Like tourists they had wandered through Longchamps Palace; like tourists they had gone especially to admire the Chapel of Charity, wrought by the famous hands of Pierre's namesake.

They had talked incessantly, but only once of Indo-China. They had been back at the Old Port, standing on a jetty amongst the bob and wash of the hundreds of small boats, looking across towards Notre-Dame de la Garde high on its hill above the city.

Pierre had spoken only in answer to a direct enquiry from his father. He had shrugged, making like of it, seeing the worry in the older man's face. 'We are all right. We are better trained, we have better arms, we are better soldiers. The Viet-Minh do not possess one single aircraft. When you are so well trained, it is possible to fight without dying.' He had slapped his father on the back and laughed.

The reality had come later, after the ten days had whirled by and the boy had left him so suddenly; standing on the steps of the aircraft waving his beret, his blond hair shining in the summer sun, and then suddenly gone into the blue, leaving his father with the lonely nights to face. Reality had been the crumpled letter brought to his door by a dark, scar-faced paratrooper called Dehez who had mumbled his clumsy words of regret to the dull, grief-stricken Puget, saluted and left.

The letter had been written in haste. It was not very long and it was typical of Pierre that it had contained no drama. It had said, simply:

I am on E2, which will fall tonight. We will pull back, but I might not be there when that happens. There are so many of them, these people. It is like one ant fighting a colony of ants. Valour counts for nothing. Training counts for nothing. They wear you down. They do not care. But I have been very proud of my men. I am honoured to command them. To fight like tigers, when you do not know for what you are fighting! I have tried to explain, in my halting words. That we are fighting for people like you. For the preservation of a way of life. But it is hard, when you are so far away from home. If I do not see you again, which I feel is likely, somehow, think only of the wonderful years we have had together. You have been the best father in the world, and I want you never to forget it. All my love, Pierre.

Puget finished the wine. He had that letter in his pocket now, its creases secured with gummed tape because they had worn away.

He stood up precariously. He felt half drunk, although he had not had all that much to drink.

'I must go, my boy. It has been wonderful, this visit. But the bloody English surround us. Nobody knows about us, and I do not want them to. This is something private, between you and me.' He shone the torch at the coffin on which he had been sitting. 'Thank Captain Paul for accommodating my backside. I am sure he did not mind. *Au revoir,* Pierre.'

He got clumsily down from the top of the tier and moved unsteadily along the lane between the coffins. When he reached the door he stopped, momentarily overcome by a different emotion. This was French, this place. Hallowed, exclusively French, a solemn tomb of young men.

'Gentlemen!' His voice echoed in the darkness of the hold. 'All you young paratroopers. I salute you. With you I would take London in a week, New York in two days. *Adieu!*'

After he had gone, the darkness was complete. A rat scuttled amongst the coffins, its nose twitching. It explored until it found the cheese that stood on the coffin of Lieutenant Puget, and began to nibble at it.

Carl Attwell pulled his shirt over his head and dropped it on the bed. It was very good quality cambric, a little frayed at the collar and cuffs now after six years, but normally full of the snap and crackle of good linen. Now it lay sodden, limp with the sweat he had poured into it over the two and a half hours since he had put it on before dinner. Then he slid his trousers off, leaving them crumpled on the floor. He stood spraddle-legged, yawning and stretching, looking across at his wife.

'I guess I'll take my drops now, honey. I'm beat.'

Mercy nodded without looking at him. She crossed to the wardrobe. There were two bottles inside, one large and one small. Mercy took them over to the dresser. She poured four ounces of colourless liquid from the bigger bottle, added two teaspoons from the small one and gave Carl the glass.

This was routine she had been practising for years. These were Carl's 'drops'. Four ounces of vodka, straight, and chloral hydrate. The practice and the procedure was a shared deceit. The vodka bottle had no label, and neither Mercy nor Carl had ever conceded that he was taking alcohol. It helped him to sleep. In the old days, in the days of the big meetings and endless tours, he had needed it. Now he could not get along without it.

'Thanks, hon.' He drank it all down at once, shaking his head, his face contorted at the bitter taste. 'Sure beats me how I tolerate this stuff.'

The face-pulling, the remark, were always the same. Bluff. The bluff that it was an ordeal. And removing the label—what was that, if it wasn't hypocrisy, or self-deception? And yet every time a new bottle was brought out, Carl assiduously soaked the label in hot water and peeled it off.

She crossed to her dresser, sat down and began to comb her

hair, jerking angrily at the soft dark curls. She could see Carl in the mirror, studying her, smiling. His eyes were bright, now. Already the liquor, taken so quickly, was getting to him. But it would be about half an hour before the chloral hydrate had its effect.

You hypocrite, she thought. You damned, insincere old hypocrite. And blind, too—so blind that he couldn't realize he was finished.

She had a sudden frightening look into the future. Carl was through, back home. In what country would they be finally stranded? In what language would they be thrown out of that last hotel, for failing to pay the bill? How long could they parody the old days? How long would Carl last once the real rot set in and, more important, how long could she?

Not long, she thought. I've had enough. I've grown up. All the rough edges have been knocked off. I've been honed down into a woman, and the only girl left in me is my young body. Carl had made a mistake showing her to the world. From Marseilles he could go his own way. She had given him all of her girlhood and so much of her womanhood since that day ten years ago when he had swept into her home town of Tiley like an avenging angel of the Lord.

The banners had been up, across Main Street. 'Welcome Carl Attwell', 'Kansas is Proud of You'. And 'Carl Attwell Spreads the Word of God'. The crowd had been too big to accommodate in the Baptist Hall, so the meeting had been held in the ball park. The whole town had gone, even the drunks who'd spent the day in the can and been released specially, even Nancy Coombs, the town whore, whom they said charged a dollar straight, or fifty cents if you were in a hurry or a college boy, but that was always standing up, in the shadows behind Collins's Drug Store.

Carl had been big news then. There was a fantastically successful tour of Britain and Australia behind him. He was a household name at home. You could buy his records anywhere, and he'd already published one book which was selling well. Tiley had been lucky to get him, but he was doing a series of one-night stands across the State while his agent hatched plans for something much bigger.

Mercy, by dint of arriving one hour early, had the best seat— in the front row, directly in front of the rostrum. She had been Mercy Lindstrom then, a virgin just turned nineteen, instructress in the Bible Class, lead singer in the Ladies' Choir, relief organist, a fervent and well-applauded speaker in the Church's Youth Debating Society, and a regular Sunday School teacher. In between all this, she worked at the Bank as a stenographer. Her knowledge of men was nil. She had gone with one or two boys in her church for a while, but this had consisted mostly of long walks while they discussed the Church and its needs. Sometimes there had been a few clumsy kisses thrown in when nobody was looking, but they had left her totally unstirred.

She had nearly fainted at the meeting. Flushed, trembling, breathless, she had spent an exalted two hours with her eyes fixed upon Carl Attwell as though she were afraid he might disappear. She had sung with him, prayed with him, laughed with him, unable to realize that her excitement was more in the man than in what he said, that the actual physical weakness she felt was a sexual stirring. But her subconscious took over, and when the meeting ended she eluded the clutching, possessive arm of her Aunt Irmgard. Hardly knowing what she was doing, she rushed to his dressing-room under the stand.

Carl had answered her knock with a curt: 'Come in!' and she opened the door fearfully to find him stripped to the waist, a towel in his hands, soap on his face.

His expression while she stood there paralysed had changed from anger to smiling surprise.

'Heck,' he said, 'I thought you were someone else.' His eyes narrowed. 'Say, I remember you. In the front row. You sing like an angel. What's your name?'

'Mercy Lindstrom,' she whispered.

'Norwegian?'

She nodded, starry-eyed. 'Way back.'

He took in the great, shining eyes, the soft dark hair, the ripe body, the long coltish legs. 'Come in, Miss Lindstrom.' He bowed, grinning like a schoolboy. 'Come right in, won't you? I reckon we've got a lot to talk about.'

Two weeks later they were married.

Mercy had forgotten her wedding—the hordes of photographers and cameramen, the press, the minister who had talked about 'a union very close to God'. It was her wedding night she remembered. She remembered the sudden realization that Carl was as terrified as she was, and the shocking discovery that he had had too much to drink. She remembered the awkwardness that had given way in her to a rising tide of delight as she instinctively guided him along the path that was leading her to greater and greater excitement. But it was an excitement that stayed hovering, unfulfilled, unslaked, a sweetness of desire that had turned bitter as he had slumped next to her, exhausted, and fallen asleep.

It had been a very long night.

'Mercy!' Carl's voice was loud and impatient. It jerked her back to the present.

She put the comb down and turned around on the stool, her hands folded, overtly obedient in the way she waited for him to speak. 'I'm sorry, Carl. Go on.'

He noticed her manner. Irritably, he said, 'If I'm boring you, forget it.'

'Please,' she said. 'You never bore me, Carl. Go on.'

This time he missed the irony. 'Shucks, it's nothing much. I was going to say that we could be in a far more serious position on this ship than we realize. We have no radio. We seem to be out of the shipping lanes. If something goes wrong when they try and fit the spare propeller, we'll be in trouble.'

She shrugged. 'There'll be an air search when we don't dock.'

'Will there? I wonder. Some say Sparks didn't send out a message at all. Some say he did, but he probably got it all wrong.'

He leaned forward. 'What I'm getting at is this. We might drift three, four days. Maybe a week. We'll be news when we're found. Get it? Publicity, handed out on a plate. The whole world, wondering where the heck the *Florence Hurst* is, with her strange cargo.'

He grinned suddenly. 'What if I work amongst the crew, while we're like this? Can you see the possibilities?' He held his hands apart, measuring. 'Headlines this size. Stories headed "How the crew of a ship found God". Get it? I'll be back in the big-time, honey.'

That damned, blind enthusiasm, she thought bitterly. Here he goes again. Aloud she said, 'Big-time Evangelism. I've never heard it put that way.'

His face straightened. 'A man has to live, Mercy. The days of the barefoot prophets are long gone.'

'Sure,' she said. 'A man has to live. And so has his wife. I agree with you, I don't call this living. But in the old days I used to hear the odd word thrown in about God, and what we planned to do for Him as well as ourselves.'

Carl's expression became sullen. 'I don't want to argue. That's all we've done ever since we got on this Goddam ship.'

His shoulders had sagged. His eyes were angry but tired. He was a ridiculous figure in his underpants. The withered pectoral muscles had turned into small flat breasts above the bulk of his belly. He turned away and flung himself on his bed, not looking at her.

Mercy felt a stab of remorse. He has only just turned the corner from goodness, she thought. It is all there. It can be recalled. There was so much in him that was the old Carl of ten, even eight years ago. Even yesterday, there might have been a chance to get it all back. But last night had put an end to any chance there might have been. Last night, and the bed, and Proctor's lean, hard body and the ecstasy that exploded in a million brilliant lights about her so that she had spent all day in a dazed, drugged dream, waiting to go back. Even now, at the thought, her stomach muscles contracted in a hard, anticipatory spasm. She felt congested with want. Trembling, she got up and moved across to the door.

The chloral hydrate was working. Carl looked at her dully. 'Going out?' When she nodded he said, 'Why don't you come to bed? You used to.'

She glanced at her wristwatch. 'It's very early, Carl.' Cruelly, she added, 'I'm not old.'

'Sure, sure.' He was nearly asleep, but his mouth twisted. 'And I am. Going to view the bridge, with Mister Proctor?'

Her quick, guilty 'No' fell into a silence broken by the sound of his heavy breathing. He was asleep.

Mercy Attwell looked at him for a long time. Then she left the cabin, shutting the door slowly and firmly behind her. It was more than just a physical act. She was shutting away part of herself.

She began to walk along the alleyway. I have passed the point of no return, she thought. There will be no going back now, ever.

The guitar had a rich, winy shine in the low light, its dark wood reflecting the red glow of the Not-Under-Command lights that seeped through the window of the lounge.

Mary Fannin's hand hung poised a moment above the trembling strings; then it flashed down in a blur of movement and the guitar exploded into the final throbbing chords of 'Cu Cu Rru Cu Cu Paloma'.

At the opposite end of the room O'Connor put down his whisky glass and clapped. 'Goddam nearly as good as Nancy Ames.'

Lincott only nodded his appreciation because Mary Fannin was not looking at them, anyway. With the song ended she remained still, staring out of the window on to the foredeck. Her body was starkly front-lit by the red lights.

Lincott took a last sip of cold coffee. 'I must go. I have to check on Sparks.'

The American had been drinking steadily since dinner. 'What about one of these?' He pointed to his glass. 'One for the road. A nightcap. Whatever you'd like to call it.'

Lincott shook his head. 'No, thanks.' He was bored and anxious to get away. And it was obvious that Mary Fannin, across from them, would prefer to be by herself.

O'Connor yawned and stretched. 'Oh, well, guess I can move, too. Got a poker game lined up.' He grinned. 'That's a great crew you guys have got. They nearly skinned me last night. I had to sign a note for thirty bucks. Anyway, tonight's the night. Revenge is sweet.'

They got up. O'Connor half-staggered and shut his eyes for a moment.

'You all right?' Lincott studied the heavy, flushed face.

O'Connor was shaking his head, grinning. 'Hell, yes. I can't take much liquor since I came off the sampan. Don't worry, healer, I'll live.'

Lincott shrugged and they walked to the door together. Quinan was coming along the alleyway.

'Hi, Admiral!' O'Connor grinned, showing big, strong, white teeth. 'Boat still floating?'

'Sure.' Quinan smiled at Lincott. 'How's our patient?'

'I'm going there now.' Lincott checked his wristwatch. 'I'm overdue, I'm afraid.'

O'Connor fidgeted. 'I'll be seeing you.' He flicked a finger and was gone.

They both stared after him. 'He's playing cards with the crew,' Lincott said.

Quinan smiled. 'You don't approve.'

Lincott shook his head. 'Don't misunderstand me. But . . . well, he is an officer, isn't he?'

Quinan studied Lincott. 'You don't like him, do you, Stephen?'

'No. Do you?'

'No.'

'Then we're *ad idem*, as the lawyers say. I sound like Proctor, spouting Latin. And another thing,' Lincott half-smiled at Quinan, 'our lifeboats aren't red, you know.'

Quinan looked down the alleyway where O'Connor had long since disappeared. 'Twice, he's said it. You think he's colour-blind?'

Lincott shook his head. 'No. It's something else. Something to do with boats. Strange bird, our Lootenant.' He changed the subject. 'How's the Old Man?'

Quinan raised his eyebrows. 'On the bridge. Alone. Says he wants to think.'

'Is he drinking?'

'Could be. There was a bottle in Sparks' cabin.' Quinan became uncomfortable. 'I think the less said about that, the better.'

'You're too loyal, Gil.' Lincott smiled to take the small sting out of his words. 'Don't blind yourself too long. Our Wal is showing strong signs of cracking up.'

Quinan looked at him sharply. His voice had an edge to it. 'How do you mean that? Do you mean that he's losing his mind?'

Lincott shook his head. 'Good Lord, no! But a nervous breakdown is very much on the cards if he goes on hitting the bottle at his present rate.'

Quinan shifted uncomfortably. 'He did some funny things on the bridge today.'

Lincott studied him. 'I heard. You're worried, aren't you?'

Quinan shrugged. 'I'm the Chief Officer. Wouldn't you be?'

Lincott nodded. 'Yes, I would. It's a damned difficult position for you. That is why I told you not to blind yourself. Watch him, but be careful. All I can say at the moment is that his drinking has made him jittery, bad-tempered, over-emotional and unpredictable. These are bad things in one who commands. But they do not add up to insanity or even incapability.'

There was a small silence. Then Quinan said, 'I had to know where I stood.'

'Of course.' Lincott looked at his watch. 'I must go.' He smiled and tapped Quinan on the shoulder. 'Don't worry, Gil.' Then he was gone.

Quinan looked after him for a moment. He felt weighed down with responsibility. Grove, he thought, is an insoluble problem. He shrugged, giving it up readily. Then he walked into the lounge, narrowing his eyes against the half-dark until he saw the still shape of Mary Fannin at the window. He walked across to her. She heard him coming and twisted impatiently in her chair. But when she saw who it was she suddenly smiled.

Quinan stopped and stood looking down at her upturned face. 'Going to serenade me?'

She had a withdrawn, introspective look. 'I couldn't serenade a mouse. I've got the blues tonight, real bad.'

He sat down on the arm of the chair opposite her. 'Why? Good Doctor Quinan will prescribe for you, but you have got to give me your symptoms.'

She shook her head. 'No symptoms. I get like this, sometimes. I get all tightened up inside, so I can hardly breathe. So I got some pills, in Hong Kong. Pills to make me relax and pills to cheer me up. Happy pills and sad pills. But I've run out of the happy ones and Doctor Lincott hasn't got any.'

Quinan studied her. She was looking away from him, out of the window. 'The death of the jet pilot on Monday, when we were in Haiphong. Has that got anything to do with it?'

She turned to look at him, her face suddenly hard. 'Not in a thousand years! I couldn't care a damn about him. I . . .' She turned away again. The guitar across her lap had pulled her dress high up on her thighs. Her legs were long and clean, firm under the sheer nylon. They were young legs, strong with youth, as young as the slender hands that gripped the guitar too hard. Only the face had its too-early wisdom.

Quinan found his cigarettes and held them out.

'Have one?'

She turned back, her expression softened, blinking against a glitter of tears. 'Say, I'm a real wow, I am, getting you all involved in my troubles.'

She took a cigarette and let him light it for her. She let the silence run while she looked at him and then she smiled softly. 'You're a heck of a nice guy, Mister Quinan. And I'm a heck of a not-so-nice girl.'

'That's a matter of opinion.'

She looked at him intently. 'You're calm. You're strong, inside. I'm not like you. We're different people, you and me.' She broke off suddenly. 'Say, you want to hear a song I've been writing? It's only half-finished.'

He nodded. 'Go ahead.'

She put the cigarette down. When she took the guitar off her lap it became part of her. She struck the strings casually and it welled a slow, sad melody, rich with chords. She sang in a soft, true voice, a little husky, a little low:

'The moon was dark, the stars were faint,
 The waves rolled endlessly,
 I lost my love so long ago,
 On the South China Sea.
 No moon, no light, the dark above,
 The night that mantled me
 I walk, I talk, but I died that night
 On the South China Sea.'

The guitar faded into silence. Mary Fannin sat looking at Quinan, her lips faintly parted from the last words of the song. In the tinted dark her face had become as young as her body, heart-shaped and beautiful.

'It is lovely,' Quinan said. 'But it is very sad.'

She got up suddenly, letting the guitar fall with a soft thump on her chair. She went and stood at the window, wide-legged, stiff, her back rejecting him.

'The world,' she said in a choked voice, 'is a very sad place, Mister Quinan.'

CHAPTER SEVEN

LINCOTT hurried his steps, mildly concerned at having left
Osgood alone this long. When he opened the hospital door his
eyes went quickly to the bed.

Immediately he let out a small sigh of relief. His main fear had
been of recurring violence. There was always the chance of this,
once the paraldehyde wore off. But the figure on the bed was still.
The sheet rose and fell with the regularity of its breathing. There
was one small light burning on the bulkhead above the bed and
in its wan light Osgood's face was smooth in sleep.

Lincott hovered in the doorway. He was undecided. He could,
by the looks of things, leave Sparks for another half hour at the
least. His diary, not yet written up for the day, lay in his cabin.
Its blank pages tempted him. But there was always the chance
that the sleeping man might wake unexpectedly.

Lincott sighed. I am a doctor, not a nurse, he reminded himself. But the decision had already been made for him by his
confounded over-developed sense of duty. He lit one of his rare
cigarettes and walked over to the bed, reaching behind him with
one hand to pull up a chair.

The hand found the chair, pulled it against his legs. In the
act of sitting, his eyes went casually to the sleeping man's face.
And then the chair fell backwards with a clatter as Lincott jerked
erect again, eyes narrowed, heart thumping with quick fright.

Osgood was ill. Very ill. The sleeping face was deeply and
violently flushed. There was a distinct circumoral pallor. A
quick hand on the forehead pulled away as it touched the burning flesh.

Lincott leant over the bed. 'Osgood! Sparks!' He patted the
man's cheek. But there was no reaction. Lincott whirled away
from the bed, got a thermometer from the cabinet, automatically
shook it down. Then he pulled the sheet below Sparks's shoulders
and thrust the thermometer into the white flesh of his armpit.
Silently he stood, his alarmed eyes on the congested face.

What a hell of a thing, he thought. What a hell of a thing to
happen. He had been watching Osgood for weeks. Day by day
he had measured the widening crack, knowing that collapse was
imminent, taking almost a perverse pleasure in it because Grove
would not heed him. So, when it came, there had been a pre-
meditated diagnosis ready and waiting. Acute alcoholism. But
the alcoholic had been ill, too.

'Every physician almost hath his favourite disease,' Lincott

thought bitterly. That nugget out of *Tom Jones* had amused him
at university. But now it applied to him. He was seeing alcoholics
all over the place, he thought, readily accepting this exaggera-
tion because of the bitterness of having to stand before the
tribunal of his own self-critical, introspective mind. And the
verdict was a condemnatory, categorical 'guilty'.

He took the thermometer out. It came away glistening. One
hundred and four. But Lincott's expression remained impassive.
Nothing would register on the schooled face even while the mind
curvetted with fright. At least, he thought, that is one thing I
have remembered.

Gently, he put his hand under Osgood's sweat-soaked head.
The pillow was soggy with it. He lifted the head, all his mind
concentrated on the resistance his hand was encountering. Stiff.
Slightly stiff. But not rigid. His mind temporarily discounted
meningitis, throwing it out for consideration later on.

He flung back the sheet all the way to the end of the bed. The
naked body lay before him, flabby, blotchily discoloured. He
stared a moment, then ran to the door. Gindle was passing by.

'Get Hookins. Quick as you can.'

Some of the urgency in his manner rubbed off on to Gindle.
'You want help, Sir? If he's gettin' troublesome again I can . . .'

'It's not that.' Lincott pushed him away. 'Run and get Hookins,
please. Sparks is ill, not violent. He's damn sick.'

'Och, poor fella. I'll get Willy quick.' Gindle turned and ran
off along the deck.

Lincott went back into the hospital. He got his stethoscope out
of the drawer in his desk and fumbled it on, never taking his
eyes off Osgood. Then he crossed to the bed, leaned over and
listened to the thudding heart. He put the stethoscope down on
the bedside locker, perplexed. The beat was eighty, which was
low and definitely not in keeping with such a high temperature.
He began to feel, to probe with his skilled hands, but they
worked automatically while his mind computed the symptoms.
Plague. Typhoid. Malaria. But there was no enlarged spleen,
which he had somehow expected to find. Bending, he searched
the discoloured skin minutely, looking for a bite, or rash, or,
what he feared most, the rose-spots of typhoid. But there was
nothing. Bertram Osgood's body was devoid of any marks other
than the pink line of an old appendicectomy scar.

Lincott stood up wearily. He took out a pocket handkerchief
and mopped the sweat that had gathered in huge teardrops in
his eyebrows and above his mouth.

The disease was a puzzle, so far. It looked like typhoid, but he
shook his head at that one. No. Far too quick, apart from the

absence of the rose spots. This man, apart from his alcoholism, had been all right yesterday. Today he had complained of not feeling well. Whatever had struck him had come swiftly—within twenty-four, perhaps forty-eight hours.

He stood back, felt for his cigarettes, lit one. The discoloration, he thought, is ante-mortem. This man is going to die, if I don't do something soon. He felt suddenly very alone, and weighed down with a particularly personal responsibility. And he had a moment of intense uncertainty, a spasmodic doubt of his own ability that made him wish for a hospital, and the wise heads he would normally have been able to turn to. But the *Florence Hurst* was not only crippled, she was dumb, made voiceless by the very man who needed all the help he could get.

Willy Hookins came into the room and stood near the door. He was dull-eyed, incurious. His eyes went from Lincott to the man on the bed, then back to Lincott. 'You wanted me, Sir?'

Lincott extinguished his cigarette. 'Yes, Willy, Mister Osgood is ill. Very ill indeed. And I don't know what it is, yet. I will need your help.' He mopped sweat again, put the handkerchief back. Hookins had a swelling on his bottom lip, he noticed. 'Get me the catheter pack, Willy. I'm going to do a urine test.'

While Hookins fumbled around behind him Lincott went to the washbasin, and took off his tunic. He bent over the basin and scrubbed his hands, a slender, neatly-built man in shorts and singlet.

Hookins brought the catheter in its sealed plastic container. Lincott opened it and they moved over to the bed. Lincott sat on its edge.

He looked up for a moment into the young face of the steward. 'You've never seen this done before. It's not very pleasant, but Mister Osgood won't feel anything because he's unconscious. All I want you to do is hold the kidney bowl. Okay?' He smiled reassuringly.

Hookins's frightened eyes met Lincott's. That was a contusion at the corner of his mouth, Lincott realized. Somebody had hit him there. Hawes, probably, or one of the guttersnipes in his entourage. He had heard the talk.

'Willy,' Lincott said patiently. 'I know you're in trouble. I will try and help you with it. But later. Right now Mister Osgood needs us. He is a very sick man.' He smiled. 'In fact, he is going to need that lucky charm of yours.'

Hookins went white so suddenly that Lincott thought he was going to faint. He backed away, the enamelled kidney bowl shaking in his hands. His eyes, hypnotized with terror, were fixed on Lincott's.

'Hookins!' Lincott was overcome with sudden anger. 'For God's sake, pull yourself together! What the hell is the matter with you, man? Are you ill?'

The steward shook himself. His eyes left Lincott's then slowly came back again, as though he were trying to read Lincott's mind. 'I'm . . . I'm not feeling too good, Sir,' he whispered.

Lincott tried to control his impatience. 'Can you manage? Or do you want to go off?'

Hookins thought about the crew's quarters and what could happen to him there. He shuddered. 'I can manage, Sir.'

'All right. But no more histrionics, understand?'

Lincott turned away quickly and began the task of inserting the catheter. It was done, finally, and Hookins took the bowl over to Lincott who made the test at his desk. It was amber clear, containing no sugar, a little albumen and a trace of acetone. Summed up, it was unrevealing. All it really indicated was that Osgood was ill.

It took him a few minutes to do a blood count, which was the next step. Here again, the test disclosed nothing. The red cells were slightly down and there was a depression more than a rise in the white cells. Once more, it told him in the strongest possible terms that Osgood was ill. But it gave him no lead.

Lincott felt defeated. He stood back while Hookins cleared away. Then he looked at his wristwatch. God! One hour he had been here. It felt more like five minutes. And all to no purpose.

He went back to the basin and washed his hands, then crossed to the cabinet and took a hypodermic needle out of the tray there. He turned to Hookins, who was standing limp and abject in the middle of the room.

'Willy, I want you to listen to me carefully. A lot depends on the help I'm going to expect from you in the next five minutes. I still don't know what is wrong with Mister Osgood. So I'm going to perform a lumbar puncture on him. In other words, I'm going to get fluid out of his spine,' he held up the needle, 'through this needle. It's not easy. You've got to hold Mister Osgood curled up, so that his spine sticks out nice and sharp. Then I can get the needle in without any trouble. Understand?'

Hookins's eyes fastened on the needle. The light from the bulk-head struck it so that it seemed to blaze silver in Lincott's hand. It stood erect, phallic. It brought back Hong Kong, the darkness, the screaming woman on the ground, Hawes advancing towards her. . . .

He covered his face with his hands. 'I can't! I can't!'

'Hookins!' Lincott sprang at him, pulling his hands away. 'I need you boy, it's damned important. Do you want Sparks to die?'

Hookins's wild eyes looked into the sweat-beaded, anxious face of the doctor. He drew back, trembling, his shaking hands at his mouth.

It was useless. Lincott saw it at once. Hookins's mind was in another place. He had withdrawn from here.

Rage took him. 'Get out!' he shouted. 'Get out, damn and blast you, you useless bastard!'

He heard Hookins's footsteps fading away. His back was already turned. He stood at the bed, shaking, trying to control his anger and his bitterness and a feeling of desperate abandonment. The needle was still clenched in his right hand.

'Well,' he said, surprised at the calmness of his own voice, 'it's up to me now, Sparks. There's no time to get anyone else. Let's see what I can do by myself.'

There was the click of high heels behind him, coming slowly across the floor towards the bed. He stood still, not turning, beyond caring.

And then the voice, soft and tired. 'I guess you've got trouble on your hands, Doc. Can I be of any help?'

For one heart-stopping moment he thought it was Mercy Attwell. But when he jerked around suddenly he found himself looking into the weary, wise eyes of Mary Fannin.

Peter Proctor beat time with a bare foot to Brubeck's piano while he poured himself a gin. He was adding ice and tonic when there was a tap at the door and Lucas came in.

'*Ave atque vale*,' Proctor said. 'Don't stay too long. I'm expecting a visitor. But you may have a drink, young man. One drink. And then you must needs depart.'

'Well, hell, thanks,' Lucas growled. He was wearing only a pair of rugger shorts, and the ruched elastic top clung to his board-flat stomach where the abdominal muscles clustered like linked chain, swelling into the breastplate armour of his massive pectorals.

Proctor gave him his drink. 'Cheers, *Similia similibus curantur.*'

Lucas sighed. 'Or loosely translated, a hair of the dog that bit you. I've heard it before. You must be careful, you know. You're becoming repetitious in your old age.' He put his glass down on the table next to the record player and began to twist clumsily to the music, capering like a bear, his big shoulders rolling, his bristly head down. It was wrinkled with muscle at the neck. 'I feel like a party, man. I'm real groovy tonight.'

'For God's sake, you'll have the ship rolling,' Proctor laughed. 'Why aren't you on watch?'

Lucas straightened, streaming sweat. The cabin was like a small, airless metal box.

He pointed upwards with a solemn forefinger. 'The Old Man is on the bridge. He kicked me off. He's communing with nature. 'You may go, Mister Lucas,' says he, all solemn-like. 'I wish to study Mister Osgood's collection of the whiskies of Scotland." '

Proctor howled. 'Good old Wally. He's going to skate down the companion-way on his chin, sometime during the night. So he's up there alone, is he?'

Lucas nodded. 'Not that he really needs anyone else. He's got the radar after all, just in case a big Yank transport decides to ram us. Actually, I think he's planning tomorrow's labours.'

'Quite likely,' Proctor agreed. 'Frankly, if I were in command, now that the radio's bust I would yell for help in all directions: rockets, siren, distress signals, flames on the vessel, the whole bloody issue. If something goes wrong tomorrow we'll be drifting around the Nan Hai for weeks like a ruddy Flying Dutchman until someone blunders into us.'

'Talking of radios,' Lucas said, 'reminds me that our worthy Osgood is reputed to be not just boozy, but very ill as well.'

'It doesn't surprise me.' Proctor sipped at his drink. 'I suppose he was doing filthy things in Hong Kong, the disgusting little man. A parody of an officer.' He lifted his eyebrows. 'The trouble is venereal, no doubt?'

'Don't know.' Lucas shrugged. 'Anyway, it will give the saw-bones something to do.'

Proctor drew himself upright. He was quite a good mimic. He produced the sepulchral, dramatic tones of a radio announcer. 'Tonight you will hear another thrilling episode in our medical series, "Young Doctor Lincott", as this dedicated medico fights dramatically through the night to diagnose a case of Lover's Nuts.'

Lucas guffawed. 'At least he'll be better occupied than peering around corners and sneaking down alleyways, making goo-goo eyes at Mrs Attwell.'

They were laughing when there was a light tap at the door and Mercy Attwell came in. Smiling at first, she saw Lucas and went suddenly still. Lucas, caught in mid-drink, stared at her through his glass.

Proctor looked from one to the other. '*Omnia vincit amor, et nos cedamus amori!*' Lying cheerfully, he translated wrongly, 'That means let's all have another drink.'

Stephen Lincott leaned over the drenched, unconscious naked body of Bertram Osgood. 'You hold him like this. He must be curled, like a foetus. The spine has to protrude.'

He wasn't bothering to mop the sweat from his face any more. It shone in the light of the bulkhead lamp. 'I hope I'm putting this across all right.'

Mary Fannin had taken off her shoes. She came beside him and took hold of Sparks's hot body. A rivulet of perspiration ran down one cheek. 'I've got it.'

She blotted her cheek by pressing it against her shoulder. 'Say, by the time we're finished we'll both be smelling like Friday afternoon in a hemp factory.'

Lincott was surprised that he could still laugh.

'I haven't said thank you yet. It's time I did. I don't know what I would be doing without you.'

The grey eyes avoided his. She looked irritable.

'You go ahead, Doc, and cut out the fancy speeches. I was bored, is all.'

Lincott smiled again. He went around the bed and collected a test tube he had placed on the next locker. Then he bent over, half-crouched behind the plump back with its little dimples of fat alongside the spine.

He was conscious of the tense rigidity of his body. Carefully he selected the place, then quickly drove the needle in between the vertebrae. There was a fractional moment of doubt. Then the clear, watery spinal fluid jetted out into the test tube. He took approximately two cubic centimetres of it, pulled the needle out and dabbed ether over the puncture. Still crouched, he studied the test tube clamped fast in his trembling right hand. Then he got up slowly, vastly relaxing, and met Mary Fannin's eyes as he stood.

'How long,' she said, 'since you last did that?'

'About two years.' He studied her with a new interest. 'You're very perceptive, Miss Fannin.'

'Sure.' She also stood up. 'You figure I can take time out for a cigarette?'

He nodded, moving over to his desk. 'By all means, do.'

'Thanks.' His were lying on the desk. She took one of them and watched in silence while he spun the fluid down in his centrifuge, made a slide and put it under the microscope.

'You British are so polite. I like it. Americans are more blunt. You figure most British are sincere, behind all the yuk-yuk?'

Lincott was focusing the microscope, but he looked up briefly. 'Do you want to know whether Mister Quinan is sincere?'

She was caught verbally flatfooted by his insight and the flash of humour in his eyes. Her face felt hot.

'What a darned cheek!'

Smiling, Lincott pressed against the eyepiece. For a long

moment he studied the gigantic magnification of the fluid. But there was nothing more than a couple of leucocytes, not the pus he was expecting.

The humour was gone. His mouth turned down at the corners and he looked up, his eyes bitter.

'Nothing, huh?' She studied him seriously. 'What does that let out?'

'Meningitis.'

He got up, hardly aware of her, pounding a clenched fist into his palm. Osgood's breathing had become stertorous, rasping heavily in the thick air. So now, Lincott thought, I fly blind. An eyeless man in a doubly dark room. This is where I go by touch. this is where I leave it to the drugs. This is where there is a very narrow dividing line between what I can do and whatever Power there is outside me who can help him. Perhaps between the two of us, we can effect a cure.

Mary Fannin seated herself on the empty bed next to Osgood, looking across at Lincott. 'He's very sick, isn't he? I mean, he could die?'

Lincott had been staring at the still, hoarsely-breathing figure. Now he raised his eyes to hers. 'Yes, he's very sick.' He was absorbed, not entirely with her. 'He's in a coma.' He did not want to go so far as to admit the proximity of death, although the knowledge of it had been with him from early on.

She took a draw of her cigarette and placed it carefully on the edge of the locker. For a moment all he saw was the tumble of half-blonde hair. Then she looked up, very directly. 'Doc. Don't kid me. I'm tough. I said, could he die?'

He nodded abruptly. 'Yes, he could.' He fluttered his hands briefly, as though he were going to add something. But there was nothing to add. He let his hands fall to his sides and repeated, 'Yes, he could die.' Then he gave her an empty smile. 'I wish you were a senior practitioner with forty years in the profession behind you.'

'I guess I don't qualify.' She bent her head to pick up the cigarette, then met his eyes again. 'Don't look for a crutch. It's you or nobody. You know what to do. I mean, you learned all this at medical school. You know, Step A, Step B, how to diagnose. I suppose you learn it like anything else. Rover has the ball. I see Rover. Like learning to read.' She shrugged. 'So you don't know what it is. Probably old Doc Kindness from Mudsville would be just as stumped. And he'd wish he had a young guy like you around to give him some new ideas.'

She had, thought Lincott, a gift of common-sense simplification, and the reassurance that accompanied it. He went to his

desk, took a cigarette and lit it. He had smoked more in two
hours than he normally did in a day. The tobacco tasted harsh
in his mouth. But it was a comfort to blow smoke, to see the red
tip glow. It was a tiny island of stability in a sea of uncertainty.

He took the cigarette from his lips. 'It is a virus of some sort.
Everything pointed at first to either typhoid or meningitis. There
was strong evidence of both diseases. The syndrome was so
similar. But it's neither. So far all I know is that, whatever it is,
it is quick and deadly.'

He gestured almost apologetically at Sparks. 'I would so much
like to help him. He's not a bad little chap—alcoholic, you know.
Sick, even before this. I recommended long ago that he should
be removed from his post. He was badly run down. Boozed up
half the time. But intelligent. An absolute authority on classical
music. And good-natured, too. He took everything that Proctor
and Lucas could throw at him.'

She said quickly, 'Oh, those two. Look, Doc, I've read about
guys like that. They used their kind to turn on the gas showers
for the Jews, during the war.'

There was a small pause. Lincott put out his half-smoked
cigarette. 'I'm going to set up a glucose-saline drip. While I'm
busy with that, I'd like you to get a basin of tepid water and
sponge him down. Continuously.'

He pointed across the room. 'Hot water there. Sponge in the
cabinet. And get the electric fan in the corner and turn it straight
on him, from about four feet.'

He started for the cupboard beyond his desk, where the drip
apparatus was stored. Halfway, he stopped abruptly and turned
to face her again. 'You don't mind?' He was awkward. 'Sponging
him down, I mean.'

The grey eyes met his, very level, almost without expression.
'No, Doc, I don't mind.'

Lincott was rigging the drip when Quinan came in quietly.
He came softly right up to the bed and it was only as he reached
it that Mary Fannin, already started on her sponging, looked up
and saw him.

'Hello there,' she said, 'come to see the patient?'

'Yes.' His eyes were friendly but worried. They went to Osgood
and then back to her. 'How bad is he?'

Lincott, turning briefly and seeing Quinan, allowed her to
answer. It was in the nature of an accolade.

'He's very ill. It's a virus of some sort.'

You needed to tell Quinan so little, she thought. He nodded
and stood next to her, looking down at the Radio Officer. And
he put a friendly hand on her shoulder, which she liked.

'He's rather a friend of mine, this chap. If there's anything I can do to help, just say so.'

She looked up at him, curious. 'He's an alcoholic, Mister Quinan. He was no good at his job.'

'I know,' Quinan said, 'but he is still a friend of mine.'

Lincott had finished rigging the drip apparatus. He brought the tubed needle around, perched on the edge of the bed, raised the anticubital vein in Osgood's arm, and inserted the needle. Then he added a hypodermic of chloramphenicol to the drip, put the hypodermic down on a tray and came and stood next to them, not saying anything.

Quinan quietly collected two chairs and brought them up. 'Sit down, Stephen. You're fagged out. Mind if I stay?'

Lincott sat limply. He covered his face with both hands and massaged it for a moment, rubbing the creases of fatigue out of the skin. Then he smiled wearily and looked at both of them in turn.

'Nothing would please me more,' he said, 'than to have you stay. Both of you.'

There was silence after that. Quinan sat back, lit a cigarette. Mary Fannin half lay on the next bed. The three of them watched Bertram Osgood, waiting to see whether he would live or die.

Lucas looked at his cards. He laughed, his teeth very white in the strong round face down which the sweat rolled steadily. 'Twenties. I'll pay twenties.' He grinned, watching Mercy Attwell.

'Darn you!' She threw her cards at him. 'I'll never learn this crazy game.' She picked up her glass from the floor. 'And I'll never find out what's nice about this liquor.' She gulped the gin and tonic, shuddered. 'It tastes like gall.'

They were sitting on the carpet, crowded together in the small space. Mercy had removed her shoes and stockings, her bracelet, her plain necklace. Her skirt had wrinkled up, and on the underside of her thighs were the red-and-white checkered welts of the carpet's rough fibre.

'Pay,' Lucas said.

Proctor took up the chant. 'Pay! Pay! Pay!' They roared.

She laughed, her lips the rich red ripeness of plums. Her teeth were white and perfect. She put a hand on Proctor's bare shoulder and stood up, teetering then gaining her balance.

'This isn't fair. What about Peter? He lost too.'

'You're working off your handicap.' Lucas reached up and grabbed her leg under the skirt. It was girl-hard with muscle, but the skin was baby-smooth at the top.

'Come on,' he urged, 'off!'

Mercy put her hands to her zip. The hesitation was only momentary. She shook from a hot, sweet excitement that she saw mirrored in the eyes of the men so that their eyes seemed ferocious with it. The gin had reduced to a dry chrysalid the inhibitions of long restraint, and the fire in her consumed them, engulfed them with a voracious impatience, leaving her mind emergent like a new pupa that would explode into a butterfly of shimmering delight.

She pulled the zip down with a sudden decisive movement. The skirt slackened its hold and fell limply around her ankles. Laughing, she kicked it into Lucas's face. Then with a quick upward fling of her hands she wrenched the blouse over her head and tossed it aside. It was the symbolic emergence of the butterfly.

Proctor and Lucas stood up. Mercy came against Proctor's chest. She held him fiercely while they moved barbarically to the rhythm of the music. Their bare feet trampled the cards, slipping on them. The edge of the bed took her behind the knees and she collapsed on to it, panting and laughing and trying to elude Proctor's grasp. Then she pushed him aside and sat up, kneeling. She looked at Lucas standing near the door. He watched her with his angry, calculating blue eyes. She let her glance travel over the powerful body. Then she smiled slowly.

'This is another game that three can play. Come here, Max.'

There were four fans now. They sucked the sluggish warm air through their blades and flung it on to the cold water that Mary Fannin was swabbing over Osgood's body. They flung it on to the cold water and the ice packed around him on the waterproof. But the ice melted and the water turned warm from the fire that was raging under the blotched skin.

The fans hummed in a thrumming monotone. Over their noise came the ragged see-saw of Osgood's breathing, slow, hoarse: In —aaaaah; out—aaaaah. On and on.

Lincott took the thermometer from Osgood's armpit. He looked at it very carefully, blinking his eyes to focus. Then he put it in the glass on the bedside locker.

'Up?' Mary's hair was streaked dark with sweat. Although she lifted her eyes, her hands never stopped the swabbing.

'Yes.' Lincott went to the cabinet and took down a small bottle. 'I'm going to try some Coramine.' He found a clean hypodermic and withdrew two cubic centimetres, sat down on the bed and dabbed ether on Sparks's arm.

'Will it help?' There were long pauses in their conversation now, because time had no meaning. They were suspended in a time vacuum. They and the dying man on the bed.

Lincott sank the needle into Osgood's arm. He emptied the hypodermic, put it down. He dabbed more ether on the puncture. Then he looked at her for the first time.

'It might.' He shrugged. 'And then again it might not.' He looked around. 'What happened to Gil Quinan?'

'He left about ten minutes ago. To relieve the Captain, I think.'

Lincott slumped into his chair. He picked up one of the three textbooks he had brought from his cabin—Price's *General Work on Diagnosis*. He began to turn its pages then abruptly slammed it shut and dropped it. He had studied it until his eyes burned.

Mary Fannin raised her head. Her eyes went beyond him, over his left shoulder to the door. Lincott twisted around quickly in his chair.

Grove came into the room. He walked straight to the bed and stood looking down at the still body of Osgood.

'I've heard about him.' His breath when he turned to Lincott was heavy with the sour-sweet smell of liquor. 'What's the matter with him?'

Lincott stood up. 'He's very ill. It's difficult to say what it is, but it is a very severe virus.'

Grove looked back at Osgood. He said dispassionately, 'You stupid, silly bastard. I hope you snuff it.' Then he turned to the girl, who was going on with her endless sponging. 'You don't mind doing that, Miss Fannin?' He let his eyes rest on her. He let her understand the clear implication of his words and read the humiliating presumption in his eyes.

Mary Fannin's expression closed up. For the first time that night her old nervousness broke through. She blinked and turned away, saying quickly, 'No.'

Grove grinned wolfishly. 'Well, that's the first bath he's had in ages.' His eyes went to her hand, which was sponging around the groin. 'And a thorough one too, I see.' When he brought his glance back to Lincott his eyes moved jerkily and Lincott read the sign. Nystagmus. Grove was a good three parts drunk, but it never showed much until near the end. At this stage all that had happened was that the liquor had rotted through the ropes of restraint that normally held him tight. He functioned, at this point, better than when he was sober. He was quick, sharp, decisive and usually cuttingly nasty.

'How long has this condition been coming on?' he asked Lincott.

Lincott shook his head. 'I can only guess. The incubation period is about forty-eight hours. Not more.'

Grove grinned again. His eyes were full of malice. 'And you didn't spot it, eh? Not until it was too late, by the looks of him.'

Lincott met Grove's eyes. 'It was difficult. When a man is drunk most of the time, it is hard to tell that he is also ill.'

Grove read the meaning in the doctor's words. Anger tautened his face. For a moment he mulled the remark over in his mind. Lincott could almost watch him think, wondering whether he was going to make anything of it. But for reasons of his own Grove decided to leave it. He turned abruptly and walked to the door. Then he paused there a moment and did one of those unbelievably unpredictable things that never failed to leave Lincott floundering. A look almost of benevolence came to his bony face. He said mildly, 'Osgood has a nice old mum. I've met her.' Then he was gone.

There was a long silence while Mary and Lincott studied each other. Then, surprisingly, she laughed. 'What a thoroughly charming man,' she said.

It was all sweet bells that tolled amongst the crashing chords that surged towards a crescendo. It was heat and ice, it was flashpoints of fire, it was an agony of flesh, it was birth and death, it was a sudden great flaring, trailing fuse that leaped within the body and exploded there in a millennium of ecstasy.

Mercy Attwell's breath roared in her ears. Her open mouth gasped for air. Her heart drummed, racing. Her dark hair clustered on the sweat-drenched pillow.

She cried out, 'Oh God, the world is lovely. The world is a lovely lovely lovely lovely place.'

Osgood's mouth also gasped for air, but to sustain life. His breathing had begun to lapse. He inhaled raggedly in a series of tortuous breaths, each one deeper than the last. Then there was total lack of respiration for long moments until on each occasion the tense, crouched Mary Fannin thought that he would not breathe again.

The four fans still blew: the four winds from the corners of his bed. The last of the ice lost its geometrical rectangularity and melted away into a variety of shapes like a hundred different pieces of used soap. Water lapped over the edge of the waterproof and dribbled in a miniature cascade on to the floor. It made a tiny, hard, rattling sound above the humming of the fans and the erratic rasp of the breathing.

Mary Fannin took the last cigarette from Lincott's box. She lit it and blew smoke, and the smoke was taken by the fans and cut to shreds. The fans made it seem as though there were a great wind in the room; as though she should be cool. But they were simply moving the hot air about in a tossed current. Sweat still

beaded her face and there were black patches of it under her
arms. Her eyes ached and her tongue was rough from smoking.
She felt as though she could sleep for a week and yet she knew
she could never sleep.

She addressed Lincott from a great void of fatigue. 'This
breathing. Is this the end?'

He said without looking at her, 'This is what is known as
Cheyne-Stokes respiration. It is the forerunner of death.'

She lifted eyes that looked huge, because the passage of the
night, and of events, had pinched her face. 'So we're beaten,
then. The virus has won.'

'No!' He said it sharply. His face shone in the light from the
bulkhead lamp. 'I am going to try some tetracyclene.'

She shook her head. 'You don't know when you're licked, Doc.'

Lincott's breath came in quick gasps. He had the hypodermic
ready. 'I am licked,' he said, 'at the moment of death.'

Mercy Attwell moved along the alleyway. She moved slowly and
haltingly, her left shoulder bumping against the hard warm steel
of the bulkhead. Her feet faltered as though she were blind.
There was no drive at all left within her. She was drained. She
was limp. Her physical tensions were gone. Only her fatigued
mind laboured on in thought.

For ten years she had lived at the very nadir of sensation.
Tonight she had been at the zenith. But the music and the ecstasy
were so quickly gone and now she knew the true depths. It would
have been better not to have been up there, she thought. If I had
been left unsatisfied I would be alive still. Always afterward, with
Carl, she had been alive, even if she had been alive to hate and
weep. It was a cruel thing her body had done. Was it like this
with every woman, to be led ever upward, like a soaring rocket,
with a sweet taste of wine in the mouth and every heave of the
body, every gasp of breath, one movement closer to a frantic
ten-second eternity until it finally came in total exaltation, way
up amongst the far stars? And then to be hurled in shattering
cataclysm down into an icy bath of awakening. Where the cabin
was a raw steel cabin and the bed had the absurd claw-marks of
her upward progress and there was the sick smell of gin and stale
cigarette smoke in the hot air.

They would not look at me, she thought, when I left. They
would not look at me, or at each other. There is this fine time,
this two-hour time. And then the shame. The body is a cheat. For
ten years I have lived with this, to find that I live within a
cheat.

A bar of light fell across her path. It stopped her with its

febrile solidity. She looked at it and then realized that a door
had opened off the alleyway. A door had opened and O'Connor
stood before her, his arms folded, blocking her path.

'Hello, you American bitch,' he said.

Her mouth opened silently. She tried feebly to move past him.
If he had been a wall of reeds, she would have failed. But he
was iron. He took her with his fingers encircling one wrist and
led her into his cabin, shoving her against the bed, and shut
and locked the door. Then he leaned against it and looked at
her.

'Like a drink?'

Her voice came out in a whisper. 'I will tell my husband.'

He laughed suddenly. 'Your poor, Goddam, son-of-a-bitch sky-
pilot husband!' He lowered his voice. 'I'll tell him too, baby.
I'll tell him what you've been doing tonight. And last night. You
think I'm blind?' He scrubbed at his mouth with the back of
a hand. The eyes in the petulant, heavy-chinned face glittered
at her. 'How he'd suffer, the poor bastard. It is a very refined
form of torture for a man to be told his wife is lying on her back
for the other team.'

He came away from the door quite suddenly and went over
to the cupboard against the bulkhead opposite his bed. There
was a bottle there, and glasses and a jug of water. He slopped
whisky into two glasses, added a dollop of water and thrust one
at her where she crouched against his bed, staring at him.

'Drink this, baby. Drink with a fellow American. All those
months in the camp, I dreamed of this. I dreamed of drinking
with a clean-cut American girl.'

She made no move, no answer. She remained rigidly impassive,
staring at him.

O'Connor came close to her. He pressed the glass against her
face. Some of the whisky spilled. It ran fire into one eye and
wasted down her cheek.

'Better drink, baby.'

She took the glass. The pain in her eye told her that she was
alive. She drank, and gagged, and drank some more until the
glass was empty.

'Good baby.' O'Connor's own glass was almost neat liquor.
He drank some greedily. 'You were wise, kid. Poor old Attwell
would have suffered, had I told him. Now I won't tell him. He
won't suffer the way I suffered.'

He bent over, almost doubled, staring into her face. 'I didn't
have his kind of torture. I got it plain and unsubtle. I got beaten.'
Abruptly he straightened. He stormed across the cabin and hammered a big fist at the door so hard that it rattled. Then he turned.

He put his shoulders against it. His body was quivering. His knuckles were skinned. He stared at the blood beginning to well out of the abrasions and then shoved the hand in his pocket. 'That's the way I got beaten. And with the boot, too. They put the boot in. In the guts, in the kidneys. Ah God, those guys. They knew nothing. They're not like Americans.'

A sob welled out of him and his eyes glittered tears. His face contorted, like a child who has been deeply hurt. 'One day they came to me. "So it's you," they said. And then they started in. Christ, I had it hard.'

He wrenched himself away from the door and went rapidly to the cupboard, turning his back on her. He added more whisky to his nearly full glass. All she could see were his shoulders, bulky but not wide, the big shaking hand and the bottle chattering on the rim of the glass.

He turned quite suddenly. The look in his eyes terrified her. 'Guys in a prison camp go raw. You understand? They shed civilization like a snake sheds its skin. Some of them stay brave and dumb. They figure they're still in the army. Others look after number one. Is that a crime?' His voice flared. 'Is it right to suffer for some Goddam stupid principle?' He lowered his voice confidingly. 'It's not, baby. Bravery is stupidity. The words are synonymous. You've got to stay in line. Play it cool. But they were too dumb to understand, those punks.' He laughed suddenly. It was a corruption of mirth. 'And yet I'm the one who's here, baby. I'm the one who got away. Funny, isn't it?'

There was a silence that seemed to her like an aeon of time. It rolled by while he stared into nothing, lost in another place. Then abruptly he recovered himself. 'Here, baby, have some of this. Have a drink with Bunny.' When he saw the dumb refusal in her eyes his voice hardened. 'Come on, baby, you don't want it in your face, again, do you?'

She read his expression. Dear God, she thought, I cannot turn to you. And I cannot scream. She put out her hand, took the glass and drank some of the whisky. It was nearly pure. It scorched her throat, made a fire inside her.

O'Connor sat next to her on the bed. He put out a hand and fingered her neck and shoulder while she sat quite still. His eyes were suddenly feverish.

'Long time no do,' he said softly. He took her suddenly and pulled her against him. The glass fell from her fingers and struck the bed, spilling whisky on them impartially. It made the only bond that existed between them as he pulled her against him.

The rising sun threw a single lance-like ray against the hospital

window. It struck the metal rim, glanced off and was flung across
the room where it made a pale bar of light on the bulkhead above
Osgood's bed.

Lincott pulled the sheet over the dead man's face. Then he
turned and looked at Mary Fannin. The night, he thought, had
purified her. It had put hollows in her cheeks and deepened the
shadows under her eyes, but it had removed the look of spurious
wisdom. It was gone from the fullness of her lips, and the deeps
of her eyes held only sadness.

She got up shoeless, creased from the long hours. She stood
looking down at the bed.

'Turn off the fans.' She kept her back to him, hearing the
click of the switch. The thrumming died away and only then
did she turn slowly to face him.

'Doc,' she said, 'I'm not crying. I don't want to cry. Is that
wrong?'

He put his arm around her. 'No. You never cry when you're
so close to death.'

They walked out of the hospital into the brilliant shining
clarity of the early morning.

CHAPTER EIGHT

SLOAN slapped his tray down and leant against the greasy table
for support. 'Fried eggs, bacon, banger, grilled tomato four times.'

The fat, friendly, sweating face of the cook loomed up. 'Comin'
up.' His eyes narrowed and he bent forward suddenly to study
the steward. 'Cor strike a light! You look proper done in, mate.'

Sloan shook his head. The cook's face blurred and then came
back into focus. 'I feel done in. Think I got the 'flu comin' on.
Been shivery ever since I showed a leg this morning. Me 'ead feels
funny, too.'

The cook went away and came back with four plates containing
sausage and bacon. 'Eggs and tomatoes'll be ready in a sec.' He
grinned. 'You should take more water with it.'

'Nah, it's not that.' Sloan couldn't even return the thrust.
'I'm ill. And what a flippin' morning I've 'ad. First I takes coffee
to the Yank. 'e's lyin' on his bunk, 'alf dead, with eyes like beet-
roots, and the cabin is stunk-up with booze smell. "Good morning,
Sir," I says, "you may not know that Mister Osgood, our Radio
Officer, died an hour ago." I was just givin' 'im the news, see?
So what's he do? 'e goes stark ruddy mad. "Course I knows," he
screams, and uses all them Yank swear-words, and starts yellin'

about the Angel of Death. I couldn't foller it all. And then he dries up and comes for me and I gets out of that cabin flippin' fast, I can tell you.'

'Ah, don't let it bother you.' The cook wiped sweat from his forehead with a galley towel. 'I think that Yank went crazy in the P.O.W. camp.' He gave Sloan a dark look. 'You know what the Communists do? They drip water on your 'ead until you go bonkers.'

He went away again. Sloan put his hand to his head. It felt searingly hot. He blinked his eyes. A sudden bout of ague took him and he shuddered. Bleedin' 'ell, he thought, I'm going to pass out if this goes on.

The cook came back with a platter and slid fried eggs and half tomatoes on to the plates with a spatula. When he looked up, Sloan was leaning against the table, his eyes shut, shivering.

'Hey!' The cook put out an arm. 'You're sick, mate. Better book off. Where's that no-good little 'Ookins? Let him take over.'

Sloan opened his eyes. 'Let me get shot of this lot.' He picked up the tray. The cook's fat face swam before his eyes.

The cook watched him sympathetically. 'Can't be much doin' at breakfast, anyway. Never known it so quiet.'

Sloan let out a shuddering sigh. 'Only Mister Quinan, the Old Man, Mister Proctor and the Froggy. The Engineers are busy. Mister Lucas is doing the meal relief, of course. He'll be down when Mister Quinan is finished. Miss Fannin worked all night in the 'ospital. She and the Doc are kipping. And Mrs Attwell ain't well. She's in her cabin with 'er ubby and they don't want breakfast.'

He turned away unsteadily. Halfway to the dining saloon he stopped and frowned. He looked down at the tray. He had suffered a complete loss of awareness. He knew vaguely that he was frightened. He moved on slowly, trembling, bemused. Then there came a very brief moment when he returned to reality. It lasted only a fraction of a second, but it was long enough for terror to take him by the throat with a vision of blackness and death. He cried silently, God help me, and then he moved back into a dark place.

It was the command-post bunker and he knew it well. A shell landed overhead. The concussion shook him and he cringed. Sand dribbled through the roof. He moved forward very slowly. Another shell struck overhead, shaking him. More sand, sand down his collar. He trembled.

'It's started,' he whispered. 'The bleedin' barrage has started again.'

Lincott swam slowly out of a deep pit of sleep. His body was drugged with it, fibreless, quiescently unresponding. But his mind came to the surface, gradually at first and then, reacting to an urgent calling, a loud insistent calling, it snapped quickly and brutally awake. It dragged his unwilling body with it so that he sat up in the same moment, his heart drumming with fright. He had been asleep for thirty-five minutes.

Usher's scared, sweat-beaded face looked down, as though from a great height.

'Sir! Sir! Doctor Lincott! Are you awake, Sir?'

Lincott stumbled to his feet. 'Sparks?' he said. 'Is he . . .' Then he remembered that Sparks was dead. 'What's the matter?' He found his creased white trousers and fumbled them on. He had been too tired when he came in to do anything more than strip to his underpants and fall on to the bed.

'It's Sloan, Sir. He's sick. Very sick. In the dining saloon.'

Lincott found his tunic. Usher was already at the door, holding it open, urging Lincott on with his eyes. Still flinging it on, he ran along the alleyway, following Usher's drumming heels.

There was a cluster of still figures in the dining saloon. They stood amongst a shambles of smashed plates, trampled tomato, the custard-yellow of broken eggs.

Lincott burst in amongst them, pushing them aside. He had a quick, panoramic view of their faces: Grove shaking, badly rattled, opening his mouth to speak; Proctor stiff-faced, with dark shadows under his eyes; Quinan holding on to the arm of Sloan who stood crouched racked with ague, his blind gaze travelling very slowly about the room.

Lincott tried to control his breathing. His chest was still heaving from the run. He said to Quinan, 'What happened?'

Grove thrust in. 'He came through the doorway carrying the tray. I happened to look up. His face had a strange expression. Then he ducked and dropped the tray. He started talking about a barrage—an artillery barrage. He is completely out of his mind.'

Lincott reached out, touched Sloan's forehead. It was very hot. He experienced a feeling of helplessness. His heart seemed to sink away within him, leaving the breathy, fluttering wings of fear.

'Let's get him to the hospital. I doubt that he can walk.' He was surprised at how normal and controlled his voice sounded.

He put his arms around Sloan's shoulders. 'Easy old chap.' Gently, he pulled the man back so that he and Quinan could take the steward's arms while Proctor and Usher took his legs. Much in the manner of Sparks, the afternoon before, they began to carry him from the room. But Grove put a hand on the doctor's arm.

'Just a minute, Lincott.' He gestured at Sloan. 'What is the matter with this man?'

Lincott stared at him. 'I don't know, yet.'

'Is it the same thing that killed Osgood?'

Lincott looked quickly around at the other faces. What was Grove trying to do—invite panic? He said, 'It may be. Until I examine him I can't say.'

Grove's mouth twisted. 'There seem to be an awful lot of "don't knows" and "can't says" in your vocabulary.'

Lincott had hardly slept. He looked into the contused eyes of the Captain and his control broke. 'I am not a bloody magician!' He shook his arm loose. 'Get out of my way, please.' Even to his own ears, his voice sounded over-loud, and shockingly strained.

The party made its way in silence to the hospital, which had been cleaned earlier. Osgood's body was gone, to be shrouded for later burial. Usher helped Lincott strip the sick man and then Loncott was alone with the memory of Quinan's hesitant parting smile and the friendly concern in the Chief Officer's eyes. He is worried, Lincott thought, as much about me as he is about Sloan.

He turned to the sick man and began a thorough examination. There was no need to record his findings, although he would do this later—they stayed indelibly engraved on his mind as each brutal fact aligned itself in turn with Osgood's symptoms: temperature, one hundred and three; deep flush; patient in a state of stupor which would probably deteriorate into coma; circumoral pallor; body skin blotchily discoloured; spleen normal; urine unrevealing; blood count unrevealing.

Lincott stopped at that stage and gave Sloan an injection of tetracyclene. There was no harm in reversing the process. Then he sat back next to the bed, lit a cigarette, and struggled against the first insidious tremors of panic.

Epidemic. The word loomed huge in his mind. An epidemic on an isolated, crippled ship, of an unknown killer-virus. It would sweep them like a grass-fire.

He tried to reassure himself. Osgood's body had been debilitated by alcohol. He would have died from it in due course. A comparatively mild illness, in his state, could have killed him. Sloan, by comparison, although older, was fitter. The disease had been detected earlier. It might run a surprisingly mild course.

I must not be so gloomy, he told himself. I am jumping to conclusions. But when he put the cigarette down, when he studied the still form on the bed again, the moment of false, self-induced hope was instantly gone. He knew with the absolute certainty of all his years of training that Sloan was very ill. Sloan would die unless he could find the cure.

He got up slowly and walked down the room, passing the empty beds. He stopped at the end and blindly studied the blank steel bulkhead. It is a lonely road, he thought, that I have to follow. He became bitter, letting a tide of self-pity engulf him.

There was a sound of light footsteps crossing the deck. Lincott turned quickly. And then the mood of hopelessness was suddenly gone, and he smiled with a great fullness.

Mary Fannin stood at the foot of Sloan's bed, the bed that had been Osgood's. She stood very still, studying him with those grey discerning eyes. A time of moments rolled by. And then she said, ' "I am licked at the moment of death." That's what you told me last night. Remember?'

He nodded. 'I had forgotten for a little while.' He came up to her. 'Thank you for reminding me.'

She smiled. 'We nurses have our uses.' A slender hand gestured at the bed. 'How bad is he?'

'About the same as Osgood was, in the beginning.'

'You figure I should start in sponging him right away?'

He looked at her. How do you begin to understand people, he wondered. Instead he said severely, 'You shouldn't be here. You've had as little sleep as I have. You're a passenger. There's no call for you to knock yourself out in a sick-room.'

A small grin tugged at her lips. 'Doc,' she said, 'I was bored, is all.'

He laughed. He couldn't help himself. 'All right, Mary. Start the sponging. The earlier the better, really. But I want to do a lumbar puncture first. Let's get going.'

They busied themselves. Ten minutes later, when the lumbar puncture had been performed and its results had proved as negative as Osgood's, Mary Fannin stopped in what she was doing and said, 'Oh, by the way. You're wanted by the Attwells. She isn't feeling too good.'

Lincott became completely still. He raised his eyes slowly 'She's not—very sick?'

'No.' Mary Fannin shook her head. 'The old guy caught me when I was passing their cabin. He said to tell you to come, but I could hear her arguing from inside.'

Lincott looked at his watch. He pretended reluctance.

'I suppose I'd better go. Five minutes away from Sloan isn't going to do any harm. You'll be here.'

He found his bag and quickly put together the few things he

needed. He was clumsy and irritable all of a sudden. He dropped his stethoscope twice and then swore when he had trouble getting the bag shut.

Mary Fannin had been watching him. 'Stephen.'

He turned impatiently, in a hurry to go. 'Yes?'

She shrugged. 'Here I go, sticking out my neck. But you're all fingers and thumbs. You're like a nervous boy-scout. Is it worth-while? Mercy Attwell is a married woman. On top of that, she's gone kind of haywire. She . . .' Mary Fannin stopped suddenly. 'It's none of my business.'

Lincott felt the hot blood rushing into his face. Anger struck him like a squall. It showed in the rigid lines of his face.

He said coldly, 'I agree with you. It is absolutely none of your business. You make a very good nurse, Miss Fannin, but you should learn to keep your impertinences to yourself.'

He turned abruptly and walked out of the room.

O'Connor came out of the alleyway and stood in the shade of the lower boat deck. He looked aft towards the gaping black mouth of Number Five hold, whiskered with lengths of cable and stubbled with gear. It had an abandoned air.

He checked his watch. It was ten minutes before eleven. The crew had been working since early this morning, shifting cargo from Number Five to lighten the stern. Now they'd had to go below to clean up for the funeral of Bertram Osgood, which was being held at eleven. He had only been dead since six, but in this climate, and this heat, things like that had to be done quickly.

He grinned. He'd seen the crew's mood. They'd had to work like donkeys in a temperature well over one hundred degrees, driven by Lucas's scalding tongue and Quinan's determination. They were smouldering with an explosive hatred that could find no immediate release.

O'Connor left the shade and went out under the brutal hammerblows of the sun. Hawes, Ludd, Draper, the long-maned Kyle and the little drunkard who was always in their company, were coming for'ard from their quarters in the stern. He went to meet them. He looked cool in more borrowed clothes: a pair of pastel hipsters belonging to Proctor that clung with over-snug determination, a cotton shirt donated by the Purser which caught him under the armpits and the same linen jacket he had worn the night of his rescue, on Monday.

They met on the after-deck, for'ard of the mast table. Hawes's group remained together, uncommunicative, suspicious of the American. They were reasonably respectable in jeans and white shirts. Draper wore a tee-shirt that clung like a second skin. It had been cut to follow the vee-shape of his trunk, and had a picture of a loaded barbell stencilled on the front.

'Hi, you guys.' O'Connor gave them an easy, relaxed smile. He produced cigarettes and offered them around. They were billed, by arrangement with the Purser, to Uncle Sam, who, O'Connor had assured the Purser, would redeem in hard cash when O'Connor was exchanged. 'I'm always early for funerals, late for weddings. Crazy, isn't it?'

'I wish they'd get the frigging thing over with.' Hawes fingered the ring in his right ear, his small black eyes studying O'Connor.

'Aah, for Pete's sake.' The American grinned, held a match to Hawes's cigarette. 'I know how you feel, buddy. When it's a guy you don't really know, it's just a funeral. Words out of a book.' He made a gesture of mock humiliation. 'Especially when it's an officer, huh? And Osgood was a punk, let's face it. A souse. Permanently canned.'

Draper leant forward. 'He was a bum-boy, you know.'

O'Connor grinned and shook his head. Draper was a Scouse, and the gabbled words had been unintelligible. 'I don't read you, Muscles. I don't get you loud and clear.'

Hawes shook his head. 'He says Mister Osgood was a homo. You know?' He made a filthy gesture.

'Oh, sure.' O'Connor grinned. 'I got it. Say, it's crazy, isn't it, we're all talking English and we can't understand each other?'

He put his hands apart, palms facing outward. 'So what? Who cares? We're pals because I know how you guys feel. It's crazy, this idea of fitting the spare prop. Grove should yell for help before they bury number two.'

'Number Two?' Hawes was thinking in nautical parlance. 'There's nothing wrong with Mister Proctor.'

'For Christ's sake!' O'Connor grinned. 'I mean the second guy to die.'

They stared at each other in silence. Then Hawes said, cautiously, 'You mean Sloan?'

'Sloan or some other punk who gets it worse.' O'Connor shrugged and eyed Hawes, watching him, waiting to see how he would respond.

Hawes had a shrewd animal intelligence. He studied O'Connor for a moment. 'Are you trying to tell me there's an epidemic on this ship?'

O'Connor chuckled. 'Hell, no. Two guys don't make an epidemic.' He flicked his cigarette over the side. 'But it's kind of worrying, isn't it? First Sparks flips. He goes crazy and smashes the radio. The Doctor finds that he's ill, real sick, and treats him right through the night, but Sparks dies. And then this morning exactly the same thing happens to Sloan. He flips, doesn't he? Starts talking about a barrage.'

Ludd's single eye flickered with interest. 'Sloan had a hell of a time in the war.'

'Sure.' O'Connor nodded. 'His mind started playing tricks. He was right back there.' He looked at them sharply. 'Have you heard the latest reports on Sloan?'

Hawes shook his head and the rest remained silent and intent. They all knew. Everybody knew. But they wanted to see what O'Connor would say.

'He's dying.' O'Connor, with his heavy face and deliberate, factual voice, had an ability to shock.

'He's lying there naked while they sponge him and the Doc injects him with antibiotics. But they're the same antibiotics he used on Sparks. Sloan can't talk or see or think. He's going exactly the same way Osgood went.'

There was a reflective silence. Hawes dragged on his cigarette. 'That makes sense. But if there's an epidemic starting, then it's a germ causing it. And it's not something picked up in Hong Kong because those two weren't mates. In fact Sparks never went ashore in Hong Kong. He was bottled all the time.' He fingered one ear-ring. 'It must be something on board.'

'I think that's about medically accurate.' O'Connor looked over his shoulder. Grove, Quinan and Proctor emerged on to the lower boat-deck, blinking their eyes against the searing glare. Grove held a black-covered book in one hand.

'I'd better go.' O'Connor gestured at the officers. 'Looks as though they're ready to begin.' He moved as though to leave.

Hawes thrust out a sudden rough hand and caught him by the wrist. O'Connor winced from the force of the grip.

'Not so fast, Lieutenant O'Connor.' Hawes's face broke into a sudden humourless smile that showed a quick confidence. It was as though he had succeeded in placing the American in some mental classification that made them equals. 'You're fast with your suggestions but not with your solutions.' They studied each other while O'Connor stood docilely pinioned.

'There's two men sick, so far, from the same disease. And one of them is dead. I might be the next one. What do you reckon is the cause?'

O'Connor's eyes looked into Hawes's face for a moment. They gave no hint of the sudden tremendous violence with which he ripped his hand loose.

He rubbed his wrist, grinning without resentment. Then he said, 'What do you figure to expect, Hawes, you carry rotten dead bodies from Point A to Point B? You reckon that's a healthy pastime?' Then he flipped a casual hand and walked away to join the officers assembled on the lower boatdeck.

He left a profound silence behind him.

The Attwells had come out and joined the group. Mercy looked exhausted. There were dark circles under her eyes. She locked glances with O'Connor for a moment and then looked away.

'Hi, everybody.' O'Connor smiled at Attwell. 'Taking the service, Reverend?'

Grove looked around sharply. The idea hadn't occurred to him. He tendered the Anglican Prayer-book hesitantly.

'By all means, Mister Attwell. I'm sorry. I hadn't thought of it.'

Attwell smiled and shook his head. 'I am not an ordained minister of any Church, Captain. I simply preach the Word of God to all denominations, sects, creeds and religions. In the absence of a minister or priest, the duty, I'm afraid, falls on you, as Master of this vessel.'

Grove was reluctant. Quinan, studying him, found that he was seeing Grove as a stranger, a haggard man battered facially by his passages with the bottle, over-thin and ridiculous in his tropical uniform that exposed the slivers of legs and the concave boniness of his chest. I have become over-critical, he told himself. It is because we are helpless, more so even than a becalmed sailing ship because if a wind came it would not help. We are caught up in each other too much on this idle, drifting vessel.

Grove turned away from Attwell and opened the prayer-book. He had two places marked—the order for the burial of the dead, and the section dealing with the burial of the dead at sea.

All the crew who were available had drifted up, including McBlain and Norton, the Second Engineer. McBlain looked tired and overwrought. He mopped at his face continually with an over-large handkerchief, reminding Quinan of the episode on the bridge yesterday. Stephen Lincott and Mary Fannin had emerged momentarily from the hospital and stood watching at a distance. Hookins came slowly from the stern, his face the colour of the white jacket he wore. He looked at no one and stood alone near the mast table.

Gindle and Gauldie appeared, walking awkwardly along the port working alleyway. They carried between them a narrow board platform, and on it was laid the canvas-wrapped body of Osgood.

Mary Fannin watched it go by. She experienced a peculiar sensation of disbelief. This was the man she had sponged last night, the man whose naked body she had held curled for the lumbar puncture, the man whose breathing she had heard deepen and flutter like the tremulous wings of a trapped moth and finally fade into a silence that was impossible death.

He is too real, she thought. The canvas shroud outlined the body instead of covering it. The lump at the feet, she knew, was the scrap iron that would take the body down into the everlasting green waters of the Nan Hai. She looked away.

Gindle and Gauldie stopped, resting the tip of the platform on the rail. They turned and looked at Grove.

Grove cleared his throat. His hands, holding the prayer-book, trembled slightly. He read straight from the beginning:

' "I am the resurrection and the life, said the Lord : he that believeth in me, though he were dead, yet shall he live : and whosoever liveth and believeth in me shall never die." '

Grove read badly. He stumbled over the unaccustomed words. When his voice stopped they could hear the silken flick of the thin pages as he turned them shakily. He saw the massed type of the Lesson taken from Corinthians and discarded it, turning abruptly to the passage dealing with the ceremony at the graveside. He studied it a moment, then turned to the other place he had marked for burial at sea, so that he could compare the passages and find a point at which the normal service had to be departed from. He did this in a quite complete silence devoid even of the normal working noises of the ship.

Then he began to read:

' "Man that is born of woman hath but a short time to live, and is full of misery. He cometh up, and is cut down, like a flower; he fleeth as it were a shadow, and never continueth in one stay." '

In the moment that he paused, Hookins began to sob. There was no other sound at all but the sudden frightening, broken sound of his crying. And he wept unnaturally erect, not bent and in penitence, looking blindly ahead while his cheeks boiled with tears and his throat uttered the harsh constricted noises of a man in grief.

Grove stayed mute. His eyes fluttered from Hookins to the book and back again as the sound continued. He looked at the crew but they stayed motionless, transfixed like Gindle and Gauldie who were holding the chip of platform on which the body lay.

Nobody moved. Grove began to read again, raising his tenor voice above the noise of weeping:

' "In the midst of life we are in death: of whom may we seek for succour but of thee O Lord, who for our sins art justly displeased?" '

Grove stopped again, defeated by Hookins's grief. No one was looking at him. Everyone stood frozen, staring at the steward.

Hookins moved forward. He took a few steps that rang hollowly upon the deck. His mouth opened, square, pulled by the puppet-strings within him:

' "Deliver us not into the bitter pains of eternal death." ' His eyes were fixed on a distant horror that showed in their dilation. 'She was not dead until the end. Until the very end. She saw. She heard. She felt. She touched. She smelt. She knew that the body is sown in dishonour, and corruption, and weakness.'

His voice had the fullness that Grove's had lacked. Time seemed to stop. The puppet-figure marched rigidly another pace. Then the mouth opened again and the damning phrases rang out across the deck: ' "It is too late to knock when the door shall be shut; and too late to cry for mercy when it is the time of justice. O terrible voice of most just judgment, which shall be pronounced upon them, when it shall be said unto them go ye cursed, into the fire everlasting which is prepared for the devil and his angels." '

He turned so suddenly that some of them drew back from his madness. His eyes had gone to Hawes, who stood a few yards away with his group. An arm went out, pointing, like an accusing robot. His voice rang out: 'There is the Devil, and the angels of Hell!'

Only Quinan was watching Hawes. He saw the ugly violence break out on Hawes's face. Hawes moved forward as though impelled by a current, but Ludd's knotty arms came from behind. They locked about his waist and held him there.

Hookins twisted. His legs seemed to give way suddenly so that he lurched. He lost sense of direction and cannoned into a fitting below the mast table, cutting his face up on the cheekbone. The blood that welled suddenly out of the gash made him look clown-like because of the whiteness of his face. He turned to Grove and laughed, while the tears still cascaded down his face. And then, quite suddenly, his eyes rolled back in his head and he pitched forward with a crash on to the hot iron deck.

He lay there in a petrified silence for a full ten seconds while nobody moved. Then Lincott was suddenly kneeling over the body. He touched Hookins. He pulled down an eyelid, put a hand briefly over the heart. Then he turned his head, looking along the deck, and nodded. His nod was to Mary Fannin, but it was correctly interpreted by all the many who stood under the scald of the sun.

Lincott stood up. He looked around and then at Grove and made a gesture at the body.

Grove held the prayer-book clamped rigidly in his hands. His eyes moved from Lincott to the nearest group of seamen.

'Hawes, Ludd. Take Hookins to the hospital.'

Grove's voice had a rusty dryness. He stood firm, holding the prayer-book. Hawes and Ludd remained still. Gindle and Gauldie were caught in tableau holding the platform on which Osgood's body lay. It seemed a wafer of wood in their unmoving hands. Lincott watched Grove. Quinan and Proctor and the Attwells and Puget and Mary Fannin at the hospital door and all the rest of the concourse gathered under the China Sea sun seemed momentarily fixed in time.

Hawes broke it. He was afraid, and his face showed it. He moved a little. Then he said, 'No, Sir. He's sick of the same thing that killed Mister Osgood, Sir, the same thing that's got Sloan dying. I don't want to touch him.'

All of them moved suddenly. There was no sound, but their bodies swayed like corn to the first puff of sudden wind. It was the impact of Hawes's words, the finality of them. And it was the shock of hearing said what was silent in all of them.

Grove let the prayer-book drop to his side. He held it in one hand while the other clenched and trembled, the fingers rubbing nervously at the sweat on the palm. His face darkened.

'I am giving you an order, Hawes. You and Ludd will take Hookins to the hospital.'

There was another short silence.

Hawes fingered an ear-ring. His small black eyes met Grove's. 'No, Sir.'

Grove studied him a moment. The hypnotic influence of Hookins's collapse was leaving him. He was no longer dealing with a strange robot figure, heedless and uncaring. Hawes was solid flesh and blood, full of calculated malice and wilful disobedience. Fury took hold of him. Quinan saw it manifest itself in the way Grove bent forward silently, the way his body trembled. He felt a sinking feeling of hopelessness. Grove was going to force the issue. Standing to Grove's left and slightly behind him, he stared at the thin, turkey-coloured neck and tried to will him into a sense of reason. But Grove plunged headlong into fatal confrontation.

'Your explanation is nonsense, Hawes. And your action amounts to wilful disobedience and insubordination.' He raised his voice, so that the next words came out in an authoritative bark: 'Take that man to the hospital!'

But Hawes stood his ground. He shook his head. 'I think my reason is fair enough, Sir. I won't touch him.'

Grove shouted right on the top of Hawes's words, so that they

were almost consumed by his voice, 'I'll log you, Hawes! I'll fine
you! Do you know what the penalty is for wilful disobedience?'

'I know. I've read the books.' Hawes's bass rumbled contemptuously. 'But I don't know but what the Union mightn't
have something to say. That man has a contagious disease. He . . .'

'To Hell and damnation with your bloody Union!' Purple-
faced, Grove allowed all control to leave him. 'Are you going to
take that man to the hospital?'

'No.' Hawes could have been carved out of stone. 'And this is
the third time of telling.'

There was a silence that seemed to stretch into minutes while
Grove struggled to find a way out, while he looked for a way
to save face. His eyes darted fleetingly to Quinan. Quinan saw
the convulsive flutter of the muscles in his cheeks, the uncontrolled spasm of agitation about the mouth. But it was too late
now to help.

Grove's glance went back to Hawes. His voice had lost its
crackle. The words seemed to burst out of him. 'That man is
lying on an iron deck. He'll fry unless you get him to the hospital.'

The hopelessness that Quinan had experienced turned into
solid despair. Grove had yielded. He had asked for quarter in
front of nearly the entire ship's company. The hatred of Grove
he had experienced yesterday in the wrecked radio room rushed
back. He conquered an insane desire to smash his fist into Grove's
face. But the rage remained bottled up inside him. He had to do
something, he had to break the tableau or they would all be here
for a thousand years.

Quinan drew a deep, shuddering breath. Then he broke away
from the group suddenly and ran out under the hard hand of
the sun to where Hookins lay. He scooped up the thin body as if
it had been that of a child. Standing, his eyes locked with Grove's
for a moment. Then he walked slowly along the after-deck, carefully mounted the short companion-way that led to the lower
boat-deck, and vanished in the direction of the hospital, followed
by Lincott and the girl.

Grove watched him go. A minute passed. Then he raised the
prayer-book. In a shaking voice he read quickly through the
remainder of the service. Then he nodded to Gindle and Gauldie.
They tipped the wooden platform, and all that remained of
Bertram Osgood slipped overboard with hardly the noise of his
body striking the water to remember him by.

Grove closed the prayer-book. The entire remainder of the
service had taken thirty seconds. It was brutally callous. But
Grove ignored Attwell's outraged stare and Puget's quizzically
lifted eyebrows. Sweat had burst out all over his face and was

streaming down his cheeks. His heart was thudding so violently that he thought it was going to break out of his body.

He turned to Proctor. 'Give my compliments to Mister Quinan and Doctor Lincott. Tell them to meet me on the bridge in five minutes.' He realized that Proctor was staring at him. He knew that his voice, even to his own ears, had had a dreadful gasping, gulping faintness. He shoved the prayer-book at Proctor. 'Here. Take this.'

He could not even wait for Proctor to leave. He turned away on trembling legs and lurched up on to the lower boat-deck, took the starboard companion-way to avoid even seeing the hospital door, rushed along the boat-deck past the starboard lifeboat and clambered up the last companion-way on to the bridge wing. Then he stumbled through the wheelhouse and chartroom and wrenched open the door to the radio cabin.

The whisky was where he had hidden it, in one of Osgood's drawers behind a thick bundle of files. It glinted darkly amber in the gloom. The cork squeaked out of the bottle and the whisky gushed into his mouth, searing his tongue and gums, running fire down his throat, springing an instant trap of spasm in his stomach so that he had to pull the bottle away from his lips and clench both hands over his abdomen while he heaved dryly. But he managed to keep it down.

He put the bottle back, found a clean handkerchief and patted his chin and neck where the whisky had spilled. Then he left the radio room, closing the door firmly, and went to the wheelhouse.

The whisky had cleansed his mouth like an astringent wash. When he lit a cigarette it tasted good, nutty and rich the way it had in the old days before his palate had soured. He drew in smoke and let it rebound from the bridge window as he stared blindly down at the foredeck.

He was so angry that he knew only the whisky had saved him from collapse. Starting with Hawes's refusal to obey his command, he had begun to pant from the fury of the rage inside him, to over-breathe so that he had starved his bloodstream with a shortage of carbon dioxide. Lincott had explained all this to him a long time ago, when they had been on better terms. The raw shock of the whisky had prevented him from fainting. It had lit a fire inside him which sent tongues of solid, reassuring warmth along his veins. The hard, clamped knot in the pit of his stomach relaxed. His breathing slowed down but his anger, if anything, increased. It was so rampant that he was unable to marshal his thoughts properly.

'Bastards!' He spat the word out aloud. He hated them, all of them, with a vicious, vitriolic hatred. Hawes and Ludd.

Insubordinate scum. **Animals.** Gutter-sweepings. Quinan, that imperturbable, holier-than-thou bastard, taking the law into his own hands by carrying Hookins away. Quinan shopped me, Grove thought. I'd have fixed Hawes's clock, by God, and Ludd's too, but Quinan shopped me. And then there was that lily-white, mealy-mouth bloody doctor, who was the cause of all the trouble in the first place because he was too damned stupid and incompetent to diagnose the illness.

He dropped the half-smoked cigarette and ground it under a savage boot-heel, as quickly fumbling for and lighting another. He had it in his lips when Quinan and Lincott appeared suddenly on the port bridge wing. The wheelhouse door opened and slid shut hollowly behind them. They stopped and stared at him.

'Thank you. Thank you very bloody much! What did you do—have a quick sleep before you came up here?'

His anger was overpowering. He was unable to realize the incredible and even terrible picture he presented in his rumpled, sweat-sodden tunic and shorts that bagged over the bony body, his eyes quite wild in a face that had gone white under the permanent puce-coloured overlay of his cheeks.

Quinan took a step forward. He was genuinely concerned. 'Wal, are you all right?'

'Don't you "Wal" me, Mister Quinan!' Grove's voice took on a wicked note. 'What the hell did you mean by butting in and taking Hookins away? You destroyed my authority in front of the crew.'

Quinan's face showed his disbelief. He was still the same Quinan, steady and rock-like and unshakeable, more concerned for Grove than angry at the treatment he was receiving, and because of this Grove, recognizing it, hated him all the more.

'Hookins is a very sick boy, Sir.' Quinan spoke quietly and respectfully. 'It seemed to me far more important to get him into bed, there and then. Hawes and Ludd can still be dealt with.'

'No, they can't! The effect is there. It has made its mark.' Grove swung his attention to Lincott. Here the real hate lay. It was difficult to argue with Quinan because he was so seldom wrong. And Grove, even in his rage, knew he needed him. But Lincott was another story.

'Doctor Lincott.' The fury bubbled up anew. But this time, with the whisky helping, he managed to inflect into it an icy note that resembled control. 'We have one man dead and two men sick. They all seem to have had the same symptoms. I don't suppose there would be any purpose in your denying that there is now an epidemic on this ship?'

'I had no intention of denying it,' Lincott said woodenly.

'So you admit that there is an epidemic on board?'

'Let's try to be rational,' Lincott said. 'I don't know whether three cases make an epidemic—in a community as small as ours, I suppose they do. But certainly three men have contracted a contagious disease, I agree.'

'What is it?'

Lincott coloured faintly. 'I don't know.'

'You don't know?' Grove repeated the words in pretended astonishment. 'Why?'

'It is an unknown disease.'

'Unknown to you, you mean.'

Lincott was now flushed and angry, but still on the defensive. 'There are many viruses. In the present case, the syndrome resembled at first both typhoid and meningitis. But it was neither. The disease is characterized by . . .'

'Don't give me your ruddy medical double-talk,' Grove interrupted rudely. 'What the hell is a syndrome?'

'A pattern of symptoms,' Lincott said.

'Very well. Now am I to understand that three men have contracted a disease of which the syndrome is the same in each case, that this disease resembles typhoid and meningitis, but is neither, and that you do not know what it is or what to do about it?'

'That's hardly fair,' Lincott protested. 'I am working in the dark. I have to try . . .'

'Doctor,' Grove interrupted again, 'have you evolved a cure?'

Lincott struggled to find words. Then he seemed to realize the hopelessness of trying to reason with Grove, of trying to explain his position. He shrugged suddenly and said, 'Not yet.'

'Ah, so.' Grove was pleased with the admission. 'Is there a possibility that more men will fall ill?'

'That is impossible to answer.'

'A great number of things seem impossible for you to answer,' Grove sneered, 'and all of them medical, oddly enough. Tell me, what preventive measures have you taken?'

Lincott was puzzled. 'Preventive measures? Do you mean . . . ?'

'Hygiene!' Grove shouted. 'Cleanliness! Goddamit, man, what is the matter with you this morning?' He thrust his face into Lincott's so that the doctor caught the reek of the fresh whisky smell. 'Do I have to spell everything out for you? Do you want me to have the rats killed? Do you want the toilet seats wiped? Do you want the crew to scrub their balls with disinfectant? Is that what you want? Or do you want anything?'

Lincott had gone white with anger and humiliation. But he tried to control himself. 'It is not the rats. You can forget about them. The men should avoid personal contact as much as possible.

And all food should be cooked. This will not stop the spread of the disease but it might help to contain it.'

'All right, Doctor. I'll see to it.' Grove dropped his cigarette and ground it out. 'But I want to make my attitude perfectly clear. I have been humiliated in front of my officers and men. The crew are afraid. Discipline shows signs of breaking down. Anything could happen if we are not careful. And for this state of affairs you will have to take full responsibility. I regard your inability to stamp out this—this syndrome as complete lack of competence on your part. Is that clear?'

Lincott stared at him open-mouthed. For a moment he was shocked beyond words. Then he laughed incredulously, but there was no mirth in the sound. 'My God, but you're mad! You've lost your mind, Grove. Can't you understand that there is *no* cure for the Hurst Syndrome? Or are you too befuddled to . . .'

'Don't you bloody-well talk to me like that!' Grove screamed.

'I'll talk how I bloody-well like!' Lincott, like Grove, had lost control. He was white-faced and shaking. 'You're too free with your accusations. I am not prepared to stand on this bridge and be insulted by a man who conceals his own lack of ability and mental deterioration behind the competence of his Chief Officer!' He turned and walked out of the wheelhouse.

'By God in Heaven!' Grove leaped out of the wheelhouse, murder written all over his face. When he got to the bridge wing Lincott was halfway down the companion-way. Grove stopped there and screamed at Lincott: 'I'll log you, Lincott! I'll have you struck off the medical register!'

Lincott stopped. He looked up. Calm had returned to him 'Go right ahead. And I intend to file a complete report on your habitual drunkenness.' Then he was gone along the deck.

Grove stood paralysed for a moment, panting. Then he stormed back into the wheelhouse, flung open the chartroom door and paused there. 'By God, I'm going to make that quack sorry!'

Quinan came up to him and put a hand on his shoulder. 'Wal, don't. You'll be cutting your own throat. If Lincott files a report on you, he'll be believed. McBlain, for one, will back him up. Don't you see?'

Grove hesitated, torn between Quinan's commonsense and his own rage. 'I've left my cigarettes in the radio cabin,' he said abruptly. He turned and walked away through the chartroom. He was gone five minutes, and when he returned Quinan could smell the fresh whisky on his breath.

But he was calmer. The frantic anger of a few minutes ago had been burnt out by the second dose of alcohol. He became suddenly brisk and businesslike. 'I have reconsidered my decision

to log Lincott, as well as Hawes and Ludd. But you must understand one thing, Gil.' He looked at Quinan with quite a strong
measure of shrewdness. 'This ship is idle and helpless. That
would be bad by itself, but on top of that we have an epidemic
of a disease on board that can kill. The crew are already afraid,
as I told Lincott. They have already defied me once. This could
lead to chaos. It is imperative, therefore, that any man who puts
a foot out of line is severely dealt with—far more severely than
would be the case in normal circumstances. And that is what
I propose to do.'

Quinan found and lit a cigarette. Then he said, 'If things get
worse, trouble will come from only one quarter: Hawes, Ludd,
Kyle, Draper and Knowles. And although the rest of the crew
might not back them up, they might also not stand in their way.
The Bo'sun has never been anything more than a figurehead.
You'll get no help from him. So if one of those rowdies gives
trouble, and you decide to act severely, how are you going to
enforce the punishment?'

Grove studied Quinan for a moment. 'What are you getting at?'

'Just this, Walter. Forget about discipline. Turn a blind eye.
What's the good of a court of law that sentences a man to death
and can't hang him? You would be in the same position. Until
we're out of this hole you'll have to play things very cool, you'll
have to overlook a lot. It's the only course open, unless you want
to lose control altogether.'

Grove looked at Quinan in silence for a long time. Quinan
could see his thoughts shuttling about by the passage of expression
across his flushed face. Then unexpectedly he smiled, and it was
that same tender, woman-like smile, backed by eyes that were
filled with an excess of affection.

'You crafty bastard!' He came up to Quinan, put one arm
around his shoulders and hugged him. 'You're right, Gil. Stone,
dead right. I don't know what I'd do without you, old strong and
silent!'

Quinan smiled automatically. Here we go again, he thought.
Wally Grove, the human weather-machine. Rain, squalls, thunder, sunshine, all at the click of a switch.

Gently, he shrugged off the encircling arm. 'I'd better be off.
We've got to get a move on with the work.'

Grove slapped him on the back. 'Good man, Gil. Hurry it up
all you can. I'll be along just now.'

Quinan left the wheelhouse and clattered down the port companion-way. Half-way down, he heard the radio cabin door being
closed. He paused a moment, shaking his head in bitter wonder-
ment. Then he went on aft, heading for Number Five hold.

CHAPTER NINE

MORNING dragged into afternoon. Lunch was poorly attended. Usher, who had been pressed into service as a steward, served it sullenly. Lincott and Mary Fannin had theirs brought to the hospital, and it was a sign of the crew's growing fear that Usher stubbornly refused to enter, and made them collect the plates at the door.

At precisely four bells, which was two o'clock, McBlain, the Chief Engineer, began acting strangely. He was talking to Savage, the Third, as they walked around the silent engines where the men were being kept busy on maintenance and minor repairs. His conversation grew more and more disjointed and interspaced with long pauses during which he stared silently into space. Savage had become uneasy. He was trying to invent an excuse for going topside and telling Lincott about it when he received a violent push in the back. They were standing next to the guard rail about one of the engines. Savage went over it and fell heavily. If the engines had been operating he would have been horribly injured. As it was, he received cuts and abrasions and was badly shocked, but by the time he had scrambled out McBlain had gone.

He was found in his locked cabin. When the door was burst open he had wrecked everything in sight. He was carried, struggling, to the hospital.

Half an hour later Norton, the Second Engineer, quietly collapsed and went straight into a coma.

The fear grew. To the crew, the disease assumed the proportions of a being, something tangible and yet intangible, lurking in the ship, ready to strike without warning. And as a being it was wicked, it must have its own origins in sin and corruption, because it made men mad before it destroyed them.

It was then that the whisperings of Hawes and Ludd and the others began to be heard. This was the reward, the superstitious whispers said, for carrying dead men. This was the revenge of men plucked from their graves. The being's home was in Number Three hold.

The fear grew greater. It became a breathy thing of panic, beating butterfly wings of terror in the bodies of the crew. The men avoided touching one another. The cook refused to receive back the plates from the hospital and Mary Fannin had to throw them overboard. Work on lightening the stern by removing cargo from Number Five slowed to a crawl.

At six bells in the afternoon Henry Norman, the Purser, contracted what Lincott had now christened the Hurst Syndrome. Norman was an ageing, aloof, debt-ridden man, an addicted and unsuccesful gambler. He became ill in the ship's lounge, where he had been reading, and pulled every book he could reach off the library shelves before he collapsed. Nobody would touch him, including Proctor and Lucas, who were called. Norman began an absurdly pathetic crawl to the hospital, watched along the way by frightened men. It was Lincott and Quinan who eventually found him and carried him away.

Usher flatly refused to return the chaotic pile of books to their shelves.

Work on Number Five hold ceased altogether.

In the hospital, Sloan was now dying. Lincott, busy administering sulfonamide to Henry Norman, found himself falling asleep with the hypodermic in his hand. He doused his head under the tap at the wash basin, finished with Norman, then excused himself and went to his cabin, where he gave himself an intramuscular injection of Dexadrine.

On the bridge, Grove and Quinan met and had a brief discussion. The crew would no longer work, and there was no way of forcing them. Even Grove, for once, was able to see the cold facts of the situation. The fitting of the spare propeller would have to be abandoned. It was decided that the *Florence Hurst* was now to be regarded as distressed and that all possible attempts would be made to obtain assistance. The International Code Signal NC, and the Quarantine Signal QL, went up to join the two black balls of the daylight Not-Under-Command sign. The two signals meant: 'I am in distress and require immediate assistance' and 'My ship is infected with contagious disease.'

All other regulation distress procedures were adopted. The foghorn was to be sounded at one-minute intervals, day and night. At night, rockets would be fired at intervals while the supply lasted. And 'flames on the vessel' would burn on the flying bridge. For this purpose the engineers erected an empty drum there, filled with cotton waste soaked in lamp oil.

In McBlain's cabin, Savage, the young Third Engineer, was making order out of chaos. He was a religious boy, and one of the few who was prepared to touch a sick man's belongings. He was convinced that he would never see McBlain again, so he had made a small pile of the Chief's personal belongings on the bed. There wasn't much—his last bank statement, showing that he was in overdraft to the extent of forty-three pounds; one or two bills; a wallet containing a picture of his wife and two daughters, both dandling his grandchildren on their knees; about twenty pounds in notes; some postage stamps; and a letter from the almoner of a hospital in Liverpool stating that Mrs McBlain was unable to write but sent her love and was feeling better.

Savage unashamedly read this letter, and wept. Then he put it on the bed and extracted the last item from the wallet, which was a small slip of paper bearing the words: 'I O U seven pounds thirteen shillings and sixpence, to be paid when the *Florence Hurst* docks.' It was signed 'B.O.C.' Savage had been upset by the letter from the almoner, and he was in any case opposed to card-playing and other similar forms of gambling. Angrily and emotionally, he crumpled the paper into a ball and threw it with the rest of the rubbish on to the floor.

In the early afternoon Grove had slept off the effects of a quarter-bottle of whisky taken in repeated trips to the radio cabin. Then he had gone boldly to Lincott and asked for vitamin B, which the doctor gave him in the form of a massive injection. At the same time he had informed Lincott that he had reconsidered his decision to log him. Lincott immediately tendered the withdrawal of the report he had intended to file on Grove, and an armed truce prevailed between them.

It was now five o'clock. Grove stood in the wheelhouse with Quinan, who was on watch. Overhead, they could hear hammering as Savage's fitters clamped the drum on the flying bridge. The foghorn's control was just outside the wheelhouse door on the port side. It emitted an ear-splitting blast every six seconds. Grove waited until the noise had stopped.

'Anything on the radar?'

Quinan shook his head. 'Nothing. We're all alone.'

'Then what's the use of blowing that bloody horn?' He went to the door and said to Usher, 'You can stop that for a while.' Coming back, he lit a cigarette and blew smoke against the bridge window. 'We're in trouble, Gil. God, what a shower! We've only been disabled for about thirty-three hours. We're not overdue. There won't even have been a search mounted, at this stage.' His eyes as he turned to Quinan had blurred with tears. 'We'll drift the Nan Hai, dying one by one. We'll be a crew of dead men before they find us.' For a moment he choked up, seized with emotion that was entirely self-pity. Then he burst out, 'Why does it have to happen to me? Why always me? I'm bloody well cursed, aren't I? Star-crossed, I said yesterday. And that's what I am. What have I done to deserve this, Gil?'

Quinan said nothing. But he looked at Grove with wonder. All I feel for you now, he thought, is contempt. Even the hatred has gone. There's Sloan dying, and decent men like McBlain and Norton dangerously ill, and all you can think of is yourself.

There was movement on the port bridge wing. Looking up, Quinan saw Hawes, Ludd and Kyle standing there.

Grove followed his glance. When he saw the men he suddenly forgot his sorrow as fury filled him. His face darkened. 'What the hell are you doing on my bridge?'

Hawes touched his forelock. It was a mockery, and Grove knew it and Hawes knew he knew. But he smiled and said, 'Begging your pardon, Sir, but these men and I have been asked by the crew to talk to you, Sir. We're spokesmen, like. We'd like to know a few things about what's going on.'

Grove swung away. 'I don't talk to scum!' Already he had forgotten his acceptance of the advice Quinan had given him after the tangle with Lincott.

Hawes's smile slipped. But he stood his ground.

'It's not for me to say, Sir, how you might feel about us. All we've ever done is to do our work, Sir, like we were told.' His eyes went to Quinan. 'But I think it might be a good idea, Sir, to hear us out, what with the Chief Officer present and these men behind me to witness my request. All we want to know is where we stand.'

Grove had placed himself in a dilemma again through his own impetuousness. He had to yield, but he did it angrily, as though he were conceding a favour. He was becoming an expert at the volte-face.

'Very well. But you will be told only what I am prepared to tell you. If I consider any question improper, or seeking confidential information, I shall refuse to answer.'

'That's fair enough, Sir.' Hawes went through his parody of saluting while his hard eyes showed his total lack of respect. 'Begging your pardon again, Sir, but could we have Doctor Lincott up here for a minute? Some of our questions are medical ones, you might say.'

Grove made as if to refuse. Then he shrugged and said, 'What the hell?' and snapped his fingers at Usher, who was standing uncomfortably to one side. 'You there. Go and fetch the Doctor immediately.'

Usher made haste down the companion-way and Grove turned his back on the deputation. He smoked his cigarette in short, nervous puffs while Quinan toyed with the dead wheel. Neither said anything.

Lincott arrived in minutes. He raised his eyebrows when he saw the men on the bridge wing, then pushed past them and went into the wheelhouse. He was breathing heavily from the short climb up the companion-way and he looked old, with tremendous dark, swollen circles under his eyes. To Quinan he seemed to have become small and frail as well. He had, Quinan realized, lost a great deal of weight in the past twenty-four hours.

Grove actually smiled at him. 'Ah, there you are, Doctor.' He waved a hand at the deputation. 'These . . . er . . . gentlemen would like to ask us some questions, and some of them, apparently, only you can answer.' He snapped his fingers again, this time at Hawes. 'Come on, man, get on with it. The Doctor has to get back to the hospital.'

Hawes cleared his throat. 'The first question is not a medical one, Sir. We simply wondered whether you are going to go on with fitting the spare propeller.'

Angry words sprang to Grove's lips. How could he, when this idiot crew were too frightened, too sheep-like, to go on with the work? And, God, he knew damn well that they'd seen the distress signals, and the drum being fixed to the flying bridge. They knew what it all meant. The question was stupid, unnecessary, and answered itself. But, for once, Grove exercised prudence. It was just an opener, it was a way of leading into the conversation, and perhaps some of them needed confirmation from the Captain himself. God knows, he thought, they're stupid enough.

He shook his head. 'No, we're not. If help shows up, we'll take it.'

Hawes nodded. 'Thank you, Sir.' He eyed Lincott momentarily. Then he brought his glance back to Grove. 'And now, Sir, the crew would like to know where they stand with this disease. We've got a raging epidemic on board. One dead, five sick. We're trapped with it. The men are scared, Sir. At this rate we're all going to die. We want to know what it is, and what's being done about it.'

Let's hope, Quinan thought, that Walter doesn't muck this one up. They're entitled to know. And Grove had done nothing about putting them in the picture. To his relief, though, Grove hung back and gestured at the Doctor.

Lincott stepped forward. The Dexadrine had begun to work, but it had produced only a surface alertness. Underneath its heady effect there was still the bone-weariness of his exhausted body.

'It's a virus, caused by a germ.' He rubbed nervously at sweat on his forehead. 'I am doing everything I can for the sick people. They are being treated with a variety of antibiotics as well as sulfonamide. Their temperatures are reduced as much as possible by sponging and bathing. I won't burden you with terminology you can't understand, but I can assure you that I am doing the utmost in my power.'

He rubbed his forehead again. 'Germs are passed by contact: hand to hand, mouth to mouth, by breathing and sneezing.

coughing and the like. That's how contagion spreads. You men must avoid personal contact, as I've said before. Keep outdoors as much as possible. Keep clean.' He stopped, looking more exhausted than before. A trickle of sweat ran down one cheek. 'Is there anything else?'

Hawes grinned. 'Doctor, you've told us everything and you've told us nothing. Very encouraging, one might say, until it's examined. And then it's nothing but a lot of words.'

Lincott flushed. What could he tell them, when he didn't know himself? It was no use spreading despondency, or generating panic. And Hawes had been shrewd enough to detect the thin fabric of his words.

He hesitated, caught in the abyss of his own unwilled ignorance. But he couldn't ignore the man. Grove was watching. So was Quinan. He said, haltingly, 'What more is there to tell?'

'Name. Origin. Cause.' Hawes's voice was emphatic. His thick forefinger stabbed holes in the air to add force to his words. 'Have you ever heard of the *Normandier?*' When Lincott, puzzled, shook his head, Hawes went on.

'She was a cargo ship. World War One. I had an uncle on her. In 1918 her crew were hit by blackwater. Just about every man on her snuffed it. They had no doctor.' He sneered. 'Not that that means anything.' Again, he pointed a thick finger at Lincott to emphasize his words. 'The point is this. Those men knew what they were fighting. They knew the enemy they were up against. They could *name* the disease. Can you, Sir?'

There was a long silence. Then Lincott said, 'No. But there are many viruses. When I was a houseman they brought a man to the hospital one day who was very ill. That was at half-past nine in the morning. Nobody knew what was the matter. He had a virus. That was all anybody could say. A team of brilliant men worked on that man. But he died at half-past two. Nobody ever found out what killed him.'

Hawes was unimpressed. 'Most interesting, Sir. But it doesn't help us, does it? The fact is, you don't really know what's hit us, do you?'

Lincott was silent a moment. The spirit seemed to go out of him. He said, listlessly, 'No.'

'Exactly.' Hawes was perversely pleased. 'And you haven't found a drug yet that will cure it, have you?'

Lincott shook his head.

Hawes grinned. He felt the same exhilaration as cross-examining Counsel, when a witness starts to crack. He hammered home his last point. 'And of course you don't know how it got in amongst us, do you?'

Lincott made no answer. He was not prepared to. The technical explanation of his difficulties would go straight over the top of Hawes's head, and it was obvious that the man did not want to listen, anyway. He wanted to talk. He was building up to something. Silently, Lincott fought down his increasing hatred of the squat deckhand.

Hawes grinned again, triumphantly. 'No answer, eh?' He waited a moment to give impact to his words. Then he said, 'Doctor, I can tell you where this disease comes from. It's as easy as falling off a log. I'm surprised it didn't occur to you, with your training.'

Lincott stared at him, hating him. The silence ran on until Grove moved restlessly and said, 'Well, where? You're so damn clever. Tell us where it comes from!'

Hawes's black eyes met Grove's. 'From those coffins in the hold,' he said softly.

The six simple words struck Lincott like a blow in the face. He heard Grove's 'Jesus Christ!' of astonishment. He detected Quinan's shocked involuntary movement. But this happened in a far-off, detached way while his mind struggled to adjust first to his total surprise, and then to still that insidious part of his mind which clamoured critically, scourging him for not having foreseen the possibility of untrained minds leaping to such a simple and, to them, likely conclusion. It should have occurred to him. He should have disposed of it in advance. He smothered this inner voice. His introspection, of course, would force him back to reckon with himself later. But for the moment he put his mind very strongly to Hawes's theory, considered it, and rejected it.

'That is absolute nonsense,' he said flatly. 'It is impossible.'

Hawes's jaw dropped. He stared at Lincott in absolute amazement. 'Impossible? Impossible?' For a moment he was unable to believe that the Doctor had rejected him. Then anger took over. He dropped his unctuous politeness like a shed cloak. His eyes blazed. 'You don't want to know the truth. You're blind and you want to bloody-well stay blind!'

Instantly, Grove flared. 'Have you lost your mind, Hawes?'

'I wasn't talking to you!' Hawes's voice became loud. 'It's this sawbones who's too bloody proud to see the answer under his nose. He . . .'

'Get off my bridge!' Grove shouted. 'Get off, you bastard, and take your guttersnipes with you!'

'I'll get off! I'll get off!' Hawes swung on Grove, quivering. 'But I want to tell you one thing first. I don't accept what the Doctor says. Nor do these men with me. He swung on Kyle and

Ludd. 'Hey, boys, do you believe the sawbones?' When they
obediently shook their heads, he rounded on Grove again. 'You
see? I don't. They don't. Nor do the rest of the crew. He's wrong
and he's too bloody proud to admit it.' He clenched a big fist.
'But, by God, by all that's holy, we know the truth of it, and to
hell with school-learning and the rest of it. It's those coffins
causing the epidemic and we want them off this ship!'

Grove couldn't believe it. Disbelief over-rode anger. 'Off the
ship? You mean jettisoned? All three thousand of them, here
at sea?' When he saw Hawes's grim nod he gaped at him for a
moment. Then he laughed. It was a distortion of mirth. 'Now I
know you're mad. You and the rest. Stark, staring, raving mad!
You must be, if you thought I would even consider such a
demand!'

'We'll see what the Chief Officer has to say about that,' Hawes
said heatedly. 'What d'you say, Mister Quinan? You was always
the reasonable one.'

Quinan shook his head. 'No, Feller. The Doctor is the only
person qualified to rule on the point. If he says it's not the
coffins, then they stay on board. You must abide by his decision.'

'Like hell I will!' Hawes was furious again. He was being let
down unexpectedly on all sides. 'Are you going to let us all die
because this bleeding quack is too stubborn to admit he's wrong?'

Lincott flared for the first time. 'For God's sake, Hawes, don't
talk yourself into something idiotic. I give you my word it is
impossible for the disease to emanate from the coffins. It . . .'

'Your word!' Hawes looked at him with loathing. 'What the
hell's the good of your word? We know the truth of it.' He almost
quoted O'Connor's words. 'What the hell do you expect, carrying
stinking dead bodies?'

'Good God, man,' Lincott burst out, 'they're fourteen years
dead!'

Ludd spoke for the first time. 'Aye, and better they'd been left
in their graves.'

Kyle shook his long black hair. 'It was a crazy thing, pluckin'
men from the earth.' He giggled obscenely. 'The dead don't like
to be moved.'

Lincott shook his head in bafflement. They were beyond him.
Grove saw it too. He said, 'We've done talking. Get off my bridge.'

Hawes stood his ground, square, rock-like. 'Captain, we've
made our decision. I want your answer straight out. Are you
going to jettison the bodies?'

'Are you threatening me?' Grove stared at him.

'Are you going to jettison the bodies?' Hawes repeated
woodenly.

'No!' Grove shouted. 'You've heard the Doctor, damn you!'

'Fine.' Hawes nodded grimly. He looked at Quinan, Grove and Lincott in turn. 'We've been pushed into this, mind. I want everyone to remember we've been pushed into it. But you give us no alternative. We'll do it ourselves, and God help the bastard who tries to stop us!'

There was a moment of shocked silence. Then Grove lost all vestige of control. 'Great God in Heaven.' His voice was a raw whisper that penetrated like heated steel, his body a fine-drawn wire, vibrating with intensity. 'Disobey, would you? Well, listen to this, Hawes. Listen carefully. You're scum, you and your mucky henchmen, and I don't give a damn whether you live or die. Touch one of those coffins and you are interfering with the lawful cargo of this ship. That's piracy, my boy, or mutiny, or both, and the moment you do it I'll dedicate the rest of my natural life to ensuring that you are hanged by the neck until you are dead.' He passed a shaking hand across his forehead. 'That's all. Now get off my bridge.'

Hawes looked long and hard at Grove. Then he said, 'The right of it is on our side,' and turned away and disappeared down the companion-way, followed by Kyle and Ludd.

Grove turned jerkily back into the wheelhouse. His face was exhausted, his eyes expressionless. The adrenalin that had pumped fiercely through his arteries drained away. The rigid tension that had strained his body collapsed. For a moment he looked very old.

He went to the telegraph and leant against it, drooping, while Lincott and Quinan stared at him in silence. Then he lifted one hand and slammed it viciously against the telegraph handle, ringing 'full ahead'. But the bells jangled meaninglessly down in the empty engine room, where only the generator hummed.

He looked at Quinan, his face twisted in despairing anguish. 'Ah God, if only it were true. Full ahead, and over the briny deep we go. A jolly crew, all bells and trumpets and naked nymphs and horns of plenty filled with bottles of gin and contraceptives. No plague, no dead men, no bastard mutineers. And we'd have a propeller, a great golden shining thing fastened to the shaft with waterproof Elastoplast . . .' He paused, staring at them. 'But it can't be that way, can it? Darkness lies upon the face of the deep. Darkness and death.' He straightened abruptly. 'Excuse me, gentlemen, I have things to do.' Then he walked across into the chartroom. A moment later came the sound of the radio cabin door opening, then slamming behind him.

. . . The noise in the Lotus Blossom had swelled from an early clamour to a din that was nearly solid, so solid that it was only if you were an *habituée* of the place that you could single out its components: the clash of the cash register which seemed to be rung up all the time, the jarring clatter of a thousand dishes from the kitchen, the ceaseless babble of the houseboys and waitresses and hostesses that was on a different key from the harsher bray of the Caucasian diners, and the uncertain wail of the saxophone that was part of the three-man band. The lobster had been cooked in Ve-Tsin and sherry and light soy sauce and sesame seed oil and ginger. It was split down its length, so that the flesh was marble white against the rich scarlet shell.

'It is my favourite, this lobster of the five flavours.' Henry Chan poured another glass of wine that was the colour of the palest feathers of the oriole. He watched the tiny tracery of bubbles rise to the surface and vanish. 'You sang well tonight.'

Mary Fannin ate a little of the lobster. She was not hungry. She was never hungry. She smiled at Henry Chan. 'In this?' She gestured at the din, at the smoke haze.

'They become quiet for you. They seem to sense your sadness—your melancholy. For you are sad, aren't you, Mary the Lost One?'

He had called her that when she first came to work for him, out of gentle affection.

'For the ills of the world,' she said, 'yes. For myself, no.' She took a sip of the wine. 'I'm not sorry for myself any more, Henry.'

'That's good.' He studied her across the table. 'I have seen you heal a little. But not altogether.'

'It's a fair repair job.' She smiled again and drank some more of the wine. If she didn't she wouldn't sleep.

He was silent for a while, watching her toy with the lobster. Then he said, 'There is much beauty in you. It is an exceptional beauty, not found in many people, because it is not only physical, it also generates from within.' He waved a sudden, accusing hand. 'Call it a current, call it a germinating seed. The metaphors tumble over my tongue. Call it what you like. But it can never fully emerge here.'

She glanced down at her dress under the concealing stole. Her full, perfect breasts were barely concealed, and from between them her white skin showed, crisscrossed with velvet lacing, all the way to her navel.

'It's your night-club, Henry,' she said dryly. 'Don't condemn it too much. But I guess you're right.'

He leant forward urgently. 'This hidden beauty, it needs to be nurtured. Now in my home, in my garden, that beauty would flower like a summer seedling wooed by the gentle hands of the sun.'

She laughed softly, so as not to hurt him. 'We've been through this before, you know. Except that each time you proposition me more beautifully.'

He looked at her solemnly. 'It is not my colour—my race—that delays your decision? One hears of these things?'

'Good heavens, no!' She was astonished. Henry Chan, sometime graduate of California Tech, rich restaurateur and amateur poet, was more of a white man than many white men she had met. 'Henry, I don't feel anything about anybody, including myself.'

He seemed relieved. 'Patience is one of the many virtues of the Chinese. A year—two years—ten! It means nothing. Have some more wine.' He sat back and they grinned at each other in mutual affection.

Mary Fannin drank the wine. Her headache was going. It was nice being with Henry. She pushed away the half-eaten lobster and looked across the room, feeling in her handbag for a cigarette. She found it and put it to her lips. Instantly, Henry Chan's hand materialized from under the tablecloth holding a lighter. He flicked it and she felt the warmth of the flame near her face.

She was still looking across the room. A man had come in and was standing on the edge of the dance floor, looking around for a table. He was in Air Force uniform, his wings glinting in the low light. He was a power-house of a man, almost as wide as he was high, pugnosed and aggressively-jawed. It was a face and figure you wouldn't forget in ten years, and it had been only eight months. Ron Sharp. Glen Erley's wing man. Randy Ron Sharp who had turned Glen in and given evidence at the court-martial. Ron Sharp who had known all about Clare and kept it to himself because of his secret desires. She could almost hear him speak as his lips framed the words to the waitress who came up: 'When does the American girl sing?' Then he was led away to a table.

Mary Fannin stood up. 'Henry, do you mind if I don't sing again tonight. This headache . . .' It had come back in full force, beating a giant drum inside her head, blinding her.

She saw the alarm on his face. 'Of course not.' He was standing up, offering codeine, offering novocaine. Henry could command almost anything. But that wasn't what she needed. There was just the quick goodbye, the lurching run up to her room, the peeling walls and the suitcase, the sound of rain outside and the long wait for a grey daylight, the newspaper with the tremendous headlines about the double murder and the tiny item that the *Florence Hurst* had docked and would be leaving that afternoon, destination Marseilles. There was the ticket bought from the small offices of the travel agent who represented the Peterson-Hurst Steamship Company (1909) Limited. There was the gangplank under her feet, the sorrow about Henry Chan, the knowledge that she was running again. . . .

Mary Fannin wiped sweat from her face. It was quiet in the hospital except for the ragged noise of Sloan's breathing.

She finished completing the printed form on her lap. It was one of Lincott's ideas. He'd had them run off on the ship's duplicator. It was something born of desperation, a searching, a seeking: Name. Age. Weight. Height. Duties. Shifts. Hobbies. Recreations. Movements for forty-eight hours up to time of committal. It was exhaustive. It stopped, she thought wryly, just short of finding out whether you were C. of E., or Cath. or Meth or Presb., and what your sins were, like whether you regularly committed adultery or masturbated or put duds into the gas meter. When Lincott did something he did it thoroughly, and the trouble was that the patient couldn't talk. You had to go around asking questions of frightened men who wouldn't talk easily and who didn't see the sense of it anyway. She sighed, clipped the form to its board on top of the temperature chart, then got up and hung it in place at the foot of Norman's bed. Henry Norman . . . Henry . . . Henry Chan. It was the association of names that had taken her back so vividly.

Lincott came in. He was sweat-streaked and rumpled. He went straight to the chart at Norman's bed and paged through it. 'Nothing about what he did on Tuesday afternoon.'

She shook her head. 'He played liar-dice with the cook for half-an-hour, lost five and sixpence. Then he mooched off. Nobody seems to know what happened to him after that.'

Lincott's eyebrows went up. 'With the cook?'

She smiled. 'Gambling knows no social barriers.'

He put the chart back and came over to her where she sat at his desk. 'I owe you an apology, you know.'

'Doc,' she said, 'I asked for it. I had no business saying what I did this morning It's just that I've been watching you eat your heart out over Mercy Attwell and I was going to tell you, before you blew up, that you're wasting your time. Proctor and Lucas . . '.

'I know,' he said. 'This is a small ship. I'm not blind.'

She studied him with more than wonder. 'And you don't mind?'

He sighed. 'Mary, retrogression in women more often expresses itself sexually than criminally. That is what has happened in Mercy's case. She's not depraved, she's sick.'

'She's also married.'

'I know. But that's the most minor of the problems. And you know something? I don't care. I'm prepared to follow her 'round the world. I'm prepared to wait a hundred years. I don't care.'

'Mary Fannin knew she could be blunt, now. 'Then get set for a broken heart. Attwell isn't going to let her go.'

'He's old,' Lincott said, callous only because of the wealth of his feeling. 'He won't last forever. I'm patient, Mary. With her I'm patience personified.'

It was no use talking to him. She shrugged. 'It's your life. And brother, you've sure chosen to make it complicated.' She changed her tack. 'How was Mercy, by the way? Couldn't have been too bad. I saw her at the funeral.'

Lincott became guarded. 'She'll be all right.' He lit a cigarette and sat gazing through the smoke, forgetting about the hospital, about Mary Fannin, remembering his visit to the Attwell cabin that morning.

She had been wearing a thin negligee and lying on the bed without a coverlet because of the heat. Attwell stood in the background, flushed, sweating and too nervously inarticulate to be much help.

'She won't darn-well talk to me, Doctor.' Without his arsenal of cliches he was not nearly as impressive as he had been when he had prayed on the foredeck. 'She just lies there. She won't look at me. And say, take a look at her eye! And I know she's in pain down . . . down below. She was in agony in the bathroom.'

It seemed almost as though it was Attwell who wanted the sympathy. Lincott wouldn't give it.

'Mind leaving us?'

Attwell was surprised. 'You mean . . . go out?'

Lincott nodded. Mercy Attwell stirred. 'Please go, Carl.' Her voice was toneless.

'Well, okay, if that's what you want.' Fumblingly, he withdrew.

Lincott sat on the edge of the bed. 'What happened to the eye?' She was looking straight across the cabin to the far bulkhead. 'I got liquor in it.'

'I guessed as much. It's badly irritated.'

'You're not . . . surprised?'

'No. What about the other complaint?'

She had not yet looked at him. 'I don't want you to examine me. You can tell things that way, I know.'

'All right.' He lit a cigarette and sat quietly next to her, his fingers encircling her wrist while he took her pulse. He stayed that way for much longer than was necessary, with this small link the only connection between them. His patience was greater than hers. In the end, he knew she had turned her head and was studying him. Then she said, 'There is nothing physically wrong with me, Doctor Lincott. Nothing important, that is. I'll get up now.'

'What are you going to tell your husband?'

'It doesn't matter.'

'It does.' He delved into his bag. 'I'll give you some drops for your eye. We'll tell him the eye is a mild attack of conjunctivitis; it does affect the eyes quite badly, actually. I don't want to go into details about the other complaint, but it's probably cystitis—that's a bladder infection—so I'll have some Citro-Soda sent to you from the hospital.'

He gave her the small bottle of eyedrops, his schooled face smooth and impassive.

This time she was looking at him. 'There is no measure of condemnation in your voice or your manner.'

'I'm a doctor, not a priest.'

She sat up so suddenly that she startled him. 'But you know, don't you?'

'Yes.' For the first time he allowed his own emotions to show. He took her hand urgently. 'Don't feel guilty! It's not your fault. Don't blame yourself.'

At last she gave way. The eyelids clamped down, and from beneath them tears squeezed out and rolled down her cheeks. Her face crumpled like a child's. 'Oh God, I'm so bloody mixed up. I just want out, Stephen. I just want out. I don't want to be me any more.'

He leant over and she clung to him. She began to sob, a hoarse, exhausted, frantic sound. 'I want out. I want out. Help me to die. Please help me to die.'

'Come on, now,' he said tenderly. 'Get it off your chest.' He put his arm around her. Her shoulder was warm against his hand and he could see the round breasts, marble smooth and russetly-nippled. She had the body of a girl, totally without blemish.

The sobbing stopped. She pulled away and looked into his face out of tear-swollen eyes. 'I've seen the way you look at me, Doctor Lincott. Stop wasting your time. I'm no bloody good any more. I even swear. That's a good British word, bloody, isn't it? Peter Proctor taught it to me. I can swear in Goddam American, too. Nice words for a religious girl, don't you think?'

He caught her arm. 'Stop it! Stop it!'

'Like hell I will!' She struggled off the bed, her face contorted. The negligee wrinkled high up over her thighs. It gaped open at the neck and bared the full breasts. But there was a sort of reckless unsexual abandonment in the way she allowed it to happen. She gained her feet and wrenched away from him, standing at the dresser, panting. 'Leave me alone, Doctor Lincott. I'm having a ball. I'm a fun-girl. Don't come to me with your bloody sad spaniel eyes shining eternal love!' She began to laugh while the tears started again and ran down her cheeks. 'I'm a fun-girl, see, and I'm at my best when I'm lying on my back. I . . .'

Lincott backhanded her across the face. The noise of the slap was shockingly loud in the small cabin. She staggered back and stood staring at him, one hand to her cheek, her eyes wide. But they were sane eyes.

'Oh, dear God,' she whispered. 'Oh, dear God, Stephen. I'm through. It shows on my face, in my eyes, the corruption. I will never be whole again. . . .'

'Doc! Doc!' Lincott was trembling. He shook himself. Mary Fannin was standing with a bowl in one hand. 'The ice has come. I'm going to work on Sloan.'

'All right.' He walked with her to the bed and stood looking down at the sick man. His respiration was failing. In the midst of life we are in death, Lincott thought. We are in death and sinfulness, depravity and corruption. This ship is evil. It has been cursed by God.

'I am going to give him an injection of corramine,' he said.

When Quinan came off watch it was full dark. A big moon, round and cheese-coloured, was hanging over the port quarter. Its reflection shivered in the broken water mixing with the blood-shine of the Not-Under-Command lights.

He stopped a moment, looking at the colours in the water. Then he walked into the hospital.

Sweat broke out on him immediately. It was hot in here. The air was heavy with man-smell: sweat and urine and faeces and vomit and impending death. There were fans everywhere, moving the foul air about without cooling it. The five sick men lay quiescent, naked, glistening upon their saturated sheets. Their parallelism, the geometrical equidistance of their beds, provided the only impression of order in a room which was a tangle of disorder: a heap of dirty linen in one corner, pools of water beneath the beds, the spider-web of electric wires from the fans to the mains socket.

Mary Fannin was crouched at the first bed. She was wearing the same shorts she had worn on Monday; but instead of the top, she had on one of Lincott's shirts. She was barefooted. She raised a hot, exhausted face. 'Hi. Nice in here, isn't it?'

He pulled up a chair and sat down. 'You'd make Hades enjoy-able, Miss Fannin.'

She laughed briefly, took a sponge out of a bowl and began to bathe the naked body on the bed. 'Sure. Shiny-nosed, haggard and unwashed. Go try your flattery on someone else.'

'It's not flattery. Mind if I smoke?'

'Go ahead.' She straightened up. 'Light one for me, too. This is coffee-break. Only there's no coffee. There's no coffee and no clean linen because they refuse to launder what's been soiled. And we're running out of drugs. Great isn't it?'

Quinan lit two cigarettes and gave her one. 'Something will turn up. It must. I've never seen the Nan Hai so deserted.'

She shook her head. 'No. There's something we've got to play out on this ship, before help comes. It's a feeling I've got.' She grinned and shrugged off the mood. 'I hear that Feller Hawes, that brilliant diagnostician, has decided that the bodies cause the disease, and intends to throw them all overboard. What will you do if he tries it?'

'Stop him.' Quinan hoped he showed more confidence than he felt.

She was sceptical. 'You and Proctor and Lucas and Grove? Don't kid me. The only muscle Grove has got is in his lungs, and Proctor can only wrestle in bed.' When he shrugged she leant forward. 'Why bother? What difference does it make to those dead guys whether they're on the bottom of the sea or planted in a cemetery in France? Anyway'—she grinned and put a hand on his arm—'if you need help, I can throw a mean right.'

Lincott came in and stood looking at them dispassionately. 'I hope I'm not breaking anything up.' He sat on the edge of the desk. 'Welcome to Bedlam.' He had developed a tic at the corner of his right eye and his face looked yellow, parchment-like, in the light.

Quinan said bluntly, 'How long since you slept? You look like hell.'

Lincott showed a trace of a smile. 'I've forgotten. And in any case, I couldn't sleep if I tried. I would appreciate it, though, if you would get Florence Nightingale here to take a breather. She has been on her feet for twenty-four hours without a break.'

Quinan took her hand and stood up, pulling her gently to her feet. 'Come on. You're going to lie down if I have to hold you on the bed.'

Mary Fannin looked at him, open-mouthed. 'Well heck, what are we waiting for?'

Even Lincott managed a grin. 'I never realized what a cheap Romeo you are, Gil.' He turned to the girl, becoming serious. 'I don't want to see you for a couple of hours. Off you go!'

'I'm not tired, Stephen,' she protested. Then, seeing his determination, she weakened. 'All right already! But when I come back, you go. You take a turn. Promise?'

'More or less.'

They started moving to the door. 'One thing,' Quinan said, 'I meant to mention earlier. Usher passed O'Connor's cabin. It was unoccupied, but Osgood's tape recorder was working. It was on "record". Usher switched it off. When he told me about it I took the recorder and put it in your cabin because it was nearest.'

Lincott stared at him. 'Why? Who wants to record nothing?'

'Because "record" is also "erase". You can erase any section of tape simply by putting it on "record", turning the volume down and leaving the thing.'

'Why erase anything?'

'It was Tommy Tucker's speech that was being erased.'

'Oh.' Lincott looked up sharply. 'Has it all gone?'

'No. About half.'

Lincott lit a cigarette. 'It's strange. But you wouldn't attach too much mystery to the affair if you had been with O'Connor the way I was, on Monday afternoon when he heard it outside the hospital. I thought the man was going to have an attack. He's probably developed an obsession about the thing. I wouldn't blame him for wanting to rub it out.'

At the end of the room Henry Norman began to moan in his delirium. Lincott ground out the cigarette. 'I'm off. Excuse me.' He got up and walked away.

They went out into the half-darkness. 'I heard about this Tommy Tucker,' she said. 'I heard about him in Hong Kong. Every country's got to have one. You British had Haw Haw. The Norwegians had Quisling. They're renegades, no matter what their nationality; they're crazy people who've got some awful twisted hate stuck away in their minds.'

They reached her cabin and she turned with her hand on the door, smiling. 'I haven't got any etchings, but why don't you come in and have a drink? I couldn't sleep in a thousand years. I only came away to please Stephen.'

'I'm suddenly very thirsty,' Quinan said.

She laughed and opened the door, switched on the light and led the way into the cabin. 'Here. Take a seat. Brandy and luke-warm water suit you?'

He sat down, knowing she was pleased at being able to play hostess. Watching her slim, competent hands making the drinks, he realized that the garish nail varnish had been removed. It was not the only thing about her that had changed. The quick, nervous way of speaking had given way to a firm contralto. The shadows had gone from the grey eyes. There was a measured confidence about her movements. The cat, he thought, had started licking its fur again.

She brought him his drink. 'Why did your wife divorce you, Mister Quinan?'

He was startled. He would have been annoyed as well if it hadn't been clear that she was not prying. He looked into the level grey eyes. 'Let's just say that she didn't like being married to a sailor.'

'You mean she didn't like being alone.'

He nodded. He remembered the way it had been at first with Pru. Ecstatic homecomings, endless love-making, heart-wrenching departures. Then the slow cool-off. The nights sitting alone, waiting for her to come home. The smouldering suspicion. The proof. Even then, he'd turned a blind eye for a while out of a strange feeling of guilt. In the end he had let her divorce him.

'How did you know about her?'

She pretended to look wise. 'I have my spies. Actually, Stephen Lincott, in addition to being a very good doctor, is by way of being a natural gossip.'

'Then you know all about me.'

She became solemn all of a sudden. 'You check out very well. I know that you're a hell of a fine seaman, and those aren't my words. I know that you can handle hard men and hard liquor and hard women. I also know that you've been carrying Captain Grove for nearly a year now, and that if it wasn't for you he'd have been on the beach, or whatever you call it, long ago.'

Quinan was perversely annoyed. 'Lincott talks too much.'

'Don't be unfair,' she said quickly. 'He doesn't, and you know it. He just happens to admire you a great deal.'

Quinan leant forward. 'There is one thing you must understand. Grove is still Master. He is God-Almighty on four hundred and ninety feet of steel called the *Florence Hurst,* and to disobey him is to break the law.'

'Sure, but don't nurse him. He's a big boy now. He's going to do something crazy, yet, and you don't want to land in the soup alongside him, do you?' She sat down on the bed and swung her slim legs up. 'My feet are killing me. Look, I knew one of these emotional guys like Grove, once. They're all the same. They're wired like a computer and you've got to be a qualified programmer to keep track of them. They're brilliant one moment, dumb the next. Their minds go chip, chop, leaping from one circuit to another. Guys like these could start a war, arrange a peace when nobody else could, invent electric light, murder children, and sweetly nurse orphans by candlelight.' She sighed and looked through the porthole at the big moon. 'The one I knew was called Glen Erley.'

Quinan thought about the way she had reacted to the jet going down on Monday. He thought about her bleak, blues-ridden mood on Wednesday night. 'Tell me about him,' he said.

She gave him a crooked sardonic smile. 'Glen Erley was more than just a man, he was a habit. I met him when I was seventeen. I was Little Orphan Annie, working in a five-and-ten since I was fifteen. Except I wasn't really an orphan. My Old Man was doing a ten-year stretch at a pen in Nebraska and my brother had joined the Marines by kidding his age. Glen Erley was Ivy League, Prince Albert tobacco and clothes out of Esquire. He didn't have to work, but he was a sharp man with a camera and with his connections he was having himself a time in the glamour game. Another Peter Gowland, but not as good.'

She took a sip of her drink. There was a mixture of bitterness and humour in the grey eyes. 'Can you imagine how I felt? It was a piece straight out of Cinderella, except the coach was an Aston-Martin and the horses were the kind that run for you with a jockey up on top. There was a yacht too, and a cute little Piper Tripacer. Glen was outdoorsy, and woodsy and horsy, provided he had a canvas chair and an umbrella and a mint julep in one hand. We used to hit Grand Junction for the Field Trials and Sebring to watch Jimmy Clark burn up the track. The only thing we never got around to was an altar. My fairy-story Glen lived in a big castle owned by a bad ogre; in actual fact it was a Georgian mansion with fourteen bedrooms, and the ogre was his mother. I really think he wanted to marry me, up to the point where he made the mistake of taking me home. But she froze me out with a seventy-two-year-old, twenty-four carat stare, and she could have frozen Glen's inheritance, too. Suddenly the picture changed. Suddenly I was in a flash apartment and Glen was paying the rent and sneaking visits whenever he could.'

She gave Quinan a look which was vulnerable and defiant at the same time. 'You don't have to believe this, but I still loved him, and I still thought I'd catch that altar. But it got a bit wearing. Life became a series of spats and make-ups. Always, Mary's lamb would come back.'

Mary Fannin finished her drink. 'This dragged itself out until Glen was called up for Vietnam. He was a reserve pilot. Suddenly he was gone. And I got a bee in my bonnet. I figured that if I could get over there, without Momma around I'd get my man. So I hunted around and came across an outfit called the Grey Ladies. It was like the Peace Corps and the Salvation Army and the Keystone Cops and your British Naafi rolled into one. It was supposed to be the working girl's chance to do something for the boys Over There. And because working girls are just naturally presumed to have very hot pants, they put us in these awful grey uniforms so that we looked like a combination between the Girl Guides and Friar Tuck.'

She waved a hand. 'To cut a long story short, I got over there, and after a few months I found him. He was lean and tanned and Whammo! My heart dropped through my boots and I was ready to start all over again. We spent that night in my trailer, and every night after that we alternated between my trailer and a tent at the airfield where he was stationed. That's where I got to know a guy called Ron Sharp, who had his designs on me. And then one morning we were found by the woman in charge of us, an old spinster known as Ma McCall. It's no wonder we were known as the Call Girls. Anyway, she paraded me in front of the other girls, with a crowd of servicemen watching, and stripped me out of my office and my uniform like something straight out of the Foreign Legion. I was taken to Saigon by jeep and dumped.'

Mary Fannin broke off. 'This is not a very nice story, I'm afraid.'

'Go on,' Quinan said.

She shrugged. 'I was there two weeks, still hoping Glen would get in touch with me. Then I heard the news. His wing man, this Ron Sharp, had snitched on him. Turned out that Glen's fearless flights into Vietnam were real safe sightseeing tours confined to the countryside. They were shooting up top-priority targets like bullock carts and peasant huts and school houses. Three schoolhouses, as a matter of fact.'

She stopped abruptly and held out her empty glass. 'Care to do the honours? Baring my sordid past is turning out to be thirsty work.'

Quinan detected the bitterness in her voice. He got up, took her glass and mixed the drinks. 'Have you ever told anyone this story before?'

'No. You want me to stop?'

He came back with the drink. 'That's the point. Don't stop. Tell it all. It can only help.'

She looked at him for a moment as though she were trying to see inside him. Then she raised her glass and said, 'Cheers, Mister Quinan. You're quite a guy.' Then she put the glass down and went on.

'Glen was court-martialled, but quickly. A real drumhead affair, or whatever you call it. Guilty, of course. There'd never been a more open-and-shut case. My hero was nothing more than a kid-killer in uniform. A real no-good soldier. He couldn't even kill himself properly. An hour after the verdict he grabbed the guard's gun and shot himself, but all he did was make a big dent in his head and they saved him with major surgery.'

She sat up and put her hands around one knee, staring straight ahead of her. 'I still couldn't get him out of my system. They put him on a hospital ship in Saigon and I wangled permission to go see him. When I found him, there was this cool fashion-plate sitting by his bedside, looking travel-stained in a careful way. Her name was Clare Erley and Glen had married her out-of-state one week before he left for Vietnam. Apparently even his mother didn't know until after I'd also gone.'

She turned to Quinan. 'That's it. Glen couldn't say much. I stood there like a fool for a couple of minutes. Then I broke and ran. But Clare followed me out. She was very sweet. She said I could give up the chase now. She said I could forget about being a rich man's plaything. Glen needed a wife, now, to look after him and win back his good name. She probably meant his inheritance. Then she suggested that I should go back to wherever good whores come from.'

She studied him out of exhausted eyes that brimmed with tears. 'I didn't know, Mister Quinan. I'd never thought of myself as a whore. I didn't know what a good whore would do. So I picked Hong Kong.'

The eyes drooped over the tears. The brandy had reached her and she was fading fast. 'There you have it, Mister Quinan. The story of my life. Ron Sharp found me in Hong Kong and I knew I had to go. I was running again when I came on board. Then I helped nurse a sick man, and watched him die; I met a dedicated doctor and a Chief Officer who's carrying a sick ship and a crazy Captain on his back, and suddenly I'm Mary Fannin again. I'm me. I can look the world in the face, and if it ever gives me any trouble I'll swing right back.' She closed her eyes and lay back.

Quinan got up and sat on the edge of the bed. He took her hand. 'I'm very proud to know you, Mary Fannin.'

She opened one eye drowsily. 'Just for the record, I'm giving you official notice that as from when I wake up I'm setting my cap at you.'

'You don't have to,' he said. He smiled. 'I'm right here.'

'Stay there.' The eye drooped shut. 'Hold my hand tight, Gil. We can talk later. Right now, I'm kinda tired.'

CHAPTER TEN

THE ATTWELLS, Peter Proctor and Lucien Puget were playing vingt-et-un in the lounge.

'The thing,' Peter Proctor said, 'is never to pull my leg too often. I'll pay eighteens.'

'Perfidious Albion.' Puget put down his cards. 'What a ridiculous game. I bow out.' He sat back and lit a cigarette. The night goes so slowly, he thought.

'Pay me,' Mercy Attwell said coolly.

Proctor raised his eyebrows. 'Well done. You've outfoxed the fox.'

'I've learned a lot.' She regarded him without expression. 'In a lot of ways.'

Proctor looked away. 'What about you, Mister Attwell?'

Attwell had been studying his wife. Now he jerked his eyes around to Proctor. 'Sorry. What was that?'

'The cards,' Proctor said impatiently. 'Do I pay you?' He was not his usual debonair self. He had had quite a lot to drink and the liquor had brought sweat to his face. Mercy's presence had made him jumpy and restless. She had crossed her legs and his eyes were being drawn continuously and irresistibly to the under-side of her thigh that showed beyond the top of the stocking. It was smooth there, he knew, and soft-firm, sprung with woman's muscle, and fever-hot there . . .

'No,' Attwell was saying. 'You don't have to pay me.' His eyes caught the direction of Proctor's glance, then slid away. 'I guess I'll never get used to cards.'

'You'll learn,' Mercy said. 'Pour me a gin and tonic, Peter.'

'Now, honey!' Attwell's voice was raggedly remonstrative. 'You know I don't like that.' He had declined in appearance. He had aged. His cheeks were haggard. He had made a bad job of shaving that morning. There were patches of steel-coloured bristle on his chin.

Mercy's eyes flashed. 'You're playing cards, aren't you? What would your worshipping multitudes say if they could see you now?'

Puget could see the confusion in Attwell's eyes.

'Really, hon!' Attwell's laugh was empty. 'That's kind of unfriendly, sweetheart. After all, the circumstances are excep-tional. We're just passing time. We're just . . .' He stopped and looked at her helplessly. The big shoulders slumped. 'Have the drink, honey. I'll have one too, Mister Proctor. A double.'

Proctor had gone to the drink table. 'Are you sure you . . .'

Attwell shouted suddenly, 'Sure I'm sure!'

They looked at him in astonishment. He took out a hand-kerchief and mopped his red face. 'Sorry. Sorry. I guess I'm a little overwrought.'

'I do not blame you.' Puget picked up his discarded cards and rattled them into neatness on the edge of the table. 'It is the knowledge of death that surrounds us. It is the fact that Hookins

and Sloan have just died.' He shrugged. 'Osgood as an alcoholic.
He was easy to kill. But Hookins and Sloan were normal, healthy
men. Suddenly the score is three, instead of one. The disease is
lethal. It takes twelve hours, approximately, to consume one. It
is what Doctor Lincott calls a killer-virus. Like the 1918 'flu.'
His wise, whimsical, unfrightened eyes considered them. 'The
beginning of a holocaust, perhaps. How many more of us will
the pestilence take, eh?'

Proctor brought the drinks. 'Let's change the subject.'

The Frenchman looked up at him. 'You are afraid?'

'Of course I'm not.' Proctor sat down. 'It's just damn silly,
that's all. We all know what's happening. We're all upset because
of Hookins and Sloan going so suddenly.'

Attwell had regained some of his calm. He said to Puget, 'I
must confess that I don't see any purpose, Sir, in dwelling on
the matter.'

Puget smiled. 'Come, come, Padre. You are a man of God. You
are not afraid of death, surely?'

Attwell went red. 'That is one thing I am not afraid of, Sir.'
He wanted to go on but Proctor prudently interrupted.

'Come on, let's play.' He dealt in silence. Only Mercy bought
cards. Then Proctor had to show his own hand.

He had nineteen. 'I'll pay twenties.'

'Pay me,' Mercy said.

Proctor coloured. 'Rubbing it in a little, aren't you?' He slid
chips across the table. 'You, Monsieur?' When the Frenchman
shrugged he turned to Attwell. 'You, Sir?'

'Way out.' Attwell wagged his head.

Puget chuckled. 'Lucky in love, Father.'

Attwell slammed his glass down. The liquid sprayed out in a
glitter of droplets, like tiny gems. 'I am not a priest, damn you!'

'No.' Puget stared at the big, choleric face. 'You are a salesman.
You sell God, huh? You are a seller of God!'

Attwell went white. He heaved himself ponderously to his feet.

'Carl!' Mercy Attwell cried. 'Sit down!'

'Please, gentlemen!' Proctor shouted. 'We're all a bit edgy.
Take it easy.'

Attwell looked at Mercy with a curious expression. 'Do you
really want me to stay, after that, after what he called me?'

'Please, Carl,' she said. 'It's not late. I don't want to go to bed
just yet.'

He shook his head in disbelief, then sat down.

Proctor dealt. They considered their cards for a moment in
silence. Then Puget chuckled. 'It is strange, how we remain
together. We do not even like each other. We are afraid so we

huddle. It is the herd instinct. We do not wish to be alone in
our cabins when the madness strikes. We are all afraid.'

Proctor stared at Puget. His face was wet with sweat. Then
his expression seemed to break apart as he shouted, 'That does it!
Christ, I'm damned if I'm going to sit cooped up with a crazy
Froggy with the death wish!' He got up violently, scattering
cards on to the floor, and went to the table where the drinks were.

Puget laughed. He was the only one remaining seated. The
Attwells had risen, too. 'Tish! The equable Monsieur Proctor.
Such language, and to a passenger! One would think he was
indeed afraid. Fear works great changes . . .'

Proctor whirled. A bottle went flying. 'Shut up! Shut up!'

Carl and Mercy Attwell got up and left the room. They walked
the alleyway in silence to their cabin. When the door was shut
Carl put his arm around his wife's shoulders.

'You afraid?'

'Not at all.'

'I am. At least I think I am. That Frenchman was right, in a
way. I do sell God. I admit it.' He snorted. 'But not for money,
the way he was implying. That's what got my goat.' He reverted
to his original theme. 'I should be out there in that hospital,
selling God, or whatever you'd like to call it. But I'm not. I
haven't gone near those sick people. Does that make me afraid?'

She moved restlessly under the weight of his heavy arm. 'It's
not fear that keeps you away, Carl.' She pulled away from him
and went to the closet. 'I'll mix your drops.' She opened the door
and took out the two bottles.

'I don't want them, honey.'

She whirled. He had taken off his shirt and was holding it in
one hand, so that it drooped to the floor. There was something
childlike about the stance, made pathetic by the patent age of
his withered breasts that drooped upon the bulk of belly.

'I figured we could . . . could get together. It's been kind of
a long time. What do you say, honey?'

She stared at him, aghast, overwhelmed with surprise. She
found herself saying, 'This is rather sudden, isn't it?' Then,
adjusting, she shook her head. The thought revolted her. 'No,
Carl. I'm dead beat. Not tonight.'

He grinned at her, trying to look boyish. 'Aw, come on, baby.
Don't be that way.' He came up to her, unexpectedly quick, and
pulled her against him, rubbing his body against hers, nuzzling
her neck. She tried to struggle, but his bulk and his excitement
made him strong. She stepped back, but he came with her. The
edge of the bed caught her behind the knees and she collapsed
across it with Carl's heavy body pinioning her while he scrabbled

at her clothing. She heard her skirt tear. When he raised himself momentarily she rolled to one side, the skirt bursting loose as her body twisted. She came up on her knees. As Carl lunged towards her she swung back her hand and slapped him viciously in the face.

He froze in mid-motion, his hand to his cheek, his eyes wide, his breath whistling through his gaping mouth. He watched her while she got slowly off the bed, shaking, and went and sat at the dresser, staring into the mirror.

Carl swung his legs off the bed. Then he put his hands over his face. His voice came out muffled and defeated. 'I'm sorry. I must have gone crazy.'

She would not look at him. 'It was my fault, Carl. You're entitled to your marital rights. I just can't help myself, that's all.' She got up and went back to the closet. 'I'll mix your drops now.'

He had lit a cigarette when she brought them to him. He drank the vodka-chloral hydrate mixture, gave her the glass, and swung his legs up on the bed. The struggle had worn him out and he looked grey and tired. She experienced a moment of deep pity. *He didn't really want to have me,* she thought. *He wanted to prove his manhood.*

She put on another skirt and walked to the door. 'Good night, Carl.'

His smile was surprisingly wry. 'Have a good time.' Then he turned on his side, his back to her, staring at the bulkhead and waiting for the chloral hydrate to work.

The flickering flames from the burning drum on the flying bridge painted the *Florence Hurst*'s upperworks in lurid gold and crimson, and the smell of oil lay heavily along the decks. The foghorn split the night every sixty seconds, making sleep tortured and conversation impossible.

Hawes stood at the stern. It's going to be a long night, he thought. He stood in a darkness that was patterned, leaping shadow from the flames further for'ard. He was smoking, looking down at the water, letting his thoughts drift the way the water drifted.

God, how calm it was. Four days it had been like this. No wind, no waves. It was like being in harbour. But there was something frightening, something unreal about it, as though either God or the Devil had put them here, becalmed them like in the old days of the sailing ships, and then sent a pestilence amongst them that brought madness and death.

It was probably God, he thought, not the Devil. God punished men for their sins. The idea made him uneasy, because he was afraid of anything intangible and therefore he was afraid of God who, to him, crouched just above the stars, angry and omnipotent and filled with militant righteousness. Uneasily, he pushed the thought aside. There was enough to worry about without adding God to the picture.

The water below him broke under the stern and lapped back, many-faceted like a gem, reflecting the broken images of the moon. The asphalt road in Hong Kong had shone the same way that night before the *Florence Hurst* had sailed, only it had been the yellow glow of approaching headlights that the wet surface had picked up, duplicating them in racing fragmented refraction so that four lights, two real and two virtual, symmetrically united, raced towards them along the dark ribbon of road ahead of the growl of a heavy engine.

The men flooded across the road. They waved and gesticulated. Draper stood on his hands and hallooed. Knowles did a doddery hornpipe, bathed in yellow light. Kyle threw back his head and sent a string of broken yelps kiting up into the weeping drizzle. They were wicked drunk, eight-hour drunk, sober-drunk, drunk beyond the point of falling down.

Wheels locked. Big tyres planed upon the slick surface. It was an Army truck, matt khaki finish, with a leviathan ticking over under the bonnet.

Hawes ran around to the passenger side of the cab, grinning, his shirt torn from an early ruckus he'd forgotten. A torch shattered the darkness but robbed him of his sight.

'Struth, put that bloody thing out!'

'Just looking you over.' The torch went out. Hawes could make out sergeant's chevrons on a bent arm that draped over the cab's high window sill. 'What do you lot think you're up to, muckin' about out here? Heading for Red China?'

Kyle came up. 'We're lost, mate. Got to get back to the 'arbour. Give us a lift?'

The torch came on for a moment, shining on Kyle. The sergeant said, 'Christ,' and put it out again.

'Come on, sarge,' Hawes pleaded. 'It's wet out here.'

The sergeant said something to his driver. The massive engine gunned. Then he put his head out of the window. 'I'd sooner have a car-load of monkeys than you mob. Sorry, chums. Times are hard.' The truck began to move forward in first gear.

'Stop him!' Hawes yelled. Draper, Knowles, Kyle and Hookins flooded across the road again, bathed in light under the slanting drizzle. Draper made obscene gestures and Kyle howled like a wolf. The truck growled to a halt.

'I've a good mind to fucking run you over,' the sergeant cried from the cab.

'Up yours, soldier boy,' Hawes snarled. 'Now hold still while we climb on the back or we'll bend your flippin' lorry around your neck. There's two of you and six of us, so use your loaf before it gets dented.'

They began to run towards the tail-gate. The sergeant put his head out of the window, twisting his neck so that he could look back. He shouted something unintelligible. The engine roared again but the truck stayed still.

Hawes reached the tail-gate and put his hands on the cold metal floor. Then he realized that he was looking at a pair of combat boots that stood inches from his hands. Above them bagged battle-dress trousers and then the skirt of a rain-slick poncho. The skirt lifted slowly and from beneath it emerged the barrel of a sub-machine gun, rising like a steel penis. The round ring of its muzzle pressed with icy tenderness against Hawes's forehead.

Hawes stood transfixed. Pressure from the muzzle pushed his head back. He was suddenly staring into the slitted, glittering eyes of a Gurkha. They stood like that for a moment that was an aeon of time. Then the Gurkha smiled.

'Letting us up?' Hawes whispered, head back, still crucified by the pressure of the gun, but with hope flooding him.

The Gurkha still smiled. Then he shook his head and stamped on Hawes's outstretched fingers. Hawes screamed and the truck moved off with a clashing of gears. The sergeant's mocking laughter drifted back.

They collected in the middle of the road. Hawes was too drunk to feel much pain, but he flung a string of obscenities after the disappearing vehicle.

'I'm going to Red China,' Draper announced. He began to lurch away into the darkness. 'I'm . . . whaddaya call it . . . I'm defecting. I'll have me four Chinese girls at night.'

He described succinctly what he would do with them and Kyle giggled.

'Not you, Shorty. I've seen ya. It's only your other muscles what are big.'

Draper stopped and turned. 'It's not what you've got, but what you do with it,' he announced proudly.

'Mucking sojers,' Ludd said. 'Gestapo, more like it. Their own kin, out in the rain and they . . .'

'Just you wait till I lay my hands on a soldier-boy,' Hawes raged. 'I'll have his guts for garters, that's what I'll do.' He put his head down. 'I'm goin' to Red China too.'

'Lights! Lights!' Knowles screamed. 'It's a car, not a truck. Play dead, Willy-boy. Play dead now, quick!'

Hookins flung himself down on the asphalt.

The car slid to a halt, its tyres swishing water. A Jaguar insignia gleamed dully in the bounce-back of its headlights. The driver's door opened and a light came on inside. Hawes saw a woman in the passenger seat. She was breathtakingly beautiful, blonde as honey, her shoulders draped in fur.

A man's voice said, 'What's the trouble?' It was a measured, unexcited, careful voice.

'My mate. He's hurt.' Hawes and the others ringed Hookins.

'Oh.' The driver was standing by his door. He said something to the woman and then walked into the glare of his own lights. Hawes saw the flat angle of a beret, the glint of a belt buckle.

'Jesus, it's a soldier boy!' A hot excitement rushed into him.

'An awficer, too.' Kyle giggled. 'Tell him about the Ghurkha, Feller.'

The man reached them as Hookins got up. They scattered and surrounded him. Sudden alarm came to his face.

'Here! What's this?' He began to back quickly away. The woman called something sharply from the car and he turned to see Draper opening her door.

'Hello, ducks. Come out and say hello.'

'Get away!' she said. 'My husband . . .'

Draper put his hand on to the low neckline of her silver dress. 'Come out, ducks.' He pulled, but the dress ripped away. She screamed shrilly in terror.

'My God! Elizabeth!' the man shouted. He hurled himself at them. Kyle intruded and staggered back from a tremendous punch over the heart. Knowles tripped, sprawling, and the officer fell over him, rolling and kicking, but Hawes came from the side and swung a boot into the soft flesh below his ribs.

'Fucking soldier boy,' he snarled.

The officer got to his hands and knees, shaking his head, hurt. He reached out and grabbed Hookins's ankles, but at the same moment Ludd kicked him very hard in the stomach. His beret fell off and he toppled over, doubled up, mouth wide and straining as he struggled for air.

Draper dragged the screaming woman into the light. Her fur had gone and her dress draped in tatters around her waist. She jerked uselessly in his arms. She was beyond hysteria. Her face was mad with horror. She was made grotesque by the blonde hair that had tumbled loose around her face to half-cover it, made garish by the chaste pearl necklace that bobbed over her **bare breasts**.

She screamed in a raw voice, all the time, 'Keith! Keith! Oh dear God!' flaying their nerves with it until Draper fought one hand free and hit her on the side of the face and she went suddenly limp.

Hawes turned away from the fallen officer, panting, looking like a devil in the hurting light. He lunged over to the woman and stood staring at her, still overcome with savagery, his barrel chest heaving under the torn shirt.

'Stuffing soldier boy's woman!' His thick hands went out and grabbed the remains of the dress and ripped it off her. She hung in Draper's arms in only a girdle and stocking and the pearl necklace.

Draper was panting too. They were all panting, all hypnotized by the sensuous white body. She stirred and lifted her head and saw them. She saw the circle of gleaming eyes, silent and intent like a ring of wolves. She began to moan.

Hawes said thickly, 'Me first,' and took her from Draper and put her down on the wet asphalt. She began to scream again but lay there while they used her in turn, her arms beating in spasmodic rhythm. When it was over Hawes saw her head turn. She was silent, but her eyes met his. There was recognition. His face changed. The woman saw it and beat at the tar, trying to get up. She managed to get to her hands and knees and crawled slowly, ridiculous in her nudity, to the side of the road while they watched in silence. Then Hawes walked up to her and began to kick. He kicked until he reeled away in exhaustion.

Afterwards they ran back to the city, silently through the rain. . . .

Hawes threw the stub of his cigarette over the stern. His arm did it, really, in a spasmodic, uncontrolled jerk. His breathing came quickly and unevenly. Sweat rolled off him. God, what madness had taken him that night? It was liquor-madness, he thought. Drink did that to him. Drink put an unreasoning animal at the controls. To do a thing like that when there were a thousand sampan women ready and waiting! And then to kill, on top of it.

He had no regret. Death meant nothing to him. He had killed before. There was the taxi-driver in Marseilles. The wide-boy in London who'd tried to cut him up over a wristwatch deal. But there had been a purpose in those actions. Reason. Even necessity. Business, in a way. But not with the Fletcher woman.

She was so bloody white, he thought. Pink and white. The pinkest part of a woman was her nipples, and those bobbing cherry nipples above the diamond-white skin, they'd sent him so crazy that he had . . .

There was movement at his side, half-body and half-shadow,

huge, alarming. Sheer fright made him hit out, his fist striking like the head of a snake. But there was only warm skin against his knuckles, no impact, as the figure moved instantly backward with the blow and the chuckle came out of the darkness.

'Hi, buddy-boy, old revolutionary. Things that go bump in the dark, eh? Got the creeps, Feller-boy?'

Hawes pulled himself together. He was shaking with reaction. 'God, there's no need to sneak up on a man!'

O'Connor laughed. 'I didn't, really. You were away, man. Real gone.'

'Like hell!' Hawes was on the defensive. 'I'd have heard you coming.'

'I reckon not.' O'Connor's voice was quite confident. 'You weren't with it. But I give it to you, you're real quick with your reflexes. And maybe I was doing my Redskin act, just a little bit. Been reading smoke-signals tonight.'

'Smoke signals?' Hawes tried to catch up. His mind had now recovered from the fright, and he had sense enough to realize that O'Connor's presence was not accidental. 'How'd you mean?'

O'Connor chuckled again. 'Aw, you know, buddy. Other Injuns signal to Chief Bunny. Puff. Puff. News. Tell-um about how maybe some dead bodies get moved, tomorrow.'

'Oh!' Hawes stared at him, trying to make out the American's expression in the darkness. Then he smiled slowly. 'You've got a good news service, Lieutenant. That's right. Going to help us?'

'Heck, no. I'm a neutral, see? This is strictly between Limeys. I'll be around, natch, to wish you well. You guys are in the right.' He reached out a hand and patted Hawes on the shoulder. 'Tell you something else, buddy-boy. Only Grove is taking you seriously.'

'What about Mister Quinan?'

'He's got his hands full. And the other two reckon it's an idle threat.'

Hawes was silent for a while. The night pressed around them. Then he said, 'Where do you fit in, Lieutenant?'

O'Connor chuckled. 'I told you, I'm a neutral. A sympathetic neutral. And also, I got me an idea.'

'What kind of an idea?'

O'Connor grinned in the darkness. 'I'll put it to you this way, if you don't mind answering one question: where would you most like to be, right now?'

Hawes didn't have to think. 'Somewhere else. Off this ship.'

O'Connor was pleased. 'Exactly. And if you go to the Captain and you say, please, Sir, may we take one of your boats, a bunch of us guys want to leave, the Captain's hardly likely to say sure, go right ahead, Mister Hawes, take your pick, is he? Nor is Quinan or even Lucas or Proctor.' He didn't wait for Hawes's answer. 'But if you force Grove to back down tomorrow, if you force him to give in and allow you to jettison the coffins, things will be kind of different, won't they? It will be like a test of strength.' He made his voice suddenly hard, wielding the words like a club. 'If you succeed in getting those coffins overboard tomorrow, buddy-boy, you'll be able to help yourself to a boat and sail away into the Goddam blue, and you know it and I know it.'

There was another long silence. Then it was Hawes's turn to grin. He slapped O'Connor on the back. 'Have a cigarette, Lieutenant.'

O'Connor smiled. 'These Limey cigarettes taste like dried grass. But I'll have one with you, buddy-boy. Like a pipe of peace, huh? Sure, I'll have one with you, old Feller-boy, old blood-brother.'

They laughed together, in the darkness.

The night was going by, becoming wearisome in its dragging passage.

Quinan came into the hospital. He went to Lincott's desk and sat there, staring straight ahead, jerkily lighting a cigarette. He and Lincott had just finished transporting the dead bodies of Hookins and Sloan to the carpenter's workshop.

Mary Fannin came up. She stood next to Quinan, touching him with her body to transmit her warmth and understanding. She studied him out of heavy, tired eyes. Her sleep had lasted half an hour, no more. She had been back here ever since. She had forced herself awake, brutally rejecting sleep, but the sleep had hung on, like the after-effects of a drug.

'Did you manage all right?'

Quinan drew on the cigarette. He nodded. 'Hookins didn't weigh much. He was a thin kid. But the effort has exhausted Stephen.'

'Where is he?'

'I don't know. We put the bodies in the workshop and then he said "You and Mary can manage for a while, Gil," and just . . . walked away.'

She put her hand on his shoulder. 'Leave him, Gil. He's probably sleeping. He was out on his feet.'

He got up and went to the first bed, the bed that had been Sloan's. Now it was occupied by the fever-racked body of Gauldie. And in the next bed was Woods, the Boatswain, one hour ill.

'They come and they go,' he said bitterly. 'When Woods and

Gauldie got it, so soon after the other two died, that really broke Stephen up. All the life seemed to go out of him.' He looked at her expressionlessly. 'The time has come when we have to start keeping the score. What is it—three dead, five sick, isn't it?'

'Don't, Gil,' she said, 'it doesn't sound like you.' She shivered. 'I know it's selfish, but I wish Stephen would come back. Old McBlain is very bad. I'm doing all I can, but Stephen's presence makes such a difference.'

They went back to the desk. For a while they sat and looked at each other wordlessly. Mary Fannin lit a cigarette. Then she moved restlessly and said, 'It's not the coffins. Stephen said it was impossible and I believe him. It's a germ causing this thing. It's a germ like a 'flu germ or a cold germ or any other kind of germ. It gets passed on by coughing or breathing or touching or drinking out of the same glass.' She pointed to a dog-eared magazine lying on a corner of the desk. 'I found that magazine in the library. There's a story in it, a true one, about a woman called Typhoid Mary. Ever heard of her?'

Quinan shook his head.

'She was a typhoid carrier. Never got it herself. For twenty years she left a trail of typhoid all over New York. She was a cook; she cooked in institutions and private homes. She changed her name all the time. She was death, and she knew it. But it took that long for the health authorities to catch up with her.'

Quinan smiled at her. 'Do you think there's another Typhoid Mary on this ship?'

She shrugged. 'I don't know. I just don't know. It could be. A carrier, in other words.'

'Have you shown that story to Stephen?'

She shook her head. 'I haven't had a chance. I will, though, soon as he comes back.' She paused to consider. 'I think his mind is working on similar lines. Or it was.' She pointed to the clipboards that hung at the foot of every bed. 'Whenever somebody becomes ill, we try and trace his movements back for forty-eight hours. But it's so darn difficult.'

Quinan got up. 'I'm going to make the rounds. Won't be long.'

She smiled. 'Still nursing Wally Grove, Gil?'

A cloud passed across his face and she was sorry she'd said it. But he shook his head. 'No. He's locked himself in the radio cabin. Says he's busy. I don't know what he's doing.'

I do, she thought. They started to walk to the door. Outside, the foghorn boomed again. They had become used to waiting for it, and speaking in the silences between its noise. They waited for it to stop but it went on and on, filling the hospital with its clamour. There was a shout nearby and feet thudded on the deck.

Quinan reached the doorway just as Savage, the Third Engineer, appeared in it. He was panting.

'It's Usher. He's gone crazy on the bridge. He's locked on to the foghorn and nobody will touch him.'

Quinan looked at him, while the noise went on. Then he said, 'I'll come. I may need help. Will you give me a hand?'

The young engineer considered for a moment. Then he shrugged. 'All right. You don't mind if I pray out loud, do you?' His grin was reassuring. It added a touch of sanity.

'I'll pray, too,' Quinan said. They walked out together.

Mary Fannin turned back into the hospital. She looked down the row of beds. There was one empty. Oh God, she thought, when is it going to stop?

There was the sound of light footsteps behind her and she turned, expecting Lincott.

Mercy Attwell stood in the doorway.

They regarded each other with mutual interest. Mary noticed the flushed face, the tilted, hard expectancy of the full breasts that pressed against her blouse. God, she thought, it's showing; even Attwell will notice it soon. This woman had a honeymoon ripeness; she was ready to be bedded at any given moment; she was halfway there before anyone touched her. Her hackles rose.

'Well,' she found herself saying stiffly, 'this is an unexpected honour. Come right in, Mrs. Attwell.'

Mercy stayed where she was, her hands against the steel sides of the doorway, one slender, perfect leg over the coaming. Mary saw the smell strike her nostrils. Her face wrinkled with involuntary distaste.

'I just wondered if I could give you a hand.' Her eyes fluttered from Mary Fannin to the inert bodies of the sick men, to the mess of soiled linen and back.

On Monday you could have, Mary Fannin thought. You would have worked, and worked well. But there was nobody sick then, and now it is too late. You're a different woman now. No. It was definitely too late.

'I guess not,' Mary said. 'Stephen Lincott will be back soon and Gil Quinan helps when he can. And I think Richard Savage is going to throw in with us. We'll make out.'

Mercy Attwell seemed at a loss. 'I've got . . . nothing to do.'

Go find Proctor, Mary thought angrily, he'll give you plenty to do. You can swop around, and burn off all that nervous energy. She shook her head. 'Thanks for the offer.'

'I just thought . . .' Mercy Attwell stopped. She seemed to withdraw into herself. 'Good night.' She turned away. The sound of her footsteps faded away along the deck.

She wanted to help, Mary thought. And I threw her out. She remembered the look of almost desperate appeal in Mercy's eyes. Suddenly filled with guilt, Mary rushed to the door.

'Mrs Attwell! Mrs Attwell!'

There was no answer. Suddenly, the foghorn cut off.

Peter Proctor awoke violently, and in terror. He rolled over on his side and scrabbled for the switch at his bedside, his sweating fingers searching like trembling feelers until suddenly there was a small click and a yellow glow pervaded the cabin. It rolled away the reluctant darkness that, even then, seemed to hang in the square corners of his cabin.

He lay there for a moment, blinking uncertainly, reassured like a child by the light. He looked at his watch. God, only two hours since they'd chucked up the cards. He'd fallen asleep quickly. Then he sat up, found his cigarettes, and sat hunched over his naked knees staring at nothing, puffing on the cigarette and waiting for the racing beat of his heart to slow.

He had walked alone, deathless, in an eternal blood-like gloom upon a dark deck that had no beginning and no end. There was no sound in all the world, and no sight ahead and no sight behind. There was a silent sea that shimmered without life, but there was no heaven and no stars, and no other life but his because all the others were dead. They lay about him. He walked between them, saw the mounds of them. They were without colour and dimension. Their lips moved silently and their fingers waved. They came out of the no-future into his present-time and receded into the no-past. But they would not end and eventually he grew afraid because he knew that they had started to follow, and so he ran upon his endless silent deck, passing more of them, and each heap would come awake and join the others until the moving dead were legion, and so he ran faster upon his forever-deck and screamed a shocking scream of silence that rebounded and echoed in silence. . . .

Proctor dropped the cigarette into the ashtray. Sweat was cascading down his legs. It seemed to burst out of the skin, trickling down through the dense, dark hair on his calves. It was not natural, he thought, to sweat like that. He got up and went to the wash-hand basin and stared into the mirror that was screwed to the bulkhead above it.

What, he thought, if I have not been asleep? Perhaps I have not been asleep. Looking into the mirror, he grew deathly afraid, and could not meet his eyes any more because they might hold a latent madness that he would recognize. Shaking, he ran water into the basin and plunged his face into its relative coolness. Then with the water still running down his neck and naked chest he went back to his bed. He sat on the edge, picked the half-smoked cigarette out of the ashtray and tried to reason with himself. He had no temperature, he was sure. He did not feel weak. He was even mildly hungry. He had nearly convinced himself that he was all right when another thought occurred to him.

The others had not known. They had not known, when the madness came. What if it had happened to him already, and he was unaware?

With this thought he grew afraid again, and angry at the same time, hating Puget with a vicious hatred because it was his insidious tongue that had brought this state of quivering fright.

He got up and began to pace the small confines of the cabin. When the knock came he stopped abruptly and stared at the door. Then he said hesitantly, 'Come in.'

Mercy Attwell entered the cabin and shut the door behind her. 'Hello, Peter.'

He could not find words for a moment. He regarded her in silence, conscious mainly of a sense of overwhelming relief at having company.

'Hello,' he said at last. 'Do come in.' He flushed at the absurdity of that remark and went on quickly. 'Take a seat. Like a drink?'

She stayed where she was. 'Peter, I only came here because I had . . . because there was nowhere to go. Carl went to bed straight after the card game packed up. I tried at the hospital, but they didn't want me. I . . . I wanted someone to talk to. That's all.'

'Well, you've found someone,' he said with false cheer. Then he looked away, getting a fresh cigarette from his box and fiddling with it, unlit. 'Actually, I never expected you to come at all, under any conditions. I didn't exactly smother you with love and fondness last night after we'd . . . we'd . . .' He trailed away.

'No, you didn't. Why?'

'Oh, it's something that happens.' He turned the cigarette over and over in his fingers, as though it merited close study. 'It's got a name. Post *coitum triste*. Sounds awful, doesn't it? It's a sort of re-emergence of the boy scout in one, making one sorry to have been so jolly naughty and dirty.'

'Guilt?'

He met her eyes. 'Yes, guilt.' He shrugged and tried to be cheerful again. 'Look, do sit down. There're two-and-a-half hours to go before I relieve Max and I certainly can't sleep because I've tried.'

'All right.' She crossed the cabin slowly and sat on his bed, back erect, her perfect legs curled under her. Her eyes met his candidly, but with a conscious embarrassment in them, like a girl who is examined by a doctor and then meets him socially.

She is a person, he thought. For the first time I am regarding her as a person, and she is a very nice person, beautiful and human and warmly touchable. It was odd, only to realize this now.

'This thing there was,' she said, 'between us. It's gone, isn't it?'

'It's gone, yes.' He said it regretfully. But it was true.

'And do you still resent me, the way you did last night?'

'I don't think it pays, these post-mortems.' He smiled at her. 'But the answer is no. I do not. Can't I get you a drink?'

'All right. And a cigarette, if you don't mind.'

'Not at all.' He went and mixed two gins-and-tonic, then lit a cigarette for her.

'Cheers.'

'Your good health.' Proctor took the only chair, facing her. 'If we ever get off the *Florence Hurst* are you going to go on? I mean with Carl?'

'I don't know.' She shook her head. 'So much has happened. We've all changed, I think. Most of us for the worse. Only some of us are showing up well . . . like Mary Fannin.'

They fell silent, without awkwardness, sipping at their drinks and smoking. There came the sound of voices, after a moment, and then footsteps drummed along the alleyway with a noticeable urgency.

'Something's up.' Proctor got out of the chair. 'Won't be a sec.' He put his glass down and left the cabin. He was gone two or three minutes and when he came back Mercy could see the dark change in his face.

'The Chief is dying,' Proctor said. 'Also, Usher's got the disease now. They're looking for Lincott.' He picked up his drink, holding it as though it were useless to him. He stared at her. 'It can't go on like this, can it? We can't just go on drifting, and falling ill and dying. God, there's three men dead already and another on the threshold. It makes you wonder when . . .' He stopped abruptly, wordless.

Mercy got up. 'They'll wake the whole ship. I'd better go.' She put her cigarette out and walked to the door. She was opening it when his words reached her.

'Mercy, don't go.'

She turned back. When she saw his expression she shut the door and came up to him, looking into his face.

'Peter, are you afraid?'

The word was torn out of him. 'Yes.'

'I am not,' she said wonderingly.

'Don't go,' he said urgently. He came up to her and put his arms around her. 'Stay here with me.'

'Peter,' she said, 'I didn't want . . .

'I know. Don't say it.'

'But I . . .'

'Please.'

She smiled suddenly. It was the first time. She put her hands on his waist. 'I'll stay.'

He kissed her. 'I could love you, you know.'

She laughed. 'Don't talk nonsense. You couldn't love anyone.' She put her head against his chest. 'Just be gentle. That's all I want.'

The foghorn sounded suddenly, for the first time since Usher had taken ill. Its roar filled the cabin, shattering her last restraint, making them suddenly frantic in their mutual loneliness.

Lincott lost his footing and plunged through darkness to the rough floor. He lay there a moment, sobbing for breath, sweat-soaked. The torch was nearby, casting a feeble glow forward. He reached for it, then stood up unsteadily. The weak beam seemed unable to penetrate the silver fog of dust motes that it's light illuminated.

Lincott stopped. He had lost himself. He had advanced further and further into the hold only because he had been afraid to start what he had come here to do.

He turned the torch on to the nearest tier of coffins. They seemed to tower upwards, and he knew he would have to climb to the top. Panting, searching out toeholds, he shakily ascended until he was kneeling eight feet from the floor, trembling, dizzy with a vertigo that the darkness made worse. The coffins were three abreast, so he could spread himself a little. He inched forward, shining the torch downwards. Then the cuff of his left sleeve touched something that seemed to tumble away without resistance. A moment later glass shattered with a heart-stopping crash. He froze for a moment. Sweat started out on his face and ran down into his collar. Then he moved the torch so that its beam picked out the pale shards of glass lying on the dunnage floor with a spattering of what looked like liquid amongst them.

He moved forward another foot and came to the next row of coffins. There was a small irregular shape lying atop one of them. He picked it up and felt it. Cheese. Dry and hard. He let it fall into the darkness. Then he felt in his pocket and brought out the screwdriver he had stolen from the carpenter's workshop. The blade blazed solitary silver in the torch-glow. He directed it downwards on to the first screw in the coffin and let the bit settle in the slot on the screwhead. He took the strain and began to turn.

There were twenty screws. When he had taken them all out, putting them one by one carefully into his pocket, the coffin lid was stained with the dark droplets of his sweat.

He put the screwdriver down beside him and gripped the edges of the lid in his hands. It moved easily, but he was suddenly afraid to lift it. A torrent of argument rushed through his mind. He let the lid go and turned his head aside, half-nauseated, his face twisted. Then he thought of the five men in the hospital, and the three who were dead. He owed it to them. He forced his head back. He laid the torch down between his knees so that it shone along the coffin lid. It made the empty screw-holes look like craters surrounding a moonlit plain. He took the lid in his hands, lifted it, and suddenly dragged it aside on to the top of the next coffin. Choking, sobbing with revulsion, he put his left hand into the coffin and stirred it amongst the warm mould, plunging as it grew more bold, touching hardness amongst the softness until the hand and sleeve were coated and immersed. But then he could stand no more. His conviction gave way. He jerked his arm out, grabbed the heavy lid and slid it back into place. He put his clean arm on it and laid his burning face upon the cloth and listened to the harsh noise of his panting in the silence of the dark.

After a minute he stirred. He sat up, found the screwdriver. One by one, tediously, he replaced the screws. It took him nearly half an hour. Then very slowly, like an infirm man, he felt his way down the tier and stumbled out of the hold.

When the light clicked on in his cabin he realized that his sight was blurred. He felt as though he were looking through gauze. There were no sharp, defined edges.

He went and sat on his bed. It was pleasant. The soft mattress opened its cushiony arms to him, beckoning but insidious. He was weary beyond weariness. God, how long since he'd slept?

He fought his way off the bed. He ran water into the basin and soaked his entire head in its lukewarm coolness. Straightening up, he had a vision of himself in the bulkhead mirror, and he shrank from it. It is not me, he protested silently. His face was yellow, haggard. The eyes were swollen and staring, unblinking like the eyes of a shock case. But the tiny muscle at the corner of his right eye still jumped uncontrollably. He looked very old. He wrenched himself away, then, as suddenly, gasping with spasm, he flung back and vomited dryly, on and on, as though his body were determined to produce something from his empty stomach. But there had been no food for a long time now, only endless cups of tea.

Exhaustion took hold of him. He recognized it and became

alarmed, a small awake voice crying warning from within the mantling cloud of fatigue. Dully, he found the ampoule of Dexadrine and the hypodermic. He took off his jacket—why had he worn a jacket, in this heat?—and fumbled clumsily until the ampoule was empty, its thin glass sides beaded with the last remaining drops. The hypodermic needle bit into his arm. Then he dropped the hypodermic, hearing it break on the floor, and went and flung himself on the bed.

'Fix it,' he mumbled, 'that'll fix it.' His voice seemed to come from a very great distance. Even now, the voice within warned him not to lie down. He sat up groggily, staring into nothing until he finally became aware that his eyes were pointing at Osgood's tape recorder. He blinked them into focus.

Music, he thought suddenly. He got up and lurched to the machine, fumbled with the controls. A small light came on and the reels started to revolve. He retreated to the bed and sat on the edge, staring at the tape recorder hynotically.

It warmed to a hum. Then, instead of the music he vaguely expected, a voice suddenly filled the cabin, coming through in mid-sentence: '—and that's how it's going to be until there shall be a victory for the People, for the little guy who has to stay in line, for the poor sucker who's done nothing but pay taxes and lick boots and send his kids off as cannon-fodder so that the rich shall inherit the earth, not the meek, the way your Bible says, soldier. The rich. You think about it. You just take your mind back home and think about the folks who had, and the folks who . . .'

Lincott's fingers found the switch and the voice cut off. There was only the noise of Lincott's quick, rough breathing in the cabin.

'You bastard! You two-faced bloody swine!' He went to the bulkhead and slammed his fist against it. Tears squeezed out through his eyelids. 'It *is* the meek who shall inherit the earth! It is! It is!'

He dropped his hand, panting. There was the noise of footsteps coming fast along the alleyway outside his door and then the drumming of knuckles upon it.

'Doc! Doctor Lincott! Are you there?'

Lincott let the breath go out of him slowly. He blinked. His vision had become suddenly needle-sharp. The sweat was drying and his body was beginning to cool. The Dexadrine was starting to work.

He crossed to the door and opened it. Savage stood there, his face jumping with alarm. 'Where the hell have you been? I looked for you here, just now!'

'I'm on my way,' Lincott said unsteadily. 'What's the matter?'
'Usher's sick and McBlain is dying,' Savage said. His expression
broke. His face contorted. He began to weep. 'McBlain's dying,
Stephen. Please come quickly.'

Lincott drew a deep breath. 'Okay,' he said. 'Let's go.'

Grove took a sip of the whisky and put the tumbler down with a
sharp smack on the desk. He sighed, blinked, rubbed his eyes.
He wondered what the time was. He looked at his wrist but his
watch was not there. He frowned, puzzled, then remembered that
he'd taken it off some time ago and propped it on the desk in
front of him.

His eyes searched the desk, but he could not find the watch.
There were books piled all over the desk. Perhaps it was behind
one of them.

'Where are you, watch?' he asked sharply. Clumsily, he pushed
two of the books. They fell off the desk without appearing to
make any sound when they struck the deck. Strange. Anyway,
there was the watch. It had been behind the books. He leaned
forward and tried to focus on the hands. Twelve-something.
Twelve thirty-five. Hell's bells, it was late! There must be
something wrong with it, he thought. He picked it up and shook
it. No. On second thoughts, that would be about right. He'd
been here a long time. All that reading to do.

Thank God, he thought, that I've stayed sober. He was as
sober as a judge.

'Sober as a judge,' he said aloud, and laughed. He felt quite
good. Cheerful. That was the best way to drink. Just have a few.
It restored the old status quo. Made one feel fine.

Jerkily, his eyes returned to the book open in front of him. It
was Volume Nine of *Halsbury's Laws of England*. All the books
piled before him, in fact, belonged to the same set. They had
been on the *Florence Hurst* as long as he had, stuck away in the
radio cabin. Nobody ever read them. They were musty, old,
published long before the war. But that didn't matter, The law
didn't change, much. Especially British law. He had been plodding through them for hours, untrained in their use, blunderingly
searching.

Now he paged through the index of Volume Nine, frowning.
God, this was no use to him. It was all Criminal Law and Pro-
cedure; the whole bloody book, just about, was nothing else.
Angrily, he turned the pages. Then his eyes caught an item:
'High seas. Offences on.' The next line read: 'High seas. Offences
peculiar to the.' Under this heading there were sub-items:
'Decoying Pacific Islanders.' God, no! Then: 'Piracy.'

Whoops, he thought, maybe that's it. I should have realized it would be under Criminal Law. Damn it, it was a crime, wasn't it?

Quickly, he turned to the pages given by the index. He read laboriously, wondering why the lines kept moving before his eyes. Then, suddenly, his face lit up.

'Got it!' he said thickly. 'I'll show the bastards!' Carelessly he ripped a page out of another part of the book and folded it as a marker. Then he got up, pleased with himself, pacing the small cabin and sipping from his glass.

'Lucky I stayed sober,' he said again. He came back to the desk and peered at the watch. Jesus! Five to one. He'd better get some sleep

He went to the locked door, put his hand on the key. Then he shook his head. No. If he came out everybody would be at him, pestering him with non-essentials. There had been all sorts of funny goings-on tonight; the foghorn booming on and on, people running and shouting. He hadn't paid any attention.

He made up his mind. I'll stay here, he thought. To hell with them. He went back to the desk and filled his empty glass. He was feeling good now. His plans were made for tomorrow—it had needed only that slice of law to round them off. The law, backed by a gun.

'Walter,' he said, 'you are a very clever fellow. I congratulate you.' He laughed. Then he began to sing, raucously:

'Here's to Walter, he's so blue,
  He's a bastard, through and through,
  He's a bastard so they say,
  He tried to go to heaven but he went the other way!
  Drink it down, down, down. . . .'

The liquor burnt his throat as he drank the glass empty. He was laughing again as he reeled across to the desk, reaching blindly for the bottle.

CHAPTER ELEVEN

FRIDAY MORNING. Four bells. Ten o'clock. The *Florence Hurst's* fifth day at sea. Her second as a derelict. Her forty-first hour shut off from the world by the wrecked radio.

In the hospital, three people sat immobile in chairs. Two, by their broken-necked attitudes, were asleep. They were Mary Fannin and Savage.

The third was Lincott. He sat very erect. His eyes, unblinking, were fixed on the blank bulkhead opposite him. The fingers of his right hand encircled his left. He had taken his pulse five minutes ago and found it normal. It was too early to tell yet, in any case, whether what he had done in the hold last night was going to have any effect upon him. But he continued to sit like that, forgetting all about the fingers that lightly held his wrist.

He was trying, unsuccessfully, to marshal his thoughts. But whenever he thought that he had all the units of his equation aligned, he would discover that he had forgotten one, or that his mind had gone entirely blank. Then he would try again, and they would pop up one by one: the data that lay in those clipboards at the foot of every bed and next to him on the desk, four clipboards on the desk, each representing a dead man; Tommy Tucker's voice on the tape recorder last night, and what he had noticed about it lost in a shimmering quicksand of exhaustion and the heady effect of the Dexadrine; the story about Typhoid Mary that Mary Fannin had given him to read; Quinan —Quinan came into it somewhere, but he could not exactly figure out where; and other parts of the equation that would come and go, suddenly, without warning. Some, or all, would be gone, and he would find himself dwelling fixedly on a non-essential, like his petty resentment of McBlain, for dying. McBlain hadn't tried. He had responded to treatment in the beginning, but he hadn't wanted to live. With his wife dying, he had just given up and let death take him. Like Hookins. With all the trouble Hookins had been in, whatever it was, there had been no particular reason to fight. He had just slipped away. Even Osgood had let him down, although in Osgood's case the mind might have wanted to live but the body had been the weak link, this time.

The material I have been given to work with, he thought resentfully, is not very good.

In one of the furthest beds Norton, the Second Engineer, groaned once out of the deep tortures of his coma. Lincott got up very slowly, holding on to his chair for a moment to steady himself. Then he moved to the bed. His gait was rigid, like a careful drunk. Automatically, he shook down the thermometer from the measuring-glass on the locker and slid it into Norton's armpit, waiting there quite motionless until the half-minute was up. Then he took the thermometer out and studied it.

It was one degree down.

He put the thermometer back in the glass. I suppose I should rejoice, he thought. I suppose I should wake the others and we should caper about with delight, because there is a chance that Norton might live. But he did not feel like rejoicing. I am too tired, he thought. He walked slowly back to his chair and

sat down again and stared at the bulkhead across the room. Once
again, he tried to assemble his equation.

In the kitchen, the cook took his fourth aspirin of the day
and then sullenly contemplated the menu for lunch. I've got it,
he thought. I've got it and nobody cares. They would care, all
right, if he ran amuck with the meat cleaver. He shrugged with
a sort of frightened indifference and thought about the menu
again. There was soup, but nobody would want soup in this heat.
They could have curry. They'd had curry yesterday but they
could bloody well have it again and if they didn't like it they
could flipping-well throw it at him. He was used to that kind of
treatment. Nobody cared a damn about him.

With increasing melancholy he began to slice onions.

In his cabin, Quinan came groggily awake. He had slept just
under two hours since he had come off watch at eight bells. He
showered, and felt the lukewarm water restoring a measure of
alertness. Then he dressed, debating for a moment whether he
should open the newspaper-wrapped parcel containing his best
uniform, the one he had had drycleaned in Hong Kong. It had
come on board literally at the last moment, thrown across the
widening gap between the *Florence Hurst* and the dock by a
panting, shrilly-determined deliveryman. But Quinan decided
against it. There was no telling how long they would remain in
their present situation. There was an older, hand-washed uniform
in his closet, so he put that on instead, and went topside to find
Grove.

The sea, in gentle swells, moved the *Florence Hurst* onward
along her meandering, aimless course, producing only the
occasional creak from the untried hull. The sun beat brutally
down upon her iron decks. Viewed from without, she would have
seemed a ghost-ship, another *Marie Celeste,* if it had not been for
the solitary figure in sharply-pressed white tropical shorts and
shirt that stood upon the canvas-covered planks of Number Three
hatch.

Lucas was in a surprisingly cheerful mood. He had dressed very
carefully to look especially smart. The white stockings that
covered the powerful, muscular calves were folded exactly one
inch under the knee. The white trousers were cut a little extra
short because his legs were brown and he liked to display the
curving definition of his quadriceps muscle. The sun didn't bother
him particularly because his cap with its snowy cover protected
his bristly flaxen head, and because he was young and fit and
supremely confident.

Apart from which, it was his birthday.

I'm twenty-five today, he said silently to himself, twenty-five

today, I've slept with many a whore, been drinking and knocking
since I was four, I don't need the key of the door, hip-hip-hip-
hooray, for I'm a bloody bad fellow, I'm twenty-five today.

What a hell of a place to have a birthday, he thought, standing
on a hatch cover like the faithful sentry at Pompeii, with a Webley
in a canvas holster strapped to his side loaded with real cartridges
so that he could shoot dead any of the crew who might try to
jettison the coffins. It was bloody absurd. They would never be so
silly. But just to be on the safe side he unbuttoned the holster
and tucked the flap back against his waist.

The gun was nearly new. Its bright, slick-blue finish blindingly
reflected the sun's rays from burly shoulders that bulked on either
side of the thick neck of hammer. It made him a little uneasy
looking down at it where it nestled against his trim side, so he
changed his mind and buttoned the flap again. Immediately he
felt better. In the past, any trouble on the *Florence Hurst* had been
capably dealt with by his big fists. There was no reason to change
the status quo.

I'm twenty-five today, he sang, twenty-five today, I've slept
with many a . . . He stopped, suddenly. The short hair bristled
on his neck and he let his hands fall to his sides and took a
deep breath.

Hawes, Ludd, Kyle, Draper and Knowles had come from the
port alleyway and were spreading out across the foredeck, turning
to face him.

They stared at each other in complete silence. Lucas listened
in an abstract way to the thudding of his heart. He wondered
where the hell Quinan was, and conquered an overpowering
desire to crane his neck back and see whether there was anybody
looking over from the bridge wing.

His eyes swept across the faces of the men and settled on
Hawes. He saw the absolute fury with which Hawes was regarding him and it suddenly dawned on him that Hawes had not been
expecting this; Hawes had been anticipated completely, and for
the moment did not know what to do.

Immediately Lucas felt better. Well, he thought, Wally Grove,
hangover and all—and my God, what a hangover—that's the
first time in your life you've done something clever, putting an
armed man on the hatch-cover when nobody else thought the
danger was anything more than an idle threat. His momentary
fright disappeared and he began to feel elated. He wanted to
crow, he wanted to express his delight. And it was inevitable that
he should direct it at Hawes.

'Wotcher, Feller!' His voice rang out in the heavy air.

Hawes's face worked. 'You think you're bleeding clever, Lucas!'

'Not at all,' Lucas said imperturbably, with a new aplomb. 'I'm doing my duty. If you want to break the law, go ahead and try.'

Lucas could almost watch Hawes think. They hadn't really expected any trouble, he could see that. All of them wore heavy cargo-handling gauntlets. They were equipped to move the coffins. They had thought Grove would back down.

There was the noise of footsteps on the port bridge wing. Lucas now felt entitled to turn and look up, and caught sight of Grove's head.

'Now listen, you men.' Grove's voice had the same rusty dryness it had contained at Osgood's funeral so many years ago that had been only yesterday. It was mechanical, expressionless, robot-like. It gave no idea of what the speaker was going through.

'I want you to listen carefully. I am speaking to you as Master of this ship. Mister Lucas was put where he is by me. You can see that he is armed. He has my full authority to use that weapon if needs be.' There was a silence for a moment and Lucas thought he could hear the rustle of pages. Then Grove went on. 'What you propose doing is a very serious breach of the law. I told you that yesterday. I have now found proof of that statement. I have here a book of law'—Lucas could picture him holding it up— 'which clearly states the position. It says, and I quote, "a seaman is by statute deemed to be a pirate, felon and robber, punishable as a pirate, who . . ."'—there was a pause as Grove read past irrelevancies—' ". . . . endeavours to make a revolt in the ship". The book goes on to state, dealing with punishment, that "the punishment for a statutory piracy is penal servitude for life or for not less than three years".'

On the bridge, Grove closed the book over its marker and handed it to Quinan, who was standing behind him. His hand shook so violently that Quinan had to snatch at the book to prevent it falling. Grove interlocked his fingers and put them on the rail in front of him to steady himself.

'You men propose to jettison the lawful cargo of this ship, against specific and very clear orders, and after having been informed of the impossibility of your theory by the Medical Officer. Your intended action constitutes, in my opinion and in the opinion of my officers, a revolt. I have warned you of the consequences. Now go to your quarters.'

The silence seemed to go on and on. Grove turned to Quinan and gave him a shaking, lopsided grin. His stomach was a twisted knot, made of iron. His heart hammered. Sweat cascaded down his cheeks. The deck seemed to tilt alarmingly. He clutched at the rail and closed his eyes. When he opened them the deck was level again and Quinan and Proctor were staring at him. I am over-breathing again, he thought. Hyperventilating. He needed a drink, but it was impossible now. Desperately, he tried to calm himself.

On the hatchcover, Lucas pushed back his cap and regarded Hawes contemptuously. 'That's fixed your clock, Feller.'

Hawes's hands clenched in the big gauntlets. He said nothing.

Lucas couldn't leave it. 'Come on Feller. Come and get the coffins. What's the matter?'

'Anybody can talk big,' Hawes said thickly, 'behind a gun.' His hatred of Lucas burned in his small eyes.

'You're chicken,' Lucas sneered.

Draper licked his full lips. 'Come on, Feller. Let's forget it. There's nothing we can do here. They've got us cold.'

Hawes stood undecided, quivering with rage. Then fate intervened on his side. From the starboard alleyway Lucien Puget emerged, tall, spare, brisk, a black beret on the silver head, half-smiling at some secret amusement. He had come four yards on to the foredeck before he awoke to the situation and stopped suddenly. His face straightened. He regarded first Lucas and then the five men ranged in front of him.

Hawes grinned like a devil. He flung out an arm. 'There's the old Froggy-bastard who brought this load of grief aboard in the first place. Fix him!'

Draper advanced toward Puget. 'Bringing your mucking filthy bodies on board a decent British ship! We should bloody-well teach you a lesson!'

In their frustration, it hadn't taken much to inflame them. Hawes shouted, 'We'll teach the old bastard a lesson, won't we, boys!'

'Yippee!' Knowles cackled, 'give him a bleeding good beating!'

Puget had stood his ground until that moment. But his confusion and alarm had rapidly increased. He saw impending violence written across the faces of the men. He broke and ran, and in his fear he ran the wrong way. In a loping, lopsided, old man's stride he went for'ard past the mast table. His beret fell off as he collided with a stay. He left the beret and scrambled onwards.

Like a pack of dogs, baying, they took after him.

'Here!' Lucas shouted. 'Stop it! Cut that out!' He danced nervously to the edge of the hatchcover, forgetting all about the revolver at his waist. His alarmed eyes darted alternately to Hawes, who only watched the chase, grinning, and to the grey head of Puget, who fell near the foc'sle head and got up again, barely eluding Draper's clutching hands. Kyle howled and yipped and Knowles cackled.

Puget's eyes were starting from his head. He ran absurdly, crab-like, the terror stamped across his face. As he came back, passing the mast table, he flung himself to one side and scrambled up on the ladder that led up to it, his desperate hands clawing at the slender rungs.

Lucas cursed helplessly. 'Over here, Mister Puget!' he called. 'Stop that, you bastards! He's an old man, he's . . .' He turned to Hawes, white-faced. 'Call them off, you bloody swine! Can't you see they'll . . .'

'You get 'em off!' Hawes laughed. But there was murder on his face, and it was not intended for Puget. 'Come off the hatch-cover and get him!'

'Ah, Jesus!' Lucas cried. Puget, clawing upwards, had been grabbed from behind. Ludd and Draper had reached him, grab-bing at his legs and trying to drag him down. He clung to the ladder with frantic tenacity, his head twisted to look down, his face contorted like a cornered animal. He felt his grip loosen as the terrible drag on his legs increased. *Non! Non! Pourquoi le faites-vous a moi? Allez-vous en!* He screamed. Then his hands gave way and he was pulled down, and the yipping of the men changed to a more savage note as they swarmed over him. The old man struggled, hitting out, all of them rolling about under the overhang of the mast table, a wild tangle of bodies.

Lucas was conscious of Hawes's grinning ferocity. Fury and desperation swept away the last of his control as he saw the Frenchman's face, masked with blood, emerge from the tumbling figures.

He jumped down from the hatchcover.

Hawes's expression changed. The grin was swept away by naked hatred. He burst into movement, running with a choppy, bent-kneed, powerful motion, angling across the foredeck to cut Lucas off from the Frenchman. As Lucas's feet hit the iron deck, Hawes slammed into him with vicious force. Lucas staggered. As he straightened, Hawes hit him low in the belly. His cap flew off and he half-buckled. In this moment Hawes hit him again with his sledge-hammer fist and blood spurted from Lucas's nose. He fell heavily on the deck just next to the hatchcover. For a second he looked at Hawes's looming figure while the blood dribbled off his chin on to his shirt. Then he came off the deck as though propelled by a current. He flung himself into Hawes and hit him twice. The noise of his fists made a thick, smacking sound. Hawes backpedalled and they skittered across the deck to the side, hitting each other viciously, ducking and lunging with wicked expertise.

On the bridge, Quinan had leapt to the companion-way with

Proctor at his heels. He had his hands on the rails when Grove's voice impaled him there.

'Mister Quinan! You will not leave this bridge!'

He stopped so suddenly that Proctor slammed into him. Grove had wrenched himself away from the rail and was staring at them, his lips trembling.

'Walter, we've got to go now!' Quinan shouted. 'You want that old man killed? You want . . .'

'You and Proctor will stay where you are!' Grove's voice was almost a scream. 'I am giving you an instruction, and deliberate disobedience is mutiny!'

'To hell with him, let's go,' Proctor cried. 'Jesus, Lucas and Puget are being torn to pieces down there!' He tried to push past Quinan but was hauled back by Quinan's iron hand.

'Walter, you're wrong. We've got to go and help,' Quinan pleaded. 'God, man, what are your reasons? Have you seen that pack of wolves down there?'

'Seen them? Of course I've seen them.' Grove whirled away from the rail. He paced the small bridge wing, panting, his mouth working. 'You're all I've got. I can't let you and Proctor go. Once I've lost you we're spent. I can't lose any more men, you understand? I can't risk it!'

Quinan experienced a sense of wild disbelief. Here was Grove talking about losing more men, as though a battle were being fought down there, as though he were a general struggling to decide whether he should commit more troops. It was a nightmare, but the horror on the foredeck was real.

He stormed back across the bridge and grabbed Grove by an arm, dragging him to the rail. 'Look down there! Are you insane? How can you forbid us to go? Ah, God, it's finished!'

Proctor ran to the rail as well. Puget lay still, near the mast table, crookedly twisted like a rag doll. His shirt had been torn off him and the puckered white of his old man's flesh was visible, streaked and spotted with blood.

Lucas was on his knees. Draper and Ludd and Hawes stood around him, slamming blows at will into his body. Only his iron bulk kept him erect. Fall, Quinan pleaded silently. But Lucas stayed on his knees. He twisted his head, looking up at the bridge. They saw his bloody lips frame the words, 'Help me.' Then his hand went to his side, his fingers scrabbled weakly at the buttoned-down holster-flap. At that moment Draper sledged a blow into his neck and Lucas went down on all fours. Blood dribbled in a stream from his nose. Hawes jumped in and swung a kick into Lucas's side and he toppled over and lay still. The men broke away and ran for the hatchcover.

Quinan felt himself being pulled from behind. He twisted and looked into Proctor's rage-contorted face. 'You bloody coward! You bloody fucking coward! Why didn't we go down when we had a chance? Why did you listen to this mad bastard?'

Quinan pushed him away, sick within himself. 'You heard the Captain. He . . .'

Proctor was weeping with rage. 'The Captain's crazy, you fool. Why do you have to be so blindly obedient?' His arm swung back to deliver a blow. Then suddenly he let his hands drop. All the fury went out of him. 'Ah, God in Heaven, we're finished on this ship!'

Quinan looked at Grove, but Grove was paying no attention. He was crouched, shaking as though with palsy, against the wheelhouse bulkhead, fumbling with the pages of Halsbury, trying to get his hands to function so that he could open the book. Finally he succeeded. The book fluttered open at the marker and Grove barged to the bridge rail just as the winch rattled, filling the heated air with its noise.

Grove's voice was shrill. He had the book poised on the rail. 'Listen to me, you men down there. Do you know what you've done? You've put your heads into a noose. The law says "Whoever with intent to commit, or at the time of, or immediately before or after committing, the crime of piracy in respect of any ship, assaults with intent to murder any person on board the ship, or who stabs, cuts, or wounds any such person . . ." '

Quinan watched him, hypnotized with disbelief. Those animals down there had beaten an old man until he was either dead or unconscious. They had beaten one of their own officers. But Grove read the law to them while the winch rattled and the air was cluttered with the noise of the wedges being struck out along the hatchcoaming and the jangle of metal on the deck. He read law while the Frenchman lay masked in blood below the mast table and Lucas, with the most infinite care in the world, like an infant at the beginning of animation, slowly dragged his hands underneath him and began to lever his body, a fraction of an inch at a time, into an upright position. Grove's tenor voice was heard as a railing background, in fragile and unintelligible accompaniment, and was ignored.

' ". . . or unlawfully does any act whereby the life of such person may be endangered, must be sentenced to death." ' Grove's voice stopped. His fumbling hands tried to close the book but he dropped it and it fell with a thump on to the wooden boards of the bridge wing deck. In the same moment he had whirled about and pinioned Proctor with his furious eyes. 'Call me a bastard, eh? I heard you. And I'm crazy, too. What would you do, you womanizing ill-gotten fool, in my place, when you've only four men who'll obey you? Get them chewed up down there? And then what? What'll you do then, you twit, after the heroics?'

'And what will you do?' Proctor shouted. 'Keep us here on your bloody little safe island until everybody's dead? What's the difference? Those people down there will stop at nothing. You want to stop them jettisoning the coffins, don't you? Well, what's stopping them now? They're doing it! And you've got that old Frenchman's blood on your hands on top of it. And what about Max Lucas?' His face writhed into a sneer. 'He was teacher's pet, wasn't he, so was I for that matter, until the propeller came adrift and people started to die. But now, poor bastard, you've abandoned him!'

Grove hardly seemed to have heard him. He was looking down at the foredeck where by now the battens had been removed from the hatchcover and the derrick was pointing its long slender snout over the square, cavernous opening to the hold. Draper, Kyle and Ludd were within, weirdly monstrous with strips of cloth bound across their faces as crude, surgical masks. The ever-present dust could be seen, rising unnaturally as though it were the dust of the graves brought with these long-dead men, sparkling in a million motes into the laser-beam of the brutal sun. The cargo-net swished down and the three men began to fill it, tossing the light coffins into it.

Grove tore his eyes away. They looked straight into Quinan's. 'Here. Here.' He was breathing so quickly that his voice was fluffy and nearly inaudible. His eyes darted away, fluttering to the foredeck and as quickly returning. He fumbled in his pocket, and in that time he continued this aberrated movement until he was thrusting a ring of keys at Quinan. 'Get a rifle from the armoury. You know where the clips are. Bring it up here and open fire on those men.' His eyes stopped and held Quinan. He was suddenly jibbering. 'You know the legal position. You are perfectly within your rights. Those men have committed a capital offence. An eye for an eye, a tooth for a tooth, the Bible says. And these men are under orders. There is discipline to enforce. Nobody's going to jettison my cargo. Nobody. Go and get that rifle and . . .'

Quinan took the keys as Grove's voice trailed away to silence, the great swollen eyes fixed on him, the chin wet with saliva, the thin chip of a body half-crouched, half-curled. He looked at the keys in the moment that the winch rattled again and he knew that the first load was coming out of the hold. The keys burnt bright silver in his palm.

'Gil!' Proctor's voice was sharp but controlled. 'Gil, look at me.' Quinan turned slowly. The Second Officer's narrow, brown face contained a look Quinan had never seen before. It was a curious admixture of sudden maturity and bitter fatalism. 'Gil, do you really intend to obey that command? You'll notice it's you who has to do the dirty work. Do you really intend to get a rifle and shoot Hawes, or Ludd, or any of the others, despite what they've done? We're Merchant Navy officers, Gil, we're not killers. Are you going to go on with your crazy loyalty? We're finished, anyway, all of us, if we ever get out of here. Too much has happened. Don't listen to him, Gil. He's crazy. He . . .'

'Shut your face,' Quinan said quietly, but he said it without insult. He turned to Grove. 'Walter, I'm very sorry, but at the moment I am not prepared to obey that instruction.' He was almost formal about it. He dropped the keys on the deck. 'Let Hawes have his coffins.' He repeated, unconsciously, the words of Mary Fannin the night before. 'It doesn't matter to dead men where they lie. And we must protect the lives of the innocent people on this ship.'

Grove stared at him, gulping for breath. Quinan had a moment of alarm because the Grove he knew had gone completely. Grove said nothing. He stayed there in the corner where the wheelhouse bulkhead met the bridge rail, deeply crouched within its protection, shaking as though in great ague. The sanity Quinan had hoped for from his ultimatum was not forthcoming; it could not, from this hunted, demoralized man.

Quinan turned away. 'Hawes!' he called.

The winch clattered again in that moment. Hawes, having won, never knew it. Quinan, about to call again, clamped his jaws together.

Lucien Puget had sat up, suddenly and without stirring, like a newly-animated marionette.

There was a darkness before the Frenchman's eyes, a great cloud that swung between him and the sun. He felt no pain. But the obstruction irritated him. It cast shade when he knew there was no cloud. He put his hand to his face and wiped his eyes. The hand came away scarlet-wet with blood. Blood? Had he fallen? He must have. But it didn't matter; it could not be of any consequence. The shadow above him was more worrying. He blinked his eyes and looked up into the still, cobalt vault of heaven and suddenly, as in the focusing of a lens, his vision cleared and he could see not far above him the tobacco-brown ropes of the cargo net and within it, bulging and straining it at odd angles, the lemon-yellow wood of its clutch of coffins.

He stared uncertainly. It was impossible. They were at sea. They could not be off-loading now. Slowly, his brain started to work. And at the same time his eyes picked out the stencilling on the nethermost coffin in the pile, facing him like a hovering long kite: *'Puget P. L. Lt. No. 3976621. Decede le 11 Mai 1954. Dien Bien Phu.'*

Puget's face contorted. *'Pierre!'* he screamed.

He struggled upright, driven by his horror. Hawes, watching the cargo-net rise, did not see him. Puget passed behind him, stooping to pick up one of the peg-shaped wedges that had been driven out of the hatch-cover. With this in his hand he passed around the high bulk of the mast table and scrambled up the ladder. Knowles, operating the winch, had his back turned.

Quinan saw it all happen while he stood stock-still, made mute by the drama below. Hawes, in that instant, saw it too. He had turned to signal Knowles. He saw Puget behind Knowles, blood-spattered, staggering, the makeshift club lifted high. He saw the Frenchman's lips twist as he said something which was lost in the noise. Hawes opened his mouth to shout a warning, but he was too late. Puget brought the wedge down on Knowles's head and Knowles collapsed over the winch, head lolling, his body pushing the lever forward. The great drum of cable unwound like a gigantic cotton reel and the cargo net and its contents crashed down on to the deck at the side of the hatch.

Like a great angry cat, Hawes leapt for the mast table ladder. At the same moment Quinan flung himself down the companion-way with Proctor hard on his heels, only to find Mary Fannin and Lincott on their way up. There was a momentary tangle. Mary Fannin's body was pushed hard up against his. He felt its warmth. He looked into her flushed, horrified face.

'Why don't you do something?' she cried. 'Stephen and I heard the racket from the hospital. That old man, they're going to . . .'

'Mind aside,' Quinan commanded. He pushed past her and pelted down the rest of the companion-way, sensing that all of them were following him. He was running as his feet hit the iron deck. When he burst on to the foredeck his mind, seeming to record in slow-motion, showed him Lucas first, almost in the scuppers, beginning to crawl ever so slowly towards them; beyond him Puget tumbling down the mast table ladder, dragged down by Hawes; and Ludd, Draper and Kyle rushing across to fall upon the old man as his knees buckled and he sprawled full length on the hot iron plating.

Quinan charged into them with such impetus that Kyle was bowled over and the other three were knocked off balance. Quinan had learned his fighting in an ugly school that counted purely on results. He was rough, brutal and dirty, but he was terrifyingly effective. Draper took a head-ringing, open-handed

slap over the ear that put him temporarily out of the fight.
Almost in the same movement Quinan caught Ludd across the
throat with his forearm. He had a vague picture of Proctor and
Kyle struggling together, but Hawes was the dangerous one. He
turned and was just in time to absorb a crushing punch from
Hawes that struck him on the right cheekbone. He heard the
flesh give, but they were outnumbered and this was no time for
backpedalling. With his head spinning, Quinan went forward.
Hawes was not expecting it. He had lowered his guard, confident
of seeing Quinan fall. It was a mistake that he had no chance
to correct. Quinan hit him twice rapidly, over the heart. It took
the breath out of Hawes, but Hawes was far too tough to go down
on that sort of treatment without being battered into submission;
and then the whole affair would develop into a thing of minutes
when, to succeed, it had to be seconds. Quinan knew what to do.
With Hawes bringing his guard up again he dropped his own
hands, stepped forward one pace and kicked Hawes in the crutch.

Hawes reacted in slow motion. The agony that was like liquid
fire travelled up from his bruised testicles, crimping him slowly
over while his face became ashen.

Quinan was already turning away. 'Come on! Come on!' he
shouted. Puget was lying inert, almost at his feet. He scooped
the old man up and slung him over one shoulder and began to
stagger off the foredeck, almost catching up with Mary Fannin
and Lincott who were half-carrying, half-dragging Lucas.

They straggled up the companion-way, panting, staggering.
When Quinan reached the bridge wing he put Puget down gently
and then crouched next to him, trying to steady himself and not
collapse while the deck spun and his breath roared in his ears.
He was aware of blood dripping in tiny red droplets on to the
honed planking without realizing that it was coming from his
own cheek. Dreamlike, he saw Lincott fling himself down on one
knee, his hand going flatly on to Puget's chest.

Proctor's voice was coming from somewhere. Quinan looked
up. 'Peter,' he gasped, 'keep them off the bridge. Take Max's gun.
Just point it at them. They won't come.'

It was all he could manage. His lungs had to suck air again
so desperately that he made a wheezing sound as he tried to
breathe. It took a minute while he remained quite still, hunched
and on all fours like a crawling infant, waiting for the exhaustion
to pass and his head to clear. Then he looked around very slowly,
seeing for the first time Lucas stretched out on the planking to his
left. He was on his side, with his eyes open. Mary Fannin was
gently mopping his battered face. His nose, by its angle, was
broken. One eye was already swelling shut. He spat bright blood

out on to the deck while Quinan watched. Then he twisted to look into the girl's face.

'I read you all wrong,' he said. 'I'm sorry.'

She smiled. 'Don't let it throw you, Max. You're young. You'll learn.'

Lucas got unsteadily to his knees and crawled the six feet to Puget's side. The others joined him, clustering around the still form and the silent Lincott.

Puget's eyes fluttered open. He looked straight up into heaven and was pleased with what he saw there. He smiled faintly. *'C'est un jour magnifique,'* he murmured. He was silent for a moment and then said, *'Je viens toute de suite, Pierre.'* Then he fell silent. His body quivered a moment, straining. As suddenly, it went limp.

Mary Fannin let out a little gasp. 'Monsieur Puget! Monsieur Puget!' She reached out and touched his arm.

'Leave him.' Lincott looked at her bitterly. 'He's dead. You expect him to stand up to what he's been through? His heart gave out.'

Mary said softly, 'I remember the night we left Haiphong, he asked Mrs Attwell whether she believed in ghosts. He made her laugh. He was a nice old man.' She started to weep silently, just the tears running down her face, no sound of grief at all.

'What did he say?' Lucas asked.

Lincott looked away from them, out across the sea. 'He said it was a beautiful day. Then he told someone called Pierre that he was coming.'

He jerked his glance back. 'He was right. It is a beautiful day, isn't it?' The muscle at the side of his eye was jumping uncontrollably. His voice rose. 'Isn't it a beautiful day?'

They were silent. Then Lucas jumped to his feet suddenly. 'You bastards!' he shouted. 'You bloody bastard murderers!' His voice rang across the silent decks and faded away while he stood staring blindly towards the bows, his big chest heaving with the force of his emotion.

Proctor said into the silence, 'Take it easy, Max. They've gone. They've left the foredeck.'

Quinan got up shakily. Only the heat was preventing the muscles in his thighs from binding up completely.

He looked down at the empty foredeck, black-mouthed with the open gape of Number Three hatch, the cable snaking in great greasy curls over the slumped cargo-net with its harvest of coffins.

'We've won,' he said wryly. 'If you could call it that. What a hell of a victory.'

The others came silently to join him, staring down. Then Lincott said abruptly, 'I can't stay. There're the living to treat.' His lips twisted. 'The pre-dead.' He turned away and clattered down the companion-way out of sight.

Mary Fannin moved. 'I must go, too. He needs help.'

Quinan put his hand on her shoulder. 'Not yet. Dick Savage is there. Stay just a little while.'

'You don't understand.' The level grey eyes looked up into his. 'Stephen hasn't slept since Tuesday night, unless you count a few minutes on Thursday morning. And he told me that on Tuesday night he couldn't sleep and read until one o'clock. Today is Friday. Figure that out. He's giving himself Dexadrine shots to stay awake, and they're making him . . . odd.' She touched his hand gently. 'I'll see you later.' Then she was gone down the companion-way.

Proctor, Lucas and Quinan stood in silence for a moment with the dead man at their feet. Then Proctor said, 'Well, either we cover Puget or take him to the carpenter's workshop. What's it going to be?'

'Get a blanket from Osgood's cabin, for the time being.' Quinan said. 'The workshop is too near the crew's quarters for my liking. I don't think any of us should go aft until we know where Hawes and company are and what they intend to do.'

'I'll get it.' Proctor started to move and then stopped again, flung about by confusing forces within him. 'Gil, I'm sorry for what I said just now. I was nearly going crazy, seeing what was happening on the foredeck.' He searched Quinan's face for a moment, fingering his bottom lip which had been cut during the struggle. 'What are we . . . you . . . going to do about Grove?'

Quinan became deliberately obtuse. He had noticed with inner amusement the way Proctor had corrected himself. 'How do you mean?'

Proctor hesitated. 'Well, you refused to obey him. What happens now? Are you going to continue in that line, or . . . or . . .' He trailed away, watching Quinan with care.

Quinan said levelly, 'Any sensible command the Old Man gives me, I will carry out.' His use of the courtesy title for Grove was noticeable.

Proctor let out his breath in a long, angry sigh. He made a disgusted sound and turned away.

'Peter!' Quinan said sharply.

Proctor stopped. 'Yes?'

'Do you want me to relieve the Captain of his command?'

The question was, at first, too blunt for Proctor. He began to say something, and checked himself. Words dammed up inside him. He had to release them. He swung towards Lucas.

'You should have seen him, Max! Cowering there in the corner, jabbering, spit running down his chin, more like an idiot than a man, fiddling for his keys, and giving them to Gil, and telling Gil to get a rifle and start hosing lead on to the foredeck!'

His own description made Proctor brave. He turned back to Quinan. 'Yes,' he burst out, 'I do! I think you should relieve Grove of his command!' Having unburdened himself, he stood staring at Quinan, breathing quickly, fingering the cut on his lip.

'On what grounds?' Quinan asked seriously.

Proctor made an impatient movement with one hand. 'You know damn well! He's mad. He's madder than a ruddy hatter!'

Quinan would not be prodded into emotion. 'This ship carries a Medical Officer. To do a thing like that I would have to have medical backing, wouldn't I?'

'You'd get it, all right,' Proctor said carelessly. 'The state of Grove's mind is obvious even to a layman.'

Quinan pursued his own point. 'Have you asked Lincott for his opinion?'

Proctor paused. 'No,' he said reluctantly.

At last Quinan allowed a note of anger to enter his voice. 'Well, I have,' he said roughly, 'and I suggest you do the same before you start making reckless suggestions that *I* have to carry out. Stephen would have told you, if you'd bothered to ask, that the Old Man is not insane, nor is he incapable of command. He's a neurotic. He drinks. There are plenty of Skippers who drink; that's not in itself a crime. He's unpredictable and jittery. He's even odd. But he is not, I repeat, unable to command this ship.'

Proctor flushed. He knew better than to impute Lincott's opinion. He tried reason. 'Almost everything that's happened to us since we became disabled is directly attributable to the peculiar things the Old Man's been doing. You can't deny that.'

'Like the decision to fit the spare propeller?' Quinan asked quickly. 'What was wrong with that? He was trying to save the Company money. It's been done before, you know. If he had succeeded he would have been a hero. It was only the outbreak of the epidemic that put paid to the work.'

He made his voice more friendly. 'Look, you two. Don't think I haven't thought about this, long and hard. So has Lincott. It's not what the Old Man has done, it's the way he goes about it. Picture yourselves giving evidence about these incidents in a courtroom. Picture yourselves in the hands of a wily barrister. Most of all, picture Walter Grove back to normal, fully fit, answering every point. How long do you think you would last?'

There was a short silence. Then Proctor shrugged and said, 'I'll get the blanket.'

He was beginning to move when the door of the radio cabin banged with a report like the blast of a shotgun, making them jump. Grove came out on to the navigation deck and walked slowly towards them, stopping at the beginning of the bridge wing. He carried a rifle over one arm.

He had neatened himself. He had tucked in his shirt and levelled the stockings on his gaunt calves. He had wiped his face clean of its ever-present sheen of perspiration. He had combed his hair. The eyes he fixed on them were dead-level. Quinan and Proctor stared at him, unable to believe the transformation.

'Is he dead?' Grove said it quite steadily. He nodded at Puget's body.

'Yes.' It was Quinan who answered.

'Are you going to leave him there until he stinks?' The blood-shot eyes fixed impersonally on the Chief Officer. Grove could have been referring to a mouse that someone had tramped on.

'Sir,' Quinan said formally, 'I think it can safely be said that order has ceased to exist on this ship. Hawes and his group have murdered a man. They are not going to sit idly by while we round them up. My own feeling is that they will make a try for one of the boats, sooner or later. In the circumstances I felt that it would be unwise for any of us to leave the bridge until the situation is clarified.'

Grove studied him for a moment. Then he nodded. 'All right. Just now Mister Proctor and Mister Lucas can take him into Osgood's cabin. First of all, though, I want to make a few things clear.'

He looked at the other two men and then brought his eyes back to Quinan. 'I agree, order is at an end up to a point. And you, Mister Quinan, contributed to this state of affairs very considerably by your total insubordination in refusing to obey my valid command that you should not leave the bridge.' He sneered. 'All you got for it was a smashed cheek and a dead man.'

His face changed to a look of stern disapproval. 'There must be a return to discipline on this ship. And it is going to start with the officers. I am afraid, Mister Quinan, that I have no alternative but to enter your conduct, and that of Mister Proctor, in the log, together with the defamatory and insubordinate remarks Mister Proctor made about me. It is unfortunate but necessary. I have to set an example.'

Quinan stood unbelieving in the heavy heat. Maybe he is mad, after all, he thought. Anybody who carries on like this must be.

Grove was talking again. 'It is now forty-two hours since we went off the air. I think it's about time a search was laid on. We won't have long to wait. And in the meantime, gentlemen, nobody is going to take my cargo away from me. Nobody is going to desert this ship in the boats, no matter what stage the epidemic reaches.'

He shifted his body and held the rifle in both hands. 'This is a .303 rifle, Mister Proctor. You are acquainted with its operation?'

'Yes, Sir,' Proctor said stiffly. His mouth was beginning to swell and his colour was bad.

'I hoped you might. I feared, up to this stage, that there was only one thing you could do properly.' He watched Proctor flush momentarily. 'We are going to regard the superstructure as inviolate, and you, Mister Proctor, are going to station yourself at the foot of the companion-way. You will let no one up except the passengers and officers. Certain other personnel can probably be trusted, but we cannot be sure.'

He turned his glance to Lucas. 'You, Mister Lucas, will station yourself aft, on the lower boat-deck. In this position you will be able to guard the remaining companion-ways, the hospital, and in addition keep an eye on the poop, and what goes on there.'

He turned to Quinan. 'You, Mister Quinan, will relieve either Mister Proctor or Mister Lucas as the need arises. There is another Webley in the radio cabin. You may have that. I will take the remaining rifle and have a sort of roving commission, mainly confining myself to watching the foredeck and making sure that nobody touches Number Three hold again.'

There was another silence. Grove said, 'Everything clear?' and was satisfied with their nods. 'Very well.' He came a little closer and extended the rifle to Proctor. 'Take it.'

Proctor took the weapon and slid back the bolt, exposing the sleek yellow cartridge held back by its spring at the top of the magazine.

'There's one up the spout, too,' Grove said. 'That means you've got eleven shots if things get troublesome.' He laughed. 'Quite enough, I should imagine, considering there're only five of the bastards.'

Proctor said woodenly, without looking at Grove, 'I can hit what I aim at, Sir.'

Lucas put his hand to the canvas holster at his side. His jaw went slack and an expression of intense surprise crossed his battered face. He looked at Quinan in wonder. 'The Webley. It's gone!'

'What!' Grove crossed to him in three rapid strides, stepping over Puget's body without even glancing at it. He grabbed Lucas and pushed him around, staring at the empty holster. 'My God, man, do you realize what this means? At least one of them, Hawes himself, probably, is armed. How in the name of God could you be so careless, you bloody fool!'

This was more like the old Grove, screaming mad.

Lucas's shock gave way to bitter resentment. 'It must have been taken while I was being . . . beaten. I was hardly in a position to stop them . . . Sir.' His insolence was patent.

'Watch your tongue!' Grove snapped.

Quinan stepped quickly into the breach. 'He can have the other Webley, Sir. If I have to relieve anyone I can always take over that person's weapon.'

Grove pondered a moment. 'All right. The damage is done. Now I want you men to take your stations.'

'May I request permission, Sir,' Lucas said heavily, 'to have my nose attended to? I don't think we need expect trouble for at least a couple of hours, considering Hawes's condition after Gil—Mister Quinan, I mean—attended to him. And I think Mister Quinan could do with a few stitches in his cheek.'

Grove looked from one to the other. 'All right,' he said abruptly. Then he turned suddenly and stalked back along the narrow navigation deck and went into the radio cabin. They heard the door shut.

Proctor exploded. 'He's bloody-well three parts cut, I swear it! He was hanging on for dear life to his senses. My God, to think we have to obey a crazy dope-artist whose only . . .'

'I don't feel very well,' Lucas said suddenly. 'I think I am going to be sick. That kick in the stomach . . .'

He broke off and ran to the side and vomited agonizingly for a minute while the others watched in silence. Then he straightened up and wiped his mouth. His eyes were swollen from the strain and he was sweating profusely. 'Christ, I'm spitting blood.' He held up a forefinger with a bright speck of blood on the point.

'It's probably from your mouth,' Quinan said comfortingly, 'but you'd better see Lincott right away. I'll come with you.' He fingered his cheek.

'What a hell of a way to spend your birthday,' Lucas said moodily.

Proctor raised his eyebrows. 'Is it really? Your twenty-fifth?' When he saw the nod he added, wryly, 'Happy birthday, old boy!'

Lucas looked at him dispassionately. 'If I thought you meant it I'd shove your face in.'

His eyes went moodily past Proctor. He stiffened so suddenly that Quinan thought Hawes's group must be making their way up from the stern. But Lucas was looking beyond the length of the ship. His eyes were on the far horizon, and he said, almost calmly, in flat, unexcited accents, 'I can see a ship.'

'What?' Proctor spun around. 'Where? For God's sake, where?'

Lucas pointed. 'There she is. Nearly dead astern. Hull down already. She must have sailed past us while the shindig was going on.'

Quinan could make out the smudge on the horizon. He ran to the wheelhouse, got his glasses and turned them on the distant ship. 'Stern on. You're right. She must have been in sight for quite a long time.'

He sighed hopelessly, and said with masterful understatement, 'Nothing's going very right, is it?'

'There's still a chance,' Proctor said excitedly. 'I think we should try the rockets. And the foghorn. They might still . . .'

'Rockets in daylight?' Lucas said sceptically.

'We'll try,' Quinan agreed.

They fired seven rockets, which was all they had. They sounded the foghorn repeatedly. But the smudge became a blur, and the blur became a pinpoint obstruction on the razor edge of the horizon. And then even that was gone, and there was nothing left to see, and nothing left to do but go about their duties and wonder when they would have a chance of burying the dead.

At precisely noon, one of Savage's men contracted the disease and was brought to the hospital. Within five minutes the Purser, Henry Norman, died.

It was almost, as Savage said, as though he had been making room.

CHAPTER TWELVE

NOON CAME. The sun attained its meridian. And the earth, tilting, gave it its illusory downward trek. Water spilt on the deck of the *Florence Hurst,* steamed, vaporized, and evaporated. A beautiful albatross, plumed in white, circled, hovered and was gone to shear other great horizons, leaving them as one tiny chip upon its vast recollections of seas and ships and oceans.

Gilbert Quinan, standing near the gaping hatch on the fore-deck, had noticed that the barometer was dropping. The gentle Nan Hai, surfeited with serenity, began to heave and dilate with moderate swell. It was enough to make the old ship creak in protest. It was enough to make him brace his legs. But it was not enough to cause worry, or make him think in terms of counter-measures.

Peter Proctor, on guard duty at the foot of the companion-way, detected the increased movement, gauged it and ignored it. He simply made his legs the gimbals of his body and continued to re-read the fire-fighting regulations pinned to the bulkhead, which he had already read twenty-three times and planned to read twenty-five times before he tried them backwards, by memory. He had also discovered that he could, by standing in a certain place where there was an old cigarette burn on the deck, eject the copper-and-yellow cartridge from the old Enfield on to exactly the same place every time he tried it. He had tired of this before he had started to read the fire-fighting rules, which he had already known, and he was in any case doing both these things because he was afraid.

He knew about Henry Norman and the engine-room hand. He felt a tremble in his belly when he realized that one in every four of them had now contracted the disease, and one in every eight of them had died from it.

It was strange, he thought, how a man's bowels could turn to water from a certain type of fear. He had stormed on to the foredeck with Quinan this morning regardless of the conse-quences, even after seeing Lucas and Puget brutally beaten. This meant, he construed, that his fear of physical violence and pain was under control. But, by the same token, Lincott and Quinan and even Mary Fannin had come with him. And these people worked day-long in the hospital. By what special soul-magic did they remain unafraid of the unseen as well? It was a far more terrifying menace.

They're strong, he thought. They have some sort of deeper reserves they can draw on. I haven't. This thing has got me by the guts and I can't shake it.

He lit a cigarette and watched his fingers tremble. Desperately, he started to read the fire-fighting regulations once more. A trickle of sweat ran out of his hairline and made a tear-streak down his cheek, but he ignored it. The rifle had become slippery in his hands. It irritated him to have to hold it. He put it down, prop-ping it against the bulkhead, and went on reading.

On the lower boat-deck, Lucas stood guard a few paces from the outer door of the hospital. He looked like some gladiator of old with his strapped and padded nose, and despite the discom-fort it caused to the bruised flesh he was smoking a cigarette. It helped to calm him after the new horror he had recently wit-nessed.

He had helped Quinan to bring Puget's body down from the

bridge wing. Then he and Quinan and Lincott and Savage had collected the other four bodies from the carpenter's workshop under the after mast table and had laid them on the deck. They had worked in silence, in the searing heat, with the smell of death and deterioration about them, a silence made more noticeable by the lifeless heave and roll of the ship and the faint groanings that came from her hull. They had wrapped the five bodies crudely in canvas, weighted them with scrap iron, and dropped them one by one over the side. And then Quinan had said: 'God help them, God bless their souls,' and Lincott, that strange, yellowed, old-young mechanical man, had begun to talk to Quinan in a flat, mechanical voice about the dead men Quinan had seen on the sampan, and this had added to the unreal quality of daylight nightmare, because his questions seemed to have no bearing on the present, and Lucas had wondered if Lincott was losing his mind.

Lucas drew on the cigarette. He experienced a sense of disbelief when he thought that on Monday, only five days ago, he and Peter Proctor had been humiliating Lincott, on the bridge wing in Haiphong harbour, in that heartlessly humorous way of theirs that stung and hurt and bolstered their own arrogance. On Monday night he had tried to force himself on Mary Fannin, grinding his big body against hers while he whispered obscenity into her ear. Yesterday, Thursday, he had refused to touch Henry Norman in his absurd crawl from the lounge to the hospital. But today he had wrapped Henry Norman in his canvas shroud. Today Mary Fannin and Lincott had dragged him off the foredeck in the middle of a riot. Today Lincott, their whipping-boy of old, was keeping himself going on Dexadrine while he slowly broke himself in his endless drudgery amongst the sick and the dying.

Lucas shook his head. I'm twenty-five today, he thought, but this time he was not singing it silently to himself, the way he had this morning, on the hatch-cover. It was a sober thought. I'm twenty-five, he thought, I'm suddenly a year older, but it's more than just that. I've grown up very quickly.

He walked slowly to the deck's edge, leaned his thighs against the rail and looked along the after-deck, past the mast table to the high jut of the poop. He was uneasy. Hawes's group were there, in their rats' nest, but they were not going to stay there. They'd killed a man. They were afraid, as well. And Quinan was right when he said they would probably make a try for the boats. They were scum, harbour-scum capable of anything, animals of the lowest order, and it had taken this state of affairs to show them up. On top of that, there was every chance that the rest of the crew, although they might not give Hawes active support, would not stand in his way when the time came. Savage, who made periodic trips to the engine room, reported that his men were asking why the ship was not abandoned. They were calling the *Florence Hurst* a hell-ship and saying that God had deserted them. The cook and his helpers and struck, on the basis that they saw no point in working when nobody else was, and the cook had retired to his cabin to get drunk with Gindle, the surviving deckhand of those not within Hawes's group or already sick. There had been a final and complete breakdown of discipline.

Lucas took the Webley out of its holster, broke it, and studied the yellow cartridge heads, each eyed with its Cyclopean copper primer. I wonder, he thought, whether I would use it. He thought he would. He began to pace the deck slowly, his eyes on the after-deck.

In the hospital, Stephen Lincott stirred from the bedside of Long, the engine-room hand. He stood up very slowly, surveying the scene about him as though it were new to him. His eyes took in the high-piled mess of filthy, fouled linen, the scattering of emptied ampoules, some crushed into powder by careless feet, the haywire rigging of the flexes from the fans. He listened to the noise of stertorous breathing, he smelled the thick air that was full of the decayed smell of long illness. Then he began to move towards the door.

Mary Fannin came from Gauldie's bedside and stopped him. She put a gentle hand on his shoulder.

'Stephen, you must sleep.' She was more insistent than she had ever been, and yet more gentle.

Lincott smiled. 'Later. Gauldie and Woods and Norton are holding on. I can't give in now. But I'm going to my cabin. I'll rest for a few moments.'

She knew why he was going to his cabin. Her face showed its sadness. But there was no way of stopping him. She watched him while he gently removed her hand and walked out.

In his cabin, Lincott opened the drawer in his dressing table that contained the ampoules of Dexadrine. Only four remained. They lay next to the automatic pistol he had bought in Marseilles two years ago.

He stared at the pistol for some moments while his thoughts laboured slowly through his mind. Then he took one of the ampoules out and shut the drawer. He had a hypodermic with him. He filled it and injected himself, then walked over to the tape recorder, switched it on, ran it back a way, pressed 'playback'. Then he went and sat on his bed, staring at the blank bulkhead opposite him, listening to the slobbering, hate-congested

voice of Tommy Tucker until it faded away into a crackle of
static and the cabin was suddenly full of the throbbing beauty
of the *Pathétique*, which Osgood had loved so much.

Lincott got up. He walked over to the tape recorder and stood
looking down at it. Quite abruptly, he bent and switched it off.

'It was the distortion,' he said aloud to the empty cabin. Then
he turned and left, heading back for the hospital.

In the radio cabin, Grove carefully stowed the brace and bit
behind the shattered main console of the radio. Some curls of
wood fell from the bit on to the table and these he gathered and
put in his pocket. He was panting from his effort of the last
half hour, but pleased with himself all the same, both at what
he had accomplished and also that he had been able to do it
undetected even by Quinan, who was prowling the ship as far
aft as the lower boat-deck and was liable to appear unexpectedly.

He sat down, getting his breath back. He seemed very weak,
and he knew that it was a long time since he had had a proper
meal. He could not remember exactly when. He shrugged the
thought aside and got the bottle of whisky out of the drawer in
front of him. He had long ago finished Osgood's supply. This was
his own, brought here secretly, to be consumed secretly.

He poured whisky into the dirty tumbler on the table and
drank some neat, letting it run a fuse of fire down his throat
before it exploded into warmth and power in his stomach.

Immediately, he felt better. He sat back and lit a cigarette,
chuckling out loud when he thought of what he had just done.
Holy God, if it came to the push, some people were going to get
a surprise! He shrugged. Let them. He had done the correct
thing, and he was quite sure the Company would approve when
they knew the full circumstances.

Surprisingly, his cigarette was finished and so was the liquor
in the tumbler. He poured more, filling the glass to its brim this
time. He lit another cigarette. Already the alcohol was beginning
to do its work. It had fixed him in time, so that he looked neither
back nor forward. He was conscious only of the present, and of
the heat in his blood and the strong excitement in his mind.
He fetched the rifle from its place near the door and, carrying
his drink and the rifle, he went through into the chartroom and
then through the open chartroom door into the wheelhouse.
There he stood at the window looking down on to the foredeck
where the hatch lay, still uncovered, with the jumble of netted
coffins next to it.

Grove swore. He went out on to the port bridge wing and put
his glass down on the deck. Then he balanced the rifle on the
rail. He laid his cheek against the gun's coaming and cuddled

the stock. His eyes lined up the sights with the grey-painted lever on the mast table until it balanced, dancing gently, upon the square tip of the front sight. I could do it, he thought. I could put a bullet into that lever five times out of five.

He brought the rifle down, bent and picked up his drink. 'Nobody,' he said thickly, looking around, 'is going to take my ship away. Nobody is going to jettison my cargo. Nobody is going to take to the boats.'

He took a gulp of whisky. Let them come, he thought, full of new bravery.

In the lounge, Carl Attwell put down his cards wearily and said, 'I'll pay eighteen.'

'Pay me.' O'Connor showed his hand. 'You make a bum banker, Reverend.'

'I am not a minister,' Attwell said montonously. His big, sagging face looked straight down at the baize-covered table. 'And I am not used to cards.'

He moved chips idly with his long, strong, square-tipped fingers. His mind was far away. It was in Proctor's cabin. He was listening to a jazz record and watching Proctor and Mercy make love on Proctor's bed. . . . Mercy was beside herself, choking and groaning with the bitch-heat of her. But suddenly she got up from the bed and came and stood in front of Attwell, her hands on her naked hips, her lower body thrust out so that he was presented with the bulge of her pelvic mound. In a matter-of-fact voice she told him quite unemotionally, almost as though he were a child, that it was necessary for her to have Proctor. Proctor could do things he couldn't do and it was only fair that . . .

'What was that?' he asked. The sweat was running down his cheeks. His hands suddenly scattered the chips so that they spilled on to the floor.

'Carl!' Mercy's voice was remonstrative, but her eyes went past him. Neither of us, he thought, is really prepared to look at each other.

'I'm sorry. I'm sorry.' He scrubbed at the sweat on his face. He looked wild and dishevelled. 'Do I pay you?'

'Please. I have nineteen.' Mercy was pale. There were dark circles under her eyes and her forehead was beaded with sweat. She looked ill.

Attwell found some chips and fumbled them across. Then he said suddenly, 'I don't know that I'm all that crazy about going on.'

Mercy said automatically, 'Rubbish, Carl,' and O'Connor looked at his watch and chuckled.

'I would if I were you, Reverend. Kind of a long afternoon

ahead of us. The cook's on strike, and you haven't had any lunch. Chances are you won't get any dinner. You're gonna be awful bored by nightfall.'

'I am not a priest. I am not a minister of religion,' Attwell intoned. He became beset with the thought of weeping, and wanted to weep, but held on to himself and struggled against it. He felt his eyes wet themselves with tears and kept his head down.

'It is a sad thing about Monsieur Puget,' he said. 'Murdered, like that, this morning. Those men must be brought to book. They are killers. There was no excuse for what they did to that old man.'

O'Connor's lips twisted. 'Nuts. Listen, that old guy was seventy. He'd had a good life. He was well off. Time had come for him to meet his Maker. He'd had his three-scor'n ten. No harm done. Not like my Old Man.' He faced them aggressively. 'You want to hear about my father?'

Mercy Attwell was looking across the lounge. How can I even be in his presence, she wondered. He is filth. But she said, coolly, 'Tell us,' and slid a glance at her husband whose wild, jerking fingers still moved the chips in rapid erratic circles about his corner of the table.

O'Connor picked up his glass of beer and drained it. 'We had this place on the side of a lake.' He put the glass down and wiped his full lips. 'We had a nice house and a jetty and a big red boat. He used to take us out on the lake in it with an old Evinrude put-putting behind. He used to sing to us kids, me and my brother and sister; he used to sing all those songs about how if you were the only girl in the world and Mister Moon was looking from above and if you were a tulip and I was sailing along, and he told us poems; you know the one about Daddy's letter is with God, about the kid who stuck the stamp on his forehead and the carriage killed him? He used to sing and recite, bellowing above the noise of the farting of that old engine. And he used to laugh a lot. He had big, crooked teeth and all I see is those big teeth and that big laugh and I can hear the engine yet.

'He could catch bass like no man ever has yet, and he was a hunting man and we had a big red setter, same colour as the boat, and this dog, man, this dog could nail a covey of Huns so he was looking down on them and making their feathers ruffle with his breath, but still they wouldn't fly.'

O'Connor got up, driven from his chair. He stormed across the lounge towards the table that had the drinks on it, but half-way he stopped. He waved the empty beer glass.

'So his business failed. He was in hardware, my old man. His business failed and he said give me time, I'll pay everybody, I'll pay everybody, I've got real estate I can sell; but Jesus no, they wouldn't give him time. They sold him up. They sold the house and the red boat, and when he saw the boat go he took the setter and his gun and went out into the fields and shot himself in the throat with number eight chilled shot.'

He stopped, panting, breathing hoarsely. 'Don't tell me about Puget. Puget had it sweet. It's a lovely day, Puget said. It wasn't a lovely day for my old man, oh no, Sir. Oh Jesus God, no, old buddy boy. He got hisself killed for the guys with the mercury blood-streams because he just didn't show the right temperature for a good investment. He got killed and they shook their heads and said selfish bastard, leaving those kids, and they went on watching the ticker-tape and totting up their shares and figuring their capital gains or whatever-the-hell you call it, the shitting capitalist bastards.'

He stopped talking suddenly, and in deathly silence he went and poured three drinks, beer for himself and vodka-tonic for Attwell and gin-and-tonic for Mercy. When he came back to them he put the glasses down on the soft, country-green baize and settled back in his chair. He gave them a big, easy grin, as though it had never happened.

'If I were you, Reverend,' he said, 'I'd elect to go on with this here card-game.'

Attwell picked up the cards slowly. He began to deal. The hours, he thought, will limp across the face of the afternoon. The sun will falter on a crutch down the western side of the sky and fall with a big molten splash into the sea. Then maybe we'll have evening.

When Quinan looked out of his porthole he saw a new night, just fallen, that, for once, did not look like a magician's stage, like a black backdrop clustered with sequinned stars. There was no backdrop, there were no stars, and the only way you could tell heaven from water was the phosphorous bursts that ran all the way to the non-existent horizon.

He turned away. He was thirsty and hungry and grubby and well on the way to feeling defeated. He remembered Monday night, so long ago, and his wish after he had left Grove's cabin that he could be a thousand miles away, in a green garden. More than ever, he felt like it. But it was still escapism. I am, he thought, so much an inseparable mixture of the practicalist and the idealist. He was cleft by his awareness of what was common-sense and what was fantasy. It was desirable fantasy to take away from Grove, poor defeated, drunken Wally Grove, the command of his ship. It was commonsense to anticipate the brisk, competent-looking Wally Grove, thoroughly dried out by the Company, who would face him with hatred across the bare Court of Inquiry, answering his charges with points that were, every one of them, arguable. This was commonsense, this was the practicalist in him, and the practicalist outweighed the idealist. He had enough sense left to be frightened by what he had contemplated, what seemed so easy when it came from his mind, or Proctor's ready lips, when Proctor would have no can to carry and would blow with the wind when the chips were down.

Thank God, he thought, I have kept my head. He grinned crookedly. There were some compensations. There was Mary Fannin, who produced schoolboy sensations in him that were adultly related, and whom he knew was probably the final end in him of a subconscious quest that had gone on since his wife had left him. This was a final joyous joy that deserved better treatment, and he was biding his time to give it that. And, he thought, although there is no probable solution to the fact that I am hungry, my thirst is easily quenched by the bottle of brandy in my wardrobe.

He got it out, smiling; it was a temporary pleasure. He poured some into a glass, but hadn't sipped more than twice when he was brought up sharp by the knowledge that he was dirty. His uniform was stained and torn from the sweat he had poured into it and by the usage it had had during the riot on the foredeck this morning. There was, though, the final dry-cleaned uniform that had come on board at the last moment in Hong Kong. It still reposed in its hasty newspaper wrapping, in the top drawer of his dresser.

It took only a moment to decide to wear it. He debated futilely the pros and cons of imminent rescue, and the breakdown of the laundry service, and the likelihood of where and how his next clean uniform would appear. But in his present mood the thought of feeling clean and crisp, bolstered as he was by the fire of the brandy, for once outweighed commonsense.

He stripped naked, showered, dried himself loosely and then brought the paper-wrapped package from the drawer and put it on his bed. He broke the seals on the parcel. The uniform was wrapped in thin plastic, so he picked it up as an entity and moved it aside, looking down with mild interest at the front page of the *China Mail*, with its banner headlines about the double murder of Major and Mrs Fletcher. It seemed so long ago, all of this. Idly, his eyes scanned the paper, moving automatically to the smudgy attraction of the Stop Press column. More about those riots, he thought. But it wasn't. The top item read:

Police anxious to interview owner, or anyone having knowledge, of article described as 'lucky charm', found at scene of Fletcher double murder. Charm is an American silver dollar, with silver wings welded on to it, and has initials 'W.H.' engraved on surface. Owner believed to be a sailor. Anyone having knowledge of this . . .

Quinan stopped reading. A chill had taken possession of his body. His skin crawled. His heart was beating suddenly faster. That charm. By God, he knew that charm. His mind went back to Monday night and to his voice saying, 'Where's that charm you always wear?' And the white, thin face of Hookins, and the frightened-rabbit eyes, and the trembling voice whispering, 'I've lost it, Sir,' there in the long silence of the alleyway.

His mind moved forward from there to Thursday, to Osgood's funeral and Hookins, mad with the disease, his voice ringing crazily across the deck. 'She was not dead until the end. Until the very end. She heard. She felt. She touched. She knew that the body is sown in dishonour, and corruption, and weakness.' And then the arm outflung, pointing to Hawes and his group: 'There is the Devil. and the angels of Hell!'

Quinan dropped the paper and it landed with a soft rustle on the bed. He found his glass and drank, then lit a cigarette and stared at the bulkhead unseeingly. Hawes. Ludd. Draper. Kyle. Knowles. God, if only he'd known earlier; if only he'd opened this parcel earlier, at least Puget might still have been alive. But it was too late, now, to do anything. Of that he was sure. Once Hawes and his group knew that their crime had been discovered they would stop at nothing. Mutiny, under these present circumstances, even the death of Puget, where there was no premeditation, were things into which a defence Counsel could get his teeth, and Hawes was shrewd enough to know it. But rape and murder, a kicking-to-death, were quite another thing.

Quinan put down the empty glass. He picked up the paper and turned to go. At the door he stopped, suddenly undecided. It had been his intention to tell Grove. It was Grove's right to know, his own duty to tell him. But a small doubt kept him back. He paced the cabin, arguing with himself, afraid of Grove's disastrous unpredictability. In the end he decided to go. I want no fingers pointed at me, he thought. If I hold this back, something worse may happen. He headed for the bridge.

Grove was on the bridge wing, in darkness, but there was enough glow from the wheelhouse for him to be seen, standing with a glass in one hand and his other hand gripping the rifle which was balanced on the edge of the rail.

Grove craned his neck as Quinan emerged through the chart-house. 'Who's that? Who's that?' The voice was sharp and nervous. The rifle came around, held one-handed, its weight making the barrel tip towards the deck.

'It's all right. It's only me.' Quinan came on to the bridge wing.

'Ah, Gil!' Grove laughed uncertainly. 'Anything the matter?' The blast of fresh whisky on his breath struck Quinan in the face. So it's 'Gil' again, he thought wryly.

'I'll show you,' Quinan said. 'Come into the wheelhouse.'

Grove fidgeted. 'Sure it's all right? You never know . . .'

Quinan interrupted wearily. 'I passed Proctor on my way up. He's still on guard. And Lucas is still on the lower boat deck. Take it easy.'

Grove propped the rifle into the angle made by the bridge rail and the wheelhouse. Then he came into the wheelhouse and saw the paper. 'What's this?'

'Read the Stop Press item,' Quinan gave him the paper.

Grove looked first at Quinan's face. 'It must be important,' he said shortly. 'This is no time to . . .'

'It is,' Quinan said seriously, 'very important.'

Grove stared at him a moment longer. Then he looked down, holding the paper away from him long-sightedly. He became very still while he read, hunched almost, his thin neck craning forward. Then, so suddenly that Quinan recoiled, he flung down the paper and stamped on it and jerked his head up to look at Quinan out of staring eyes.

'Them! Those fucking bastards!' He was suddenly panting with rage. 'That's Hookins's charm. I'd know the bloody thing anywhere. So now I've got rapists and murderers amongst my crew, eh?' He was still staring at Quinan. 'Why the hell am I only told about it now?'

Quinan told him the circumstances of his discovery. But Grove hardly seemed to listen. 'By God, now they'll hang. Now there's no doubt about it. By Jesus, they'll hang now, Mister Quinan!'

Quinan became afraid. 'Keep it quiet, Walter. We'll probably be found tomorrow. Then they can be rounded up without any fuss.'

Grove looked at him in disbelief. 'Are you mad?' His face was working. 'By God, I'm going to tell them I know—that we know. You'll see them crawl to me like little woolly lambs, begging for mercy on their stinking hairy bellies!'

'For God's sake, no!' Quinan heard himself shouting. 'It will drive them to something they mightn't otherwise do. For the love of heaven, Walter, don't rush off without thinking . . .' But Grove had gone, storming out of the wheelhouse on to the bridge

wing, snatching the rifle from its corner. Quinan heard the bolt
clatter as it was rammed home.

'Grove!' He rushed out on to the bridge wing. 'Don't, Walter.
Don't tell them. Believe me, I understand them better than you
do. Only disaster will come of it.'

It was darker here, but Grove was side-lit by the light from
the wheelhouse. It showed his contorted face, the quick rise-and-
fall of his thin chest. 'You're in my way, Mister Quinan. I'm
going aft on this bridge. I'm going aft and you're in my way.
So move aside.'

He is mad, Quinan thought. He took a deep breath and stood
firm. 'You're not going to tell them, Walter. I'm not going to
let you.'

Grove stared at Quinan. For a moment there was only the
sound of his breathing, quick and short. Then he said in a strange,
unnatural voice, 'So it's like this morning, is it, Gil? Or is it
worse . . . are you relieving me of my command? You nearly
did it this morning, I could see it written all over your face.
Is that what you're doing now, Gil?'

Quinan's voice was hoarse. 'Walter, listen to reason. Just listen
to reason. I can't let you tell those men you know. That's all
there is to it.'

Grove shook his head. 'No, it's not. In any case, it amounts
to the same thing.' He chuckled. 'Ambitious Gilbert Quinan.
Old strong and silent. I never knew you had it in you. Or has
Peter Proctor put you up to it? There's a Cassius, that one. Or
maybe it's that Yank bitch you've been bedding. You're all
against me, aren't you? Even my officers. I can see it.' He was
almost gibbering. 'I can see it. In the faces. In the eyes.' His voice
trailed away and then came back with sudden, renewed energy,
sharp and brittle with decision. 'Mister Quinan, I still command
my ship! Now step aside.'

The muzzle of the rifle reflected a deadly ring of light. It rose
slowly, disembodied, dancing in the darkness from the unsteadi-
ness of Grove's hands.

Quinan took a deep breath and lunged below it. He landed
on his hands and knees, scrambling forward, clutching at Grove's
legs, but they slipped through his grasp. Wildly grabbing,
Quinan's left hand caught the stock of the rifle. Again he lost
his grasp, but it was sufficient to slow Grove down. Moving very
fast for his size, Quinan jumped up, half-collided with Grove
so that the smaller man stumbled into the wheelhouse. Hoping
to corner him there, Quinan raced after him but Grove was
already at the opposite door, recovered, with the rifle in his hands.

'Come on, Mister Quinan!' He grinned crazily at Quinan.

'Come on, ambitious Mister Quinan, come and relieve me of my command!' The words came gasping, distorted by the way his breath was rasping through his open mouth. Then he was gone again, and Quinan heard the sound of his light footsteps going aft along the navigation deck.

'Grove! No!'

Desperately, Quinan went after him, plunging through the wheelhouse and seeing the thin figure, now distant, pull to a halt. Quinan was still racing along the deck when he saw the rifle go to Grove's shoulder as he stood garishly illuminated by the flames from the flying bridge. A shot thundered out, deafeningly loud. A shower of blue sparks fountained off the iron deck near the stern and the bullet howled out into the sea-darkness.

'Hawes!' Grove's voice was a thin wail. 'Hawes, do you hear me?'

Quinan reached him. He grabbed at the thin body but Grove, impossibly strong, struck him wickedly with his free hand on the cheek Lincott had stitched that morning and Quinan staggered back, momentarily paralysed by the pain, turned sick and dizzy by it. He was trying to claw his way back even as Grove's thin tenor voice screamed, fatally, 'Hawes! I know what you did in Hong Kong, you and your cut-throats! You murdering, rapist bastards! I'm giving you half-an-hour to surrender yourselves for trial in due course by law. Do you hear me, Hawes?'

Vicious, uncontrollable anger replaced Quinan's pain. Blind with rage, he reached Grove. He saw his fist chop down brutally hard on Grove's face. The rifle fell with a clatter and Grove sprawled beyond it, dazed, still harshly outlined by the flames, rumpled and absurd with his mouth open and blood trickling down his chin and his thin hair on end.

'You hit me.' The voice had no iron in it. It was as frail as the body, slow, shocked, unbelieving. 'You hit . . . your superior officer.'

Quinan looked down at him for a long moment. Then he said, 'You bloody, crazy fool,' and walked away towards the bridge, shaking, to find Proctor and explain what had happened.

There was one chair in the Attwells' cabin. Mercy sat on it, hunched, staring at her nyloned knees and beyond them at the threadbare carpet. She was wearing only her thin negligee and the stockings and a tiny girdle she had bought in a fleeting moment of temptation in New York, two years ago.

She felt strange. Exalted, almost, within a heavy, weary body, as though her mind wished to take flight but was imprisoned by her physical fatigue. It had been a strange, terrible day, culminated just now by violence between the Captain and Quinan. She had heard the rifle shot, the excited talking near her door. Then things had quietened again.

She put a hand to her forehead. It felt hot. I am not ill, she reassured herself, just exhausted. But there is a cure. Carl uses it. The Captain uses it. The world uses it. I have used it. She got up and went to the wardrobe and took out the bottle of vodka, innocuous without its label. She poured some into the glass on the dresser and drank it quickly, choking over its breath-taking strength. Then she went to the mirror and shrugged off the negligee and let it fall to the floor. She stood examining her body, standing there without pose or poise, flat-footed, facing the glass.

She was still beautiful, still perfect.

I found out too late, she thought. She studied the slender column of neck, the moulded shoulders, the cherry-nippled breasts that thrust out without a single line of sag against the rib-case, the soft-firm belly dimpled with navel, suggestively girdled by the scrap of step-in, the long, slender, thoroughbred legs.

A thought came to her, unexpectedly: 'Your body is the temple of the Holy Ghost.'

She turned away from the mirror and picked up the negligee and put it on, hurriedly. First Epistle of St Paul to the Corinthians, Chapter Six, verse nineteen. The words burned into her soul. But not into my body, she thought. My body has been sundered, and the Holy Ghost had fled, leaving it as clay. My body is worthless and I am worthless and I cannot ask forgiveness.

The door opened and Carl came in. He shut the door and stood against it, looking at her in a strange, expressionless way with eyes that seemed to have been shuttered.

There was a long silence. Then he said, slowly, 'Five days. Five years. A lot of changes, huh, honey?'

She said nothing. He came further into the room, two slow paces, and stopped again. 'God put us on this ship for an examination of our souls. You figure that could be right?'

She hadn't moved. 'It could be,' she said softly.

'It is.' He grinned at her. 'Find out anything?'

'Yes.' The words were snatched out of her by her own mouth.

'So did I. Took a bit of getting used to.'

Those blind eyes frightened her. A sudden headache raged within her skull. She was cold. When he came further into the cabin and sat down slowly, gruntingly, on the edge of his bed, she trembled with relief. This was more like Carl.

'Usher has just died.' He said it factually, without inflexion.

'I'm sorry'

Carl turned his head to look at her over one bulky shoulder. 'He was a good boy, so they tell me. A clean-living boy. He hadn't sinned.'

'Carl,' she repeated, 'I'm sorry.'

He turned away, bent down and unlaced one shoe, cocked his leg over the other and dragged the shoe off. It trembled in his hand and he threw it suddenly away from him. When he turned his head again his eyes had unshuttered and she saw the hate in them.

'The wages of sin is death,' he said.

Mercy moved almost violently, checked herself, and walked to the wardrobe. She forced herself to speak normally. 'It's time for your drops, Carl.'

She opened the wardrobe and took out the two bottles, turned, and saw him advancing towards her, his eyes seeming to bulge within a head that quivered and shook with an ague of emotion. She screamed and dropped the bottles and they shattered on the floor.

His bulk was irresistible. He took her by the shoulders and whirled her about, grabbing one wrist and twisting it cruelly up behind her shoulder-blade so that she was forced on to her knees.

'You are a wicked woman, Mercy Attwell.' The voice was categorical, a final judgment.

Mercy cried out with the pain. 'Oh God, Carl, let me go!'

'To give me my drops?' He laughed. 'My God, what a bitch you are. Give me my drops, Mercy, and wait until I fumble and sleep, and go to Proctor's cabin!'

'Carl!' She wailed her fear. 'Carl, I'm ill. I don't feel well, Carl. Please, oh God please, let me go.'

He looked down upon her, categorical in his judgment. ' "The whore that sitteth upon the waters." Scarlet woman, full of abominations and filthiness of her fornication.' He smiled. ' "For her sins have reached unto heaven, and God hath remembered her iniquities. Therefore shall her plagues come in one day, death, and mourning and famine; and she shall be utterly burned with fire; for strong is the Lord God who judgeth her." ' He twisted the slender wrist more, so that in agony she arched her back, forced to stare into his face. 'You took my life and my dedication and threw them in my face. God will bring his judgment upon you, through me.'

A madness took hold of her. She became filled with an insane strength. Like a snarling cat she·writhed away from him, wrenching her wrist free. The negligee flew open as she twisted and got to her feet and she faced him, panting, wild-eyed.

'You dare to talk of God! You! You talk of dedication, you!'

Her fury shook him physically. Her hatred made him drop his
arms. 'Yes, Carl, I am a whore and a tainted woman. I have been
going to Proctor's cabin. I am ashamed, and I could die for it.
But I did it because there was nothing—nothing, you hear me?—
in you that I could find to substitute for the woman in me that
was being destroyed. Women have smothered their disappointment before, a million times, and turned that energy elsewhere.
With you, I could have lost it in your faith, Carl, because the
just shall live by faith—Epistle of Paul to the Romans, chapter
one, verse seventeen.'

Mercy Attwell seemed to grow tall. She seemed to attain a
sudden vital dignity. 'If you had had one grain of faith, I would
have been by your side, the two of us walking hand in hand into
the sunlight of the greater glory of God. But there is nothing in
you, Carl. Nothing but cheap self-gratification. You've climbed
on God's band-wagon, Carl, for the records and the albums and
the reviews and the money that rolled in, and now you've slipped
you've used Him more and more, fraudulently, hiding under His
name. Puget was right. You're a cheap salesman.' She spat the
last words at him. 'You sell God!'

They stared at each other for a moment. Then she said, very
sadly, 'What I have done is unforgivable, Carl, but I withered in
your lack.'

She turned away suddenly and sat down on the bed. She said
in a small voice. 'Carl, I am ill. I am without God, and I am
afraid.'

Attwell stared at her, shaking. He saw the skull-like tautness
of the skin about her face, the depths of the appeal she turned
towards him. He stared at her on and on, his eyes locked with
hers, his body feeling the heat that was radiating from her.

It dawned on him suddenly, the extent of her illness. Then
something within him snapped. He tore his eyes away and ran
clumsily for the door, hearing her voice, hearing her cry, 'Carl,
don't leave me!' fading into infinity as the door slammed behind
him and he stood quivering, huge, frightened, staring about him.
Then he heard his voice, his terrified voice: 'Mister Proctor!
Mister Proctor! For Christ's sake come, Mister Proctor!'

Footsteps scrambled on the companion-way and Proctor was
there, panting, the alarm showing on his face. 'What the hell is
the matter?'

'It's my wife.' Attwell began to weep. His voice was broken by
sobs. 'It's my wife, Mister Proctor. Oh, God help me, she's ill!'

Somehow or other they were back, the two of them, in the
cabin. Mercy lay on the floor next to the bed, still, curled up,
looking very alone.

Attwell turned a tear-stained face to Proctor. 'She's got the disease. She must go to the hospital at once.'

Proctor had gone ashen. He stared at the still figure on the floor. Absurdly, he still held his rifle in one hand. He said nothing.

'Take her, Mister Proctor,' Attwell was out of control. 'Take my Mercy to the hospital!'

Slowly, Proctor straightened from the crouch in which he had been staring at the girl. He looked away. Sweat was running in streams down his face.

'I'll call Lincott,' he said.

There was a moment of heat-laden silence while Attwell studied him.

Surprisingly, he smiled. 'Not any more, eh, Mister Proctor? You're not prepared to touch her any more? She's no good to you this way, is she?'

Proctor stayed silent, paralysed by his weakness. A shadow appeared at the door and Quinan came in, the words he was about to say remaining unsaid when his eyes went straight to the woman on the floor.

He looked first at Attwell, then at Proctor. His realization showed suddenly on his face, and then his contempt. He bent down and picked Mercy Attwell up gently, standing for a moment with her in his arms while his cool eyes went again to each of them in turn.

'Stalemate, gentlemen,' he said, and left them, kicking the door shut with his heel as he walked out.

Mercy Attwell seemed very light in his arms, as though in her illness she had lost substance. Quinan carried her aft along the port alleyway to the inside entrance to the hospital, standing there a moment adjusting to the different light, to the forms that moved and those that lay still, to the conglomeration of beds and equipment and mess.

Lincott appeared before him. He stiffened and went still when he saw Mercy Attwell. His eyes went from Quinan to her, and back again to Quinan. He stared at Quinan in complete confusion, tongue-tied, changing colour so drastically that Quinan could see it even in the dull light. But he had been imprisoned in the hospital for so long that he could still react automatically. Mary Fannin, appearing behind his right shoulder, was the same. She was numbed by everything that had happened.

Lincott said mechanically, 'I suppose she's got it?' When Quinan nodded, he pointed towards the far end of the hospital. 'Put her down there, Gil. We have two empty beds. One has just been vacated.' He meant Usher.

Quinan walked to the bed. Mary Fannin hastened before him

and pulled back the covers. The bed had been re-made, but the sheets had clearly been used before. Quinan put Mercy Attwell down and stood back.

Lincott came up. 'We'll have to strip her.' He lifted her and between them he and Mary Fannin took off the thin negligee, the nylons and the step-in. She lay naked on the white undersheet.

Lincott produced a thermometer and slipped it into Mercy Attwell's left armpit. Then the three of them stood in the congested, drumming silence for thirty seconds until he took it out again.

'One hundred and four point one. She's very ill.' Lincott was still behaving like an automaton. He was exhibiting less feeling than on Wednesday night, with Osgood.

He gestured at Mary Fannin. 'We'll set up the drip. Long has it. Take it out. You know what to do by now. Bring the fans from Long's bed, as well.' He turned to Quinan. 'Perhaps you would do that, Gil.' He passed a hand very slowly across his forehead. 'We're still making ice, thanks to God and Dick Savage. Mary, I'd like you to collect some after you've set up the drip. We'll do the lot: the drip, fans, ice. We must get that temperature down.'

Neither Mary Fannin nor Quinan moved for a moment. Then she said, 'You'll kill Long, Stephen.'

They listened to the humming of the fans for a very long moment while Lincott studied her impersonally. Then he said, half-turning to Quinan, 'You don't know Long, Mary. Gil knows. If he dies, the people most delighted will probably be his wife and children. His hobbies are drinking, whoring, and bashing in people's heads. He is an animal.'

She said stubbornly, 'I don't think that matters. Not when you're trying to save lives. Long was responding. You can't . . . can't murder him.'

Lincott shrugged indifferently. 'Then I'll set up the drip. I'll move the fans. I'll get the ice. I'm still the Medical Officer, and I'm still in charge of the hospital.'

Quinan said, 'Do it, Mary. Do what he says.'

She looked at Quinan out of exhausted eyes. 'I'll move the fans. But I won't change the drip.'

Lincott watched her. He reached out blindly, without looking, and took Mercy Attwell's hand. 'I will do everything within my power to make her well. She will lack nothing, at anybody's expense. I will treat her with all my ability, and with God's help.'

His eyes moved between them. His voice was calm. 'I would prefer it, frankly, if both of you left. I will not neglect the others.

Dick Savage is in the engine-room. Tell him not to come back, either.'

There was absolute finality in his manner. He stood like a statue, holding Mercy Attwell's hand, waiting for them to go.

Both Quinan and Mary Fannin saw it. They turned away without saying anything, and left the hospital, and when they were in the alleyway they heard the door close quietly behind them.

They continued to walk down the alleyway. And then halfway along Mary Fannin stopped. She turned to Quinan and flung her arms around him, put her head against his chest and began desperately to weep.

CHAPTER THIRTEEN

PETER PROCTOR looked dully at his wristwatch. It showed ten-fifteen. Then he wiped his sweating face, scrubbing at it impatiently with the back of one hand. It didn't really help because as fast as he wiped it away, the sweat returned.

In the glass that covered the fire-fighting regulations he could see himself with that expression of frozen horror that had remained stamped on his face ever since Mercy Attwell had fallen ill. If he looked hard enough, the reflection changed—it became her, yellow-skinned, skull-like, staring at him with those huge eyes the way she had on Monday night at the Captain's cocktail party, except that now, instead of a rising expectancy, he saw only death.

Desperately, he tore his eyes away from the glass. He found a cigarette in his pocket and lit it with trembling fingers.

We're all finished now, he thought. We haven't got a snowball. He had heard about Hong Kong, and what Hawes and his group had done there. He knew that Grove had screamed his knowledge of it over the ship and that Quinan had struck him.

That's put paid to Quinan, he thought, if ever he gets out of this. His career was finished. And Grove's too. Since that incident an hour ago Grove had become a shambling, babbling drunk, sitting in the lounge with Attwell, who stared into space and drank desperately from a bottle that had no label, but who was being cheated somehow because whatever he was drinking was not having any effect.

And then there's Proctor, Proctor thought. Me. Suave, debonair. Quoting Cicero and Catullus to the manner born. Very public school, old chap. But God, if only they knew, if the people on this ship knew, if the legions of women he'd used and abused knew, that he had been born in Stepney, and that his parents owned a fish shop and he'd spent his boyhood years in an all-pervading odour of fish and fat and the smelly smoke of chips frying. The Latin had been boned up over endless hours from a dictionary of quotations. The smile and the manner had been practised before a mirror. The accent had been erased gradually and subtly over the years, but it had been easy because he was a natural mimic. And all of this had been done, in the beginning, in the secret of his cubby-hole bedroom. It was above the shop and had the same smell. Its walls were too thin to exclude the sounds of the never-ending, mutually Pyrrhic battle that raged everlastingly between his mother and father. They fought in the shop, exchanging blows and epithets even while serving customers. They fought in the flat. They even fought in bed. Proctor, the only child, was fed, and clothed, and grew, and passed his examinations, but was otherwise purely a presence in the place, a detached ringside spectator, as unreal and unloved to them as if he had been an extra-terrestrial visitor.

But in the silence of night, when the shop was still, he would creep quietly downstairs and look at the still, moulded forms of the fish lying under the counters, he would admire their stream-lined bodies and the air they had, with their wide-open eyes, of latent life, and the coolness of them that spoke of green and peaceful depths where only the currents played and tugged idly over the vast undersea plains of pastel colours that were sometimes lit by the penetrating sun.

It was inevitable, in his circumstances, coupled with these nocturnal visits, that the sea should call him. And with his first uniform, grudgingly paid for by his father, with his battered suitcase that had contained his few possessions, he had taken along his social aspirations and driving ambition, and they had proved his biggest assets.

Promotion had come quickly, at first. But, somewhere along the line, he had lost his goal. He used his hard-won social graces for the conquering and subjection of an endless conveyor-belt of women, and this became his ambition as well, as though he achieved, out of each conquest, each humiliation, a savage retribution that belonged in reality with the screaming, unloving, domineering virago who had been his mother.

In the process, inevitably, his career suffered. Promotion ground to a halt at Second Officer. And he was left leaderless, with only his old pastime to turn to.

I missed, he thought bitterly, in not getting on to the liners. That's all they want there—a tanned body in a tailored uniform, who dances well. I'd have been a swinger, I'd have married an American heiress and that would have been the end of the matter.

It's no good moaning, he thought. I'm here, there is no escaping it, stuck on an old tramp. Brought to sea in the first place by a cold cod. Shallow Peter Proctor. Frightened Peter Proctor. My dream is going to come true. We are all going to die, and the dead will lie in mounds on the decks, but as retribution I will be the last alive. I will walk amongst them until they become animate, and follow me, and as fast as I run, so they will run faster, until they catch me on that nightmare treadmill deck, and then I will die, too.

The cigarette had burned down in his fingers to the extent that it scorched him suddenly. He whirled about, cursing, and found himself staring at the fat face of the cook, and Gindle, the red-headed deckhand.

They were both drunk. He saw that at once. The cook even held a gin bottle in one hand. But they were trouble-bent, too. It was written all over their faces.

'What the hell do you want?' Proctor asked sharply. There was nothing cool about him now. They had given him a fright and his heart was hammering.

'We're gonna launch a boat,' the cook said thickly.

' 'Sright,' agreed Gindle. 'Gonna get off this hell-ship.'

'Git outa the way.' The cook began to push past Proctor, heading up the companion-way. With his enormous belly he brushed Proctor aside but Proctor, light on his feet, leapt backwards like a cat. He scrambled three steps up, getting ahead again and barring the way.

'Like hell you are!' He was panting. Over his shoulder he called upward, 'Gil! Gil! Come here,' trying not to make it sound as though he were afraid.

'Get him,' Gindle prodded the cook. The cook, his face twisting with drunken rage, suddenly swept up his arm and flung the bottle, overhand, straight at Proctor's head. Proctor ducked. It struck the bulkhead next to him and shattered, showering him with gin.

'Christ!' Proctor lost his temper. He swung a long and whip-like arm and caught the cook flush in the face.

The blow made a solid, meaty sound as it connected. The cook staggered back and became entangled with Gindle. Together they sprawled on the deck.

Proctor went after them. But Gindle, surprisingly quick for a drunken man, got to his feet and swung at Proctor. They clinched, hammering blows into each other, but even while this was happening Proctor sensed that the cook was up and coming around behind him. He tried to tear himself loose, at the same time desperately shouting, 'Max! Max! Quinan! For God's sake, help!'

Dimly, with the reek of Gindle's breath in his nostrils, he heard pounding footsteps. Then there was the sound of a blow and Gindle sagged, leaning on Proctor. Proctor pulled away in time to let Gindle fall, and to see Lucas, capless and looking like a Greek warrior with his nose-guard and pale hair, heading past him for the cook. But the cook, who appeared to be retreating towards the shelter-deck, suddenly swung about holding Proctor's rifle in his fat hands.

Proctor screamed 'Look out!' and flung himself to one side. The rifle went off with an ear-shattering explosion in the confined space and the bullet howled about like a leaden squib, caroming off fittings until it buried itself with a solid plunk into the wooden companion-way.

The cook fumbled clumsily with the bolt action. He saw Lucas and Proctor getting to their feet and gave it up. Berserk now, he swung the rifle like a club as he came towards them. Lucas ducked under the flail and hit the fat man solidly in the stomach. The cook went white and dropped the rifle just as Proctor flung himself back into the fray. The three of them fell to the deck.

'It's okay,' Lucas shouted. 'He's out. Get off my bleeding back, damn you!'

Proctor rolled to one side. He and Lucas were scrambling to their feet, still on their knees, when a shadow loomed in the opening and Hawes stood there, grinning like a devil, black against the harsh outside glare. He held the Webley in one hand, and it bucked as he fired straight into Proctor. Then he was past them, shouting orders, heading up the companion-way as Kyle, Ludd and Draper poured in behind. They swarmed over Lucas. Kyle swung a cosh, and they were running for the companion-way even as Lucas toppled next to Proctor.

Quinan met them as he was beginning to come down. Hawes was in the lead. He was so close to Quinan that when he fired the powder stung Quinan's wrist; but the bullet went wide and then Quinan, too, was overwhelmed by the rushing, determined tide of bodies. Draper's fist caught him on the side of the neck, jarring him and making his head spin, and then Kyle's cosh hit him a glancing blow on the head. He collapsed just outside the double glass doors of the lounge, half-conscious and hearing Mary Fannin's scream as he fell. She rushed towards him, but Hawes and his men burst into the lounge and she was barged roughly to one side. She staggered against a small table and fell.

'You stay put, there.' Hawes pointed the gun at her like an

admonishing finger. Then he switched his glance to the other two
occupants of the lounge, Grove and Attwell, who sat near each
other. He laughed. 'Well, God dammit. They're both drunk!'

Attwell had his bottle of vodka on the low table before him.
He poured a measure into his glass and looked up calmly. 'Hail,
horrors. Hail, infernal world, and thou profoundest Hell, receive
thy new possessor!'

He took a sip of his drink while they stared at him. 'That,
gentlemen, is one of Milton's gems, rather apt in this particular
case, don't you think?'

'You watch your bloody lip.' Hawes turned to Grove as the
Captain struggled to his feet. Grove's hair was on end, his eyes
glassy. His face was sunken and his uniform dirty and crumpled.
He was a parody, even, of Monday's man.

He swayed as the ship rolled, nearly losing his balance. The
drink he was clutching emptied itself down his front. Whisky
stained his tunic a tea colour but he did not notice.

'So you got past them,' he said thickly. 'Knew you would.
Useless, all of them. My officers. Useless.' He fought to focus
his swollen eyes. 'No loyalty. Won't back up the Old Man. Gonna
log 'em. Gonna log the whole lot of 'em. Disloyalty. Very heinous
offence.'

He lost his footing on the next roll and fell back on to the
couch, really unaware of what had happened to him. 'Gonna
take the boats now, huh?' He managed a sneer. 'Rats. Jus' like
rats.' He laughed.' Good luck. Good luck, rats.' Something
seemed to amuse him, because he laughed on, until the laugh
turned convulsive and he choked, eyes bulging, spittle running
down his chin.

'Let's not waste time on him.' Ludd tugged at Hawes's shirt.
'Let's get going.'

'Okay.' Hawes shoved the Webley into the waistband of his
jeans. 'Dike, you take Rummy to the starboard boat. Cast off
the gripes, check the bung. Get her to deck level. Then call us.'
He swung on Draper. 'Bring Proctor, Lucas and Quinan in here.
And don't forget their weapons.'

The men ran out. Hawes pointed a finger at Mary Fannin,
who still half-sat, half-lay on the floor. 'You. Where's Savage?'

'In the engine-room,' she said stiffly.

'He'll keep.' Hawes grinned, then turned as Kyle and Draper
came in, panting, carrying Proctor. Proctor was very still, and
the left side of his shirt was a startling scarlet against the remaining whiteness. They put him down unceremoniously on the floor
next to Mary Fannin, who put her hand to her mouth and
stared at him, rigid, fixed in horror.

'My God! Haven't you done enough, without killing him, too?'

'Murderers,' Grove said thickly from his seat. He was staring straight in front of him. 'Murderers, thieves, rapists. Bastard mutineers.'

'Shut up!' Hawes shouted. 'Open your flipping silly mouth again and I'll shut it for you!'

Mary Fannin went on her hands and knees next to Proctor, tugging at his shirt. She got it up above the wound, but when she saw the big, ugly-looking slash torn by the bullet she went white and turned away.

'Please. Can't I get the Doctor?'

Hawes hesitated. 'Okay. But I'll give you three minutes flat to bring him back here, and don't try any tricks.'

Mary Fannin got up and fled from the lounge. Quinan was sitting up and she stopped when she saw that he was conscious. 'Gil, for God's sake, don't do anything silly. They've shot Peter. They're going to take one of the boats. Just let them do it.'

Hawes appeared in the door. 'Get on, you silly bitch!' he stormed. When she went on he gestured at Quinan with a thick finger. 'You can crawl if you can't walk. Into the lounge.'

Groggily, Quinan got to his feet. He lurched into the lounge and knelt next to Proctor. The Second Officer's eyes were open.

'Hello, Gil.' The wry mouth twisted. 'Sorry I let you down. The cook and Gindle were drunk. I was so busy with them I didn't think about Hawes.'

'Forget it,' Quinan said. 'It wasn't your fault.'

'It was.' Proctor's eyes were on the ceiling. 'I called Max. He'd have seen them coming if he'd stayed where he was. But instead he was nursing me.' He smiled faintly. 'You know, I was terrified of the epidemic. I was so sure I would get the disease. Just goes to show, doesn't it? Fate's a hell of a funny thing. So I get a bullet instead.'

Feet came past them. Lucas was put down, sitting on the floor but with his back against the bulkhead. He was facing them. His head lolled and he groaned as consciousness returned.

'That's the lot.' Hawes nodded his satisfaction. 'Flesh, you and Kiddy stock the boat. Grub, water. Water's the main thing. As much as we can carry.'

Draper was holding Lucas's Webley in one hand and Proctor's rifle in the other. He put them down on the table. 'Keep an eye on these, then.'

He was turning to go when there was the noise of shouting. Feet clattered down the companion-way. Hawes snatched the Webley from his waist. Everyone went still, but it was Ludd and Knowles who burst in, panting.

'What the hell's the matter?' Hawes stared at them.

'The matter? You ask what's the matter?' Ludd's single eye glittered with shock and rage. 'Somebody's sunk us good and proper, tnat's what's the matter. The bloody boat is riddled with holes!'

'Like a cheese, she is,' Knowles chipped in, 'and that much good for sailing, I can tell you. She wouldn't last a minute.'

Hawes had gone pale. 'The port boat? Did you check the port boat?'

'Aye.' Ludd's eye swept the room. 'She's as bad, or worse.' His glance came back to Hawes. 'We're done, Feller, aren't we?'

Hawes was trying desperately to adjust. 'Like hell we are! Can it be fixed?'

Ludd shrugged. 'I reckon so, given a few hours. The holes can be plugged, like.'

'A few hours!' Hawes stared at him. He made a disbelieving, impatient gesture. 'God, I'd better have a look myself. You take care of this lot.' He swung on his heel and was gone.

Ludd looked around the room. His eye settled on Quinan. He picked up the Webley from the table where Draper had put it, and pointed it at the Chief Officer. 'No false heroics, Mister Quinan. I'll shoot you just as dead as Hawes would.' The eye circled again. 'What I want to know is, who drilled those boats? God help the man when I find him.'

Draper and Kyle had stayed behind. There had been no point in going for food to stock the lifeboats after the news Ludd had brought. Now Draper licked his lips, his face shiny with sweat, the tremendous chest bulging against the thin fabric of his shirt. 'I'll kill the bugger with my hands, I swear it. So it's hours we've got to wait now, when we could've been gone. More time to get sick, to catch the disease. More time on this bloody hell-ship.'

Attwell spoke solemnly from his seat. 'You will get it, son, rest assured. You will sicken and you will die.'

'Shut up!' Draper screamed. 'Shut your mucking mouth!' He wanted to barge forward but Ludd's knotty arm held him back.

'Take it easy, Flesh. Take it easy. He's drunk, the old coot.' He walked forward and picked up the vodka bottle that had no label. 'What's this, Reverend?'

'Fire-water,' Attwell said, 'for the sick and the damned.' Wearily, he added, 'I'm not a minister of the Gospel, Mister Ludd.'

'You don't look it,' Ludd said candidly. He flicked the Webley's big muzzle at Quinan just as a reminder. 'I'm watching you, now. Even through the glass I'm watching you.' Then he lifted the bottle and swigged a few mouthfuls, passing it on to Draper. 'Here, have a pull.'

'God, I need it.' Draper drank greedily, coughing and choking
as he handed the bottle on to Kyle who drank in his cold, prissy,
deadly way. When he put it down the bottle was empty.

' 'Ere, what about me?' Knowles was indignant. 'You've copped
the lot, you sods!'

'There is more,' Attwell intoned, 'in the kitchen. Brandy,
whisky, gin, maybe even vodka. Help yourselves, gentlemen.
And give me a touch, too. I am a mite thirsty.'

Ludd laughed. The liquor, quickly taken on top of the excitement, had done its work. 'Good lad! Thee's a fine sky pilot if ever
I saw one, and the best I saw were mostly drunk!' He gestured
at Knowles. 'Get the bottles, then, Rummy, if you're so thirsty!'

Knowles scuttled off. Grove had been sitting with his hands
clasped across his stomach, staring at the carpet between his feet.
Now he looked up glassily. 'Drink the lot,' he said thickly. 'I
give you my permission. A present from the Peterson-Hurst
Steamship Company nineteen-hundred-and-nine Limited. Drink
it all, by God, and you'll put to sea in a beautiful pea-green boat.'
He pointed crookedly at Draper and Kyle in turn. 'And you'll
be the Owl and you'll be the Pussy-cat. And you'll dine on mince,
and slices of quince, which you'll eat with a runcible spoon.
And hand in hand, on the edge of the sand, you'll . . .'

The rest of his words were lost in the slapping pop of Draper's
big, open hand against his chin. Even as a clout it was enough
to knock Grove over sideways on the couch.

'Christ, I've had enough!' Draper's voice was high and uncontrolled. 'What the hell are they talking about, talking in riddles,
always riddles!'

'Easy, Flesh, easy.' But Ludd was laughing. 'It's some poem
thing he was reciting. Not that I mind what you did. Scum, he
called us, up on the bridge yesterday. And look at him now.
Motherless, for God's sake!'

Knowles came running in with an armful of bottles. 'He
wasn't half kidding, the old coot. Lookit this!' He put them
down with a clatter on the table in front of Grove.

Grove had picked himself up. He was hunched over as he had
been before Draper had struck him, staring at the floor. The
world was swimming. The carpet was threadbare beneath his
feet, and it revolved, it went around and around in tiny con-
centric circles which was confusing, because dimly, forever losing
the thread and regaining it, he was trying to remember where
the other rifle was.

'Well now, there's no harm, seeing we've got to wait this long,
in having another drink.' Ludd grabbed a bottle of brandy off
the table and wrenched the cap loose. There was a lot of latent

violence in him. This is the stuff. A real wog's drink. Puts steam
in a man.' He had tucked the Webley in the top of his trousers,
but now he took it out again and waved it at Quinan. 'Don't
think I've forgotten you down there, Mister Quinan, or what you
can do in a fight. Real powerhouse, you are. But I'm watching
you, I am.' He drank and passed the bottle on to Knowles. 'Here,
Rummy, suck on tha' tit for a while.'

Quinan ignored them. He was still dizzy and sick from the
blow on the head, but he had carefully unbuttoned Proctor's
shirt and was studying the ugly blue-grey bullet-mark on his
left side.

At that moment Mary Fannin walked back through the double
doors. She moved like a sleep-walker, rigidly over-controlled in
her manner. She went straight to Quinan and knelt next to him.
'Gil, Stephen won't come. He's locked both the hospital doors.
He won't come. He just says he's busy.'

Quinan studied her taut, strained, exhausted face. Mary Fannin
had had more than enough. She had a look of fever about her
that was pure fatigue. She was on the edge of collapse.

He put his arm around her shoulders, holding her very tightly,
trying to squeeze reassurance into her. It did more than that. The
strain in her snapped. She put her head against his chest and
began to weep violently, the sobs tearing themselves out of her
throat.

'Let it go,' he said. 'Let it all go, kid.'

For thirty seconds the pent-up tension of all the nights of toil
and sickness poured out. Then she stopped and wiped the tears
away. 'I'm sorry, Gil. I couldn't take any more.'

Proctor, very pale and struggling against the nausea of shock,
made an attempt to smile. 'I don't blame Lincott. He's got more
on his mind than me. See what you can do, Gil.'

'I've already had a look.' Quinan touched the lips of the wound
gently. 'It's not too bad. I think the bullet sliced along your side,
maybe nicked a rib, but that's all. Trouble is, it needs stitching,
and that I can't do.' He turned to the girl and spoke gently.
'Think you can manage a short trip? Peter's cabin is the closest.
If you'll bring a sheet, and the first-aid kit he keeps there, I'll
patch this up well enough to prevent infection. It will keep till
later, when we can persuade Lincott to have a look at it.'

She got up and left. Ludd saw her go, but he made no move
to stop her because he'd heard the conversation. She was back
within minutes and together she and Quinan did what Proctor,
very white and trying to grin, called 'fairly thorough, amateur
repair-job'.

They had just finished when Hawes returned. His mood showed

on his face. He came barrelling into the lounge, the Webley
still jammed into the top of his jeans. When he saw the liquor
he snatched up a bottle of brandy and drank deeply, then lowered
the bottle and stood staring around him. He looked at Ludd
first.

'I've got two of Mister Savage's men repairing the starboard
boat. It's going to take time, though. I've promised them a free
ride if they hurry, not that they'll ever get it. The bloody gutless
fools. We'll have to take turns, checking on them. Beat the
bastards if they work too slow.' He took a deep breath. 'Now—he
examined each face in turn—Grove, Attwell, Quinan, the others.
'I want to know something. Who holed those boats?' The voice
was rough, brittle with anger.

Nobody answered. He looked at each of them in turn, but they
stared back at him, silent.

Hawes took the Webley out. He pulled back the hammer with
one big thumb and in the silence they heard it click as it cocked.

'I want to know. Who holed those boats?'

His voice fell away and the silence came back again. And then,
absurdly, Grove began to laugh. It sounded at first as though he
were choking, because he was bent forward over his knees, staring
down at the threadbare patch beneath his feet. But then he
straightened, he lifted his body, and they saw the hideous mirth
on his face, the clown-mouth that laughed below the crazy eyes.
The laughter went on, never abating, until Hawes lost control
and stormed across the room and lifted Grove out of his seat
with one big fist clutching him by the stained lapel of his tunic,
holding him, quivering, a few inches from his face.

'You!'

'Certainly.' Grove did not appear in the least afraid. 'An
extremely simple operation. Even the ambitious Mister Quinan
never knew. A one-and-a-half-inch auger, new, sharp as a razor.
A carpenter's brace. Didn't take long.' He let out a compulsive
giggle. 'You'll never leave this ship. You'll die here, Hawes. Die
here.' He repeated the two words, his head wobbling loose on his
shoulders. Then he cocked an unexpectedly ribald eye. 'Unless
you use that bee-yootiful pea-green boat, and put to sea with
the owl, and the pussycat.' He laughed again, quite overcome
with mirth, tears streaming down his cheeks. 'You're fools, you
lot. Outsmarted you, didn't I? Bloody scum, you are. Haven't
the brains of the arse of a . . .'

Hawes hit him. He hit Grove very hard on the side of the jaw
so that even his hair flipped with the force of the blow. He held
Grove, slumped and inert, as though he were a child. He held
him while he swore a torrent of obscenity, and then hit him

again, low down on the body this time, holding him and shaking him like a rag doll.

'Give him here.' Draper dropped the bottle he'd been holding. It fell on the carpet and brandy seeped out and made a dark stain. Draper's cheeks were streaming sweat. 'Give him here and let me have a go.' He snatched Grove from Hawes and swung a fist violently into him, so that Grove was catapulted across three yards and fell in a sprawl next to Quinan and Mary Fannin and Proctor.

Quinan stared at the limp form. One of Grove's eyes was so badly injured that he did not want to look at it. Bright arterial blood was trickling from his mouth. He looked boneless, still, without any animation, even respiration.

'Cut it out!' He got to his feet. 'Leave him alone.' He did not know that it was possible to feel such hatred as he felt for these men.

Hawes grinned, his barrel chest rising and falling sharply from the quickness of his breathing. 'Silly of you to stick your nose in. I owe you a score too, Mister Quinan. I owe you a kick in the nuts. I owe you one hell of a Goddamned beating, you bastard!'

He gave the Webley to Draper. 'I'm not funning now. Shoot him if he puts up a fist.'

He waited until the Webley was clutched in Draper's big hand and then he moved in and hit Quinan so hard that, even although he moved with the punch, it pitched him headlong past Proctor. He swarmed over Proctor and swung a kick into Quinan's side, hearing the breath driven out of Quinan by the force of the blow. He was going to kick again when Mary Fannin made a small, despairing, moaning sound and threw herself across Quinan's body, covering him with herself, hunched, waiting for the vicious kick.

Hawes stopped and licked his lips. The memory of the soldier's wife in Hong Kong came back when he saw her like that. It made him want to be sick. He could not do it.

'You can have him, you bitch.' He turned away and grabbed Grove's loose form, lifting it, holding the man upright so that his head lolled on his chest. 'We can have some fun with this one.'

Kiddy Kyle giggled. 'Not 'alf. We've got time to waste. Shove him 'ere, Feller.'

Hawes hit Grove on the chest. Grove was propelled backward until Kyle caught him and hit him too, without as much power but with a vicious precision. Draper took him then, and then Ludd, and they beat the scarecrow, bloodied form about the room until Grove was no longer recognizable. Then, because they were exhausted with their efforts, they flung him out into the alleyway and went back to their drinking. The neat liquor revived them.

Kyle looked at his watch. ' 'ow long before the boat's ready?'

Hawes put down his bottle. He had a wild, crazed expression. He was already drunk. 'Two hours. Maybe three.'

Kyle yip-yipped like a dog. His eyes had kept darting to the girl. 'Let's 'ave a concert, Feller. The bird can sing for us. She plays the guitar, you know.' He giggled. 'What about a strip-tease?'

With the exception of Draper, the others howled. Draper shook his head. As he had drunk, so he had become steadily more silent, more wild-eyed, more afraid of this time they were spending in this place of sickness.

'Later,' he said. 'First, I want some salvation. I want protection from the pestilence.' He fixed his eyes on Attwell. 'Say a prayer for us, Father.'

Attwell heaved himself upright, swaying to the motion of the ship. ' "Thou shalt not be afraid for any terror by night; nor for the arrow that flieth by day. For the pestilence that walketh in darkness: nor for the sickness that destroyeth in the noon-day." '

He laughed, looking at Draper. 'Are you afraid, son? Are you afraid of the noon-day sickness?'

'Pray for us, you bastard!' Draper's great moon face quivered. He jumped across the intervening space and knocked Attwell down. 'Pray for us. Don't quote from your damned Bible!'

Attwell picked himself up off the floor. He was on his knees, a bloodied contusion at the corner of his mouth.

Even Hawes began to enjoy himself. He pointed a threatening finger at Attwell. 'Pray, sky-pilot. You're good at praying for the dead. Now let's see what you can do for the quick!'

Attwell stared at them. Then he turned his head and looked desperately at Quinan and Proctor and Lucas and the girl. 'I cannot pray.' He seemed to gain courage from this. He turned back to the mutineers. 'I cannot pray!'

'Oh, by God, you will!' Draper was more serious than any of them realized. He still had Hawes's revolver. Now he pointed it at Attwell. 'Pray, Father.'

Attwell smiled faintly, wearily. 'I am not a priest, Mister Draper.'

'I don't care a stuff!' Draper screamed. 'You know what it's all about. You've got a bloody hot-line to up there, haven't you? Now pray before I kill you!'

Attwell was moved by forces within himself. He saw the great round tunnel of the gun-barrel pointing at him. The drunkenness left him suddenly and he was afraid. He began to tremble, a palpable ague that communicated itself to every part of his body so that he shook, on his knees there on the floor.

'Put up your hands,' Draper said softly. 'Put up your hands to pray!'

'I can't!' Attwell cried. He put his hands up, clasped. His grey face streamed sweat; its agonized lines were an appeal in themselves.

'Now pray,' Draper said. 'How do you start? "Oh God in Heaven". That's the way you start.' He shook the revolver at Attwell. 'Say it!'

'Oh God in Heaven,' Attwell repeated, mechanically. Then something inside him broke. Tears burst out of his eyes and streamed down his cheeks. 'I can't! I can't go on!' He began to sob, huge, agonized sobs that tore through his body.

Draper screamed, 'You'll go on! You'll go on, by God, or I'll kill you!'

'No,' Attwell said quickly. 'No. No, no, no, no. I can't go on. Kill me if you like. Kill me if you like, but I can't go on.'

'Why?' Draper spat out the word.

Attwell threw his hands apart. His body swelled. His face strained and shook. But suddenly the words were out. 'Because I have no faith! Because I have no faith! Because I have no faith!' The demoralized sobbing started again. 'I have no faith in God, whose name I have taken in vain.'

He had become a shambling, pathetic figure. On his hands and knees he crawled over to Mary Fannin and collapsed, his face in her lap. 'God help me, I have no faith. And she's dying because of it.'

The heat in the hospital had gone up ten degrees because both doors were shut. The bulkheads wept with the humidity, streaming moisture to the deck. The air, already impure, had become foul.

Lincott had left only one light burning because of this. It was above Mercy Attwell's bed and when he moved even slightly his shadow gyrated enormously upon the opposite wall. In shadow he was a gigantic doctor, made omnipotent by illusion, overflowing the bulkhead even, so that his head and shoulders were upon the ceiling, increasing the impression of tremendous, encompassing power.

In reality, he thought, I am very small. I have injected this woman with antibiotics. There is a drip working itself into her system. There are fans blowing upon her from the corners of her bed. There is ice packed about her to cool her body, to reduce the temperature which I am afraid to take. I am small because

I have done all these things and now there is nothing more to do but crush the sweat-wet fingers of her right hand in mine, and hope, and pray.

He held her hand so tightly that if she had been conscious he would have hurt her. But she was in another world. In her delirium, her mind had followed the course of Wednesday night and her face had reflected her agony. She spoke aloud, often. Her face was washed with perspiration but her lips were dry, grey-coloured, like snakeskin. The teardrops of sweat clustered all about, on the dewy-soft skin above the upper lip, on the down below the bottom one. But the lips stayed dry. He had wondered at it, and wiped them often with the wet towel he held in his free hand; but immediately they went dry again.

The snakeskin lips writhed back from the small, impossibly-perfect teeth. She panted from the disturbing forces within her. The clockwork voice had told Lincott so many things; in jigsaw fragments it had given him the pattern of her married life, but his schooled face had reflected nothing.

Now it spoke again, unreal, from within a doll.

'Bluey? Bluey? You beat him, Bluey? You and Cockett?'

The voice switched again from dialogue to description. 'Bluey and Cockett did it. He was cheating on the rice weigh-out.' The voice was small, scratchy, like a poor recording.

Lincott squeezed his eyes tight shut. He gripped her hand harder. 'Who? Who? Who was cheating?'

'He was.' The great eyes that had been staring at the ceiling switched spasmodically in his direction. They could have been looking at Lincott but they had no focus. They went on past him.

Lincott closed his eyes again. 'Bluey was cheating? Was it Bluey cheating on the rice weigh-out?'

There was a long pause. The dry lips closed while he hung on to her hand and thought for a desperate second that she was going to slip away from him. Then the lips parted again, almost popping apart from the gum that had suddenly accumulated. He wiped them quickly.

'No, no.' She rambled a moment, meaninglessly. Words trembled on his tongue and he was about to speak when she said suddenly, 'No, it wasn't Bluey, or Cockett. They caught him. He'd always cheated. All his life he'd cheated. Anything to look after number one. But that was before Haiphong.'

In the sudden silence he could hear the stertorous breathing of Long, the engine-room hand. Long was going to die, and Lincott didn't care a damn. His wife and kids would have a bloody Guy Fawkes celebration, he reminded himself absently. They'd tell all the neighbours in whatever crummy slum they lived, whoopee, the old man's dead and gone.

'Why Haiphong?' He made his voice stern. 'Why before Haiphong?'

Again, he was afraid she might go. But somehow or other he was getting through to her. He saw her face contort and knew that an ugliness was passing through her mind. He wiped her lips again.

'They were afraid, after Haiphong. It was all different, after Haiphong.' A tinny laugh rattled in her throat. 'You know how sentries can turn an eye? Well, brother, boy, did they turn it, oh yes, buddy boy. they turned it for him and the other three finks. oh Jesus yes, did they and were they only too happy . . .'

Her voice faded away. She went quite silent, her face clay-like, utterly still. He was bending towards her, frightened, when the eyes opened with mechanical precision, as though the doll had been tilted up to the point of counter-balance.

'You all thought it was the guards, you silly buggers.' She was talking British-English now, some rub-off of what she had learnt on the ship. 'But it wasn't, at all. It was Bluey and Cockett. It was Bluey and Cockett beat him.'

Her eyes seemed to register, suddenly, on the shadow-shape, the half-Lincott she saw on the ceiling. It frightened her. She saw a febrile, accusing shadow that was part-Wednesday; it had Wednesday night in its menace. She threw her free hand to her mouth and cowered back, cringing on the bed.

'Mercy,' Lincott said urgently, 'Mercy, what happened on Wednesday night?'

She made no answer, and he knew it was useless going on. She just lay there, fixed, her great eyes on the shadow, trembling.

The turn-table revolved with a hypnotic regularity. By moving his head in tiny circles, Draper tried to read the label of the long-player. It made him dizzy and he had to stop. I'm drunk, he thought, I only do that when I'm drunk.

His right hand held the pick-up, poised above the grooves that glistened like black oil. His arm was extended and he could see the sweat hanging in blunted stalactites from the underside.

That's a good forearm, he thought, pretty good musculature. I never worked it much, other than a few reverse curls; they'd always said the forearms would develop on their own from picking up the weights and from the bent-arm pullovers and forward barbell raises, things that worked your pecs and your deltoids, but you picked up the forearm development on the side. And of course the upper arm was great, sixteen-and-a-half inches of it, a swell of bicep like a halved tennis ball, with a great solid hang of tricep underneath. It was the French curls that had done the tricep, very good they'd done it, and after all the tricep was a good two-thirds of the upper arm. Chaps paid too much attention to the bicep just because it looked good when you posed, and it made the girls randy.

It is a very good arm altogether, he thought, but it's trembling so badly because I'm drunk and I'm afraid and that rather spoils things.

No, he corrected himself, I'm afraid, and I'm drunk because I'm afraid. And the others are drunk, too, because they're also afraid. Our time has come. When we found that the lifeboats were holed we should have sat back and waited to die the way Osgood and Sloan and Hookins and McBlain and Norman and Usher have died. Every breath I take, he thought, I'm breathing in more germs. I could get into that lifeboat when it's finally fixed. I could sail away, and we could land on some God-forsaken island in this God-forsaken sea, hell, the place was littered with islands, and yoo-hoo we're away, we're off the hell-ship and out of trouble with the cops, and the next thing, suddenly I'm dying and bugger-all chance of being saved in some slimy-green jungle.

He let the pick-up go, suddenly, so that it fell on to the record. There was a snort of broken grooves, and then the record player was blasting out a trumpet piece, full of wild horn. He had blundered away from the player and was standing in the middle of the room in the fog of cigarette-smoke that hung in striated layers, and he was staring at the huddled group that sat on the floor near the sliding doors of the dining saloon.

Quinan, Mary Fannin, Lucas, with Proctor stretched between them. Attwell, huddled in a corner, staring at the blank bulkhead with its peeling veneer. Lucas had concussion; you could see it in the vague unreality, the myopia of his glance; but Quinan and Mary Fannin were very much awake and even Proctor, in pain and white from shock, was looking around with sharp, angry eyes as though he were just waiting for something to go wrong so that he could lay his hands on one of the guns.

Like hell, Draper thought angrily. He was developing this thought when he found Hawes at his side, looking at him out of his wicked, red-shot eyes.

'You lay off the bottle, you son-of-a-bitch.'

Hawes stabbed him in the solar plexus with a stiff forefinger. It was excruciatingly painful, and Draper gasped. God, Hawes and Ludd and Kyle, they'd had as much but it never seemed to affect them. They walked straight and they spoke without slurring. All that really happened was that they got so Goddamned vicious it frightened you.

He pulled himself together. He had to. He could see it in Hawes's eyes, an unspoken thought that if Draper wasn't capable he'd miss that free ride, he'd miss death in the Philippine jungle, yo-ho.

'Okay, okay,' he said. 'How long for the boat to be fixed?'

Hawes looked at his wristwatch. 'Another hour, at the most.' He'd been coming and going, Hawes had, him and Kyle and Ludd, awful careful they'd been, only one at a time, and although they'd been drinking, God, they had never lost sight of the guns or taken their eyes off Quinan, who was the only real threat to their chances.

Draper blundered to the middle of the room. 'You, ducks.' He pointed at Mary Fannin. 'Get your guitar and give us a tune.'

'Leave the girl alone,' Quinan said sharply. Like all of them, the sweat was pouring off him in the close, stuffy atmosphere.

Draper produced the Webley, which in his untutored hands was always lethal. He pointed it at the girl. 'It's her I'll shoot, not you, Mister Mate. In the kneecap, I will. So button your lip.' To Mary Fannin he repeated, 'Get your guitar.'

Hawes and Ludd and Kyle came up. 'You heard the man,' Ludd said. 'We'll have a song while we wait. Go on, lass.'

The girl got up quietly. As she reached the door a figure loomed in it, blocking it. It was O'Connor, blinking his eyes at the cigarette fog, grinning, always at home. He let the girl go past and strolled into the room.

'Salaams, El Capitano.' He bowed to Hawes. 'Some folk-singing until we leave? That'll be great. Something to pass the time. That girl is good, very good.'

He saw that Hawes's expression hadn't changed. He grinned again. 'Got me a ticket to go on that old red boat of yours.'

Hawes didn't like the confident tone. 'Since when, Lieutenant?'

O'Connor threw his hands apart, a pained expression on his face. 'Since I learned to navigate, buddy-boy, old revolutionary.'

Hawes thought a moment. 'You can navigate, eh? That's right, is it?' His small black eyes dwelt on O'Connor, studying him.

Ludd moved restlessly. 'Didn't see you around when the fighting was going on. Haven't earned your ticket, it seems to me.'

O'Connor could not be ruffled. 'Natch, I wasn't around. I'm a neutral, see? An officer of the United States Navy can't take sides in a tribal fight between Limeys can he?'

He caught Quinan's eyes on him and turned. 'Sorry to have to leave you, Admiral, after all your courtesies. Bunny's got itchy feet.'

Quinan studied the heavy face. 'What's the matter, O'Connor? Don't you want to be picked up?'

O'Connor laughed and looked away. 'I want to try me out a new line in craft. Sampans I know. Cargo ships I know. I feel like a change.'

Proctor spoke from the floor. 'He's a great boy, is our Bunny, for playing both ends against the middle.' He twisted his head so that the American could see the loathing in his eyes. 'You don't happen to number Benedict Arnold amongst your ancestors, do you?'

O'Connor changed colour. He stared at Proctor with a vicious hatred. Hawes and the others, although they didn't understand the reference, detected the slur, and laughed.

'If you weren't lying down,' O'Connor began, 'I'd Goddam . . .' but he did not finish the words. He was interrupted by the return of Mary Fannin with her guitar.

She stood woodenly before them, just in front of Quinan and Proctor. She held the guitar rigidly across her body. Her eyes were unafraid. But Quinan, seated behind her, could see the tiny tremble in the long legs, and knew what she was going through.

She was wearing another of Lincott's white shirts, hanging out over the shorts she had worn the day before. The shirt, in its maleness, accentuated her femaleness. Her breasts thrust against its thin fabric. The spectacle brought excitement to Hawes, and the men with him.

Kyle giggled. 'First take your shirt off, love. Folk-singers should be bare. Give us some sex, baby.'

Mary Fannin shook her head, silently. She had gone pale.

Hawes pointed the Webley at Quinan. 'You like him, don't you? And I owe him a score. I owe him a kick in the nuts. You want me to do that?'

'Don't do it, Mary.' Quinan scrambled to his knees. What these men had done in Hong Kong was fresh in his mind. It was fresh in theirs, too. He could see it on their faces.

The girl also saw it. Fear filled her. Like an automaton, she opened the top two buttons of the shirt. Kyle's obscene, dog-like howling filled the room. His eyes glittered.

'Come on, come on,' he urged.

Draper licked his lips. 'More, more. Get a move on.'

Mary Fannin tried to smile. It was a parody of a smile. Through stiff lips she said, 'Easy, boys. Let's take it slow.' Quickly she struck a chord on the guitar, and began to play. Then her voice, soft and husky, filled the room, singing an old blues number, sad, nostalgic, full of melancholy. The mutineers went silent, staring at her.

Time, she thought while she sang, time is what I need before I'm raped by these animals, time in which some miracle will occur. But that love I lost on this sea, well, I've found another one, a better, stronger, surer love, than even a love can be reckoned to be. And so I want to live, I want to stay alive. I don't want to be kicked to death like Elizabeth Fletcher in Hong Kong. So maybe the age of miracles hasn't passed, and something is going to happen and I'll be all right.

God, she prayed, please God, help me . . .

The wooden steps had a way of moving away from him, as though they were made of rubber. He had to snatch at them with both hands. He had to feel them hard and solid under his palms before he could drag himself up a little more, resting, panting, wondering at the bright red spots on the wood, wondering where they came from.

In a little while I'll be there, Grove thought. Three more steps. And he was pleased, not only because of that, but because of the triumph of finally remembering where the other rifle was. This had taken a lot of thought, painfully retracing in his mind his movements from the time Quinan had hit him and sent him sprawling on the navigation deck next to the ventilation housing. But he had finally reasoned it out, absurdly pleased with himself, and begun this terrible upward crawl to the radio cabin.

He put out his hands, feeling for another stair. But they struck only a flat smoothness. God, he thought, I'm there. I've done it.

On all fours he crawled unevenly around into the radio cabin. When he got there he was again filled with triumph but he had to wait, panting, head hanging down, for his breathing to slow.

He half-choked on something and spat out a warm liquid on to the floor. God, he thought, that's blood. Must have bust a tooth or something. But there was an easy remedy. He reared up, like a bear pawing, and scrabbled open the desk drawer. The bottle was there, thank God, and there was whisky left in it.

With shaking fingers he fumbled the cork out, put the bottle to his lips and drank until his hand let the bottle go. It fell in front of him without breaking. Whisky leaked out on to the worn floor. But he'd had enough. The old fire—fire-water Attwell had called it; that was a bloody good name—was coursing through him. His strength was coming back.

He was not prepared to try standing. Instead he crawled to the radio table. On it he could see the ridged butt of the rifle and the brass cap set into it. If you lifted the cap you could slide out a little brass bottle that contained gun-oil. The brass bottle still had the broad arrow stamped on it, like the rifle itself, and the date, 1923.

Forty-five years ago, he thought, surprised at how sharp his mind had become. But we haven't learnt much since then, really. The man who made that rifle is probably dead, but the rifle stays on, and the rifle can go on killing. They never die, these things. They will always be needed.

He slid it towards him. It was cool in his hands; the blue steel was cool to the touch. He held it in his right hand and crawled out of the cabin again, passing the whisky bottle on the floor. I'll need a bit more, he thought. He tried to reach for the bottle but his hand seemed clamped to the rifle and he didn't want to reach over with the other hand because he might fall. And if he fell he would not be able to get up again. So he left the bottle and went on dragging the rifle, panting, drenched with the sweat that rolled off him in steady waves.

He reached the top of the companion-way. Hell, it's steep, he thought. I suppose I can slither down it on my belly, but I will have to be careful with the rifle because if I let it go it will slide down and make a bloody hellishing racket.

He lay down and inched his way on to the stairs. Immediately, the rifle developed a will of its own. The stock swung around and wanted to slide forward. And his body, too, wanted to go quickly and suddenly. He had to fight to slow his descent, reversing the rifle so that it went butt forward. The blood rushed into his head and the lip of each step bit into his chest and stomach, so that they felt more broken than before.

He slipped into a wild world of sliding, slowing himself with desperate, sweat-wet hands, and sliding again. The staircase seemed never-ending. He could hear music from somewhere. That's a harp, he thought wryly, I'd better get a move on.

It took him ten minutes to negotiate the steps. And then he emerged too suddenly into the open space outside the lounge. He became urgently aware of how tremendously exposed he was. Without looking, he slithered past the doors and stopped in the entrance to the dining saloon. He was hidden, here, from anyone in the lounge, unless someone came out.

He pushed the rifle forward. Gradually, he inched forward until he could see into the lounge through the partitioning glass doors. He could make out, close to him, Quinan's back, and Lucas's back, and Proctor stretched out on the floor between them. Close to them, standing, also with her back turned, was the American girl. She was holding her guitar and her arm was moving.

Bitch, he thought, I was right, she is a damn bitch, entertaining those swine after what's happened. For the first time in many minutes, fury came back to him. I could shoot her first, he thought, to punish her. But no. She wasn't worth it. It was Hawes he wanted. More than anything in his life, he wanted Hawes, and Hawes was there. Hawes was facing Grove, he and Ludd and Draper and Kyle. They could have seen Grove, but they were looking at Mary Fannin, and Grove was a flat shape on the deck, half-hidden by the pillar.

Grove trembled. He put the butt of the rifle to his shoulder and looked along the sights. The rear sight was U-shaped, and the straight bar of front-sight stood rock-like in its middle, aligned on Hawes's chest.

He reached out his right hand and slid the bolt back. He had a vision of a brass cartridge nestling in its magazine bed. Then he pushed the bolt forward again, hearing the click-clack as it closed. Now, he thought, I'm ready. He was bearing down on the trigger when a sudden thought struck him.

God, he thought, there's glass between us. The bloody doors are shut. The bullet will smash the glass and deflect to hell-and-gone.

He shut his eyes. I'll have to fire twice, he thought. Make a hole with the first bullet and put the second one through it. Can I? he asked himself. Already the sights were dancing. Hawes's body seemed to sway beyond them. There is something wrong with my eyes, he thought. Bugger it. It was now or never.

He nestled down and squeezed the trigger.

The guitar music ended. The last echo of the chords faded away.

'Take tha' bloody shirt off,' Ludd demanded. His eye glittered.

'Come on, ducks.' Draper was weaving. He'd had more to drink despite Hawes's threat. He could see the tops of her breasts, the beginning of the valley between them.

'Another song,' Mary Fannin said. Her arm had begun to tremble and it communicated this shake to the hand poised above the strings.

'Not before you've taken the shirt off,' Ludd said. 'Or I'll rip it off you.'

Quinan tensed himself. There was a chance, he tried to convince himself. A very small one, but it was there. The rifle was still lying on the coffee table in front of where Grove had sat. The bolt was down and the cocking piece was back. If Ludd came forward to rip the shirt off there would be enough small confusion to make it worth the try.

He looked back, tensing himself. He wanted to gauge how far the dining saloon doors were, so that he could use them for impetus to propel his body forward.

Immediately, he saw Grove. The Old Man was lying just
beyond the doors with the rifle against his cheek. His whole upper
body was swaying, jerking. The unbloodied eye was already half-
closed. Grove was going to fire through the glass.

Quinan flung his head back. He was shaking with sudden
excitement. 'Don't!' he said sharply. 'Don't, Mary. Don't listen
to them.' He stood up quickly, drawing their eyes to him.

'By God, haven't you learned your lesson yet?' Hawes lifted
the Webley and began to move towards him.

Now, Quinan thought. Now, Walter, do something properly
for once. But nothing happened, and he dared not look around.
Then he realized that Grove had probably been held back
by the fact that Hawes was moving. He had to stop Hawes
moving.

He fell to his knees, pulling the girl down with him. 'Don't
shoot!' He put panic into his voice.

Hawes stopped. He laughed suddenly. 'Not you? By Christ,
is the great Mister Quinan showing a yellow streak, at last?'

O'Connor came up next to Hawes. His eyes were narrowed.
'Don't believe it. This bastard is as tough as last year's jerky.
He's trying to throw you. He's seen something.'

His eyes roved, darting, quick. He was looking for a threat
that was not a threat. Inevitably, therefore, he looked at Proctor,
and inevitably, with his eyes at deck level, he saw the shape of
Grove beyond the dining saloon doors.

O'Connor's eyes widened. His mouth opened, and for a moment
no sound came. Then his 'Christ, look out!' came in the same
moment that he was flinging himself sideways, in the same
moment that the rifle exploded thunderously, and glass clattered,
and Draper flung his hands to his forehead where a third eye, a
red-rimmed eye, had appeared out of nowhere. Then Draper
was falling, toppling like a great tree. But even while he was
falling, Hawes had lifted the Webley and was firing at the doors,
the glass starring and shattering under the impact of the bullets.

Quinan was already at the coffee table. The rifle came up in
his hands, swinging around, but Hawes had seen the threat. He
grinned and brought the Webley down.

'Look out, Gil!' Proctor cried from the floor.

'Here's that kick in the nuts, Mister Quinan,' Hawes said.
His big index finger jerked the trigger. But even as the hammer
was going back a great force took him and flung him over backwards into the high-piled mess of library books that Norman had
pulled down from the shelves so long ago. The Webley fell with
a thump somewhere behind him, unfired.

Hawes tried to get up. He was sprawled absurdly on the books, making it hard to rise. He bent his thick column of neck, contorting it so that it quivered with the effort.

There was blood on his chest. Must have got nicked, he thought. He couldn't see Quinan anywhere, and everything had gone still. Bugger Grove. Trust Grove to try and wreck things to the last. But Grove was dead. He was sure at least one of his bullets had connected. And Quinan was down.

Let's cut out all this nonsense, he thought. Let's forget about the girl and the liquor and get that boat launched. Just goes to show, you can never relax.

'Let's get to the boat,' he mumbled thickly. He struggled up on his elbows, the books moving like hard-edged, shifting sand beneath him. Something seemed to erupt within him. Bright arterial blood poured out of his mouth. He saw it and his eyes widened. Everything had gone quiet and there was Quinan after all, looking down at him as though from a great height. Hell! He should have known the bugger was indestructible.

Well, it looked as though he'd been wrong. They'd got him after all. It was funny, in a way, how things caught up with you. All the little coincidences that you could never anticipate mounted up and . . .

He grinned through the blood. 'Man's a fool all his life,' he said. Then there was a great rushing sound and he was gone into a place of darkness.

Grove lay with the stock of the rifle under him. His cheek was on it as though he'd fallen asleep. None of Hawes's bullets had hit him. When Quinan turned him over he opened the unmaimed eye and tried to smile.

'I got him? I got Hawes?'

'Yes.' Quinan nodded. 'Hawes and Draper. The others have chucked it in. Proctor's watching them.'

Grove's smile faded. He was silent for a long time. The single eye studied Quinan. Then he said, 'Old strong and silent. I've made a proper bugger-up, haven't I?'

'No,' Quinan said quickly. 'No, Walter, you haven't. Things worked out that way. It wasn't your . . .'

He stopped. He studied Grove. Grove had gone very still. It took Quinan a moment to realize that life had fled. Then he stood up slowly. Grove looked very peaceful. Quinan felt tired beyond words. He looked down at Grove. Well, he thought, wherever you've gone, Walter, I hope you'll find some peace at last.

Lincott had hung a cloth over the face of the bulkhead lamp. It had made the room darker, it had made the room seem even hotter, but it had disposed of the dark, mammoth reflection of himself on the ceiling.

He had finished with his writing. The diary lay on the bedside locker with his pen next to it. It had been difficult, writing with the book on his knee while he sat on the edge of Mercy Attwell's bed, but he was sure it was all legible and reasonably comprehensive. There were about thirty pages of it, all told, a detailed assessment of the Hurst syndrome.

Lincott took Mercy Attwell's hand again. With his free hand he swabbed her naked body around which the ice lay half-melted, like a cluster of hailstone.

Her breathing had lapsed badly. It was not yet Cheyne-Stokes but it was stertorous, labouring. Live, he prayed. Live, Mercy Attwell.

Her eyes flicked open suddenly. They studied the ceiling a moment and then switched to him.

'Stephen, I feel clean.' The voice was clear, no longer mechanical, but thin, untimbered, like a little girl.

He bent over her, filling her vision. 'You are. You are clean.' He squeezed her hand tighter than before.

'I do not feel corrupt any more.' She struggled for breath and tried to smile. Her lips were gummed but he wiped them quickly and they opened.

She is smiling. She is smiling at me, he thought. 'You were never corrupt,' he said intensely.

She shook her head minutely. 'I was. Oh, I was. I took a wrong turning. But I'm back now. You brought me back. It was your faith in me.' The gasping speech stopped. She panted for breath.

'I love you,' he said into the world that was just the two of them.

'I know. I know. I saw it. I saw it and ignored it. It was so wrong of me.' The smooth, sweat-slick face contorted a little. Tears came out of her eyes.

'Don't cry.' He was hushed. He was panting too. 'Don't cry, my Mercy.'

She smiled through the tears. 'Given time, I guess I could love you, too. You did so much for me. Just seeing you, knowing how you felt. It's kind of funny, though, when you're strong. You chuck a thing like that aside. But when you're weak it means so much. And now I'm weak.'

Her breathing fell off again. He was about to speak, but she shook her head, again that tiny sideways movement that hardly stirred the wet black hair.

'Carl said . . .' she struggled again, fighting for breath, 'Carl said the wages of sin is death.'

'It is not!' Lincott said fiercely. 'It is . . .'

'Hush!' It was an old word from her childhood. 'I know what you think. You're sure I've . . . I've purged myself of it, Stephen?'

'I'm sure, I'm sure,' he breathed. He took her hand in both of his. 'God help me, I'm sure.'

'Will you kiss me?' She fought again, this silent struggle. Then, 'So much death all around us, and you never got it. You know why I got it, Stephen?'

'Yes, I know.'

She managed a true smile, full of the goodness which had never really left her. 'Then I guess kissing me isn't going to hurt you.'

He leant a little further and put his lips against her dry, fiery ones. When he straightened she was smiling.

'You've convinced me.' She managed to bring her free hand to touch his. 'Now I know I'm all right. There's nothing to fear, I'm sure. "Mercy and truth are met together: righteousness and peace have kissed each other. Truth shall spring out of the earth; and righteousness shall look down from heaven." '

Her eyes closed. 'Psalm eighty-five, verses ten and eleven.'

Lincott was overcome. She had slipped away into unconsciousness again. A great trembling spring within him suddenly broke. He laid his head upon her naked breasts and wept.

CHAPTER FOURTEEN

THE BODIES belonged to Usher and Hawes and Draper and Grove. The rain struck the canvas that wrapped them. It bounced off and ran in little streamlets from the valleyfolds of the canvas on to the iron deck, where it collected in a shallow lake until there was enough depth, with the rest of the rain, for it to run off through the scuppers.

It was Saturday morning. A grey morning. A morning of silence, of reaction to violence and death. A morning to consider things in a world that seemed to have only one colour. The swell had increased, but not enough to promise a storm. The rain had come instead. It drummed straight down out of the heavy-bellied clouds, without a wind to slant it.

Quinan stood on the after-deck, holding the prayer-book flat against his chest to keep the rain off it. When he looked around he saw present every member of the crew who was not either dead or in the hospital. He had seen to it that they were there, and Quinan was a man people listened to. Mary Fannin stood next to him in a borrowed slicker. Carl Attwell stooped nearby, staring blankly out to sea. Proctor was on the lower boat deck in a chair

out of the rain but within earshot. Even O'Connor hulked nearby,
a tall, bulky figure in a black slicker, standing at the mast table
where Hookins had stood on Thursday morning.

Quinan addressed them. 'I am now acting Master of this ship,'
he said. 'This ship will revert to its normal discipline and routine,
within the circumstances of what has happened.'

He looked at the cook and Gindle, who stood next to each
other with Lucas beyond them. 'Certain members of the crew
have acted in a foolhardy manner, which is going to be overlooked.' He turned his eyes to the canvas-wrapped bodies. 'Others
have committed crimes for which they have already paid, or will
pay when they are returned to Hong Kong.'

He cleared his throat. 'This is primarily a funeral service. But
I had to say what I have just said. You all know that we have been
struck by an epidemic which has already claimed six lives. Some
of us are still ill. Some of us may yet fall ill. But there is every
reason to believe that within the next twenty-four hours we will
contact assistance. This ship has been off the air now for more
than sixty hours and I am confident that a search is under way
to locate her. Once we are, in fact, located, our problems will
be at an end.'

He moved the prayer-book slightly. 'We are burying, today,
our Captain, Walter Leslie Grove. At the same time, we are
burying the two men who helped to kill him. The fourth is your
friend, young Graham Usher.' He looked in the direction of
Attwell. 'I am assured that in the eyes of God, all these men are
equal. I do not dispute this fact. There is nothing more I can say
about John Hawes and Norman Draper except that you are all
aware by now that they committed murder in Hong Kong, as
well as here on the *Florence Hurst*. It was a dreadful murder.
Let us hope God forgives them. Graham Usher does not belong
in their class. He was a decent lad who lived cleanly and was a
victim of the epidemic.'

Again Quinan cleared his throat. Why the hell, he thought,
irreverently, am I so emotional today? 'About the Captain, I
want to say one word. He was a good man. He never cheated.
He never lied. Whatever he did, he did in the conviction that it
was right.'

Quinan stopped. What more can you say, he thought. That's
all there was to Walter. These men never liked him. He was just
the Old Man. They've all served under a dozen Captains or more.
He was just a remote figure up on the bridge. They didn't know
the agony that went on within him; the torment that tore him
apart.

He lowered the prayer-book. Quickly, he read through the

burial service. The words, he thought, were so apt. 'We commit their bodies to the deep, to be turned into corruption.'

When he had finished, the thin page was pulpy from the rain. He closed the book and held it firmly clenched in one hand while the four bodies were tipped overboard. They slipped over silently, far less troublesome in death, three of them, than they had ever been in life.

The last body, Draper's, had gone, when they heard the hospital door slam. It slammed with a hollow, final note. In complete silence there came the sound of footsteps on the lower boat deck and then Lincott appeared at the top of the short companionway that led to the after-deck where they stood.

He came slowly down the ladder. His feet rang on the metal steps. He was wearing his tropical uniform, white shirt and short trousers and long white socks and white shoes, and by the time he reached them he was quite drenched with rain. But he did not seem to notice it.

Quinan felt a physical shock, seeing him. He looked old. He looked sunken about the face. His eyes were far back in their sockets. The yellow tinge of exhaustion in his skin had increased.

But his movements were sure. He stopped a few paces from Quinan and looked around briefly at the assembled, slickered figures. His voice, when he spoke, was clear.

'Mercy Attwell has just died.'

Carl Attwell moved, but did not turn. He seemed to grow smaller. He seemed to hunch within his slicker. But his face stayed pointed out to sea.

'I am sorry, Mister Attwell.' Lincott's voice held no particular inflection. 'I did everything I could.' To the rest of the assemblage he went on, 'You know that Mrs Attwell was one of the passengers. That's all you know. You do not know how seldom the world sees a person like this. I am not going to try and convince you.'

He fell silent for a moment. Then Lincott said, 'Mercy Attwell walked all her life with God. She is with Him now. For one brief moment she left His shadow, but it was a small thing, of no consequence. Largely, it was brought about by other people. By uncaring people.' His eyes touched briefly on Attwell's back, which seemed to feel the contact, and hunch more. They went on to dwell only momentarily on Lucas and Proctor. Lucas looked down at his feet. His shoulders shook. He began, quite suddenly, to weep. The boy that still occupied most of him took over and held control for a while. Proctor looked away, out to sea. It was impossible to tell what went on within him.

'When she was ill,' Lincott went on, 'she was still God's servant.

She managed, without knowing, to help me. She managed to help me diagnose and define the Hurst syndrome.'

Nobody, amongst the slickered figures that stood shiny-wet like draped marble tombstones, moved.

'There has been a very great evil amongst us,' Lincott said. Again, there was no particular inflection to his voice. A surgeon, excising a boil. 'This disease was brought to us by a carrier. You all know what a carrier is. It is a person who has a disease, but never sickens from it, and passes it on to other people who might die.'

He paused a moment. 'The evil, in this case, was the fact that the carrier knew. He knew what he was. He knew what he was doing. He saw people sicken and die, and he didn't care. From fear or insanity, I am not sure from what cause, he didn't care.'

There was a tight silence filled with the drumming sound of the rain. Quinan's eyes were fixed on Lincott. The rain ran off the Doctor's short hair and cascaded down his face and neck and wept through his clothing, but he did not notice it.

'I was, in a sense, blind,' Lincott said. 'Of all people, I should have detected this person. But he was a base person. He had carried this disease amongst his fellows. On top of that, he was a traitor to his country.'

When Lincott's voice trailed away the noise of the rain took over, drumming frenetically on the iron deck, bouncing off the fittings, gurgling away through the scuppers, but this sound was broken by the high cry of O'Connor, who had squeezed himself up against the mast table as though for shelter, a dark, straightened figure in his black slicker, the small eyes glittering, the full lips trembling.

'Jesus, Jesus! To be caught in the middle. Oh God, to be caught in the middle! They would have killed me in the camp. They caught me cheating on the food. All I wanted to do was to stay in line. All I wanted to do was to stay out of trouble. But they would have killed me, those guys. And then when the Viets found out, then they came to me, and they wanted me too, and all I did was stay in line, I said the things they wanted me to say, over the radio.'

Lincott seemed almost to smile. 'You make it sound so pathetic, Tommy Tucker. You forget the twisted hate in your guts, the revenge you wanted to take for what happened to your father.'

O'Connor's mouth twisted. 'I got my share. I got my own back, there. By Jesus, I tell you, I got my own back on those Goddam bastards; they sold my Pa up, by God I got them back, I got their sons gutless, the way I talked. I got them careless, so they got killed. I got them worried about home.' He laughed suddenly, the full lips parting, the big teeth showing, crooked teeth like his father had had. 'By Christ, yes, healer, you're right, I got a hate twisted in my guts all right!'

'But you got so twisted, it didn't matter to you any more, the people who died.' Lincott put out a hand. He beckoned. 'Come here, Tommy Tucker. You didn't ask for this germ, I know it. You got it in the camp and somehow it stuck to you. It killed people there, and then when they took you to Haiphong to broadcast, it killed them in droves. It closed down the radio station, didn't it? And when they sent you back to the camp, they knew, didn't they? The Viets, I mean. They knew you were a carrier. And the men in the camp had put two and two together, hadn't they? And so had the sentries and the camp command. So they let you escape. They let you escape with three other no-goods who were also collaborating, and God help us, we picked you up.'

O'Connor shrugged. The wildness seemed to have left him. He came towards Lincott, aware of the sudden murmuring of the crew. 'You got it about right there, buddy-boy. I guess you've got it all sewn up, Limey. Except you don't know what it feels like, to be a Martian, to go on watching people die, and knowing you killed them. You don't know what that feels like.' He came and stood before Lincott. 'So what's the cure, buddy-boy, old healer?'

'If you'd told me about it when you come on board,' Lincott said, 'it might have made quite a difference. I could have isolated you, and in due course we might have cured you. I think the hate got mixed up with the sickness, there. You didn't care, any more.'

'You're too Goddam right, I don't care,' O'Connor spat. 'So there's no cure, huh, healer?'

'Yes, there is.' Lincott put his hand in his trouser pocket and brought out the automatic he had bought in Marseilles. 'When you gave up your regard for people, O'Connor, when you did that to Mercy Attwell, that's when you asked for this.'

Quinan found himself paralysed. He wanted to move, but he could not. He saw the little weapon extend in Lincott's right hand and marvelled at Lincott's lack of feeling, and the expression of peace that seemed to cross O'Connor's face.

O'Connor took a deep breath. 'Okay, so all right, already. Which ear you want it in, old buddy-boy?'

'I wish it was number eight chilled shot,' Lincott said. He pressed the trigger and flame spurted briefly from the muzzle of the little gun. O'Connor said 'Oh,' and fell down on his knees on the deck, his face blank. Lincott fired again three times. All the bullets went into the big body. Then O'Connor toppled slowly on to the deck, his heavy body falling with a crash, the way Hookins's had done.

Lincott dropped the gun on the metal deck. It made a dry clatter. His eyes flicked briefly to Quinan's. 'Give me five minutes, Gil.' Then he turned about under the rain and walked back across the after-deck. Nobody moved, nobody reached out an arm to touch him. He mounted the companion-way, moving past Proctor in his chair. The hospital door slammed.

Quinan turned like an automaton. He met Mary Fannin's shocked eyes, staring at him out of a rigid body. 'No, Gil!' she cried. 'No, no, no!'

When they got the hospital door open Lincott was lying next to Mercy Attwell on the bed. As a doctor, it had been so easy. He had given himself an intravenous injection of five grams of pentothal, and the drug had quietly reached his heart and killed him.

What Quinan marvelled at, so particularly, was the expression of tremendous, lasting peace on his face. All the withering of fatigue was gone. He looked young. He looked fine, and well, as he had in the old days. The slim, slender fingers of his right hand were entwined with hers.

Quinan wrenched his body around and looked at the faces clustered in the hospital doorway. He spoke in a clipped, slow, careful way. 'Don't let me ever hear the word suicide. It does not apply. Don't let me ever, ever hear that word.'

He slammed the door, suddenly. Only he and Mary Fannin were there, alone in the gloom with the very sick and the dead.

He flung himself into the chair at Lincott's desk. He struggled to find words in a body that had begun to strive with emotion. The look he gave her was totally vulnerable.

'Mary, don't talk to me.' His hand reached for hers and found it. 'Just stay here. Don't go. Just stay here.'

She took his hand, but looked away while he dealt inwardly with the loss of his friend. She looked towards the far bulkhead and remembered Thursday morning when she had seen Lincott there, blankly studying it. She remembered everything that had occurred.

A time of moments rolled by.

CHAPTER FIFTEEN

IN THE AFTERNOON they picked up a blip on the radar. Gindle saw it first, and called Quinan. It was at extreme range, forty-five miles. But as they shortened the field so the blip stayed with them, closing steadily, homing dead on to them.

An hour later a big amphibian came out of the sun and roared overhead. They could clearly see the American stars on its wings.

The amphibian dipped in salute. Somebody waved from the cabin and then it was gone, growling low over the sea, leaving them the way the albatross had done.

But they were not alone for long. The silhouette of a warship appeared on the horizon. It corrected its course and became a slender, minute, typewritten V, bow on.

Quinan was on the port bridge wing, with Mary Fannin and Proctor and Lucas. Richard Savage was relieving her in the hospital. All of them had been watching the oncoming vessel through their glasses, with Mary Fannin borrowing haphazardly to study its progress.

'I'm pretty sure she's a cruiser. Australian.' Quinan put his glasses down. He was calm. There was finality in his movements. At last, help. God, they needed it. Long was dead. They'd found him there in the hospital. Who knew how many more might still have been contaminated? From what Stephen Lincott had written in his diary the holocaust would have seemed to have run its course. But there was the chance of more cases.

Mary Fannin nearly read his mind. She took his hand. 'We've been through more, in a week, than many people go through in a lifetime. We're all right now, Gil. There will be a doctor on board that ship.'

Quinan smiled at her. 'I know.' He looked at the others. Proctor stood remote. He looked away from them out to sea, his thoughts deep within himself. But Lucas was aware. Lucas, Quinan thought, had come out of this rather well.

He looked at Quinan with his clear blue eyes. 'When did Stephen know—about O'Connor, I mean? When was he really sure? You haven't shown us the diary.'

Proctor emerged momentarily from the shell within which he had encased himself. He had been thinking about Mercy Attwell, and Lincott, and himself, and a host of other complexities. His side still ached, although he was more mobile now. He was experiencing difficulty in aligning his thoughts. They came and went, vaguely, spinning out of reach as soon as he thought he had something within his grasp.

'I would like to see the diary, Gil. There might be something prejudicial to . . . to . . .' He stopped. He stared at Quinan. 'I think I am entitled to see it.'

'I'm sorry, Peter.' Quinan shook his head. He realized how formal they were being with each other and smiled. 'I sound like a lawyer. But there is nothing in it that will damage you particularly.'

Proctor said nothing. He seemed to lose interest. He turned away and studied the oncoming warship.

Quinan said to Lucas, 'Stephen was only sure on Friday night, late. His diary is jumbled, chronologically speaking. He goes forward and backward in time, as points occur to him. But it appears that he did not suspect anything on Thursday. I'm pretty sure of that because he was desperate enough, and cold-bloodedly brave enough, to go down to the hold and try to contaminate himself with mould from one of the coffins just in case he was wrong, just in case it was the bodies after all. But two significant things happened on Thursday night, although he was in no position to appreciate this significance at the time. One was the article on a carrier called Typhoid Mary, which he had read while blinded with fatigue. The other was that after he came back from the hold, in a shockingly nervous, exhausted and overwrought condition, he switched on Osgood's tape recorder and thought he recognized the voice of Tommy Tucker. Don't forget, he was on the brink of collapse. On top of that he had just given himself another injection of Dexadrine to keep going. The next day he could remember very little of the incident. He feared that it had been an aberration. But he went back to his cabin, gave himself another injection of Dexadrine—he had to, at this stage—and played the recording again. Immediately the insight of the night before returned. He recognized Tommy Tucker's voice as being that of O'Connor's.'

Quinan paused. His eyes went from one to the other. 'This was shattering. Stephen was quite sure of his identification. It meant that on board was a man who was a traitor to his country. It stamped O'Connor, it put him aside as something especially unpleasant. It brought all Stephen's attention to the man. And then suddenly, things started to fall into place. The first, following on Stephen's identification of O'Connor as Tommy Tucker, was the recollection that Puget told us on Monday in Haiphong that the radio station had closed down. The second was that there had been dead men on board the sampan when we picked O'Connor up. As a matter of fact, he asked me about them when we buried Puget and the others. It shows the way his mind was working. And of course following on the sampan thought was the logical and very important follow-up—namely that O'Connor had come on board just a little more than forty-eight hours before the first case. That was the third point. The fourth was provided by the story about Typhoid Mary. And the fifth came when Stephen went back to the hospital and re-studied all those particulars he and Mary had taken about the sick men. He sifted through them minutely, but this time he knew what he was looking for: he found that all except two of the patients had either drunk or gambled with O'Connor. And when people gamble they usually drink. There is close, intimate contact. Osgood, Hookins and Sloan had all drunk with O'Connor. The rest were the card players, even young Usher. O'Connor, of course had no social barriers. There was a great deal of twisted hatred in him—hatred for authority, hatred for wealth—which had all started when his father had killed himself through bankruptcy. But he concealed it to a large extent with his sly, obsequious, homespun, buddy-boy manner. He would play cards with officers or crew, it didn't matter a damn to him.'

Quinan frowned. He lit a cigarette while they waited in silence. 'You must remember the state Stephen was in. It must have been difficult to think at all, let alone think coherently. And yet he makes no mention of this fact in his diary. He blames himself for his blindness. He mentioned that this morning on the after-deck when he . . . when he killed O'Connor. And one of the reasons for this self-condemnation was the fact that O'Connor had a temperature when he came on board; he spoke often of our lifeboats as "red" boats. Stephen attributed both these things to other causes, but in fact, of course, they were brought about because O'Connor had a mild form of the virus, the way carriers often have, complete with minor hallucinatory spasms. The "red" boat was the boat he and his father were so proud of. But this point—whether it was blindness on Stephen's part, whether any other doctor would have picked it up, doesn't matter—was the sixth damning piece of evidence against O'Connor. Stephen was now just about positive, but he lacked background, and this was finally provided on Friday night, by Mercy Attwell.'

Quinan stopped again. His eyes went to Lucas, fleetingly, and then to Proctor. They dwelt on Proctor a moment and then passed on. Quinan became almost uncomfortable.

'Friday night clinched everything. Mercy Attwell was very sick, dying really, and Stephen was constantly at her side. She talked a great deal in her delirium. Stephen has recorded in detail what she said. Apparently she had been through a most unhappy experience on Wednesday night. She had become wayward through her realization that Attwell had no faith in God. It had momentarily deprived her of a basis for existence. She . . . she had been having an affair. It had turned into a drunken thing, involving more than one person, and when she headed back for her cabin she was in a very low state, mentally. O'Connor knew—of course a lot of people knew; this is not a heavily-populated ship —and he got hold of her on her way back.'

Sweat was running down Lucas's face. 'I was one,' he said. He said it very clearly, as though labouring to make his guilt clear. 'Peter and I. She'd been with us.'

Proctor spoke as though his lips and his cheeks and his tongue were stiff. 'That's great. The confessions of Fanny Hill. Keep talking, you twit.'

They ignored him. Mary Fannin made a little sound and turned away.

'O'Connor got drunk,' Quinan said quickly, wanting to finish the story. 'Mercy learned a lot, although in the state she was in it did not add up. She found out that O'Connor had been cheating in camp. He'd been in charge of a food detail and had been cheating to help himself. The two Australians in the camp, Cockett and Smith, found out. These two chaps had become the backbone of resistance in the camp. They beat the hell out of O'Connor, to put it plainly.' Quinan looked at Mary Fannin. 'You remember how upset O'Connor got on Monday night, at dinner, when he mentioned them? You remember how he told us he was beaten? We all thought it was from the Viets, but it was from his own side.'

He flicked his cigarette away, down over the rail to the rain-dappled Nan Hai. 'The Viets found out, of course. They latched on to O'Connor as a likely stooge. He became the meat in the sandwich. To stay in camp meant further beatings. And doing his Tommy Tucker act meant good food, staying in line, looking after number one. Except that, at that stage, the epidemic in the camp had begun. When he moved on, when he went to Haiphong and people fell ill in droves amongst the radio personnel, O'Connor was quick to catch on. So was everybody else. They sent him back, hotfoot, to the camp. But the camp knew—the prisoners and the command. His escape was literally connived at. They almost let him go, together with three other no-goods who were either prepared to take their chances or were too stupid to realize what was happening. On Wednesday night O'Connor raped Mercy Attwell. Or at least he obtained her consent by threats. Same thing, really.'

He looked away, at the homing cruiser. 'I don't think O'Connor was all right, mentally. Nor did Stephen. And I think all of you know that Stephen was in love with Mercy. He finally knew why she had got the disease. He knew why she had got it so badly. Direct, intimate contact—like Osgood and others sharing a glass or bottle with him, like Mercy Attwell's kind of intimate contact —produced a more serious form of the sickness. It produced death, in fact. That's why he killed O'Connor, this morning.'

He turned to look once more at Proctor. 'I might mention that Kyle told me, not long ago, that it was O'Connor who suggested that the disease emanated from the bodies in Number Three hold. He was obviously trying to keep attention away from himself.' He shook his head once more. 'It must have been hell, in a way, to be in that position. But O'Connor was too crooked, too devious, too mentally warped to disclose the true state of affairs when he came on board. It might have made all the difference.'

There was a long silence. Then Proctor made a small meaningless sound. He looked at them, rigid, as though he were about to speak. But he turned about and walked away down the companion-way, looking thin and angular from behind.

Quinan turned away. 'I'm going below, to the foredeck. We've got to provide a welcoming committee.' He put his arm around Mary Fannin. 'Come along.'

They went together. The foredeck was nearly deserted, in the rain. They stood at the rail. After a while she said, 'Did Stephen ever know what the disease really was?'

He nodded. 'Yes. He thinks it was a mutation of Asian 'flu. There're influenza germs around all the time. Every now and then you get a mutation. Asian 'flu was a mild example. The 1918 'flu was a holocaust. It killed millions. But it was apparently nothing more than a mutation of the same thing. Even going far back, to the time of the Plagues, this is the same theory. Given time, given a laboratory where the germ could have been isolated and an antibiotic found that would destroy it. Stephen would have been all right. But the antibiotics we had on this ship, excellent as they were, did not destroy it.' He paused a moment. 'And as you know, Stephen had no time.'

Attwell appeared, suddenly, looking old and hunched. He had heard about the cruiser. He was wearing a grey suit and a bulky, cold-weather raincoat, and his cheeks were dew-speckled with raindrops. He put a suitcase down and stood next to them. His eyes hardly touched them. They were on the other ship, watching it grow close.

Quinan was stirred by pity. Attwell looked so old. He was alone now, for the first time in many years. Alone and on the down-grade.

'What are you going to do now, Mister Attwell?' he asked kindly.

Attwell sighed, blowing out his cheeks, making it long and audible. Although, patently, there was no life left in him, it was there, stirring, latent, a new enthusiasm kindling.

'I'm going to Africa, Mister Quinan. I am going to seek God.' He shrugged. 'I've been without Him for kind of a long time. Maybe I'll find Him, but even if I don't, I'll see out the rest of my years in His service.'

They studied him. Silly old man, Mary Fannin thought. He stands there with his suitcase, ready to go aboard, not knowing whether they will take him, not knowing whether they will strip the *Florence Hurst* and take us all on board, or tow us, or put us all into quarantine once they hear the story. And what he'd said was as stagey as on Monday, when he'd prayed on his bony knees there on the hard iron of the foredeck. You're at it again, she thought, and you're just as insincere. And then she scolded herself. No. It was so difficult to tell. Maybe he had changed. Maybe this time it wasn't for the money. And the plaudits. Maybe she was wrong.

She turned to Quinan. 'I'm not going to Africa,' she said. 'I'm not going anywhere that isn't where you go, whether it's on land, desert, jungle, or, God help me, the sea.'

'Not on the sea,' Quinan said. He put his big arm around her. 'Not here, any more.'

On the cruiser, the M.O. had been called up to the bridge.

'Better get ready to go on board, with your little black bag.' The Captain grinned at him. 'It's the *Florence Hurst,* all right. Guessed as much, when the blighter didn't move.' He pointed, lifting his glasses. 'See that signal, QL? That means, "My ship is infected with contagious disease".' He frowned. 'I wonder, though, why the hell they didn't send a radio message?'

The M.O. had borrowed a pair of glasses. He read the signal. Then he put the glasses down. He was thinking in medical terms. 'I wonder what the deuce is wrong. Plague?'

The Captain shrugged. 'Search me.' They were close enough now that one could see the figures at the rail. 'There're some of them alive, though, you can see the buggers.'

'They're awfully still,' said the M.O. As their ship gained, he studied the figures at the rail—a big man with a girl standing next to him, and another big man who seemed elderly because of the way he stooped, detached from the other two. Other figures appeared, waving. But the three figures at the rail stood still. They're the ones, the doctor thought, they're the ones who will know the whole story. There was a quality about them that made him think of statues, but at the same time they had a presence about them, they were filled with meaning, and they grew larger as the cruiser closed.

'I think that's the skipper there, that big bloke standing next to the girl,' he said.

The Captain looked at him. 'It's a fellow called Grove, just so's you know.'

'Okay.' The doctor shrugged. His mind was filled with unknown complexities. He turned away. 'I'll get ready to go on board.'

The cruiser homed in, arrow-true, towards the *Florence Hurst.*

THE DOMINATOR

Andrew York

'The Dominator' is published by
Hutchinson & Co. Ltd.

The Author

Andrew York was born in British Guiana and, although he now lives in the Channel Islands, he still considers himself a West Indian. Naturally enough his favourite sport is cricket, although he plays a keen game of chess. His spare time is occupied with reading history— but for relaxation he turns to stories of the supernatural. Under his own name, Christopher Nicole, he is the author of seven novels with West Indian settings and of *The West Indies: Their People and History*.

'For now I see
Peace to corrupt no less than war to waste.'

JOHN MILTON
Paradise Lost, Book II

PART ONE

THE KNIGHT

CHAPTER ONE

CHAD WAS NEVER SILENT. The rains were still some months away, and the lake was low. The island was only a mound of sun-dried mud in the centre of a vast bed of reeds. Yet the *harmattan* whined, deposited its endless layers of sand on tree and hut, hair and clothing and flesh. It whipped the distant waters, soughed through the grass, kept the creatures of Chad awake and irritable.

Inger heard them, as she sucked Kanem against her, bruised her teeth on his. She identified the bullfrogs in the mudfields surrounding the island, the louder rumbles of the hippos enjoying their interminable baths. Noisy nights and silent days. This was a backwards world, a world which, even after two years, she found the most exciting she had known. Her mind reached for the sounds she could not hear, the scorpions lurking in the dust, the crocodiles gliding through the shallow water, the silent ecstasy of Serene.

Kanem lay flaccid, his weight pinning her to the sweat-stained blanket. Fodio continued. Fodio was the slow one. Inger stretched out her hand, touched Serene's shoulder, slid her fingers down until they were trapped between Fodio's chest and Serene's nipple. She could feel the heart pumping, inches beneath her palm. She thought, if I had the strength to drive my fingers into this soft flesh, I could tear this pounding muscle free, and throw it to the crocodiles. She often dreamed of Serene at the moment of death, awoke in an ecstasy for which Kanem could never hope.

Fodio left the blanket, crawled to the door of the hut, drew the flap to allow a shaft of moonlight to penetrate the darkness, gazed at the empty compound. The island slept. If any of the Followers of the Lord suspected the existence, much less the purpose, of these midnight meetings, they were wise enough to keep their suspicions to themselves.

Kanem rolled on his back, between the two women, crushing Inger's arm. 'I have spoken with the Lord,' he said. 'It is to be Zobeir. He will announce it to the Followers before the year is out.'

Inger smiled. Kanem wanted her so badly, needed her so badly, he had been afraid to break the news earlier, in case she had become angry and refused him.

'He must be stopped,' Serene said.

'Who can stop the Lord?' Fodio sat beside her. 'The Followers would cast out the one who defied him.'

'Have you nothing to say, Inger?' Kanem asked. 'This means that you have failed.'

She freed her arm, sat up, dried sweat from her forehead with the edge of the blanket. She looked at each of them in turn, her face expressionless. Inger's face never showed emotion. It existed, every feature exquisitely shaped, exquisitely related to every other feature, the whole framed in a cascade of straight-ash-blonde hair which lay on the white shoulders, doubly startling in this brunette world. Inger belonged in the frozen north, not the burning south; even her eyes were grey glaciers, half concealed beneath long golden lashes.

'I agree with you,' she said. 'I have failed to influence the Lord sufficiently. But if he will not be persuaded, he will have to be eliminated.' She waited for their reactions. Kanem, her Kanem, so like his brother Fodio, was a Kanembu, tall and broad-shouldered, with a high forehead, and bold chin and nose and lips. They were two of the handsomest men she had ever known; naked, they represented human muscular perfection.

Now they looked afraid, for all that she had merely put into words their own innermost thoughts. If Kanem had had the boldness of mind to equal his boldness of appearance, the coming holocaust would never have been necessary. She thought this without bitterness. She still intended to use him, when the time came.

'And how do you propose to accomplish that?' Serene's voice was quiet. The Fulani girl was short where the German woman was tall. Her hair, as long and as straight as Inger's, was the colour of midnight. Her features, as small and as delicate, were moulded rather than chiselled, and thus gave an impression of softness, of a mind behind the liquid black eyes which would yield. Her breasts were small, and pointed, where Inger's swelled and sagged; her thighs were slender as a boy's, where Inger looked capable of welcoming the world and his brother into her bustling love forest. Even Inger, for all her experience of men and women, had once made the mistake of thinking of Serene as a child. It was not a mistake she intended to repeat. Here in the centre of Chad she had found her true home, physical and spiritual. It could not be shared with Serene.

'The Followers would avenge him,' Fodio said.

'They would tear the guilty one to pieces,' Kanem said.

'The guilty one,' Inger said.

'Well?' Serene insisted.

'I have worked for a great many people in my life,' Inger said. 'The Germans, East and West; the Russians; I worked for Gunnar Moel; and for several years I worked for the British. I know where there is a man who kills, for money. And for other reasons.'

'And he will kill for you?' Kanem asked.

'For me. Yes.'

'And afterwards?' Fodio demanded. 'He will have been in our employ. How will you stop him betraying our part in this?'

Inger lay down, her head a glowing white aureole on Kanem's stomach. 'You will have to trust me, Fodio, and believe that there will be nothing to connect him to us. And after he has killed, as you say, he will be destroyed.'

'Words,' Serene said, half to herself. 'How will this assassin of yours accomplish his purpose, Inger? There are no weapons in the Centre of the Universe, and none will be allowed.'

Inger smiled. 'This man does not use weapons. He kills with his hands. You will see, Serene. You will have a part to play, when the time comes. An important part.'

'A man who kills with his hands. And he is a friend of yours, Inger?'

'Not a friend,' Inger said. 'Never a friend.'

CHAPTER TWO

'STOP HERE, MR. WILDE.' Benton rolled down his window. 'You'll get a good idea of how easily she takes the ground.'

Wilde braked the Alfa, opened the door and got out. He was a big man, two inches more than six feet tall, with broad shoulders which tapered down to hips narrow enough to suggest that he was very fit. His face was long; the gaunt cheekbones and prominent chin were like rocks under the tanned flesh; only the tenseness of his flat mouth seemed out of place beneath the deceptively mild blue eyes. His dark brown hair was receding, but there was no grey visible as yet. He was a man to trust on sight, or to fear on sight; those who could actually like him were rare.

He buttoned his topcoat, walked across the dock. The tide was out, and the little harbour was gloomily damp beneath a cold and grey May sky; the catamaran remained on her mooring, upright on the mud, like a bird awaiting only a disturbing noise to flap its wings and fly away in tremendous haste.

Benton stood beside him. The salesman was short and plump. He looked good-humoured and well fed. He smoked a pipe, regarded the world with a tolerant sophistication. But Wilde puzzled him. 'Ever sailed a cat?'

'No.'

'But you *have* sailed?'

'A great deal,' Wilde said. 'Is that firm enough to walk on?'

'Oh, indeed. And we've lots of time. The tide won't be back for a couple of hours.'

Wilde followed him down the stone steps, closed his right hand on the iron rail, and winced. It was an involuntary reaction, now. The cartilages, shattered by the K.G.B. rifle-butts on that unforgettable night in Moscow a year ago, had all healed. So he had been told, and there were X-rays to prove it. And yet to grip, to squeeze, sent rivers of pain seeping up his arm and into his shoulder. To hit something with that hand was unthinkable.

Benton's shoes crunched on the wet sand. 'I'm using a thirty-five-horsepower outboard. Pushes her along at six knots, quite economically. You need a good engine around here, I always say.'

'Yes.' Wilde buried his hands deep in his coat pockets. Masts, ships, the sea, brought back memories like a flooding spring tide; *Regina A.,* foundering in the raging seas off the Hanois Lighthouse, with Marita Kostic and a dead Stern in the cockpit; *Halcyon,* resting, as was this catamaran, on a mud berth, her slight list warning him that Kieserit's assassin was hiding in the forepeak. Since *Halcyon* he had abandoned the sea. Now he was back. Because of his hand, and because Mocka had not called on him for over a year. He did not even know if the commander was in England, or was still freezing in Siberia. He did not know if the Elimination Section had been wound up. He suspected that when it was, no one would waste his time informing him.

Benton climbed the boarding ladder, stepped into the huge cockpit, nearly ten feet wide and six deep. He unlocked the hatch, pushed it back. 'She's a bit tiny amidships. But there's full headroom in each of the hulls.'

Wilde ducked. She was a trim boat, a comfortable boat, he estimated, and she did not remind him of the others. 'Much heel?'

'Five degrees maximum. See those bottles? I left them on the table last night. All opened.' Benton grinned. 'It's a ploy, of course, Mr. Wilde. But they haven't shifted an inch, much less fallen over, and there was quite a bobble on this morning.'

'Very effective.' Wilde went down the two steps into the galley, made his way forward to the sleeping cabin, which extended the width of the centre hull. 'You said three thousand.'

'Complete, Mr. Wilde. And there's pretty near a thousand's worth of extras. That R.D.F.'s brand new, and the engine has had an overhaul. I'd say you're getting a bargain.'

'Subject to survey.'

'Oh, you won't find any soft wood. She's sheathed in fibreglass.'

Wilde returned on deck; the sea was just lapping through the harbour mouth. 'The surveyors will be in touch with you some time this week.' He leaned on the cabin roof, wrote a cheque for three hundred pounds. 'That suit you?'

'Oh, indeed, Mr. Wilde. And she's yours the very second you see your way to letting me have the balance.'

'I'll be down as soon as I get a clean report.' Wilde climbed over the side, walked back to the dock, Benton hurrying at his heels. 'Can I give you a lift?'

'Ah, no, thanks all the same. I have one or two things to do, don't you know.'

'Well, then, I'll be seeing you, I hope.' Wilde got behind the wheel of the little Alfa, put the car into reverse, ran along the dock and swung through the mud-tracked drive of the boatyard. He braked at the gates opening on to the main road, turned into the stream of traffic, allowed himself to relax, both hands on the wheel, shoulders well back, feeling the power of the car surging upwards through his legs to meet whatever it was that came seeping downwards from his brain.

Relief? It was a step he had contemplated for so very long, had rejected again and again. Not only because of the memories. Because, when he returned to the sea, it had to be for good. There had been other times when he had known a desperate urge to get out, to put a bag over his head and run blindly into the night, away from what he was, from the people who had created him, who made him dance to their tune. Not in the beginning. To the ex-commando the idea of working with a team of highly-trained and utterly brilliant men had been absorbing, even if their end product had been death. He had still been a soldier, a soldier's life is concerned with death, whether he does it by pressing a trigger or silently with his hands. Instinctively his right hand closed around the steering wheel, and as instinctively he winced.

A soldier doesn't quit, he thought, so long as he is fit enough to be used. He goes on working until he is worn out or is himself destroyed. This was the crux of the matter. He was making his plans for Wilde to slip into oblivion, not because he had kicked his heels for a year—there had been similar gaps in the past, and it was an encouraging omen for current international relations—

but because he knew, and they knew, that he was finished. He had seen it in their eyes, heard it in their voices. When a man has been taken by the Russians his usefulness is at an end. His hand throbbed like toothache.

He pulled off the road into the forecourt of a lonely public house, standing at one end of an equally derelict cluster of houses, opened the glove compartment, lit a Belfleur cigar and blew smoke at the roof. Another sign of the times. Jonas Wilde drank as he used women, and cars and aircraft and ships, as aids for reaching his targets silently and without arousing suspicion. But recently, come noon, he needed a drink. The noon drink lowered a grey cloud over Moscow, shut out Kieserit and Lynn Langtree and Odalie Pearson, and the girl called Nona. Most of all, the girl called Nona.

He slammed the door, went into the saloon bar. It was empty, a cavern of gloomy, dark polished wood, and no less gloomy highly polished brass. The licensee liked horses, or assumed that his customers did.

He pressed the bell. 'Shop!'

The woman was young, with curly black hair resting on the straps of her white apron. But for a poor complexion and a general air of untidiness she would have been pretty; there was a great deal of round flesh under the apron. She smiled at Wilde. Women invariably smiled at Wilde, those who liked men because of the latent energy they could sense in his movements, those who disliked men because of the cut of his clothes.

'Good morning,' she said brightly. 'What will you have?'

'I feel exotic,' Wilde said. 'Filled with the faint zephyrs of tropical breezes. I think we should make it a Zombie.'

'And very nice too. What is it?'

'It's a cocktail, sweetheart. Do you have any decent white rum?'

She surveyed the shelves. 'There's Bacardi.'

'That's a shade *too* decent for a Zombie. But it'll have to do. Could you put two ounces into a cocktail shaker?'

She poured, sniffed. 'It's going to be strong.'

'Which is the object of the exercise. Now will you squeeze a lemon?'

She did it expertly. Wilde glanced along the bar, saw a newspaper, remembered that there was a daily ritual he had observed for the previous twelve years, but had neglected all this week. He put it down to a quite juvenile excitement over the catamaran.

'Then what?' asked the barmaid.

'The rest is easy. One ounce of Orange Curaçao, one ounce of Jamaica rum, a dash of Pernod, and an ounce of orange juice.

Then some cracked ice and a good shake. But don't strain it. And do you happen to have today's *Times*?'

'Does that go into it too?' She did not seem surprised.

'That is for me to peruse while I wait for your concoction to register.'

'We don't take *The Times*. But there's a newsagent's shop down the road. I'll have this ready by the time you come back.'

'Good girl.' Wilde stepped outside, hurried along the windswept street, bought the paper. He tucked it under his arm, regained the warmth of the saloon bar.

She was just pouring. 'Does that look right?'

'A Zombie never looks right. Only the taste matters. Mmmm. Yes. That tastes very good indeed.' He discarded the business section, ran his finger down the Personal Column, wondered why he still bothered. Perhaps this would be the last time. He completed two columns, started on the third, drank some of his Zombie, and swallowed a piece of ice.

'IN CASE OF NEED telephone the Dream Club and ask for Love.'

'Something wrong?' asked the barmaid.

'A one Zombie morning has suddenly become a two Zombie morning,' Wilde said. 'Would you mind mixing the same again?'

(ii)

Traffic was heavy; Wilde did not regain London until three. He garaged his car, enjoyed the buffet lunch at the Playboy Club, spent the afternoon over a roulette wheel. He found it impossible to concentrate, either on the spinning ball or the Bunny. His orders usually came in writing, together with an advance on his fee, and were picked up from some discreet General Delivery. A personal contact sounded like an emergency, and he was in no mood for emergencies. Love also sounded like a woman, and he felt even less inclined to receive orders from Felicity Hart this evening.

At seven-thirty he dialled the Dream Club. 'Put me on to Love, will you?'

'Oh, yes, sir.' He listened to clicks and metallic thumps, voices shouting in the distance, high-pitched laughter. No music, as yet. He cradled the receiver between chin and shoulder, lit a cigarette.

'I'm Love.' High, thin, slightly foreign. Definitely not Felicity Hart. 'You'll have to give me your name.'

'Oh, come now, darling. The name is Wilde.'

'Let's be intimate.'

'Jonas.'

'I'm so glad. You have no idea. But you mustn't come here. Do you know Whitten Street?'

'Earls Court.'

'The fourth house from the corner, on the right. I'm in the top apartment. If you'd happen along sometime after eleven, you can come straight up.'

'Eleven,' Wilde said.

'That's the earliest I can leave here. See you.'

There didn't seem much point in deep thought at this stage. The treadmill was moving and he was being carried to a destination. He dined in the V.I.P. room, felt appropriately pampered, and returned to the tables. This time he played blackjack, made back some of his earlier losses. He left the club at ten.

The wind had dropped, and a fine rain was falling. Wilde took a taxi to the corner of Whitten Street, turned up the collar of his topcoat, thrust his hands deep into his pockets, counted the houses. It was one of the more seedy parts of Earls Court.

The fourth house had a light on in the hall and in one of the downstairs front rooms. The top floor was in darkness. He went past, crossed the street, selected a dark doorway, stepped inside. He stood absolutely still, his hands deep in his coat pockets, watching the rain slanting on to the pavement; waiting was an important part of his business and tonight, at least, he was not waiting to kill.

Half an hour passed, and he watched a woman come down the street from the direction of the Tube station. She was an African, tall and slender, erect in a manner beyond the reach of a European. Her mouth was wide, her nose small. Her straight hair was lacquered and peeped from beneath a wide-brimmed felt hat. She wore a white raincoat and thigh-length black boots.

She turned into the fourth gate, and he crossed the street. She was already mounting the steps, heard him seconds before he reached her, turned her head as he gripped her elbow. 'You must be Mr. Wilde.' Her black eyes danced with amusement.

Her accent added to her complexion made it quite likely that she was genuine. Which made even less sense than anything else which had happened today. He had been in Africa only once in his life, and that had been Kenya, seven years ago.

'I came early.'

She nodded. 'You look like you could use a drink.' She inserted her key into the lock, smiled at him. 'I'm Aimee Bosquet.'

'Does that mean you prefer to receive than to give? Or does the name mean something different in French?'

She led him through a linoleumed hall, climbed the stairs. She had thin legs. 'It's just a name, Mr. Wilde. It has to do with love, I suppose, so that's why I chose it. I must apologize for the place, but I'm not stopping. Although maybe you expected something like this?'

'Should I?'

'Don't you have prejudices?'

She was too good-humoured, too brimful of confidence. She did not know who or what he was. But she knew his name, and that alone was too much.

'I gave up those kind of prejudices when I left kindergarten. And you'd look just right anywhere.'

'That's charming of you, Mr. Wilde.' She reached the top landing, only a little out of breath, took another key from her pocket.

'Allow me.' Wilde put his left arm round her waist, pulled her against him, while with his right hand he took the key from her fingers.

Her hat touched his shoulders, and tilted. Her hair smelt of jasmine. 'Why, Mr. Wilde, I believed you.'

He unlocked the door, pushed it in with his foot. He carried her forward, found the light switch, illuminated an unattractive bed-sitter. It was empty. He closed the door, and still holding her tight, thrust his right hand into each of her armpits, then slid it down the front of her raincoat, under her skirt and round the tops of her boots.

Aimee Bosquet drew a very long breath. 'I know it's a bit whorish, but were you really expecting to be rolled?'

'Put me down as a suspicious character.'

She removed her coat and hung it on the door. She wore a white minidress. 'Shall I take yours?'

He handed it to her. 'Smoke?'

'Thanks. And can I fix you a drink?'

Wilde sat on the bed. She was the sort of woman he could watch for hours; she moved like a cat. When a woman attracted him he thought of her personality as a colour; Aimee Bosquet was a bubbling rose pomadour. 'You wouldn't by any chance have Bacardi?'

'I'm so glad you asked for that.'

'I'll get it.' He stepped past her, opened the cupboard. There was an unopened half-bottle of rum, four cans of Coca-Cola, two glasses. There were a few toilet articles, a change of underwear, and a quite expensive coat. 'You seemed pleased to hear my name, too.'

'Well, this is the third day that advert. has been in the paper, you see, and I was beginning to give up hope.' She touched glasses. 'Of getting the right man, anyway.'

'You've had other applicants?'

'I think there's a type of person who answers advertisements on a matter of principle. I even had a visit from a woman. A visit, mind, not a telephone call.'

'Tell me about her.'

'I think she was a butch type, although she didn't look it. But she just sort of sized me up and then left. She was a blonde, kind of surprised-looking. Very pale-skinned. We'd have looked good in bed together.'

'But right now you're sure you have the right man?'

'The name was right. And the drink was the clincher.' She offered him a cigarette from a flat gold case, took one herself. 'I suppose you know who sent me.'

'I'm afraid I don't.'

'You answered the advertisement. She said it was special to you and her.'

'Oh, it was. But there are so many hers, don't you know.'

Aimee Bosquet smiled. 'You look the type, Mr. Wilde. Well, I'm afraid that's it. She asked me to get in touch with you. She said you'd be glad to hear from her. She wants you to visit with us.'

'She being?'

'Inger Lieberstein, Mr. Wilde.'

'The only Inger I ever knew was a Mrs. Christopher Morgan-Browne.'

His mind was receiving only, at this moment. To remember Inger, to attempt to work out what she might be at now, would get him nowhere.

'She has been married. She's a German lady, too good-looking to be true, if you know what I mean, with white hair and an awful lot of brain.'

'I know exactly what you mean. Why couldn't she come herself?'

'I got the impression that she's not entirely welcome in Great Britain.'

'So where is she welcome?'

'Right this minute she's living in Chad.'

'I'd say you might come from around there.'

'That's right, Mr. Wilde. But Miss Lieberstein isn't in Chad, the country. She's in Chad, the lake. You know, it's quite a big piece of water, separating Chad from Nigeria, amongst other places.'

'And she's doing what? You'll pardon my curiosity, Aimee, but the Inger I'm thinking about never believed in wasting her time.'

'It's a long story, Mr. Wilde.'

Wilde finished his drink. 'That was a fresh bottle.'

She got up, poured, offered him another cigarette. She unzipped her boots, dropped them on the floor. She lay on her back, on the bed, wriggled stocking-clad toes. 'Have you ever been to West Africa?'

'As a matter of fact, no.'

'And you know nothing about it?'

'Let's see. Slavery, once upon a time, tsetse-flies, forests, maybe even a bit of desert, but I wouldn't swear to that, big rivers, big rollers on the Atlantic coast, Tuaregs, walled cities, malaria, heavy rain, a certain amount of domestic discord, cannibal kingdoms, jujus . . .'

'I find that all Europeans make the same mistakes, about Africa. Same as they do about the States, or the Soviet Union, or Australia, or India. They can't visualise the size. Nigeria, which is the country we're talking about, is just a fraction smaller than France and Germany put together, so you want to get rid of the idea that the people living in Lagos look, think, or talk the same as the people living in Kano, any more than you'd expect someone living in Marseilles to be the twin of someone from Berlin.'

'I sit corrected.'

'So, for instance, that Biafran business hasn't really affected the Northern Region all that much, except that there's no Federal money available, right now. There's not much malaria left, either. And the cannibals have just about called it a day. At least officially.' She gazed at him. 'My grandfather was a cannibal, Mr. Wilde. History has a habit of being rather recent in West Africa.'

'My great-grandfather was hanged for stealing sheep.'

'But there is still slavery, although you would never notice it. And there is still juju. Do you know what juju is?'

'Magic? A talisman, maybe, around which you build a secret society. I hope you're not trying to tell me that Inger Morgan-Browne has joined some West African secret society. I thought they didn't go for women?'

'This is a rather special kind of secret society, Mr. Wilde. Women are very welcome. And it is not confined to West Africa.'

'Things into which Inger dips her dreamy fingers are generally international. Tell me about it.'

'It is a *secret* society.'

'And you are a member?'

'Of course.'

'And on behalf of Inger you wish to involve me?'

'You will use my name as an introduction. Because you will have to have an introduction, and Miss Lieberstein does not wish it to be known that she is a friend of yours.'

'That would be a disaster, I'm sure.'

'Yes, Mr. Wilde. So, if you are agreeable, I will initiate you into the ranks of the Followers of the Lord. This will take us about a week.'

'Sounds like fun.'

'Then you will take a plane to Kano, which is a city in Northern Nigeria. It is well served by airlines. Nigeria is like that. A country of the utmost contrasts.'

'I'll keep that in mind.' Wilde refilled his glass.

'In Kano you will visit the house of a Mr. Chwarism. It is well known. You will pay Mr. Chwarism a thousand pounds, which is your fee for initiation into the Inner Court. There are several stages to be negotiated before you can achieve full membership, and this final step can only be accomplished in the presence of the Lord himself, hence the necessity for your journey. In ordinary cases the initiation fee, or a proportion of it, is returnable to drop-outs.'

'But you wouldn't regard me as an ordinary case?'

'Miss Lieberstein has no doubt that you will be capable of becoming a member of the Inner Court. You do not have to worry, it is all legal. We have some very well-known members from the entertainment world and the business world and even some politicians.'

'And this is the only way I can visit Inger?'

'The only way, Mr. Wilde.'

'You'll have to convince me it's going to be worth it. I don't really go for secrets.'

'Secrecy is not necessarily evil, Mr. Wilde. Its purpose here is anonymity. The society is dedicated to a magnificent and wholly worthwhile objective, which I can best sum up as the achievement of world peace through the liberation of the human mind from centuries of superstition and doubt, brought about by an excess of what you might call civilisation.'

Wilde sat beside her, leaned on his elbow across her legs. 'Is your mind liberated?'

'Of course, Mr. Wilde. You will find the society is unique, in its methods, in its approach to the problem.'

'I'm sure it is. Well, Aimee. I want you to tell Inger that I'm touched by her anxiety to have my mind freed from superstition and doubt and I do understand that she, and you, I know, have only my welfare at heart. My trouble is, I've just bought myself a boat in which I intend to wallow even deeper in superstition, so I don't think I shall be able to take up your kind invitation. Particularly if it is going to cost me a thousand quid.'

'Miss Lieberstein will be terribly disappointed.'

Wilde finished his drink. 'She survived me once, more literally than you might think, and I'm sure she'll do so again.'

Aimee Bosquet sighed. 'Is it the money? Should you accept her invitation, I'm authorized to advance you the thousand.'

'The answer is still no. But I tell you what, Aimee. I know a place where the action never ceases. What about you and me going along there and getting to know one another.'

'If that is what you wish.' She pulled on her boots. Wilde took their coats from the hook, heard the floorboards creak on the landing.

'Company,' he said, wrenched the door open.

A young African stood there. He wore a soft hat and a heavy coat. His right hand held a silenced Browning automatic pistol. The gun hardly made a sound. Aimee Bosquet, still sitting on the bed, her right leg across her left knee as she reached for the zip of her boot, gave a gentle cough. The white minidress had turned crimson.

CHAPTER THREE

THE PISTOL swung towards Wilde. The young man's face was tired, perhaps even a little sorry. But he was going to shoot again. And, Wilde realized, there was nothing he could do about it. His action should have been taken half a second earlier. He should have been propelling himself through space with all the energy and decision which had kept him alive for twelve years. Instead of which he was only conscious of the throbbing pain in his right hand.

The knuckle tightened, and a woman stepped against the young man, from behind. He gave a gasp, and his mouth opened. The hand holding the gun contracted, but the arm had already drooped. The bullet smacked into the floor at Wilde's feet.

Felicity Hart pushed the dead man away from her, and Wilde caught him, laid him on the floor. Blood streamed from his back. Felicity unscrewed the silencer from her point-two-five Walther and restored the tiny pistol to her handbag. She dried her right forefinger with a Kleenex. She looked surprised, but, then, Felicity Hart always looked surprised. It had something to do with her features, every one of which—chin, mouth, and nose—was tilted slightly upwards; her short golden-brown hair was back brushed. She was wearing the same sheepskin jacket as the last time Wilde had seen her, concealing the flat chest which was her only drawback as a woman, and a short skirt which allowed a pair of long, nylon-clad legs to be inspected before he reached the brown knee-length boots. Her voice, like her appearance, was breathless. 'I'd say you nearly bought it.'

'And I'm *almost* glad to see you, darling. Did you drop from heaven? Or scramble up from the other place?'

'I've been following your girl friend around London for three days, Jonas. And when the company became a crowd I thought I'd better even the score.' She knelt, turned the dead man over, went through his pockets, found nothing. 'How is she?'

Wilde laid two fingers on Aimee Bosquet's neck. 'Quite dead. And she was the sort of girl I knew I was going to like.'

'Not if this character is typical of her friends. Has she anything worth looking at?'

'Not now.'

'Then I think we should leave, just as quietly as we came in.'

Wilde switched off the light, closed the door, followed her down the stairs and into the rain. Felicity Hart turned down a side street, and then another, unlocked her Mini. 'I assume your fingerprints aren't on file at Scotland Yard?'

Wilde sat beside her, lit a cigarette. 'But you have them, I'm sure.'

She put the car into gear, eased it on to the street. 'We won't be handing you over to the civil police for a little while yet, I hope. And we have *so* much to talk about.'

'If there's one thing which really frightens me, it's a bossy woman who's also good at her job.'

'But, darling, one of us has to be good at our job or where would the country be? For instance, apart from Commander Mocka, and myself, and Sir Gerald, Jonas, you are the only person in the world who knows the In Case of Need code. Or so we thought, before the appearance of Miss Bosquet. It has occurred to us that you may have got tired of doing nothing, or even that you may have run out of money, and be offering your services on a free-lance basis.'

'And you also reasoned that I would be unintelligent enough to use the Elimination Section's call sign to contact my customer. How Great Britain has managed to preserve its independence with your crowd running its affairs will always remain a mystery to me.'

She drove very fast, threaded the little car in and out of the

late-evening traffic, ended up in a mews garage in Chelsea. He
followed her up a flight of stone steps, through a door, and
found himself on the mezzanine floor of a studio apartment,
carpeted and curtained in glowing crimson. The bedspread and
the upholstery were also red; but the walls and ceiling were
painted a gentle off white; Wilde had a distinct impression that
he had been turned into an ant and deposited in a large bowl
of strawberries and cream. And he had evaluated Felicity Hart
as Eton blue.

'I'd say you have a complex.'

'Several.' She threw her sheepskin jacket on the bed, went
down the spiral staircase to the living space. The television set
was on, as was a tape-recorder. Felicity turned the recorder back,
increased the volume. 'You can pour, and then come and listen.
This'll prove we've been here since six.'

Wilde located a refrigerator bar built into the headboard
behind the bed, removed a bottle of Krug. 'You knew I was
coming.'

'It's been there for three nights. What kept you?'

'A dream.' He left his coat beside hers, collected two glasses,
went down the steps. She lay on her stomach, her woollen dress
a splash of green on the blood-coloured carpet, her chin propped
in her hands. 'Here's to us.' He let the cork go, handed her a
glass, held her left wrist for a moment. 'Nice ring. Do I get to meet
Fred, or is it protective colouring?'

'Sandy died six years ago. But he's worth remembering. I
think so, anyway.' She sipped. 'You must listen to this. It's a
variety programme, and we should be able to remember one
or two of the performers, and some of the numbers.'

He sat on the settee, above her. 'I've never been able to watch
TV non-stop for more than five minutes. I'm sure we'd have
been doing something else as well.'

Felicity Hart sat up. 'Do you regard all women as semen
banks?'

'Do you do it often? I mean, shoot people in the small of
the back.'

'As little as possible.' She handed him her empty glass.

'The unfortunate Aimee Bosquet suggested there was a
certain amount of butch in your make-up.'

'Hasn't everyone? I'm as good as any man. I proved that
tonight.'

She reminded him of a misplaced suffragette. 'For which I
am truly grateful. But I think that poor kid was a better analyst
than most.'

'One would suppose you were sorry for her.'

'If I hadn't been quite such a yob about that door, she'd still be alive.'

'You don't think her job was to decoy you to that room?'

'No. Tell me about Sir Gerald.'

'You don't ever want to start discussing complexes, Jonas Wilde. He employs me, and you, and a whole lot of other people. Unlike us, they mostly think he's a fairly important civil servant. But as we know better, we also know enough not to go on about him.'

'What exactly does he employ you for?'

She got up, lit two cigarettes, gave him one. 'I'm his confidential secretary. And his bodyguard, when he needs one. And his trouble-shooter, here in the U.K., just as you do his dirty work in the rest of the world. Oh, he takes me out to dinner, at least twice a week, and then comes back here afterwards, so the world at large, like you, Jonas, will suppose I'm his mistress. But he really is happily married to a stunning member of the aristocracy.'

'And so he never lays a finger on you?'

'Quite literally, darling. He has never laid a finger on me in his life. I have an idea that he feels to touch a woman is a little bit dirty. I don't know what arrangement he's come to with the Honourable Catherine, but I have never seen him touch *any* woman.'

'I always knew I was in a funny business.' Wilde emptied the bottle.

'So you see, I'd just adore to give you a whirl, Jonas. You're one of the most attractive men I've ever met. But you know what they say about office romances, and I'm quite hopeless at the in-and-out bit.' She gazed at him. 'You'd have to see it my way.'

Wilde looked past her to where a key was turning in the downstairs lock. 'This just isn't my night.'

(ii)

The man was of average height, perhaps two inches under six feet. He was not thin, but he didn't look fat, either. He wore a blue suit and a black coat, had just taken off his bowler hat and held it in the same hand as his umbrella. His shoes were highly polished, and glistened with water. He gazed into the room with a disinterested expression, closed the door behind him. His face was utterly devoid of distinguishing marks. The nose could perhaps be described as Grecian, but it fitted so discreetly between an average mouth and an average forehead, was overlooked by two so cowlike brown eyes and protruded exactly as far as an unremarkable chin, that it could hardly be called a feature. The dark hair was smoothly brushed, and was neither too short nor too long. Wilde, rising to his feet, wondered if this man had been picked for his job because he was so totally unmemorable or if he had groomed himself after his appointment.

Sir Gerald placed his hat on a chair, leaned his umbrella against it. 'It is an unpleasant night, Felicity. I will have a glass of dry sherry.' He sat down, crossed one knee over the other. 'You're overweight, Wilde. How's the hand?'

'Healed, I'm told.'

'And Miss Langtree?'

'As instructed, I kept her in protective custody for as long as possible.'

'Which was?'

'Until she got tired of me, and blew. A difficult girl to entertain, Lynn Langtree. One needed the virility of a sixteen-year-old boy and the approach of a forty-year-old hedonist.'

'And you were only able to supply the one.' Felicity returned with a laden tray. 'I hope you don't mind putting Bacardi on top of champagne.'

'I enjoy putting Bacardi on top of anything, darling. Now you can tell me what happened to Commander Mocka, Sir Gerald.'

'We got him back from the Russians eventually. He wasn't in a very good mental state, but we are hoping for a complete recovery in time.' Sir Gerald sipped his sherry. 'Now I wish to discuss this evening. Felicity?'

'I located the advertiser, as instructed, and kept an eye on her. For three days. This evening Wilde appeared. So I telephoned you, and went back on duty.'

'Wilde?'

Wilde related the events of the evening from his telephone call to the Dream Club.

'Inger Lieberstein. Felicity?'

Felicity gazed at the cream ceiling. 'Inger Lieberstein. Born Dresden, Germany. 16th December 1935.'

'So that's why we never got on,' Wilde said. 'We're both Sagittarians.'

'Middle-class parentage,' Felicity said. 'Early revealed an abnormal intelligence. Spoke nine languages by the time she was four, possessed a photographic memory and a remarkable grasp of mathematical theory. Considered to have an adult I.Q. of 183. Exhibited by the Nazi government as an example of what the Third Reich could produce. Captured by the Russians in 1945, exhibited by the East German government. Escaped from Berlin in 1951—it wasn't difficult in those days—with the assistance of

Swedish agent Gunnar Moel. Worked with Moel's Scandinavian
System for some years. Came to Britain, naturalized British subject.

'Worked with the Atomic Energy Commission as a physicist,
found duties uninteresting, eventually was recruited by the
Special Services to operate an escape route out of Central
Europe. Oh, I forgot, because she was so well known as a child
she underwent plastic surgery, at Gunnar Moel's expense, after
coming west. Not an especially good-looking girl, she opted for an
unnaturally beautiful set of features. Married to Christopher
Morgan-Browne, her associate in the route. Operated successfully
for several years. Seconded to the Elimination Section to assist
Jonas Wilde in reaching Gunnar Moel, when it became apparent
that Moel was taking the Scandinavian System out of Nato and
over to the Warsaw Pact. During the course of this assignment
Wilde learned that she was actually a double agent. As a result
of this development, her husband was killed, but she disappeared.
This is the last entry in her file, and is dated just over three years
ago.'

'Having identified her as a traitor, Wilde, I wonder you did
not think it necessary to, ah, eliminate her.'

'My brief was Gunnar Moel. Once that was done, my only
ambition was to leave Sweden as rapidly as possible. Swedish gaols
may be the most civilized in the world, but once you're in you still
can't get out.'

'I suspect you were more affected by Mrs. Morgan-Browne's
unusual personality that you'd care to admit. Tell me about this
secret society the woman Bosquet mentioned.'

Felicity resumed her inspection of the ceiling. 'West Africa is
riddled with secret societies. I would say she was referring to a
character named Ukuba, whose headquarters are supposed to be
on an island in Lake Chad. You may remember that he toured
the world a couple of years ago, airing his views that the only
thing wrong with humanity was excessive civilization and technology. Not original, by any means, but Ukuba was at least
prepared to practise what he preached. The papers gave him a lot
of space when he took an entire floor at the Royal Oak, had the
furniture and fittings moved out, and slept on the floor in the
middle of his followers. Apparently he made quite a few converts.
People go to see him, and presumably are the better for it. I must
say, though, the sect has never had any political significance. He
is regarded as a second-rate Guru.'

'I'll have another sherry, Felicity,' Sir Gerald said. 'Now tell
me, Wilde, does Felicity's description of this, ah, Nigerian sect
complement what the woman Bosquet told you of it?'

'She didn't tell me much of it. But it view of the entrance fee they don't sleep on the floor from necessity.'

'And did Inger Lieberstein ever strike you as the sort of woman who disliked civilization?'

'In a manner of speaking, yes. But not to the detriment of her personal comfort. My principal memory of Inger is a white mink.'

'Yet she is so involved in this peculiar community that she wishes to do business with her old friend Wilde, a man she has seen in action and therefore has been able to sum up at his exact worth, and who also neglected to kill her the last time they saw each other.' Sir Gerald smiled, briefly. 'Of course, she may have decided that a spell of, ah, primitive living would do you good, Wilde. And I agree with her.'

'Presumably she means to use the sect for her own purposes,' Felicity said.

'Of course. But it occurs to me that her plans have fallen through and, indeed, that she could be in trouble. It may well be that the citizens of Northern Nigeria, and in particular the menfolk, are not receptive to her Nordic charms, while the ability to speak a dozen European languages and discourse on molecular interrelationships is probably considered irrelevant by the majority of the inhabitants of such a backwards society. And, of course, in so fiercely nationalistic an atmosphere, any interference by a European would be fiercely resented. Yes, indeed. Frau Lieberstein is under restraint. Obviously someone out there can understand that she is a valuable piece of human merchandise, so he is keeping her alive, but she is unable to leave. So what can she do? She is a woman who all her life has made enemies rather than friends, has relied on her artificial beauty and her remarkable brain for survival, and who now finds herself stuck in the middle of a large mudhole. In her desperation she remembers the man who, although they may officially be enemies, revealed a weakness for her when last they met. She despatches her faithful handmaiden to summon Wilde to her aid. But the wicked caliph who is holding her has learned of her plans, and sends *his* faithful manservant to stop them, and in the very best traditions he reaches the unhappy girl just after she has blurted her tale to our gallant hero.'

Wilde finished his drink. 'You never mentioned the name of your publisher.'

'It is rather a gorgeous romantic plot. Yes, indeed, I see Frau Lieberstein as a damsel in distress, and I see you, Wilde, as a bold knight setting forth to rescue her. You will make a good knight, Wilde. Under their guise of religious fervour, by all accounts, they were quite as amoral and as vicious and as deadly as yourself. Felicity will arrange your passage.'

'Come again?'

'You do intend to answer such a *cri de cœur*?'

'Whatever else Inger may cry for from time to time it will never be assistance.'

'But you *are* going to her succour, Wilde. I insist upon it.'

'Commander Mocka at least gave me reasons for his more distressing decisions.'

'It seems to have escaped your remarkable perception that Frau Lieberstein remains a traitor to this country. What is more, she is a traitor who for several years was employed in British Intelligence, and we have already established that she possesses a photographic memory which would make Felicity's accomplishments reminiscent of a three-year-old learning its alphabet. Frau Lieberstein has given us an example of her, ah, total recall in the ease with which she remembered your code sign and habits, and sucked you into her orbit. God knows what else she may do, what else she had already done, to disrupt our affairs. For the past three years I have had two highly trained agents doing nothing but attempting to locate this unpleasant young woman, without success. Now she has made the error of disclosing her whereabouts to us. Why she wishes you to come to her is of no relevance whatsoever. We have here an opportunity for you to atone in some small measure for your mistake in permitting her to survive Gunnar Moel. You will catch the first available plane to Kano, as instructed, and there you will join this sect, and you will make your way into the presence of Frau Lieberstein, and once *there* you will break her beautiful neck.'

(iii)

Wilde sighed. 'I suppose you'd turn nasty if I refused.'

'I can be extremely nasty. Do you have any funds on the premises, Felicity?'

Felicity drew one of the crimson drapes on the outer wall, revealing not a window, but a large safe.

'We'll need twenty-five hundred pounds,' Sir Gerald said. 'Wilde's usual down payment of half his fee, and a thousand to pay for the initiation. I assume your various, ah, shots are up to date, Wilde?'

'I try to please.'

'So why did you think of refusing?'

'Killing women isn't really my forte.'

'But you have done it?'

'Twice deliberately, once by accident.'

'It was the woman Kirby who upset you, wasn't it? My dear boy, you may have been conceited enough to suppose that she was in love with you, but her sole mission in life was your destruction. And now we have the woman who deserted you for Gunnar Moel. You should have no compunction in destroying her. Felicity, who do we have in Nigeria?'

'Several people, including one in Kano.' Felicity continued counting five-pound notes. 'But his function is observation, not field work. We have never considered Nigeria as a possible threat to British or Western security.'

'And you are apparently expected to use your real identity, Wilde. Yes, Miss Lieberstein's demise will have to be an accident. Take your time. She has invited you, and when you arrive she will not look for any other motive than self-interest on your part. You will assume the role of a retired British agent, unwillingly put out to grass with insufficient funds to continue the way of life to which, I am informed, you have become accustomed. Getting out of Nigeria after the completion of your mission must be your responsibility.'

'Yes,' Wilde said.

'And I think you should abandon any idea of driving across the Sahara. Even nowadays such a venture requires as much preparation as sailing a yacht across the Atlantic Ocean, and it also remains several times as dangerous. You will have to make sure that no one has any reason to arrest you, at least until you are safely back in this country.'

Felicity placed five neat bundles of notes on the coffee table. 'I'm afraid I did not complete my report on the events of this evening, Sir Gerald.'

'Indeed?'

'I have never seen Wilde work, but according to his file he takes top ranking in caution, speed and concentration. Tonight he not only opened a door without making sure just who was on the other side, but when he discovered his mistake, he froze.'

'A year on the beach, you know,' Wilde said.

'It was the hand, I presume. Dr. Malaine said the trouble with such an injury was far more likely to be psychological than actual. Felicity is suggesting that you are no longer capable of carrying out your duties.'

'Well,' Wilde said. 'As a matter of fact . . .'

'But if it is in your mind, the sooner we get you back to work the better. However, in these circumstances, and having regard to the identity of your target on this occasion . . .' Sir Gerald finished his sherry. 'I think it would be a good idea for you to accompany Wilde, Felicity. A certain amount of clean living might not do you any harm either.'

'Oh, can I, Sir Gerald? Oh, you darling man. I've always wanted to visit Africa.'

'You have just got to be joking,' Wilde said.

'I never joke, Wilde. It has occurred to me that such small success as attended your Russian mission was because you had a female assistant, however unsuspecting she may have been of your true purpose. And there can be no question that a man and a woman travelling together are far less suspicious. And, as you must have realized, Felicity is efficient. She will make sure that, ah, *nothing* goes wrong.' He put on his bowler hat, picked up his umbrella. 'I will leave you now to, ah, work out your *modus operandi*. And perhaps at some stage in the operation you may find an opportunity to wish Miss Lieberstein my fondest regards. Good night to you, Felicity.'

'There are just two little points,' Wilde said. 'Aimee Bosquet suggested there is a certain amount of preparatory indoctrination required before one is allowed near the sect itself. And then there's the bloke with the gun. Or, more important, the bloke who sent him.'

'Regarding the first point, I'm afraid you'll have to play it by ear. As for the dead man, I shall request Scotland Yard to hush up the unfortunate events of this evening, at least for a while. The gunman's employer will therefore presume that his man is still following Aimee Bosquet, waiting for her to carry out Frau Lieberstein's instructions. You will have to use Miss Bosquet's name as an introduction, of course, but this should not in itself cause suspicion as she would appear to have been a *bona fide* member of the sect.'

He closed the door behind him. Felicity looked at her watch. 'It's nearly five. I won't be able to do anything about our passages until nine. Would you care for some breakfast?'

'I am going home to bed,' Wilde said. 'And, darling, the bowler hat is quite wrong, you know. Lynn Langtree was like an albatross hung round my neck, and was almost entirely responsible for the endless trouble I encountered in Moscow. Besides, try to figure out Inger's reactions if I show up with an almost equally attractive blonde.'

'Jonas, I do love you, really. Especially for the word almost. But I'd really like to meet her. And in any event I couldn't possibly disobey Sir Gerald. He'd probably have me shot. You run along and change, and be at the B.O.A.C. Terminal Building by nine this evening. There's a flight at a quarter to eleven.'

'To hear is to obey, O mistress,' Wilde said, and caught a taxi to Kensington Square.

Mrs. Bettin was taking in the milk. 'My, how you do pop up, Mr. Wilde. Did you buy your boat?'

'It's being surveyed. I'm afraid I have to rush off again this evening, Mrs. B. My boss wants a prospective site surveyed. I'm catching a plane at eleven.'

'What an exciting life you lead. I wanted my nephew to be a surveyor, you know, and he said he wasn't going to spend his life working for some borough council. However did you get an appointment like yours?'

'I often wonder.' He cooked himself a breakfast of steak and mushrooms, packed a suitcase, went to bed. He was very tired. Besides, there was nothing to think about, at this moment; he had already come to a decision about his most pressing problem. He awoke at seven-thirty, scrambled an egg, showered and dressed, went along to the Terminal, found Felicity Hart in the bar, drinking vodka. She had discarded her sheepskin jacket for a check raincoat, wore a beret, and carried an overnight bag.

'For a while there I thought you weren't going to make it,' she remarked. 'I've checked us in. Here's your boarding card. I also changed half of your money into local currency.'

'Where are the tickets?'

She kissed him on the nose. 'In a safe place, darling. But of course you wouldn't dream of trying any funny business, would you?'

'Like Sir Gerald, I'm beginning to lose my sense of humour.' He ordered Bacardi. 'I feel I should point out that people who tag along with me usually wind up very dead.'

'I know. There was a girl called Julie Ridout, once. And then the poor commander, sent to get you back out of Moscow, and finishing up in Siberia. Do you think you're a gremlin, Jonas?'

'Every time. I keep brooding on the mess poor Sir Gerald is going to be in if we both disappear into the sunset. It could happen, you know.'

'And I keep thinking that maybe you have a death wish, especially where this white-haired bitch—sorry, I did mean witch —is concerned.'

'Your solicitude is reducing me to tears. I think we have just sufficient time to powder our respective noses before the coach is called.' He finished his drink. 'Coming?'

'I'm your nursemaid, remember?'

He went to the Men's, took a long time washing his hands while the room emptied. He stepped outside, found her waiting for him. Behind her the huge building bustled, but no one was interested in a stray couple. 'I want you to know, Filly,' he said, 'that I am touched by your remarkable devotion.'

'You say the sweetest things.' She leaned forward, and Wilde closed his right fist and allowed it to travel the three inches between their respective chins. 'Just testing.'

Felicity gave a gentle gasp, and her eyes closed. He held her tight, kissed her mouth and cursed silently while a party of young men went through the door behind him, was still kissing her when they re-emerged, whistling at the lovers.

Wilde turned round, so that he was between Felicity and the rest of the room, stepped through the door and into the first vacant loo. He sat her on the seat, decided against hitting her again, instead took off her coat and dress, gazed in surprise at a creamy white complexion, undisturbed by the slightest blemish, mark, or article of underclothing. It occurred to him that maybe he had been just a little hasty in judging by her exterior, but it was too late to change his mind now. A hasty flick through her bag found both their tickets; hers he tore into tiny pieces, flushed it and her boarding card. He replaced her on the seat, propped her against the wall, kissed her on the forehead. He tucked the coat and dress under his arm, stepped outside again. Flight 279 was just being called, but so was one to Sydney. He spotted a ground hostess wrestling with a carry-cot, joined the queue, smiled at the Australian baby.

'I wonder if you would tell me if I'm in the right place?' He produced his ticket and boarding card.

The hostess read, frowning, and Wilde deposited the rolled clothes at the foot of the cot. The baby blew a bubble.

'This is the Sydney flight,' the hostess pointed out. 'You're supposed to be at that gate over there.'

'Thank you ever so much. I felt there was something wrong.' Wilde hurried across the room. Behind him, someone in the Men's was shouting.

CHAPTER FOUR

WILDE AWOKE when the jet landed at Frankfurt a few minutes after midnight. Here all his fellow first-class passengers departed; apparently the end of May was not the ideal time for visiting Nigeria. But no sooner had he taken his seat again than the forward part of the aircraft was once more crowded, although only two people actually came on board. But to settle them required the combined efforts of both stewardesses, one of the stewards, several members of the ground staff, and at last the captain himself. Wilde put his pillow over his ears, got back to sleep just before the plane left the ground, awoke at four, to gaze through his window at a brilliant dawn.

Presumably they were over the Sahara by now. But however bright it was up here it was still dark down there. And he was awake. There was a nuisance. Wakefulness brought thoughts. Conscience? Hardly. He had always accepted that peace was a term relative only to war, that nations had always waited only the accretion of sufficient physical strength to browbeat their weaker neighbours. In the second half of the twentieth century, because most of the weaker neighbours had grouped themselves under one or other of the superpowers, the process of gaining an ascendency took longer than ever before. But it was continuing, day in and day out, physically and economically and morally. And in the course of fighting this unending secret war people had to die, as they would die in far greater numbers if the shooting ever again became general. So the business was best left to the professionals, who performed their duties quickly and efficiently, silently and unobtrusively, and as painlessly as possible. He was still a soldier after thirteen years.

Wilde's great value was that he could turn himself into a machine, fix his concentration upon a single objective, and keep going forward, no matter what was happening around him, until that objective was reached. This was the power that was, perhaps, failing. The power of hatred. Perhaps only young men are capable of true hatred. Old men are too tired, and in real terms Wilde was very old.

He looked at his fist. Hitting Felicity Hart had caused him no pain. But he had not been killing Felicity Hart. And but for her he would now be dead. He had had a mental blockage, and he had always known that his first such blockage would be his last, had almost welcomed the prospect. He lived by the law of the jungle; it was fitting that as soon as he lost his fangs he should himself be cut down. It made a sort of gruesome sense out of all that had gone before. Oh, damn Felicity Hart.

Was that the reason for disobeying an order? He could argue that going on an assignment with Felicity Hart would be like taking your wife to Brighton for the week-end. But that wasn't the reason, either; he had no doubt that should the going become rough she'd be worth every ounce of her weight. So the reason was Inger Lieberstein. But to think about Inger, to remember the three days they had spent together, alternately sating their mutual physical attraction and venting their psychological antipathy, was like breaking his hand all over again.

She had sent for him. To ask for his aid? Or to offer him employment? She had offered him employment once before and he had refused. She might well have reasoned that after a further three years of his ghastly existence, working for people who loathed him and did not even really trust him, who used him because there was nobody better at his peculiar profession, he might be ready for a change. And, as usual with Inger, she would not be very far wrong. Right or wrong, she had sent for him. Surely there was honour even amongst thieves. Oh, certainly, he thought bitterly. But not amongst assassins.

But surely Inger would also have changed, in her three years, and for the worse. She must have lost that veneer of beauty and confidence, utter contempt for humanity, ice-cold and computer-like mental processes which had made her at once deadly and irresistible, and become what she was in reality—a vicious, amoral animal. Surely. It was even possible that Aimee Bosquet *had* been nothing more than a bait, to suck him out of hibernation, to die with him by the gun of Inger's hireling. Except that the Inger he remembered would never waste her time carrying a personal feud to those lengths.

He raised his head. A woman was staring at him from farther down the aisle, on the other side. At least, he presumed she was a woman; she wore a yellow trouser suit. The face itself was sex-less, dominated by a massive chin and a long nose, and the black hair above was cropped like any schoolboy's. It was an ageless face in repose, but the utter weariness of the brain behind had been accumulated over too many years, showed in the fish-like stare from the dark eyes, the deep shadows under them, the tight lines which began by her nose and curved downwards past her mouth. Wilde frowned. It was a face he had seen often, and thus knew very well, without knowing it at all. It was a mental image on his retina, as was his own washbasin, his own alarm clock, his own reflection in the mirror, for that matter, something that was constantly seen but never actually committed to memory. Faces like that troubled him. There were too many out of his professional past which might at any moment reappear to haunt him.

The face sighed, and turned to look out of its window. He gazed at her profile instead. He had on occasion seen photographs of it, made up to look quite unusually handsome. But after an hour's uncomfortable sleep it merely looked bad-tempered.

He got up, went to the toilet, still couldn't be sure. And he had to be sure. He stood above her. 'Good morning,' he said. 'You wouldn't by any chance be Cynthia Boraine?'

She looked at him, closed her eyes.

'Ssssh!'

The man was lying on the next seat. He was extraordinarily small, scarcely five feet tall, and wore horn-rimmed spectacles. His hair was fair and cut short; he reminded Wilde of a koala bear.

'Can't you see she's trying to sleep?' he hissed. 'She's *very* tired.'

'Then I'll apologize.' Wilde retreated to his seat as the chief stewardess bustled through the curtain from the tourist cabin, gave them all bright smiles.

'Good morning, everyone. Time for breakfast. We'll be down in an hour.'

'Isn't that Cynthia Boraine?' Wilde whispered.

'Why, sir,' she whispered back, 'we never discuss our passengers.' She smiled. 'They say she's the wealthiest woman in the world.'

'And what caused all the trouble last night?'

'I know they say she doesn't drink, but last night she behaved as if she'd taken aboard all the gin in Frankfurt. Nothing on her breath, mind. Look!' She leaned across him. 'Isn't that tremendous?'

Wilde disentangled his nose. The sun was just beginning to reach the land beneath them, and there were no clouds. They were flying over the most lunar of landscapes, coloured an inhospitable light brick. To the far south there was a line of darkness, like a distant sea. But that would be forest.

'It gives me the creeps.' The stewardess poured coffee. 'In a sexy sort of way.'

'Like imagining coming down in it,' Wilde said. 'Where would Lake Chad be?'

She thumbed eastward. 'Maybe four hundred miles away. Mind you, it's not much to look at right now. This is the very end of the dry season, you know, and the lake is just one great big mudhole. But it could start to rain any day, and when it does watch out.'

(ii)

It occurred to Wilde that of all the sacrileges of which twentieth-century civilization was guilty, dumping an international airport within even five hundred miles of Kano was probably the most heinous. Certainly it was comparable with the best in Europe. His porter assured him that Kano handled some forty flights a day, and looking at the signpost outside the terminal building, with its impressive list of distances which culminated in New Zealand, he could well believe it. Yet it left him with a feeling of depression.

Perhaps it had something to do with P.C. Wren. John Geste's tragic wanderings across the Sahara had finally brought him here, as Lawrence and de Beaujolais had passed through it on their way to the coast and the mystery of the Blue Water. He expected the Americans, Hank and Buddy, to be standing outside the Customs hall, and he was disappointed at not being greeted by an escort of mail-clad lancers, their faces bound in flowing white robes. The robes, the all-enveloping *haik* of the desert Arab, were there, and for a very good reason. By the time Wilde reached his taxi, a pre-war Opel, the soughing wind had already driven a fine layer of red dust down his collar, and the city itself seemed to be shrouded in a driving, brick-coloured cloud.

'You have a hotel booking?' asked the driver, no Arab this, but clearly a Hausa, tall and aggressive, whose left hand seemed attached to his horn by an invisible wire.

'I wish to go to the house of a Mr. Chwarism. Do you know it? If not, I imagine we could do worse than follow that Mercedes.'

For Cynthia Boraine had been met, as if she were a queen, which he supposed she was, in her world of breakfast on Waikiki, lunch in San Francisco, tea in New York and a floor show in Montego Bay febrility. This morning she had donned a rope of pearls, each one of which could easily have paid her fare, and a pigeon's blood ruby solitaire on the index finger of her left hand which would probably have purchased the Comet itself.

The driver guffawed. 'Oh, yes, that is Mr. Chwarism's car. Oh, yes.'

'Then let's go, MacChaka.'

The driver's amusement bubbled over the steering wheel and out of the window to include various passersby. He allowed his horn to lead him through the Town of Strangers and under a low gateway into the city itself, scattered like a child's mud village around the founder's rock, where the red dust streets ended disturbingly in European give-way signs, and the crumpled walls, thick, dark, loopholed—or perhaps windowed—suggested a perpetually beleaguered city, and the bicycle-riding Fula, their magnificent robes always about to become entangled in their rear wheels, seemed to be outriders for the Saharan caravans which imagination suggested would at any moment appear over the northern horizon, and which—so Wilde's hastily read guide book assured him—still accounted for most of Kano's prosperity. Kano had to be romantic, but it was also unattractive and dirty, its drabness, relieved only by the white-walled and green-domed mosque, effortlessly beautiful in a way no Christian church has ever been able to approach, which reminded him that in Africa the Moslem world represented the future.

The Opel negotiated a succession of narrow streets, emerged into a square, stopped before a high, windowless red house, the front of which was pargeted in symmetrical black designs, while from the roof the dogs' ears gutters leaned forward like medieval sentries about to deliver a bucket load of boiling oil. Despite the early hours the square was packed with people, donkeys and dogs, and was supervised by two blue-clad policemen, their waists bound in wide red sashes, and red tassels hanging from their blue fezzes. The Mercedes had disappeared. The driver got out, banged on the door. 'Gentleman to see Mr. Chwarism,' he said into the darkness, and handed over Wilde's bag.

'Keep the change,' Wilde suggested. The entry hall, a gloomy, low-ceilinged cubby-hole lit by a single oil lamp, had a peculiar smell, and the woman who picked up his suitcase as easily as if it were an empty basket, was veiled.

'We were not expecting you,' she said in perfect English.

'It's a long story.'

The veil rippled. She could have smiled. Or she could have blown a raspberry. 'Then you must tell it to Mr. Chwarism.' She led him down a corridor, opened a door, 'You will wait in here, please.' She departed, still carrying his bag.

The room was small. There was a jalousied inner window, and through this Wilde looked into a courtyard, in the middle of which there grew a red-barked acacia, its yellow leaves drooping as they waited for the sun. He lit a cigarette, sat down on a lattice-work settee, got up again as the door opened.

"I am Chwarism.' He was, Wilde decided, a Tuareg, with a European paleness of skin. His mouth half-smiled constantly, and his eyes never rested for more than a second in any direction. His robe was deep red. 'You have come to see me, Malharbe says.'

'My name is Wilde.' Wilde held out his hand, and Chwarism hesitated for a moment before taking it, again as a European might. 'I wish to become a Follower of the Lord.'

Chwarism gestured to the settee, sat beside him. 'I do not understand you, Mr. Wilde.'

'Aimee sent me. Aimee Bosquet.'

Chwarism frowned. 'It is customary to write, to make arrangements.'

'Ah, well, you see.' Wilde assumed his most fruity voice. 'It all happened rather suddenly. I was at this place, the Dream Club in Soho, don't you know, and I got talking with Aimee. Saw quite a lot of her, I did, and at last she suggested that I should pay you a visit. I didn't take her seriously, at first, thought she was pulling my leg. But she did keep on about it, said it would do me a world of good to live rough for a while, don't you know, and all of a sudden. two nights back, I turned to her and I said, All right, my girl, I'm going. Well, as you just said, she wanted to write and make arrangements. But I like to do things right off, don't you know. No backsliding. So I told her, It's either now or it's never. So she said just to use her name. So here I am, what?'

He gazed at Chwarism while he spoke; presumably anyone he met from here on could have sent the young man after Aimee. But Chwarism stroked his chin and looked definitely sorry for any man who could be such a bloody fool.

'Aimee Bosquet does work at the Dream Club in London, certainly. She has already sent us more than one client from there. But I'm afraid, Mr. Wilde, that the Followers cannot be joined on the . . . How do you say in England? The spur of the moment, eh? Nor can such a step be undertaken lightly. For one thing, there is the expense . . .'

'One thousand pounds in cash,' Wilde took the money from his jacket pocket.

Chwarism turned the bundle over, riffled the notes. 'I see you are indeed a man of decision, Mr. Wilde.'

'Aimee did say that if I didn't like it I got my money back.'

'Oh, yes, of course, Mr. Wilde. But a man like you, oh you are most certainly the sort from whom we select the Followers of the Lord. You have my word on that. But as to the refund, you understand that there are certain expenses which we are forced to accept from the very moment you set foot in my house.'

'Just so long as the whole bundle doesn't go up in smoke the first day, don't you know?'

'Well, then, Mr. Wilde, you must come and meet Miss Boraine, the lady who arrived just before you? Or perhaps you have already met her. She is travelling with a Mr. Loman.'

'I saw them on the plane.'

'Of course you did. Miss Boraine is a most charming lady.' Chwarism's tone was doubtful. He led Wilde across the hall and into another room, considerably larger than the waiting-room, but also looking on to the centre courtyard. Here there were no chairs, but several rugs on one of which sat Cynthia Boraine, while her spectacled friend occupied another. They were drinking the local coffee, which was brewing on a table in the corner, and which Wilde now discovered accounted for the scent pervading the house. The only other furniture was a roll-top desk.

'There's the man again!' Loman exclaimed. 'Cynthia, do you think he's following us?'

Cynthia Boraine glanced at Wilde. 'Are you following me?' Her voice was curiously brittle.

'My dear lady, I could ask the same thing of you.'

'He's a reporter,' Loman declared. 'He has to be a reporter. Some snake in the grass blabbed.'

'A reporter!' Miss Boraine stood up. She was very nearly as tall as Wilde.

'I'm not, you know. My name is Wilde, Jonas Wilde.' Wilde held out his hand 'I've read a great deal about you, Miss Boraine.'

'A reporter,' Cynthia Boraine said again, and dropped her coffee cup. Carefully she trod on it, ground it into the rug, then, without hurrying she turned to Loman. He handed her his cup without a word, and it also became part of the rug. Miss Boraine then crossed the room, placed her foot against the table, pushed it over, and kicked the coffee pot against the wall. Black liquid oozed across the floor.

Cynthia Boraine selected a so far untarnished rug, sat down again. 'Now get him out of here.'

Wilde and Chwarism gazed at each other, and then both looked at Loman, who was mopping his brow with a green and white handkerchief.

'I didn't really want any coffee, anyway,' Wilde said.

Chwarism stroked his chin. 'Are you a reporter, Mr. Wilde?'

'Good lord, no.'

'Because you understand that the privacy of our guests is very important to us.'

'I'm trying to rid my mind of, ah, centuries of superstition and doubt, don't you know. Just like Miss Boraine. Of course I know who she is. I've seen her photograph in the newspapers. But I've never met her before this morning.'

'If you're not a reporter,' Cynthia Boraine said, 'I apologize. Pay for the crockery, Conrad.'

'I'm sure Mr. Chwarism will put it on the bill,' Loman said. 'Miss Boraine has been under a great strain since her last divorce,' he explained.

'And I didn't come several thousand miles to sit around a . . .' she wrinkled her magnificent nose. 'A room smelling of sub-standard coffee.'

'Of course not, Miss Boraine,' Chwarism said. 'But there are certain formalities to be gone through. First, I must ask you to give me your valuables.'

'Why?'

Chwarism opened the desk, took out a printed sheet of paper, carefully dipped a straight pen into a bottle of purple ink. 'I will give you one of our official receipts. Let me see, one pearl necklace, and one ruby ring. Will there be anything else?'

'Miss Boraine didn't come all this way to hand over her jewellery, either,' Loman said.

'Miss Boraine has come to Africa to be saved from herself.' Chwarism spoke in a hushed tone. 'She will leave Nigeria a new woman, a woman whom the misfortunes of the world, the attacks of unthinking critics, the advance of age, whom nothing will be able to affect. She will shine like a star amongst her friends, glitter like the sun amongst her enemies. Life will have taken on a new meaning, a new purpose, and she will find all she needs there in her heart.'

'If I believed you,' Cynthia Boraine said, 'I'd *give* you the damned pearls.'

'Whereas all I am asking is for you to deposit them, here in my safe, to be reclaimed when you leave Kano again. In the Centre of the Universe there can be no such thing as jewellery, or privilege, except within the ranks of the Followers, and you understand that you will be commencing as a novitiate.'

'I think . .' Lomas began.

'Well, don't.' Cynthia Boraine removed her pearls and her ring. 'We decided to give it a whirl, Conrad. So we'll give it a whirl.'

'You are indeed a woman of wisdom, Miss Boraine,' Chwarism said. 'Have you anything else? Mr. Loman? Mr. Wilde?'

They gave him their watches, received receipts.

'Now. I have here some medicine for each of you.' Chwarism unscrewed a bottle, took out three large yellow capsules. 'It is to protect you against malaria, you understand.'

'I thought there was no such thing nowadays,' Cynthia Boraine said.

'It is virtually extinct in Kano, certainly. But in Chad, who can say. It is for your own protection, Miss Boraine.' He clapped his hands, and the veiled woman entered, carrying a tray with three glasses of water. 'If you would take them now, please.'

They obeyed. 'Ugh!' Cynthia Boraine said. 'You're sure you don't just mean to poison us.'

Chwarism smiled. 'Now you must change your clothes. You have brought suitable things for the bush? Good. Malharbe will show you to your rooms.'

The woman led them up a gloomy staircase, opened the first door on her left. 'You will change in here, Mr. Wilde. There is no hurry; you do not leave Kano for an hour.'

Wilde entered a small, windowless room, strongly suggestive of an oven, and lit by a smoky oil lamp. There was a table, on which waited his suitcase, and a straight chair, but no bed, although there was a blanket on the floor. It occurred to him it was possible to carry the pursuit of simplicity a shade too far; the quinine still filled his mouth. He sighed, closed the door, and discovered that he was not alone.

(iii)

The small figure had been waiting behind the door, totally concealed in a white *haik*, the upper fold of which was wrapped round her head and face.

'Welcome,' Wilde said. 'I had a feeling everything was proceeding in an altogether too orderly fashion.'

She unwound her head-dress, revealed a mass of glossy black hair, falling straight on either side of a brown-yellow face, with features so delicately rounded he felt that to touch her would be to lose her. Like most Arab women she looked older than her actual age, which he thought might be sixteen.

'I am Serene,' she whispered.

'That would be disappointing. I'm Wilde.'

'That I know. Inger sent me.'

'I think she made a mistake.' Wilde opened his case. 'Do you mind if I change?'

'I should like it.'

She was immediately behind him now, exuding a scent which he could not place, but which was as nostril clogging as the dust on the street, although a great deal more pleasant. He turned, and she put both arms round his neck. She did not so much kiss his mouth as possess it. Her tongue drove all the way back to his throat, and she seemed to project her saliva, almost as if exchanging it for his. His hands closing on her shoulder blades, slipped all the way down to her thighs on the rough woollen cloth, only halted when the convex became concave.

'Is this included in my initiation fee?'

'Do I please you? Inger said that I would please you.'

'I have no doubt at all that you're going to please me, darling. But right now I have to catch Chwarism's transport.'

'You do not trust me.'

'Once upon a time Inger would have been keen on pleasing me herself.'

Serene smiled. When she smiled the mask of childlike softness dissolved and became instead a mosaic of passions. He thought that if she ever did get around to pleasing him he would not forget the experience. But he also thought she would smile when her enemies died. And if she was a friend of Inger's she would know about death. Her colour was maroon. 'Inger is old now.'

'Is that a fact.' Wilde folded his suit, put on khaki slacks and a bush shirt.

'You do not believe she sent me?'

Wilde decided to try a shock tactic of his own. 'I believe you, sweetheart. Do you know a girl called Aimee Bosquet?'

'Aimee is my friend. She was to tell you about the Followers of the Lord.'

'She mentioned them. And Inger, of course. Which is why I'm here. But she didn't have time to say much else. She was shot by a countryman of hers. Right there.' He prodded her gently in the navel.

Serene made a round O with her mouth. 'But you?'

'His brief was the both of us. Which is why he waited until we were together. But he didn't quite make it.'

Serene looked delighted. 'You killed him. Yes. With your hands. That is what Inger said, that you will use your hands.'

Wilde closed the suitcase, sat on the table. 'So you tell me what Aimee didn't.'

'I cannot tell you about the man who tried to kill you. But Inger will know.'

'So tell me about Inger.'

'She needs you, Mr. Wilde. She has work for you to do. Work which only you can do. She will be so happy that you have come.' She smiled at him. 'We shall see much more of each other in the Centre of the Universe.' She opened the door, glanced into the corridor, and disappeared.

(iv)

Wilde attempted to analyze exactly what had just happened. So Inger *was* offering employment. His memory took him back to a bedroom in Stockholm. On the bed lay a man with the upper half of his head missing, and beside him stood Inger, a smoking pistol in her hand. She had never needed anyone just to kill for her. And on the face of it, his recent visitation, however charming, seemed utterly pointless. But Inger had never made a pointless gesture in her whole life. He felt like a cigarette, retrieved his case and lighter from his jacket pocket, was frowned at from the doorway by Mr. Chwarism.

'Oh, no, no, Mr. Wilde. Of all civilization's vices, tobacco is perhaps the most odious. Come, my car is waiting.'

'Next thing you'll be telling me there's no liquor in this universal centre of yours.'

'But of course there is liquid, Mr. Wilde. Water, the staff of life.'

'I'll have to settle for the dancing girls.' Wilde put on dark glasses, followed him downstairs and on to the street. The girl Serene was already sitting in the front of the Mercedes; she did not look round. A moment later Cynthia Boraine and Conrad Loman arrived. Like Wilde, they had changed into khaki bush shirts and slacks, to which Miss Boraine had added a white silk headscarf.

She glanced at Wilde, got into the back seat. Loman hesitated. 'You won't say anything to upset her, Wilde,' he whispered, and sat beside her. Wilde squeezed in. Malharbe stared at them from the doorway; a crowd of assorted races stared at them from the street. Chwarism himself took the wheel, and following the prevailing custom of driving behind his horn, soon had them out of town and back at the airport, where a six-seater Bell helicopter waited.

'That must have set the Followers of the Lord back a shilling or two,' Wilde remarked.

'The Lord lacks for nothing, Mr. Wilde. Why should he? Can I assist you, Miss Boraine?'

Cynthia Boraine ignored him, climbed the step, peered into the cabin. 'That!' she said. 'Move it.'

'Ah, this is a poor old beggar who has requested assistance in reaching his home. I could not refuse him. I do beg you to be generous, Miss Boraine.'

Loman mopped his brow with the green and white handkerchief, looked apprehensively at Wilde. But surprisingly, Cynthia Boraine seemed to have momentarily exhausted her temper. 'He can sit at the back.'

'But of course, my child,' agreed the old man, who, judging by the length of white beard which escaped his *haik,* was certainly very old.

'I didn't know he spoke English.'

'Do not let it concern you, Miss Boraine,' Chwarism said. 'He will not take offence; it is against his religion.' He gave Serene a hand up; she went to the rear of the cabin, sat beside the old man.

'Now in you get, gentlemen,' Chwarism said. 'And I will wish you a pleasant journey.'

'You mean you're not coming with us?' Wilde asked.

'My duties keep me in Kano. But you will be well taken care of. The pilot is very good.' He slammed the doors, and within seconds they were whirring high above the city, from the air even more suggestive of something created by an imaginative child at low water.

'Now this is a bit more civilized.' Loman polished his glasses. 'Don't you think so, Cynthia? I really thought we were going to be stuck in one of these local trains from now until next week.'

'Shut up.' Cynthia Boraine closed her eyes. Wilde brooded at the empty, dustswept landscape beneath them. The country was hypnotic. For a while they followed a railway track, bearing east over a brick red plain, undulating as they reached it, although from a distance it gave the impression of being flat. There were tracks, but no surfaced roads, and there were scattered trees and a great deal of scrub, interspersed with enormous ant hills, constructed like miniature forts, and, he calculated, several feet in height. There was little water to be seen, and almost as few people, except for the occasional tiny village, each with its small herd of cattle which even from the air could be described as scrawny. But soon these dwindling evidences of humanity disappeared, and they flew over semi-desert, in which the lonely acacia represented vegetation, and the red dust rolled beneath them like a blood-coloured sea.

And as the morning advanced, so the temperature increased. They were flying at not much more than five hundred feet, Wilde estimated, and seemed to be roasted between the burning sun and the scorching scrub below. Loman produced his green and white handkerchief and mopped sweat, and suddenly his mistress awoke with a start, tore the scarf from her head. 'God! God! God! I can't stand it. You!' She turned round to look at Serene, who remained sitting absolutely still, as she had done since their journey began, huddled beneath her *haik*. 'What do you do to get cool? You!'

Serene made no reply. Her eyes were open, but she might have been asleep.

'Give her a shake, Conrad,' Cynthia Boraine instructed.

'Yes, Cynthia.' Loman unfastened his seat-belt.

'You are going to seek the Lord?'

The words were so unexpected that all three of them stared at the old man with their mouths open.

'Isn't he supposed to address you as memsahib?' Loman whispered.

'I don't think he means to,' Wilde said. 'Yes. We are looking for the Lord.'

'The Lord is good.'

'He'd better be,' Cynthia Boraine said.

'He will make a new woman of you, my child.'

'I've heard that one already.'

'He will say, You must give your innermost thoughts to me. Release your mind. Tell me what you dream of when you awake in the small hours of the morning. in the warmth of your bath, at the moment of orgasm.'

'Now look here,' Loman said. 'No nig-nog's going to be rude to Cynthia Boraine.'

'It is you I am addressing, Miss Boraine,' said the old man. 'Tell me, what has disgusted you with life?'

Cynthia Boraine raised her head. Her cheeks began to fill with blood.

'If you throw a temper tantrum here you will doubtless kill us all. That cannot be your objective, and you know as well as I that your famous outbursts are usually deliberate, induced by a childish desire to be the centre of interest. But why are you ashamed to speak about your problems? To admit them, even? Is this not why you are here? And are your problems not known to everyone? You are Cynthia Boraine. Your father died and left you a fortune, and nothing else. So you have devoted your life to an inconsequential search for pleasure, and in your civilization the ultimate pleasure is presumed to be found in sexual excitement. So you have spent a lifetime searching for that magic elixir, that moment of ecstasy which will transcend all others, through eight husbands, and uncountable lovers, until at last you understand that such a moment is unobtainable, and so you find yourself going mad, because now nothing any longer gives you the slightest pleasure.

'But why be ashamed of having lived such a life? At least it was part of a scheme for living. which so few people ever achieve, and now that you have decided to put it behind you, it should be possible for you to look back on it with no emotion greater than interest. Miss Boraine, I tell you there can be no such thing as shame in the intelligent human being. To be ashamed presupposes that one is worse than one's fellows, and this is impossible. For we are all foul in the sight of heaven.'

Cynthia Boraine stared at him. The colour had drained from her facc. 'I don't discuss my personal affairs in public,' she said. 'I'm tired. So tired. I was told I could rest in this Centre of the Universe place. That's all I want, a rest.'

'The Lord will do better than give you a rest, my child. He will rejuvenate you, make a new woman of you. Because so much of your trouble is compounded by your age. Ah, yes, forty-five is a difficult age for a woman, but not for the Lord.'

'Forty-five?' Cynthia Boraine's cheek's reddened again.

'That is the best of all ages to be. Old enough to have ceased behaving like a fool, young enough to know a great happiness in your later years. But to accomplish that, it is necessary for you to give your mind into the Lord's keeping, to confess to him your innermost thoughts, to become as putty in his hands.'

'Go back to sleep,' Cynthia Boraine suggested. 'Conrad, I'm likely to be putty in anybody's hands if I don't get something to eat.'

'I'll see if I can find our cases, shall I?' Loman asked 'I've some chocolate.'

'Your cases are in Kano, Mr. Loman,' said the old man.

'In Kano?'

'Now you mention it, I didn't see anyone putting them on board,' Wilde agreed.

'You will have no need for them in the Centre of the Universe. And as for food, it will be there when you land. For what is a few hours' hunger?'

Cynthia Boraine's face was a glowing crimson ball. 'Let's get this straight. You mean that Chwarism character forgot our luggage?'

'Not forgot, Miss Boraine. He never sends the suitcases.'

'But what about our clothes? How long do we spend in this Centre of the Universe?'

'Who knows, Miss Boraine? It may be weeks, it may be months.'

'*Months? With no change of clothing?*'

'The Lord will provide, Miss Boraine. And what are clothes? Will it rain? Then the bare skin is best. Will it be cold? Then a blanket will suffice. Will the wind blow? Then you will shelter. Do you think it necessary to conceal your nakedness? Then there is no better garment than the *haik*. Now come, I have some sweetmeats here which will allay your hunger.' He produced a round box, opened it, held it out.

'It looks like Turkish Delight,' Loman said.

'That it is not. But you will certainly find it delightful. And I should be honoured were you to partake with me. See?' He placed one of the soft sweets in his mouth.

'They do look rather good.' Cynthia Boraine tasted one.

'Yes, indeed,' Loman said.

'And you, Mr. Wilde?' invited the old man.

Only Serene's eyes were visible, staring at him from above the fold of her robe. He took one of the sweets. It had a most distinctive flavour, vaguely reminiscent of marzipan. 'Very nice.'

'I knew you would appreciate it, Mr. Wilde. And you, my child?'

Serene accepted one of the sweets.

'Now we shall all feel better,' the old man said. 'Tell me, Miss Boraine, you have heard of *borbor*?'

'No.'

'It has several ingredients, but the main component is the juice of the plant you would know as *caloptropis procera*. A white liquid, extracted from the bark. Do you know, Mr. Wilde, it is used by the women of the desert to destroy their enemies?'

'Eh?' Loman swallowed.

'Oh, yes, indeed, Mr. Loman. A single drop of undiluted *borbor* in the eye, for instance, will blind a man instantly. Or a woman, of course. Taken internally, the liquid consumes the brain, takes away the will, makes the subject a mindless lump of clay.'

'Oh, my God,' Cynthia Boraine said. 'I've eaten it.'

'There is nothing for you to be afraid of, Miss Boraine. The mixture you are digesting will do you no permanent harm; it has been carefully prepared. And the Lord needs your brain, in order to reshape it into a proper appreciation of what life is about. He will restore it to you in due course, you may be sure of that. No doubt it is already having a soothing effect upon you, removing your fears, your ingrained suspicions, making you more willing to trust me, to confide in me, to surrender yourself to me.'

Wilde realized he was right. He seemed to have no weight above the neck. Desperately he tried to get up, but really it no longer seemed very important. With a gigantic effort he fought the swirling clouds which rose from the base of his brain, gazed into the smiling eyes which gloomed at him. He summoned all his strength, leaned across the seat, seized the old man's beard, and tugged.

'Now, Mr. Wilde,' said the old man. 'Why did you do that?'

Wilde's mouth moved slowly, opened and closed with an enormous reluctance, and his tongue seemed filled with lead. 'I wished to look upon the face of the Lord,' he said.

CHAPTER FIVE

UKUBA SMILED. As Wilde had guessed, his beard was false, but he was certainly old enough to have owned one of that length and colour. His skin was pale, his forehead high. He had a large, straight nose, separating two enormous dark eyes. His face was a mass of lines, and the flesh sagged away from his cheekbones, but the eyes were alert and amused.

'You are strong-willed, and perceptive, Mr. Wilde. Yes, I am the Lord.'

'You wouldn't consider the use of the name just a little blasphemous? Whether you call Him Allah, or Jehovah, or God.'

'I do not ape the Creator, Mr. Wilde. The word lord means one who has power and authority. I have power and authority. I like it best in its Latin form, *dominus*, from which we can deduce that a lord dominates those around him. I dominate those around me, Mr. Wilde.'

'I didn't mean to be rude, Mr. Ukuba.' Cynthia Boraine's face was unusually soft. 'I didn't know who you were. I hope I didn't hurt your feelings.'

'Now, Miss Boraine, how could you possibly hurt my feelings? Do the thoughts of the ant, crawling over the floor at your feet, ever trouble you? Now tell me the most secret of your desires. Take me down into the very bottom of your mind.'

Cynthia Boraine smiled. 'Crowds,' she murmured thoughtfully. 'Lots and lots of young people, all reaching for me, tearing pieces off my clothing. Crowds. Horrible, lovely people. Crowds.'

'Was that not easy to confess, Miss Boraine? And your wish shall be granted, you may be sure of that. And then, perhaps, we shall be able to plunge ever deeper into your subconscious. Mr. Loman?'

'Trains,' Loman said. 'Trains, rushing over the tracks, at a hundred, a thousand miles an hour. Tons and tons of metal under my hand, Toot-toot. Up and down.'

'Truly Miss Boraine, you have made a strange choice of a travelling companion. And now you, Mr. Wilde. What about you?'

Wilde stared into Serene's eyes as waves of drowsy relaxation spread through his system. He was aware of anger, that he had been tricked, but clouding his judgement was the pervading sense of irresponsibility, which made his job no less than his personality seem irrelevant, summoned up instead black shapes from the depths of his subconscious. To think, to compose ideas, to turn ideas into words and make the words say what he needed, required all of his willpower. And yet his goal remained poised in front of him, and because of his anger its attainment became essential.

'Girls,' he said drowsily. 'A girl. The most beautiful girl in the world. All alone. An island. Palms. Water. Just her and me.'

'Really, Mr. Wilde, your normalcy is almost as frightening as Mr. Loman's childishness. Is that your most passionate desire?'

'Must be alone,' Wilde muttered. 'Her and me. Nobody else.'

'What would such a romantic idyll be like, with more than two people? But tell me, Mr. Wilde, your idea of beauty, would it be fair, or dark?'

'I like them fair. The blonder the better.' He gazed into Serene's midnight eyes.

'Then you shall have your desire, Mr. Wilde. The most beautiful blonde woman in the world. But perhaps you would also be kind enough to tell me something of yourself. Miss Boraine I know. Mr. Loman is acceptable as her secretary. But you are a man of mystery, arriving in Kano unheralded, uninvited, even. You say Aimee Bosquet is sponsoring you?'

Think, Wilde begged himself. Think. This man has virtually founded a religion, which has attracted some pretty unusual people. Therefore he must possess the arts of the politician as well as the emotional appeal of the fanatic. The question gave no hint that Ukuba might expect Aimee by now to be dead. But *someone* in the Centre of the Universe must be wondering if the gunman had been successful.

'Met her in the Dream Club,' he muttered. 'Go there often.'

'And when you are not in the Dream Club? What do you do then?'

Wilde shrugged. 'Private income. Rich uncle, don't you know.'

'His name?' This time the question was sharp.

'Gerald,' Wilde replied as quickly. 'Uncle Gerald. Pays me just to keep out of trouble.' He grinned. 'Good old Uncle Gerald.'

'Indeed, he must be,' Ukuba agreed. 'Now, we shall be flying for some time yet. Why do we not all try to get some sleep?'

Wilde closed his eyes. To keep them open longer was impossible, to keep his brain working doubly so. To rest, to sleep, was all he desired. Perhaps this too was part of the *borbor*. Beside him, Loman snored, and Cynthia Boraine gave little puppy-like grunts of contentment. And behind them the Lord smiled, at peace with himself and the world, never glancing at the girl beside him, and then seemed to leave his seat and enter their minds, so that the image of Inger and Wilde, so close, so intertwined, was separated by the elderly, smiling face, and it occurred to Wilde, deep in the depths of his dream, that Inger was going to be the least of his problems.

And then he was awake, his mind clear, and more free from tension and anxiety than at any time in the previous thirteen years. Still the rotor blades whirred overhead, but the sun had now passed its zenith and they had flown out of the semi-desert into what appeared to be a vast swamp, in which enormous reed beds were interspersed with long rivers of mud and slime, and only occasional patches of water.

'What a ghastly mess.' Cynthia Boraine had also woken up. The very last of her hostility had disappeared.

'This is Chad,' said Ukuba.

'This is a lake?'

'The fourteenth largest lake in the world. At its fullest extent it covers an area of approximately eight thousand square miles. Think of that, Miss Boraine.'

'And all of it is swamp?' Wilde asked.

'There are large open areas towards the centre. You see it now at its lowest, because we are at the end of the dry season. Any day now the weather will break, and in four months' time, perhaps before you are ready to leave us and resume your place in the world, Miss Boraine, the level will have risen by twenty feet or more. Then you will be flying over water, even now. Mind you, it is true to say that the lake is shrinking. A century ago there were great cities on the banks of Chad. Now they are huddled heaps of ruins, the nearest water five and ten miles away. Even Maidugari, which is the capital city of the province of Bornu—it is some distance to the south of us, now—used to be close to the lake. It is the desiccation, Mr. Wilde. But then, once upon a time, as I'm sure you know, all of North Africa was fertile beyond imagination, and indeed, perhaps from Kano to the Tibesti mountains on the borders of the Soudan, was one vast inland sea. There are beautiful lakes at the foot of the Tibesti, Mr. Wilde, their waters a kaleidoscope of colours because of the salts and minerals they contain. But they too are shrinking.

'What caused such a change? What causes it to go on changing? Because it is doing that, you know, Mr. Wilde, turning Nigeria and Chad and other countries in this region into desert. Was it a climatic upheaval? Or was it endless aeons of man himself, chopping down his trees for firewood, turning the good earth into sand by his abominable cultivations? One could envisage the dustbowl of the United States becoming a similar Sahara were the Americans not wealthy enough and technologically advanced enough to keep the water flowing. But, for all their efforts, the world is drying out. Is that not a terrifying thought, Miss Boraine? This vast ball, which the scientists tell us contains more water than land, has been drying since time began, and has at last been overtaken by man's wastefulness.

'If we were to draw a graph, one line, declining very, very slowly from left to right across our paper, would represent the level of usable water in the world, the other, rising so steeply in recent times as to be almost perpendicular, would represent our requirements, based not only upon the explosion of the population but also upon the fantastic liquid consumption of this so-called civilization of ours, which demands at once a cleanliness natural to no other animal species and at the same time bases all its industry upon water power of one kind and another. Man is literally sucking his planet dry, Mr. Wilde, and, alas, he has not yet ascertained whether there is any other suitably wet planet within his easy reach. I look forward, perhaps ten thousand, perhaps only a thousand years, to when the Atlantic itself will look like Chad in the dry season.'

'You're a cheerful soul, Mr. Ukuba,' Cynthia Boraine said.

'I'm starving,' Loman remarked. 'Do you know when last we ate, Ukuba? Six o'clock this morning, on the plane.'

'We shall soon be at my home, and there you shall eat your fill, I do promise you.'

Wilde gazed down at the interminable morass. There were no causeways, no roads, nothing to suggest that any human being lived down there, or, indeed, had ever set foot in it. Nothing to indicate how, having completed his mission, he was going to regain Kano; piloting helicopters had not been included in his training. How simple it all seemed in a London flat. Hop a jet, find a girl, wait for the right moment and make sure she falls from an upstairs window, leave again. He wondered if Sir Gerald really thought of it like that, really thought of his executioner as some sort of indestructible machine. No, that was wrong; Sir Gerald did not care whether his machine was indestructible or not. No doubt a successor was already in training.

Ukuba was gazing at him. It occurred to him that even mind-reading might not be beyond this unusual old man. He wondered how long it took for the effects of the *borbor* to wear off. 'Why did you choose to make your home in such a wilderness?' he asked.

'I live there now because it gives me, and my guests, the in-estimable boon of complete privacy, Mr. Wilde. But in the beginning my family was forced to it. We have lived in Chad for a very long time. How old would you say I am?'

'Eighty?'

Ukuba smiled. 'You do me a slight injustice, although you are close. But yet when I was a boy, Mr. Wilde, this country was the kingdom of Bornu. At its greatest it dominated West Africa. By the time I was born it was already in decline, beset by the slave general Rabah. You have heard of him?'

'Some.'

'He marched west from Egypt, Mr. Wilde, in 1880. My family looked upon him as a saviour. For I, and Serene here, am decended from the first of all Ukubas, Mr. Wilde, in a direct line. Did you know that Serene is my great-grand-daughter?'

'She never told me,' Wilde murmured. The certainty that he had jumped with both feet into a monumental mess clung to him like the Kano dust, and yet did not seem important beneath the influence of the drug.

'So who *was* the first Ukuba?' Cynthia Boraine asked.

'Ukuba commanded the first Fula armies ever to march into West Africa, Miss Boraine. More than a thousand years ago. You could say that we were the Normans of Nigeria, Mr. Wilde and in that context I trace my ancestry back to the Conqueror him-self. But, alas, the Fula never really established themselves in Bornu. We did not conquer it until the turn of the nineteenth century of the Christian Era, only to be in turn driven out by the Faki, Mohammed el-Amin el-Kanemi. My family fled to the remoteness of Chad, to preserve the purity of our blood no less than our independence. And then came Rabah with his regiment, three thousand of the best fighting men in the world, fleeing the fall of his leader, Zobcir Pasha. In thirteen years he fought his way across Africa. A prodigious feat of arms, Mr. Wilde. He would have made Pizarro seem insignificant, but for one thing. Pizarro was conquering a world which would not match his technology. Rabah fled from the monstrous effects of a superior technology, only to find that same technology waiting for him. Fifty years earlier he would have been a name to conjure with, like Chaka the Zulu, or Lobengula, or our own Idris. Instead he met the Germans, pushing up through the Cameroons, and the French, pushing south through the Sahara, and behind them were already the British, spreading north from the coast.'

'He was a bit of a blighter,' Wilde said, 'according to the history books.'

'He saved my family, Mr. Wilde, although certainly he was a dark and cruel man. Alas, when he was cut down by French bullets we again had to flee to Chad. But by then we had money, and so my father decided that if I was ever going to amount to anything I must adopt the ways of the white man. What is it your classical desert chieftain never omits, Mr. Wilde? His three years at Oxford. Oh, yes, my father was very classical, although he himself had never left Bornu. He sent me to England, to study under a tutor, with Balliol as my destination. But that was the summer of 1914, and I was overtaken by events and also by a certain innate romanticism. I received my education in the manners and morals of the European at Loos, and thereafter, Mr. Wilde.' He turned to the window, pointed down. 'The Centre of the Universe.'

(ii)

Out of the reed forest there had appeared several islands, denoted by thick clumps of trees, and they were now approaching the largest of these, on which there was a small wood; beyond was a pasture dotted with cattle, then several acres of cultivated land, and at last, close to where the reed beds started again, a large cleared area containing a village of grass huts.

'My God!' Cynthia Boraine said. 'I thought the chopper meant things were looking up.'

'The helicopter is necessary because there is no other quick way in or out of the Centre of the Universe, at least in the dry season,' Ukuba said. 'During the rains it is possible to make the journey to the mainland by boat, but even then what have you accomplished? It is two hundred miles to Ngura, and the nearest railhead. You will observe, Mr. Wilde, that while I detest everything about the twentieth century, or the nineteenth, for that matter, I have no intention of being left behind by the more obviously useful aspects of its technology. Unlike Rabah. Now we must prepare to land. Will you refasten your seat-belts.'

The helicopter settled, the blades ceased whirling, and a vast silence drifted through the cabin, ending, when the door was opened, in the whistle of the wind, twice as strong as in Kano, scything through the reeds, floating red sand particles endlessly across the island.

'The *harmattan*,' Ukuba said. 'It is with us always, until the rains start. But you will get used to it.'

A European face appeared in the doorway. The owner was a muscular young man, with a complexion the colour of the dust and wearing a khaki bush tunic over khaki shorts, khaki stockings, and a bush hat. He had pushed his goggles up on his forehead, and smiled at them with blue eyes. 'Let me give you a hand, Miss Boraine.'

'My pilot, Captain Anderson,' Ukuba said.

'South African?'

'Rhodesian, Mr. Wilde. Several of his countrymen visited Nigeria during the recent troubles in the south, to fly the planes, you see. Some of them stayed. But you are a man of insatiable curiosity.'

Wilde followed Cynthia Boraine and Loman to the ground, turned his back on the stinging, scorching wind. 'A thousand pounds is a lot of money to me, Ukuba. I feel I've quite an investment in this scheme of yours.'

The prophet smiled. 'Scheme? What a strange way of putting it.' He turned away from the helicopter, raised his arms. 'The Lord is good.'

From the huts, and the wood, had come perhaps forty people, who now knelt and touched their foreheads in the dust. It was impossible to decide either their sexes or their nationalities, as they were all dressed like Ukuba and Serene, in rough white tunics and trousers, over which flowed their *haiks*. And despite the heat, which Wilde estimated as close to one hundred degrees Fahrenheit, the universal material was wool. He was aware of a feeling akin to acute indigestion; Inger could now be within a few feet of him.

'Friends of yours?' Cynthia Boraine inquired.

'These are the Inner Court of the Followers of the Lord,' Ukuba said. 'Most of them, at any rate. We have several novitiates already in residence.' He clapped his hands, and the head raised. 'Zobeir!' One of the tallest of the Followers stood up and came towards them. Like his leader, he was beardless, thus aggressively declaring that he no longer accepted the Moslem faith. In other respects he was entirely Egyptian, with a large, slightly hooked nose and glooming eyes, and a spare physique. 'You may remember that Rabah's leader under the Mahdi, and, indeed, his foster father, was Zobeir Pasha,' Ukuba said. 'The first Zobeir was the most infamous slave trader of all history, Mr. Wilde. Far more beastly than your own John Hawkins. My Zobeir is a descendant of his. He is my assistant, my right-hand man.'

Zobeir bowed. 'Welcome to the Centre of the Universe.'

'It's our pleasure. I hope,' Cynthia Boraine said.

Wilde watched the Followers of the Lord fade away, back to the wood, to the field, to their huts. He wondered if they had any weapons? But why should they? This was obviously nothing more than a gigantic swindle, so far as he could see. But Aimee Bosquet was dead.

'This is Miss Cynthia Boraine,' Ukuba was telling Zobeir. 'And her secretary, Mr. Conrad Loman. You will remember, Zobeir, that we were expecting them.'

'Oh, yes, indeed, my Lord. And this gentleman?'

'This is a Mr. Jonas Wilde, Zobeir. He arrived unexpectedly. It seems that he has been sent to us by Aimee Bosquet.'

Wilde cursed the *borbor*, silently; he could not make up his mind if Zobeir's eyes had flickered.

'You mentioned something about food when we landed,' Loman said.

'Zobeir will see to your wants,' Ukuba said.

'You don't eat?' Cynthia Boraine demanded.

'Alas, my child, when you are my age so many of the pleasures of the flesh must be forgone. One picks amongst them, anxious to preserve one's strength for the more important tasks. I take my meals alone. But I will soon be with you again.'

'Come.' Zobeir led them away from the helicopter and across the baked mud of the compound to the largest of the grass huts, clearly an assembly point, for before the door there hung an iron triangle. The gloom within, after the glaring mid-afternoon sun, combined with the sudden cessation of the whistling, heavy air, was breathtaking, and instantly they were assaulted by a cloud of mosquitoes which had them stamping and slapping. As their eyes became accustomed to the dim light they discovered that the hut was devoid of furniture except for a pile of blankets in the corner, but it was larger than Wilde had supposed, and the rear of the building was lost in darkness.

'Well, really,' Cynthia Boraine declared. 'I paid a thousand pounds for this?'

'Here in the Centre of the Universe,' Zobeir said, 'we are concerned with the mind, not the body. But we know the body must be strong, to feed the mind. Pray be seated.'

'On the ground?'

Zobeir sat down, crossed his legs. 'The earth is the source of all things, for good and for evil, in this world.'

'Well, having come so far, I suppose.' Cynthia Boraine sat down. She slapped her face, left splodges of blood on the pale skin. 'You're sure it's us who're supposed to be eating? I'll tell you, Mr. Zobeir, I have no objection to camping out, but I'm damned if I'm going to let these things take me apart.'

'They will soon become tired of you, and you will soon become used to them.' Zobeir clapped his hands, and two of the Followers entered, carrying between them a large earthenware tureen. Wilde decided they were women, and probably Africans, but the probable girl who followed, holding a jug, gazed at him with blue eyes. The tureen was placed in front of Zobeir, the pitcher next to it, and the three women withdrew, shuffling softly through the dust.

'They forgot the plates,' Loman said.

'We use our fingers.'

'You mean we all dig from the same bowl?' Loman cried. 'Without even washing our hands? You must be out of your tiny mind.'

'What is it, anyway?' Cynthia Boraine asked.

'It is a *couscous*, really. But as we are unrestrained by outdated beliefs, the main ingredient is beef, rather than lamb. We have our own breed of cattle in Chad. Very tasty. And the stock is a porridge made from guinea-corn, with some vegetables added.' He scooped out three fingers of the stew, deposited it in his mouth. 'If you prefer not to eat, the decision is yours. Alas, we have nothing else. Except this wine.' He handed the jug to Wilde. 'Try some. I'm sure you will enjoy it. It is *merrisé*, that is a liquor made from the date palm. Or there is sour milk.'

'I'll try the wine.' Wilde said. The drink, which could easily have been a too recent muscadet with half a bottle of Scotch thrown in for good measure, to a certain extent made him less aware of the mosquitoes.

'Give me some of that.' Cynthia Boraine wiped the neck of the jug with her sleeve, drank deeply. 'God! I'm a teetotaller. Or I thought I was.' She handed the jug to Loman, raised her eyes to heaven, dipped her fingers into the pot. 'It's not bad. Or maybe I'm just too hungry to care. Okay, Mr. Zobeir, I'm beginning to get the message. So tell me what happens next.'

'Oh, you will not be bored, Miss Boraine. There is much to be done. The Followers of the Lord all have their part to play in the Centre of the Universe, whether it is the care of the cattle, or the tilling of the earth. And then there is much discussion. This occupies our evenings.'

'No meditation?' Wilde asked.

'No meditation, Mr. Wilde. The followers are a group, not an accumulation of individuals. We believe in discussing everything.'

'Sounds like fun,' Cynthia Boraine said. 'Well, you can put me down for the cows, Mr. Zobeir. My dad had a farm, well, actually, he had seventeen, and I used to holiday there from time to time. I like milking cows.'

'All in good time, Miss Boraine. For firstly, as novitiates, you must become part of the spirit of the community, and this demands that you must share. Everything you possess.'

'Here we go. But Babs Walton did say even to think about this place gave her goose pimples. Nice goose pimples.'

'Of course, Mrs. Walton is your sponsor. But now you will appreciate why Chwarism insisted you leave your valuables in Kano. You would have been unhappy had you arrived here to have your jewellery divided amongst the rest of us.'

'Unhappy! You sound like a British politician.'

'But the sharing of oneself, one's mind, is the most important function of the Followers of the Lord. Even our domestic arrangements are subjected to this rule. For instance, you will have observed that there are twenty-four houses in our village. This one is the eating house, and beside it stands the cookhouse. There are twelve houses for those of our members who have decided to couple.'

'What a repulsive expression,' Cynthia Boraine remarked.

'How can words be repulsive, Miss Boraine? Words are there to be used, for the conveying of meanings, and when a man and a woman decide that their happiness lies together they form a couple, in every sense of the word.'

'I'm surprised you recognize marriage,' Wilde said.

'Our own ceremony, Mr. Wilde, with its own laws, certainly. Because the female of our species can bear but one offspring at a time, as a rule, mating for the human animal must be an event of much seriousness and some permanence.'

'You're going to have me bewailing the fact that I'm not a grub,' Cynthia Boraine said. 'What about the other ten houses?'

'They belong to the bachelors of our community. You will share one of them, Miss Boraine, with three other female novitiates.'

'I share a house like this with three girls?'

'A smaller house than this, of course,' Zobeir pointed out.

'Of course. What time did you say the chopper went back to Kano?'

'*That's* what has been bothering me,' Loman said, with the air of a man just beginning to understand Einstein's theory. 'If you believe in marriage and, er, all that sort of thing, how come there aren't any kids knocking about the place? Most African villages are crawling with kids.'

'No doubt the Lord will be happy to explain that, and anything else which may be troubling you.' Zobeir stood up as the doorway darkened, and Ukuba entered.

'You have enjoyed your meal?'

'I didn't think I would,' Cynthia Boraine confessed. 'But I'm really quite replete. On the other hand, the more Zobeir tells me about this paradise of yours, the less I like it.'

'You are naturally conservative, Miss Boraine, and therefore instinctively dislike social conditions to which you are not accustomed. Give us time.'

'Yes,' Cynthia Boraine said thoughtfully. 'Well, first thing, Mr. Ukuba, I'd like to have a word with you, in private.'

'We are in private, Miss Boraine. There are no secrets in the Centre of the Universe.'

Cynthia Boraine removed a dead mosquito from inside her tunic. 'I suppose, if you put it that way. The fact is, Mr. Ukuba . . .

'You must address me as my Lord, here in the Centre of the Universe, my child.'

'Oh, very well, my Lord. I just wanted to say that in my opinion you played us a nasty trick on board that chopper. You may not believe this, but I can remember every word I said while that *borbor* thing was messing me about.'

'Of course you remember, Miss Boraine. It would be catastrophic were you to forget.'

'Well, that's the point. I think we should all forget it. I didn't mean any of it.'

Ukuba smiled. 'You meant every word of it, Miss Boraine. In fact, I would say it was one of the few truthful statements you have ever uttered. And here in the Centre of the Universe it is our first duty to cater to our guests' innermost wishes.' He clapped his hands, and two large Followers came in.

'These are my adopted sons, Fodio and Kanem,' Ukuba said.

'Miss Boraine's immediate desire, Kanem, a not unnatural one for so confused a young woman, is to be torn to pieces by that vast public which reads about her in the gossip columns and gapes at her when she drives by in her Bentley. Obviously we cannot indulge her to that extent, but it will do to let her work with the group from the House Number Six. Take her to them.'

(iii)

Cynthia Boraine scrambled to her feet. 'You don't lay a finger on me. I told you, Ukuba, just forget it.'

'Remove her, Kanem.'

'Conrad!' Cynthia Boraine shouted. 'Are you going to let these nig-nogs have a go at me?'

'Well, now, look here, Mr. Ukuba.' Loman also got up.

'Join us, my child,' Ukuba said. 'This is Serene, my great-grand-daughter, Mr. Loman. But you have already met. She travelled with us on the helicopter.'

The Arab girl stood just inside the doorway, her robe shrugged back from her head. Wilde wondered if she was even sixteen. She gazed at Loman, a half-smile on her lips.

'Conrad!' Cynthia Boraine shrieked, as the man called Kanem laid her across his shoulder. 'Conrad! Help me!'

'I assure you, Mr. Loman, it is what she really wishes, deep in her heart,' Ukuba said. 'You heard her say so. Now, Serene will show you over our island. I am sorry there are no trains here, but she will keep you interested, I am sure.'

'Well . . .' Loman took off his glasses and polished them with the green and white handkerchief.

'Come!' Serene extended an arm.

'Conrad!' Cynthia Boraine screamed. She sounded very close to tears.

'Come.' Serene stepped outside.

'Well, I suppose this what we came for.' Loman followed her.

Kanem also went to the door. 'Wilde!' Cynthia Boraine wailed, and then disappeared.

'Are you sure she's going to enjoy this?' Wilde asked.

'I promise you, Mr. Wilde, that the next time you meet she will be an altogether different woman. You may even begin to like her. So there remains only yourself. And your wish will not be difficult to satisfy, as I promised. But first we should speak with one another. Some more wine?'

He thought the *borbor* might just about have worn off. But if ever he was going to need a clear head now was the time. 'Not for me, thanks. Supposing, just for the sake of argument, that she isn't a different woman? She's quite well known, you know.'

'You are considering what might happen if, for instance, she charged me with assault?' Ukuba smiled. 'She came here of her own free will, Mr. Wilde. She was introduced to us by a friend of hers, also a wealthy socialite, who also required a certain rejuvenation of a tired spirit. I assure you there is absolutely no risk of her not responding to treatment. Her resistance is not so much that of an ordinary woman, which she is far from being, but rather that of the habitual dominator, through her extraordinary wealth. But all the while the *borbor* is eating away at her inhibitions, at her strength of will. That one sweet will go on working for some time.'

'And you can always give her some more,' Wilde said thoughtfully. 'How come you're not affected by it?'

'Like most poisons, one achieves an immunity, in time. All the members of the Inner Court have immunity.'

'So you use the stuff just to prepare your initiates for their sex ration. Funny, though, I'd have thought that Cynthia Boraine could get all the sex she wanted, straight or stirred, on the scene in Europe or the States.'

'Sex? You think that is what I provide for my guests? Perhaps you look upon the Centre of the Universe as some kind of gigantic, open-air brothel, hidden away in the swamps, where jaded appetites can perpetrate nameless excesses. My word, no doubt you assume that Miss Boraine is at this moment being raped. My dear Mr. Wilde, no member of the Inner Court would dream of touching her, as a woman, without her consent. Mind you, this is by no means so impossible as you may think. Many novitiates find a mutual attraction while they are here; it arises from the sharing of our thoughts, of our labour. But for the moment all we will demand of Miss Boraine is her labour. Oh, no doubt, as she is the junior member of the group, she will be to a certain extent, how do the Americans put it, hazed? But this can only benefit so intransigent and spoiled a personality.'

'And suppose she doesn't care for it?' Wilde asked.

'Then they will persuade her. And soon enough she will find a real pleasure in labouring, not for reward, but for the sheer joy of helping her fellow man.'

'Sounds too good to be true.'

'You mean you doubt your own ability to achieve such a goal? Of course it is harder for some than for others. But it is impossible for no one, given time, and thought, and patience. Let me tell you my own experience, Mr. Wilde. My philosophy found its impulse, as you may well imagine, in my horror at all the things civilized man appeared to hold dear, during my sojourn in

Flanders, and it grew when I attempted to understand civilized humanity in the London of the twenties. Of course, I was far from unique or even unusual. Different people attempted different ways of coming to terms with those monsters of social convention and mechanical limitations and urban requirements and national demands. I decided to reject it utterly. The more I probed, Mr. Wilde, the more I became sure that I was right. In every possible way.'

'You use helicopters. And civilized medicines.'

'I use those products of civilization which I choose, but I use them selectively. It is the *enslavement* of the human mind by the soulless necessities with which man has surrounded himself that I resist. That I think is dangerous. Let me give you an example. You sleep on a soft bed, and by the time you are forty you have back trouble. I sleep on the ground, and my back is as strong as it was in my youth. Your women seek to make themselves more and more beautiful with cosmetics, and by forty their skins are like unpolished leather; my women wear nothing on their faces, and not even the mosquitoes can affect their beauty.'

'Their complexions may be just fine, but surely you'd admit that primitive women age faster than most.'

'You are thinking of the swollen bellies, the sagging breasts, normally associated with primitive females. Such distortions are the results of inordinate childbearing. Now, it is the function of the female to bear a child, certainly. But one child only. That is the law of the Lord. To bear one child, to suckle one child, does no harm to any woman. It but gives her a desirable aspect of humanity. Those of our women who marry are expected to discharge this duty in the first year of their shared life. Oh, you will find no children here, just as you will find no domestic pets. Such sentimental pleasures distract the adult human being from more important tasks. For the offspring of the Inner Court I maintain an orphanage in Switzerland. There too, for the sake of their health, I am prepared to accept some of the so-called benefits of civilization, but in the main, and almost without exception as regards adults, those blessings are in time debilitating, and too often downright evil. So in Miss Boraine's case, as you will see. Her world is dominated both by her sex and her wealth. Here we shall convince her that neither of those things are of any importance, while we probe deeply into her subconscious, turning out all those hidden fears and desires which are the truly dominant part of every human being's personality, Mr. Wilde.'

'And then what?'

Ukuba smiled. 'Then we shall have a human being standing truly as God created her, unafraid, untainted, knowing only her-

self, but knowing herself in a sense which cannot be understood
by the greatest of the so-called philosophers. Is that not the oldest
and best of all admonitions? Know thyself? Know thyself, Mr.
Wilde, and you know all, the secrets of man and the secrets of
God.'

'And Zobeir here, and the other Followers, all know themselves?'

'The members of the Inner Court have each achieved that goal,
yes.'

'Fifty-odd people is a poor return for a lifetime's work, Ukuba.'

Ukuba continued to smile. 'Fifty people, Mr. Wilde? Fifty
people? Shall I tell you how I started? It was in 1919, and I lived
in London, and I discovered that there were others similarly
disenchanted with that destruction which seemed to us to be the
sole end product of man's ten millenniums of progress. We were
also, and rightfully so, mistrustful of his abilities to change his
ways, his inevitable march towards destruction, at this late stage.
We met, we talked, and eventually we practised. We bought a
house, Mr. Wilde—in Dorset it was, an empty, ramshackle place
—and we lived there, without furniture or heating, for over a
year. There were twelve of us. A nice number. A number which
has its basis in other religions.'

'You were sort of prototype hippies,' Wilde suggested. 'But
eventually you got fed up and went home.'

'Eventually I was called home by the death of my father. I had
to come, for I had a responsibility to my family, as I was the eldest
son. And so, as you say, we broke up. But sitting here, surrounded
by the silence of the lake, the vastness of the desert—for the Sahara
is closer than you may realize—I had little to do but think. We
owned a fine house, then, Mr. Wilde. Right where we are sitting,
in fact. One day I and my sons destroyed it, and in its place we
built grass huts. I then contacted my late companions, in England,
and found that they too, or, at least, eight of them, still yearned
for the life we had barely touched upon in our year together. I
invited them to come here and stay with me for a while. Here we
discussed and formalized our beliefs, and then they went out into
the world to proselytize. They are all dead now, alas, but the
movement has grown. For many years it made slow progress, for
we were less active than we could have been. But two years ago
I was persuaded to declare myself to the world. I undertook a
tour, and the results were staggering. It is estimated that several
millions heard, and understood, and believed.

'Of course, few of the Followers visit Chad. Only those we consider would make suitable members of the Inner Court come
here, and serve for periods which may vary from a few months
to a year, and then depart to spread the word. The vast mass of

our followers are merely those who have imbibed our precepts without even, perhaps, truly understanding the implications. But I can best give you an idea of the number of the Followers if I tell you that there are more than ten thousand members of the Inner Court.'

'At a thousand pounds a head? I make that ten million quid. So the helicopter set you back a hundred thousand, maybe.' Wilde looked around him. 'Where do you keep the rest?'

'In a Swiss bank account, Mr. Wilde.'

'For the Lord's old age, perhaps?'

'I am seventy-eight years old, Mr. Wilde. How long do you think I should wait? Besides, as you must realize, only a proportion of the members of the Inner Court can afford the fee. We accept the wealthy, like Miss Boraine, like yourself, perhaps, searching for some mental armour with which to face the tensions of their lives, in order that they may pay the way for those who undertake to work for the movement.'

'The work being?'

'Our cause is that of international peace, Mr. Wilde. And we believe that peace is jeopardized, as it has always been jeopardized, by governments, by authority, by laws which are in the main created to keep the masses in servility rather than for the improvement of mankind. But come, we have talked sufficiently. I have enjoyed speaking with you because I will confess to you that you are totally unlike the usual novitiate. You have an analytical and inquiring brain, not one which has found the world too heavy a burden, and you are a man of the utmost personal confidence, as can easily be discerned from your movements. Additionally, your resistance to the *borbor* is quite remarkable. I look forward to learning why you really came here, Mr. Wilde, because, of course, that absurd desire of yours to be alone with the most beautiful girl in the world was obviously selected from some of the more banal examples of Western literature. However, as you have expressed the wish, it is my duty, and my pleasure, to grant it.' Ukuba stood up. 'The most beautiful woman in the world, Mr. Wilde. My wife.'

CHAPTER SIX

WILDE reached his feet in a long bound. The woman had come out of the darkness at the back of the hut, could have been there all the time.

'Your wife?' He felt as if a large horse had just kicked him in the navel.

'Certainly, Mr. Wilde,' Ukuba said. 'Her name is Inger.'

The grey eyes, glooming from the white shroud of her *haik*, had always reminded Wilde of icicles embedded in the eaves of a snow bound cottage. In two years the face, chiselled by some latter-day Polycleitus, had been given an almost mahogany tan by the African sun, but otherwise she was untarnished, as he knew the straight platinum hair and the almost perfect body would also be untarnished, even if in that time, as Ukuba had suggested, she had borne a child. And if the face and the body had not changed, neither would the brain. It occurred to Wilde that on the plane he had been indulging in so much wishful thinking; Inger had not changed. Inger would never change, until she died. Her colour was glacier blue.

'This is the man, Inger,' Ukuba said softly. 'Tell me of him.'

'Yes, my Lord.' Even her voice had not altered, so low his ears instinctively strained, so clear it was impossible to miss a word. 'I know this man, Jonas Wilde. He has come here to kill you.'

There was a moment's silence, disturbed only by the slither of Zobeir withdrawing to the doorway. Then Wilde threw himself forwards. But she knew what his reaction must be to her denunciation. She faded from in front of him, and he blundered into the darkness at the rear of the hut. He spread his legs, balanced on the balls of his feet. Behind him there was movement, and he glanced over his shoulder, saw the two young men who had earlier removed Cynthia Boraine.

Time was running out. He reached into the darkness, touched the rough wool of her robe, tried to close his fingers, slipped, and fell to his hands and knees. He turned, saw her dart between the four men who were behind him.

The killing hate, which he had earlier been unable to create, came bubbling out of his subconscious. He tensed his muscles, transmitted his hundred and eighty pounds of weight from his thighs into his right arm, throwing the edge of his hand out and upwards from his body, in a swinging backhanded blow, struck the nearest upright, smashed the thin wood as if it were cardboard, parted the grass curtain, thrust his fingers into the aperture and ripped the side of the hut open, stepped into the compound.

The Followers of the Lord were waiting for him. Four of them, including the pilot, stood by the helicopter. The rest formed a group of silent figures, immediately in front of the eating house. There was no sign of Inger.

He ran into the nearest of the sleeping houses. It was a reed-walled igloo, containing a pile of blankets and an army of mosquitoes, but no humans. He ran outside again. Still the Followers stared at him. The next hut was also empty. And now

Ukuba, accompanied by Zobeir and his two adopted sons, had left the main hut.

'Come, Mr. Wilde,' Ukuba said. 'There is nowhere for you to go. Surrender yourself to me.'

The Followers moved forward, two steps each, making a semi circle around Wilde, cutting him off from the remainder of the buildings. He glanced over his shoulder. Behind him the baked mud sloped down to the reeds, but on this side the reed bed was only twenty yards wide, and beyond there was open water. Chad, he thought. Remember about Chad. Chad is nowhere very deep, except in the centre. In the dry season the average depth of the lake is four feet, and this was the very end of the dry season.

The watchers came closer, two more steps, a wall of white-robed bodies and glooming eyes. He could not kill all of these people. Even were he armed with a machine-gun, he could never gun down these devout believers in the peace of the primitive life.

Still facing them, he retreated round the hut. Would any of them follow him into the reeds? They would be committing suicide. He was Jonas Wilde, code name Eliminator, the man whose life was dedicated to death, who had been trained in every aspect of the art of killing, even with his bare hands. They must know that; they had seen him burst through the side of the hut. They must be aware of the latent strength which he could command, the power of concentrating all his weight into his hands at any given moment.

He frowned. He had never had to remind himself of his assets before. It came to him, slowly and for the first moment almost unbelievably, that he was afraid, with the mindless, ever deepening fear of a young girl alone in an empty house.

He shook his head in an attempt to clear his mind. He had known fear before. But fear had always come in the shape of a problem. There is a man with a gun; I must reach him before he shoots me; if I do not, I shall be dead. A problem with an answer, one way or the other. But he could not say, there are fifty unarmed people, advancing on me. If I do not attack them before they close around me, they are going to . . . he did not know. He could not imagine.

'You can go no farther, Mr. Wilde,' Ukuba said. 'Behind you is only the water. It may be shallow, at this moment, but it is not empty, and it extends for a very great distance. Even could you escape the crocodiles, you could not wade more than a thousand miles, Surrender yourself, Mr. Wilde.'

Once again Wilde looked over his shoulder. He was trapped by the unknown. He had been trained to fight men, not reptiles, and not ideals. And not the *borbor,* eating at his willpower.

He clasped his hands on the back of his neck, walked up the slope towards the waiting people.

'He is yours,' Ukuba said.

He kept his hands high, moved into their midst, and was consumed. The mass closed on him, pressing their bodies against his, shoulders, thighs, legs crushing together like some slow-moving yet inevitable football scrummage. Not a finger was laid on his person, and yet he was conquered, the breath driven from his body and the thoughts from his brain. He saw only eyes, black and brown and green and blue and grey, surrounding him like angry stars, moving ever closer, until without warning they receded, and he found himself lying in the dust, his breath coming in great gasps.

'There is your murderer.' Ukuba's voice seemed to come from a vast distance away.

"He is not so helpless as he looks,' Inger said. 'He is a dangerous man.'

Wilde lay on his back, surrounded by feet. He spat dirt from his mouth, blinked his eyes to clear away the dust, watched her come through the throng. She had pulled her *haik* from her head; her white hair shimmered in the afternoon sunlight.

'So it is as you warned, my child,' Ukuba said sadly. 'Had I not the evidence of my own eyes, I could never have believed it. I found him a man I could like.'

'That is part of the secret of his success,' Inger said. 'To earn respect, and liking from his intended victim. Even love, on occasion. And the girl?'

Breathe, Wilde reminded himself. Let the dust clear, breathe, and keep control. Above all, keep control.

Ukuba sighed. 'There also, my child, you were right and I was wrong. There also. Believe me, that is the heaviest burden I must bear.'

'I do not understand.' Zobeir knelt beside Wilde, stared at him. But there was no hatred in his eyes, only bewilderment. 'You know this man, Inger?'

'I met him once, years ago.'

'And you say he came here to assassinate the Lord? But that is unbelievable. Who could wish for such a thing?'

'Who indeed, Zobeir?' Inger said. 'But we shall ask Serene.'

(ii)

The dust rose again from the scuffing of innumerable feet. Serene was hurled through the crowd, to kneel at Wilde's side. She looked over her shoulder, not at her great-grandfather, but at Inger, an expression of mingled fear and horror on her face.

'No,' she whispered. 'No . . . it was not I. You must listen to me, my Lord.'

'Hush, child.' Ukuba turned away from her, faced the waiting people. 'Members of the Inner Court of the Followers of the Lord, listen to me. What has happened this evening has grieved me more than I can say, grieved me because it is the first discord ever to disrupt the peace of the Centre of the Universe, grieved me because I was warned it was going to happen, by the good woman to whom I have bound my soul, the mother of my son. This man, this creature,' he stirred Wilde with his toe, 'is one who sells his strength, his brain, his soul, for money. He is here not because he wishes to join our ranks, to absolve himself of the many terrible crimes which lie on his conscience, but because there are those who would seek to destroy me. My own grand-daughter is one of them.'

'No!' Serene scrambled to her feet, and Zobeir seized her round the waist and threw her to the ground again. 'No,' she whispered.

'No?' Ukuba asked. 'You would lie to save your miserable life?'

Serene's tongue circled her lips. 'You must listen to me. Oh my Lord, you must listen. Grant me that privilege. Alone. I beg this of you.'

'You went to Kano. You begged my permission to spend some weeks in Kano. I did not inquire why. You are my own flesh and blood, a direct descendant of the first leader of our people. So I refuse you nothing. What did you do in Kano, Serene?'

'Listen to me,' Serene begged. 'Listen to me.'

'She went there to await the coming of this man. And when he arrived she crept into the room where he was changing, offered herself to him. Yes, Serene, my child, I watched you. Chwarism gave Wilde that room on my instructions.'

'You watched,' Serene cried. 'But you did not hear what we said. You could not hear. Because I was obeying instructions.' She threw out her arm, her finger pointing. 'Her orders.'

'And do you not think Inger warned me you would say just that, Serene? You stand condemned out of your own mouth.'

'And yet,' Inger said, 'she speaks the truth, my Lord, at least in a fashion. Serene could never have evolved such a horrible plan. And if she had, she would have not known how to find such a man as Wilde. Has she ever been farther afield than Kano or Fort Lamy? And again, my Lord, in every crime there has to be a motive. Who would stand to gain most from your death?'

'I wonder,' Wilde said, 'if I might be permitted to get a word in edgeways.'

'Assassin!' Inger hissed, crouching beside him.

'Lady Macbeth really isn't up your alley, darling. This whole thing reminds me of a farce I once saw.'

'You!' She pointed above his head. 'Help me.'

Before Wilde could move, two of the men were standing on his arms, pinning him to the ground. Inger herself knelt on his chest, a white-robed succubus. Her head was bare, and her platinum hair hung on either side of her mahogany-tanned face with perfect symmetry. 'Now force his jaws,' she said.

Wilde tried to kick, but two more men were standing on his feet. Another man knelt behind his head, and his fingers ate into the base of Wilde's jaw. His mouth opened, and Inger scooped up a handful of dirt, thrust it in. Mud filled Wilde's mouth, his throat, seeped up into the back of his nostrils. For a terrible moment he thought he would choke, and desperately he raised his head, drawing a minimum of breath through his clogged windpipe.

'But surely *he* will be able to tell us what we wish to know,' Ukuba said.

'Wilde?' Inger's tone was contemptuous. 'I know this man, my Lord. He will repeat whatever it may be that Serene has told him to say. If he has a virtue it is loyalty to his employers. So for the time being he will merely seek to follow her example, and accuse me. Let us give them both time to reflect on their sins, their crimes, their likely fate.' She stood up, faced the Followers. 'We are not a violent people. We believe in peace. But we must learn the truth about these two criminals, discover which amongst the Inner Court have been plotting the overthrow of the Lord. What is the sentence of the Followers of the Lord?'

The eyes were back, glooming at him. 'Let them be crucified,' someone said, and the cry was taken up. 'Let them be crucified.'

Once again the horde fastened itself on to Wilde, this time like a swarm of locusts, each grasping for some portion of his body or his clothing, and half carried, half marched him across the compound. He was reminded of a lynching, and realized that he was not so very far wrong at that. He heard Serene screaming. One cannot be lynched with dignity. Strange how this thought crossed his mind, upset him more than his physical danger.

They reached another shore of the island. Here the sloping earth ended in shallow water, which stretched into the fading evening light. He was thrown to the ground, while the angry Followers hunted him once more, stripping off his clothes as small boys might dismember a fly, tearing each article to shreds, so absorbed in their task that he wondered if human beings had ever been intended to look deeply into their own subconscious selves, because of what, inevitably, they must find lurking there.

He was stretched on a wooden frame, already waiting and obviously well worn, to suggest that the Followers were experienced at this mode of punishment. His arms were extended and secured to the transverse bar at each wrist and again under the armpits. His ankles were tied together and then to the upright, and the cross was lifted and held erect by three men, its base in an already prepared hole, which was now filled until the upright was immovable, and he was left hanging from the arms and shoulders, his feet just clear of the ground.

But there were two holes, and the Followers had also brought Serene to the shore, were stripping her as well. The Arab girl seemed to have collapsed with fear and exhaustion, allowed her limbs to be tossed to and fro. Another cross was produced, and she also was bound to the wooden frame by wrist and shoulder and ankle. In a few moments she was erected, facing Wilde and only a few feet away from him, a small-breasted, thin-hipped golden brown wisp, her black hair trailing past her shoulders, her eyes shut tight as if by so doing she could exclude the horror of her surroundings.

'Now let us leave them,' Inger said, 'to consider the consequences of their actions. Let them hang here until they are ready to confess to us the author of their crimes. Kanem, you will remain to make sure they do not manage to free themselves.'

'Free themselves from the cross?' Ukuba asked. 'No one has ever accomplished that.'

'You do not understand the resources of this man Wilde,' she said. 'You must not forget, my Lord, that I have seen him work. You will remain here, Kanem, and should he even attempt to move, you will prevent him. Fodio will relieve you.'

She led them back to the village, and as if their departure had given a signal the night was filled with the whirring of insects. The sun sank behind the trees of the wood, plunging the lakeside into darkness, and the mosquitoes rose from the reeds like a coven of minute witches assembling for a sabbat. And this night the appointed meeting place was Wilde's body. They caressed him, explored him, penetrated every orifice, thrust their stings deep in his flesh. He thought that by sunrise they might very well have sucked him dry of blood. He shook his head, tried rotating his body, but that caused the ropes to cut into his shoulders, and he understood that this would soon become unbearable, even if he kept still. He could not shout; it was all he could do to breathe without choking on the earth which still clogged his nostrils. In any event, one could not disperse mosquitoes by noise. Or could one? He wondered at the number of things he did not know, irrelevant bits of knowledge which had suddenly become very relevant indeed. He thought that when he got down from this cross, breaking Inger's neck was going to pose no problem whatsoever. If he got down from this cross. It was a very large word. And there were other thoughts hammering at his brain. Observations, events, which taken separately made no sense at all, but which, if he could but add them together, suggested a tremendous amount of sense.

'Kanem!' Serene whispered. 'Kanem! Listen to me.'

'Be quiet, woman.' Kanem squatted on the ground, his back to them, gazing out at the lake.

'You cannot leave me hanging here, Kanem, to die of hunger and thirst. You cannot, Kanem. I am your foster sister. Is that not so? And your woman? Have I not shared my body with you, even as I shared it with Fodio, aye, even as I shared it with that she-wolf? Kanem! You cannot desert me now.'

Kanem got up, stood against her, forced her jaws apart.

'Kanem!' she gasped. 'No, Kanem.'

He thrust the stone into her mouth. Wilde could hear her teeth grating. Kanem left them, went up to the village, returned a few minutes later with a blanket. He resumed his seat, wrapped himself in his *haik*, added the blanket to his shoulders. With good reason. Within an hour the *harmattan*, which had dwindled to a gentle breeze at sunset, had risen almost to gale force, and become amazingly chill when compared with the scorching heat of the day. Great shivers racked Wilde's body, causing the rope to sear his armpits, his head to pound against the wood of the upright. Six feet away Serene's teeth chattered on the stone. Thoughts raced through his mind, of the man with the gun, but who had sent him? Of Inger denouncing him, but who had sent Aimee Bosquet? Of Ukuba, so apparently wise, and perceptive, accepting every word that fell from his wife's mouth as the truth.

He lost track of time. Existence became a continuous, immediate agony, and he had no means of judging the passing of the minutes. He even thought he dozed, now and then, awoke with each renewal of the pain in his shoulders. But perhaps it was only once, and when he opened his eyes he saw Inger standing in front of him.

(iii)

Her hands were clasped before her; she looked incredibly peaceful and unnaturally beautiful. Both the brothers waited behind her. 'Kanem,' she said softly. 'Fetch me some water.'

Kanem went up the slope. Inger slapped Wilde on the chest.

The blow cut his freezing flesh like a knife, but it also destroyed six mosquitoes. She held her hand in front of her face, looked at the blood splashed across it. 'They must like the alcohol in your system.'

Wilde gazed above her head, and the brilliant moon just beginning to droop towards the trees. He figured it must be quite close to dawn; there was no feeling left in any of his limbs.

'What do you think of crucifixion as a punishment, Jonas?' she asked. 'It has long been popular in West Africa. They learned it from the first Portuguese missionaries, oh, four hundred years ago. Before then they would cut off a leg, and leave the victim to bleed to death. That remained the punishment for slaves. But for people of importance, crucifixion was far more suitable. You can watch your prisoner die slowly, day by day, hour by hour, if you choose. And then, for three days, as a rule, you can change your mind, and cut him down, and nurse him back to health, and, of course, put him back on the cross again. That is far more interesting than just cutting his head off. The British put a stop to it about fifty years ago. That is the true hallmark of the British colonial period, you know, Jonas. An ending to all satisfactory local customs. The creation, perhaps, of an emotional vacuum.'

Wilde gazed at her.

'You are angry. Oh, so angry. But more than that, you are confused. Everyone is confused. Poor Ukuba is confused. He cannot believe that such a thing could happen, much less that his grand-daughter could be involved. Zobeir is confused. He does not understand what is happening at all. And as for Serene, she is half mad with confusion. Eh, Serene?' She reached up, slapped the girl hard across the face. Serene's head jerked, struck the wood of the cross, slumped again.

'I have the water, Inger.' Kanem stood in the darkness. 'She begged me to help her, as she has been my woman. Mine and Fodio's.'

'I am your woman now, Kanem. Yours and Fodio's, for always. Is that not what you wanted?'

'Then let her die quickly when the time comes.'

'I do not mean her to die at all. Presuming only that she is not stubborn.' She took the jar of water, stood against Wilde, held it to his lips. 'Do not swallow, Jonas. That earth will turn your stomach, and you have enough to contend with. Rinse, and spit.'

Wilde obeyed. The spittle struck the breast of her robe. Inger smiled. 'You owe me that one.' She gave him more water. 'Again.'

This time he hit her on the shoulder.

'Now this time you may swallow. I would, Jonas, in preference to aiming for my face. You will get no more.'

He swallowed. His mouth tasted like the inside of a sewer, but at least he no longer felt he would choke on every breath.

'It is good to see you again.' She stroked one finger down the line of his jaw, touched his lower lip. 'So good. I would like to kiss you, Jonas, but I'm afraid you would bite off my tongue. I would like to hold you in my arms.' She dragged her fingers down his body, caressed him, and when he responded, dug her nails into his flesh. 'But I must just look at you, it seems. I enjoy even doing that. Your presence reminds me of Hamburg, and Copenhagen, and Stockholm, and London. Of lace pants, and fast planes, and comfortable trains, and expensive motor-cars. Of guns and intrigue. I miss the tension of life in Europe, Jonas. Do you know, I have not seen a pistol in two years, much less fired one? I wonder if I could still shoot straight?'

'So why don't you go back?' Wilde asked.

'Oh, I mean to, in due course. But you'll agree that I couldn't stay there, after what happened in Stockholm. When one has betrayed both Nato and the Warsaw Pact in immediate succession one has to choose one's friends very carefully. Tell, me, Jonas, what do you think of Africa?'

'I'm an optimist, so I keep believing it must improve.'

'I like Africa, Jonas. I only came here because Europe was barred to me, so you could say it was an accident. But a most fortunate one. I was cowering in Paris, barely able to keep myself alive, when Ukuba came there on his world tour. I was persuaded to visit him, out of curiosity, more than anything else. But he fell in love with me, with my brains as much as my face, and I allowed him to bring me here. I have stayed for two years. Do you know, Jonas, even I was no more than one in a crowd in Europe? There are so many brilliant people, so many beautiful women. Here I am unique. Besides, I think there must be a considerable amount of the primitive in me. I like the forests, the remoteness of civilization, the physical strength of the people. But you, Jonas, you are are out of your depths here. I could see it, the moment I laid eyes upon you. You are a creature of the jungle, like me, but it is a different jungle. When I first sent for you I knew I was going to enjoy watching you flounder, away from your planes and your cars, away from the people who would take you at your face value, and become your ready victims when you chose to reveal yourself. How does it feel, Jonas, to be just one of the crowd?'

'I only wish I were, just now. But you sent for me. You're being brilliant again, sweetheart.'

She smiled, turned to Serene. 'Remove the stone, Kanem.'

Kanem forced Serene's mouth open; the stone popped out

like a fruit pip. Painfully she ran her tongue round her lips. 'Why?' she whispered. 'Why?'

'But this was our plan, Serene,' Inger explained.

'For all of us. For the four of us. Fodio! You cannot do this to me.'

'You are the Lord's own flesh and blood,' Fodio said. 'The Followers would have chosen you in his place, rather than us.'

'And would I not have shared my power?' she cried. 'I believed you, Inger. I trusted you. You sent me to Kano, to wait for Wilde. You sent me, Inger. I shall swear that, and I shall continue to swear it, no matter how long you leave me here, until the Lord believes me. He will believe me. He trusts me. He has always trusted me.'

'He will never believe you now, Serene,' Inger said gently. 'You cannot understand, can you? Ukuba loves me. It is a word which has never had much significance for me before now. But it is something that he needs, desperately. For all of his life he kept himself aloof from emotional attachments, because he wished to be all things to his Followers. But never to desire is unnatural. When forced beneath the surface of human consciousness it bubbles like a volcano. So when the Lord met me he exploded with love for me, with desire, and admiration, and tenderness. There is my strength, Serene, redoubled now that I have borne him a son.'

'Kanem's!' Serene hissed. 'How will you defend yourself against that charge, Inger? Is it not the law of the Inner Court that adulterers shall be exposed on the cross, for three days, and then expelled? You will hang here like me, Inger, and then the Followers will thrust you back in that world from which you fled.'

'Will you accuse me of adultery? Where is your proof, Serene? The evidence of your own eyes? But only your eyes. The boy looks like me, and the Lord knew that I was not a virgin when he married me. But you, Serene, you he still regards as a child, unknown and unknowing. What will he do to you, when you are examined by the women, under my direction? Is not fornication classed with adultery as a crime? Think well where your own best interest lies. For it is the same with Wilde. You cannot prove that *I* sent you to Kano to wait for him. But you were there.'

'How could I have *known*?' the girl wailed.

'If you co-operate with us now, do as we wish, then your life shall be saved. It will even be possible for you to resume your proper place, in time.'

'I do not understand. Oh, if I could understand.'

'You see, Jonas.' Inger said, 'she thought our plan was to

eliminate both Zobeir and Ukuba. For you to eliminate them, Jonas. Because Serene is a simple child, who has never left the neighbourhood of Chad. Would such a plan make sense to you, Jonas?'

'I never knew you to need a hired hand.'

'But you came, in response to my summons. Why did you come?'

'I wanted to see you again, I suppose. And they had put me out to grass, after Stockholm. Funds were low.' He frowned. 'I wish I could figure why you wasted the time looking for me.'

She smiled. 'Even you, Jonas, allow your thoughts, your conceptions, to be limited. Supposing you lived in Maidugari, over there. If I wished to use you I would send for you, and you would come. But you happen to live in London. Don't you realize that you can get to the Centre of the Universe quicker from London than from Maidugari? In this modern world of ours what is time? What is space? We are hurtling towards an understanding of the fourth dimension. These people I live with, they are not stupid. Their horizons are limited by the trees, and the lakes, but their intelligence, in certain cases, matches my own. What they lack is my experience. So were I to intrigue, here in the Centre of the Universe, they, Ukuba, certainly, would see through me quickly enough. Unless my intrigue were to be conceived on a scale to which no one here has ever aspired. So they, like you, Jonas, are forced to say to themselves, would she have searched the world over for an assassin, only to denounce him the moment he sets foot on the island? Does that make sense? Of course not. If there is one innocent person in the Centre of the Universe then it has to be Inger, who at the risk of her own life warned her husband of his danger the moment she became aware of it.'

'But who, then, will kill the Lord?' Serene asked.

'What a ghastly thought, Serene. Truly you are at heart a little savage. Why should anyone wish to kill the Lord, when he is an old man who will shortly die, in any event? My wish is merely to influence the succession, and in such a fashion that no suspicion can possibly fall upon either my nominees or myself.'

'But why then seek to sacrifice me?' Serene asked. 'I would never have betrayed you. I went to Kano on your instructions.'

Inger sighed. 'Now you see, Fodio, why I could never have trusted her. She is as lovely as a rising star, but she is also as devoid of brainpower. Of course *I* sent you, Serene. But you will tell the Followers of the Lord that it was Zobeir.'

(iv)

'Zobeir?' Serene asked.

'He will be cast out,' Kanem said. 'For why should you accuse him were he not guilty?'

'And who has the most to gain from the death of the Lord?' Fodio demanded.

'Zobeir is well known as an impatient man,' Inger said. 'He is the very one who would seek to expedite his succession.'

'Zobeir,' Serene whispered. 'But should I accuse him, I will still be tarnished with having been his accomplice.'

'You will have to trust me,' Inger said softly.

'And if you do that, sweetheart,' Wilde pointed out, 'you need your head examined.'

Inger glanced over her shoulder. 'You like the taste of our sand, Jonas, darling?'

'I shan't utter another word.'

'Listen to me, Serene. Certainly you will be accused with Zobeir. But you are the Lord's own flesh and blood, and, besides, I, and Kanem and Fodio as well, will intercede for you.'

'This we swear,' Kanem and Fodio said together.

'So that, while you will have to appear to be punished, for the benefit of the Followers, it will not approach Zobeir's in severity. Your sentence shall be banishment from the Centre of the Universe. But I will see that you are well supplied with money, and you will live in perfect contentment, wherever you choose, until the Lord has passed away, and either Kanem or Fodio succeed to his place, when you will be recalled.'

'You mean I could leave Africa?' Serene's eyes shone. 'I could go to London, or Paris, or New York?'

'You may go wherever you choose.'

'Zobeir.' Serene wrinkled her nose. 'There is something . . . something the man Wilde said to me, in Kano, which could well concern Zobeir.'

'I never mentioned his name,' Wilde said, 'because I'd never heard it before.' Whoever had been employing the gunman was Inger's problem now.

Inger smiled. 'It is of no matter. But I will offer you your life as well, Jonas.'

'Now I know you're pulling our legs.'

'Why should I do that? You gave me my life in Stockholm. I am but discharging a debt. Besides, you have served my purpose, and, who knows, I may need you again one day. You can never harm me here in the Centre of the Universe; you would need an army even to return, without my permission. Similarly, I am immune from the British government, or even those all powerful American friends of yours. The Nigerian government knows the size of the Lord's following, and are happy to leave him in peace, so long as he pays his taxes. I do not wish you to support Serene's tale. You could not, convincingly. I merely ask for your silence. So you will have had a brief, and I am sure interesting, holiday in Africa. You will have seen how the other half lives, Jonas, and also you will have learned that there are still places in the world where you are utterly helpless to influence the course of events. I am sure that such a lesson will do you good. It may even make you more efficient. And as Aimee will have promised you, I will refund your expenses.'

'I told you, I won't utter another word.'

'Serene?'

The girl licked her lips. 'Yes,' she said. 'Yes, I will accuse Zobeir.'

Inger pointed at the lake, which was changing from black to deep blue as the first rays of the sun crept across its surface. 'Then let it be done, and quickly.'

Kanem ran back to the village, where he seized the steel rod, and beat the triangle which hung outside the main building. Again and again he clanged the bars, and slowly the Followers of the Lord, their eyes still heavy with sleep, emerged from their huts, one after the other, the tall figure of Zobeir and the grey head of Ukuba amongst them, but neither, Wilde observed, Cynthia Boraine nor Conrad Loman.

'What has happened?' Ukuba wrapped himself in his *haik* as he came through the throng. 'That was the alarm signal. What has happened? Inger? Why were you not at my side?'

'I could not sleep, my Lord,' Inger said. 'I wished to question the man Wilde more closely. And it is fortunate that I did so. We have uncovered a most hideous plot, aimed directly at your life, as I suspected and warned you.' She threw out her hand. 'Serene has confessed.'

Ukuba stood before the cross. 'You have not harmed them?'

'The Followers of the Lord shall offer no violence to their fellow humans except in self-defence. Serene hangs as you left her, my Lord. But I have spoken with her, impressed her with the horror of the crimes she planned, against the man who is her only remaining blood relative, and all in the cause of her own ambition.'

Ukuba gazed at his grand-daughter. 'You wish to confess the name of your accomplice, my child?'

'I have sinned most grievously, my Lord,' Serene whispered. 'I wish to atone for that sin, no matter what the cost.'

'Then you retract the statement that the authoress of your mis-
deeds was Inger?'

'I was told to say that, and I obeyed. But I can obey no longer.
The traitor is standing beside you, my Lord.'

Ukuba turned his head. 'Zobeir?'

'She lies.' Zobeir made to move, found that Kanem and Fodio
had taken their places behind him. 'My Lord, Ukuba, you know
that cannot be.'

'I know that it should not be, Zobeir. You and I have been
friends for many years. I have grown to love you like a brother,
and I have grown to trust you as my eventual successor. But I
have never allowed my love or my trust to blind me to your faults.
I had hoped that with increasing age and experience you would
learn to overcome them.'

'My Lord, you cannot condemn me upon the evidence of a
young girl, unsupported.'

'The evidence of my own great-grand-daughter, Zobeir. And
as for support, she admits her own guilt. Certainly, someone had
to send her to Kano to meet the man Wilde.'

'Someone, my Lord, but why me? She has already accused your
wife.'

'But that was obviously false, Zobeir. What could Inger possibly hope to gain from my death? Indeed, my departure from this
life can only mean the end of her own authority here in the
Centre of the Universe. Even did she not love me, and I know
she does that, it would be in her every interest to keep me alive.'

'Whereas you, Zobeir,' Inger said, 'stand to gain the very
pinnacle of your ambitions by my Lord's death.'

'Do I not also gain those by waiting?' Zobeir cried.

'Who knows, old man? Who knows?' Kanem shouted. 'As my
foster father has truly said, your faults of character, your impatience and your rashness, are too well known amongst the
Followers of the Lord.'

'Serene, my child,' Ukuba said. 'Do you swear, by the memory
of your dead mother, that Zobeir sent you to Kano?'

Serene gazed at Inger, and then at her great-grandfather. 'I
swear, my Lord.'

'And you, Mr. Wilde,' Ukuba said. 'What can you add to this
sad business?'

'Not a thing.'

'But you admit to being a professional assassin?'

'It takes all sorts to make a world.'

'And what did Serene say to you, in Kano?'

'I'd say her principle objective was to make sure I was the
right Wilde.'

'What instructions did she give you?'

'She said I would receive my instructions when I reached the Centre of the Universe.'

'But she led you to understand that your employer was Inger?'

'Otherwise I wouldn't have come.' Wilde grinned. 'We worked together, briefly, on a previous occasion. Like you, Ukuba, I formed a high opinion of her capabilities.'

'She has told me of her past,' Ukuba said. 'And I believe you. Zobeir, the circumstantial evidence against you is overwhelming. You had the motive, and God knows you had the opportunity. Apart from Inger and myself, only you amongst my close associates has travelled sufficiently, and has experienced enough of the outside world, to have come into contact with this man.'

'It is a lie, my Lord,' Zobeir said. 'I swear it.'

'On your knees, murderer.' Fodio seized him round the neck and threw him headlong. 'He stands condemned, oh, Followers of the Lord. He must be placed upon the cross.'

Slowly, Zobeir got to his feet. He kept his gaze fixed on Ukuba's face.

'What do my Followers say?' Ukuba asked.

'He must be crucified,' they said.

'It is but what he deserves, my Lord,' Inger said.

'Indeed, my child, I know that you are right, as always. But our entire movement is dedicated to peace, and so I shall use my prerogative as Lord of the Followers, and spare his life. But I banish him from the Centre of the Universe, and I cast him out from the Inner Court,' He pointed at the lake. 'There is your road, Zobeir. Take it.'

Zobeir gazed at them, at Inger, at Kanem and Fodio, at Ukuba himself. Last of all, he stared at Serene for a long moment, and the girl shut her eyes. Then he took off his *haik*, dropped it on the ground, turned away from the waiting people, and walked slowly down the shore. He hesitated for a moment on the edge of the water, not blue here, close to the land, but brown, turgid, impenetrable. By now the sun was well clear of the horizon, and the brilliant light streamed across the calm waters of Chad, illuminated the shore, the two people hanging from their crosses, the white robes of the Followers of the Lord, the man standing alone.

Zobeir waded into the lake. They watched the brown water rise about his ankles, lap at his knees, suck upwards to his thighs, soak his woollen tunic. He was now a hundred feet from the shore, not looking back, thrusting through the water in the direction of the clump of trees which marked the next island. And now the water had stopped rising.

'God is good,' Ukuba said. 'Zobeir is strong, and healthy, and determined. He will find his way from island to island, and in time he will even regain the mainland. He knows Chad very well.'

'Always providing the crocodiles don't get him,' Wilde said.

Ukuba smiled. 'You are thinking of my warning to you, Mr. Wilde. Oh, there are crocodiles in Chad. Less than there were, but still sufficient to make bathing dangerous. But now, when the lake is low, they lie buried in the mud. Only when the rains come will they again roam the waters. Zobeir will survive. But he must no longer be counted amongst the Followers of the Lord. Anderson, on your next visit to Kano you will instruct Chwarism to inform every member of the Inner Court, no matter where he might be, that Zobeir is no longer one of their number.'

'Yes, my Lord,' the Rhodesian said.

'There remains Zobeir's two accomplices,' Ukuba said. 'Take them down.'

Kanem stepped up to Wilde, released first his feet, and then his wrists and shoulders. Wilde kept his balance with an effort; he had very little feeling in any of his limbs. Fodio released Serene; she knelt and then sat, her hair clouding her face.

'What punishment do the Followers of the Lord decree for these people?' Ukuba demanded.

'Have mercy, my Lord, I beg of you,' Serene said.

'Indeed, my Lord,' Inger said. 'It would be fitting, both because she is your own flesh and blood and because she was nothing more than a tool in the hands of Zobeir.'

'She yet must be punished.'

'Of course, my Lord. Like Zobeir, there can be no place left for her in the Centre of the Universe. But surely this is punishment enough.'

'So be it,' Ukuba said. 'And I thank you, my child, for your generous heart. And the man?'

'He has committed no crime, my Lord.'

'He is a self-confessed murderer. He came here to kill me.'

'As for his past, my Lord, surely his future will punish him for that. For the present. he did not know why he came here. He was sent for, with an offer of employment, which he presumed came from me. He has told me that things have not gone well for him in Europe, and so he sought a position as my bodyguard, assuming that I was still engaged in my youthful activities. That, being the man he is, he would have accepted Zobeir's commission is un-doubted. But it is against all the tenets of justice to condemn a man for what may be in his heart. He has committed no crime, here in the Centre of the Universe. Let him also be sent forth, never to return.'

Ukuba turned to the waiting people. 'What say you, members of the Inner Court?'

There was a moment's hesitation, while Wilde watched Zobeir's head, no more than a dark blob now, as it bobbed on the water. He was not sure they would be doing him a favour; he had no prospects of walking back to the mainland. Yet his instincts told him that trusting Inger was his only way out of here; she was the most treacherous of women, but she was also as arrogant and confident as ever. She genuinely considered him harmless, to her, and possibly again useful at some future date.

The Followers seemed to practise much of what they preached. The agreement came in murmurs.

'Then let it be done immediately,' Inger said. 'But they are not so guilty as Zobeir, nor so familiar with the country. My Lord, I beg you to permit them the use of the helicopter.'

'Gladly, my child, but for a fear that the man Wilde might attempt to take over the machine.'

'There will be no chance of that,' Inger promised. 'Fodio, fetch them clothing.'

Two *haiks* were produced, together with a tunic each, and a pair of the ill-fitting trousers. *Nail* sandals were thrust on their feet, the strap passing between their first two toes. Wilde attempted to wrap his head in the *haik*, discovered there was more to it than he had imagined.

Inger allowed him a brief smile. 'You will have to look to Serene for instruction. Now extend your wrists.'

He hesitated, staring at her. She was close enough for him to touch, and Kanem was four feet away. He could complete his mission now, if his muscles would react, after their night on the cross, if he was prepared to die. If he was prepared to kill Inger. If he had ever been prepared to do that. And she, with the carelessness of a spendthrift, had just tossed him his life, as she might throw a coin to a beggar.

He placed his wrists together, and she bound them, then did the same to Serene. Fodio and Kanem marched them across to the plane. 'We will accompany them on the flight,' Kanem said, 'to alleviate all of your fears, my Lord.'

Ukuba frowned. 'But you have heard the judgement of the Inner Court, my son. No harm must befall them. Their sole punishment is to be set down far from the Centre of the Universe.'

'I heard, my Lord,' Kanem said. 'And it shall be so.' He pointed to the step, and Serene climbed into the cabin.

'Give my love to Miss Boraine,' Wilde said. 'I hope her night was more enjoyable than mine.' He clambered in, sat beside Serene. Kanem and Fodio sat behind them, and the door was closed. The rotors started immediately, the helicopter left the ground, circled the island once.

'I can't say I'm sorry to be leaving,' Wilde remarked. 'I can't remember a place I've liked less.'

'You have seen enough.' Fodio drew the curtains across the windows, left the cabin in darkness.

'We have a right to know where you are taking us,' Serene said.

'You will know that when we arrive. But I can tell you that it will be neither Fort Lamy nor Kano. We do not wish you to be able to find your way back to civilization too quickly. But it is no matter; you have each other.'

The brothers seemed to find this amusing. Serene gazed at Wilde for some seconds from behind the folds of her *haik*, but even in the gloom he could tell that the expression in her eyes was quite different from the careful seductiveness of the previous morning. Then she curled herself into the ball she had emulated during their last flight together. Wilde considered his wrists. Inger had tied them, and what Inger had tied would take some unfastening. Besides, it was not worth the effort. She had kept her word, and now he could allow himself to understand just what had happened to him.

It would be pleasant to assume that his utter *débâcle* had been caused purely by the *borbor* still affecting his system. Or perhaps because Ukuba had made more of an impression on him than he was prepared to admit, and Inger wore the protective mantle of his wife. Pleasant, but hardly honest. He wondered what he would do when next she snapped her fingers. Because, however efficient he was, however fast-thinking and quick-moving, however fit and however ruthless, he was only as good as the people behind him, the people who employed him. Inger made Sir Gerald and Mocka resemble a couple of average carthorses. So if he was nothing more than an assassin, now and for ever, he would survive longer by working for someone at least superior to himself. Supposing she *had* offered him employment, what then? Or was he irrevocably handicapped by being one of that totally outdated species, a patriotic man?

But she had not offered him employment. And he was well aware that his value to the British government lay only in his reputation for never having failed to complete a mission.

The helicopter started to descend. Kanem unstrapped his seat-belt, took a thick white cloth from the seat behind him, wrapped it into a band, passed it round Wilde's eyes, secured it at the back; Fodio was doing the same for Serene.

'You're assuming we won't like it where we're going?' Wilde asked.

'You will find it very restful where you are going, Mr. Wilde.'

The helicopter touched the ground, settled. Wilde listened to the door opening, heard nothing but the soughing of the wind.

'Come.' Kanem apparently took Serene first. Then he touched Wilde on the shoulder. The brothers dragged him to his feet, pushed him across the cabin and through the door. The ground on which he landed was soft, and he fell to his knees. Sand scattered across his face, like a fine, brittle powder, stinging the flesh.

The door slammed above him, the rotors regained full power, and more sand clouded around him, sucked upwards by the down draught. The noise of the engine grew fainter.

'Mr. Wilde ' Serene asked. 'Where are you?'

'Right beside you, sweetheart.'

'Then help me take this off. Quickly.'

There was a note of alarm in her voice. He moved towards the sound, soft sand clogging his feet. He bumped into her, ran his hands up her shoulder and over the back of her head, fumbled at the knot holding the blindfold, released it. 'Now what about me?'

There was a moment's hesitation before he felt her hands on his head. The bandage fell to his shoulders, and he blinked. The glare was tremendous, and it was some seconds before he could see clearly. Then he stared at nothing. Nothing but reddish-brown emptiness, a sea of sand-dunes, undulating in every direction, their crests blown into sharp edges by the unending wind. There were no houses, no trees, no rocks, no mountains, no water. There was only sand.

'So let's have the punch line.'

'We are about two hundred miles north of Lake Chad,' Serene said. 'This is a sand sea. Even the caravans fear it, Mr. Wilde. This is Inger's mercy. She has set us down in the Sahara Desert.'

PART TWO

THE DAMSEL

CHAPTER SEVEN

WILDE figured it could not be much later than ten in the morning. Already the heat welled up from the sand at his feet, and the glare closed his eyes to narrow slits. Sweat started from his neck and trickled down the inside of his woollen tunic, tickled his thighs. He had an awareness of helplessness, of total defeat, he had never before experienced. As Inger had said, Africa was too much for him.

'Will you untie my wrists?' Serene asked.

He tugged at the rope, gazed into her eyes. After her initial alarm she had regained the indifference of her name. Whether or not she *had* foresworn Islam, she remained a fatalist; presumably, when one grew up in a country like this, there was no other way to look at life.

Her hands were free. She rubbed them together, unfastened his in turn. She squinted at the sun, then sat down, legs drawn up, and gave the fold of her *haik* a further turn completely to cover her face.

He knelt beside her. 'I'd like you to know that I'm sorry you got involved in this mess, even if you were planning to do the old boy in.'

Her eyes reappeared. 'Sit down and save your strength, Mr. Wilde. It is at least four marches to the nearest water, providing we travel in the right direction.'

'There's always something, isn't there.'

'I know which way we must go, Mr. Wilde. But as I said, it will take us four days.'

Incredibly, she seemed to be offering him life. 'Sweetheart,' he said, 'we have no food, and no water, and this is a very hot sun.'

'You must have faith in me, Mr. Wilde. Inger supposes that we are certain to die. But she knows nothing of the desert, and the Kanembu, who are Kanem and Fodio's people, are creatures of the forest. My father was a desert Arab, who taught me how to survive the sun and the sand. The Tubbu, the people of the Tibesti, sometimes make journeys of up to a week without once tasting water. But we have to preserve the moisture in our bodies. So you must sit as I am doing, and you must keep still. If possible, you must sleep. At dusk we will move off.'

'Supposing one simply has to leak?'

'Then do so. Once the water reaches your bladder, it is of no more use to your system. But we must not talk any more, Mr. Wilde.'

She disappeared once again beneath her robe, and was still, a small statue shrouded in a dust cloth. Wilde sat beside her. The sand was hot enough to send waves of weariness surging through his body. He wound the ends of the *haik* loosely around his face, wished he'd gone in for Yoga. He thought about Serene for a while, and then about Inger. Kanem and Fodio would have regained the island by now, and Inger would know that her plans had been brought to fruition. He wondered at the tortured mental processes which must be circulating through that remarkable brain. Presumably, it went something like, I love Wilde, and I hate Wilde; I want Wilde to die, but I cannot kill him myself, and I cannot watch him be killed; but when he dies, it must not be something quick, like a gun-shot or a knife-thrust; it must be slowly, of thirst, cursing me with every last bit of strength in his body. Well, he did not doubt that she would have her wish. But if Inger really thought like that, then she had changed. She was halfway round the bend. The Inger he had known in Stockholm would no more have allowed emotion to interfere with her judgement than a rattlesnake.

He thought about very long drinks of rum and coca-cola, in a glass half filled with ice. Surprisingly, he was not very interested in food at this moment. That would be an added complication.

He thought about other people, other places, about swimming in the tumbling surf off the Cobbler Reef in Barbados, about being locked in the refrigeration plant in Stockholm, with Inger beside him. A naked Inger, her white flesh assuming a shell-pink tinge as the cold got to her.

He thought . . .

Serene shook his shoulder. His head jerked, and he tried to move, but his arms and legs seemed to have solidified. Serene pulled the cloth away from his face, and he found the sun was behind him, sinking into the sand as a blood-red ball. The heat was gone, too, from the air, but it remained trapped inside his clothes, a *mélange* of sweat and dust and sand and mosquito bites.

Serene helped him to his feet. 'The stiffness will wear off when you walk. And we must travel far tonight, while we have all our strength.'

'Where?'

She pointed at Venus. 'We keep that on our right hand. Soon there will be others.'

She set off with an almost military gait. It was like walking along the sea-shore, and if the foot was left on the ground for more than a second it sank ankle-deep into the sand. It was exhausting, but not a fraction so exhausting as just looking. The fading light made very little difference to their ability to see; the night was brilliant, and the dunes were etched in perpetual waves, undulating into the distance, in front of them, behind them, and to either side of them.

Serene looked over her shoulder. 'It will be easier when we leave the sand sea. Perhaps tomorrow night, if we are lucky.'

Wilde placed one foot in front of the other. Tomorrow night was not a practical objective. The wind was rising now, whipping the sand into stinging spurts, and the temperature was dropping like a runaway elevator, plunging the night into a cold which had been unapproachable in Chad.

They walked, and shivered, and stumbled through the sand. Wilde even thought he slept, from time to time, staring at Serene's back. Damsel, he thought. Damsel in distress. My damsel.

He was on his knees; his body had turned to lead from the waist downwards. The wind accumulated the sand into drifts against his thighs. He watched Serene walking away from him, into the brightness, for the moon had risen, and hovered above them like a frozen sun. Then she stopped, and turned, and came back.

'No, no, Mr. Wilde. We must keep on walking until dawn.'

'Anything you say.'

He stood up, wondered why she cared.

Dawn came as suddenly as had dusk. Serene sat down without a word, wrapped herself in her *haik*. Wilde made the mistake of attempting to lick his lips, found his tongue sticking to the roof of his mouth. Even breathing was difficult, because of the dryness of his throat, and now rumbles of wind filled his belly, had him shivering and shuddering. The memory of the foul-tasting water Inger had offered him seemed like nectar. Coherent thought was impossible. He gazed at Inger's hair, which seemed to have become part of the desert and the sun, and coiled and swung in shimmering whiteness, round and round his body, between his legs and under his arms, filled his mouth. Inger's hair was real. It was the only real part of her. Serene's hair was real too. But it was black and wiry, not soft and clinging. One would not choke on Serene's hair. But if one had to choke on a woman's hair, Inger's was the best going.

'Come,' she said. Not Inger, Serene. Or perhaps they were both here, dragging him onwards. It was night again, and cold. He had survived two days and one night without water, without food, perhaps without life. The sand was growing softer and deeper with every step. But it wasn't really sand at all. It was Inger's hair, spreading across all of North Africa, stretching its tentacles upwards towards the Mediterranean and Europe. It might be possible to walk out of the sand sea, but not out of Inger's hair.

Serene stopped. He did not notice, and walked into her. She made no sound, caught him, steadied him, made him stand still while she knelt and gazed at the sand. There was a moon again tonight, glistening out of a cloudless sky. And there was scuffed sand, stretching north, stretching south.

Wilde dropped to his knees. 'A caravan?' The words sounded like an unintelligible blah.

'Many camels, certainly. Going north.'

'We'll follow them?'

She shook her head. 'These are two days old, Mr. Wilde.'

'But there will be others?'

'Maybe, Mr. Wilde. Maybe tomorrow, maybe next month. We cannot wait.'

'I tell you what, sweetheart. You go on, and I'll wait.'

She stood above him, so close he could smell her sweat. 'You will die if you stay here, Mr. Wilde. No man should willingly die before his time.'

'And you don't think my time may have arrived? Ever read *The Talisman*?' Strange he hadn't thought of this before; when he talked, saliva flowed. He could talk forever.

'No, Mr. Wilde.'

'It's about a king of ours, of England, named Richard. Rather a Bad Thing, really. He used to rush around this part of the world, chopping people with his sword. It was a very big sword. Until one day he met a chap called Saladin.'

'I have heard of Salah-al-Din, Mr. Wilde.'

'I thought you might. So Richard said, I'm better than you, darling, and proved it by clobbering a bit of iron into two pieces with his big sword. Maybe, Saladin said, but can you do this, and he chopped a piece of silk in two with his scimitar. So it occurred to our boy Richard that there are some people who belong in the desert and others who belong in the fog. So he went back to his fog. And stayed.'

'But first he had to survive the desert.' Serene held his cheeks between her hands, kissed him on the mouth. She still had saliva. It tasted like nectar.

'Tell me why?'

She smiled. It was the smile he had seen in the room at Kano, that century ago. It was not a smile to forget.

'You are a man who kills. And Inger is afraid of you. I could tell it, from the tone of her voice, the way she looked at you, the way she wanted you. I have never seen Inger afraid, before you. Come.'

They walked, and stumbled, and staggered through the sand. But now he could think only of Serene. Of Serene's smile.

He sat, his legs crossed, his arms folded, his head sagging. He no longer felt thirsty, in recognizable terms. His mouth was filled with cotton wool, which, if left undisturbed, by opening or by speaking, was not positively unpleasant. The rest of him had no existence. Only his brain, hovering above its layer of cotton wool, was actively painful, actively unhappy with its situation.

'It will be easier tonight,' Serene said. 'Look yonder.'

Wilde raised his head. There was no alteration in the colours in front of them, but the texture was different, and the shape of the landscape had changed, too. It sloped upwards, and at no great distance erupted into outcroppings of rock, towering into the air, carved into grotesque shapes by the wind and the ever eroding sand, hovering and cowering, seeming about to overbalance.

'Then what are we waiting for?'

'We still have a great distance to travel. Now be quiet.'

His mistress had spoken, and he was silent. But this was real servitude, not psychological. Without Serene he had no being.

Another day, but today, surprisingly, he found it less easy to sit still, to sleep, for all that he had never before today truly understood the meaning of exhaustion. Instead of resting, his brain raced. It occurred to him that he knew he was going to die, this time, that he was not going to survive more than one night. That Serene would have to go on alone. He envisaged her as some sort of spirit, wandering across the desert, carried by the wind, seeking her revenge. In the desert it was easy to believe in ghosts.

'Come,' she said. It was still daylight, but the heat was fading from the sun. 'We will find the walking easier now.'

He got to his feet. He reminded himself of a donkey. If he were a donkey, she could ride him, from time to time, take the load off her feet. He thought it would be rather pleasant, to spend the rest of his life clamped between those golden brown thighs. But she would be a cruel mistress, and he would make a poor donkey. So he was a dog, tired but faithful, incapable of thinking for himself, obeying her voice, the only voice he knew.

Perhaps the going *was* easier. The sand thinned, but instead there were stones. It would become easier when he became used to kicking against things instead of extricating his feet, if he had the time to become used to it.

He was on his knees, and his knees hurt. Serene stood beside him. 'You must get up, Mr. Wilde.'

'Not this time, sweetheart.'

Serene knelt. This time she did not kiss him; she seemed able to evaluate accurately the condition of his responses. She sank her teeth into the lobe of his ear. Possibly, he thought, she bit it right off. He was glad to be rid of it, an extra, heavy, useless piece of flesh.

She pulled at his tunic, exposed his neck, sank her teeth into the flesh of his shoulder. Now she hurt him, and he was angry. He struck at her, but she caught his arm as easily as if he were her child. 'Get up, Mr. Wilde.'

He reached his feet, and started moving. He kept his gaze fixed on the small of her back, on the bulge of her buttocks, as they moved, rhythmically, under the woollen cloth. He made himself see through the cloth to the golden-brown flesh, with sweat dribbling across it, cutting ravines through the layers of sand, because there was sand and dust everywhere; there could not be a single portion of their bodies, inside or out, which was not coated with sand.

She stopped, throwing out her arm to arrest him in turn. The moon was still bright, but was already sinking into the horizon. They had walked most of the night. 'We must be careful,' she said softly. 'There are people.'

(ii)

For a moment the words meant nothing to him, and then he stumbled forward. She caught his arm. 'In the desert, Mr. Wilde, no man knows his friends at a distance. Be patient. Just a little while longer.'

Now he could hear sounds, lost in the shadows of the large rocks in front of them. A voice spoke.

'*Kallahani?*'

Serene answered. 'It is peace.'

'*Lo barko?*' asked the voice.

'Our jeep is dead. In the sand sea. We have walked for three days.'

'*Ndi durummi?*'

'We have seen the sand, and the sky, and the wind. We have seen neither food, nor water, for three days.'

Now he could see them. Three men, armed with what looked suspiciously like modern rifles. One of them walked towards them, carrying a gourd. 'Drink,' he said in English, and offered it to Wilde.

'After the lady.'

'No, no, Mr. Wilde,' Serene said urgently. 'You are a European. They know that, even though you are dressed as an Arab. We will receive better treatment if I appear to be your servant. But take just a little.'

Wilde rinsed his mouth, allowed some of the water to trickle down his throat. It was warm and rusty, but it tasted like vintage Cockburn's. He handed the gourd to Serene, who drank, and then returned it to the man. He beckoned them, led them between the rocks and into a ravine, gouged by some long dry river. Here there was a fire, and then a tent, while farther away several camels were hobbled together, stamping and snorting. Another, older man waited for them in front of the fire; behind him there were two women, huddled close together, staring at the newcomers.

'This is not good,' Serene whispered.

'Eh?'

'These are not Tubbu. These are Tuaregs.'

'So?'

'But the women are not, Mr. Wilde.'

The leader of the party came towards them, said something, pressed the palm of his hand against Wilde's in the desert greeting, and pointed to a large pot.

'Couscous?'

'We are going to have to take our chances, sweetheart,' Wilde said. 'I'm hungry.'

'You must eat only a little or you will be sick.' She helped him to sit down, stood behind him. Three of the Arabs sat opposite him. The other had disappeared into the darkness.

'No, no,' Wilde said. 'My servant must eat now.'

The oldest of his hosts smiled, nodded. Serene sat down.

'That is good,' Wilde said. 'Now, if you gentlemen will excuse me.' He took three fingers of lamb stew, chewed, every movement of his jaws pure delicious agony, smiled at his host, and fell asleep.

He awoke just after dawn, and already the stony wilderness was beginning to scorch, although the encampment in the gully was still shaded. He lay on the ground, some distance from the tent, and Serene was beside him, also sleeping. Their hosts were seated around the *couscous* pot, having their morning meal, while the women were engaged in stamping out the fire.

The old man, seeing Wilde's eyes open, beckoned him over. Now he was definitely hungry. He accepted a drink of water, attacked the food. In the daylight he decided they were a father and three sons. They wore green *haiks*, and in addition to their rifles, which turned out to be ex-British Army Lee Enfields, and cartridge belts, each carried a lethal-looking knife. But they

seemed friendly enough. No doubt they were gypsies, and therefore unreliable, but obviously he had nothing worth stealing.

They watched him in silence for a while, and then the men
exchanged words between themselves. Wilde wiped his mouth on
his sleeve, allowed himself to belch, hoped these were the right
sort of Arabs. 'I think we should have a chat,' he said. 'I'll wake
up my servant, shall I?'

'I am speaking English,' said one of the young men. 'And she
sleeps well.'

'Oh, she does that, all right. Well, firstly, I wish to thank you
all most sincerely for saving our lives.'

'It is the will of Allah,' said the young man. 'It is hard for us
to know how you are in the sand sea, alone with your servant.'

His reply was important, from their obvious interest. He
decided to build on Serene's beginning. 'We are with a caravan
for Nigeria. But there was a storm, and we became separated. My
friends will be searching for me.'

'Ah,' said the young man. 'We are going to Agadem. There.'
He pointed.

'Which is where, exactly?'

'North. It is in Niger, across the border. Several days, yet.'

'Then where are we now?'

'We are in Chad. Your friends will not cross the border to look
for you.'

This also was important; the young man's eyes were no more
than dark slits. 'Oh, indeed they will,' Wilde said. 'The caravan
was dividing, and half was going to Fort Lamy. They may well
come this way. So my servant and I will keep on in that direction.'

'It is many, many days,' said the young man. 'And you are not
strong. Agadem would be better.'

'This Agadem; it has an airport?'

'Sometimes.'

'Point taken. We will go south. How far is the nearest water to
the south?'

The young man shrugged. 'Two days on foot. But we will give
you a camel. And food and water.'

The old man said something.

'And a rifle,' said the young man. 'That is good?'

'That is out of this world. *Beau Geste* was never like this. I
have no money to pay you with.'

'It is nothing. We still show you the way to go, so you will no
longer need your servant.'

'I sit corrected.' Wilde wondered how weak he really was. He
tucked his right hand under the folds of his *haik*, buried the
fingers in the top of his trousers, so that his knuckles made a

distinct bulge. 'Tell you what, I won't accept the rifle. As for the girl, you wouldn't like her. She is too thin. And as lazy as they come.'

The young man grinned. 'Thin, yes. We have looked, while she slept. But she is still young. She will grow plump. And she has a face a man can remember. We will accept her.'

Serene was awake, gazing at them with anxious eyes.

'I think this young fellow is making you a proposal of marriage, in a roundabout fashion,' Wilde said.

'They would sell me, Mr. Wilde. This is their trade, and I am beautiful.' It was a very simply made statement of fact.

'So what do you think we should do? You're the local expert.'

Serene sat up. 'You have no option, Mr. Wilde. As he says, you are not strong enough to walk farther. A camel will take you wherever you wish to go.'

'And you?'

'I will become some sheikh's concubine. Or perhaps a dancer. There is much money for pretty girls farther north.' Still she gazed at him; but he was not her foster brother, and she would never beg him as she had begged Kanem.

'So I've heard.' He smiled at the young man. 'Well, old sport, I'll tell you. I'd trade the old bag in like a shot, for the camel and the goodies. Trouble is, I'd be breaking the Shopkeepers' Act, or whatever it is they have in your part of the world. She's no good.' He patted his crotch. 'She's had the sickness. Still has, as a matter of fact.'

The young man gazed at Serene. 'There is no evidence.'

'You didn't look far enough.' Wilde moved his right hand, just a little, as if freeing whatever he was clutching. 'So we'll go our way, and you'll go yours. I'm sorry, but there it is.'

The young man spoke with his father and his brothers, then all four of them got up and went farther down the gully. The women continued their work, taking down the tent, occasionally glancing at Wilde. He moved over to sit beside Serene.

'That was good of you, Mr. Wilde. But there is nothing to stop them taking what they wish.'

'We'll put our trust in the rumoured disorganization of your down belows, and the possibility that I may have more than one weapon in mine. Anyway, here they come.' He stood up, and Serene stood behind him. How strong? But why should he be any weaker than these four, who had also just crossed a fair piece of desert?

'So be it,' said the young man. 'We must go, to Agadem. But as it is written in the Koran, so we shall leave you food, and water.'

'In that case I'll take back what I was thinking. And if I manage to lay hands upon a whole bit, I'll send you a wire.'

The women were loading the camels, cursing and shouting to make the animals stand. The men bowed to Wilde, and mounted; there was a beast for each. The women walked, gazed at Wilde as they passed, went up the gully and disappeared.

'I propose we finish our breakfast,' Wilde said, 'since they were kind enough to leave it for us. And then I suppose you'll say we should doss down for the rest of the day.'

'We must make haste today, Mr. Wilde. They are going to come back. They only left us the food to make sure that we would remain here for a while.'

'Very probably, darling. But just where were you thinking of hurrying to? They're the cavalry.'

'They are four men, with guns, Mr. Wilde.'

'And you have no idea what a pleasant feeling it is to be back in my version of civilization.'

'They will kill you.'

'If they were thinking of doing that, why leave us at all? I think they're worried about my supposed pistol.'

'They know you are not armed, Mr. Wilde. They will have looked, while you slept. But they wish to make sure that the rest of the caravan you spoke of is not close by.'

'How long before they reappear?'

'If we *are* alone, and without transport, they know we will only travel by night. They will give us time to go to sleep. Two hours.'

'Then we've time to eat.'

She gazed at him for a moment, sat down, helped him finish the *couscous*.

'Isn't that better? I could go on eating for the next few years, and never feel stuffed.'

'You are strange. Inger told me that you are a professional assassin. That you kill silently, and without mercy or pity or conscience. But you do nothing but joke, and seem happy.'

Wilde extracted a piece of meat from between two teeth. 'Try figuring what conditions would be like inside my skull if I didn't, darling. Tell me, how does your complexion stand up to this sun?'

'I do not enjoy the sun, Mr. Wilde.'

'But it doesn't actually lay you out, over short periods. Let's hope the same can be said for me. Would you like to undress?'

She looked up the gully once again. 'There is no time, and I am unclean.'

'I'm thinking of various movies I've seen. Family viewing, too, believe it or not. Ever go to the cinema?' He stood up, took off his clothes.

'There are no such things in the Centre of the Universe. But Inger has told me about them.'

'I suppose you could look at them as a perpetual university of useless and generally inaccurate knowledge. They rely on the premise that for everyone who is an expert at anything there are several millions who are not.' He knelt, arranged his pants and tunic and sandals in a long line, thrust stones inside to simulate the presence of bones and flesh underneath the cloth, draped his *haik* over the lot, selected a large stone for his head and placed it inside the folded cloth. 'For instance, I've never actually fought Apaches in the great south-west, but it occurs to me that our Tuareg friends may not have had that experience, either.'

Serene pulled off her *haik*, dropped her tunic and trousers on top of it. 'The ambush.'

'Precisely. If I can keep my mind on my work long enough to arrange your things the right way. Isn't it remarkable how the first square meal in three days can cause the sap to rise?'

'But what will we use for weapons?'

'When pushed, I can generally find something. Now I figure they will come over the top of the gully, up there, in order to shoot down on us. That's what they'd do in the movies.'

'Oh, no, no, Mr. Wilde. Cartridges are too expensive. One man will go up there to give them cover. But the other two will come down the gully itself, to use their knives.'

'Darling, I could kiss you. But there were four of them.'

'One must stay with the women.'

'Now I simply have to. Let's get up top.'

She nodded, but instead of leading him out of the gully to the easier slope, turned and bounded several feet up the almost sheer rock-face, her bare toes and fingers discovering cracks where apparently none existed, and then just as suddenly she halted, hanging above him, legs and arms spread wide, while the rivulet of sweat which coursed out from her hair and followed the ravine of her backbone hung for a second from her buttocks before dripping on to his upturned face.

'Four men,' she said. 'They will surely kill you, Mr. Wilde. But if you were to go on and leave me . . .'

'One would suppose you *wanted* to spend the rest of your life dancing. If we go, we'll go together. Now get moving.'

She disappeared over the lip, some twelve feet above the floor of the gully itself, and he began his ascent. It took him considerably longer, and was extremely painful. Serene knelt above him, waiting to grasp his arms and drag him to safety. He lay on his back on the burning rocks, gasping for breath, while she crouched over him, her hair acting as a sunshade.

'You are hurt. There is blood. Here.' Her fingers were very soft.

'I'll survive. I hope.'

'The men of the forest, who go without clothes, wear a sheath. It is composed of plaited grass, and hangs by a cord from the waist, and protects the organ from thorns and such things when they are in the bush.' She completed her investigation. 'You are not damaged.'

'I'd have thought that was obvious. Now let's find a bit of shelter.'

She led him to a boulder from beneath which there peered a stunted bush, situated some twelve feet from the lip. She squatted, her backside half an inch off the ground, and stared at him. Little beads of sweat clouded her forehead and her cheeks, pitting the soft sand dust which coated her skin. And now that she was still, the ever present flies gathered, crawling over her lips, clustering on each nipple as they might on two lumps of strawberry jam, seeming to possess her. She ignored them, although the constant tickling had him slapping and scratching. And yet, incredibly and disturbingly, the presence of so much living filth actually increased her animal attraction. They gazed at each other for some time, and then she stretched out her hand, rested it for a moment on his cheek, and withdrew it again. It occurred to him that could he snap his fingers and transfer this girl into a short skirt and nylon underwear and a sheepskin jacket and a red and white decorated Chelsea apartment, he might have the answer to the quest on which he had been engaged ever since the death of Jocelyn Kirby.

'Tell me about Inger. And you.'

'She came two years ago, as she told you. My parents were dead. She was as a mother to me. But more. She taught me about life, and love. I was a virgin when she came. I believed my great-grandfather that fornication was a sin, that a woman should go to her husband untouched by other men. She seduced Fodio and Kanem, and had them seduce me.'

'All this while married to Ukuba?'

'She makes a great show of worshipping him. But in her heart she despises him, and all he stands for, Mr. Wilde.'

'And you hate her for this? For destroying your innocence?'

'I loved her, Mr. Wilde. I served Fodio and Kanem only to please her. But I was too apt a pupil, perhaps. Everything she wished to teach me I was eager to learn. And so she became jealous of me. And I learned to hate her. And yet I loved her. I love her still, Mr. Wilde. But I hate her, too.'

'And you wish to avenge yourself upon her?'

Serene's face closed, as it had done when Inger had been tormenting her upon the cross. 'They have come back.'

Wilde heard nothing for several seconds, and then a stone moved, some feet away. He touched his lips with his forefinger, held her arm, and pressed it down. She nodded, made room for him to pass her and kneel at the corner of the boulder. He understood that he was on trial, that having heard so much about him from Inger, and having seen so little, she was sceptical. He closed his right first, opened it again. His hand hurt.

A man came up the slope from the desert below, his rifle thrust in front of him. His face was invisible behind the rolls of woollen cloth, but he was clearly one of the three sons. He came slowly, carefully, but yet with a sense of urgency; his brothers would not wish to act until he was in position.

He reached the lip, knelt, peered into the gully. Serene's fingers ate into Wilde's arm. But the others would still be waiting, and watching.

The man raised his left hand above his head, moved it to and fro, lowered it again. Wilde counted to ten; the gully was at least fifty yards deep. He stood up. The last time he had killed a man while in the altogether he had been freezing. Now he was burning; the sun seemed to redouble its strength with every minute as it approached noon, and it pounded down on his exposed head. He sucked dust-filled air into his lungs, walked quickly across the red-hot rocks, allowed his shadow to fall on the man's arm.

The Arab's head jerked, and he rose to his feet, turning as he did so. Wilde had already side-stepped, placing himself between the man and the lip, and had anchored his feet, transferring every ounce of his hundred and eighty pounds from his thighs and up into his shoulder and thence along his right arm, throwing the arm out from his body in a backhanded, upwards sweep, the weight now concentrated in the edge of his hand, which crashed into the base of the Tuareg's skull.

The rifle slipped from the already lifeless fingers, struck the rocks with a clatter. The Arab's knees gave way, and he followed the gun to the ground with a dull thud. Wilde was already on his knees, ignoring the stinging pain in his hand, wrapping his fingers around the trigger guard as he looked over the edge, saw the other two young men, on their bellies, unaware of what had happened above them as they wormed their way towards the silent bundles of white cloth. Both had their rifles slung across their shoulders; as Serene had said, they were going to rely on their knives. He felt rather than saw her beside him, knew she was investigating the dead man's clothing. She made no sound.

The first man reached Wilde's clothing, reared like a striking snake, his knife glinting in the sunbeam which reached the floor

of the gully. Wilde stood up. 'Drop it,' he said. He figured he was
speaking a universal language when backed with a gun.

The leader had already plunged his knife through Wilde's
haik, once, twice, the second blow a reflex action even after he
knew he had been tricked. He turned, looking up and pulling
the rifle from his shoulder in the same instant. Wilde squeezed the
trigger, and the green robe exploded into crimson.

The second man fired, the bullet whining away into the morning air. Wilde squeezed the trigger again, and nothing happened.
Only then did he realize that his weapon had apparently never
encountered grease in its life. He dropped to the ground, working
the bolt. 'Stay down!' he snapped at Serene.

But she remained on her feet, a golden-brown fury, her midnight hair just disturbed by the gentle breeze, the long knife she
had taken from the dead man's belt held between the thumb and
the first two fingers of her right hand. As the third Arab turned
his rifle towards her, she laughed, a bubbling explosion of pure
glee which accompanied the whipping motion of her arm.

It occurred to Wilde that looking over the lip to observe the
success of her throw was as pointless as dreaming of her in a
Chelsea flat; she had, after all, been trained by Inger.

CHAPTER EIGHT

SERENE peered over the edge. 'He is dying,' she said with satisfaction. 'And the other man is already dead. And this one is dead.
This was superb.'

'Don't you believe in any of your great-grandfather's prin-
ciples?' Wilde asked.

'The Fula have always been a fighting race, Mr. Wilde. We did
not need the Prophet to make us into conquerors. Ukuba's world
is impossible to achieve, even were it desirable. It is but a dream,
which binds the more gullible of his Followers to him.'

'Now she tells me. Don't you think we should do something
about the other bloke?'

'He has heard the shots, and will suppose that you are dead.
Even now he will be coming to us.'

Wilde at last managed to free the bolt on the rifle. 'I don't
think much of the care they take of their weapons.'

'But you cannot grease guns in the desert, Mr. Wilde, or the
sand would stick to them, and they would become useless. And
you do not need a rifle. This man . . .' She stirred the corpse with
her foot. 'I could not believe it, the way he died. Inger told me

and I could not believe it then, either. Tell me how he died, Mr. Wilde.'

Wilde scooped the crisp black hair from the nape of her neck, kissed the furry down on the base of her skull. 'Under there is something called your medulla. It controls your breathing, your heart-beat, every automatic function of your body. It's well protected, of course, by a thick piece of tissue called the occidental process. But if you hit someone at just the right angle and with sufficient force you can drive this protective tissue into the medulla itself. And that's it.'

'Silent. Immediate. You must teach me how to deliver this blow.'

'You stick to your knife, sweetheart. You have to hit pretty hard. Would that be our friend?'

Serene looked into the gully. 'It is the father.'

Wilde stood up, the rifle butt against his shoulder. 'Stop!'

The old man checked, looked up at the rocks.

'Tell him to unsling his rifle, and throw it behind him.'

Serene gave the order, and the old man obeyed.

'Now, can you handle one of these things?'

She nodded. 'My father taught me. I told you, when I was a little girl, every year for three months he would take me into the desert, so that I could learn the skills of my people. He believed in Ukuba's teachings, but he said that we must be prepared for anything that might happen.'

'There's nothing like an indulgent father. Down you go, collect a rifle, and keep the old chap covered until I get there. Covered mind.'

She laughed, stooped, rolled the dead man over the edge of the rock, watched him plummet downwards to strike the ground at the feet of his father, and then followed, as graceful as any trapeze artiste. Wilde waited for her to reach the floor of the ravine and pick up one of the discarded weapons, then he checked his rifle-bolt again, walked down the slope, the sun's heat smashing into his head like physical blows, the stones sharpening themselves on his bare feet. At the bottom of the hill he came upon the camels, hobbled together. In front of them squatted the two women; their wrists had been bound behind their backs and then secured to a stake driven into the ground, so they could not stand. They gazed at the naked white man in alarm, mingled, he suspected, with amusement, and then with one movement they shrugged their *haiks* from their heads. One was a Tubbu, plump and loose-mouthed, the other was a Negress, tall as any man, dark-skinned and disdainful; both were young, and worth a second glance in any company.

He untied their wrists, but kept his rifle handy. 'Come.' He beckoned them into the gully. They hesitated only for a moment, and then followed him, leaving the camels grunting and spitting at one another. Serene had regained her *haik*, and sat cross-legged on the ground, her rifle across her knees, cleaning the blood-stained knife. The old man stood opposite her, his hands clasped on his neck, gazing at the bodies of his sons.

'Tell these ladies that we mean them no harm,' Wilde said, 'that they are at liberty to go where they please. We will take two of the camels, and half of the food and water; they may have the rest.'

Serene translated, and the Tubbu woman answered. 'They say that they have nowhere to go, Mr. Wilde, except with us.'

'Eh?'

'They say that they have lost their maidenheads, and will not be welcomed back by their own people.'

'Well, suggest something.'

'It would be simplest to shoot them, Mr. Wilde.'

'Try again.'

'They are of no value to us.'

'It wasn't their value I was thinking about, sweetheart.'

'I do not understand you, Mr .Wilde. You have killed two men this morning already. What are two more, and women at that? You are going to have to kill the old man, in any event.'

'I don't think that will be necessary. And if it's any consolation, the whole thing doesn't always make sense to me, either. But the answer is still no. You tell them that we have no use for them, and that they must go their own way.'

Serene shrugged, addressed herself to the Arab woman once again; the Negress screamed with laughter.

'That sounded good.'

'I have told the Tubbu that you spit on her, because her breasts are shrunken like dried dates, and her buttocks are bony like those of a cow, and she has the smell of a she-goat, and that if she does not take herself and her companion off, you are going to shoot her in the belly.'

The Arab woman had already removed her *haik* and her tunic, was shaking herself to dispose of the first point, was obviously about to attend to the others.

'Not dried dates, darling.' Wilde said. 'Overripe pumpkins, maybe. But I'm sorry.' He shook his head.

She scowled, made a few remarks to Serene.

'She says if you ever wish to lie upon my belly you must be mad, because anyone can see at a glance that I am a syphillis-ridden whore,' Serene said.

'That's how these unfortunate rumours start. Tell me, why are they so interested in me?'

'It is because you are without clothes, Mr. Wilde. They have never seen a man naked in the desert. It is against the teachings of Islam.'

'Oops.' Wilde dressed himself, slung one of the rifles and two of the cartridge belts, pointed the other rifle towards the two women, shook his head once more. 'You tell them that we are going now. We will leave them two camels, as we promised. But if either of them attempts to follow us up the gully I *am* going to shoot her. Tell them they can bury these men.'

'They will never do that,' Serene said, but she translated.

The Negress sighed; the Tubbu rolled her eyes, and made a suggestion. Serene smiled, and then laughed. The old man dropped to his knees, both hands clasped in front of his face, babbling at Wilde.

'She says, leave them the old man, and they will stay behind.'

'He doesn't seem too pleased at the prospect. What will they do to him?'

'They hate him,' Serene said. 'He has been very cruel to them. He has beaten them every day, and when they would not obey him he had his sons drag them through thorn bushes. They wish to kill him. Slowly.' She placed her sandal against the old man's shoulder, pushed. He fell over, apparently still praying. 'It is what he deserves.'

She put on the remaining cartridge belts, slung the fourth rifle, tucked her favourite knife into the waistband of her trousers, stepped over his prostrate, gabbling figure.

'Where is the next water to the north?' Wilde asked.

Serene shrugged. 'Two days, maybe.'

'Then tell the old boy to beat it.'

She frowned at him. 'This man would have cut your throat, Mr. Wilde.'

'So I'm offering him sore feet.'

'Oh, he will get to the water,' Serene said. 'He knows the desert as you know your own face. But he will not thank you for your mercy. He will hate you for killing his sons.'

'I'll add him to the bottom of the list. Now tell him.'

Serene sighed, spoke to the old man. He gabbled something at Wilde, leapt to his feet, and scuttled up the gully.

'I will go and make sure he does not turn the camels loose.' Serene glanced at Wilde. 'I could shoot him. That would be quick.'

'Let him walk.' Wilde faced the two women, who were shouting at him, and gesticulating. 'I'm sorry, darlings. Now you just

shut up and sit down or I'll change my mind about the camels.'
He pointed at the ground. 'Sit!'

They glowered at each other, sat down.

'*Ciao*,' Wilde said, and followed Serene.

(ii)

The old man had disappeared. Serene had already selected the
two best camels, hobbled them separately. Now she was going
through the packs, transferring what she wanted into the one they
were going to use. 'There is money. Chad currency.'

'Bring it along. I'm sure we'll find something to spend it on.'

She dropped it into the bag. 'And there is more ammunition,
and some dates, and dried meat. And tea. Only a little water, but
there is water close to us, now.' She strapped two French Army
surplus jerry-cans to the larger of the camels. 'It is to the south.
You still wish to travel south, Mr. Wilde?' She continued to delve,
without looking at him.

'That's why I sent our friend north.' There was a great deal of
water to the south. Lake Chad.

'Then let us make haste before those women try to follow us.'

Wilde went over to the camels, and around them at a safe distance, still managed to have what might have been a hose directed
at him. 'You're going to have to teach me about these beasts,
sweetheart. Do they do everything backwards?'

'Everything fundamental, Mr. Wilde. Two camels copulating
make a most interesting spectacle. But this is not the breeding
season.'

'Thank God for that. It seems to me that if there is anything
wrong with this country it's that all life is a shade too fundamental. What do I do?'

She shouted at the larger camel, added a few pokes and
thumps with the butt of her rifle, and he sat down, gazing at her
with undisguised venom.

'Now you get on to the saddle, Mr. Wilde.'

'Famous last words. How's this?'

'Forward a little more. That is very good. Now kick him.'

'I wouldn't dream of it. Not while he's down there and I'm
up here.'

'You must show him that you are his master.' Serene swung
her rifle, struck the unfortunate animal a savage blow across the
rump. It stood up so promptly that Wilde nearly kept on going.
Serene scrambled on to hers, took the lead.

He copied her as best he could, but within half an hour had
come to the conclusion that he had not really been intended as

a camel jockey. Presumably it beat walking through the sand sea; his legs no longer suffered. But his stomach sagged and lurched along with his saddle, and sitting down was going to be difficult.

The rocks and boulders became larger and more numerous, and their progress began to resemble a drunken corkscrew. But now the vegetation was also increasing. They passed several suitable camping sites, and the sun dropped into the western horizon, and still Serene jogged along, head rising and falling with unchanging rhythm.

'Don't you think we could call it a day?' Wilde shouted at last.

'We must reach the water. It is not far.'

'We've enough for tonight. Surely.'

She looked over her shoulder, only her eyes showing above the fold of cloth which covered her mouth and nose. 'It is written that when a woman goes to a man first she must wash herself clean.'

Wilde scratched his ear.

'Do I not please you, Mr. Wilde? Up there, while we waited for the Tuareg, I know that I pleased you.'

He supposed he should feel complimented. But there was no affection in Serene.

'It is here.' She pointed. It was quite dark now, and for some minutes he saw nothing, although his camel was certainly moving faster. Then they entered another of the long, narrow gullies between the rocks which were clear proof that once this area had been fertile.

'How do we get off these things?'

'You make it sit, like so.' She kicked and shouted at her mount, and it sank to its knees. Wilde tried the same intonations, without success, until she came to his aid. 'I will see to the camels and the tent. You would like to drink?'

'Where?'

'Just follow the cut, Mr. Wilde.'

He descended the gently sloping rock passage, came to open ground, with black earth, a scattering of palm trees, and a hole in the ground. He wasn't sorry it was dark. This was just water, and whether it was green or brown would not be apparent until morning.

He lay on his face, rinsed his head and neck, drank, wondered if he had sunstroke; his scalp seemed to be lifting and falling again with every breath. Serene knelt beside him with the water-cans. She filled them, then drank in turn.' Come.'

He followed her back to where the tent was pitched, inside the gully itself; the camels were hobbled about fifty feet away, brows-ing on an incautious bush.

'This is the only oasis for some distance, Mr. Wilde, so we will not light a fire. In this ravine no one will know that we are here.' She undressed, poured some water from the jerry-can into the drinking gourd, and with great care washed herself between the navel and the knee. 'Now I will please you,' she decided. 'And if you will come here I will wash you also.'

'Be my guest.' He stood in front of her. 'You don't think it would be simpler just to have a bath in the pool?'

'Water is for drinking, Mr. Wilde. Not for wasting. Do you know that you have a growth of beard, and it is grey? When it is longer it is going to make you look very old.' She stroked the bristle. 'It is already getting soft. Does that not feel good?'

'It feels marvellous, darling. I tell you, though, we Europeans are a kinky lot. May I indulge in a fancy of mine?'

'I am yours to command, Mr. Wilde.'

'Then close you eyes.' He poured some more water, washed the dust from her face and neck and ears. Then he washed her breasts as well; he couldn't get the flies out of his mind.

She smiled. 'Inger has told me how her menfolk prefer to caress the breast more than anywhere else. Is that not strange, Mr. Wilde? I cannot give you milk.'

'Live in hope, die in despair.'

'I do not understand you. I do not understand anything about you.' She crawled into the tent, spread one of the blankets. 'Lie here.'

Wilde obeyed. She knelt beside him, stroked his face. Her hands drifted down his chest, plucked the hair and tickled the nipples, explored the crevasses of his groin. 'Do you not wish to possess me, Mr. Wilde?'

'It's a thought, for a rainy night.'

'But you will not touch me.'

He put his hands behind his head. 'For the time being, you're working hard enough for both of us.'

She frowned at him. 'You are afraid that you will wish to keep me, once you touch me. You wish to find a woman you can keep, Mr. Wilde. You are very lonely. I have read it in your eyes. I saw it even when you looked at the rich American. She is not beautiful, but she is a woman, and for all her wealth she is a lonely woman. You knew this, and your eyes were hungry. Not with lust, but with longing. And yet you are a handsome man, and strong, and you know how to kill. You are a man any woman would be proud to know and to love. Why do you not have a woman, all of your own?'

'It's a long story.'

'There was a woman once,' she said thoughtfully. 'Yes. You

are no longer a young man. But when you were young there was a woman. There had to be a woman. She left you for another man.'

'She didn't have the time.'

'Then she died? Alas. How did she die, Mr. Wilde?'

'I killed her.'

Serene's mouth formed the round 'O' he found so attractive, and for a moment her caresses ceased.

'I killed her because she was going to kill me. That was her reason for coming to me in the first place.'

'And so she deserved to die, Mr. Wilde.' She lay on his chest, imprisoned him between her thighs. 'We have been travelling south, all day. But tomorrow, if you wish it, we can travel southeast, to Mao.'

'Don't tell me he's mixed up in this, too.'

'Mao is a town, Mr. Wilde. From there you will find transport to Fort Lamy, and you can return to England.'

'You sound as if you'd like to offer me an alternative.'

She kissed his mouth, explored every tooth with her sharp pointed tongue, worked her body against his, used the walls of her prison as an assault force. His hands closed on her shoulders, searched downwards to her buttocks. Her skin was like velvet. And he had wanted her for so very long. For ever, perhaps, without even knowing. But possession would only come when she was ready.

'There's a shame,' he said, as soon as he got his breath back. 'And as you've just reminded me, I'm no longer a very young man.'

She laughed, slipped from his body, and washed herself all over again. 'Neither are you a very old man, Mr. Wilde. You will soon be ready again. I will make you ready. And then I will be ready too. I am ready now, but I prefer to wait. Waiting increases pleasure. Your true lover can wait for ever.'

'I've read the *Kama Sutra*. In Europe we've always inclined towards a more balanced life. You know, a little of what you fancy rather than a succession of banquets.'

'You English, in particular, are overly concerned with time.'

'You haven't met many modern Englishmen, darling. Their point of view is very close to yours. Tell me about tomorrow.'

'Our alternative route lies due south, Mr. Wilde. That way there is nothing between us and Lake Chad.'

'And then what?'

'There is still much water to be crossed, for the Centre of the Universe lies towards the middle of the lake. We will need rain. But the rain is overdue. I will be your guide.'

'And then what?'

'There are no weapons in the Centre of the Universe, Mr. Wilde. We have our rifles. They will not find it so easy to tie us to the cross this time.'

'And Inger?'

'Inger condemned you to a lingering death in the desert. She deserves to die.'

'I won't argue with that.'

'Inger has loved you. But she has loved me as well. So with her I am a child. By myself. Together with you it will be different. But you do not wish to kill her.'

'I'm beginning to doubt my ability in that direction.'

'Together we are stronger than she, Mr. Wilde, because we can draw strength from each other. That fable you told me, about the king and the sultan. You are the king, I am the sultan. Together we can deal with iron or silk, can we not? Or both, in combination. It is a matter of wanting.'

She sat silent, immobile, as she had done each day in the desert, waiting for him to join her pact of revenge. And why did he hesitate, even for a moment? He was in Africa to eliminate Inger Lieberstein. And now that he had been outwitted and humiliated, used and discarded, left to die in the desert after having been contemptuously promised his life, surely now destroying Inger was not going to pose any problem. Even his instincts had been driving him south, before Serene had mentioned the matter. And he knew she would be as good as her word; however long it too, she would guide him back to the Centre of the Universe. So his only remaining obstacle was the Inner Court of the Followers of the Lord.

He had never supposed that he was a particularly brave man. He happened to have lived in the presence of sudden death for a very long time, and every man is bold enough when he has confidence in himself and his weapons; all military training is based on this one simple tenet. Wilde's confidence arose from his experience, the deadly power in his right arm, his charm, his ability to think at tremendous speed when he had to. So when he had known fear in the past it had been the nervous reaction of a pilot who has temporarily lost control of his aircraft, who knows death, for himself and perhaps for others, is hovering very close, but who also possesses all the skills needed to regain command of the situation, if it is at all possible to do so.

The Followers of the Lord were outside his experience. He thought that circle of silent, white-robed figures, slowly advancing towards him, was going to haunt him for the rest of his life. He looked through the doorway of the tent to where the rifles were stacked. He did not doubt that Serene was as good a shot as himself, and they had well over fifty cartridges. But to open fire on fifty unarmed pacifists . . . Sir Gerald would call him a fool. So would Felicity Hart.

The alternative, after reaching Inger, was to die. Because the next time he found himself on the cross he would be there for good. And the operation seemed so utterly pointless. He had, often enough in the past, been prepared to die to accomplish his orders; but always he had been able to persuade himself that something of national importance was at stake. The internecine machinations taking place for the control of a group of mystics seemed about the most absurd thing in the world for which to commit suicide.

Serene was kneeling beside him. 'Help me, Mr. Wilde. The Centre of the Universe was my home, my only home. I have no other, and now it is barred to me. I have no friends, no relations. I have nothing, except you. Help me to destroy Inger, and Fodio, and Kanem, and I swear to be your woman. More, I will be your slave. I will be your slave forever, Mr. Wilde. I will follow you always, do your bidding always. And I will keep my word.'

Wilde sighed. 'I'm afraid your people are a little out of my class.'

She frowned. 'But they are only men, and women, Mr. Wilde. You fought those Tuaregs. You pitted your bare hands against four rifles, and you won. I do not understand you, Mr. Wilde.'

'Men with guns, fine. Men with ideas which may just be right, no. I've always wanted to visit Mao.'

She got up and dressed, served the dates which were to be their supper.

(iii)

Wilde was awakened by a blaring of horns, found the gully blocked by two jeeps and half a dozen Chad policemen, armed with rifles, and commanded by a Frenchman. Serene was gazing through the doorway, her face cold. 'They will take us to Mao,' she said. 'They will arrest us. Even if they permit us to continue without papers, by this afternoon they will find the dead men, and then they will come after us.'

'In which case, you had better leave the talking to me,' Wilde suggested. She gave him a scornful glance, and retired behind her *haik*.

'The top of the morning to you,' Wilde said in French, stepping clear of the tent.

'My God!' The police officer was at once tall and plump. He

wore his cap at a rakish angle, and his revolver was slung low on his hip. 'But you are a European.'

'English. My name is Smith. John Smith. I'm a scientist. Quite well known, as a matter of fact. Perhaps you've heard of me?'

'John Smith. The name has a familiar ring to it, certainly. But . . .'

'My jeep broke down in the sand sea. I'm afraid our papers as well as my equipment are still there.'

The Frenchman frowned. 'I'm Faure.'

Wilde shook hands.

'But we were not informed you were coming,' Faure said. 'That is not right.'

'Ah, well, you see,' Wilde explained. 'We were making south, for Yo and then Nigeria, don't you know. We hadn't planned to enter Chad territory at all. But when the old jeep packed it in, my guide said she knew the way to the south-east, and so we walked this way.'

'You walked out of the sand sea?'

'I thought our number was up, too. But she's very efficient.'

'She?'

Faure peered into the tent. 'Your guide is a woman?'

'Serene!'

Serene removed the robe from her head, came outside. 'I am Mr. Smith's guide,' she said in good French.

'Truly, Mr. Smith,' Faure said in admiration, 'you must have remarkable powers. How you persuaded any Fulani to part with this young lady . . .' His frown returned. 'You did not by any chance buy her?'

Serene tossed her head. 'I am not for sale, Captain Faure. I am of the family of Ukuba.'

'Then I apologize, young lady. I only mentioned the matter because this is not a routine patrol. We are on the track of a most notorious slaving gang. A father and three brothers who have been selling women to the desert sheikhs. You are most fortunate to have avoided them, for our information was that they were travelling this way, and they will certainly have stopped at this water-hole. But I cannot understand where you obtained your camels in the desert. They are fine beasts.'

'As a matter of fact,' Wilde said, 'we took them off the men you're chasing.'

'You took them off the Tuareg.' Faure nodded. 'Oh, yes, I understand, Mr. Smith. I have met Englishmen before. During the war. Now, I have a bottle of wine in my pack. Two, in fact. It is hot, and not very good vintage, but it is drinkable. Let us sample it while my men fill their canteens, and we will speak

about this adventure of ours.' He smiled at Serene. 'And I would
be honoured if you would join us, Princess.'

'I shall be pleased to do so,' Serene agreed.

'Silly of me, I know,' Wilde said in English. 'It never really
occurred to me that you're a princess.'

'Then, Mr. Smith, you must have met some uncommon com-
moners in your time.'

They breakfasted with the captain, and Wilde recounted their
meeting with the three brothers and their father. Faure listened
with the utmost gravity. 'This is the truth?' he asked Serene.

'It is what happened.' She glanced at Wilde. 'He is good with
his hands.'

'No one will ever believe such a report.' Faure opened his
second bottle of wine. 'That a man and a girl, unarmed, liqui-
dated a slaving gang. Believe me, Mr. Smith, my life is composed
of reports, and red-tape, and endless arguments with the people
in Fort Lamy over what is, and what is not, possible in the desert.
I have a proposition to make to you.'

'That's extremely decent of you,' Wilde said, 'but I'm afraid
I'm committed to Serene.'

'Oh, you are a funny man, Mr. Smith. You are also a very
lucky man to have such a woman at your side. My proposition is
that we say you had these camels with you all the time, walking
behind your jeep, eh, because you are a careful man, eh, and have
driven in the desert before. And later on today I will visit the
place you have described, and find the bodies of the three Tuaregs,
and assume that they were attacked and murdered by some rival
band. Oh, yes, Mr. Smith, the desert is still very much of a frontier.
As for the old one, no doubt he is across the border by now, in
Niger. But he is nothing without his sons.'

'And the women?' Serene asked.

'I expect we shall find them easily enough. But, in truth, women
like those, unable to return to their families, unwanted, are nothing but a nuisance. They will go to a home while the government
tries to find them employment, and in time they will leave the
home, and soon they will be on the streets, which is where they
would have found themselves had we not interfered in the first
place. It is a sad business, but none of your concern. I will give
you a paper, which will allow you to continue on your way to
Nigeria. Perhaps you would be good enough to tell me your first
destination?'

Wilde grinned at Serene. 'We had been planning on visiting
Lake Chad.'

'Ah. Of course, you are the famous naturalist. There is much
wild life around Chad.'

'I suppose you could say that I'm a bit of an anthropologist as well,' Wilde said. 'I study human beings, as well as animals and bugs. Serene keeps suggesting we should visit the Centre of the Universe.'

'And she is a descendant of Ukuba. Then she is a relative of the Ukuba who is called the Lord.'

'A distant relative,' Serene said. 'But I know how to get there.'

'Do you know the place?' Wilde asked.

'By reputation. It is easier to approach from the Nigerian side of the lake.'

'Which was our intention, as I told you. But that was before my jeep broke down.'

'To take a jeep into the sand sea at all, that was a dangerous business. But, of course, you had your camels along as a safety measure, eh? Very wise.' He chuckled to show that he was as capable of making jokes as the next man. 'But you can still go. It is simply a matter of crossing the lake. You have arranged for a boat?'

'I leave that sort of thing to Serene,' Wilde said.

'It would be a difficult journey at this moment, because there is little water. But soon the rains will come. It always rains, eventually. You will also be returning this way, Mr. Smith?'

'I have no idea. I could, I suppose. Why?'

'I would like you to come to Mao and pay me a visit. I would like to learn what you have found in this Centre of the Universe.'

'Why haven't you been there yourself, if you're so interested?'

'The island is situated somewhat in the Nigerian portion of the lake, and it would not be good for a Chad policeman to go invading, eh? Besides, many people, and my superiors are amongst them, dismiss any sect which can give its headquarters such an absurd title as not worthy of even our contempt. But it is my opinion that the Followers of the Lord are a group about which every policeman, but more especially those in Equatorial Africa, should learn. I would greatly appreciate your views.'

'I understood they are a pacifist organization.'

'Oh, indeed, very pacifist, Mr. Smith. But do you not find something disturbing about pacifism today? Something sinister? It is concerned with disarmament, with opposing imperialism, with peace between the nations of the world, or, rather, I should say, the governments of the world. These are certainly admirable objectives. But it also condones a terrifying amount of personal violence, and violence to property. I wonder if pacifism today is not just a cloak for anarchy, Mr. Smith?'

Wilde scratched his ear.

'And the Followers of the Lord, as you say, are a pacifist group *par excellence.* Just how far the group extends, how many members it commands, is not known, but certainly it is widespread in Africa. And still we cannot be sure how widespread. Once upon a time, you see, the police reports from all the British colonies and territories would have been correlated, and could easily have been compared with all the reports from the French territories. Now we have more than a score of rival nations, all determined to preserve their integrity, to guard their own archives, regardless of the cost. And the cost may be high. This man, this Ukuba, has thousands, perhaps millions, of lives to play with, when he chooses to use them. Or when his successor chooses to use them, for he is reputed to be quite an elderly man. And his successor, whoever he may be, is sure of victory. For when his people march, what can the authorities do? Nothing? Then their country is overrun. Open fire? Then they mow down thousands of unarmed men and women, and perhaps even children, and are immediately condemned by world opinion. This is a new kind of warfare, Mr. Smith, waged with human bullets. Who knows, perhaps it has already begun. Who can say how many Followers of the Lord have been involved in the protest marches of the past half-dozen years? There is only one fact which is certain: Our reports indicate that the number of Followers is increasing, almost every day, and the number of protesters in the world is also increasing, almost every day, and principally amongst the young people. Ukuba's doctrine, that all the evils of mankind are to be found in twentieth century science and technology, appeals to modern youth.'

'That's quite a nightmare you have there,' Wilde said.

'Let us hope it remains only a nightmare, Mr. Smith. To reassure myself, I would like to discover the true nature of the Followers of the Lord. I would like to learn where they are going, what is their ultimate aim. I would like to stop them, if that is possible. So you come to Mao, on your way home from the Centre of the Universe, and we will talk.' He stood up. 'And now we must be on our way, to visit the scene of your victory, eh? I will bid you goodbye. And to you, Princess Serene. You have made the day bright indeed.'

They watched the jeeps roll out of the gully and away into a dust cloud. 'Miserable French bastard,' Serene remarked. 'I do not like policemen, Mr. Wilde. But you handled him very well; it would not have occurred to me merely to tell him the truth.'

She wanted nothing but revenge, because that was her nature. The dark forces of her subconscious had been carefully nurtured and brought to the surface by her great-grandfather. Ukuba thought he had been releasing them, but instead he had gathered them in a dark stain across the surface of her character, and left them there to accumulate whatever emotions were passing on the wind. Her case was worse than most, because in his ignorance Ukuba had for two years exposed her to Inger, which was corruption enough for any human being. But when Ukuba died the entire sect was going to be exposed to Inger. It was going to be dominated by Inger. Domination was the Lord's own word.

And the solution? In the jungle of ideologies and loyalties in which he moved there was only one solution. Solutions must always be final. Even when they involved innocent people.

Serene took the jerry-cans to the water-hole. He sat waiting for her to come back. 'It is several days to Mao yet,' she said.

'Suppose, just for the sake of argument, sweetheart, that I opted for Chad, instead?'

Carefully she put down the jerry-cans, stood up, shrugged the *haik* from her shoulders.

'You're sure this scheme of yours is practical? We can get there, I mean.'

'It may take us a long while, Mr. Wilde. But we will get there, eventually.'

'And time is the one thing we have a lot of. All right, sweetheart. Target Inger.'

'I knew you would agree, Mr. Wilde.' She was against him, and on top of him, and underneath him. He had to do very little; she was self-perpetuating. Perhaps a great deal of her excitement was faked. But it was none the less real to be on the receiving end. She exuded sex from every inch of her body, in the way her toes stroked, her fingers manipulated, her tongue explored. Inger, whose responses had always been reluctant, could never have taught her a technique as thorough, as Eastern, as this.

At last she spoke. 'Now I am truly yours, for ever, Mr. Wilde.'

But it occurred to Wilde that she had it backwards, and that she knew this, and that this was what he had really feared all the time.

CHAPTER NINE

THEY LOADED the camels and made south through the stone desert, riding all day, and camping for the night beneath the shelter of a clump of acacias, which surprisingly seemed able to exist without any visible water supply. They scarcely spoke; it did not seem necessary. But Serene was as attentive as the most loving of wives.

Before dawn they were awakened by a thunderstorm. The jagged shafts of lightning seemed to plunge into the desert not a hundred yards from where they lay, and the thunder was as continuous as a bombardment. Serene opened the tent flap to gaze at the brilliant display. 'There will be wind,' she said. 'But the storm is good; it means rain.'

She was right about the wind. It rose, steadily, until it was blowing a gale. They spent the morning huddled inside the tent, although for all the protection it gave them from the driving dust and pebbles they might have been in the open.

Towards noon the storm blew itself out, and Serene went looking for the camels. She returned within half an hour with both animals, and they repacked and were ready to move again when she unslung her rifle and ducked behind the trees. Wilde followed her example, saw a solitary camel, accompanied by two robed figures on foot, perhaps a hundred yards to the north.

'This is the most populated bloody desert I have ever crossed,' he remarked. 'Think they mean trouble?'

'It is those women. I told you that you should have shot them.'

He squinted into the glare, realized she was right. And the camel they had lost in the storm had carried their water. 'You'd better invite them in.'

'They will be both hungry and thirsty, Mr. Wilde. And therefore dangerous.'

'How far is it to the next water?'

'We should be there tomorrow.'

'Then we can spare them a drink. We're the ones with the guns, remember?'

Serene slung her rifle, stepped out from behind the trees. She cupped her hands round her mouth, shouted. After a few minutes the women came towards them. Serene ostentatiously cocked her weapon, pointed to the dates and one of the jerry-cans. The women smiled at Wilde, and then attacked the food, using the knives they had taken from the bodies of the dead Tuaregs. Watching them, it occurred to Wilde that he was in the presence of three of the toughest females even he had ever encountered; the two slaves lacked Serene's terrifyingly amoral deadliness, but possessed instead the aggressive physicalness of women used to manual labour and used, too, to disposing of their rivals with their hands rather than their tongues. Properly commanded, they could be a source of tremendous strength, supposing they could be commanded at all.

'I wonder if you'd do some translating for me,' he said. 'I'd like to talk with your fat friend.'

Serene gave him a very old-fashioned look. 'And can I not

satisfy you, Mr. Wilde? Truly you must be a man of vast appetites.'

'Stop grumbling, and listen. Inger is our enemy. I have no wish to fight with your grandfather and his people. As I told you yesterday, I respect them, what they are trying to achieve. I think I can talk us in and out of the Centre of the Universe, but if I can't the Followers of the Lord are more likely to be impressed by four people with guns than by two. We have four guns, and now we have four people.'

'You would trust those two with rifles?'

'Providing our tactics are right, the need never see a live bullet. But only you and I will know that.'

'Truly, you are a man of resource, Mr. Wilde. Yes. Four people armed with rifles would be an obstacle even to the Followers. To feed two more, that will be difficult. But soon we will be in more fertile country, and they will be useful when we reach the lake. Yes. It is not the food which is important. They must be made to follow you, and you only.'

'I was afraid there'd be a catch.'

'It is the fat one we must dominate.' Serene's eyes glinted. 'She is the leader in all things. She has established herself as superior to the dark one, and the dark one will do as she says. It is necessary to make her obey you.'

'I'm open to suggestions.'

'You can flog her. But you will have to beat her very hard, and then she will hate you, as she hated the old man. Oh, she will follow you, and obey you, but only until you meet your master.'

'And then it's me for maenad party. Isn't there a less painful way?'

'You are a man of infinite charm, Mr. Wilde.' Serene's eyes became bottomless.

'Oh, to be in England, in the rain and the fog and the frigidity. You won't be jealous?'

'Of that cow? To lie on her will but make you desire me the more. Retire into the tent. I will arrange it.'

Wilde sat in the tent, listened to gales of laughter. The flap lifted and Serene came in, accompanied by the plump Arab woman. 'She has agreed to hold a conversation with you.'

The woman smiled. Her teeth were actually the most attractive part of her. She was even younger than he had supposed, now that he looked at her more closely, but she was both overweight and dusty. She reminded him of his first-ever visit to a brothel, as a National Serviceman over twenty years earlier. Serene pointed to the blanket, and the woman took off her sandals.

'She is called Fatimah,' Serene said.

'Oh, come now.'

Serene smiled. 'I have given her that name, Mr. Wilde. Hers is not so attractive. Nor, in your tongue, so descriptive. The Negress I have called Joanna. It is a name I have never liked.'

'Ask her how she got here.'

'They have been following us, Mr. Wilde. They would have come up with us sooner, but first it was necessary to overtake the old man.'

'You have got to be joking.'

'I knew they would not let him live, you should have let me shoot him. It is the way of our people, Mr. Wilde. We do not forget an injury. They are very happy with the way he died. It took a long time. And then they had to hide to avoid the police patrol.'

'Why ever did they wish to do that?'

'It is as Captain Faure told us, Mr. Wilde. They have no wish to be sent to a home, and then found employment by the government.'

'Yes. Well, you tell her the conversation is off. I have a distinct pain in my gut.'

'You cannot turn her away now, Mr. Wilde. Then she will hate you more than the old man. He was going to die, anyway. There is no room for mercy in the desert. Now you know that, you will be stronger, eh? And we need them, Mr. Wilde. I also was worried as to how only two of us would successfully regain the Centre of the Universe.' She sat down, cross-legged, on the far side of the tent. 'I will stay here and make sure it goes well.'

'Your sense of humour kills me.'

'Oh, it will not affect me in the least. I will find it interesting. And Fatimah will not mind.'

'Maybe she won't. But I can tell you who it'll most certainly affect. It already has. Between you and the old man, I couldn't raise a sigh.'

'This is to the good. She will assume you are deliberately holding yourself in, for love of her. She is an ignorant desert whore. But it were best to begin now.' She said something to Fatimah, who gave a guffaw of anticipatory laughter, and lay down, her sand-coated toes reaching upwards to stroke Wilde's chest.

'You did say something about cleanliness.'

'I am a princess,' Serene pointed out. 'She is a slut.'

(ii)

The next morning they met a caravan out of Mao, and learned that there had been a tornado in the south which had flattened

houses and caused a wide sweep of destruction. But as yet there
had been no rain. Serene merely smiled, translated Wilde's greetings, and used some of the money they had taken from the Tuaregs
to buy food. That evening they camped in a real oasis, shaded
by a copse of date palms, and inhabited by a semi-resident family
of Arabs, who invited them to dinner, served them lashings of
merissé, and exchanged sly giggles behind their hands.

'I have told them that you are a mad Englishman,' Serene
explained, 'travelling across Africa with your harem. Which is
true enough. Joanna wishes to come to your tent.'

'I'm saving my strength.'

'But I have promised her, Mr. Wilde, and Fatimah has told her
great tales of your prowess. It cannot be until tomorrow, of course.
I have explained to them that I am your number one woman, and
am required on alternate nights.'

'You have no idea what a load that takes off my mind. What's
that?' A large object splashed on the back of his neck.

'It is the rain. I knew it would come.'

Within an hour the rain was falling steadily. It pattered on
the tent all night, and next morning the world was quite startlingly wet and grey. Serene cursed and screamed and finally drove
Fatimah and Joanna outside with promises of a road only a few
miles to the south. It was there, a dirt track trailing between the
rocks; the rain turned it into a nightmare. The water fell straight,
flooding each footstep, splashing on head and shoulders and back
and chest, exploding upon impact, not heavily, but with a terrifying relentlessness. Soon Wilde's haik was a sodden and, he suspected, shrinking garment. It took only a few minutes longer for
his tunic and trousers to be similarly reduced, and from then on
he existed in a soaking cocoon. His camel snorted and splashed,
and in front of him Serene rode with bowed head. Even Fatimah
and Joanna, arms tight around one another as they shared the
third saddle, endured the wetting in miserable silence.

The vegetation brightened almost visibly, but the road itself
disintegrated as quickly, the loose earth draining down the shallow
parapets, and huge gutters appearing with every alteration in the
level of the surface. Their progress slowed, and again, as the
camels picked their way through the muddy soup, and camp that
night consisted of huddling together beneath the dripping tent
while the ground grew ever more liquid. Lighting a fire was out
of the question; they ate dates and drowned their sorrows in
merissé after which even Joanna apparently felt conditions were
too uncomfortable for anything more violent than sleep.

Next morning Serene and Fatimah engaged in another long
argument which ended in a crisp slap, delivered by Serene.

Fatimah uttered a shriek of rage, lowered her head, and butted her rival in the stomach. They fell together, rolled through several inches of mud, and became an indistinguishable flurry of arms, legs, and high-pitched anger. Wilde hastily unclipped the sling from his rifle, showed the heavy leather strap to Joanna, who seemed inclined to join the action, and then swung, once, twice, three times. Fatimah gave a howl of pain, tried to get up, slipped, and received two more welts across her ample backside.

'You as well, sweetheart,' Wilde said, and rolled Serene on to her face with his toe. She took the beating in silence, got up, attempted to brush mud from her body, and only then winced. 'Now tell me what Fatimah was suggesting.'

'She wishes us to remain in camp until the rain stops. She says it will soon slacken. But we must go on.'

Certainly they were so wet there did not seem much point in hanging around. 'Then tell her that those are my wishes,' Wilde agreed.

Serene translated, and Fatimah shrugged, began loading the camels. Amazingly, neither of them seemed angry with him. 'A man must dominate his women,' Serene explained. 'And you whipped me as well, so she is not jealous. It is good.'

'I simply must introduce you to a friend of mine,' Wilde said.

It was too dangerous to ride, so they walked throughout the day, eventually leaving the road, or perhaps the road left them, and entering woods which provided a limited shelter from the teeming rain. The ground had grown softer, and by evening there was not much to choose between this swamp and the sand sea, except that where the sand sea had been uncanny in its silence, this was disturbing in its constant squelching.

They saw little wild life, except for the odd snake. 'Once there was lion here, and giraffe, and every kind of antelope,' Serene said. 'But now they either die of thirst or they drown. So they have moved south. There is still lion beyond the lake.'

Another sleepless night, spent huddled under the trees. As Fatimah had predicted, the rain eventually stopped, but the foliage continued to drip, and in place of the rain there returned the thunder, accompanied by brilliant sheets of lightning. At dawn Serene and Fatimah enjoyed their now habitual argument, punctuated by many references to Wilde with both look and gesture. And once again Fatimah eventually gave way.

'I thought you said they would follow me anywhere?' Wilde asked.

'And so they will,' Serene said. 'But they need to be reminded of your prowess, and of what you are going to do for them.'

'And what's that?'

'Promises cost nothing,' she pointed out.

'Providing I'm not around when they want to collect.'

By mid-morning the rain was back. Wilde no longer had any idea as to just how long his journey had taken. Life ended when the helicopter had dropped him in the sand sea. Was that a week ago? It had returned, briefly, in the oasis during the conversation with Faure and immediately afterwards. Now it was gone again, and he was plodding through eternity, following a girl who hated, towards an execution. To prevent a greater execution. Perhaps. How irrelevant it all seemed. That was the secret of Africa; it made life itself irrelevant. But Africa was the reality, Europe and North America and even Asia the artificial creations of mankind.

'We have arrived,' Serene said, and he heard other voices. Soon there were people as well, moving through the trees, naked men and naked women, surrounding them, touching Wilde's sleeves. 'This is a family of Badumi,' Serene said. 'The people of Chad. They live by fishing, mostly. They will sell us a boat.'

Again he had that uneasy feeling of being surrounded by incalculable numbers of people, curious, dispassionate, totally unsympathetic. They left the bog for higher, drier land, and he could see a village of grass huts. Here waited the father of the clan, wearing a penis-sheath and a string of beads.

'These lake people are amongst the most primitive in all Africa,' Serene explained. 'One has to visit the pygmies of the Congo or the bushmen of the Kalahari to find their equal.'

'But you have been here before.'

'Chad is my lake, Mr. Wilde. Without me you would be nothing.'

The chief asked questions, and Serene replied, waving her arms, the low, guttural intonations sounding strange in her throat. Fatimah and Joanna held hands, casting anxious glances at the people around them, obviously assuming them to be cannibals.

'He says,' Serene translated, 'that this is the start of the fishing season, and their boats are expensive. I will offer him the camels as well as money. They are no more use to us now, and he will be able to sell them in Mao.'

'Anything you say. But I don't think he's happy about it.'

The chieftain had finished consulting with his sons, and was doing some gesticulating in turn.

Serene shook her head, and the father raised his eyes to heaven and turned his palms outwards.

'What's he want now?'

'He demands our rifles as well as the camels. We will have to go

on and find another village. This man is a profiteer. And he knows
it is not legal to sell rifles to the Badumi. Especially modern
weapons like these. What the government would do to someone
who practically *gave* them . . .'

'Darling, you're a scream. So we'll bend the law a little. Offer
him one gun, and twenty rounds of ammunition.'

'How can we go back to the Centre of the Universe with only
three rifles, Mr. Wilde? Suppose your plan goes wrong, and the
Followers seek to kill us?'

'In that case, I don't think we'll miss one rifle at all. Offer him
the gun.'

She chewed her lip, began arguing again. But the chieftain
merely kept on shaking his head and looking at the massed clouds
in the sky, and at last she unslung one of her weapons and threw
it and a cartridge belt on the ground. The chieftain smiled. His
sons were more appreciative; they picked up the rifle and
examined it carefully. The chief addressed Serene once again; his
tone was an octave lower.

'He invites us to spend the night,' Serene said contemptuously.
'To share his miserable pot.'

'A good night's rest on top of a square meal won't do any of
us any harm. We don't want to be droopy when we talk with your
great-grandfather.'

'It is my opinion that we should keep going, but if that is what
you wish, Mr. Wilde . . .' She smiled graciously at the chief and
Fatimah and Joanna immediately sat down with heavy sighs. It
was only after dinner that Wilde discovered what was bothering
Serene; as he had escaped the previous couple of nights, it was
Joanna's turn at last.

(iii)

Dawn brought about as perfect a morning as Wilde could remember. The sky was a brilliant and cloudless blue, it was too early
for the sun to make itself a nuisance, and around them the forest
gleamed, like a young girl who has just left a refreshing shower.
Only Wilde no longer had any desire to think about young girls,
refreshing or otherwise.

The entire clan escorted them to a rickety wooden jetty, situated
at the head of a small creek which wound its way between the
trees. Here there were three boats. Each was about twelve feet
long, with no seats or decking; they reminded Wilde of collapsible
lifeboats only half erected. In any event there was no water into
which to launch them; the jetty stood in a glutinous mud which
made Bembridge Harbour suggest an asphalt playground.

'How long will it take them to get a boat ready?' he asked
Serene.

'It is ready now, Mr. Wilde. These boats are made of grass.'

'That's what must be bothering me.'

'Oh, they are very good, strong but light, and therefore easy to
pole along. Their frame is wood, you see, but the grass makes
them pliable; if they are butted by a hippo they just bend, where
an all-wooden boat would be stove in or capsized.'

'Did you say butted by a hippo?'

'Oh, yes, there is much hippo in the centre of the lake. These
boats have only one fault; they absorb water.'

'Sweetheart, don't you think it would be safer to chop down a
few trees and build a raft?'

'But they only take the water slowly, Mr. Wilde. The grass is
porous, you see, and in time it becomes filled with water, and too
heavy to float. And then, of course, the boat must be thrown away
or it sinks.'

'Your grasp of physics terrifies me. Supposing you happen to
be in the middle of the lake at the time?'

Serene laughed. 'That would be very careless of you, Mr.
Wilde. It would also be a very great tragedy.'

The chieftain extended his arms, and made a speech, praying
for his guests' safety, Wilde hoped. His family applauded, and
then four of the young men loaded a pot of *couscous* and the
two jerry-cans of water into one of the boats, and, to the accompaniment of much hissing and stamping of the feet from their
sisters and cousins, placed the craft on the mud.

'Now what?' Wilde asked. 'Does Mohammed go up to the
mountain, or do we wait for the mountain to drift our way?'

'I do not understand you, Mr. Wilde. The followers of the
Lord do not pray to Allah or to His Prophet. They find their
strength in their own hearts.' She placed the rifles and the cartridge belts beside the jerry-cans, removed her clothing and placed
it on top of the rifles, embraced the chieftain, and climbed down
from the jetty, promptly sinking up to her thighs. Fatimah and
Joanna did likewise. Wilde also undressed, shook hands. The
chieftain seemed delighted. So did the mud, which welcomed
Wilde as if it had been waiting since time began to get hold of a
pair of white legs.

'You must come to the front with me, Mr. Wilde,' Serene said.
'We will show these whores how to work.'

'Give me time.' Pulling one leg out of the mud and replacing
it was a monumental operation, not made any easier by his utter
uncertainty as to what his toes might encounter on their downward journey.

'Now take hold of the rope.' Serene looped the grass fibre painter round his shoulders. She took her place immediately behind him, gave a whoop, and they set off, Fatimah breaking into a West African version of 'The Volga Boatman'. They squelched through the mud, surrounded always by other splashes and rustlings from the reed-lined banks, gasped and panted, but kept the boat moving, and the Badumi villagers, who still clustered on their jetty, clapped hands in approbation.

'How far?' Wilde asked. Already burning pains were seizing the muscles of his thighs.

'Not far,' Serene promised; she was shoulder-deep in the mud.

'Well, you can use the pole.' He held her round the waist, extracted her from the swamp with a gigantic sucking noise, and deposited her into the boat. 'How does it look?'

She shaded her eyes. 'There is water just over there.'

They rounded a bend, and the creek became an estuary. The nearest clump of trees was a hundred yards away now, and from mud-level they seemed to be entering another desert, brown and odoriferous. They followed Serene's directions, and she thrust one of the long poles over the side to help them along. 'Soon now,' she assured Wilde.

But before they could reach the water, the water reached them, in the form of a downpour. The sun disappeared as if someone had drawn a curtain, and the rain came down in almost solid sheets.

'Quickly,' Serene shouted, leaning over the side, her fingers sliding on the mud which coated Wilde's shoulders. 'Come on board.'

He sucked himself out of the bog, swung one leg over the gunwale, while the boat listed dangerously. Serene threw both arms round his thighs and tumbled him into the bottom, where Fatimah and Joanna joined him as rapidly as possible. Wilde sat up, and understood Serene's anxiety. The mud was dissolving before their eyes, dissipating into huge pools of water, and he could feel the boat moving, as on a flooding tide.

'How come we didn't just wait for rain?'

'Because when it stops, the mud will come back again. It takes much rain to drive this away. Now we must make haste.' She handed him one of the poles and gave him an encouraging smile, while the rain pounded on her head, drained through her hair and dripped on to her shoulders, deposited the mud in a pool between her legs. 'We are doing very well, eh?'

'If you say so, sweetheart.'

'Oh, now that we have got out of the creek we will make good time. You have poled a boat before?'

It occurred to Wilde that the Cam had never looked like this. 'No.'

'Then you must copy us. Like so.'

To his amazement, before commencing work, the three women dressed themselves, dragging their tunics over their mud-stained bodies and wrapping their *haiks* around their heads. Then Fatimah resumed her chorus, the long poles were thrust over the side at the bow, and each girl marched aft, always seeming about to hang on too long at the stern and be left suspended like a monkey on a stick, but always jerking the pole clear in time, to return to the bow and resume all over again. Wilde joined in, ineffectively at first, but soon gaining something of their rhythm; the boat slithered across the last of the mud, and within minutes was floating. He watched his companions in growing admiration. With mud dripping down their legs, and smooth muscles rippling in their arms, they put forward the strongest argument he had yet encountered for the physical equality of the sexes.

By noon the downpour had stopped, the clouds had cleared, and Serene called a halt for a meal. They drifted, a mile from the shore, bobbing on the surface of an utterly calm sea on which the sun played like a spotlight. Fatimah and Joanna gabbled happily at each other while they consumed dates and *couscous* and drank *merissé*, until Wilde felt the inside of his mouth was going to be permanently puckered. 'Where from here?' he asked Serene.

She stood up, shaded her eyes. 'We go that way,' she announced, as if she had seen a signpost. 'Two, maybe three days.'

They poled, ceaselessly, throughout the afternoon. At night they drifted, resumed poling with the first light. They endured at least two rainstorms in every twenty-four hours, avoided various groups of spluttering hippopotamus, disturbed colonies of birds, pushed their way through unearthly reed morasses, sudden sprouting out of the water. From the depths to which the poles entered. Wilde figured the lake was nowhere more than eight feet deep, and they kept the line of trees always on their right hand. They did not bathe, and they performed their natural functions as they came to mind. They drank *merissé* in preference to water, and existed in a condition of perpetual half inebriation. Blisters appeared on their hands, and were ignored, and Wilde suffered agonies from sunburn. Sometimes Fatimah sang, and sometimes she and Joanna muttered at each other. And they smelt. Wilde decided he would never be able to touch a woman again without feeling, and smelling, mud, and a variety of other things besides. Even Serene became nothing more than a walking ball of mud and sweat and slime and energy.

He could no longer doubt that he had either sunstroke or malaria; his headache was constant, sometimes almost unbearable, so that he could hardly open his eyes when the sun was shining, sometimes nothing more than a dull reminder that every tooth in his head was loose. He suffered from diarrhoea, but so did his crew, and at night, when the temperature dropped almost as alarmingly as in the desert, and the wind turned the placid waters of the lake into a tumbling millrace, he shivered incessantly. He was either very wet or unnaturally dry, but above everything else he was dirty, in a sense he had never known before, even in Korea. And this massive exercise in self-mortification was being undertaken solely in order to execute a woman with whom he was disturbingly close to being in love.

Soon after dawn on the third morning the raucous timbre of Fatimah's song, the slurp of the poles, the constant rustle of the water, and the gruntings of Joanna, were disturbed by an entirely new sound, at once harsh and, to Wilde, reassuring. 'Quickly,' Serene said. 'We are fishing.'

The boat drifted, the women lined the gunwales, leaning over, appearing to be dragging a net. Wilde joined them, glanced over his shoulder at the helicopter which sailed out of the forest to their right, not troubling to come out of its way to take a closer look at the lonely craft, but still near enough to tell what they were doing.

'Anderson?' he asked Serene.

'Who else, Mr. Wilde.'

The aircraft disappeared behind the trees, and they resumed poling. By noon they had left the lake proper, and were negotiating a series of narrow creeks between small islands. The water was once again very shallow, and now they were terribly aware of the forest closing about them, huge and silent, shutting out the sun, always wet from the last rainstorm. Serene called a halt an hour before dusk, turning the prow of the boat so that it ran into the reed beds extending from one of the islets.

'The Centre of the Universe is but an hour away,' she said. 'You remember Zobeir, Mr. Wilde, walking through the shallow water to another island? That is it, over there; he would have to swim now. Beyond that is the home of the Lord.'

He was surprised to discover that he was nervous. He had been travelling for so long the realization that he had at last got back to where he had started came as something of a shock. Perhaps because he had never really expected to get this far at all. And even now it seemed incredible.

'Please congratulate Fatimah and Joanna,' he said. 'How you got them to work this hard is a complete mystery to me.'

'It was simple, Mr. Wilde. I have told them that when you have finished your business at the Centre of the Universe you are going to take us all to England and keep us in a big house. They have heard about England and are very excited about it.'

'Not half as excited as I am. I don't happen to have a big house.'

'You need not worry. I will help you to escape them afterwards.'

'But you *do* intend to come along?'

She smiled. 'You need me, Mr. Wilde. Without me you are nothing. Now you must tell them what you want them to do.'

'Well, listen very carefully, darling, and remember that I want to get us in, and out, in one piece, and without having to shoot everyone in sight.'

'It shall be as you desire, Mr. Wilde.'

'So you'll leave any talking that has to be done to me. Now tell Fatimah that we are going to leave herself and Joanna somewhere snug, and all they have to do is sit there until we come back to them. But they'll each have a rifle, and if they hear a shot they're both to start shooting, and not stop until we get back to them or they run out of ammunition.'

Serene frowned. 'And you claim you do not wish bloodshed? I do not understand.'

'You leave the strategy to me. Now tell me where is the best place for us to land without being noticed.'

'That would be on the forest side, Mr. Wilde. To the west of the village. If we go through the forest they will not even be sure where we have come from, and the boat will be safe.'

'And how long will it take us to reach that side of the island?'

'It is a good way. Perhaps four hours.'

'So what time do the Followers of the Lord usually bed themselves down?'

'Within an hour of sunset, Mr. Wilde. They will be eating their evening meal now.'

'Then we'll just take it easy for a little while, eat the last of this muck, and be on our way. Tell the girls that it is my custom to pray before a battle, and that I have to be alone. Only you may approach me.'

Serene raised her eyebrows, but Fatimah and Joanna appeared to understand. Wilde retired into the bush with the three cartridge belts and Serene's knife, sat down, and removed the bullets from all the cartridges in two of the belts, replacing them with wads of mud. Serene stood above him, her mouth a round 'O'.

'If there's any killing to be done I intend to do it,' he said.

'You are a man of infinite resource, Mr. Wilde.' But she was thoughtful. She went down to the water's edge, and for the first time in three days took off her mud-stained, sweat-stained *haik*, folded it, stowed it in the boat, and washed herself, paying particular attention to her breasts. It looked like a good idea, and Wilde joined her. She smiled at him. 'I have taken you out of the desert, Mr. Wilde, and I have guided you through the forest. I have kept you and fed you and provided you with women. And now I have brought you back to the Centre of the Universe. Are you not pleased with me, Mr. Wilde?'

'More than I can ever show you, sweetheart.'

Serene laughed, with that bubbling emanation of delight he did not think he would ever forget. 'Oh, you will repay me amply, Mr. Wilde. You will begin this very night when you kill Inger Lieberstein.'

'I suppose I shall.'

The amusement left her face, and it was very solemn. 'Because if you do not, Mr. Wilde, I will kill you.'

CHAPTER TEN

THE BOAT made no more sound than the swish of the poles through the water. It was several hours past midnight, Wilde figured, and although the moon had not yet set, its brightness was shrouded by cloud. The swamp was noisy in a uniquely tropical fashion. Frogs croaked, insects seethed, and there were other, more sinister sounds as well; the rain of the last week had wakened the jungle from its drought-induced hibernation. Memory dragged him back all of twenty years. He supposed this was, in essence, a commando raid. The strangest commando raid of all time.

The boat entered a reed bed; the stalks closed around it like a living forest. Wilde slapped mosquitoes, gazed at the dark curtain of trees only a hundred feet away.

'We can go no farther,' Serene whispered.

'How deep, do you think?'

'Four feet, here. But it will become shallower.'

'And what about the beasties?'

She shrugged. 'They are there. But not everywhere, Mr. Wilde.'

He presumed that a sleepy crocodile could be approximated to a land-mine, sighed, and jumped over the side, his rifle held above his head. The water was surprisingly cool, and came to his waist. 'Remind the girls to keep their powder dry.' The reeds sliced at his arms and chest as they parted in front of him. The ground shelved. He stumbled and bruised his toes amongst the pebbles and roots, and his heart bounced like a yoyo every time he struck something hard and sizable. Behind him Serene waded silently, Fatimah and Joanna whispered and giggled. This was the culmination of their adventure, if they even counted it so high. In front of them lay their promised visit to faraway places. There is no honour amongst assassins.

The water lapped at his ankles, and he was in the trees. He was out of the world of the crocodile and into the world of the snake. He wasn't sure about African water snakes, and now wasn't the time to find out. 'Which way?'

'Come.' Serene took the lead, feeling her way from tree to tree. He glanced over his shoulder, and Fatimah gave him an encouraging smile. His feet were a mass of cuts and bruises, and thorns scraped the flesh from his shins. He understood why the forest Africans went to so much trouble to protect their most vulnerable organ. But before them lay the pasture, where the cows huddled close together, heads turned inquisitively towards the invaders.

'There is a bull, and he will make trouble,' Serene said. 'We must go round the edge.'

Wilde nodded, signalled Fatimah to move to the right. They bent double, although against the background of the trees they would be quite invisible, even supposing any of the Followers of the Lord might be out for a midnight stroll.

He could see the circle of huts. Serene squeezed his hand, and at the same moment dropped to her knees. He obeyed, and the two women followed their example.

'Ukuba's house is the small one beyond the eating house,' she whispered.

'Then the girls have come far enough. Tell them to snuggle down here, and stay awake. Remember, they go into action at the first shot.'

Serene translated, and Fatimah grinned, worked the bolt on her rifle.

'It is as well they cannot do themselves an injury,' Serene remarked. 'It will soon be light now.'

'Then could we get a wiggle on?'

She crawled into the darkness. They crossed the vegetable garden, passed behind the circle of houses, silent, sleeping, peaceful, and Wilde decided the Lord had made a mistake in rejecting pets. Serene halted. 'We have arrived, Mr. Wilde.'

He stood up, walked round the front of the small house, parted the flap and stepped inside. He stood still, his rifle thrust forward, waiting for his eyes to become accustomed to the utter darkness, inhaled human sweat, felt Serene behind him. He held her shoulder, moved her to the right of the doorway, took his place on the left. Now he could see the blankets, the dark mounds beneath. He said, 'Ukuba!'

There was a movement, and the Lord sat up. 'Who is there?' 'The name is Wilde.'

Ukuba tossed off the blanket, scrambled to his feet.

'Wilde?' Inger sat up, pulled her blanket to her throat, let it drop again.

'What is it you wish, Mr. Wilde?' Ukuba asked. 'It was wrong of you to return, and with a rifle. What do you mean to accomplish with that? The sentence of banishment, when imposed by the Inner Court of the Followers of the Lord, is not to be taken lightly.'

'Wilde!' Inger said again, in a lower tone, 'you are mad.'

'I brought him back,' Serene said.

'Serene?' Ukuba asked. 'Is that you? My child, you have committed a most grievous sin. The Inner Court will not be pleased.'

'*I* have sinned?' Serene demanded. '*I*? My Lord . . .'

'You were going to let me do the talking,' Wilde reminded her, and listened to the clanging of the triangle. 'Someone's a light sleeper. Let's join them.'

He jerked the rifle towards the door. Ukuba hesitated, and then stepped outside. Inger, wrapped in her blanket and looking almost as youthful as Serene, seemed too surprised to move; but Wilde knew better. Her brain would be whirring like a broken mainspring, choosing her moment as much as her tactics. He held her arm, pushed her through the door. She glanced at him, then faced the Followers of the Lord as they flooded out of their houses, headed by Fodio and Kanem.

'Wilde?' cried a well-known voice, and Cynthia Boraine pushed her way to the front. 'Say, whatever happened to you? They told me you didn't approve of the set-up, and left.'

'I've decided to come back.'

'It is the assassin,' Kanem shouted. 'He has defied the wishes of the Inner Court, and returned. That traitorous girl has brought him. And they have dared to blaspheme against the teachings of the Lord by introducing firearms into the Centre of the Universe. What will be the verdict of the Inner Court upon those who would ignore their commands?'

'Fire the gun,' Serene said. 'Let us kill her and run for it.'

Inger's head jerked. But she made no effort to free herself.

'Play it cool, sweetheart.' Wilde raised his voice above the sudden babble of sound. 'Listen to me, members of the Inner Court. Yes, I have defied your commands and returned to the Centre of the Universe, and yes, Serene has guided me. I made her do this. I have returned to complete the mission with which I was entrusted. I did not lie to you when I admitted that I had killed, that I was paid to do so. But I am not for sale. I am an agent of the British government. I was sent here to arrest the woman Inger Lieberstein and return her to England for trial. I wished to do so without disrupting the harmony of the Centre of the Universe, but that is now impossible. So I have a demand to make of you: Hand this woman, who is more criminal than any of you can possibly imagine, over to me, and I shall leave your island, and yourselves, and your movement, in peace. This I swear to you.'

'Oh, you bastard, Jonas,' Inger said softly. 'Oh, you bleeding bastard. But you won't do it, my sweet. Do you think these people give a damn for the British government?'

'She is right, Mr. Wilde,' Ukuba said. 'We of the Centre of the Universe obey our own laws, and not those of tyrannical civilization. Inger has confessed her crimes, to me and to all of us. She has told us that once she was a spy, that she worked for both East and West. But East and West do not exist for the Followers of the Lord. Perhaps you will charge her also with murder. But she confessed that, too, that in the course of her earlier life she was compelled to defend herself. This was forced upon her by that very civilization which does so much harm to mankind. All of these things my wife has confessed, and for them all she has been forgiven, by me, and by my Followers, here in the Inner Court. She no longer bows to the jurisdiction of any government in the world.'

'She's a great confessor,' Wilde agreed. 'I'm sorry, darling, but this is for keeps. I wonder, Ukuba, if she'll also confess that she's been cuckolding you with your foster sons, that she and they have hatched a plan to rule the Followers of the Lord once you are dead? That she looks upon you as a dying man already? That inviting me here was part of her plans to rid herself of Zobeir, her one rival, without attracting any suspicion to herself. That Serene was telling the truth when she said Inger sent her to Kano to meet me, in order to implicate her, to blackmail her into accusing Zobeir. That Zobeir was innocent of any intention to harm you.'

'Those are all lies, my lord,' Inger said. 'I swear it. Why did not Wilde speak up like this ten days ago?'

'Why, indeed,' Ukuba said. 'I shall be interested to discover that, my child. But, of course, they are not lies, and it grieves me that you should stain your soul yet again with such a crime. Do you not think I am aware of what you planned?'

(ii)

The night was sibilant with the shuffling of more than fifty naked pairs of feet.

'You knew?' Inger whispered at last. 'But that is not possible.'

'All things are possible to the Lord, my child,' Ukuba said gently. 'Explain it to her, Kanem.'

'I told the Lord everything that was said between us, Inger. Everything that was done.'

'You?' She turned. 'And Fodio?'

But Fodio was no longer present. A nervous tic began throbbing at the back of Wilde's brain. There was more intrigue on this small island than he had encountered in all Russia.

'Are we not brothers?' Kanem asked. 'And are we not also adopted sons of the Lord?'

'I found you missing from my blanket one night, my child,' Ukuba said. 'And it was not difficult for me to discover where you had gone. My sons were not unwilling to confess to me. But I forgave you that, and you may believe me I would even have preferred to prevent you incriminating yourself by insuring that Wilde never answered your summons. There, apparently, I failed. When he arrived here I was forced either to let you appear to carry out your scheme or to denounce you to my Followers. I chose the former course, and Kanem's warning was proved true in your every action.'

She gazed at him, her face, which had, just for a moment, showed at once anger and fear, resuming its normal impassive cast. 'Then I must ask your forgiveness once again, my Lord. But I beseech you, as you love me, do not send me away with Wilde. He does not lie when he says that he works for the British government. But he is not a policeman. He is their executioner. They would not dare put me in a court; I know too much about them. That is why they have sent him, instead of another.'

'This I understand, my child,' Ukuba said. 'And you may rest assured that I shall never deliver you to your enemies.'

A slow rage began to burn in Wilde's belly, a fury composed of many things, but centring on the spreading crimson on Aimee Bosquet's white minidress. And he had refused to contemplate the destruction of the Lord and what he stood for. Yet vengeance still had to wait, to be controlled, to be accurately directed. 'I'm in a bit of a fog,' he confessed pleasantly. 'Knowing all the while that she's been plotting against you, planning to do for Zobeir and create God knows what other kind of mayhem after your death, you intend to let things go on as if nothing had happened?'

'But of course, Mr. Wilde. I do not expect you to understand. You are a young man, and you live by the strength in your right arm. You are intensely virile, as I recognized the moment I saw you. For you, perhaps, women have always been but the play-things of an idle hour. But I, Ukuba, have devoted my life to sterner tasks, have deliberately turned my heart away from the solaces of a woman's love.'

'And you think Inger loves you?' Serene demanded. 'She is as cold as a block of ice.'

'But I love her, my child. Just to look on her fills my heart with gladness. To have her smile on me is more important than to eat.'

'And yet you share her with your foster sons?' Wilde asked.

'And in your concept of civilization that is the height of depravity. But here in the Centre of the Universe moral judge-ments are made by me. To have her come to me from two men such as they but makes her the sweeter.'

'And Zobeir? You drove him out just to keep her as your bed-fellow? You sent Serene to her death?'

'I expelled Serene from the Centre of the Universe, Mr. Wilde. She was guilty of participating in a plot which she assumed to be directed against my life. And she is my only living blood relative. I was as lenient with her as I could. As for Zobeir, he understands not only my needs, but that a power struggle to establish my successor would destroy the entire sect. It had already been decided between us that he would go into voluntary exile for the duration of my life; your appearance but made it necessary for us to indulge in some play-acting. He will return in due course. I am an old man, Mr. Wilde. Regardless of what you or others might say, I am content that I have spent my life wisely, that I have con-tributed to the good of mankind. Now, in my declining years, while I wish to see my movement grow, I also wish to enjoy some personal happiness. I find my happiness with Inger. I shall con-tinue to do so until I die.'

'And then?'

Ukuba smiled at his wife. 'Then she must again fend for her-self. But she will do well, I am sure, Mr. Wilde. However artificial, her loveliness qualifies her to fill even your false description as the most beautiful woman in the world. I am sure my adopted sons will never permit her to want.'

Inger knelt. 'My Lord, your goodness overwhelms me. That I have sinned against you will always lie heavy on my heart.'

'Then rise, and stand here beside me. It may even be possible, Mr. Wilde, that your attempted interference in the affairs of the Followers of the Lord has been all to the good, in that it has brought my wife and myself a greater understanding of our natures. So I no longer have the heart to punish you. Perhaps I am weak, and there will be those of the Inner Court who will wish to reproach me. Nevertheless, I decree that once again you shall be banished. Serene will go with you, as for ten days she has remained by your side. But this time, Mr. Wilde, do not attempt to defy me and return, or you shall learn that when it is a matter of protecting their own members the Followers of the Lord can be harsh indeed.'

'Point taken,' Wilde said. 'I watched Aimee Bosquet die.'

'Aimee?' Inger cried. 'Aimee is dead?'

Ukuba turned to Kanem. 'I instructed you to prevent their meeting. Not to kill.'

Kanem's face was a dark shadow. 'It was the only way, my Lord. You do not stop a man like Wilde with words. But I cannot understand why Kumane did not complete his mission.'

'He tried,' Wilde said. 'And then there's the small matter of Serene's and my banishment. The first one, I mean. We were taken into the middle of the desert, and left there.'

Ukuba gazed at his wife. 'You ordered this?'

'No, my Lord,' Inger said. 'I swear it.' She turned to Wilde. 'Do you honestly suppose I would go to such unnecessary trouble to kill you, Jonas?'

'Frankly, no. But I intend to find out who did.'

'It was I, Mr. Wilde,' Kanem said. 'I gave those orders.'

Ukuba regarded his adopted son with a mild frown. 'Do you seek to overrule my authority, Kanem?'

'It has become necessary for me to question your ability, my Lord. And not just in regard of this murderer and his accomplice. You said just now that Zobeir will return. How is this?'

'Zobeir has committed no crime. I had intended to establish this, at an appropriate time, but the man Wilde has done so for me. Chwarism is my faithful servant who understands my intention, and will ignore Anderson's message concerning his expulsion. On my behalf, Zobeir is undertaking a journey to visit the various cells of the Inner Court, to give them greetings from their Lord. Then he will return here, and succeed me, as Lord of the Followers.'

'As Lord?' Kanem shouted. 'You said . . .'

'I told you that you were to say as much to Inger, to force her to declare herself, so that I could understand what she was about.' Ukuba smiled. 'I was telling her the truth. Did you not realize that, my son?'

Kanem stared at him. 'No,' he said at last. 'I did not realize that, Ukuba.'

'But who could possibly be my successor, save Zobeir, my oldest living associate in the movement?' Ukuba frowned. 'Surely you did not consider yourself, young and inexperienced, and, as you have just revealed, hot-headed and not yet sure of our true purpose, suitable for a position of such immense responsibility? Oh, no, my son. That can never be.'

'You think so?' Kanem demanded. 'It is you, old man, living in your world of dreams, who is wrong.'

'Be quiet, my son,' Ukuba said. 'You have confessed to procuring a murder, to planning two more, including that of your foster sister. These are terrible crimes. Now you are about to utter words which cannot be withdrawn. You will force me to call upon the Inner Court of the Followers of the Lord to pronounce a judgement against you.'

'No, no, my Lord,' Kanem said. 'They have already pronounced a judgement, against you. They have grown weary of your inane decrees, inconsequential decisions. They are contemptuous of your doting fascination for this white-haired intriguer. They know Zobeir for what he is, but a relic of yourself, similarly out of touch with the forces at work in the world of today.'

'And you are in touch, Kanem? You, who have never left Africa, who depends for his knowledge of the outside world upon the reminiscences of the woman he has just described as an intriguer?'

'Perhaps to judge from a distance is the best way, my Lord,' Kanem said. 'I am at least sufficiently a realist to know that this Wilde is not the sort of man you can turn loose at will, supposing that he will tamely obey your wishes, as your Followers have done for too long. He must die for trespassing upon the Centre of the Universe. And the traitress Serene must die with him. Aye, and your foul-spirited wife. What say the Inner Court of the Followers of the Lord?'

'Let them be crucified,' they howled. 'Let them all be placed upon the cross.'

'We can't stand for that, Conrad!' Cynthia Boraine cried.

'Oh, I do agree,' Loman's voice came out of the centre of the crowd of white robed figures. 'That's pitching it a bit strong, I do agree.'

'I entirely agree with you.' Wilde brought up his rifle. The avenging of Aimee Bosquet was a luxury he could not afford; in any event, Ukuba and Kanem could be left to destroy each other in the eyes of the Followers far more efficiently than he could do it with a bullet. 'This is all very interesting, but you chaps are going to have to sort out your own domestic problems. I am leaving now, and I am taking both Inger and Serene with me, and anyone else who may care to come.' He glanced at Cynthia Boraine. 'I don't think you really belong in this mess, sweetheart.'

'You know what, I'm beginning to think you could just be right. You coming, Conrad?'

'You will shoot me, and those of my Followers who would try to stop you, in cold blood?' Ukuba demanded.

'I'm an assassin, remember? So use your nut, Ukuba. You have problems of your own, with your young Turk here, without getting involved with me. And as Inger suggested, I've brought reinforcements. They're looking at you now, from the edge of the pasture.'

'Yet we will stop you, Mr. Wilde,' Fodio said. He stood on the right of the crowd, and the dying moon glinted from the barrel of a Sheppard and Turpin machine carbine.

(iii)

To turn was to die. Wilde dived for the shelter of the nearest house. He landed on his hands and knees, heard the chatter from behind him, watched a spurt of dust tear the earth not a foot to his right. He rolled to his left, struck a body, lay on his stomach, fired. But Fodio had also taken cover, and the bullet screamed into the night. He regained his knees, conscious of the woman moving beside him, and the machine-gun fired again. Inger gasped, and fell. Wilde threw the rifle into the doorway, caught her shoulders, dragged her with him into the darkness, lay still while bullets crackled through the grass walls of the hut as if they were not there. By now the firing had awakened Fatimah and Joanna, and from the far side of the vegetable garden a fusillade rang out, an accompaniment for the screams of the Followers of the Lord as they scattered, in bitter testimony to the probable success of Wilde's strategy had he not allowed himself to be deluded by Ukuba's preaching. In seconds the compound was empty, save for the helicopter, but the night remained a bedlam as Joanna and Fatimah continued to blaze away in the general direction of the village.

'Jonas,' Inger whispered. 'Jonas. I'm hit.'

He stroked the darkness, found the fine silver threads of her hair, touched her face and moved the blanket to find her shoulders, damp with sweat, slid down across the breasts to her belly and then her groin and buttocks, came to her thighs, and his fingers were sticky.

Her breath came in little gasps.

'The right hip,' he said. 'But it's missed the bone, I think.'

'Jonas! I'm bleeding to death.'

He tore the blanket into strips, found the wound with his fingers and by listening to her panting become the whimpers of a frightened animal in pain, pressed material into the torn flesh, bandaged her as best he could. Now he could almost see. She lay on her back, pillowed on her hair, both hands pressed to her mouth, legs wide, belly pulsing. 'You'll hold for a while,' he said. 'I'd bet on blood poisoning, if I were you.'

'Jonas!' Her fingers closed on his shoulder, tight, biting into his flesh. 'Jonas! To feel you . . . Jonas, I didn't mean to send you to the desert. I meant to save your life.'

'I told you I believe you. You owed me that much.'

'But you came here to destroy me. You lied about having left the British.'

'We all have our faults.' He tied the last knot, tested his rifle-bolt, his blood-wet fingers slipping on the metal. He eased himself into the doorway. The firing from close at hand had stopped, and a blanket of silence lay over the village. But still the edge of the garden was seared by flashes and explosions. 'How many weapons have your boy friends got?'

'I don't know. I didn't know they had the Sten.'

'Oh, what a tangled web we weave . . . I'm still in a bit of a fog. So you seduced our two all-African boys, and laid one of your deep plans for seizing control of the sect when the old man died. Bit hard up for material, weren't you?'

'Have you any idea what it is like to be penniless and afraid, Jonas? In Paris, where once I dined on champagne every night? Have you any idea what it is like to have tied yourself to a man more than twice your age, and who believed in the most old-fashioned of marriages? And those two boys were so eager. So anxious to learn.'

'To learn,' Wilde said thoughtfully. 'But not to accept you as their leader. So they spilt the beans to the old man, and Ukuba gave them a turn by seeming to wish to leave matters right there. It seems to me the both of you just didn't know what kind of fire you were playing with. They really had it made, with you intriguing against the old man, the old man and Zobeir coming to a quite ridiculous arrangement just to let him keep his hands on you for the remainder of his life, and the Followers gradually becoming restive as they realized their Lord was nothing more than a doting senile delinquent. And I always thought European politics were bad.'

'Kanem,' she whispered. 'Kanem. Leave that one to me, Jonas.'

'They do say hate's as good as anything for keeping alive on. Our problem is, where did they get that gun, and how many have they got.' Cautiously he stuck his head through the door, had one question answered. A heavy-calibre automatic pistol exploded too close for comfort, and dust flew into his eyes. He

sank back into the darkness. If the Sten had gone, then Fodlio
was worrying about the rest of the invading force. But rescuing
Fatimah and Joanna meant settling with the pistol, first.

'Jonas?' Inger whispered. 'Are you hurt, Jonas?'

'No.' He turned, his fingers tight on the trigger, as a scraping
sound came from the side of the hut. He felt Inger moving,
holding on to his legs to drag herself across the floor. He gave
her his hand, and she crawled behind him, pushing herself into
the recess of the hut, pressing her body against his back. She
glowed with heat.

'Mr. Wilde?' Serene whispered. 'Are you there, Mr. Wilde?'
Inger's fingers were like talons, willing him to be silent.

'I'm here. How did you get in?'

'I have my knife. I wish I had the rifle we gave to the Badumi.'
She lay beside him. 'Ukuba is with me.'

The prophet crawled into the hut. 'What calamity have you
brought upon my people, Mr. Wilde? No guns have ever been
allowed in the Centre of the Universe. But now there are automatic weapons, and people will be killed . . .'

'You've been sitting on a small volcano for God knows how
long,' Wilde pointed out. Inger's hands stroked up and down his
back. She was trying to talk with her fingers, to win him back
without revealing her presence to the others, bargaining with
every ounce of her ebbing consciousness. 'Those adopted sons
of yours must have been planning this coup for some time; you
don't find machine-guns growing on trees.'

'My God! My God!' Ukuba said. 'This will be the end of the
sect, of my people.'

'Of us as well, if we don't get a move on.' Cynthia Boraine
wriggled through the hole in the wall.

'Any more?' Wilde asked.

'I don't know where Conrad has got to. I don't know what's
going on at all, Wilde, but I'd rather have you up front than
that trigger-happy Kanembu. Give us covering fire to reach the
chopper and I'll save you a seat.'

'You can fly that thing?' Lips caressed his shoulder. Hungry
lips. Inger had never found it necessary to hunger for any man.

'For God's sake,' Cynthia Boraine said, 'I own one.'

'I always had a feeling you were going to turn out to be my
favourite woman. My trouble is, I've got a couple of sidekicks
on the other side of the meadow.'

'Seems to me they can take care of themselves, judging by
their fire-power.'

'They're using blanks.'

'Now he tells us. You too?'

'No. The idea was to avoid bloodshed. Don't bother to kick me; I'm doing it to myself. I honestly believed these people might turn the other cheek.' Now her whole body was glued to his, from toe to mouth, her arms locked round his waist. He could feel every pulse in her arteries, just as he could feel the blood seeping through the bandage to soak his legs. Helpless and hurting, she was, after all, nothing more than a frightened little girl. But to start thinking about Inger Lieberstein in terms of pity was to prepare himself for calamity.

'Serene?' he asked. 'You were in on this revolution when it was on the drawing-board. How many of the Followers are backing Kanem and Fodio?'

'I do not know, Mr. Wilde. But if Miss Boraine can fly the helicopter I think we should leave. Fatimah and Joanna are only slaves.'

'What about Inger?'

'After what has happened we can leave her to the mercy of Kanem and Fodio and the Followers of the Lord. They will crucify her, Mr. Wilde, as she crucified us. Only they will not take her down from the cross. Do you know that it takes not less than four days to die, hanging on the cross?'

The succubus moved, sliding against him. The small white teeth scored his flesh.

'We'll have to get hold of Conrad, though,' Cynthia Boraine said. 'Say, what's all that silence?'

The firing from the pasture had stopped, even the echoes had drifted away into the night, and the setting moon played upon the deserted compound.

'Talk about the Chinese rope trick,' Cynthia said. 'Not half an hour ago there were fifty people out there.'

'They're still around,' Wilde reminded her. 'But they don't know how many people I have up my sleeve, either. I think your best bet is to leave. Maybe you could circle back in half an hour, and see if there are any pieces to be picked up. Take the old man and Serene with you.'

'No,' Ukuba said. 'I will stay with my people. I will put a stop to this. Those bullets made me afraid. But the Lord cannot be afraid. I will go out there and speak with my people, and they will disarm my sons. And their accomplices.'

'You're going nowhere at all, except to that plane,' Wilde said. 'Your dreaming days are over, Ukuba.'

'He's right, you know,' Cynthia said. 'But if you don't mind, Wilde, we will hang around. You go dig your friends out of trouble. We'll sit tight, and keep our heads down.'

Inger's fingers were like claws.

'I will come with you,' Serene said. 'I have my knife.'

'All this talk, of death and dying,' Ukuba said. 'Here, in the Centre of the Universe. I have failed. My God, how I have failed. I must speak with them.'

'You cheer him up,' Wilde suggested to Cynthia Boraine. He reached behind him, squeezed Inger's arm. They were right, of course. They had always been right. He was not going to kill her. He had never had any intention of killing her. His problem now was saving her life. 'We'll be back,' he said to the darkness. 'But first we have to settle our watchdog. Don't come until I call, Serene.'

He pushed the rifle through the door, was halted by a sudden outburst of fire in the distance.

'Fatimah?' Serene asked.

'That's the Sten. I hope to God those kids have enough sense to keep *their* heads down.' He drew a long breath, stood up, ran outside, and hurled himself flat again as the pistol exploded. He rolled, over and over, chased by another bullet, reached the shelter of the next hut.

'Wait!' he shouted, as Serene's head emerged. The pistol barked, and she disappeared. Wilde fired at the flash, and again, and again, reached his feet, still firing. He ran across the open space, kicked the body of Anderson; the pilot had taken two thirty-thirty bullets in the chest. Behind him, in the darkness, there was whimpering.

'You hurt?' he asked.

The woman shook her head. Five minutes earlier she had shouted 'Crucify them!' with the rest. Now she was alone in the night, with a dead man and his murderer, and she was afraid. Wilde thought this whole operation was an interesting study in psychology. Or lack of it. He picked up a nine-millimetre Lüger, gave it to Serene. 'There'll be a couple of rounds left in there, I imagine. You go round the edge, I'll cross the field. But be careful.'

'They will not kill me, Mr. Wilde,' she promised. 'It is good that again we fight together, eh?'

'I can't think of any ally I'd rather have. Now move.'

He went between the houses. There were people around him, cowering in the gloom, hiding in doorways. Not all of the Followers of the Lord had turned against Ukuba; or, if they had, they were waiting to see who was going to win this particular battle first. He ignored them, ran for the vegetable garden. The firing from the pasture had stopped at the heavy exchange from the village, but now another burst broke the silence, and this time he saw the flashes. He dropped to his knees, took careful aim, fired twice, lay down to reload. There was no reply, and he got up again, ran forward. The night was noisy with its silence, and now the rain poured downwards, obliterating the last of the moon, splashing on to the pitted earth, cannoning off his head, covering the island and the night with its water mist. He reached the edge of the pasture. The cattle had accumulated in a huddle on the far side, and lowed anxiously. There was no need to fear the bull now. He turned to his left, skirted the edge of the vegetable garden, and found the women.

CHAPTER ELEVEN

JOANNA lay on her face, her fingers still wrapped around her useless rifle; she had been firing even as she died. Fatimah had understood the worst; her rifle was discarded, and from the mangled talons which had once been fingers, coupled with the exploded death-mask of her face, she had held her hands in front of her eyes in a vain effort to resist death.

The anger, so long controlled, bubbled upwards through Wilde's system like an electric shock. Self-anger, at the way he had been taken in, because he so desperately wished to believe that somewhere in the world there could be a group of people dedicated to peace and non-violence. A world from which men like Jonas Wilde could be for ever excluded.

He stood up, gazed at the line of trees, over his shoulder at the houses, listened to the cattle, the heavy whisper of the rain. For the first time the water felt cold.

Fodio stood behind him, not twenty yards away. He said 'Drop your weapon, Mr. Wilde.' The Sten gleamed in his hands.

But he had not invited the two women to surrender. Wilde turned, his rifle levelled, and Fodio understood his bluff would not take. He threw the empty machine-gun to his left, dived to his right. Wilde fired, knew he had missed, moved forward.

Mud splashed behind him, and he threw up the gun, held in both hands, to act as a block to the clubbing arms. Kanem grunted, and they fell together, but Kanem was on top, and a series of swinging blows knocked the rifle from Wilde's hands, sent Wilde himself rolling through the mud and into the dead women.

He sat up, shaking his head. Kanem was about six feet away, scrabbling in the soaking earth for the discarded weapon. Fodio was on his feet again, and coming forward. They were two very large, very strong, very fit young men, and there was no element of surprise available. Except for Serene. But Serene had not arrived.

He got up, ran forward. Kanem sidestepped, swung the rifle, struck Wilde on the shoulder and sent him cannoning into Fodio. Both men went down, Fodio's arms wrapped around Wilde's chest, holding him tight. Kanem knelt on his back, raining blows on his head, fortunately without knowing what to aim for. It occurred to Wilde, as consciousness ebbed and flowed behind his eyes, that too many years of enforced peacefulness had built up inside them an insatiable desire to destroy, and to *feel* the destruction. They were delivering themselves into his hands. Perhaps. If his hands *were* healed, and his system not sufficiently debilitated by his ten days' crawl through the desert and the forest.

He threw his head to one side, drove it downwards, thrust his teeth deep into Fodio's shoulder. Fodio screamed, and his arms relaxed long enough for Wilde to free his own and send his fingers questing for Fodio's testicles. The scream became a howl, and Wilde was rising, ducking his head once more and shrugging his shoulders to send Kanem, carried by the impulse of his next blow, tumbling over the both of them and into the ground.

Wilde regained his feet, head swinging from Kanem's punches, breath coming in great gasps, but now the raging anger was gone, and in its place was the killing fury he had spent so many hours learning to harness. The two young men, Kanem also standing again now, Fodio kneeling, massaging his groin, knew it too, knew that they had aroused something with which they were unfamiliar, with which they had not been prepared to cope. And yet they did not run away. They knew, but they could not believe. They were two to his one, and their brains told them that their instincts had to be wrong.

Fodio stood up, said something to his brother, moved to his right. Kanem came forward, bending slightly from the waist. Wilde calculated the distance, turned to face Fodio, and checked. The night became filled with a noise, a wailing cry which cut across the pre-dawn darkness like the beam of a searchlight, and which ended in a stomach churning sob. It had come from the wood at their backs, and it had been uttered by a woman.

For another moment they gazed at one another, and then Wilde was upon Fodio, closing his right fist to drive it hard into the Kanembu's belly, spinning him round in the hopes of setting him up for a killing swing. But Fodio had been warned by Inger, and instead of straightening he allowed himself to go on falling, throwing both arms around Wilde's thighs, drawing him close and using his teeth to repay the injury Wilde had earlier inflicted. Wilde grunted, a growl of agony mingled with anger, brought his hands together down on Fodio's neck, was himself struck a numbing blow from behind. He fell, still held by Fodio, and once again they hunted him like a pair of savage dogs, and with no more understanding of how to destroy a man as opposed to merely inflicting a beating. Blows thudded on his head and back, Fodio's fingers and teeth ranged his groin, tearing and snapping. Painfully Wilde turned, his body slippery with the continuous drizzle, and with sweat and blood as well, found himself on his back, beside Fodio, with Kanem kneeling on his stomach, drove his hands upwards, arrested one powerful blow, failed to stop the next, which laid his cheek open as if he had been struck with an axe, then lodged the fingers of his right hand in Kanem's eye.

Kanem flailed with his hands, closed them both on Wilde's wrist. Wilde drove his fingers deeper, ignored the burning sensation from his genitals, panted, closed his left hand on Kanem's throat, forced his iron hard fingers onwards into a world of unthinkable softness, felt Kanem's fingers relax as the young man gurgled with pain.

Kanem fell over, both hands pressed to his blinded eye. Fodio rolled away from Wilde, rose to his feet, stared at his brother in horror. Wilde was on his knees, great waves of pain commencing in the pit of his belly and seeping downwards through his legs, leaving the stinging of his lacerated face no more distracting than a mosquito bite. He crawled over Kanem, once again seized the unprotected throat. Fodio hurled himself forward, and Wilde swept him away with a single thrust of his right arm, never easing the pressure on the collapsing windpipe beneath the fingers of his left hand. Kanem's body heaved, once.

Fodio circled the two men, bending low, searching for a weapon. The night swung around Wilde's head. Each raindrop was like a blow with a club. The ground beneath him rose and fell, sagged sideways and bubbled back again. He vomited, and kept on squeezing. In the distance he heard another of those appalling death screams, and dimly, out of the corner of his eye, he traced Fodio's progress, scraping through the soaking grass, churned now into mud. But Kanem was dead. Kanem had been dead for seconds.

Fodio got up, a rifle in his hands. Which rifle? It did not matter. Life and death had been for so long a lottery. One fought, and one killed, or one was killed, and one did not much care which, except that to live meant a continuance of problems, and heartaches, and physical pain, whereas death meant nothing more than oblivion. Wilde turned towards the black muzzle. Fodio gazed at him, nostrils dilated. The rifle rose and fell, but its target remained Wilde's body, chest to legs, legs to chest. Fodio concentrated, drawing a long breath. Wilde waited, also attempting to control his breathing. Death or life, life or death, depended upon a twenty-five per cent chance.

Fodio squeezed the trigger. The click was louder than any thunder-clap. Fodio stared at the useless weapon in his hands, threw it at Wilde, and ran for the trees.

Wilde followed. He moved with alarming slowness, stumbling over the wet ground, keeping his eyes fixed on the dark shadow in front of him. Only his brain raced. His heart summoned him to the screams. They could not have come from far away, and his instincts told him exactly where they had come from. But his instincts also told him to ignore them, to ignore them now and always, that to answer that belated summons for assistance would be to scar his memory with something permanent. His brain came to his rescue, telling him that Inger, living, dead, or dying, was no longer an enemy, just as she had never been a friend. But Fodio, living, remained dangerous. Deadly. No, Fodio had never been deadly. He had not been taught the art of deadliness.

Fodio reached the trees, paused to glance over his shoulder, tripped, and fell to his hands and knees. Wilde went on trotting like an overweight business executive forced out for a morning constitutional by an over-eager wife. He wheezed for breath, and his throat was dry all the way back to his lungs. The gap had closed.

Fodio regained his feet, stepped into the trees, became another shadow in a world of shadows. But Wilde could hear the frightened panting, the squelching, stumbling footsteps, the crackling of the branches. Fodio, a forest African, was destroying himself through his fear.

Wilde slowed to a walk, allowing some of the gut-pain to dwindle, his head to clear. Fodio was in front of him, unable to divert, to twist, to turn, even to change direction. Fodio could only go on, and they were already ankle-deep in mud and water. He paused, listened to the whisper of the rain on the trees, the larger plops of leaf-accumulated drops of water sliding through the branches to hit the swamp beneath. For a moment this was all he heard. Fodio was also standing still, also holding his breath. But his terror was too great, and a moment later there came a gasp that was almost a hiccup, followed by a splash as he tried to run again.

Wilde drew himself forward, brushed aside one branch, and then another, scarcely felt the serrated wood burning his face, struck Fodio on the shoulder as the African attempted to duck behind a tree, lost his balance, and pitched head foremost into several inches of water.

He sat up, dazed, unsure where he was. He thought it possible that he fainted, sitting in the water, his head against a tree-stump. When he opened his eyes Fodio was waist-deep in the lake, wading for the next island. The rain had stopped, and it was dawn. The sun peeped above the still waters of Chad like a single gigantic bloodshot eye, and its first heat summoned up moisture mists from the swamps and lagoons, reed beds and mud beds. Wilde was enveloped in a thin white vapour, which ate through his flesh like acid to rot his bones, had him shivering so that he could hear his teeth chattering.

And Fodio had escaped. The young man was now some fifty yards clear of the shore, wading strongly, not looking back. He could not be caught; Wilde knew that for him to venture into that turgid water would be to die. Even if Fodio did not turn back against him he would drown. There was hardly sufficient strength left in his body to lift his head.

Fodio had escaped. He wondered if it mattered. He watched the strong, dark body in front of him, entering deeper into the lake with every step, moving almost quickly, his chest cutting a deep bow wave which spread behind him across the still water like a perfect arrowhead. How strange, Wilde thought. His eyes, having picked up one arrowhead, now discovered another. No, two more, one on either side of Fodio, and still at a distance. But these had to be optical illusions because there was no visible cause. Whatever was closing on Fodio was swimming immediately beneath the surface.

Blood pumped through Wilde's veins as if his heart had exploded. There had been a week's rain, and the mud banks had dissolved. He cupped his hands around his mouth. 'Fodio!' he bellowed. 'Come back!'

His warning gave the doomed man nothing more than an unnecessary few seconds of mental agony. Fodio glanced over his shoulder, hesitated, looked to his left. He tried to run, absurdly in chest-deep water, tripped, and went beneath the surface. He reappeared, made a sound. Intended as a scream, it reached Wilde as nothing more than a gurgle. The ripple disappeared, and in their place the water boiled. For an instant a tail, long, scaled, slimy, powerful enough to break a man's leg with a single blow, whipped the surface, and then that too disappeared. But the water was no longer placid; there were unseen convulsions going on at the bottom, and the ripples raced to the shore to set the reeds trembling. The attempted revolution in the Centre of the Universe was over, and there was nothing between Wilde and the scream.

(ii)

The sun was higher, struggling upwards into a momentarily clear sky. It was time to go. Somewhere. Away from blood and the stench of death. As if Wilde could ever escape the stench of death.

He got to his feet, and water ran down his arms and thighs. His belly was a puff of air, his throat a gravel surfaced desert, his brain a tumbling, horror-filled jungle. Because he was not yet finished with death. Or perhaps, even more terribly, with life. There was no sound, but he was close to the reed beds, from where he had placed the screams, how long ago? One hour, two? Fifteen minutes?

He splashed through the shallow water, leaned against trees, tripped and fell to his knees, saw the grass boat embedded in the reeds, and came upon Inger.

She was tied to a tree, kneeling, the rope round her chest holding her body clear of the water, so that she was submerged only to her thighs. Her head sagged, and was obscured by her hair, a cloud of silver-white threads which trailed on to her shoulder, suddenly lifeless and almost ugly. Wilde thought this was as well. Her body, too, was obscured, its gentle tan hidden by layers of mud and blood, while the blood had mingled with the water in which she crouched to surround her with a brown-pink lagoon. This too was as well. Some of the blood had come from the wound in her leg. But most had come from the death wound in her throat.

Wilde knelt, in the brown-pink water. He could no longer vomit; his body no less than his brain was drained of substance. Inger had been right, after all. He was out of his depths in Africa. But, then, so had she been.

He listened to soft splashes, did not turn his head. He had half a hope that she might kill him as well. He knew she stood just behind him. He wondered if she still held the knife in her right hand.

'Kanem?' she asked.

'Kanem is dead.'

'Fodio?'

'Fodio is dead.'

'And now Inger is also dead. You are a man who kills, Mr. Wilde. But you would never have killed her.'

Wilde said nothing.

'I knew she was there, in the house, with you. I have lived with Inger, loved Inger, breathed Inger, for two years, Mr. Wilde. I could smell her, in the darkness. She had a peculiarly sweet smell. So when I left you I went back to the house. I knew you could deal with both Kanem and Fodio.'

'I wish I had your confidence. But she followed *you*?'

'I told her you were going to kill her, that you had promised me so, when you had done with her lovers. I told her that I was her only hope of escape, that I knew where our boat was hidden, that I could take her away from here. So she came with me. She was very frightened of you, Mr. Wilde.'

'Yes,' Wilde said.

'And as she was wounded, so she depended upon me for support. To tie her to that tree was a simple matter. She screamed, for you, Mr. Wilde. But she was too weak to resist me.'

'She did not send us into the desert,' Wilde said. 'Kanem did that. She spoke the truth, Serene.'

'I know she spoke the truth, Mr. Wilde. I killed her for betraying me in the first place, for using me and then throwing me aside.'

'That called for this?'

'Vengeance is a law with my people, Mr. Wilde. At least, before civilization rotted their virility. And I am not civilized. This is the teaching of the Lord. And I spared her the horror of mutilation. This, too, is a law of our people, Mr. Wilde, and where the wrong to be righted is a grievous one, it is done upon the living victim. When Inger understood my intention she screamed again. And then she begged me to spare her beauty. And this I have done, Mr. Wilde, because I knew that you would come here, and I know that you loved her. But for that very reason I had to destroy her, because of you, because you would not have done it, would even have saved her life, and would, eventually, have been destroyed by her.'

'And you?'

She touched his cheek. 'You are badly bruised. But I would never harm you, Mr. Wilde. I adore the ground on which you set your feet. I told you this, in the desert, and again in the forest. You are lonely, and afraid. This I can see in your eyes. Oh, you are not afraid, as other men know fear. You fear only for yourself, what you have become, what you will become, increasingly, with every year. But as you truly said to Ukuba, the world of man is composed of many facets, as is the world of nature, for are we not all animals? Perhaps you are the mamba, moving silently through the grass, deadly to all things which step too close, hated by all living creatures, great and small. But nature elected to allow the mamba a place upon this earth, Mr. Wilde, and we are in no position to doubt the will of nature.' She smiled. 'And even mambas have their mates.'

Wilde stood up. 'What will you do now?'

She gazed at him, and slowly her face closed. She had discarded both her knife and her pistol; he wondered if she regretted that.

'We live in different jungles, you and I,' he said.

'No, Mr. Wilde. There is only one jungle. The difference is in our hearts. Come. '

She led him through the forest, and across the pasture, where the cows still huddled anxiously together, and the bull stamped its feet and bellowed, and kept its distance.

On the edge of the vegetable garden she paused, searched amidst the bodies and the long grass, found a rifle which worked.

'Will you give me your bandolier? We may have need of it.'

He gave her the bullets, and she loaded the gun. They crossed the vegetable garden, and came to the huts and the Followers of the Lord. They stood in a group, some gazing at the still figure of Anderson, other watching Cynthia Boraine and Conrad Loman, who waited by the helicopter. But most stared at Ukuba, who stood alone.

'The fighting is over, my lord,' Serene said. 'Kanem and Fodio and Inger, those who have rebelled against your authority, all are dead.'

'You did this thing, Mr. Wilde?'

'He and I together,' Serene said. 'We have saved your sect and the peace of your island, my lord.'

Ukuba gazed at his Followers. 'No one can do either of those things, now,' he said. 'Tell me, Mr. Wilde, was what I attempted to do so very criminal?'

Wilde shrugged. 'Someone once wrote that young men dream dreams and old men see visions. You attempted to do both at the same time. What will happen now?'

'I have fallen from favour in their eyes. They will destroy me, and you, if you do not leave quickly.'

'Which is the general idea.' Cynthia Boraine produced the pistol Wilde had taken from Anderson. 'Get into that machine, Conrad.'

'Anything you say.' Loman mopped his brow with his green and white handkerchief, scrambled into the helicopter.

'You'd better come along with us as well, Wilde,' Cynthia Boraine said.

'We will all leave.' Serene cocked the rifle. 'Get into the plane, grandfather.'

'You cannot desert us,' someone said from the crowd. 'That would be the ultimate betrayal.'

'My grandfather abdicates,' Serene said. 'He gives you the right to choose his successor yourselves. And if one of you moves so much as a finger I will blow his head off. Get into the plane, Mr. Wilde.'

'They are right,' Ukuba said. 'I cannot desert them. Not now.'

'You have taught them the meaning of life,' Serene said. 'You have taught them to exist of themselves. If they wish to leave, then they will build themselves a boat. There is a boat in the reed bed beyond the forest; they may take that as their example. As for deserting them, grandfather, you did that two years ago, when you first saw Inger. Now hurry.'

Ukuba got into the helicopter. Cynthia Boraine tossed the pistol to Wilde, followed. The engine started, the rotors turned. Serene climbed aboard, and Wilde followed her, slammed the door. The Followers of the Lord gazed at them, bereft of leadership, of the power to act of their own volition. Until they could discover a new leader. But he would not possess the Lord's stature, and by the time Zobeir attempted to pick up the pieces the Centre of the Universe would be a deserted lump of mud in the middle of Lake Chad, and the millions of the Followers scattered across the world would be like a giant snake whose head had been cut off; no doubt they would twitch spasmodically for a while, but every movement would further dissipate the dwindling strength of the body.

'I have no idea where I'm going,' Cynthia Boraine shouted down into the cabin.

'Fly due west.' Serene buckled Ukuba's seat-belt. 'We will go to Kano. Chwarism is loyal to Ukuba, and no one else.' She smiled at Wilde. 'There we will say goodbye, Mr. Wilde. But I shall always count our ten days together as the most important of my life.'

'You have not told me what you will do.'

'My great-grandfather is very rich. And I am his only blood relative. I shall look after him, be as all things to him.' She stroked the grey head; Ukuba's eyes were closed. 'And in time I shall become civilized, like you, or Miss Boraine. In time I may even be as wealthy as she. Oh, we shall not meet again. And if we should, I will take care that you shall not recognize me.'

'I let you down,' Wilde said. 'Why did you not kill me, as you promised?'

'You could not kill a woman you loved. I could not kill a man I loved. But, please, it would be better for us not to speak.'

Wilde climbed the ladder, sat beside Cynthia Boraine.

'I wish I could figure out what really happened back there,' she said. 'You know, that first day I thought I'd been conned into a sort of voluntary Devil's Island. They beat me, you know, with some kind of cane. Me! Brother, was I wild. Pardon the pun. I swore I'd have the law on them, and I swore some more when they took away my clothes and gave me these winding sheets. And then they put me out to work like some coolie. But all the time they talked, and we talked. And there was no malice. No . . . no nothing, maybe. Just peace. I think I'd have understood what it was all about in another week. What everything is all about. Now I've the strangest feeling that between us we've just axed what could have been a coming religion.'

'If it's any consolation I have a feeling it destroyed itself.'

'Um. You know what I'd give a few dollars for? A single puff on a Turkish cigarette. Turkish! My God! I must be out of my tiny mind. Say, was that blonde zombie really a twenty-two-carat baddie?'

'She was on the wrong side.'

'And in your book that's all that matters.' She glanced at him. 'So it's back to the old cubby-hole in Whitehall. But they must give you *some* time off, I figure. Especially after a beating like the one you seem to have had. I figure I'm going to be at a loose end, too, for a while. Life will seem sort of dull, don't you think?'

Wilde looked below them at the desert. It occurred to him that he had been happy in the desert.

Cynthia Boraine consulted her instruments, adjusted their course, sighed. 'Well, I guess you can always find me in a gossip column.'

(iii)

'I will have a dry sherry, thank you, Wilde.' Sir Gerald opened the french doors from the bar, chose the table at the end of the balcony, laid down his hat and umbrella, looked along the valley at the stream, and beyond, at the meadow dotted with cows. 'I must say, this is a most delightful spot. However did you find it.?'

Wilde placed the tray on the table, sat down, drank deeply. 'It's one of those little hideaways which, despite the pylons and the motorways, reminds one of how beautiful England can really be. How civilized, maybe.'

'Oh, indeed, I do agree.' Sir Gerald unfolded one of his two newspapers. 'There is a report here about Nigerian Federal police having been flown into the Lake Chad district to investigate some sort of ritual massacre which took place amidst a religious sect known as the Followers of the Lord. Of course, these things do happen in Africa, more often than anywhere else. It didn't even make the television news. But it seems that the leader of this sect, someone called Ukuba, an Arab, I believe, has disappeared.'

'I should think he kept a numbered bank account in Switzerland.'

'These chaps generally do. The police discovered several bodies, including, apparently, that of a white woman.'

'Her name was Inger Lieberstein.'

'Of course. You've just come back from a visit to Africa, haven't you? Tell me, what do you think of the dark continent?'

'I don't think about Africa,' Wilde said. 'Africa is one of those places that you feel. I have never felt so insignificant anywhere in my life. Or wouldn't you know what I mean?'

'Oh, indeed, my dear boy. I imagine it must be rather like waiting to go into bat for Harrow at Lord's. Yes, indeed. And I was only twelfth man. But you managed to find your damsel in distress.'

'No,' Wilde said. 'She found me. Or I wouldn't be here.'

Sir Gerald frowned. 'Do you know, Wilde, a great deal of the time I have absolutely no idea what you are talking about? I must say, you're looking well on your, ah, holiday, despite that rather nasty bruise you've accumulated. You've lost that extra poundage, and your tan is positively Bahamian. Tell me, did you manage to learn anything about these Followers of the, ah, Lord? I had occasion to discuss them with the Foreign Secretary while you were away, and he showed some interest.'

'If, on top of their other troubles, the Federals have moved in, then the sect is dissolved. Take my word for it.'

'Oh, I shall. And I'm glad to hear it. Yes. We knew rather, ah, more about them than I was prepared to disclose to you before your journey, for obvious reasons.'

'What obvious reasons?'

Sir Gerald finished his sherry, peered into the little glass. 'Obvious to me, Wilde, and that is sufficient. Whitehall has quite a file on this Ukuba. By the way, what did you make of him?'

'Like so many of these lofty characters, his feet were firmly stuck in the mud.'

'Ah, yes. But we didn't know that, unfortunately, and frankly, the Foreign Office were wondering what to do about it, in view of the alarming reports as to the growing size of his, ah, following. Once upon a time we would have sent a battalion of the King's African Rifles up the, ah, creek to disperse the core of the sect. But of course we no longer have any jurisdiction in that part of the world, even supposing we still possessed the King's African Rifles, and the Nigerian government, quite understandably, are at the present time reluctant to consider sending troops in any direction except home. I will admit that our superiors have been a little worried about the possible ways in which such a situation might develop. So they came to me.'

'Who else?'

'Quite. Not that even I could immediately come up with a solution, of course. But no sooner had you appeared with your peculiar problem, than I realized I had found a possible answer. It occurred to me, that failing the said battalion of soldiers, to introduce you into the midst of that happy band of primitives would cause the Lord at least to reappraise his programme.'

'Lucky for you I happened along.'

'In a manner of speaking, of course, Wilde. But to every problem in life there appears, eventually, a solution. One must merely be at all times ready to seize the opportunity when it occurs. So in my business, during my daily consideration of the various, ah, abrasive areas which could possibly threaten the security of either this country or Nato, I work in the confident knowledge that sooner or later I shall be enabled to insert one of my, ah, men, into the heart of the would-be opposition, and observe what profit can be gained. In this case, things have turned out better than I could possibly have hoped. Yes, indeed. In the circumstances, I am prepared to overlook your conduct in, ah, ditching Mrs. Hart. Although whether she will be prepared to do the same, in view of the embarrassing circumstances in which you abandoned her, remains to be seen. Have you seen this?'

Wilde took the other newspaper, glanced at the marked passage.

'THE CASE OF THE NUDE IN THE MEN'S LAVATORY.

'At Bow Street yesterday morning, Mr. Nigel Atkinson-Brown, Q.C., on behalf of his client, Mrs. Felicity Hart, pleaded guilty to a charge of behaving in a manner calculated to disturb the peace at the British Overseas Airways Corporation Terminal Building in Victoria on Thursday last. In mitigation, Mr. Atkinson-Brown stated that Mrs. Hart, who is a senior secretary in the Civil Service, had been working extraordinarily long hours for some weeks previous to the incident, and was actually on her way to a well-deserved holiday in Africa when she suffered what appears to have been a blackout. She remembered having a drink in the bar prior to the departure of her coach for Heathrow, but she had no recollection of what happened afterwards, and, in particular, of removing her clothes and entering the Men's Lavatory. Nor could she account for the whereabouts of her clothes, which have not yet been found. On awakening, she without thinking opened the door and stepped outside, only then realizing her condition.

'Commenting on the obvious excellence of the heating arrangements in the building in question, Magistrate Mr. Thomas Brudenell imposed a fine of five pounds, and recommended that Mrs. Hart enjoy a long rest.'

'Which she is now doing,' Sir Gerald said.

'I don't suppose you'd believe me if I told you I wasn't aware of her unusual sartorial habits?' Wilde asked.

'Frankly, no. She's an altogether unusual young woman, as I'm sure you've found out. Well, thanks for the sherry. No doubt I'll be in touch.' He took an envelope from his inside breast pocket. 'That contains fifteen hundred pounds.'

Wilde lit a Belfleur cigar. 'There's just one thing. Am I to understand that you were not really interested in Inger Liberstein, after all?'

'My dear boy, I have always been interested in Inger Liberstein. I mean, who could fail to be? But I will confess that I have not actually been, ah, looking for her. Those two agents I spoke of were, ah, figments of my imagination. As you should have understood, were I to send agents after every British operative who has ever defected, I wouldn't have anybody left at home, would I? But I had no doubt, from my knowledge of Frau Lieberstein, that she would be well placed in the hierarchy of this, ah, religion, and so whatever reception they accorded you on arrival would soon turn to resentment when you, ah, eliminated her, which would in turn provoke you to the mayhem we have just been discussing, and at which you are such an adept. Thus I would be killing two birds with one stone. Yes, I am very pleased with you, Wilde. You have no idea what a struggle I have on my hands, with every government which takes office, and, indeed, after every review of our financial situation, to persuade them that having a man like you on our, ah, payroll, is either necessary or desirable. But you are considerably cheaper to maintain than a battalion of the King's African Rifles.'

'You know,' Wilde remarked. 'Every time I see you I think to myself what an utterly detestable man. But then I always wind up thinking I'm rather glad I work for him, after all.'

Sir Gerald smiled. 'Now isn't that remarkable, Wilde. My emotions as regards you are identical. Except, of course, as you say, that you work for me.'

(iv)

Wilde finished his drink, got into the little Alfa, drove down to the south coast. It was one of those afternoons which make June the best month of the year, warm and sunny, with none of the weariness of September. It was an afternoon to appreciate being alive, rather than to brood on those who were dead. But it was impossible to do one without the other.

He parked his car on a dusty high street, found the right office. 'Mr. Benton,' he said. 'Sorry I didn't get back to you sooner. Is that boat still available?'

'Waiting for you, Mr. Wilde. Waiting for you. But, of course, your agent took care of everything. She's ready to sail away. The cat, I mean.'

'I've been abroad the last week, so I didn't know just how far things had gone. Thanks very much.' Wilde lit a cigar, got back into the Alfa, drove down to the dock. The tide was in and most of the yachts were out. The catamaran bobbed to her moorings, not fifty feet from the shore. He hailed a young man messing about in a dinghy, got a ride, went on board. Felicity Hart lay on a mattress in the cockpit; she wore a bikini and dark glasses.

'Why, Jonas,' she said. 'What a pleasant surprise. But I knew you'd show, eventually. I've been just lying here, watching the clouds. You have no idea how relaxing it is.'

Wilde went below.

'Oh, she's ready to go,' Felicity said. 'I've stocked the galley with enough food for a month, and lashings of liquor. And a nice boatman took me over to the yacht club and filled the petrol tanks. I explained that I was waiting for my husband. You owe me two thousand, seven hundred pounds for the boat, and a hundred for the grub.'

'Put it on the slate.' Wilde found the working jib, went on deck. Felicity Hart leaned on the hatch cover. 'Tell me, how did you find out about the ship?' he asked.

She smiled. 'I followed you that afternoon. Back to your little Kensington hideaway? So when you left me behind I went round and introduced myself to Mrs. Bettin. I explained that we're engaged, officially, and got your mail off her. There was a letter from the surveyors saying you were on to a good buy.'

'Your efficiency frightens me.' Wilde hoisted the mainsail, released the topping lift, stowed the boom crutch; the catamaran made little runs into the wind, brought up against her mooring chain. 'By the way, can you swim?'

'Like an absolute bloody fish,' she said. 'It's my one athletic accomplishment. Tell me, Jonas, where are we going first?'

Wilde took her in his arms, swept her feet from the deck, dropped her over the side with a gentle splash. 'The dock is that way,' he said, and went forward to cast off.

THE BLACK CAMELS
OF QASHRAN

Ronald Johnston

*'The Black Camels of Qashran' is published
by William Collins, Sons & Co. Ltd.*

The Author

Ronald Johnston, born in Edinburgh, joined the Merchant Navy at the age of sixteen and remained for thirteen years—long enough to get his Master's Certificate. He eventually came ashore to become general manager of a booming company but threw it all up to take on the job of professional writer—with a family to support, a desperate gamble but one which has most decidedly come off, now that he has written half a dozen successful novels.

CHAPTER ONE

THERE WERE TWELVE CAMELS. All black. They came slowly up the last steep slope to the crest of the dune. They stepped carefully on the soft, moving sand, the riders leaving the reins loose, letting the animals pick their own way in the darkness. Twelve black camels. Twelve of the legendary four hundred, the sacred herd of Qashran.

Rasul smiled as his camel came over the ridge. They were right on course. Ahead, the desert was suddenly flat, the sand coarser and less yielding underfoot. Ahead, five miles away, a spread of lights shone brightly in the darkness, marking the target. Sheikh Rasul reined in his beast and waited for the others to join him. He felt good. He had that tight feeling of expectancy in his stomach, that feeling he got watching one of his falcons closing in on a desert bustard, that feeling he sometimes got close to a favourite woman. That feeling he used to get in the old days when he ruled undisputed over Qashran, when he used his cunning to balance the forces in the tribe, to play oil company against oil company, to set foreign government against foreign government, to get the most and give the least.

But the old days had been over for three years. Three long years in the alien luxury of exile in Europe. Now that was over. Now Rasul was back in Qashran and soon everyone would know he was back.

He looked round. His men were all up out of the last dune, sitting their camels easily, waiting for his signal. Yussuf was there close behind him. He had been Rasul's faithful slave all his adult lift. Yussuf was easy to pick out in any group of Bedouin. The cloak and the head-cloth could not disguise his huge Negro body. Hamid Babrah was there too, poised, confident, checking his watch and nodding congratulations to himself. Rasul had never liked Babrah. He was Egyptian and Rasul did not like Egyptians. They called themselves Arabs but were not Arabs. For Rasul, the only Arabs were desert Arabs. But Babrah was good at his job. His job was training men to fight and to destroy. There would be no fighting this time, just destruction, massive destruction, a sign of the sheikh's return to his homeland, a portent of what was to come.

Rasul urged his camel forward. He headed east of the lights, making for a shallow depression a mile away from the wellhead.

He felt the change in the camel's gait, firm, confident, not tentative as it had been all the long crossing of the singing sands. That had been like crossing a sea, mile after mile of soft sand, soaring and diving in a confusion of crests and troughs, moving, shifting, and all the time groaning and murmuring and calling up thoughts of the spirits of the desert. Even the Bedu kept clear of the singing sands. That suited Rasul. He had known his way through them since boyhood. The singing sands were the back door into his land, and his escape route south into the wastes of the Empty Quarter and his base camp there. The maps said that the sands and the Empty Quarter were in Saudi Arabia but that meant nothing to Rasul. The desert belonged to those who crossed it.

They rode down into the depression, dismounted and couched the camels. Rasul walked up to the lip with Hamid Babrah to inspect the ground and check over the details. The Egyptian uncased a pair of binoculars. The sheikh's eyes needed no help. He could see all he wanted to see. There, a mile away, etched in the glare of the floodlights, lay Qashran Number One. This was the target; the source of Rasul's wealth, the reason for his exile, and now the first victim of his vengeance.

It was called Number One because it was the first well in the state to strike oil in commercial quantities. There had only been dry holes and traces before. Number One was now a producing well. There was no derrick, no chains and tackles and tongs and stands of drill pipe, no clatter of steel on steel, no rattle and whine of winches and wire. There was just the silver painted wellhead assembly and the huge pipeline leading from it across the sixty miles of flat desert to the coast on the Persian Gulf now diplomatically renamed the Arabian Gulf. But Number One was not just an isolated, unmanned, producing oil well in the desert. It was the hub of all Inoco Oil's programme in Qashran. The whole complex was now known as South Base but Rasul still called it Qashran One. The site spread over a hundred acres of desert. There was a pumphouse, a gas separation plant, a generating station, tank farms, workshops, stores, all in course of expansion ready for the new wells in the west soon to be brought on stream. There was an office block, a big dormy house for the European staff, another for the Pakistani clerks and engineers, and one for the local workers. Air conditioning was everywhere. Round the whole site ran a twelve foot high chain link fence which affronted Rasul more than anything else.

It was that fence that held his attention. A fence in the middle of the desert. It meant nothing to him that the site was close to the disputed border with Saudi Arabia and therefore wide open to raids and sabotage. When Rasul led Qashran, he knew how to control the border. It meant nothing to him that herds of goats and camels could cause chaos if allowed to wander at will through the complex of buildings and equipment. The goats and the camels and the Bedu herdsmen had been there for centuries before the oil men. The fence was to him a symbol of all he had fought against, and lost, and now was going to fight against again. He spat in the sand and grinned. He would never understand these British and Americans. They build a fence to keep strangers out. They put guards on every gate and note down every man and animal and vehicle that passes through. Then tonight, because young Kassim is celebrating his latest lunacy, they leave the whole place empty but for half a dozen men. And the man on the east gate was one of Rasul's.

Babrah was ready to move. The sheikh just nodded. There was no need for talk or discussion. Everything had been planned down to the last detail. Babrah would ride forward with three of the men. That allowed for the arrangements inside the fence having been altered at the last minute. There was nothing unusual about four Bedu stopping to exchange gossip and sip coffee. If everything was still as planned, these four and the man on the gate could easily deal with the rest of the skeleton staff. The one place where they could afford no mistake was in the control room. There must be no chance of the radio link being used.

The four rode up out of the depression. They would be invisible from inside the fence almost until they were up against it, but Rasul could pick out every step, silhouetted against the floodlights. He pulled at his beard and wet his lips with his tongue. Praise be to Allah. They were inside the gate. He smiled. His eyes rested on the feather of flame flaring from the tall stack above the gas separation unit. What a puny flame. Kassim deserves something better than that to celebrate the opening of his new *suk*. But Rasul could not smile for long when he thought about Kassim. He glowered across the desert and his mouth and eyes hardened. The gulf between Kassim and his uncle was unbridgeable. It was not only a gulf of age, though they were separated by close on forty years. It was a gulf of tradition, of education, of belief.

Qashran, like the other Trucial States, had come late into the search for oil. Iran, Kuwait, Saudi Arabia and Bahrein had kept the oil companies busy for years. The Trucial States were primitive, the land inhospitable, the prospects for oil less promising. The companies had staked their claims, of course, by paying annual fees for exploration rights. The sheikhs were glad to have the money. There was very little activity and the Trucial way of

life went on as before. The money let the sheikhs buy their tribes-
men's loyalty. It let them buy better falcons to hunt with and
better rifles to fight with. Preserving one's boundaries, annexing
neighbouring territories, extracting tax from the desert people,
dispensing justice at the daily *majlis,* that was the Trucial way of
life. And praying. Especially in Qashran where they were Wahhabis, Allah's Puritans.

Rasul had been the leader for a long time. He was only in his
twenties when his father was killed. There had been no doubt
about the succession. His name, Rasul, the chosen one, summed
it up but the succession was his because the tribe already knew
that he could ride faster and further, shoot straighter and plot
more astutely than any of his uncles and brothers. There had been
no threat to his leadership until oil was found in the neighbouring state and Inoco suddenly decided to exercise the exploration
rights they had been paying for for years. That was not to say
that there had been no attempts to unseat Rasul. There had been
many but Rasul was well informed. Plotters in Qashran were
accident-prone. Half a dozen of the sheikh's relations had con-
firmed the legend that no member of the ruling family ever died
peacefully in his bed.

The lights along the fence snapped off, on, off, on again. Praise
be to Allah. He called the rest of the men. They mounted and
rode out. Rasul stayed where he was. He was not needed over
there. Hamid Babrah was the expert. But the sheikh was not
alone. Yussuf had stayed behind too. Yussuf was always there,
waiting, watching. He had been there three years ago and had
tried to warn Rasul that his friend, Troy Sahib, and the elders
and Inoco were plotting to replace him with Kassim. The sheikh
had beaten Yussuf senseless with a camel stick.

Ben Troy had been the British Political Agent in Qashran for
an unusually long time. He had come immediately after the
end of the Second War. Troy was not just a trusted adviser, he
was a friend. He had helped Rasul to retain his independence, he
had advised him how to deal with the oil companies and the neighbouring sheikhs. He spoke the Gulf Arabic that Rasul used. They
talked together, they hunted together, they were like brothers
but without the rivalry that usually meant in the desert. But
Yussuf had been right. Rasul was ousted. He was not killed, just
sent into exile. That had been a mistake.

Rasul had made that mistake once; when Kassim's father, the
sheikh's younger brother, had been killed. Then he had listened
to his friend, Troy Sahib. He had listened and been convinced
that, to make plain that he had nothing to do with the killing,
he should look after the boy, send him off to school, first in Bah-

rein, then on to England. Maybe even then Troy was preparing the ground for his palace revolution.

The sheikh had never really understood the English. They were ruthless and capable. Even a limited knowledge of history proved that. But they had this peculiar feeling that, though almost any political intrigue could be justified, it was not right to resort to the simple final solution of killing off those who no longer served any useful purpose. They should have arranged an accident for Rasul. That omission was now going to cost them dearly.

There was an hour of waiting for Rasul to relish all his hates. It was a long list. It had been a long time brewing. This was not the dislike, the suspicion that had made him ruthless and effective in command. This was real hate, hate fed on impotence, hate nurtured in that villa by the lakeside in Switzerland, with plenty of money, his own servants, his wives, and never a sight of the desert, or the feel of the blistering sun, or the challenge of argument in the *majlis*, or the threat from a relative with a taste for power. It was the kind of hate that destroys unless indulged. He stood there and savoured his hate for Kassim, for Inoco and its chief in Qashran, Carl Banner, for his own choice as chief of the Defence Force, John Negley, for the elders, for the merchants, for everyone who had applauded his overthrow and exile. For Troy, friend turned traitor. No, not for Troy. Troy Sahib had done what he had to do. He was a servant of his government. You could not hate a friend who had been forced to betray you. But you could be disappointed, you could feel a sense of loss; you could return and fight and make him come and admit he had been wrong.

The sheikh smiled grimly as he remembered the day Hamid Babrah had come to see him in that villa. From that day Rasul had started to live again. The hate no longer gnawed at him, it stimulated him, for then he knew he had the chance to take his revenge.

It had taken time. It had been frustrating. First, the planning, then the secret departure from the villa, most of his staff staying behind to ensure that everything seemed as before, the plane trips, the night crossing by dhow, the long trek through the mountains and down into the sands of the Empty Quarter to the place only he knew existed. Long ago he had discovered that place; a huge valley surrounded on three sides by immense dunes rising almost a thousand feet up, the other side a great crag of black basalt; and deep inside the rock a torrent of sweet water. He had kept the knowledge of that place secret. It was not in his territory. He owed no favours to the Saudis.

It had taken time to trek in food and arms and ammunition. It had taken time to recruit and train the men. Then two months ago there had been that first expedition. Up out of the singing sands to round up and drive away the sacred herd of black camels. Rasul smiled briefly. That had been a good first expedition. It had his style about it. The aftermath had been disappointing. The only place the herd could have been taken was over the border into Saudi Arabia. Rasul had hoped there would be a diplomatic row, maybe even some incidents on the border. He had miscalculated. He had forgotten that young Kassim had very little time for the traditions of Qashran. The whole thing had been hushed up. Thinking about it, Rasul saw Troy's influence. Troy would not have missed the significance of the raid. He would be quick to suspect the truth, to advise Kassim to pretend it had never happened, to start checking up on that villa in Switzerland. Now it did not matter what had been discovered there. Soon, very soon, everyone would know that Sheikh Rasul was back in Qashran. It would not even matter if Troy had discovered Hamid Babrah's plans for the revolt. Rasul had his own plans.

There was movement over at the fence. They were coming back. The sheikh walked down and mounted his camel. It lurched to its feet and he rode up out of the depression. He stopped and waited. Qashran One looked quite normal. The lights were on all round the fence, the flare was still lit above the gas separator. The thud and hum of the generators still reached out across the desert. The returning camels were trotting, the roped captives running to stop being pulled off their feet and dragged across the sand. The sheikh walked his beast towards them. As they came near, the riders ran their camels round in a tight circle, snaring the men from Qashran One in a tangle of rope. Yussuf walked forward and flashed his lamp on the struggling heap. He tightened a rope here, tied a knot there, then stood back and held the prisoners in the full beam.

Rasul stopped his camel only inches from the men. He stared down at them for almost a minute. Then he unsheathed the great scimitar and held it close to the nearest struggling head. All movement stopped. Staring, frightened eyes were fixed on the scimitar, its blade gleaming, the jewels in the handle picking up the torchlight and glowing red and green and blue. That sword was more eloquent than any speech. The Great Sword of Qashran, once emblazoned on the state's green flag, discarded by the new sheikh. To these men on the ground, the sword meant justice, desert justice. It had a long history. Taken as loot from the Turks at the turn of the century, it had spilled a lot of blood.

Blood from hands and feet chopped off, blood from heads rolled in the sand. It gleamed and glittered over their heads in silent menace.

'Tell them, tell them when they come to mourn over their oil well. Tell them that Rasul, the chosen one, prince of Qashran, lord of the desert, friend of the great spirits, servant of Allah, tell them that I have returned. Tell them to read the Holy Koran. "Wait for the day when the sky will pour down blinding smoke, enveloping all men; a dreadful scourge." Tell them that the Sword of Qashran will lift that scourge and cleanse the desert with blood.' The blade quivered and the nearest head strained back into the captive heap.

Then Rasul raised the sword high and spurred his camel forward. He sheathed the sword and took his camel stick in his hand. The stick jerked the black camel up to full speed. The sheikh crouched into the wind of the camel's race across the sand. He was excited as he had not been for a very long time. He was back in Qashran. He had revealed himself. He had seen the terror in those eyes gazing up at the sword and the man on the black camel. His great final adventure was really begun. He thought he could hear the plaintive anthem of the singing sands. It sounded in his ears like a battle hymn.

He reined in and stopped his mount on the crest of the first dune. Yes, the sands were singing; moaning, hissing, shuffling, sighing, harmonizing with the hoof beats of the camels racing up behind. Rasul turned and looked back across the flat desert. His men slowed. He signed to Yussuf to lead off down the steep slope. Only Babrah remained beside the sheikh. Rasul barely glanced at him. The Egyptian was peering at his watch. He always seemed to be peering at his watch, or his compass, or through his binoculars. He was not a Bedu. He was an instrumented Arab.

Babrah nodded to himself. One minute. He was relieved to be there on the edge on the dunes. There would be little enough time to escape when his charges started to blow. In seconds the pumping station on the coast would realize something was wrong. In minutes the southern sky would reflect the scale of the disaster. In half an hour a helicopter could be whirling down close to the site. Babrah knew his business. He did not share the sheikh's penchant for melodramatic speeches and sword waving. He was a soldier, a revolutionary soldier.

'Just a few seconds now, Your Highness.'

Rasul nodded. He enjoyed hearing Babrah use these words—Your Highness. He knew the Egyptian found them difficult to say. He knew his feeling about royalty. He knew that Babrah had fought against the royalists in the Yemen. He knew he had helped to force the British out of Aden. He knew he had trained the guerillas in Jordan to raid across the river and stop any chance of the king talking to the Israelis. It pleased Rasul to have this anti-royalist call him 'Your Highness', to know that he did it only because he was using the sheikh for his own ends, to know that Hamid Babrah was yet to discover that this revolt was a Bedouin revolt and would be played out according to Bedouin rules.

The view across the desert was normal. The lights at Qashran One still glowed, the gas flare still flickered. It was the same view Rasul had seen as he crested the dune on the inward journey. It was as if the last two hours had never happened.

When it did start, it was a disappointment. The sheikh had visualized it a score of times in advance. He had seen the desert erupt in a mass of smoke and flame, he had heard the night shattered by enormous explosions. He had seen the black smoke climb up into the flame-lit sky, billowing and swirling, then forming and hanging there as a symbol his people would recognize better than any word.

The first explosion was faint, a mere thud which seemed to travel through the ground rather than the air. Rasul looked round. In the darkness he could see the Egyptian's outline, binoculars up to his eyes. You had better improve on that, Hamid Babrah, or I'll roll your head in the sand. He fingered the hilt of the sword. Then he smiled. Or, as the English would say, 'I'll knock your block off, old boy.' The sheikh's long exile had not dulled his macabre Bedu sense of humour.

Two more explosions, heavier but still muffled. Rasul looked back. For a second he lost his bearings. All the lights were out. The desert was lit only by the glittering stars.

Babrah was checking off the destruction in his mind. First, the emergency power plant. Then the generator house and the switch room. He moistened his lips. Next the transport depot and the fuel tanks.

The sheikh watched and waited. This time he spotted the flash. The noise of the new explosions, unconfined, reached out across the desert with pleasing intensity. As it hammered on Rasul's ears he could see the flames growing up the silhouetted fuel tanks, collapsing as the tanks exploded and crumpled, spreading to the workshops and the transport park, leaping like a giant firecracker among the vehicles, consuming them, firing their fuel tanks, jumping on to the next line, all the time fed by the gallonage pouring from the ruptured storage tanks, pouring through the carefully breached fire walls round the tanks. A spreading sea of flame. A long drum roll of explosions. Babrah deserved his reputation as an expert.

More explosions. More fire. Rasul could see now the shapes of the dormy houses and the control centre. All the window spaces gleamed as the incendiaries scattered inside burst and spread their flames. Quickly the windows shone like rows of bright lanterns.

The puny flare above the gas separator was still burning. Then the plant exploded and the severed chimney fell into the debris. A tower of flame jumped skywards and the roar of the blast scythed out for miles across the sand.

Rasul felt his palm wet on the hilt of the sword. He wiped it dry on his cloak but it was already damp again when he returned it to the sword. He could not take his eyes from the scene of this first victory. The mass of flame had pushed back the darkness. He could pick out small details; the shape of a crumpled tank, the ribs of mangled buildings, debris being tossed in the air. The light was red and orange, like a desert sunset. Even the haze was there, not purple like the sunset, but black like a woman's clothes. Black and billowing, a horde of Bedu women dancing madly above the flames.

A rat-tat-tat of small explosions. The fire walls in the crude oil tank farm. Then two, three, four heavy blasts, and the scene at the transport park was repeated on a grander scale. The storage tanks exploded, the crude oil caught fire. The flames leapt from tank to tank, ran on the running liquid through the breached barriers, into buildings, over equipment, everywhere. Even the sand was burning.

The sheikh was entranced. In all his imaginings he had never thought it could be like this. He had seen fireworks in Europe; this put all that to shame. He shifted in his saddle. He was restive for the grand finale.

He missed the blast that severed the wellhead assembly from Qashran One. It was not a huge explosion. It was nicely calculated to do its job and not to spoil the aftermath. But he sensed the rumbling overture deep underground. The well had been freed from its captivity. The rumbling grew till it was not only felt but also heard. The sheikh's camel made to turn away. He reined it in, his eyes fixed on the eastern extremity of the site.

The pent up oil soared suddenly up out of the ground. It grew like a magic black tree, straight, limbless. In seconds it had climbed hundreds of feet up through the air. Its triumphant swishing roar overcame all other sound. Then, as its force was spent high above the ground, the black column seemed to grow tendrils and leaves. At once it shed them and they dropped back to earth in a fire spray. They fell back into the raging pool of flame already surging round the well. They fell back and added to the flames, feeding them an endless charge of volatile crude. The sea of fire advanced on the wellhead like a racing tide. It was all around the gushing column of oil. Suddenly the black tree disappeared. In its place there was an awesome pillar of flame. Qashran One had been fired.

Even miles distant, Rasul could feel the scorching heat. The sulphurous stench was in his nostrils and the noise roared in his ears. The camels were panic-stricken. They swung from side to side, straining against the tight reins, rolling their eyes wildly, flaring their nostrils, snarling and baring their yellow teeth. It was time to go. But Rasul fought his beast. He wanted more time to feast his eyes on Qashran One.

Now it stood high up into the sky, swirling and roaring like a giant dust devil sucked up by the desert wind. But there was no wind. All around the sand was still. There was just the towering black cloud growing up out of the inferno where the wellhead had been, making insignificant the lake of fire still burning across the whole site of South Base.

Suddenly there was wind. Just a faint whisper at first but soon a chill breeze. Rasul felt it on his back, saw his cloak stir. He was afraid. The wind was coming from the south, up out of the singing sands. That could not be. There was never wind from the south. The sheikh knew nothing of science. He did not know that the fireball he had made was sucking in new air from every point of the compass, greedily gulping in fresh stocks of oxygen. But he was not afraid for long. He soon found an explanation. It was just as it had been in his dreams. All the affronted spirits of the desert were swarming in to join him in battle, to hoist a great sign in the sky over his land. He looked up at the huge black cloud, already blotting out the stars. Yes, there it was. The Great Djinn of Qashran. Now they would know that Rasul was back. In the name of Allah and supported by all the ancient spirits. The Bedu would know, Kassim would know, Troy would know, Banner would know, everyone would know.

He let the camel turn its head away from the heat and the stench. He was surprised to see Babrah. He had forgotten all about him. The Egyptian turned his beast. He sat high in his saddle, proud of his expertise, waiting for praise.

The sheikh fingered his sword. 'Praise be to Allah, The Compassionate, The Merciful, King of the Last Judgement.' Then he walked his mount forward over the lip of the dune and down into the singing sands.

CHAPTER TWO

IT WAS A PARTY people would talk about for months. The setting made all the difference. Kassim's new *suk* had the right kind of scale.

The new bazaar was a devastating blend of architectural forms. From the outside it looked vaguely Venetian, each long side a succession of deep-set arches fronted by a broad walkway. Each arch was a basic shop unit. Above these arches ran a balustraded gallery in front of another tier of small arches; more shop units. The ends of the *suk* were huge square gateways with studded wooden doors in the style of a desert fort. And above each gateway rose a tall Persian wind tower to collect and distribute the breezes to and from the sea. The wind towers had seemed plain and simple, so they had been capped with copper mushroom domes in the Turkish manner. The whole structure was roofed with low-pitched concrete beams separated by sheets of glass tinted in various colours to tame the harsh glare of the sun. The area round the building was reserved for cars. The *suk* was, in fact, a Qashrani one-stop shopping centre.

By day it was impressive from the outside in a vulgar way. Now, by night, floodlit and with the lights from inside etching the arches and painting the glass roof in all its rainbow colours, it was exciting. But it was inside that the *suk* took the breath away. The whole enclosed area was floored in intricate mosaic. Down each side were the shop units made by bringing the arches through from the outside. At each end a broad stairway with carved wooden banisters led up to the gallery which ran round the inside of the building. Up there, the shops were reserved for the luxury trades. In the well, under the glass and concrete roof, there were fountains and gardens.

The project had cost a great deal of money. It was not being launched with a lavish party, a well-organized public relations exercise to sweeten the pill the merchants and traders had had to swallow. They were happy enough in the old bazaar which had grown up higgledy-piggledy along the edge of the creek. Sheikh Kassim now wanted that land for a new development with a luxury hotel and apartment blocks set in their own parkland overlooking the creek which would become a marina when the dhows and fishing boats were banished to the new harbour already growing out from the shore.

Kassim had a gentlemanly ruthlessness which owed much to the unusual pattern of his education. First Bahrein, then Eton and Oxford, followed by post-graduate studies at the London School of Economics and the Harvard Business School. It was one of his party pieces to describe himself as a socialist Bedouin capitalist.

He had handled the merchants' objections to the high rents in the new *suk* in a straightforward way. He guaranteed them space if they agreed to all his terms by a stated date; and added that the day after that date the bulldozers would start flattening the old site. They agreed. They knew that the high rents were realistic. Kassim's vast development programme was bringing them in a lot of business. They also knew that Kassim was as good as his word.

But the party was not only for the local merchants. Kassim had cast his net much wider. Two chartered VC 10s had flown in with a hand-picked selection of bankers, property developers, contractors and industrialists. Carrots were being dangled in front of each group. For the bankers there was the normal funding business from any growth area and there was also the gold market which Kassim planned to wean from its current haven at Dubai. For the property men there was the hotel and marina scheme; for the contractors there was all the new construction; and for the industrialists there was the chance of establishing businesses locally under generous tax advantages. Kassim saw his desert sheikhdom as a glittering jewel attracting business men and tourists from all over the world. There was a rumour that the idea took root when he visited Las Vegas and saw what could be conjured up out of a stretch of sand. He did not visualize a dependence on gambling but he was in a hurry to import the West into the Middle East. On these chartered planes he had also imported some of his friends from Europe and America. They were all female, young and very good looking. Life at the top could be lonely in Qashran City.

Ben Troy leaned on the balustrade round the gallery and watched his protégé. Kassim was his protégé though he had not chosen him. Troy had had the new sheikh wished upon him; by his masters in Whitehall, by Inoco, by the merchants, by the elders. But as the Political Agent, Troy had organized the succession. It had been smooth and trouble-free; his knowledge of the country and of Rasul's character had ensured that. After almost three years he was still sometimes not sure he had done right. The first mistake had been to underestimate Kassim. Everyone had thought the young sheikh would be a puppet, following the Inoco line on oil and the Whitehall line on politics. But Kassim had turned out to be more of a puppet master.

There he was, manipulating the strings as he came up the stairway at the far end of the gallery. Troy watched. This was Kassim giving his usual polished performance to two of the visiting businessmen and a trio of girls. It all seemed very natural, unforced. It was a convincing impression of a gay, good-looking young nobleman enjoying the fruits of a wealth he had done nothing to create. It was not Kassim but it was one of Kassim's favourite impersonations. It was a feint that often succeeded in lowering people's guards. He had been at it throughout the reception—champagne cocktails, and the lavish buffet supper with champagne. Kassim's way with drinks said much. Champagne cocktails and champagne were not his favourites but they had a touch of glamour about them and it was efficient to deny people any choice. 'Speed and plenitude are the criteria.' If the volume of chatter and laughter welling up from the main floor was any kind of yardstick, he had been right.

Not everyone who came to Qashran thought it odd that Kassim enjoyed a drink. It was surprising how many men travelled abroad to do business and never troubled to learn anything about the places they were visiting. Qashran was not just Mohammedan, it was Wahhabi. In Rasul's time, alcohol was forbidden, even to Europeans. Some thought that was one of the old sheikh's big mistakes. But Kassim's background was not Wahhabi, it was British with a leavening of ideas from Europe and America. He took a drink, he hardly ever took too much. To those who asked him how a Moslem could drink and still be a Moslem, he gave back a question. 'Can you quote me that part of the Koran that forbids alcohol?' Then, indulgently, he would explain that what was forbidden was excess. Very few visitors were knowledgeable enough to argue. Those who were, men like Troy with a lifetime's experience in the Gulf, did not waste time in argument. They thought about the significance of the attitudes behind the posture. They thought about the political effects of a ruler of a Trucial state who was only nominally a Moslem, a ruler who thought that the old religious order was holding back the development of his country. They thought about the effects of a Trucial Attaturk driving his people into the twentieth century, whittling away the old ideas that had maintained a semblance of primitive order. These men noticed that the other Trucial rulers were not at this reception. They worried about a ruler who could roar with laughter when a European announced that what he liked about Qashran City was that you hardly ever met an Arab. They worried because they knew the Middle East. They could see the pattern. The Yemen, then Aden, then the announcement of the coming Brtish withdrawal from the Gulf. All the states bordering the Gulf were rich prizes long sought after by Arab nationalists.

Kassim's radical developments made Qashran odds-on favourite as the first flashpoint in the Gulf.

The young sheikh had listened to all the arguments. He was not convinced that a slower rate of advance would keep the revolutionaries at bay. In fact, he thought it would make their job easier. He always ended with the suggestion that the answer lay, not in his slowing down, but in the neighbouring states trying to keep pace with him. Kassim dealt in logic. It would have been a brave political attitude anywhere; in Trucial Oman, it seemed foolhardy.

But for nearly three years the prophets of doom had awaited the explosion in vain. Instead they had seen Kassim's plans bear fruit. They had seen Qashran City start to take on a shape that made its new name seem almost appropriate. They had seen first a trickle, then a flood of Bedu deserting their herds and coming up to the coast to go to school and learn to be truck drivers and mechanics and oil men. They had heard the complaints of the elders about the end of the old traditions like the daily *majlis* but they had noticed that the complaints were quickly muted. Kassim knew how to dispense wealth and privilege strategically. They had heard from outside the grumblings of the rulers of the neighbouring states. But they only grumbled and bought a few more Cadillacs. They had heard the crescendo of abuse pouring through the transistors from Cairo Radio. But they knew that Cairo was still recovering from the Israeli thrashing. At Kassim's party to celebrate the new *suk*, everyone seemed to agree that nothing was going to happen to slow the economic miracle.

Everyone but Ben Troy. He had always been uneasy at the pace of Kassim's expansion. But he had been able to explain that unease. His long experience of the country and his feeling for its traditions. His guilt about the overthrow of Rasul. His diminishing influence with the young sheikh. Maybe even a feeling of lost purpose in his career.

But his unease that night had less complicated origins. It stemmed from an instinct. He had learned to trust his instinct. There was no proof, just vague rumours filtering in from the desert, nothing he could discuss with anyone, just a certainty that the party would not end as smoothly as it had begun. It was two months since the black camels had disappeared. Troy had been sure then that that was Rasul's work. Four hundred black camels were not easily hidden but they had vanished as if swallowed up by the sand. The only place they could have gone was across the border into Saudi Arabia. There they could disappear and nothing might be heard of them for years. But Rasul had never been a favourite of the Saudis. Of course, Arabian politics made strange bedfellows. To advance their claim to the whole of Trucial Oman, the Saudis might be supporting Rasul. But why assume that Rasul was involved? The Saudis might have taken the herd as part of their constant pressure on the Trucial sheikhdoms. They might have hoped to rekindle the tension along the disputed 1955 border. With the new oil finds not only on-shore but also off-shore, Trucial Oman had become a rich prize. That was Kassim's reading of the incident. That was why he insisted on ignoring the disappearance of the sacred herd. He was glad to be rid of it. It was an anachronism which drank a lot of precious water. And there was the other evidence. Troy had reported his suspicions to the Resident in Bahrein. The Foreign Office had been asked to inquire. The intelligence people reported that Rasul and his entourage were still in Switzerland. Troy remained unconvinced. He knew the evidence was against him but he was sure that Rasul was close by and that soon he would make his presence known. The party was tailormade for the purpose. Ben Troy felt there was an inevitability about it all. He was uneasy only because it had not yet happened. When it did happen, whatever happened, he would welcome it. There would then be no more wondering or worrying. He would have a real job to do. It would be his gift to Qashran. It would be more difficult this time. Rasul was a shrewd old fox and Troy would be without the weapon of trust. He felt that in winning the battle against his old friend, he might lose the war.

He shook himself and stood up straight. People were being rounded up and moved towards the stairways up to the gallery. Kassim was beckoning from the far end. Troy walked towards him. The girls and the businessmen had been left at one of the bars. The man with the sheikh was tall, stooped, with a strong face and a mane of white hair. He had to be a politician. His suit marked him as American.

'Come on, my dear chap,' said Kassim. 'You seem to have been hiding all evening. Anything the matter? Is the food not up to scratch? The champagne not cold enough? Or are you just out of sorts because your wife's away for the summer?'

'Which question shall I answer first?'

Kassim grinned. 'None of them. I want you to meet Senator Coney. Senator, this is Ben Troy. He's the British Political Agent. He tells me what to do. Makes sure I run Qashran like an outpost of empire.'

'Hallo, Mr. Troy.'

'Senator.' The handshake was firm but painless. Practice makes perfect. Ben knew about the senator. Ben was a very good diplomat. He had had a rundown on every name in the guest list.

Coney was a Southern Democrat and a hawk, in the new jargon. He was on record as deploring the British decision to leave the Arabian Gulf. He saw no alternative but an American presence to ensure the stability of the area.

'You've sure got an impressive outpost of empire here, Mr Troy.'

'Not really. That's one of the sheikh's jokes. I only advise. He makes the decisions. You may already know that my advice and his decisions don't always coincide.'

'So I hear. Maybe that's just as well. You folks aren't going to be around too much longer.'

Troy smiled. 'So it seems. I'm sure all the Trucial sheikhs will be offered help by other governments.'

'That's just the point. Which other governments?'

'Isn't that why you're here, Senator?'

'No. I'm just a member of the Senate. I'm only fact finding.'

'And that,' broke in Kassim, 'brings us to the point. The senator is going down tomorrow to look over South Base and the new sites. When he gets back, I want you to put him in the political picture. The Gulf, the Trucial States, you know the kind of thing.'

Ben nodded.

'There you are, Senator,' said Kassim. 'It's all arranged. You'll get it straight from the fountainhead. No one knows more about local politics than Troy Sahib.'

Coney smiled his thanks. 'What's with this sahib business, Mr Troy?'

'That's a relic, Senator. A relic of what's called Britain's Imperial past. The Gulf used to come under the India Office, so everything here is still a bit Anglo-Indian. We don't have garden parties, we have durbars. We don't eat lunch, we have tiffin. It's served by boys who are grown men. And I get sahib tagged on to my name. It doesn't mean anything.'

'Don't you believe him, Senator.' Kassim was enjoying himself. 'It means much the same as pasha further west in the Arab world. You ask him about his father. Troy Pasha was quite a character. It's all terribly significant, you know. The British are very strong on professional elites. The Troys are part of a very special elite, the Arabists. They know more about the Arabs than the Arabs.' The sheikh smiled. 'Not that that means very much.' He laughed at his own joke, rocking back and forward on his heels.

'We must talk some more about that, Mr Troy.'

'Whatever you say, Senator.'

Kassim took Coney's arm. 'Now come along and I'll pick you a nice partner.' A band had just started up. 'Are you going to dance, Ben?'

'Not me, Your Highness. I'll watch from the sidelines.'

'That's in character. Watch and wait and plan and plot.' Kassim grinned and towed the senator away.

Troy turned away. Yes, I'll do that, Kassim. And you may yet be grateful for it. He was surrounded by a noisy jostling mass of guests. He wanted to be by himself but not alone. He wanted someone close by just as a presence to stop him indulging his premonition of disaster, someone who would not insist on chat. There was no familiar face in the sea of hot happy faces round him. He felt trapped. He pushed himself rudely against the tide. Then he saw the broad familiar back bent over the balustrade of the gallery. He struggled through the throng and squeezed himself in beside Carl Banner.

'Hi, Ben. You don't look too full of the party spirit.'

Troy shook his head and sucked in a few lungfuls of air. 'Never could stomach cocktail parties. But this, this is the absolute end. It's as if the whole world is here.'

'And there's more to come.' Banner pointed down into the well. An army of caterers had already cleared away the tables. Carpets and cloths were now being unrolled for the traditional Arab feast.

'At least the food will smell right. The people too.'

Banner chuckled. 'You really are in your Garbo mod, Ben.'

'Maybe. All I know is that I'd enjoy myself a lot more down there than I'm doing up here.'

'So why don't you go down and grab yourself a hunk of camel and a few sheep's eyes?'

'They call it protocol, old chap. That was all right in Rasul's time because Rasul expected it. It's not the done thing now because Kassim would object.'

'And that, my friend, is one of the many things I have Kassim to thank for. I never did get to like these mutton grabs.'

Troy smiled. It was his thin, polite smile. He did not want to talk. He stared down into the well, identifying the food as it was trundled in. Kassim had ordered a special feast for his people. There were six camels each stuffed with a baby camel. Fifty sheep, fifty goats, countless chickens, a dozen gazelle and a couple of dozen desert bustard. There were huge platters of rice, boiled, fried, and curried. There were dishes of goats' milk butter, of cheese, of hardboiled eggs floating in sauce, of paper-thin omelettes. There were trays of hard, unleavened bread. There were bowls of fruit, peaches, pears, figs, and pineapples; there were tureens of nutmeg-dusted custard and dishes piled high with sickly sweetmeats. There were crates and crates of Pepsi-Cola. And all this was only for the influential few, the elders and those Qashranis with some sort of rank at the palace or in the police, the civil service, or the Qashran Corporation. Elsewhere in the city and the near desert other feasts were already under way. Everyone with a mind for it would have a full belly that night.

The scents of the food reached up to the gallery. Troy's nose twitched. He felt hungry. Other guests had caught the scent too and were straining against the balustrade to peer down into the well. Ben wondered how strong that balustrade was. He smiled as he pictured a cascade of well-dressed guests pouring down into and on to that mass of Arab food. Then he noticed their faces and felt sick. He was trapped there in the front rank. There was no escape. He was going to have to stay there and watch them all staring and giggling at Kassim's cabaret.

The Qashranis were led into the feast by the elders, all minor sheikhs, and by the senior members of the palace staff. The procession was orderly and dignified. Everyone was turned out in his best clothes. The babble of talk died in the gallery. The senior elder stopped at the foot of the stairway and bowed to Kassim at the top. Kassim bowed in return and the file broke ranks and squatted down on the carpets round the piles of food. The guests above were immediately forgotten. Hands dipped into the food, lips were smacked in relish and the murmur of appreciation and recommendation soon became a sustained roar. Talk was animated, argument fierce and friendly, there was much laughter. Neighbours exchanged sought-after titbits. The piles of food were reduced at alarming speed.

Troy felt the press of spectators ease. He looked around. The gallery guests were drifting away, to the dance floor, to the bars, forming little groups, introducing, being introduced, chatting, laughing, doing all the pointless things that made a good party. Their fascination with the Arab feast had been shortlived. It had been killed by Bedouin dignity. A circus was not worth watching if the performers ignored the audience.

He stayed there watching the feast but not really seeing it, aware of Banner still beside him but not yet ready to talk to the American. Ben found he was thinking about his wife. She would have enjoyed this party. He had been surprised when she did not stay for it. But Helen ran her life on a strict pattern. She always left Qashran early in May. 'Darling, the heat is unbearable in the summer. Of course you can stay inside in the air conditioning but why live like a packet of peas in a deep freeze when you don't have to.' She came back in the autumn for six weeks but returned to London for Christmas. 'Darling, Christmas is a time to be with the family.' Her husband was not one of the family.

Her family was their two sons and her three brothers. She had never really given up her maiden name of Baston. There were catty people who claimed that she only became Helen Troy because she believed she had the kind of face to launch a thousand ships. She certainly was a powerful personality. The only daughter of a famous admiral, her three brothers had followed the armed forces tradition of the family. Eldest son into the Navy, second son into the Army, third son into the Air Force. They were all now in senior posts. Helen's contribution was to marry into the Foreign Office. It should have completed a very influential Baston quartet; the three services and the FO. She could not have been expected to know that Ben Troy was not that kind of career diplomat. His background and his inclination had made him an Arabist. Not just the academic expert, rather the kind who loved the desert and the desert Arabs, who valued their attitudes and traditions, who found themselves inevitably at odds with their political masters because they believed it to be their duty to protect the primitives from the tainting influence of the West. Helen Baston-Troy had tried very hard to mould her husband's career. She had had no success. Ben and Rasul had matched her every move. With Rasul's overthrow, all her hopes had gone. Ben had organized Kassim's succession. He had to stay and make it work. And the British Government had announced its decision to withdraw from the Gulf. Ben Troy's career would end in two, maybe three years.

But turning disasters into triumphs was Helen's greatest asset. She was already planning for an active retirement. Ben shuddered every time he thought of it. No more the long shimmering desert horizons. Instead, damp vistas of green and brown. No more the thrill of flying falcons off against the desert bustard. Instead, chill moors and the blasting of driven birds. No more the poetry round the camp fire, the argument, the laughter. Instead, the stilted talk at the tea table and the frenetic chatter of cocktail time. No more the satisfying gorging at a feast. Instead, the dainty dyspepsia of the British dinner table. Never again the plaintive cry of the *muezzin* calling the faithful to prayer and the sight of men worshipping their god on their knees, wherever they happened to be. Instead, the well-scrubbed congregation at the village church, bellowing the hymns, not comprehending the vicar's wordy sermon, but showing a proper respect for those sitting apart in the Baston family pew. Ben held hard to these images. He was secretly afraid he might enjoy retirement in England; and that would only confirm him in his feeling of guilt at having helped to destroy the land and the people he loved best. He shuddered and searched about for a brighter thought. He smiled. Yes, that was

worth thinking about. He would have to follow that up. Helen
had not flown off from Qashran Airport as usual. She had begged
an overnight trip to Bahrein on her brother's ship. Yes, it would
be worthwhile hearing Vice-Admiral Rodney Baston on the chaos
his sister had caused on that brief journey.

Ben knew he would also hear about her from the Resident in
Bahrein. But that report would lack the malicious venom of her
brother's story. The admiral was the one Baston with whom Ben
got on. It was as if the sea and the desert had something in
common. He was known affectionately throughout the fleet as
Bastard Baston. It sounded different when said in Whitehall. The
admiral believed in the Navy. He believed particularly in aircraft
carriers. He was now flying his flag in one of the last British
carriers, leading a hotch-potch group known as the Gulf
Squadron. In London, the Ministry of Defence (Navy) was praying that nothing would happen to give him a chance of proving
his theories on the effectiveness of a carrier-led task force. In his
two days of flag-showing off Qashran he had impressed and
deafened the city with his new American Phantom jets. Ben
smiled again to himself. Yes, he would like to hear Rodney on
Helen.

'What's so funny then?' It was Banner. 'Don't tell me you've
come round to laughing at your pet Arabs?'

'How do you mean?'

Banner nodded down into the well. The main feast was over,
the whole area was now swarming with servants and others, stuffing food into their mouths, grabbing what they could and stowing
it away in their clothes. It was the way at all Bedu feasts.

'No, no, it wasn't that. I hadn't really noticed. It was something
else altogether.'

'Want to share it with me?'

'Not really. It was personal.'

'Fair enough. I just wondered if you'd been watching the
colonel and his lady.'

Ben looked puzzled.

Banner pointed. 'Over there. The colonel and his lady friend.
John Negley and Susan Shaw.'

Troy followed the finger. He smiled. 'I see what you mean.' It
was an odd romance, if that was the right word. It had, according
to the social sages of Qashran City, been blowing hot and cold
for two years. At one party the word would pass around that the
colonel had popped the question. At the next party you would
hear that Doctor Shaw was demanding to be made an honest
woman. But nothing ever happened. They went on with their
jobs; they huddled together at the occasional party; they visited

each other now and again. It was difficult to believe that they shared anything more than middle-aged frustration.

Colonel Negley had been in the Gulf a long time. He first came out during the war. Later on he was seconded to the Trucial Oman Scouts and was based in Qashran when Sheikh Rasul asked him to recruit and train a small army cum police force. He had taken the job to avoid the redundancy waiting for him at home. He had done well. He had built a small but efficient force. Then came Kassim and his plan to expand the force into a proper Defence Force. Negley had organized that, even the three patrol boats and the fleet of helicopters. Troy often wondered how long the colonel would last. He was not really a big enough man to handle Kassim and his plans. More important, he did not like the Bedu. He wore their headdress, he spoke their language, he knew their history and their traditions. They appeared to respect him. But he was not one of them, he did not love them. There was about him an aloofness that was a solid barrier against real contact.

Susan Shaw seemed to have breached that barrier. But maybe she just happened to be on his side already. They were both European misfits who had found themselves and each other in the desert. Doctor Shaw's work among the Qashrani women was already famous. She was a highly qualified gynaecologist and pediatrician with an infinite dedication to her profession. She shunned the magnificent facilities of Qashran City Hospital because there she would have few patients. She had a tented hospital at Madaira oasis and travelled out into the desert from there. A pundit had once said that what was needed to investigate Trucial women was a woman doctor of peculiar and unique ugliness. Susan Shaw came like a gift from Allah. She was not really ugly but she was peculiar and unique. She was very large. She always wore slacks, which seemed to add to her size. Her hair was straight, pulled back and tied untidily at her neck. She was short-sighted and peered out at the world through thick spectacles. She had a big mouth and a long straight nose. She was so unusual that she was rather attractive. Maybe arresting would be a better way of putting it. She was never happy in strange company. She suffered then from a breathless shyness quite unlike the forceful personality, incisive thinking, and brilliant technique she displayed when talking to friends or practising medicine. Ben liked her a lot.

'D'you think they'll ever do anything about it?' asked Banner.

'About what?'

'You know. S-E-X.'

'Maybe they have,' suggested Ben. 'Or maybe it's not that kind of friendship.'

'There's some other kind?'

'So they say.'

'Who says?'

'People. An old Greek started the idea.'

'Old—that makes sense. Greek—I don't believe it. I know Greeks. Oversexed, the lot of them. Lovely people.'

Ben grinned. 'You need a spot of leave, Carl. You've been out in the desert too long.'

'That's for sure. Not this summer though.' Banner sucked on his cigar, flicked the ash off and watched it falling down among the frenzied throng in the well. 'That's the Doc's trouble, I guess. How could she get romantic when she spends her life guddling about inside these Bedu women?'

'I don't suppose Bedu women's insides are any different from any other women's insides.'

'So?'

'So there are lots of doctors around the world with perfectly normal sex lives.'

'I don't believe it. And if you're right, they must be schizos.'

'Aren't we all?' asked Ben.

Banner grinned and puffed on his cigar. He and Troy were good friends. They had different backgrounds, different attitudes, but they understood each other. All their conversations followed this pattern of question and answer, thrust and parry. They were like a dog and a cat brought up together. They fought all the time but it was just fun. As a team, they were formidable.

They looked round as the lights dimmed and a fanfare rang out from the band. Spotlights played on the roof and huge clusters of balloons and paper streamers were released and drifted down.

Ben shook his head. It's like the old Chelsea Arts Ball. Same effect too. The guests were stretching up to grab the balloons, bursting them, laughing, reaching for more, winding themselves up in the trailing streamers, laughing, enjoying themselves. They ignored the squares of white paper drifting slowly down against the rising warm air. The white squares seemed to have been concentrated in the roof above the well. There, they were like a snowstorm of gigantic flakes. One settled on the rail beside Troy, wavered, then slipped off and away. One quick sight of it brought back all his forebodings. He leaned out over the rail and grabbed at another of the flakes. He caught it and felt himself being pulled roughly back from the rail.

'Ben, what the hell're you up to? Have you caught the party spirit or something? You could've nose dived right down there.' The lights were back on. Banner's face showed his concern.

Troy was staring at the paper in his hand. 'I'm all right, Carl.'

He shrugged off the American's grip. 'Have a look at that.' It was crudely printed on one side. There was no writing. Propaganda is best in pictures for illiterates. The drawing was of the Great Sword of Qashran.

'Well, I'll be—— What the hell'll that Kassim get up to next? He must be nuts.'

'No, Carl. This is one thing Kassim didn't organize.'

'Then who?'

'Kassim will say it's been a practical joker. He'll be very annoyed but he won't show it. Tomorrow he'll instruct John Negley to find the culprit. He won't find him because we know who the culprit is, and he's very good at not being found.'

'Ben, you've got a bee in your bonnet about Rasul. He's still in Europe. You told me yourself. And even if he isn't, what can he do? Rustle some mangy camels, dish out handfuls of leaflets.'

'That bee in my bonnet is buzzing very loudly, Carl. I know that bee very well. I think it's about to start stinging.'

'So maybe it stings. So we swat it.'

'I hope you're right. Look down there.' Troy pointed down into the well. The Bedu were all holding the leaflets and chattering excitedly.

'They sure got the message, same as you.'

'Let's go and join our young lord and master. He'll soon be pressing the button to start the fireworks display. Who knows what might happen?' Ben was suddenly almost in high spirits.

Banner growled. He was thinking. He was thinking that Qashran crude oil was extremely volatile.

They pushed their way along the gallery through the happy crowd. They were surrounded by people quite unaware of the threat that had just dropped around them and was now being trodden underfoot. Kassim caught sight of them as they came near. His look said it all. I know and I don't want it mentioned. The senator was standing beside him. The sheikh handled it very well, inviting them to join him on the outside gallery to watch the fireworks, still apparently the life and soul of his own party.

It was a superb fireworks display. After the first flurry of rockets, screaming upwards and bursting and showering glowing stars against the backdrop of real stars, came huge cascading fountains of fire. Then the set piece displays; the camel taking shape, fading, being replaced by a sleek motor car; the Arab dhow, dwarfed and extinguished by a super-tanker; an oasis disappearing under a flood of water from an immense faucet; then an oil derrick, then two, three, four, a dozen, all with brilliant gushers soaring up into the sky. And all the time there were rockets and whizz-bangs and whirling Catherine wheels and the crash and crackle of hundreds of giant jumping jacks. Ben smiled wryly as he recalled that Kassim had brought a team of experts all the way from Switzerland to set it all up. He wondered where that other recent resident of Switzerland was. He wondered what he was doing, what he was thinking.

It was not long before he got his first clue. The display was moving towards its climax. Kassim's controversial new state flag was being painted in fire. It was the sheikh's own design. A Scotsman on his staff had pointed out that the saltire, the cross of St Andrew, was usually only associated with Scotland, or maybe Greece. Kassim's only comment was that he hoped both these countries would be honoured to have Qashran as a partner. The flag was emblazoned diagonally with crossed bands of silver—the pipelines that carried the new wealth; the triangles at hoist and fly were green—the old, the background colour of Rasul's flag; the triangles top and bottom were bright red—the colour of change flooding over the ancient land. The glowing fireworks flag was acclaimed with a fresh fusillade of rockets. The light blinded the eyes, the din stunned the senses. But through it all Ben caught the wail from the refinery across the creek. Carl Banner too separated it from the fun noises. They both stood quite still, making sure. The American moved first. He turned and ran back inside, making for the stairway.

Troy ran in after him. 'Carl, wait. I'll come too.'

'You wait here. Might not be much. I'll let you know.'

They were at the top of the staircase. 'It's bad and it's not local. Look.' Ben pointed. From where they stood the fireworks flag was hidden by the close set arches of the building. Through one of these arches they had a clear view to the southern horizon. The view was a semi-circle of redness.

'Good God. That's South Base. Looks like the bloody lot's gone.' Banner leapt down the stairs four at a time. 'I'll take the chopper,' he shouted as he reached the bottom and sprinted across the mosaic floor still strewn with the debris of the Bedu feast.

'I'll catch you up,' yelled Troy. He looked once more at the view south and hurried back to the sheikh. The fireworks had just died and everyone was pointing at the glow in the south. Scattered phrases reached Ben's ears. 'Must be the sunrise.' 'Can't be, too early.' 'Wrong direction.' 'What's that awful siren for?' 'Part of the show.' 'Amazing. Don't know how they do it.'

The sheikh was looking south too. His shoulders were stiff.

Troy took his arm and spoke quietly. 'Your Highness.'

Kassim looked round, then turned back to his guests. 'Excuse me, please. Something I must attend to.' He stepped back then turned and came quickly inside. 'How bad is it?' That was Kassim. No beating about the bush. Straight into the meat of the business.

'It looks bad, Kassim. Very bad. Banner's going down in the helicopter. I'll go with him. You go to the Corporation building. We'll report in there as soon as we know what's happened. I'll get Negley to spread his men through the town.' He stared hard at the sheikh. 'Have you got all that?'

'Of course. All very sensible. You'd better be on your way.'

Ben turned and sprinted along the gallery, looking for the colonel.

'Troy Sahib,' Kassim called after him.

He stopped and looked back.

'Thank you for not saying "I told you so".'

Ben nodded and ran on, calling out for Negley. 'John, John. Colonel Negley. Colonel.' He had run the full length of the gallery when the colonel appeared. He looked a bit sheepish. God, what a time to be canoodling.

'What's all the fuss?'

'It's South Base. Bad fire. Not an accident.' Ben was short of breath. 'I'm going down with Banner. Kassim's going to the Corporation building. Use your radio link to him. Get your men spread through the town. Guard every important spot. Have you got that?'

'What's all this about? You're getting very bossy, Ben. Some fire in the oilfield and you start bellowing . . .'

'It's about Rasul, Colonel. Rasul's back in Qashran.' He did not wait. He ran down the stairs at that end and out into the car park. He knew Negley would stir himself. Rasul's name had brought a look into his eyes. The colonel had always been afraid of the old sheikh.

CHAPTER THREE

THERE WAS NO ONE near the parked cars. Everyone was round on the other side of the *suk* watching the glow in the southern sky. The only sound was the plaintive screaming of the siren.

Troy backed his car out fast and sped for the gates. They were open and unattended. The tyres screeched as he swung the car on to the road. He took the new road passing south of the old bazaar and skirting the creek. He put his foot down and the car leapt ahead. Airport or refinery? He juggled with the problem. The big helicopter usually used the airport. Had Banner gone straight there? But any information would be at the refinery. Banner would go there first. Carl was the methodical type. He would want to know all there was to know before he went to look at South Base. Whatever had happened down there was not going to be better or worse in the few extra minutes taken to sort things out at the Qashran City end. Probably better. It was plainly a major disaster. It would take a deal of organization to quell that fire. The junction came up in the headlights. Left to the airport, right to the refinery. Ben pulled the car round to the right. The tyres squealed again and the car lurched. The sound of the tyres hung in his ears as he pushed the car at full speed down the broad concrete highway. He realized that the sound was loud because the other sound had died. The siren had stopped. That convinced him he was heading in the right direction. Banner must have arrived. That was the first thing he would have done. 'Shut that bloody noise, will you.' Ben was aware of the lights of the city on his right, the reflections from the surface of the creek, but all his attention was on the lights of the refinery ahead. It was not a big plant, just enough to serve the local market, but big or small the flood-lit tower of a cracking plant at night always drew the eye.

The car was almost there before Troy thought about Rasul. The car slowed as his foot lifted from the throttle. It was as if the thought of the old sheikh had made him suddenly more cautious. The car slowed more as Ben wondered if the fire at South Base might have nothing to do with Rasul. There was no firm evidence. It was just assumption. It might be nothing more than coincidence. His premonition, the leaflets dropping like huge confetti amid the balloons, the disaster at South Base. Come to think of it, the timing was almost too good to be true. And I convinced then all; Banner—that doesn't matter, there's a big fire whatever the cause; Kassim—he doesn't forgive easily, especially if it has sown seeds of doubt among his visitors; Negley —he won't like having put the town under a security cloak if there's nothing to it. Don't be stupid. Of course it's Rasul. It must be. That fire at South Base couldn't be an accident. It's too big, too widespread. That's obvious without even seeing it close up. It must have been set. If it was set, Rasul set it. Ben was surprised at his own thinking. He realized he wanted it to be Rasul. He had waited almost three years for this chance. He had to fight his old friend again. This time it had to be a fair fight, a fight on Rasul's terms. That meant a fight to the death. The car coasted up to the refinery gates. That's funny. A fight to the death and I'm quite calm. It's as if I'd welcome death. It would cure a lot of problems; no retirement, no more Helen, no more guilt. Just peace and quiet, forever. No, death won't be so easy to come by. Maybe it will be Rasul who dies. That will please him. In the tradition of his family, violent death. Death in battle against the infidel. And then the Moslem Paradise, dancing fountains, sumptuous tents, glorious clothes, groves of date palms, fig trees, pomegranate trees, frankincense and acacia, all peopled with a host of obedient virgins. Better than life, better than the Christian heaven. Odd though, that host of obedient virgins. Funny idea for Paradise. Ben grinned as he stopped the car. Henry VIII had summed it up—Better the rhythm of a well-laid whore than the spasmodic jerks of a virgin.

The two Pakistani guards behind the steel mesh gates were shouting and waving. Ben flashed his headlights and stabbed the horn button. They shouted more loudly and waved more vigorously. He got out of the car and walked forward. 'Come on, come on, open up. You know who I am. Open up. Mr Banner's expecting me.'

'No, sahib. No come in. Banner Sahib say no one come in. No one but no one, he say.'

'I know, I know. But he didn't mean me. Now open up.'

The two guards shook their heads.

Troy was getting annoyed. 'All right, go and phone. Go and ask the Banner Sahib. Go on.'

They looked at each other, then one turned and went into the gate office. Ben walked up and down, then got back into the car. With time on his hands that feeling of urgency came back. He started to imagine that Banner would take off before he reached him. He revved the engine in his frustration. The guard behind the gate watched him. Ben twisted round in his seat to look south. The horizon was shortened by the gradual slope up from the coast to the edge of the flat plain of the desert. But the sky was coloured. It was shaded in pink and red, shimmering, pulsating. That really was a fire. He turned away.

The man came out of the gate office, running. He shouted to the other man and they both began unlocking the gates and hauling them open. Troy's car was through with only inches to spare before the gates were half open. He drove straight to the main office block. He ran up the steps, ignoring the guard. All of a sudden there were guards everywhere. Wonder where they were when Rasul hit South Base? Inside, Banner stood in the middle of the room firing off instructions at the four men round him. They all had a hang-dog look but they were listening. The fire at South Base had obviously interrupted a good going party.

'Hallo, Carl.'

'Hi, Ben. I'm just about through here.' He turned back to his staff. 'Now, have you all got all that?' They nodded. 'I hope so. One slip-up and I'll crucify the lot of you.' He left them staring at their boots. 'Come on, Ben. Let's get going.'

They strode quickly across to the helicopter pad. The small helicopter was standing in the floodlights, its rotor blades whirling. 'Stoned,' growled Banner. 'Stoned to the eyeballs. Stoned, the bloody lot of them.'

'It was a party night, Carl. They seemed to be sobering up pretty quickly.'

'Bloody better had. I tell you, I told them, I'll crucify them if there's one slip-up.'

'Yes, yes, you said that already.'

'Who the hell's side are you on?'

'Save your breath, Carl. Clamber up into the cabin.'

They squeezed into their places. There was not much room. Banner was in the seat alongside the pilot. Troy was crammed in behind, packed round with odds and ends of equipment hurriedly collected and slung on board. Ben was still fumbling with the straps when Banner told the pilot to take off. The engine roared and the plane lifted. Carl pulled on a head set and passed one back to Troy.

Banner talked at once to the pilot. 'O.K., Harry. Take her right down the road to South Base. And fast.'

The pilot nodded and called the airport tower for a clearance. There was nothing else in the air.

Banner switched channels. 'Banner calling Queen Charlie. Banner calling Queen Charlie.'

Troy smiled to himself. The Qashran Corporation call sign certainly had impact. Maybe Queen Charlie was just about right. It was a bit of a hermaphrodite organization. The Queen was deigning to reply.

'Queen Charlie to Banner. Receiving you loud and clear. Please report your position.'

'Hallo, Queen Charlie. Banner here. I'm in the small Inoco chopper. Troy's with me. We've just cleared the airport and we're starting down the south road.'

'Have you any information or instructions?'

'No information. I'll have that in half an hour. I left instructions at the refinery. They'll be in touch with you. Over and out.'

From his seat at the back Troy had to move his head around to get a view. The plane was flying at only a hundred feet. The white ribbon of the concrete road stretched out ahead to the red-crowned horizon. The road showed up clearly in the darkness against the darker colour of the desert. The silver pipelines showed too, alongside the road, the huge girth of the crude line from South Base to the coast dwarfing the slender pipe carrying fresh water south from the distillation plant at Qashran City. Banner said nothing. He sat hunched up in his seat staring ahead at the glow. Already that glow had form. Its greatest intensity was on its eastern edge. It was less bright to the west and lower in the sky. Banner knew what that meant. Qashran One was on fire. And most of the rest of South Base must also be alight; the storage tanks, the fuel stores, the transport park, everything. But Qashran One would be the problem. The rest would burn out, might even be extinguished. The well would be the problem. It would take specialists to snuff that. Carl knew about wellhead fires. He had worked on a couple. He knew it took time, lots of time. Weeks if they were lucky, maybe months, even years. He sat and stared and went over it all in his mind. He knew what had to be done. Survey the whole thing, report to New York, get them to hustle up the experts. In the meantime, put out what could be put out, isolate the well, lay on water and cranes and bulldozers and workshops, pull in all his drilling crews from the new wells being sunk elsewhere. He was going to be busy. He was already so busy that he never gave a thought to how it had all started. His job was to put it out.

Ben Troy was not thinking about the cause either. He was thinking about the consequences. He could not visualize as expertly as Banner what it would take to put out the flames and get the oil flowing again. But he could see that no oil would flow for a long time. He knew what that meant. No income, no confidence in the hitherto booming Qashran economy, no investment. He could see the political effects only too clearly.

The horizon dropped and exposed the seat of the fires. Suddenly the glowing sky gave way and became a panorama of leaping flame, pools of flame, stalks of flame, ribbons of flame, all dwarfed by the tower of flame roaring up for hundreds of feet above Qashran One. It was brilliant red, streaked with yellow, and capped with a billowing mass of black smoke. 'Good God. Good God.'

There was no reply on the intercom for almost a minute. Then Banner spoke to the pilot. 'Take her round to the west, Harry. Don't get too close or we'll melt.'

'I won't. The turbulence in there could toss us out of the sky.'

The plane canted round, aiming to clear the western edge of the base, but still closing. Banner scanned round with his field glasses. He took his time. 'You were right, Ben. It's a set piece for sure. Every fire wall round every tank's been blown. Your pal must've gone to school in Switzerland if he set that lot.'

'Experts can be bought.'

'He sure bought a good one.' His eyes swept over the sea of fire that was destroying five years of his life. 'Never did like that lousy old Arab bastard. I tell you, Ben, you'd better get to him before I do or I'll hand you him in little bits.' His voice fumbled with the words.

'Finding him's going to be the problem, Carl. Can we go round to the south and see if we can pick up a trail? He'll be over the border now but we might get a lead.'

'Take her round to the south, Harry.' Banner wiped at his face. The cabin was uncomfortably hot.

The pilot nodded.

Troy took over. 'Run straight down to the border. That's the beginning of the dunes. Then fly along the edge of the dunes. As low as you can get. Have you got a searchlight?'

'How's that?' Harry switched on the belly lights and dropped the helicopter.

Troy strained forward in his seat till he could see the twin pools of light chasing across the sand just ahead of them. 'That's fine. As slow as you like after you reach the edge of the dunes.'

Banner was calling the refinery. 'It's just what I thought. Number One's alight. Most everything else too. Get that gear moving down the road. Everything you can lay your hands on. Foam, lots of foam, d'you hear. Explosives. Crawlers, bulldozers, tractors, everything. And every man there is. I'll give you an hour.' He listened. 'I know it's better than sixty miles. There's no speed limit. I want the first trucks in an hour. That's more like it. Just keep saying O.K. Next, the pipeline crews on that crude line. Give them the big chopper. I want every valve reversed down the whole length. Got that? Good. Next, the refinery crew on that sea intake. I want these cooling water pumps hooked up direct into the crude line. Got that? Good. Get to it then.'

The plane was at the border and turning east. Troy was watching for signs in the sand. The pilot had the helicopter very low and slowed right down. Even so it was difficult to pick anything out. There were shadows everywhere. Shadows from the plane's lights, shadows from the fires to the north. Several times Ben almost spoke but held back the words. Then he saw the tracks. 'Hold it, hold it there.'

The pilot brought the plane up, hovered, turned round and hovered again with the chewed up sand held in the searchlights, the sand stirring in the downdraught from the rotors.

'That's it, Carl. Not too many. Maybe a dozen, dozen and a half.'

'So where are they now? They can't be far away. It's only been an hour.'

'Far enough. They're out there in the singing sands. Safe, south of the border, as they say in the best westerns.'

'Very funny. Well, they can't stay there long. No one can live down there.'

'Rasul can, Carl. He knows that place like the back of his hand. He's got secrets down there no one else has.'

'Not even you, his old buddy?'

'Not even me.'

The pilot interrupted. 'Say, you guys, d'you want that I stay hung up here all night?'

'Sorry, Harry. Take her away.'

'Where to?'

'What about following these tracks north,' suggested Troy. 'O.K.'

The plane turned and faced the fire again. They all screwed up their eyes. After the darkness over the dunes, the glare was blinding. Harry turned the helicopter north-east to follow the tracks. The glare drifted to the left and eased.

'Must be pretty damned hot down there, close up,' said Banner. 'Noisy too, I'll bet. Can't hear a thing with these earphones on but it must be noisy.'

Ben watched the tracks in the sand as the plane traced them back. They were less distinct now on the harder sand away from the edge of the dunes.

Carl was calling the refinery again. 'Send this cable to New York. Make it top priority. Here's the text. "Qashran One sabotaged and on fire. Grade One emergency. Send best fire-fighter soonest." Sign it "Banner". You got that? Read it back.' He listened. 'O.K. Get it off right away.'

'There. Down there,' said Troy. The aircraft hovered. 'There's the change in direction. They came here and turned west for the base. Then they came back and took off for the border.'

'So what does that tell us?'

'Nothing, I suppose.'

The pilot broke in. 'Wait a minute.' He drifted the plane over the depression in the sand. 'There. See that. Thought I saw something. Down there. There's three or four of them. More. Five. Six.'

'Well, I'll be,' breathed Banner. 'No, that's not them. They're from the base. Six of them. That's about right.'

The men on the ground were looking up and waving frantically. They had freed themselves from the ropes just as the well caught fire and had scurried for cover in the depression.

'Can you land here?' asked Troy. 'They'll be able to tell us a lot.'

'They can wait, Ben. I want to get back on to the road and be ready for these trucks. There's a loud-hailer in the back somewhere. Find it for me. Harry, I'll tell them to wait, then you take us back to the road, drop us, and come back for them.'

'It'll take two or three trips.'

'You got something else to do?'

Troy passed across the hailer. Carl pulled off his head set and slid open the door. The noise struck at his ears. The roar of the engine and the rotor blades above was just part of the greater roar of the blazing well. He shook his head and poked the hailer out of the door. He bawled down to the men on the ground to wait, told them the plane would be back for them soon. They waved frantically, not wanting to be left alone again. He slid the door shut and waved the pilot away. The plane turned and headed for the road north of the base.

Banner pulled on his earphones. 'What a bloody racket. Try about a mile and a half above the well, Harry. We don't want to melt and we do want to hear ourselves think. Ben, you help me offload the gear. Then Harry can ship you back to the city when he's collected these strays. O.K.?'

'Yes, that's fine. There's not much I can do down here.'

They were over the road. Pinpoints of light showed far to the north. 'That's better,' said Banner. 'Looks like the first of the trucks. Set her down, Harry.'

Banner had the door open before the helicopter landed on the road. The noise hit their unprotected ears and the heat, even at that distance, was stifling. The air reeked with the stench of burning oil. Troy started handing out the gear. There was a lot more than he had realized. Lights, water carriers, a radio set, two revolvers, a rifle, map case, first aid kit, a duffle bag. He felt around to make sure he had not missed anything, then crawled out of his seat and clambered down on to the road. The heat and the noise and the smell were worse there. 'You forgot the kitchen sink,' he roared.

'What?' yelled Banner.

Troy waved the question away and slid the plane door shut. The chopper rose at once, the rotors fanning a hot draught down on to the two men. Without the engine noise there was only the roar of the fire to din their ears. They were far enough away to hear each other if they huddled together.

'Grab these lights, Ben. We'll lay a marker for Harry.' They walked twenty yards up the road and set the lights in a square. They switched on the red flashers and walked back to where they had left the rest of the gear. They stood for a minute watching the blazing base, forcing themselves to scan west over the smaller infernos, finding their eyes drawn back irresistibly to the enormous pillar of fire and smoke reaching up from the well. 'Over here, Ben,' Banner walked off the road, dropped to his knees and smoothed out the sand with his hands. 'I'll show you how I plan to play this. You can let them know when you get back up north.' He marked the sand with a cross. 'That's Qashran One. Here's the rest of the base.' He sketched it in. 'The well has to wait. Need experts for that. I'm going to concentrate on the rest. Douse the fires, salvage what I can. Then isolate the well. Drive a firebreak right through here.' He gouged out a line between the well and the base. 'Use explosives if need be. Then get ready for the experts. We'll need water, millions of barrels of it. Going to bring it down the crude line from the sea. Use the cooling water intakes for the refinery, hook them into the crude line, switch the valves all the way down and we've got the whole Gulf right here.' He looked up at the fire. 'Maybe need most of it too.' He turned to Ben. 'Any questions?'

'Just one. How long?'

'How long what?'

'To put out the fire. To get the oil flowing again.'

Banner flung his arms in the air. 'You're a wow, Ben. You really are. If I knew the answer to that I'd be up there with God or Allah or whoever.'

'All right. I know you've got a big job on. I've got a job to do too.'

'That's for sure. Your job's to find the joker that lit this lot.'

'Certainly. But not just that. My job's also to keep this country running. That means oil. How long, Carl?'

The American stared at him then gave him a crooked grin. He squinted up the full height of the well fire. 'I don't know. Two weeks, three weeks to get the fire out. If we're lucky. Maybe the same again to get the well back on stream. Say a couple of months. If we're lucky.'

Troy just nodded. Long enough. And what if you aren't lucky? The old Qashran did without oil. The new Qashran can't. Too much has changed. It's away past the point of no return. I wonder if Rasul realizes that. Can't. He never could see the need for change. He thought the desert and the book were everything. Romantic primitive puritan fool that he is.

'Here's the chopper, Ben.'

'Good. I'll talk to them.'

'Here.' He tossed Troy a water-carrier. 'See if that loosens their tongues.'

Ben walked up the road and stood beside the winking lights as the aircraft came in. He was suddenly thirsty himself. He took a drink. The water was warm and tasted flat but it refreshed him. The plane hovered then subsided neatly on to the road in the marked square. He ran forward and pulled open the door. The three passengers scrambled out and crouched there uncertainly. They were terrified. Troy waved the plane away and shepherded the men to the side of the road. They were all Bedu, their clothes disfigured by the addition of the brass buttoned drill jacket that marked them as Inoco guards. He pointed to the water carrier and they drank greedily.

He spoke to them in their own language. 'Tell me what happened.'

They all started talking at once. He let it go for a while, letting them run off their fear, picking up the threads of the story. The word that was repeated time and again was Rasul. So it was Rasul. I knew it. I knew it. He quietened them and asked them questions in turn. He got the whole picture. He told them to wait where they were and to leave some water for the others. He walked slowly back down the road.

'I was right, Carl. It was Rasul.'

'Old bastard.'

'He left a message to say he was back. He quoted a piece from the Koran.' Ben glanced up at the black cloud ballooning above the well. 'Very appropriate too.'

'He would. Bloody old hypocrite.'

Troy did not argue. 'Estimates varied from a dozen to fifty of them. All on black camels.'

'Right again, eh. He did take that mangy herd.'

'They were all Bedu but one. He was dressed like a Bedu but he didn't speak like one. He was the expert.'

'That one I'd like to myself for half an hour.'

'Here's the chopper back again. I'll tell them you'll send them back up on the first truck.' Ben put his hand on Banner's shoulder. 'Good luck, Carl.'

'I'll need it all. And good hunting to you.'

Troy saw the men out of the plane, cut short their stories, and told them to wait for the first truck. He pointed down the road to where Banner was peering at maps and plans in the light of the fires. They calmed down, knowing that someone was staying with them. Ben got on board and Harry lifted the aircraft and followed the road north.

Ben felt tired. He looked at his watch. It was just after two.

Can't be. Damned thing must have stopped. He peered at it.
No, the second hand's still circling. Less than two hours since
that fabulous fireworks party. Seems an age. He shook his head,
stared at the sleeve of his jacket and grinned. Still got my dinner
suit on. That's ridiculous. You don't do this kind of thing in
a dinner suit. That's taking the Sun Never Sets idea a bit far.
Watch it, Ben. You're tired and starting to think silly. Got to
think straight. Think about Rasul. Yes, that wakes you up.
Rasul's back. The game's begun. You've played him before.
You know him better than anyone else. Watch every move.
Think it all through. You've beaten him before. You can beat
him again.

Maybe. But sometimes the old fox cheats.

CHAPTER FOUR

THE QASHRAN CORPORATION building dominated the city. It
had none of the flamboyance of the new *suk*. It was a stark steel
and concrete tower block. It dominated by its sheer bulk. Its
fourteen storeys dwarfed its nearest competitor in height, the
muezzin's tower at the mosque, and its broad frontage of windows
and coloured cladding stared north over the Gulf and seemed to
peer into every corner of the town. At night it was even more
overpowering, its banks of brightly lit windows making a solid
slab of light rising up out of the city, and right on top the huge
flashing neon of the corporation sign which served as a leading
light for approaching ships.

The sign was a golden Q surrounding the new state flag. It was
significant because it symbolized the role of the Corporation.
That role was nothing less than the control and administration of
the state. The Corporation was young Sheikh Kassim's creation,
a commercial holding company taking the place of a civil service.
It was a novel development of the theory of partial nationaliza-
tion. Every major foreign company wanting to operate in Qashran
had to set up a new company as a subsidiary of the Corporation,
the ownership being 50/50 between the Corporation and the
company. There was already Qashran Oil, the Inoco operating
company, Qashran Contractors handling public works, Qashran
Water running the desalinization plants, the Qashran Bank,
Qashran Cold Storage and so on. The idea had taken time to
appeal to foreign investors. It smacked too much of state control.
But Kassim had been vindicated by performance. He encouraged
profits, did not tax money reinvested in the country and only

taxed exported profits moderately. The Corporation's share of profits was used to promote new industry and to subsidize non-profitmaking sectors such as health, education and welfare. Kassim had seen the effects of high taxation in Europe and America. There was no personal income tax in Qashran. Everything bought carried a sales tax, everything saved was tax free. It had turned out to be a very good system. It made people wealth conscious. It attracted the foreigners needed to develop a country with a small, largely illiterate population. It also made them conscious of the country in which they lived and worked. Every new Corporation subsidiary had a recognizable symbol—the state Q encircling the existing company sign of the foreign investor. Smaller businesses escaped participation by the Corporation but were licensed and taxed on a different basis ensuring that they enjoyed no special advantage. Kassim's system was evolving all the time. It was attracting more and more attention. It was one of several reasons for his unpopularity with his neighbours who still followed the age-old system which gave all the revenue into the hands of the ruling sheikh as personal income.

As Ben Troy walked into the building and waited for the elevator up to Kassim's office, he thought about the foreign investors and about the neighbouring sheikhs. The investors would be worried when they heard about the sabotage at South Base. Suddenly capital and profits would not seem so secure. The sheikhs would be delighted at first to hear of Kassim's misfortune Then they would wonder about their own positions. Could the same kind of trouble cross their borders? Ben shrugged. That was their problem. He had two of his own. He had to advise Kassim on how to handle the South Base disaster and what followed, for Ben was sure that more would follow. And he had his own feud with Rasul. He felt that that feud was somehow at the centre of the whole affair.

He watched the indicator light as the lift came down. He felt quite calm. He even wondered if he was imagining the whole affair to be more important than it really was. He discarded that notion. He knew it was an illusion brought on by the change of scene from the chaos at Qashran One to the ordered quiet of the city in the early hours. It was a quarter to four in the morning.

Ben had dozed in the helicopter on the way back from South Base. He was met at the refinery by Davidan who had traced his car there and was waiting to drive him home. Davidan, everyone called him David, was unusual for a Bedu. He had been with Ben throughout his twenty-five years in Qashran. He was valet, butler, cook and chauffeur. He was competent at all these jobs. He enjoyed being a servant. That morning he was in great form. He had just recently come out of the sulks. Mrs Troy's visits marked the low points in his life. He had enjoyed the feast at the *suk* and the fireworks and all the talk. And now there was the great fire down at the oilfield and exciting talk that maybe Sheikh Rasul was back in Qashran. There had been too little excitement for too long. No hunting trips, no evenings at the palace, nothing. He plied Ben with questions all the way back to the Residency. The noncommittal answers only excited him more. He turned on the shower, laid out fresh clothes, heated coffee. He insisted on driving Troy Sahib into town. He would wait there in the car park until he was needed again.

Ben got into the lift and pressed the thirteenth floor button. He had phoned from home. 'Of course I want to see you. As soon as possible. In the office.' The whole thirteenth floor was reserved for Kassim and his personal staff. The unlucky number amused the sheikh. That floor was convenient to the vast penthouse which topped the building. The sheikh had moved out of the palace as soon as the Corporation building was ready. The palace was now reserved for a host of relatives and old retainers, and the concubines he visited from time to time. Kassim was in no hurry to marry but he was virile enough. The Bedu judged a man on his courage, cunning, wealth and manliness.

Kassim was alone in the big conference room. He was studying the huge model of the city, showing all the planned developments as well as those completed. He looked up. 'Tell me the worst. I've had the reports from the refinery. It seems pretty bad.'

Troy walked over to the wall map. 'It's certainly bad. Qashran One's on fire and most of South Base has been wrecked.'

'Not an accident, I suppose.'

'Not that, Your Highness.'

'Was my dear uncle involved?'

Troy nodded. 'Yes, Rasul was there, in person. Waving the Great Sword and quoting the Koran. "Wait for the day when the sky will pour down blinding smoke, enveloping all men; a dreadful scourge." '

'A bit melodramatic, don't you think?'

'Maybe. Do you know the rest of that quotation?'

'Of course I don't. You can't keep up with the Koran when you're being educated at an English public school.'

'It runs, "Then they will say; Lord, lift up this scourge from us. We are now believers." What your uncle did say was that the Sword would lift the scourge and cleanse the desert with blood.'

'He's a man out of his time, Troy Sahib. He would have done terribly well in the Victorian theatre.'

'He might do quite well here. He had Bedu with him. They were all on black camels.'

'So you were right again. Congratulations. I suppose that means the rebirth of The Honoured Ones. You see, I may not know my Koran by heart but I do know my local legend.'

'The legend's based on fact, Kassim. The Bedu still believe in it.' Al Shuruf, The Honoured Ones, had a long history. They were the four hundred Qashrani fighting men chosen to ride the sacred black camels into battle. They could not be harmed when mounted on the sacred beasts. They were assured of victory in every battle. And when their fighting days were over, they were assured of a place in the Muslim Paradise.

'They won't believe in it for long. Legends won't do too well against machine guns and helicopter gun buses.'

'First find your target, Your Highness.'

The sheikh stared at the map. 'Where is he?' he asked quietly. 'How many men? How much help?'

'There's only one place he can be.' Troy pointed. 'Down there in the singing sands or beyond in the Empty Quarter.'

'A base? It's a logistic nightmare down there. Water alone would keep a squadron of transport planes flying all the time. Even the Saudis couldn't afford that sort of help.'

'I don't think he's getting any help from the Saudis. I don't think they even know he's there. But you're right about water. That's the main problem. He must have a water source. He must have known about it for years. He used to disappear down there from time to time for days, sometimes weeks. That's one of the secrets he always kept to himself. If he's got a good water source, the rest is no problem. Caravans trek through the Buraimi Oasis all the time for Saudi Arabia. There's no check on them. His could just leave Buraimi and divert to his base wherever it is. And there have been odd rumours from time to time these last few months.'

'Yes, yes, I know, Mr Troy. And you reported them to me and I told you to forget about them. How many men?'

'Can't tell. Not more than twenty tonight. But he could easily recruit a few hundred Bedu.'

'I suppose he could.' Kassim studied the map again. 'But now he's shown his hand. We know he's down there in or beyond the sands. He's bottled up. We can fly patrols along the border.'

Troy nodded. 'True. He must know that too. So what will his next move be? My guess is that, having punched you in the stomach at South Base, he'll try a few jabs at your head.'

'You mean here, in the city. It's been quiet so far.'

'There's plenty of time. Plenty of targets. Plenty of Bedu too for once. Your feast brought them in in their thousands to eat your food and watch your fireworks. He's chosen his time well.'

Kassim paced the length of the room several times. 'You don't think we're reading too much into this? You don't think that this attack on South Base was once and for all?'

'Do you?'

'I'm asking you, Mr Troy.'

'No, I don't think it was once and for all. Think of all the money and organization that's gone into this so far. That could mean nothing if it was just Rasul. It might be an angry gesture against his exile and the changes in Qashran. But others are involved. That attack was far too expert for Rasul. He was there. His men were there. But they had expert help. That kind of help only comes on a long term basis.'

'Yes, of course. I should have realized that experts were involved. Not the Saudis, you say. Who?'

'I can only guess. But it's not too difficult. There are Arab countries further west who don't approve of kings and sheikhs.'

'And now they've been encouraged by the British decision to withdraw from the Gulf.'

'Touché. But you do have your own Defence Force, Your Highness, and there is the new mutual defence pact with your neighbours.'

Kassim laughed. 'You know as well as I do that that pact's just a piece of paper. And anyway, I'd never let any of my neighbours on my territory.'

Ben said nothing.

'Tel me, Troy Sahib, off the record, of course. What would your government's reaction be to a request for troops?'

'I imagine that they would prefer that you handle this yourself.'

'But if I couldn't?'

'We still have a treaty obligation for a year or two yet.'

'That's a pretty lukewarm assurance. Maybe it's just as well that Senator Coney is still here.'

Troy smiled. 'Maybe. But I don't think you'll need him, Kassim. I think the die is already cast. If Rasul and his friends want to fight you openly, they will do that. If, on the other hand, they want a direct confrontation with British forces, they will arrange that too. It all depends on what they want to achieve. They can't have a very big force. It's almost certainly not very sophisticated either in men or equipment. So, whether against your forces or the British, in a straightforward battle they would lose.'

'So we can ignore the pitched battle idea and concentrate on security here in the city and out in the oilfield.'

'I think so,' Ben said slowly.

'You don't sound convinced. It was your theory, you know.'

'I know.' He pulled out a chair from the big table and straddled it, his arms folded on top of the back. He stared at the map on the wall. He looked up suddenly, then made to rise. 'Oh I'm sorry. D'you mind if I sit?'

'Be my guest.'

Ben settled again. 'You don't play chess, Kassim. Your uncle does. So do I. We've played each other hundreds of times. He's very good.'

'When do we get to the point?'

'That's the problem. The point is to divine your opponent's motives. Rasul's made the first move. We're marshalling our forces to counteract that move. We think we know what his next move will be. We're preparing to meet it. We may be making the mistake of thinking we know what his motives are.'

'His motives are obvious. He wants to wreck everything that's been done since he was flung out. He wants vengeance. He wants to turn Qashran back into a wilderness. He wants to see all the Bedu down on their knees mumbling towards Mecca five times a day. He wants to stop the world and make it spin backwards. I'm not going to let that happen.' It was the first time Kassim had shown his anger.

Troy thought for a bit before replying. 'I think these may be his aims. I don't think they're his motives.'

'Now you're playing with words. Aims, motives, what's the difference?'

'Kassim, your uncle is a very proud man. Exile, particularly exile the way it happened, was a great shame on him. I think his motive may be a desire to wipe away that shame. If we think about that we may be better able to make the right decisions.'

'And they are?'

'We can't know yet. But remember that Rasul is not alone. He has others helping him, advising him. Their motives are certainly not the same as his. Their aims may be similar. They may even appear at this stage to be identical. But if I'm right, the difference in motive can be decisive.'

The sheikh looked sceptical. 'You may be right. On the other hand you may be wrong. You have a weak spot, Troy Sahib. You still like my uncle. You like a lot of what he stands for. You believe the legend of the noble savage. I don't. I hate Rasul. Correction, I despise him.'

Troy said nothing. There was some truth in what Kassim said.

'Now let's deal in facts, Mr Troy. Did Banner give you any idea of how long it will take to put out that fire?'

'Nothing definite. He's already cabled New York for a specialist to deal with the well. Meantime he's mobilizing every man and machine he can lay his hands on. The road south's packed with trucks and equipment.'

'So I've heard. But he must have some idea of the time it will take.'

'His estimates were pretty vague. He did say that with luck it might be three or four weeks. But he also mentioned months. That was to get the fire out. After that he has to get the oil flowing again.'

Kassim banged the table with his fist. 'Damn Rasul. Damn, damn, damn. Banner will have to do better than that. It's not just the loss of revenue. It's loss of confidence. There are several big deals in the offing. I can't afford to let them go sour. I'll give him two weeks for the fire and another two to get the oil moving. A month. That's the limit.'

'That may be asking the impossible.'

'So? I'm just giving Banner a chance to prove that famous Inoco motto. "The difficult we do immediately, the impossible takes just a little longer." A month seems to me to be a generous "little longer".'

'We'll see,' said Troy, getting to his feet. 'That's not my province. No doubt you'll discuss it with Banner and his experts when they arrive.'

'I will. Now, about security here in the city. That's nearer your province. I'd like you to be here when I go over the plans with Negley. I'll call him in on the radio. Will you stay?'

'As you wish. Troy stood there after Kassim had gone, looking round the big room, the walls hung with maps and charts telling hour by hour, day by day, the progress of the new Qashran. There was an unreality about it all. It seemed to have little to do with what was going on outside. It was all facts and figures, convertible into money. Nowhere was there any chart telling why people thought what they thought, did what they did, risked what they risked. It was an accountant's world, a computer man's world in which individual human beings were only statistics. It was not Ben Troy's world.

He walked across and stared down at the huge model of the city. It was a planner's dream, already on the way to becoming true. All the main roads were already laid, all broad enough to handle ten times the expected volume of traffic, all dual or triple carriageways, no cross roads, all interchanges and flyovers, complete separation of vehicles and pedestrians. The new *suk* was now ready, the marina plan for the east side of the creek was in the pipeline. The huge desalinization plant was working twenty-four hours a day turning the water of the Gulf from salt to fresh. It ran now on oil but would soon be converted to use the gas being burned off at the refinery and down in the oilfield. The pilot plant for an even bigger fresh water scheme using the heat of the sun as power was already running. The latest thing in sewage treatment would soon replace the old sea disposal system. West of the creek, beyond the refinery, the power station was being enlarged and the area round it was reserved for industrial development, away from the city but an easy travelling distance and close to the two main sources of power. The new Bedu township, predictably Kassim-town, was starting to take shape to the east of the city with the old place as its focal point, fronted by a great square, and looking down from its vantage point on the slope up from the shore to the start of the desert plateau, down over the rows of houses, the mosque, the market, the cinema, the schools, the technical college, down to the sports stadium and the open air pool built out into the Gulf. Up on the desert the airport could already take the biggest jets and extensions were planned to handle the jumbos to come. There too, Kassim's new air arm was based, the first half dozen of a fleet of dual purpose helicopters, big enough to carry men and supplies and fitted to mount a terrifying armoury of rockets and machine guns. Close to the airport, strategically sited overlooking the city, were the barracks where Negley had his headquarters. Growing out into the Gulf in front of the city was the new port area and beyond that the long finger of the oil jetty. Later on, even further out, there would be the single point moorings for the new mammoth tankers.

It was a thrilling model but it was just a model. On the ground there were still acres of sand waiting for the bulldozers and the graders, the steel and the concrete, the men and the money. Most of all, the money. There were two areas where there were fewer spaces than elsewhere. The business district was already well built up and the residential complex with its villas and ranch houses was growing steadily outwards from the Gymkhana Club at its centre. But it was not an exclusive British and American community. In that wealth-conscious society there was a healthy leavening of business and professional people from other countries; from most parts of Europe, from India, from Pakistan, from Iran, from the Lebanon. One of these villas would have been housing an Israeli if Kassim had had his way. It was soon after he came to power that he chose the man to head his research · and development into irrigation. He ignored Troy's advice.

'I'm not interested in his religion or his nationality. I want him to grow cabbages and grapefruit, oranges and lemons. I want him to plant trees. I want him to change the climate and turn the desert into a garden. I don't care if he's a pagan or an atheist.'

The Six Day War saved the situation. Not that it changed the sheikh's view. The Israeli had more important things to do.

The growth in the business and residential areas marked Kassim's priorities. He needed foreign expertise and foreign capital. For that he had to provide showers and air conditioning, electricity and sewage, all in a spacious community development, with a good school and a club.

Ben stretched out a finger and placed it on a solitary block away from all the new building. That was his home, the Residency. He smiled. It was very ordinary; in white plaster, square, built round a courtyard, with verandahs looking down from the upstairs. The wind tower rising above the front door made it look like a church. It had been his home for twenty-five years. He had brought Helen there when they were married. His first son had been born there. That had been a good year or two. It had never been the same again. He shook his head. Not really Helen's fault at all. I shouldn't blame her. It was no place for a young wife and family. It still isn't, though there are plenty here now. I should have taken the transfers she organized. I might have been an ambassador now. That's a joke. Me, an ambassador. I'm not the type. I suppose that's why I never tried. All I ever wanted was the desert and the Bedu. They've got a new name nowadays for the likes of me. Drop out. True, I suppose. Less unkind than that older diagnosis: 'Gone native, y'know, poor fellow.' No, I had to do it my way. At least this way I'm where I want to be though the world is catching up with me even here. And Helen is happy too in her own way. She commutes from here to London, from London to Paris; she meets her friends, she sees the boys, she's near her family. It's a pity, of course, that we don't have a marriage any more. But how many do? How many are bored with each other and still pretend to have a marriage? At least we have each pre-served some individuality. And sometimes, together, we have a good day, even two days. Never as long as a week. That would be asking too much.

He lifted and laid down the little wooden block that was his home as his eyes wandered over the model of the city. It was difficult to believe that all this had grown and was going to grow out of that stretch of parched sand he had landed on in the last year of the war. That arrival had been nothing like the storybook idea of the arrival of a British Political Agent. His predecessor could not meet him; he had died up there in that solitary white house with the Union Jack hanging exhausted from the flagpole in the suffocating heat. Troy's reception committee had been a few old fishermen clustered together at the edge of the creek, and further back, near the little village of *barastis,* a group of Qashrani women, dressed in black from head to toe, their faces covered with the stiff blue-dyed beaklike masks of Trucial Oman. Ben's Arabic was fluent but it was not Gulf Arabic. Only one small fourteen year old boy tried to understand. He explained to the men who Troy was and that he had to get to Sheikh Rasul at once. The boy was Davidan. A camel was brought. Ben made a good impression. He had been riding camels since he could walk. David walked beside him to the Residency, then later took him on to Rasul's mud palace. Two lifelong friendships in one day. David, still his servant and his right hand; Rasul, friend, then friend betrayed, now foe.

Rasul had kept the new Political Agent waiting that first day. He had never thought much of the last one. He expected nothing better. But it only took seconds for him to know that this man Troy was different. He did not speak Rasul's Arabic but he spoke Arabic like an Arab. He knew Arab etiquette. Soon it was all clear. Ben's father, Troy Pasha, was a name known even in that remote land. From that day forward they respected each other and Ben's influence was quickly recognized in Rasul's less aggressive attitudes to his neighbours. It was recognized too in the *majlis* where every Qashrani had the right to air his grievances and seek justice. It was recognized most in the change in Rasul's character. He was less forbidding now he had a friend to talk to, to play chess with, to vie with in composing poems, to race against on camels, to fly falcons with after the desert bustard.

Ben's marriage did not please the sheikh. It kept him away from the palace and from hunting trips. But the woman soon had a child and went back to England and was only seen occasionally after that. In Qashran the world was standing still. But not in the rest of the Gulf. Oil was pouring out of Kuwait and Saudi Arabia and the waters of the Gulf were busy with tankers. Rasul had been happy to accept the small income offered for an option on exploration rights. It was easy money. Everyone knew there was no oil in Trucial Oman.

Then the oil men came with their strange sand trucks and caravans. They went south and drilled holes in the desert and found nothing. They went on looking and drilling. Then Banner came and drilled far deeper than anyone before him, and brought in Qashran Number One. Rasul's troubles had begun.

Money, the kind of money that an oil strike brought, meant nothing to the sheikh. At first he insisted on being paid in the specially minted Maria Theresa dollars which were the only currency universally accepted in Arabia. One payment convinced even Rasul that that kind of money could not conveniently be stowed in a saddle bag. He took Ben's advice and opened bank accounts in Britain and Europe and America. He knew the importance of wealth. It was an essential tool for any Bedu leader in ensuring allegiance. But the scale of his new riches was beyond him. The responsibilities they brought with them were even more difficult to grasp. It was his money, his alone. It did not belong to a state or a government or a nation. If these things existed, they existed in the person of the ruling sheikh. His friend, Troy Sahib, guided him. The mosque was worth the money. The mosque would help uphold the Wahhabi faith against the infidels. The small hospital was justified too. It would make his people stronger against the temptations of the alien cultures. The school was a good idea. It would ensure that there would be Qashranis fitted to sit in council and argue with the oilmen. He even agreed to relax the Muslim laws on alcohol within the Inoco compound. Rasul's progress was cautious but for him and for that part of the world it was quite spectacular. Ben Troy's slightly tarnished reputation at the Residency in Bahrein and the Foreign Office in London was being burnished. There was even talk that the Baston-Troy woman might have been right all along. But of course Qashran was a special case. Teheran, or Baghdad, or Cairo would be something quite different. Events made any further talk of a promotion for Troy unnecessary. From being the one Trucial state with a fairly liberal regime, Qashran suddenly became the centre of a vicious Wahhabi revival.

Sons and heirs are greatly prized by the Bedu. Abdullah was Rasul's only son. He had been groomed since birth to succeed his father. Tutors had given him some formal education. He spoke English well and was a favourite with the oilmen. He joined in one of their parties one night in the compound. It was a wild party. Abdullah got very drunk. He decided to show his Western friends how the Bedu celebrate. He charged round the compound on his horse firing off his rifle in a noisy *feu de joie*. It got out of hand. He killed one and wounded two others. They came from the palace and took him away. He was never seen again. Some said that Rasul himself had shot him. Others that the sheikh had beaten him to death. What was certain was that the sheikh never spoke his son's name again. But he did act. Alcohol was forbidden to anyone in Qashran. Strict observance of the Wahhabi faith was enforced. Local custom was applied to everyone. Western women were forbidden to wear sun suits or bathing costumes or short dresses in public. The pool at the club was drained. Simple courtesies like opening a door or holding a chair for a woman were not allowed. The place was still too primitive for a woman to stay in permanently. Now even a short holiday was unendurable. The women travelled out only as far as Bahrein. Their menfolk were given leave to join them there. There were two ways round the alcohol prohibition. One was to distil it secretly. Discovery meant instant deportation. Few tried it after one engineer miscalculated and blew himself and his bungalow to bits. The other way was to take a trip to Bahrein on the plane that was quickly christened the Booze Express. A posting to Qashran was soon known to be like a prison sentence.

Rasul was set fair on a collision course with the businessmen and politicians in London and Washington. He refused Banner permission to go ahead with his drilling programme, he refused permission to develop the pilot refinery. With only Qashran One producing oil, and that at a reduced rate, Inoco's investment had no hope of earning its keep. Architects and planners and builders and entrepreneurs still came and submitted plans. They were all turned down. But the plans were not torn up. They were put into the suspense file while the businessmen sought out sympathetic ears in the corridors of power. Questions were being asked in the Senate about the treatment of American nationals. Questions were being asked in Parliament about public executions and mutilations being carried out in a country where Britain was the protecting power. Newspapers were running exposées on Rasul's reign of terror. The stage was being set. Troy got his instructions from Whitehall.

It was very easy for him. He was one of the few people whom Rasul still trusted. It was easy too because he understood that a sheikh remains sheikh only while he is respected for his courage and his wealth and feared for his retribution. Ben was practised in the devious ways of Bedouin diplomacy. On wealth, he reminded the elders that there would be much more wealth when more wells were drilled and oil was allowed to flow as fast as it was needed. There would be more wealth when the builders came and the businessmen came. There would be opportunities for the Bedu to start businesses and make their new wealth create more wealth. That wealth could only come if certain men had the courage to change things inside the state. Of course, Qashran was never named, nor was Inoco. These ideas only come up in conversation, talking about hypothetical problems in hypothetical countries. It was just mental exercise. Another hypothesis was examined: how terrifying could a ruler be when stripped of the power to enforce his decisions? For instance, if a ruler had a Defence Force and that Defence Force refused to take orders from him.

It came to a head at a *majlis*. Rasul was there, his negro slave behind his chair as always, holding the great scimitar, the elders were all there, Troy was there, and John Negley and Carl Banner. The coffee was poured, drunk, refilled, drunk again. The American had a request. For the umpteenth time he asked permission to raise the pumping rate on Qashran One and start drilling again elsewhere. Rasul refused. The senior elder rose. He was frail and he was afraid. His white beard trembled as he said his piece. Maybe the sheikh would think again. More oil would mean more wealth for the people. It was truly said that Allah had put this treasure under the desert as a gift in exchange for the piety of the Bedu. Surely the great Allah must have sent the infidels to dig holes and reveal his gift. Was it Allah's wish that, having revealed his treasure, it should now be denied to his people?

Rasul sat quite still and stared at the old man. The words meant nothing. The important fact was that they had been said. He looked slowly round the hall. Another rose to his feet, then another, and another, then they were all on their feet, shouting and waving their arms. He let them exhaust themselves. When they were all silent he told them calmly that he had heard their advice but had not changed his mind. They could go now. No one moved. He said it again, louder. There was some foot shuffling but they stood their ground. He stood up and bellowed at them. There was fear in their eyes. He shouted for his guards to open the doors and drive them out. The doors swung open. There were not just three or four guards. A whole company of the Defence Force was drawn up outside. Doors opened at the side of the hall. More troops. The old elder stepped forward. The knowledge that he was making himself a place in history gave back strength to his voice.

'Rasul, you are no longer our ruler.'

The sheikh did not need to hear the words. He looked from face to face, as if marking in his mind every feature, every name. He looked long at Banner and Negley. He looked longest of all at Troy. There he saw signs of emotion but no sign of weakness.

Ben felt only contempt for himself. He had done his job, he had done it well, he had done it without bloodshed. It was not difficult to betray a friend. He walked forward and led the way out of a side door. The palace yard was lined with troops. He checked his watch. On schedule. That alone made it a *majlis* to be remembered. A plane was whining down along its final approach to the airstrip. The plane was a few minutes ahead of schedule. In a couple of hours it would whisk Rasul away into exile in Europe. Tomorrow the new sheikh would arrive in the land he had last seen as a four-year-old boy.

'Sorry to keep you waiting, Mr Troy.' Kassim was back. 'Come in, gentlemen.'

It took Ben a few seconds to adjust, to remember that he was in a skyscraper block standing where a minute before he would only have seen sand. He nodded to the others. 'Hallo, John. Robinson.' Robinson was the chief of police, still part of the Defence Force but destined for a separate existence. Ben had never liked the man. Efficient enough. Good on traffic and petty crime. Supposed to be good at riot control. Plenty of experience. He had served with the colonial police in several parts of Africa, then in Aden. Ben had always wanted to ask him if it was a coincidence that every country he served in gained its independence.

'Over here, gentlemen.' The sheikh walked across and stood facing a wall map of the city. 'I hear all's quiet, Mr Troy. That's right, isn't it, Colonel?'

'Yes, Your Highness. We may be making too much of this. Are we sure that Rasul is back?'

Kassim pointed to Troy.

'Yes, John, he's back. He was there tonight, at Qashran One.'

'There's nothing going on here, that's for sure,' said the policeman. 'Lots of excitement down in the native quarter but just talk.'

'In the where?' snapped Kassim.

'Sorry, sir. Your Highness. Down in Kassimtown.'

'I should jolly well think so. Right, gentlemen, let me hear your plans.'

Negley and Robinson had been thorough. They had men posted at all the important utilities. Patrols were covering the docks, the airport, and the built-up areas. There were plans to fly the helicopters on patrol across the desert, checking the oilfield, the pipeline, the oases, and the grazing herds. It was thorough but when it was totted up it was clear that the Force had no spare capacity. Any sustained trouble, or a lot of small incidents spread through the city and the desert would overstretch Negley's miniature army. No one spelled it out. Nothing might happen. They had to wait and see.

Kassim pulled back the curtains. It was daylight. From that window they could see southwards across the desert. The single cloud seemed to grow out of the horizon. It was black. Even at that distance it seemed big. It had an odd shape all of its own.

The sheikh gave a tired smile. 'Well, Troy Sahib. You're the expert. What is it? A desert *djinn*?'

'Funny you should say that, sir,' said Robinson. 'That's what they were saying earlier on, the Bedu I mean.'

'Exactly what were they saying?' asked Troy.

'Exactly? I'm not sure. It was when they were all watching the glow from the fire. Something about a great *djinn*.'

Ben nodded. 'You should try and find out who started that rumour, Chief. Someone started it. Someone was told to start it. That story wasn't spontaneous.'

'What's the point?'

'The point, Chief, is the legend of the Great Djinn of Qashran. It's what, in your previous engagements, may have been called strong ju-ju. The Bedu may be Muslim and Wahhabi but they hold hard to a fair slice of paganism. The Great Djinn is the friend and helper of the great warrior sheikhs. The Djinn's last acknowledged friend was Sheikh Rasul.'

No one said anything. They all just stared out at that black cloud fouling the horizon. That was real. The planning on the map suddenly seemed too neat, too like a board game with a predictable ending. They wondered what would happen next; where and when.

CHAPTER FIVE

THE BLACK CLOUD writhing above Qashran One looked different from where Banner stood a mile and a half north of the well. There the column of fire and smoke dwarfed everything else, the heat made the desert dawn hotter than high noon, and the sustained roar of the flames overcame all speech that was not a bellow close to the listening ear.

The desert on both sides of the road was littered with parked trucks and piles of equipment. Men were unloading, sorting, checking. Everyone seemed to be too busy to take any notice of the well. These men knew there was no use peeing on a volcano. The only thing that would snuff Qashran One was days, weeks, of organization and planning, then some inspired calculations and a large slice of luck.

Banner walked back to his new headquarters. This drilling team had been only a few hours away. The drilling trucks would be useful later on but, for now, the three big trailer caravans gave him offices and accommodation for his senior staff. The generator truck was already working and the air conditioning made him shiver as he stepped into his trailer. But that was only for a few seconds. The coolness and the comparative quiet quickly revived him. He ran some water into the basin and wet his face and neck. Better still. He cleared everything off the long map table, smoothed out a big sheet of paper and started sketching a plan of South Base.

He had been right round the site in the first jeep to arrive. There was a chance of salvaging some equipment. A few vehicles had escaped destruction and one of the main workshops did not seem to be too badly damaged. Small compensation but he knew he would need everything he could lay his hands on. He marked his plan to show how he wanted the fires in the base attacked when water and foam arrived. That would keep the men busy while he went back to the refinery to hurry things up at that end. He called up on the radio and asked for the helicopter. He had the senior men in and explained what he wanted. They checked over the equipment lists together. They were a competent crowd; a mixed bag, American, British, and Continental, owing allegiance to oil and money rather than to any country. Mixed talents too; drillers, engineers, geologists, riggers, roughnecks and roustabouts. Carl knew every one of them personally. That was the way he ran his company.

That was the way he thought of the company, his company. Not the local offshoot of the giant international Inoco, not the subsidiary of the Qashran Corporation; just Carl Banner's own oil company. It was very much his own creation. When he first came to Qashran as a toolpusher with a reputation for successful wildcatting, the Inoco records showed a dismal succession of dry holes.

In his first few months he added some more. But when the company decided to pull out he asked to be left to try a new approach. So he and his team were all there was of Inoco in Qashran when he brought in Number One. Carl had picked up some knowledge of business in Texas and California and Venezuela. He had been filling in the spaces for years from a trunk of books he carried with him. He had an answer ready for anyone who asked how he had managed to get to the top from a lowly start. 'The only difference between me and the others is that I can read.'

It was not his reading but his instinct that told him to move fast when he brought in Qashran One. He knew that New York would waste no time in sending someone to get an exclusive contract with the sheikh. Carl moved faster. As far as the sheikh and his British PA knew, he was Inoco. The news of his oil strike reached New York with a copy of the letter of intent he had exchanged with Sheikh Rasul. New York did not send him champagne; they liked initiative but they liked it kept within bounds. They did, however, put him in charge of the Qashran operation. He soon discovered it was not plain sailing. The old sheikh was difficult and got worse after the trouble with his son. Carl's political education had begun. He learned fast. He deserved most of the credit for organizing the pressures which led to Rasul's exile and the new era under Kassim. Standing there on the road waiting for the helicopter, he knew why Rasul had chosen Qashran One as his first target. Not just because it was the most obvious and the easiest, but because it was Banner's well. Bloody Bedu bastard. Bloody Rasul. That would be the pattern. Vengeance. Who would be next? Negley, the elders, the merchants, Kassim? Then Ben Troy. He must rate a special revenge.

That was their problem, not his. Banner was going to save his well, his base, his oilfield, his company. His planning was already far ahead. He had even decided how much explosive the expert would need to blast out the well fire. Carl was not a fire-man but fire was a standard hazard so he had learned all he could about it. He reckoned it would take five or six hundred pounds of TNT to snuff the fire. It had to be a nicely calculated blast. Too little would not do the job. Too much could make it worse. He took a last look at the fire as the chopper settled on the road. Couldn't make it much worse, he thought.

Carl catnapped during the half hour trip back to the refinery. The first thing he did there was take a shower and change into fresh denims. Two mugs of strong coffee completed his revival. He was pleased with the work on the bypass to feed sea water south through the trunk pipeline. The manager expected to be finished by late evening. Reports from the crews switching the valves down the length of the pipeline showed that they would be ready by midnight. Good. Very good. Limitless water by midnight. The whole of the Arabian Gulf on tap to damp down the wreckage of South Base and isolate the blazing well. Back at the office there was a message from Kassim asking Banner to call him. He decided to go over in person. Kassim would be pleased to hear that things were running on schedule. Maybe he would then commandeer all that contractor's equipment Banner needed.

The cable from New York arrived just as he was leaving. He read it and swore. He read it a second time. He cursed again and again, beating time with his huge fist on the car bonnet. The Pakistani driver was alarmed and despondent. He hoped the panel beaters would be able to straighten out the dent in his lovely car.

There was a cable for Ben Troy when David wakened him just before noon. It was only an acknowledgment of the one he had sent to the Resident in Bahrein but it had about it the usual faint air of disapproval. That was not surprising. Ben had a rather picturesque turn of phrase for a diplomat.

'Qashran One oilwell afire. Oilfield base destroyed. Skilful sabotage. Witnesses confirm presence ex-Sheikh Rasul. Reference previous reports suggest intelligence sources Switzerland extract digit forthwith. Further suggest alert Gulf Squadron anticipation Kassim requests assistance.'

Ben sat on the edge of his bed sipping the mug of tea. David answered his questions. No, nothing had happened since he turned in. The town was quiet. Yes, something would happen soon, more than one thing. No, he didn't know what would happen, just that it would. Yes, all the Bedu knew that Rasul had come back. No, they were not afraid. They were excited. They were all good Wahhabis. The mosque had never been so full. Yes, it was maybe true they were being careful. What was wrong with that? The important thing was to be ready to join whoever won the battle. No, they were not sure that Rasul would win. But he had won the first round.

Ben smiled and emptied the mug. The Bedu were being realistic. Picking winners was a desert tradition. He looked again at the short cable from Bahrein. The Resident would be hedging his bets too. He knew the Gulf. He might disapprove of Troy but he knew his assessments would be reliable. The Gulf Squadron would already have been alerted. Ben grinned at himself in the shaving mirror. Admiral Baston would be delighted. The razor nicked his face. He grimaced. Not really funny at all. Too many people with too many axes to grind. Axes are sharp. They can cut deep. He dabbed at the nick with a tissue and studied the red smear.

The squadron was already on course for Qashran. The admiral was not delighted. He had been enjoying sitting on the tails of a Russian cruiser and two destroyers bound for Iran on a courtesy visit. Baston believed that the Gulf was British waters, had been since the Navy cleared the pirates off the Trucial coast, should remain so. Anyway, it had been good to turn the tables on the Russians, shadowing them, flying his aircraft over them. Tit for tat. The admiral had had a bad time from the Reds when he was with the NATO fleet.

He stood on the bridge complaining to the carrier's captain. 'I tell you, man, it'll turn out to be just another of these false alarms. Always the same nowadays. Some damned Arab coughs and we've got to come running. It'll be nothing. Nothing, I tell you. Haven't flown a plane off in anger since God knows when. Best we can hope for is to land a few of these Tommies from the assault ship. Better have that Major Whoever-he-is brought on board for a briefing.'

'I'll do that now, sir.'

'Don't know what the hell we'll tell him. Don't know anything. Give him something to do, I suppose.'

'Yes, sir.' The captain turned to order the signal to the assault ship.

'Damned silly, y'know, having these Tommies in a Navy task force. What's wrong with having the Marines? Don't suppose there's any left with this shower in Whitehall cutting down on the forces. Damned silly.'

'Yes, sir.'

'Anyway, have to tell him something. Tell him to make ready for a bit of desert warfare. Shake out his corduroys. Brush up his suede boots.' The admiral roared with laughter then peered at the captain. 'Don't get it, do you? Eighth Army. Desert Rats. No, of course you don't get it. Weren't in the war. Can't make that out. You not being in the war.'

'It had to do with my age, sir.'

'Hmm. Suppose it had. Damned odd. What do we know about this Qashran place? Ah, yes, we were there just last week, weren't we. That young sheikh chappie. Yes, and my brother-in-law's there. Political something-or-other. That might be useful. Did you know I had a brother-in-law in Qashran?'

'Your sister did mention it, sir.'

'My sister? Helen? Oh, yes. She was here, wasn't she. Yes, she would mention it. Odd girl, my sister. Talks too much. Not a bad sort though. Heart's in the right place. Yes, she's married to him. The political fellow. Don't think they get on too well. He's not a bad sort either. I rather like him. He'll put us in the picture when we get there. When do we get there?'

'In about eighteen hours, sir. Dawn tomorrow.'

'Hmm. Pity about having to break off harrying these Russkis. Tell Communications to listen out for them. Maybe pick them up on the return trip.'

'Yes, sir. Can I send that signal now, sir?'

'What's signal's that?"

'To Major Kirk, sir. To come aboard for a briefing.'

'Good God, man, haven't you sent that yet? Have to do better than that. We're on an alert, y'know.'

Tony Kirk was away ahead of the admiral. As soon as they had changed course and gone on alert he had his officers together and briefed them. Not that there was much he could tell them. What he did tell them was much the same as he told them every day. Check equipment, drill men. Re-check equipment, drill men some more. Today there was something extra in that it might not be for a dummy run; this could be the real thing.

The major was excited. This would be the first blooding of his special force. It had been his idea to form this unit. Not that he got the credit; the army did not work that way. But he had got command and that was what he wanted.

Major Kirk was a fighting soldier. He had still been at school when the war ended but he had made up for missing it. Malaya, Korea, Cyprus, Borneo, he had wangled postings to all these places when the troubles were on. He had collected a DSO and and MC. Starting in an infantry regiment, he had chased after every special course in the book. He was a glider pilot, he had an ordinary pilot's licence, he had just recently trained on hovercraft; he had done a stint with the Parachutists, special training in demolition and espionage techniques, and his expertise in handling civil disorders had been remarked on in Aden. He was a crack shot, a good horseman, and a Judo Black Belt. His proudest boast was that he could, blindfolded, identify, strip and reassemble every infantry weapon in use anywhere in the world. He had very few friends.

He sat in his cabin lovingly oiling his ·375 Mannlicher. It was the only concession to his buccaneering spirit. No corduroys, no suede chukka boots, no silk scarf at the throat, no rakishly angled cap. He always dressed strictly according to the book. But he carried the rifle everywhere. It was his trade mark. In his hands it was a deadly accurate weapon. He fondled the gleaming metal and the polished wood as another man would fondle a woman. His mind was already out ahead of the squadron, seeing pictures of landing craft running up beaches, helicopters hovering, scout cars stirring clouds of desert dust, well-led men clearing buildings, rounding up suspects, searching, destroying. As he saw the pictures, his mind's ear listened and thrilled to the symphonies of battle.

In the barracks beside the airport Colonel Negley was seeing different pictures and hearing different tunes. The colonel was not an imaginative man. Nor was he an optimist. He had lived a long time with the knowledge that he was a failure. True, he commanded the Qashran Defence Force. True, he was an extremely able administrator. But it was also true that he was a very English Englishman who lived in exile because his country did not need him. Also true that his exile was in a land he disliked, among people he disliked, in command of men he did not trust. It was also true that, in more than thirty years as a soldier, he had never been in battle.

It was this knowledge that was uppermost in his mind as he studied his maps. He had disposed his men well. It was the

kind of exercise that, done on a sand table at a staff college, would
have earned high praise. This was different. This was a city on
the edge of a sand desert. The property was real, the contours
were real, the people were real, the responsibility was real. The
colonel was not sure that he would make the right decisions if
things started happening. He had tried telling himself that nothing would happen, that it was all a scare, that the sabotage at
Qashran One was an isolated incident. But he could not believe
that. He could not believe that because he knew that Sheikh
Rasul was behind it.

Negley had been brought up on loyalty. He had never rid
himself of the guilt of betraying the sheikh. It was not a question
of whether it was right or wrong for the country that Rasul
should be deposed. The colonel had taken an oath of allegiance
to Rasul. He had broken faith. Now he wondered if it was just
guilt. Maybe it was fear. He had always been afraid of the sheikh.
He had seen Rasul's kind of retribution. He wondered how his
debt would be settled. A knife in the belly, a bomb through his
window, a shot in the back, poison in his food. He pushed away
the remains of his breakfast.

Something else was worrying the colonel. His friendship with
Susan Shaw had reached a crisis. He was confused and dispirited.
He had grown accustomed to her forthright way of speaking.
It had been different last night. It had been personal. He had
been happy at the party, happy in her company, sitting close to
her, away from the crowd, holding her hand. It had been like
recovering an old dream of when he was a child and sat like that
with his mother. Then it had all gone wrong.

'John, don't you ever feel you need a woman?'

'I beg your pardon.'

'You heard me. Well, do you?'

'Really, I . . I . . .'

'You mean you don't. That's a pity. I sometimes do. Feel I
need a man, I mean. You'd have done very well. It's better if
people can talk too.'

'But . . but I never thought . . .'

'You never thought of me as a woman. No, I don't suppose
you did. Not very many people do. Can't blame them. Ugly
bitch, aren't I? That's no drawback, mind you. I've seen some
awfully ugly women much sought after. They have to try harder,
you know. A lot of men like that.'

'Susan, I . . I don't know what to say.'

'You've already said it, John. Don't pile on the agony and
try and get worked up about me. I'll get over it. Don't worry. I
won't go rushing off to the Club and seduce one of these louts

at the bar. It'll pass. Has done already, I suppose. It was probably too much champagne. It's a depressant, you know. Not a stimulant. It depresses the higher centres of the brain. Brings out the animal in one.'

Troy had butted in then with news of the fire at Qashran One. Susan had been gone when he got back to their alcove. When he had time to check up he discovered that she had gone back to her hospital at Madaira. Now that worried him too. If trouble started, she would be without protection out there. Patrols would pass through. They could check up. But often she went far out into the desert, chasing after the real nomads. Nomads like the Shotras, fierce, proud, savagely Wahhabi. She was accepted by them now. They trusted her. The colonel did not believe that any Bedu could be trusted, least of all primitives like the Shotras.

I'll bring her back. That's what I'll do. I'll send out a patrol and bring her back here for her own protection. I'll take the patrol myself. One of the new helicopters. That's it. Fast, easy to find her, set down, pick her up. He stood up and stepped across to the door. He was alert. He had made a decision. He paused with his hand on the doorknob. She won't come back. Not for me, not for anyone. Certainly not for me. I must be mad. The thought of it. Me, kidnapping that huge, fearless, wonderful woman. I couldn't even lift her off the ground.

He leaned his head against the door. God, what a bloody mess I'm in.

Ben Troy sensed the tension as soon as he entered the conference room.

'Come in, Troy Sahib,' said Kassim. 'You're just the man we need to pour oil on troubled waters. Come to think of it, that's an unfortunate choice of metaphor in all the circumstances. Mr Banner and I are having a difference of opinion.'

'I see. Hallo, Carl. What's the problem?'

Kassim held out the cable Banner had got from New York. 'This is the problem.'

Ben read it. 'Regret inform you all firemen committed at least six weeks. Isolate and contain wellhead fire meantime. Report circumstances and extent of damage soonest." He laid the paper on the table. 'That's longer than you expected, isn't it, Carl?' Banner nodded. 'Pity, but there's nothing to be done. You just have to wait.'

'Thanks. That's what I've been trying to tell the sheikh.'

'And I have been telling Mr Banner that I will not wait six weeks. I can't afford to wait. Here are Mackintosh's figures. They say it all.' Mackintosh was the Scots accountant who was the

corporation's comptroller. 'The whole of our development programme depends on the flow of oil. The loss of revenue is serious
enough. But the loss of confidence, the effects on projects still in
the pipeline, doesn't bear thinking about. And don't you look so
smug, Troy Sahib. I know you've always said I was going too far,
too fast.'

'I'm sorry, Your Highness. I wasn't thinking about that at all.
I was just wondering how we find an expert to put out Qashran
One when Inoco in New York can't find one.'

'I've already found one. Isn't that so, Mr Banner?'

'No, it bloody well isn't.'

'And there, Troy Sahib, lies our difference of opinion.'

'So I see. But who is this expert you've found whom Carl
doesn't approve of?'

'There isn't one,' snapped Banner. 'He wants me to snuff
that well.'

Ben looked from one to the other. 'Can you?' he asked Carl.

'No. It's a job for an expert.'

The sheikh was holding out a manilla file. The tag had
Banner's name on it. Ben took the file and opened it. The sheet
on top was a photocopy of a feature in an oil magazine. The
picture showed one of the famous firemen with his arm round
Banner. The headline was in quotes and ran: 'This one could
be the best ever fireman.' The story told how Carl had helped
to tame a wild well in Venezuela. Ben closed the file and looked
at the American.

'Just reporter's talk, Ben. It doesn't mean a thing. It's easy to be
a helper. It's different when you're making the decisions.'

'That sounds like a fair comment, Your Highness.'

'It sounds different to me, Mr Troy. Let me list the induce-
ments I've offered Mr Banner.'

'I don't like being threatened,' growled Carl.

'You don't have much choice, Mr Banner. Now, the induce-
ments. One, Senator Coney has been trying to break down my
door all morning to hear what's happened at South Base. The
senator is very active in the oil lobby in Washington. I don't
think he would like to hear that an American oil man was not
co-operating. Two, Qashran Oil is a 50/50 partnership between
me and Inoco. But I, wearing my Corporation hat, make the
laws here. It is possible that awkward laws could be made. Three,
the Inoco contract comes up for renewal next year. Four, all
foreigners need a visa and a permit to work here. All that gives
me a fairly strong hand, don't you think?'

Ben studied the two men in turn. 'Aren't we jumping the gun
on all this?'

'Ah, there speaketh the diplomat,' said Kassim with a smile.

'After all, there's a couple of week's preparatory work as I understand it before any attempt can be made to put out that fire. Let's get on with what has to be done. By then maybe New York will have found an expert.'

'Very sensible. And if they haven't, Mr Banner will then put the fire out himself.'

'Carl?'

'I'll get things ready of course. That's all started.'

'So that problem is solved,' announced the sheikh. 'Thank you, Troy Sahib. Now, Mr Banner, about these two new wells. How soon can we get them on stream?'

'We can't now. They were scheduled for next month and the month after. I can't spare any men.'

'You must find a way to spare the men.'

'What's the use? If I did manage to get the pipelines finished, we can't use them. They're going to feed into the main trunk line from South Base. That line's being switched to take water south.'

'I know that. But that will only last till the fire's out. Then if the new lines are ready, they can be hooked up and the new wells can come on stream immediately.'

'You're just never satisfied, are you. And don't say, "The impossible takes just a little longer." I could screw whoever thought up that motto.'

The phone cut off Kassim's reply. He walked over and picked it up. The other two men watched and listened. The jangling bell had sounded like an alarm in their ears. It had suddenly reminded them that, while they were talking and arguing in the cosy quiet of the conference room, the city outside had been awaiting Rasul's next move.

'Yes—I see—What happened?—Find out then—And let me know at once.' He put down the phone. 'There's been an incident out at the end of the jetty. They don't know exactly what yet. Seems to have been an underwater explosion. Near the stern of a tanker.'

Ben pulled up the venetian blind in the big window. The harbour, the jetty, the sea were in plain view. He swung round the telescope that stood there to let the sheikh check up on the progress of his projects. 'Can't see much. A few men standing around looking down into the water. The ship seems to be all right. There's no smoke. No flames. Some chaps are at the stern, leaning over the rail, looking down.'

'Let me see,' said Banner. 'She's about 50,000 tons, deep in the water, must be fully loaded, or almost. There's a jeep going out along the jetty now. Looks like John Negley.' Carl stood up straight. 'Maybe it's a false alarm.'

'I wish you sounded more convinced,' said Kassim.

They waited twenty minutes before the phone rang again. The sheikh took the message. 'That was the harbour-master. I think we can assume that my dear uncle has struck again. That tanker has had its propeller blown off. It can only be repaired in a dry dock. And there's no dry dock big enough within a thousand miles.'

Banner was the first to speak. 'I don't get it. It doesn't sound like Rasul. It's not spectacular enough for him.'

'Maybe it was supposed to be more spectacular,' suggested Kassim. 'Maybe he intended to blow that ship sky high.'

They all turned and stared out of the window, wondering if that might still happen.

'One thing,' said Banner. 'We're sure of a good fuel supply. We'll have to discharge that ship back into the tank farm. We might be thankful for that crude to feed the refinery before this is all over.'

'Good for you, Mr Banner. You've just made a triumph out of a disaster. I like that.' Kassim turned to Ben. 'You're not saying much, Troy Sahib.'

'Sorry, I was thinking. I was trying to see if there's a pattern yet.'

'And what did you decide?'

'Nothing. Except that things are going to be a lot worse before they're better.'

CHAPTER SIX

IT STARTED to get worse that night.

Kassim studied the reports as soon as he got up. He went out on to the penthouse patio and looked round his city. There were no obvious signs of the night's sabotage. Far below a patrolling jeep shattered the dawn with the wail of its siren. The sheikh went back inside and poured a fresh cup of coffee. He leafed through the reports again then uncapped his pen and opened his diary.

'Day 2. Uncle Rasul and his friends were out and about during the night. Half a dozen incidents if one counts the stampeding of a herd of goats through the market and into the city. At least that suggests my enemies may have a sense of humour. The Defence Force has been kept busy. No arrests but plenty of noise. The Bedu do love firing guns. The night's casualties were three goats and a camel killed and two soldiers wounded, probably by other soldiers. Several complaints from European residents about the noise disturbing their children's sleep. It seems likely that they will have more to complain about before long. Cairo Radio is already screeching about the freedom fighters in Qashran.'

Hassan walked to work as usual that morning. But the route he chose was not direct. He wanted to check up on the night's work. Not that he expected to see anything spectacular. Last night had been a trial run, just to judge the effectiveness of the bombs he had made and the organization he had helped build up over the past twelve months. At the sea water distillation plant a gang was already working to repair the main pipeline shattered by the explosion. Good. In the city centre a filling station was charred, the forecourt flooded with foam. Good. That runaway lorry with the incendiary charge had hit the pump island dead centre and set fire to the spilling petrol. Further on, a gang from the power company was disentangling the wreckage of a distribution box. That bomb had blacked out four streets. The posters and the crudely painted scimitars fouling all the walls and windows proved that the darkness had been well used. Here and there walls were chipped and windows broken where the soldiers and police had blazed off into the darkness. Down in the new harbour a crowd was staring at a bulldozer and a mobile crane, both half submerged in one of the docks. Good. Very cheap piece of sabotage. Just release the brakes and let them roll over the edge. Round in the creek, the tip of a derrick sticking up out of the water marked the grave of a contractor's barge. Very good. That was a big bomb. It probably blew the bottom right out of the barge. Very good. They won't salvage that one.

There seemed to be police and army patrols everywhere, stopping, searching, questioning. That was good. That was what the orders called for. Widespread incidents to stretch Kassim's forces to and beyond the limit.

Hassan arrived at his desk a happy man. That morning he had no feeling of inferiority to the British staff of the bank. He was excited but he knew he must not show it. At long last all the training and all the waiting was starting to pay off.

It was more than twenty years since Hassan had become a refugee from Palestine. He had only been eight years old then. Ever since he had been involved in some way with the struggle to win back his country. He had been in Qashran for almost two years. He never asked himself how a revolt in this desert state could help restore him to the land he could barely remember. He was using his skills and indulging his resentments.

The assistant manager was speaking to him. 'Come on there, Hassan. What about opening all these envelopes? We'll have to put one of these bombs under you to hurry you up.'

'Yes, sir. At once, sir.' He smiled. It was one of those British jokes. Quite funny, this morning.

'Day 2, PM. Senator Coney was in this morning sounding off about the protection of American property and nationals. I'm sure he would reverse the priorities in an election speech. He could be a useful ally so I sent him down to South Base by helicopter to look over the damage. He got back not long ago and says it proves his point that, if the British leave the Gulf, then the Americans must accept the responsibility. He sees Communists under every grain of sand.

'Neither Negley nor Robinson has found any of those responsible for last night's incidents. Not surprising. The bombs probably had time fuses so no one would be around when they went off. The other incidents would need only one or two men. Tonight will be a better test not only of the opposition but also of the Defence Force.'

Sulaiman was a high-spirited youth. He made his living in a variety of ways. He ran errands, cleaned cars, collected and sold empty bottles, and was not above an occasional theft. He and his friends were always on the lookout for new and exciting things to do. The man who had come to buy the Pepsi bottles told thrilling stories. Now Sulaiman and his friends had a commission.

The broken-down mud house reeked of petrol. Sulaiman was on the last bottle. Half fill it with petrol, drop in one end of the wick, plug the neck of the bottle and, hey presto, a Molotov Cocktail. Very effective. Select a target, light the wick, throw the bottle. Bottle hits target, bottle smashes, petrol spills out, flame from wick ignites petrol. Six youths, six bombs and a box of matches each. Two youths to Kassimtown, two to the city centre, one to the docks and one to the old bazaar by the creek.

It was dark outside. They split up The patrols did not worry them. They had been avoiding the police for years.

Sulaiman waited too long after throwing his third bomb. He had smashed the window of the travel agency first. He aimed the bottle beautifully. It broke against the counter and fired at once. Instead of running, he waited and watched the flames licking round and consuming a cardboard display of a big jet in flight. As the stand burned the plane heeled over and dropped as if falling out of the sky. He grinned. The jeep coasted round the corner then accelerated as he was spotted. There were shouts and a couple of shots. He ducked and ran, round the corner, up the steps, across the piazza, down the steps. The three remaining bombs swung and clinked as he ran. A siren screamed behind him. He looked round. No one. He ran on. Down steps, round a corner. A shout and a shot. There were two soldiers that way. He turned. Under the steps, across a courtyard, round a corner. It was a cul-de-sac. He was trapped. He heard the soldiers shouting as they searched. He heard their running feet on the paving. He pulled out a bottle from under his robe. He fumbled with the matches. The wick was burning. Now come and get me, policemen.

He ran at them as they came round the corner. The first shot hit his shoulder and bowled him over. The bottle smashed, the petrol drenched his clothes, the wick set him on fire. He jumped up, screaming, and rushed at the soldiers. They had plenty of time to aim. Their automatic rifles pumped five bullets into him before he dropped. The other two petrol bombs smashed and completed Sulaiman's cremation.

'Day 3. Damn, damn and damn again. My guests have all suddenly remembered previous engagements in countries where the nights are not disturbed by fires, explosions and gunfire. The postponement of the marina deal is a great disappointment. Of course it's not an official postponement, just a delay while they go back and check some figures in London. But I got the message. You get this country of yours under proper control and then maybe we will risk our money. Everyone of any interest flew out this morning, to check figures, reappraise plans, consult with principals. Even the senator decided that discretion was the better part of valour and has left. He announced that he would stop off in London and tell the British how he saw their responsibilities. I don't expect much of that visit.

'Last night was bad. More than twenty incidents, mostly fires but three or four explosions too. Quite a bit of damage but spread thinly over the city. It seems that Ben Troy was right. The attack here is going to be of the little-and-often pattern. I won't mind too much if Uncle Rasul keeps on with his attacks on the old *suk*. The fires there burned down one whole line of shops. That's doing my job for me. Now all I need is to get these developers back with their money.

'The Defence Force had some successes. They killed three last night, one youth throwing fire bombs and two desert Bedu who refused to stop and identify themselves. I don't imagine they understood what it was all about. The jail is bulging suddenly with suspects but most of them seem to be there to convince me that Chief Robinson is doing his job. He says he'll get information out of them. He says it with such relish that I dare not think what methods he will favour. I've sent a couple of the elders down there to stop him starting another war. If Robinson is enjoying it all, Colonel Negley certainly is not. Already he looks worn out. Many more nights like last night and he'll crack up. He keeps harping on about the tribes out in the desert. That's the one place which is quiet. Ben Troy says that Negley is really only worried about Doctor Shaw. It seems that the gossip about their romance is not all gossip. I can't understand what he's worried about. That woman could wipe the floor with the whole herd of The Honoured Ones. Which brings me neatly to this persistent rumour Uncle Rasul is having spread. Everyone questioned claims to have heard it from someone else. Naturally. But what is significant is that they all retell it. It proves that the old fox still understands the Bedu. Add a legend to the legend he is himself and all the wonders of science stand for nothing out here. It all seems so stupid. Four hundred mangy camels against armoured cars and machine guns. But Troy Sahib says it fits the pattern. He's very quiet about what that pattern is but I trust him. If anyone can out-fox Uncle Rasul, he can.

'He's not so good with TV men. They arrived by this morning's jet. He wanted to have them refused entry. Said there was no worthwhile news here. I still don't believe there's such a thing as bad publicity. I sent them down to South Base to take pictures of Qashran One. Banner wasn't very pleased. He radioed in to complain about them getting in his way. But the producer was very appreciative. Now I'll get them to do a programme on what I've been trying to do here.'

Sheikh Hithlan had been a merchant all his life. He started as a boy with his father buying and selling camels and goats and horses. He was old now but not too old to move with the times. He now owned a fleet of lorries, two ocean-going dhows, and a laundrette. These businesses were run by his sons. His own time was divided between the Moslem courts where he was a respected judge and his carpet shop in the old *suk*. He was a great authority on carpets. The fires the night before had been at the other end of the bazaar. He had been lucky. Allah had smiled on him. Tomorrow he would move all his stock into his new shop on the gallery of Kassim's new *suk*. It was wise to take precautions. He knew Rasul well. He had been one of the elders when the old sheikh was deposed. It was not that Hithlan regretted what he had done. He was sure it had been the right thing to do for Qashran and the Qashranis. It had certainly been the right thing for Hithlan. Allah had smiled on his labours. His small savings had become a small fortune.

His nephew was not handling these two customers well. They were Arab, well dressed, obviously well off, and interested in some of his most expensive Persian carpets. He shooed the boy into the back shop and apologized for not recognizing his visitors. They told him not to rebuke himself. He could not know them. They came from over the border. They had been recommended to his shop by a mutual friend. Ah, even better. It was always a pleasure to serve friends of a friend. Who was this friend? There were so many.

'An old friend. He sends his blessings on you and your house.'

'Allah be praised. There are no friends like old friends.'

Well said, Sheikh Hithlan. We bring you greetings and blessings from Sheikh Rasul.'

The old man jerked upright, his mouth opened, he stepped back. But the huge curved dagger pierced him below the ribs, turned upwards and sliced open his heart.

Dr Sallal was a very good dentist. He had trained in London. There, as well as winning several medals, he had discovered that English women liked having their teeth repaired by a good-looking Syrian. Sallal was suave as well as competent. He had built up a very good practice in Qashran. He had three assistants, a superbly equipped surgery, a fine house, a Mercedes 300 SL and was a member of the Club. He knew that some of his patients thought of him as nothing more than a well trained wog but when you make your living inside people's mouths you quickly learn not to rate their opinions too highly.

Sallal had trained in medicine first. He took to dentistry when he discovered that, once the techniques were mastered, the work could be done without any intellectual effort. Sallal had more important things to think about than ill-kept mouths. Mrs Gorley was his last patient of the day. She was being very brave, just gurgling now and again as the suction pipe drained away her saliva and the water from the high speed drill. Dr Sallal was thinking how well things were going. Everything was happening almost exactly according to plan. The sabotage and fire-raising by night, the intimidation by day. The poster pasting, the wall scrawling, the disruption of traffic and work as the Defence Force searched and arrested and got rougher and tougher like all frustrated policemen.

'Just rinse, please, Mrs Gorley. That's the worst part over.'

Now Phase Two was launched. A few well chosen assassinations, more bombing, looting. And he still had some pet projects up his sleeve. Yes, it was all going very well. His old friend, Hamid Babrah, must be delighted with his work. Another week like this and Kassim would have to call in British troops. Yes, very good work. And no personal risk. None of the operators in the city had the slightest idea who was giving the orders. As he plugged the cavity in Mrs Gorley's molar he wondered if it might be an idea to have his own Mercedes bombed. It would be nice to get some sympathy at the Club. Anyway, he had had the car almost a year. It was time for a new model.

'There you are, Mrs Gorley. All finished. Your mouth's as good as new.'

She smiled nervously and struggled to sit up straight. He lowered the chair and helped her out. She smiled again, more confidently with her feet on the floor. Dr Sallal really was a first class dentist. And such a gentleman too.

'Day 4. A bad night on top of a bad afternoon. Two cold-blooded murders in broad daylight. Both victims were involved in Rasul's overthrow. The message is clear enough. There will be more and they may not all be Rasul's enemies. The Bedu will not be slow to recognize a chance to settle old scores.

'The night curfew does not seem to have had much effect. Two bombs in the main sewer and another shattered the water main from the desalinization plant, underground this time. Five cars set on fire, three of them in the driveways of houses. Mounting evidence of intimidation, high absenteeism, demands for more protection, complaints about the Defence Force, rumours of strikes and demonstrations. It has even penetrated the hospital. Bedu patients are discharging themselves and the old medicine men in Kassimtown market are doing a roaring trade with their branding iron cures.

'It's obvious that there is a pattern. The pattern seems to be to stretch my forces to the point where I call in British troops. I suppose there is some political advantage for Rasul to be pitted against the British but I can't follow his thinking. With the British here the rebellion will be contained. I had assumed that the point of a rebellion was to win. Troy Sahib does nothing to clear up this contradiction. He keeps on saying that it's like a game of chess; you have to try and work out your opponent's aims and motives. It's as if he is unaware of what is going on here in the city, as if it's nothing more important than the first few moves in a needle match between him and his old rival. Oddly enough I still trust him. He has the kind of detachment which goes with making the right decisions.

'I hope Banner is making the right decisions down at Qashran

One. He is not very communicative. That's probably a good sign. At least he's not saying it's impossible to put the fire out. Quite apart from wanting to get the oil flowing again, I want to be rid of the sight of that column of black smoke standing high over the desert. It's like a sign, a rallying point. Today, in the palace square, I watched the Bedu on their knees at their devotions. They are all suddenly strictly Wahhabi. I suppose it's coincidence that Mecca is roughly in the same direction as the oilfield but I had the feeling that they were doing their praying not to the holy city but to the Great Djinn my uncle has hoisted into the sky.'

'Let's get wet again.'

Banner shivered as the water from the hose spilled over him. Not that the water was cold. It had started warm away back up north in the Gulf and had heated up all the way down through the pipeline under the baking sun. But it was still cooler than his sweat-drenched body.

The three bulldozers were in line abreast half a mile from the wellhead. Their blades were raised, holding up the steel canopies welded to them to form heat shields. There were three men on each of the two wing dozers, a driver and two hosemen. Carl made the fourth on the centre dozer. They had perfected the technique over the past three days as they cleared debris from the area round Qashran One.

A branch pipeline had been laid in to half a mile from the well from the main pipeline carrying water south from the Gulf. Six hoses were spurred off, two for each machine, their lengths flaked out carefully on the sand to be dragged out behind the advancing dozers. The hosemen on the outside machines poured water over Banner's machine, while his hosemen kept the wing dozers drenched. Coming back was tricky. They had had some trouble with the machines reversing over the hoses. But they had cured that with winches and crews back at the pipeline spur to drag in the hoses as the dozers retreated from the fire. They had had trouble with waterproofing the engines against the flood of water. That too they had cured. The difficult we do immediately.

It was late afternoon. The sun was low in the west but the light was still good. At least now they only had the heat of the fire to fight. And the noise of course. The noise of the diesels soon disappeared in the greater noise of the roaring fire. All control was by hand signals and a deal of instinct. The bulldozers crawled forward. This was the first real test. This time they had to get close in to the wellhead, find any wreckage and drag it clear. There could be no attempt to snuff the fire till all debris was removed. Hot debris could fire the well again even if a charge put out the present fire. Loose debris blown about by an explosion could wreck any chance of capping the well quickly.

Banner stood behind the driver, his eyes screwed up against the cascades of water, squinting ahead through the narrow slit cut in the shield as a sight hole. The sand was red, shadowed black, shimmering as it reflected the towering fire he could not see. His eyes were fixed on that short black stalk dead ahead, the gushing crude oil pouring up out of the desert. A quarter of a mile. It was already breathlessly hot, as if there was no air left to breathe. Gulping air through nose and mouth he could taste the salt in the warm Gulf water. He checked around. The other bulldozers were keeping station well, the hoses stretching out behind them as they crawled ahead. He turned his eyes back to the view through the slit. There should be a cool spot right in at the well head, comparatively cool, where the updraft was strongest. Carl was going right into that cool spot. He wanted to see exactly what the state of that wellhead was. What he found out would decide how he fought the fire from then on. Not just how he fought it. How he put it out. He was obsessed now with the well. He had argued with Kassim about trying to snuff the well without expert help. That had been the right thing to do. It was a job for experts. But the sheikh had come very near to the truth with his careful research into Banner's career. For years Carl had wanted to tackle a big fire himself. He had seen the experts at work. He thought he could beat them at their own game. It was a matter of time. If he could get all the preparatory work done before a fireman arrived, then he could try and snuff out Qashran One.

A hundred yards. It seemed no hotter. What can be hotter than hell?

Fifty yards.

Twenty yards. Banner could see the base of the black column now but it was shadowed. He bent down and switched on the dozer's headlights. Better.

Fifteen yards. All stop. Even with ear pads on the noise was almost unbearable. It seemed to permeate every muscle and bone of the body. Now for it.

Carl signalled to the hosemen and jumped off his machine. He had the winch hook in his right hand. The hose jets chased him as he ran the few yards and dived on his belly on to the sand. He was only feet from the roaring column of black oil. He squinted up. It was difficult to judge but the fire looked as if it started ten, maybe fifteen feet above him. That was critical. That was where the charge would have to go. Bang on the spot where the oil stopped and the fire began. He blinked his eyes and shook his head to clear his vision. Christ but that saboteur was good. The wellhead assembly had been nipped off right at ground level. That meant excavating when the fire was out. But the main valve assembly had been blown off in one piece. That made this bit easy. He squirmed forward and snagged the winch hook in the great spoked wheel of the main valve. Cool spot be damned. He pushed himself backwards, still belly down, through the sand. Then he heaved himself up and ran, crouching, back to the sanctuary of his bulldozer.

Engines in reverse, easy does it, take up the slack on that wire. That's it. Good. Good. The wrecked wellhead assembly was moving, gouging a huge furrow in the sand as it was dragged clear. Carl took a deep gulp of air and choked on a lungful of salt water. It was a long slow half mile drag back but now he knew all he needed to know to tame Qashran One. It would not happen tomorrow, or the next day. But it would happen. The impossible takes just a little longer.

'Day 5. Sudden spate of diplomatic activity. All my neighbours want to help me. I was terribly polite in turning them down. They all seemed rather upset when I asked if by any chance they were harbouring Uncle Rasul inside their borders. It's very old fashioned, I know, but if I need help, and I'm sure I soon will, I'll stick to the British. At least they're not eager to get a foothold in Qashran. They're very touchy about their imperial past nowadays. I must look for a chance to excite their sympathy.'

They were talking at the Round Bar in the Club. The six of them always stopped off on the way back from their offices. It was just like being back in England, dropping in at the local. Better really. The Gulf had let them graduate from half pints of bitter to large gins and tonic.

'I tell you, man, I saw it with my own eyes. In broad daylight. Just after tiffin. This Arab fellow was walking along the street in front of me, pulled open a car door, slammed it and took to his heels. I knew something was up so I took off after him. Then, bang. The damned car went up in a sheet of flame. Dashed nearly burned my hair off.'

'You mean he'd bombed the car, in broad daylight?'

'Yes.'

'Things really are getting out of hand. Did you catch him?'

'No. I got such a fright he was away before I could catch my wits.'

'None of Negley's lot about?'

'Not then. Later. They wasted ten minutes asking me for a description. What can you say? He was just another Arab. They all look the same to me in these nightdress things.'

'Whose car was it?'

'Don't know. It was a big American job.'

'It's getting a bit much, you know. We had three cars bombed near us last night.'

'Was that near you?'

'Yes. One hell of a mess, I can tell you. They were all burned to a cinder.'

'I had a claim in for one of these this morning. Sallal, that dentist chappie.'

'That's right. His Mercedes was one of them.'

'Very upset he was.'

'Wouldn't you be?'

'No, I don't mean that. Upset when I told him we probably wouldn't pay. Riot and Civil Disorder clause. Absolutely livid he was. He said he'd sue.'

'I don't blame him. You insurance men are a shower of sharks.'

'Come off it.'

'Will you stop arguing and get the next round?'

'Sorry, old boy.'

The Goanese barman put up the drinks.

'Cheers.'

'Cheers.'

'Chin-chin.'

'Good luck.'

'No. I must say the whole thing's becoming a bit of a nuisance. We had no water this morning in the bungalow. And the power's always being switched off. It plays hell with the air conditioning.'

'The lift in our office was jammed all day.'

'You're still a new boy. That's not sabotage. All the lifts in Qashran are like that.'

'But it's not really funny, is it? I'm thinking of sending the wife and kids home.'

'Not really?'

'Yes.'

'But you can't do that, old chap. You can't let the side down. You can't let a few Arabs upset everything. Don't worry. It'll blow over. And if it doesn't Kassim will bring in dear old Tommy Atkins. He's got a treaty with us.'

'Is there still a British army then?'

'Just.'

'My boss told me today that there's nothing to worry about. He got it from Mr Troy.'

'Got what?'

'About the British troops.'

'You mean Troy said British troops were coming in?'

'No, not exactly.'

'What then?'

'Well, my boss asked Mr Troy about British lives and property. And what was he going to do about it. Mr Troy said there was nothing to worry about. Everything was under control and he was sure that if the sheikh needed help he would ask for it.'

'That sounds more like Troy.'

'He's a cold fish, isn't he?'

'He's an old timer. He knew the place when it was all sand. He preferred it that way.'

'Don't you believe it. I reckon he stays out here to get away from that wife of his.'

'How does he manage that? My wife won't leave me alone.'

'You're bragging again. My glass is empty. It's your round.'

'So it is. Well, let's drink and be merry. Who knows when we'll get the next one?'

None of his friends had ever thought of him as a prophet. That remark was to be long remembered. Two hours and twenty minutes later the liquor bond in the harbour was blown to bits. It burned throughout the night with all the alcoholic incandescence of a gigantic, well soused Chrismas pudding.

It was early afternoon, the hottest part of the day. It said a lot for the organizers that they could pack the palace square with demonstrators at siesta time. It was orderly at first, even good-natured. The vocal backbone of the crowd was from the technical college. The students were bent on enjoying their afternoon off. The forest of placards spelled out a bewildering variety of causes. 'Rasul In—Kassim Out.' 'Yanks Go Home.' 'British Keep Out.' 'Better Buses for Bedu.' 'Qashran for Qashranis.' 'There is No God But God.' 'Stop Illegal Immigration.' 'Palestine Is Arab.' 'Death To the Infidels.' 'We Want Free Pepsi.' There were huge portraits of Nasser and Lenin and Mao. There was one of Che Guevera and the group holding it were chanting 'Che Che Che Che Che.'

Kassim and Troy watched through binoculars from the patio of the penthouse.

'I like the Che group,' said Kassim. 'It proves how well international communication works nowadays.'

'I don't like any of it. It's got all the makings of a very nasty riot.'

'Of course. That's what it's all about.'

'I'm sorry, Your Highness. I don't share your approval of all these kids and the desert Bedu being used that way.'

'Come down off your high horse, Ben. You're the one who is always telling me it's like a game of chess. These are the pawns. We could have stopped the demonstration before it started. What would that have achieved?'

Ben did not reply. It was a pointless discussion. They both knew that the rally would not stay peaceful for long. All routes out of the palace square westwards into the city and the residential section were blocked by Negley's men. It was only a matter of time.

The wait was longer than expected. For almost two hours the crowd chanted and cheered and waved banners in the baking heat and listened to speeches from white-bearded hot-gospelling Wahhabi *ulemis,* from students, from an Egyptian schoolteacher, from coast Bedu and desert Bedu. The trouble started with an attempt to form a procession to the Corporation building. The way was blocked. There were scuffles. A soldier was knocked down. Truncheons swung. Fighting spread. A jeep was overturned and set on fire. The troops withdrew and pulled on gas masks. White puffs marked where the tear gas grenades fell. The crowd in the square surged away from the gas, was forced back by the throng behind, surged open again, broke and tried for escape through the other blocked streets. More troops and police. More gas. The crowds ran back. The troops advanced. Shots. A few scattered shots from inside the crowd. A soldier fell. A volley of shots, over their heads. Another volley, lower. There were bodies in the dust now. The crowd broke and ran, out of the square, eastwards, into Kassimtown. They wrecked as they ran. The troops did not follow. The crowd was frightened and angry, hot and brimful of rebellion. They wrecked and looted. Shops, stalls, houses, garages, workshops. They fought each other. They tore their town apart. By nightfall the purple western sky was balanced by the red glow against the east as the town burned. The technical college, the schools, the cinema, the stadium, all were blazing.

Kassim watched impassively. There was just a trace of emotion in his voice when he spoke. 'Tell me, Mr Troy. Do you think that will convince your government that I need their help?'

Ben cleared his throat. 'I think so, Your Highness.'

CHAPTER SEVEN

THE ADMIRAL growled with satisfaction. 'High bloody time too.'
He peered at the message form again. 'Yes, high bloody time.
Roust them out, laddie. Every man jack of them. I want the
squadron cleared away to action stations.' He checked the clock.
'For o6oo hours.'

The sub-lieutenant stood where he was, transfixed by the sight
of the hairy creature in front of him.

'What's the matter, laddie? Never seen a naked admiral before?
Lucky you. Now you can spread the word that I'm well endowed.
After you roust them out.'

'Yes, sir.'

Admiral Baston took his time. He had a shower and dried off
under the fan as he combed his hair and brushed up his beard.
No use rushing up there and getting in the way. Let them get
on with it. Time enough to bawl them out if everything's not
ready when I get to the bridge. He dressed and picked up his
cap. He gave himself a final inspection in the mirror. 'High
bloody time too.'

It was still dark outside but the eastern sky was lightening all
the time. 'Morning all.'

'Good morning, sir.' A chorus.

The carrier's captain was already there. 'Good morning, sir.
We're round on course. Major Kirk's ready to fly off. We're in
VHF contact with the shore.'

'You're an early bird, Captain.'

'I did hear there was a signal for you, sir.'

'Had a peek at it too, I'll bet.'

A petty officer pushed a mug into Baston's hand. 'Your coffee,
sir.'

'Ta.' He looked at the man. 'You'll get on.' He sipped noisily.
'That's better.' Another gulp. 'I'll have a word with Kirk,
Captain.'

'He's on this mike, sir.'

'Ta. Morning, Major. Sorry to get you out of bed. Twenty-
four hour day in the Navy, y'know. You know the plan. Keep
in touch. Remember the rules. You're advising and assisting.
Our political agent fellow will keep you right. Give him my
regards. He's my brother-in-law. Best of luck.'

'Thank you, sir.'

Baston handed back the microphone and watched Kirk's
helicopter rise from the assault ship astern and whirl away, past

the carrier, towards the shore. He tugged at his beard. Damned shame. We're only really troop carrying. And all these lovely jets lined up down there. Must have a word with Ben Troy. See if we can work something out.

The helicopter pad outside the barracks at the eastern end of the airport was lit up. Colonel Negley came out of his office and walked across to Ben Troy who was stamping his feet in the hard sand to keep warm in that cold hour before dawn.

'About fifteen minutes, Ben.'

Troy nodded. 'Mixed feelings, John?'

'I suppose so. It's not easy to face up to being a failure at my age.'

'Nonsense. You've done a good job. This had to come. You must have known that since the beginning.'

'I tried not to. I hoped we could contain it. You build a force, you train men, you think you're doing something worthwhile. Then at the first sign of trouble you have to call in outsiders.'

Troy smiled. 'That's a new name for your own countrymen.'

'You know what I mean.'

'Yes.' Troy wanted to tell him that what he needed most was a sense of humour.

'I know my limitations. I'm a good desk man. A good administrator. I'm no fighting soldier.'

'Thank goodness for that. I'm deeply suspicious of fighting soldiers.'

'Of course you are. You're a politician. Soldiers feel the same way about you.'

'I'm no politician, John. I'm a diplomat. There's supposed to be a difference.'

'It's only a difference in style.'

Ben grinned. 'Very perceptive.'

Negley stamped out his cigarette and immediately lit a fresh one. He puffed at it nervously. 'I'm—I've decided to resign when this is all over.'

'I see.'

'No, you don't. You don't see at all. You love this country, Ben. You love the people. This is your whole life. I loathe the place. And the people. I've got a bit put by. Maybe I'll get a part-time desk job.'

'Are you going home?'

'No. No, I haven't really got a home. England's not the same any more. I think I'll try Australia, or South Africa.'

Ben just nodded. It was all very surprising, this dawn confessional. The past week had taken its toll.

'I know what you're thinking, Ben. You're thinking I'm going there just to get into a white society. Well, you're right. I've had my bellyful of black, brown and khaki. I can't help it. I feel I'm different. I know. Not just different, better. So what else can I do?'

'You could blow your brains out.'

'I'm sorry I spoke.'

'It's me who should apologize, John. It wasn't a serious suggestion. I never realized. It must have been hell for you all these years.'

They did not speak for a minute or two. The faint snarl of a helicopter came in on the breeze off the sea.

Ben stamped his feet two or three times. 'Does Susan figure in your plans?'

'Susan?'

'Yes, Susan. You two seem to be pretty close. I was wondering if you were taking her with you.'

'No, no, I don't think so.'

'Have you asked her?'

'Well, no, I haven't actually. It wouldn't be any good. I'm too old for that sort of thing, for marriage.'

Ben waited.

'Anyway, she's dedicated to her job. She loves it.'

'She can practise medicine anywhere in the world.'

'No, Ben, that's not the point. It's not that kind of friendship. We just like being together, talking, listening to music, we like the same kind of books.'

'That sounds like an ideal formula. You should ask her. Anyway, how is she? I heard you were worried about her being out in the desert on her own.'

'She's all right so far. The helicopter patrols have been checking the oasis regularly. It's all quiet. But it's these trips she does out into the desert. She disappears for days on end. I don't like it. Anything could happen.'

'Stop worrying. She'll be all right. Just ask her the next time you see her.'

The colonel grunted and ground out his cigarette in the sand.

The helicopter was overhead, hovering, descending, stirring the sand into little whirlwinds. The door opened as soon as it touched down. Men jumped out before the rotors stopped.

'Over here,' called Troy.

The first man ran across and came to attention. The twilight was still too deep to see any detail. 'Mr Troy?'

'That's me. This is Colonel Negley, Qashran Defence Force.'

'Sir. Colonel. Major Kirk, Q Force.'

'Good morning, Major. Let's get inside where we can see each other.' They walked towards the barracks.

'The admiral sent his regards, Mr Troy.'

'Thank you. How is he?'

'As usual, sir. Rather pleased at this do.'

'I dare say. And you, Major. Are you pleased too?'

'Of course, sir. This is what it's all about, isn't it.'

'Is it?'

'Sir?'

'Never mind.' They were inside Negley's office. 'Oh, I see you're Army. That's a surprise. We expected Marine Commandos.'

'No, sir. Q Force is strictly Army.'

'Hmm. Why Q?'

'Well, sir, the Commandos were really Army, originally. The Marines pinched the name. So we needed a new title.'

'I see. But why Q? Quite suitable, mind you. Q for Qashran.'

'No, sir. Q for Quell. Revolutions, rebellions, brush fire wars. We quell them.'

'I see. You deserve something better, Major. Why not, let me think, yes, Kirk's Crusaders? Or Baston's Bastards?'

Negley cleared his throat. 'The maps are over here, Major.'

'Thank you, sir. Excuse me, Mr Troy.' He turned away and unslung the Mannlicher. He laid it carefully on Negley's desk and walked over to the map table.

'Let me put you in the picture,' said the colonel. He began to explain the layout of the city and the disposition of his troops and police.

Kirk listened for a minute or two. Then he broke in. 'Excuse me, sir. I wonder if you would agree that the first priority is to sort out the details for landing my force. They're due off the city in less than an hour.'

'Yes, yes, of course.'

'Colonel, I have worked out a provisional plan. Maybe the best way is for you to run your eye over it and put right anything I've got hopelessly wrong.'

'Well, eh, yes.'

'Good. Here we go then.' The major opened his map case and brought out a sheaf of papers. 'Two landing points, sir. Most of the men via this jetty in the creek. Transport and stores on to this beach here.'

'That's the lido.'

'Yes, but I don't suppose anyone will be sunbathing so early in the morning.'

'No, but you could come into the harbour. There are cranes and everything there.'

'A bit too slow, sir. If we can run the landing craft up on to the beach we can have the transport and stores ashore in no time at all. Is that agreed?'

'Yes, yes, I suppose that's all right.'

Troy sat on the edge of Negley's desk, watching the other two. The major knows what he's doing. A fighting soldier. Attack, attack, attack. The best form of defence is attack. The best form of attack is attack. He hasn't taken long to winkle out John's inferiority complex. He's got the initiative and he's going to keep it. Ben studied the rifle lying beside him on the desk. Doesn't look like Army issue. More like a game gun or a target rifle. Probably very accurate. Beautifully made. Beautifully kept. He smiled. Kirk's Corrective. I shouldn't smile. It's not really funny.

The major was talking about headquarters, billets, a transport park. 'This seemed to me to be the ideal spot. It's a new building, I know. Is it completed? Is it occupied?'

'But that's the new *suk*, the new bazaar.'

'Oh, that's what it is. Is it in use?'

'Not yet. It's just been opened. None of the merchants are in yet but that's all arranged.'

'Good. Very good. If it's still empty, you can commandeer it for me, can't you? It's ideal. Space under cover for headquarters, billets, stores. Plenty of space round about for transport and assembly. Can I take that as agreed, Colonel?'

'No, you can't, Major. I can't just commandeer at will. Especially not that place. The sheikh will have to decide about that.'

Troy caught the colonel's eye and nodded. 'I'll arrange that, John. It will be all right.'

'Oh, will it? Well, if you say so, I suppose it's all right.'

'Excellent,' said Kirk. 'It's very well sited, tactically. Ideal. Now, Colonel, just one more point. Can I have transport and driver/interpreters for my two beachmasters? They should get started right away.'

'That's easy. I'll have two trucks round in a couple of minutes.' Negley went through to the next room to organize the transport.

Kirk walked over and pulled open the outside door. 'Lieutenant Price. Lieutenant Cox. It's exactly as planned. Transport will be there right away. You know the communication channels. Keep them open. I'll be in touch.'

Ben watched him as he walked back into the room. 'Nice rifle, Major.' He patted the stock of the gun.

Kirk's eyes lit up. 'You know about guns, sir.' It was not a question. He ran off the rifle's pedigree and dismantled it in a few deft movements. It was a better trick than most magicians come up with. 'Beautiful workmanship, Mr Troy. A deadly weapon.' He put it together again without even looking at it. He handed it over to Ben. 'Feel it, sir. Perfectly balanced.'

Ben weighed it in his hands. 'Your own?'

'Of course, sir. I'm afraid the Army doesn't rise to anything like her.'

'No, I don't suppose it does.' Ben was interested in the sexual substitution. He laid the gun down. 'Very impressive.'

John Negley was back. 'They're off, Major. If you like, I'll take you down to the *suk* and see you settled in. I'll be able to put you in the picture from there.'

'Thank you very much, sir.'

'What about you, Ben?'

'No thanks, John. I've got my own car. When everything's under control, bring the major along to the Corporation building. He should meet the sheikh.'

'That's a good idea. Maybe about noon?'

'That should be fine.' Troy eased himself off the desk and lifted the rifle. 'Don't forget your girl friend, Major.'

Kirk smiled and slung the gun. 'I'd never forget Poppet, sir. She goes everywhere with me.'

'Poppet. I suppose that's quite a good name for a gun.' He stretched out his hand. 'Best of luck, Major.' Kirk's handshake was brutally tight. Ben flexed his fingers. 'One word. Iron fist but velvet glove. There's been enough killing already. We're after law and order.'

'Don't worry, Mr Troy. Q Force won't let you down.'

Ben watched them away in the jeep. I do believe you're right, Major. You're probably very good at your job. But I'll keep an eye on you and your fighting soldiers. You've got too many medal ribbons for a youngster. Yes, I'll keep an eye on you and your Poppet.

The city woke up to new sights and sounds. The Gulf Squadron was standing off, the first landing craft were putting men ashore in the creek and the lido beach was scarred with wheel tracks as more craft offloaded jeeps and armoured cars and trucks. Overhead, Baston's Phantoms were shrieking to and fro in an aimless display of low flying. The admiral was going to make the operation as naval as possible.

Before the rush of workers to shops, offices, workshops and plants, Kirk had his first patrols on the streets, relieving the

Defence Force for a much needed rest, breathing a new sense of discipline and control throughout the city. The patrols had muscle; an armoured car in the lead followed by a lorry load of troops. The men were fresh and keen, good-humoured but firm. Their orders were simple. Get to know the street layout, check the vulnerable spots, show you mean business, no rough stuff. The last instruction was unnecessary. The Kassimtown riot seemed to have stunned all the locals. They had seen each other tear their own town to bits. That morning they went to their jobs, they cleared up the mess in the streets, they sent their children to school in the classrooms saved from the fires. At the technical college the students gathered and helped with the clearing up and the salvage. The destruction had been sudden and unexpected. The demonstration had been fun to begin with. They were going to suffer for it for a long time to come. All enthusiasm for Rasul's revolt seemed to have evaporated in the flames.

But the scorched shells of buildings were everywhere, emphasizing the resentments and superstitions and ignorance which had started it all. Now there were foreign troops, infidels, in the streets. Surely that proved that Rasul was to be feared. There were warships off the harbour and jet planes in the sky. Surely that proved that Kassim and his British and American friends were still afraid. By noon the new rumour was passing swiftly through Kassimtown, through the refinery, the power station, the distillation plant, the harbour, everywhere where Bedu worked or gathered.

'When the Great Djinn sinks back into the desert from whence it came, then Rasul and The Honoured Ones will rise up and sweep the infidel soldiers from Qashran.'

Troy heard the story first from Davidan. Ben nodded and sipped at the tall glass of iced lemon juice. The pattern was forming now. All that had gone before was just to drag a British force into Qashran. After that the pattern was still confused. To get the British in was a predictable gambit for the Arab nationalists helping the old sheikh. But to commit themselves to a pitched battle, that was out of character. Their strength lay in the bomb and the knife by night, the swift guerilla attack. No, if the rumour was inspired, and Troy never doubted that it was, the implication was obvious. Rasul had gone along with his friends when their object was the same, but now that that was achieved with the arrival of Q Force, the old Sheikh was launching his own campaign. So they had fallen out. But that was not the important thing. Troy drained his glass. No, the important thing was that he knew Rasul was not fool enough to think he could beat Q Force with a few hundred camel-mounted Bedu armed with rifles. It would be a massacre. It was that thought that made Ben realize the old fox had played himself into an almost unbeatable position. Motive was the key to it all.

Ben said nothing about it when he met Kassim just before noon. The sheikh was at his desk working on more plans for the future. He never even considered the chance that there might be no future. Rasul was an unpleasant and annoying incident which had slowed his plans and cut off his main source of income temporarily. Kassim was using the time to perfect bigger and better plans.

Troy stood at the big window and watched the Gulf Squadron patrolling out beyond the big new pipeline. He watched a jet landing on the carrier, then another taking off. Rodney Baston was keeping up his show of force without a thought of economy. A solitary landing craft was making for the shore. The fishing boats were keeping well clear. A big ocean-going tug was alongside the oil wharf preparing to tow away the crippled tanker, now empty and riding high in the water. The gutted ruin of the liquor warehouse was framed against the new harbour.

It was exactly twelve o'clock when Negley arrived with Kirk and Robinson, the police chief. Kassim welcomed them and listened attentively as they explained how the landings had gone and how Q Force and the local troops were dividing up the work. Kirk's men were taking over in the city and Kassimtown, the police sections were returning to their normal duties, and the Bedu troops were going to concentrate on patrolling the desert with mobile columns, the helicopters doing the reconnaissance. Troy listened. It all seemed very sensible. It meant that Kirk effectively had the town to himself.

'You must be wondering, Major, why we called you in,' said Kassim. 'Things seem to have been very quiet since you arrived.'

'That's probably just a lull, sir. It happens like that. I'd like to suggest we use it, sir.'

'How?'

'By going over to the attack.'

'You mean that we haven't been doing things the right way up till now.'

'No, sir, certainly not. It's just that there are now enough troops to let us change our tactics.'

Ben smiled. The major had quickly found out that Kassim was a different man from the colonel.

'Tell me about your plans, Major,' said the sheikh.

Kirk opened his map case and spread a town plan on the table. 'We can assume that the sources of the trouble are down here in Kassimtown. So we section it off and take one section at a time. No warning, cordon the area, then search. House to house, identity checks, personal search, a fine-tooth comb effect. It doesn't really matter what we find. It creates an atmosphere. Takes them off guard. Gets them on the run. Flushes them out.'

'It sounds reasonable. What do you think, Colonel?'

'Yes, Your Highness. Very good, I would say. Now that we have enough men.'

'That's agreed then, Major. When do you start?'

'Right away, sir. This afternoon, after most of the workers get home.'

'Good. Anything else, gentlemen?'

'There is one thing, Your Highness.' It was Robinson. 'Major Kirk wants me to release all the detainees. I haven't had time to interrogate most of them.'

'You'll probably never have time, Chief. Anyway you wouldn't discover much. They're a close mouthed lot when it suits them.' He turned to Kirk. 'What's your thinking, Major? Let them go and those who have anything to hide run straight back to it. Then you can flush them out. Good thinking. Let them go, Chief. On my orders. It may polish up my image a little.'

Everyone nodded. Kassim had said it all.

'Best of luck, gentlemen. I won't keep you.'

Ben grinned as the others filed out. 'Was I included in that dismissal, Your Highness?'

'No. I wanted to discuss something with you.'

'I see. What did you think of the major?'

'He seems to know his job.'

'You make that sound unflattering.'

'Do I? That wasn't intended. He compares favourably with Negley. He seems capable of making decisions.'

'Are you thinking of offering him the colonel's job?'

The sheikh smiled slowly. 'That's an idea. Negley is getting a bit long in the tooth.'

He walked round the table and stood at the window. 'It's an odd thing about professional soldiers. They all seem to have a juvenile streak in them. Did you notice that rifle he had with him? It seemed out of place to me.'

'That's his trademark, Kassim. He calls it Poppet. A deadly weapon, so he says. I believe him too.'

'Hmm. Yes, I suppose it's in character. He's obviously the type that enjoys war. That's what I mean about the juvenile streak. As if it's still cowboys and Indians, goodies and baddies. Mind you, it must be very frustrating to be trained to fight and then hardly ever be allowed to fire a shot in earnest. It's like training a doctor then telling him he can never prescribe for a real patient.'

'I'd never thought of it that way. It's not true of the major any--

way. He didn't collect all these medals on exercises. He's one of the fighting soldiers.'

Kassim smiled. 'Now you're being unflattering.'

Ben shrugged. 'Was this what you wanted to discuss?'

'No. But it has to do with another dedicated fighting man.' He was staring out of the window. 'What do you make of Rasul's latest announcement?'

'About the Great Djinn of Qashran?'

'What else?'

'I hadn't realized you had heard about it.'

'I try to keep myself well informed. Just in case any of my advisers forget to tell me everything.'

'Am I being chastised?'

'No. Just reminded. What do you make of it?'

'I'm not sure. Assuming it's not just a wild rumour, it seems to lay down a timetable. As soon as the fire at Qashran One is out, we can expect Rasul to attack.'

'A pitched battle. you mean. Not just the sabotage we've had to date.'

'That's what it seems like.'

'And how would Rasul and his Honoured Ones fare against Major Kirk?'

'They wouldn't.'

'That's what I thought. Well, if my dear uncle has a death wish I'll be happy to oblige him. This time there won't be any exile. This time I'll stick his head on the palace gates in the true Bedu tradition. Does that shock you, Troy Sahib?'

'I'm not easily shocked, Kassim.'

'But you don't want to see your old friend minus his head.'

'I want to see this country at peace. I share your dreams for Qashran. That end justifies any means.'

Kassim stared at him for a long time. 'That's a very careful answer but I believe you.' He turned away. 'I wonder how long Mr Banner will take to put out that fire?'

There was a pile of coded messages waiting for Troy when he got back to the Residency. He plodded through them. They added up to the fact that Whitehall was in a state of alarm. The alarm was not about Rasul or the revolt. It was about the British involvement.

Having agreed to stand by its treaty obligations, the government seemed anxious that the involvement should be minimal, that the troops should be used only to support local police action, that the sheikh should be encouraged to accept help from his neighbours. Whitehall wanted to have its cake and eat it.

He filed the messages away. Troy knew better than anyone what the real issues were. And everything turned on Rasul's motives. He had to be sure.

'David,' he called.

His man came. 'Yes, sahib.'

'David, I want to meet Sheikh Rasul. Can you arrange that? Soon.'

'Of course, sahib.'

CHAPTER EIGHT

THE ROAD SOUTH WAS BUSY. Troy's car was tucked in behind a convoy of lorries. David was at the wheel, anxious to pull out and overtake, but frustrated by the steady stream of vehicles coming up the other way. His language was atrocious. Ben took no notice. There was plenty of time. He sat with one arm out of the window, channelling the hot air in on himself. It was not only hot. It stank with the exhaust of the truck up in front and was full of the fine dust thrown up from the concrete. But it was moving air and that was something on that scorching morning. Ben was of the old school. He would have been uncomfortable in an air-conditioned car even if Whitehall had provided one.

He stared out at the desert. He was excited at the prospect of his trip. It was a long time since he had been out there in the sand. He tried to remember how long. Certainly not since Rasul was deposed. It must have been three years. The last time must have been that last, long hunting trip with the old sheikh, in the spring when the intrigue and the planning were still secret. But that had been a good trip. He wondered if Rasul had changed, how he would look, how he would behave face to face with the old friend who had betrayed him and sent him into exile. He wondered once again if he should be on this journey. He even wondered if he would come back from it. He was surprised that prospect did not frighten him. Why should it? It was easy not to be frightened when still inside Qashran and excited at the idea of a desert journey. It might be different out there beyond the singing sands, face to face with Rasul. But he knew he would be safe there. He was a guest. Bedu hospitality would protect him. He was not so sure he would come back any wiser. The span of time and mistrust was immense; the sheikh had new friends, maybe new values. Maybe new attitudes to desert warfare. That was a terrifying thought. All Troy's thinking had turned on the unchanging traditions of the desert Bedu. But what if his new friends had given

Rasul new ideas, new equipment, new expertise? If that was so, then the threat of an all-out attack when Qashran One was snuffed out might not in the event turn out to be as vain-glorious as he had thought. No, that was ridiculous. No one could hide away a sophisticated modern army in the wastes of the Empty Quarter. Or could they? One thing was certain. Rasul had a modern communications system. Troy had talked to Davidan only last evening. All the details of the journey had arrived with his morning tea.

The car swung out into the northbound lane and accelerated past the line of trucks. A lorry coming north blazed its headlights but David kept his foot down. He made it back to his own side with inches to spare and the offending trucks behind him. He grinned. Ben relaxed and breathed the hot, exhaust-free air.

Troy's eyes were fixed on the desert and his mind was full of practical questions. Could he still ride a camel? How long would the journey be? How would his body stand up to it after the years of soft living? Should he tell Banner what he was up to when he stopped off at South Base? Would the helicopter patrols spot him as he made for his rendezvous on the edge of the singing sands? So many questions. But none of them lay long in his mind. Troy trusted his instinct. That told him this was the right thing to do, the only way to achieve what he saw as his duty. He would try to talk Rasul out of returning to Qashran to do battle with Q Force. He knew he would fail in that. He would then arrange the battle as if setting up the men on a chess board. He would seek proof that his judgement of the pattern was right. Then he would find a way of betraying his old friend a second time.

The bang brought him back to reality. He looked ahead, startled, his ears ringing with the blast. The great pillar of smoke and flame from Qashran One was there in front of him, maybe five miles away, dominating the flat scenery, already sounding like a giant, uncontrolled fountain. But it was no different than it had been for a week. Ben looked out to his left. A herd of goats was stampeding wildly across the parched sand, chased by two shepherd boys. Then he saw the plane, high, small seen from behind, changing shape and becoming recognizable as it banked and turned. It was one of Baston's Phantoms, ranging deep into the desert, looking for rebels who were not there, blasting the wits out of that herd of goats as it broke through the sound barrier and scoured the sand with its sonic bang. Troy watched the plane as it sped north. He shook his head. Boys. Silly Boys. He was surrounded by them. Baston, Kirk, Rasul. That was the terrifying thing about war. It made boys of old men.

The car was almost at the end of the road. There were barricades ahead and huge arrows diverting traffic to the transport park out on the hard sand. David swung off and called over one of the soldiers. He wanted to drive on beyond the barricades to put Troy down near Banner's caravan. The soldier would have none of it. He had his orders. He made no exceptions. Ben told David to park the car. That was another thing about war. Judgement was not encouraged. Orders were orders.

Ben walked the two hundred yards to the caravans. The sun was hot enough but with every step it was added to by the heat of the flaming well. Every step brought nearer too the constant roar of the fire and the cloying stench of oil. A man at the caravan pointed to a group huddled together nearby. Banner looked up and recognized him as he came near.

'Hi, Ben. What brings you down here?' He spoke loudly, almost shouting to overcome the noise.

'I was just passing. How are you getting on?'

'So so. We're trying to work out a problem.' He pointed to some metal and wire set up in the sand. 'How d'you put a quarter ton of TNT bang on the right spot in that furnace down there?'

'I doubt if I can help, Carl.'

Banner took his arm. 'Let's get inside. Can't talk out here.' They walked back to the caravan.

It was chillingly cool inside. Banner got two cans of beer out of the fridge, pierced them, and handed one to Troy. 'Try that for size.'

Ben drank and shivered. 'That's better.' He emptied the can. 'Do you think you've solved that problem?'

'I don't know. I won't know till I fire the charge. If it snuffs the fire, I've solved it. If not, I haven't.'

'When's the moment of truth?'

'A couple of days yet, at least. I'll show you how I plan to do it.' Banner went over to the map table and picked up a pencil. 'Here,' he drew on the paper, 'is the well. A hundred yards out north and south I'm going to spud in a test rig. A wire will run up through the top of one derrick and across and down through the top of the other. The middle of the wire will pass plumb through the oil coming out of the wellhead, below the fire point. O.K.? Then I'll hook on the explosive, all done up in asbestos, maybe water too, and drag it along the wire. Like an overhead conveyor. Simple, so far. The problem is that as the weight comes on the wire, it sags. So I have to be able to tighten the wire, to lift the charge so that when it reaches the well it's at exactly the right height, where the gushing oil stops and turns into burning oil.'

Ben was smiling.

'What's so funny?' asked Carl.

'You. Last weekend you were telling Kassim that on no account would you try and put out that fire. Now you're just itching to have a go.'

Banner grinned. 'Fair comment. It's true what I told Kassim. It's a specialist job. But I've always wanted to try one myself.'

'Kassim will be delighted. You're away ahead of schedule.'

'I'm not there yet, Ben.'

'You will be. Two days, you say?'

'Maybe three. I want to be sure. When everything's ready I'll do a dummy run. If that's O.K. then I'll try the real thing.'

'And all hell will be let loose.'

'How d'you mean?'

'You haven't heard? When you snuff out Qashran One, you're not putting out a fire. You're assisting at the famous disappearing trick of the Great Djinn of Qashran. And that will be the sign for Rasul to attack.'

'Are you making this up?'

'No. It's the latest news we have.'

'He must be off his rocker. You've got British troops in now, haven't you.'

'Yes and no. Yes, we've got British troops in. No, I don't think Rasul's off his rocker.'

'Tell me. What kind of army has he got tucked away down there beyond the dunes?'

'We don't know. We're only assuming he is down across the singing sands. But that's pretty certain. We don't know his strength but we don't think it can be all that great.'

'So why do you think he's going to come charging back into Qashran to get blown to bits?'

'That's what I hope to find out.'

Banner took time to digest that. 'Wait a minute, Ben. What are you really doing down here?'

'This is off the record, Carl. I'm going to see Rasul.'

'You must be nuts. He'll cut your liver out before you can say *salaam*.' Carl shook his head in disbelief. 'Nuts. Crazy. D'you know where he is?'

'No. But it's all arranged. Don't worry, Carl. I know the Bedu. Nothing will happen to me. They don't turn on their guests.'

Banner kept on shaking his head. 'I wish I could be sure of that. Is Kassim in on this?'

'No.'

'I thought not.' He went over and took two more cans out of the fridge. 'This calls for a drink. I just hope it's not your last.'

They drank the ice cold beer slowly. Carl emptied his can before he spoke again. 'Why are you really going, Ben?'

'I told you.'

'So you did. And I don't believe you. At least I think that's only part of it.'

'And the other part?'

'You want to see your old buddy again. You want to try and make your peace with him.'

'You may be right, Carl. We can't ever know for sure why we do anything.'

'I'm sure of one thing. I don't miss that old Arab bastard one little bit.' Banner buckled the beer can in his fist. 'And that's what I'd do to him if he was here right now.' He tossed the can into a waste bucket.

Troy finished his beer. 'Will you do me two favours, Carl?'

'That depends.'

'I want to be dropped off later on, down near the edge of the dunes. It might be safer in one of your trucks. In case there are any patrols about.'

'Can do.'

'And could you delay snuffing out that fire until I get back?'

'You've got three days.'

'That should be enough.'

Q Force was making its presence felt in Kassimtown. The cordon and search sweeps were phased to follow quickly one after the other. There was to be no rest for Rasul's supporters. Major Kirk was pleased. His men had not found much in the way of supplies; some plastic explosive, a box of grenades, some rifles and ammunition. But they had flushed out half a dozen Bedu who tried to run rather than answer questions. Two dead, four captured, two of them wounded. It was an encouraging beginning.

The major stood behind the armoured car with his field glasses up to his eyes. 'You're sure that's where he is, Lieutenant?'

'Yes, sir.'

'Is your chap badly hurt?'

'He got it in the thigh, sir. He'll be all right.'

'Good.' He let the glasses hang and studied the map, then looked round to check his bearings. Problem. One sniper holed up on top of the *muezzin* tower next to the mosque. Can't escape. Square's cordoned off. Knows now we're here in force so he'll keep his head down. Answer. Some tempting bait. 'Who's your best sharpshooter, Lieutenant?'

'Corporal Harrison, sir.'

'Get him over here.' Kirk checked the map again as he waited.

'Sir.'

'Ah. I've got a little job for you, Corporal. There's a sniper up there on top of that tower. He's just put a bullet in one of your mates. I want you round in the next street, up on the roof of that tall building. Take a walkie-talkie with you. Report when you're in position. Then we'll give him something to shoot at down in this side of the square. That balcony up there's solid so he'll have to put his head up if he's going to shoot. Don't miss him, Corporal.'

'No, sir.'

Kirk put his glasses on the tower again. Not a sign of life. He swept round the roofs on the far side of the square. Nothing. 'Lieutenant, call up my jeep.'

'Can I go in to draw him out, sir?'

'No, Lieutenant. I'm going in. You had your chance before I arrived.'

'I'm sorry, sir.'

They waited in the unnatural quiet of the deserted square. It was very hot. Kirk took a mouthful of water and patted away the sweat on his brow and round his neck. His uniform was wet and clinging to his back. Then Harrison came on the radio. He was in position. He had a good view. He could see no one on the balcony.

'Your jeep, sir.'

'Thank you, Sergeant. Are you driving?'

'You bet, sir.' They had been together a long time.

Kirk climbed in and stood up, a loud hailer in his left hand, the Mannlicher slung as usual on his right shoulder. 'Tell your chaps to keep their eyes skinned, Lieutenant. There may be some others around.'

The jeep moved slowly into the square.

'Keep her on this side, Sergeant, in the shade at first.'

'Yes, sir.'

Kirk lifted the hailer. He had some Arabic from his time in Aden. 'Up there. You can't get away. Give yourself up. You can't escape. Give yourself up.' No reaction. No sign. He spoke down to the sergeant. 'Tell Harrison to watch out now. We should get something when we come out into the light at this next street.' He heard the message being passed on the radio as he kept his eyes on that balcony. He smiled. The jeep would be much nearer the tower when it came into the light. The sniper's angle would be steep. He would have to stand up straight to sight down over the balcony.

The radio spoke. 'There's something now, sir. Not much though. Like the top of one of these turban things.'

The major bent down. 'Don't hurry it, Corporal. He's only watching us. He'll have to get up if he wants a shot.'

'Right, sir.'

The jeep crept forward towards the wedge of sunlight streaming out into the square from the street, unobstructed by buildings. The light was on the bonnet. Kirk screwed up his eyes against the coming glare.

It all happened very quickly. A sudden sight of a head and shoulders and a gleam of metal above the balcony, a shot, Harrison's voice on the radio, 'Got him, sir,' another shot and the hailer was wrenched from the major's hand. Kirk's head came round quickly, his eyes searching for the second sniper, the Mannlicher already up at his shoulder. He picked him out almost immediately. The youth was running along a roof across the square. The major's first shot killed him. His momentum carried him over the edge of the roof and spreadeagled his body in the dust.

'Let's go, Sergeant. We'll pick up my one. I'd like to check where I hit him.'

It was a marvellous sunset. Troy sat in a hollow on the edge of the dunes and watched. At first he thought he had never seen anything so beautiful in all his life. But as he thought back he realized that the end of the day was often like this out in the desert. It was just that he had been away from it for far too long. The evening sky could be superb in Qashran City but this put that to shame.

The sun had already dropped low, turning from blinding white to orange then red, seeming to get bigger all the time, when Banner had dropped him off and turned the truck back towards South Base. The red orb had sunk slowly, throwing throbbing banners of cerise and gold up into the sky and out along the horizon, turning the dull yellow of the sand into a glowing cloth of gold. Lower still and the horizon began eating away at the roundness of the sun. The colours became denser but more brilliant. There was only a scarlet segment left, the sky was crimson and the gold of the sand was shading quickly towards purple. Suddenly the sun was gone, the whole western sky was bathed in red light from the hidden source, the land was obscured in a haze of purple. Then darkness and the dome of stars.

Only in the northwest was there anything to interrupt the rapture. The flaming pillar of Qashran One. Even at that distance it added its rushing and soaring sound to the other desert sounds, the stirring of the sand in the small breezes of evening and the sighing and wailing of the moving sands to the south.

It was not other Qashran sunsets that Troy remembered. His mind was drawn back almost half a century to his first memories of the desert, memories peopled with a strange mixture of Arabs; town Arabs, farming Arabs, desert Arabs, Moslem Arabs, Christian Arabs. Memories dominated by that odd man who was his father.

Troy Pasha was a welcome guest throughout the Levant; in Damascus, in Jerusalem, in Amman, in Beirut, especially among the nomads on the western fringes of the great Arabian desert, more than a thousand miles from where the son now sat, but the same great desert. Troy Pasha made his name in the first war when all these lands were under the Turks. He was not with Lawrence. He was ahead of Lawrence, inside Turkish territory, preparing the way for the revolt, feeding back information. When the war was over and the maps were redrawn, creating new countries and new dynasties, he stayed on, moving freely across borders, honoured and respected, taking up again his work on history and language, steeping himself in the traditions and cultures of these lands which were more home to him than England. But he clung to his English loyalties and sent back to London a stream of intelligence. He was a free-ranging, independent but very reliable one man spy network. His greatest asset was that he was trusted and unsuspected. It was an odd background for a growing boy. It left Ben with an intense respect for and understanding of the Arabs, it induced a feeling of guilt when, in Army Intelligence in the second war, he uncovered evidence of his father's double life. It gave him a sense of real purpose, maybe of repaying that debt of guilt, when he came to Qashran and found a Bedu people still primitive and untainted by Western ideas. It rekindled that guilt when he found himself the linch pin in betraying these Bedu traditions he admired. He had never doubted that what he did was right; the conflict was within himself, between head and heart.

He shivered in the sudden coolness of the evening, wrapped himself more tightly in his cloak and pulled the trailing edges of his head-dress under his chin. That was good. To be once more in Bedu clothes. That was one part of one side of the coin. The other parts, the pleasure of the long missed solitude and beauty of the desert at night, the anticipation of a journey never before made, the thought of meeting an old friend, the hope that he could turn that friend away from disaster; these parts made the coin bright, shining, inspiring, inviting. The other side was different. There a hand was offered in friendship, accepted in friendship, a plea was made, a plea was ignored, battle was joined, won and lost. That side was dark, forbidding, depressing, repellent. But he knew before he ever started on his journey that when the coin was tossed it would land with the bright side buried deep in the sand. That seemed inevitable. The unanswered question was who would win the battle and who would lose.

'Salaam.'

Troy sat up straight. The voice came from behind him. It was deep and hard edged. He held himself quite still, sensing the dagger held ready. He remembered the voice.

'Yussuf?' He turned his head slowly. All he could see in the darkness was a vague cloaked outline. The size of the silhouette answered his question. No Bedu had the giant body of Rasul's Negro slave. 'Salaam,' said Troy.

'Come.' A huge hand grasped his arm, traced it down and took hold of his wrist.

Ben let himself be led. Yussuf was not in a talkative mood. He was not one to argue with. It had been Yussuf alone who ensured that the Great Scimitar went into exile with Rasul. He had been holding it that day in the *majlis*. He had carried it out of the hall when Negley's troops escorted Rasul away. He had carried it with him on to the plane. No one had dared tell him to put it down. It was to be a peaceful revolution. No one had worried at the time. It seemed best that the symbol of the old regime should disappear for ever. Now it was back.

The camels were crouched close by. The Negro helped Troy into the saddle and prodded the beast to its feet. Its protests sounded appallingly loud. Ben found himself looking round to see if there was anyone to hear. Yussuf carried a lead rein to his own beast and mounted. It was only a few steps to the edge of the dunes. That plunge down the first steep slope reminded Troy that he had not been in a camel saddle for a long time. He clung to his precarious perch, swaying, trying to balance himself. Even in these first few minutes his back and shoulders, his legs and thighs, his hands and wrists started to protest against the unaccustomed strain. It would have been difficult to sit a camel easily after three years if the going had been level and the light good. Here it was dark and the dunes were like an angry sea, soaring high to crests, swooping low to troughs, giving beneath the beast's feet, making it stretch and shorten its steps, lifting its shoulders, dropping them, raising its rump, lowering it. Troy let his mind dwell on the pain in his muscles so that the sickness in his stomach would not rise up and make him retch. In ten minutes the discomfort was unendurable; in twenty, it seemed separate, recognizable but taking place in a body not connected to his brain; in half an hour he had relearned his forgotten lessons, was sitting his beast more easily, his body adjusting, intense concentration no longer needed.

Now he had time to look around, to pick out ahead the dark shape of Yussuf's camel, to peer down the slopes of the dunes. He could peer down into pools of darkness on both sides. They were travelling along the crests, following the secret route south through the dry quicksands. It was a marvel of navigation. The sky was velvety black, sprinkled with stars that gave a faint light. He was warm inside his cloak, even hot with the effort of holding himself in the saddle, but the air on his face was cold. All around the sands moved and whispered their melancholy symphony.

It was only then that he realized the finality of his commitment. There was no turning back. He had put himself in Rasul's hands. He had no way of knowing what kind of man the old sheikh had become after three years in exile. There was the evidence of Qashran One. He twisted round. There it was. That spilled ruthlessness. There was the evidence of the troubles in the city, the bombs, the fires, the murders, the intimidation. That spelled ruthlessness. But Rasul had always been ruthless. More important, there was evidence that he wanted to preserve the Bedu traditions against Kassim's dilution. He had invited Troy to talk with him. He would not harm him. Ben smiled. If he got back safely, Kassim's anger would be far greater than his uncle's. Young Kassim would not be amused at his political adviser sneaking off to treat with the enemy. Troy would have to have a very good story. Whitehall would not be amused. The diplomatic problems could be embarrassing. Ben was now in Saudi Arabia. The Saudis would not be amused. Ben grinned. His spirits were improving. He was not without experience of people in high places not being amused.

There seemed no end to the journey. He checked his watch. Two hours. It seemed like a lifetime. There was a lifetime of lifetimes ahead. He played games with himself to drive away the fatigue. He searched the sky, naming the constellations, trying to remember the names of individual stars, counting the red ones, then the white ones, then the blue ones.

Three hours. He searched back in his mind for all the legends he had ever heard about the sky.

Four hours. He thought about the desert, about Kassim's greatest plan. To turn back history, to make the desert fertile again, to change the climate, to irrigate the sands, to plant trees to hold the soil and bring more water with the rain. It was fantastic. It was impossible.

Five hours. The impossible takes just a little longer. He thought about Carl Banner, sitting in the shadow of his wild well, planning how to tame it with a home-made bomb.

Six hours. Home. He thought about his wife. He had had a letter from Helen that morning. She was back in London. He tried to remember every inconsequential item of her news. She had written: 'I hear you are having a spot of bother from that dreadful old man, Rasul. I never did like him. Thank goodness you have Rodney and his squadron there if you need help.' The Bastons for ever. Dear Helen, how I love you when you're there and I'm here.

Seven hours. He thought about the admiral. He tried to imitate his voice. He barked a few orders to his ship of the desert. Easy, Ben. Take it easy. You're tired, very tired.

Eight hours. Sailors. That's it. Remember that second mate on that troopship? He had a cure for tiredness. He said he kept himself awake thinking about sex. What an odd thing to do. But it was easy. He surprised himself. You're a dirty old man, Ben. He thought about Negley and Susan Shaw. That wasn't sexual. Could it be? He liked Sue.

Nine hours.

There was light in the east. Pale, grey light, cold light, striking through the eyes down into the stomach, stirring up the nausea that came in that hour before dawn. Troy tightened his lips and looked away. There was something different about the camel's movement. He concentrated on that. The gait was steadier, less strained. He listened. There was the rushing of the beast's breath, the bubbling of saliva from its mouth. There was the regular sifting hiss as foot followed foot in the sand. But there was no other sound. The night-long background music of the dunes was silenced. They were through the singing sands.

He looked back to the east. The grey light was tinged with warm bars of gold and orange. The bars shimmered, joined, blended, reddened. The light grew and revealed the endless horizon. This was the Rub al Khali, the Empty Quarter of Arabia. Hundreds of miles of sand desert. It looked almost flat, just undulating gently like a ground swell on a vast ocean. But it was not so. Troy could look down to his right, down into a huge valley gouged out of the sand. Yussuf led on farther into the desert.

The approaching sun painted the whole eastern sky almost to the zenith, and the west picked up reflected slivers of red light. Then the sun was there, a scarlet spot, a segment, a semicircle, the whole disc. The red sky faded before the rising sun giving way to the advancing blue of the day. It was suddenly hot.

Yussuf pulled up his camel. Troy's beast walked in the length of the lead rein. Ben could see nothing. He stopped alongside the Negro. They were there. Below and beyond was a vast canyon, round, five miles across its diameter, a thousand feet deep at its mid-point. Down there, specks moved on the yellow sand. People and animals.

Yussuf urged his camel over the crest and down the slope. Ben followed. All his fatigue drained away with the new sights. Three-quarters of the perimeter of the gorge was steeply sloping sand. The rest was a vertical cliff of black stone. As they neared the bottom, Troy caught the smell of scented clover. He searched the sand. There were the little sap-filled desert plants, there was broom and clover, tamarisk and camel thorn. There were outcrops of rock layered with moss. It all meant water, lots of water, but there was none to be seen. It must be underneath, close enough to be seeping up and nourishing the plants. He saw the black camels, the whole sacred herd, with some recent additions. Other camels, too, and goats. He could smell the dried dung cooking fires. There they were, almost invisible close to the base of the black crag. And tents. Rows and rows of Bedu tents. The old fox of the desert had hidden his army well.

The lead camel stopped. Ben searched ahead for a sight of the man he had come to meet. Yussuf slipped to the ground and brought Troy's beast to its knees. Ben flexed his muscles, suddenly aware of the stiffness of the long journey, concerned that he should not collapse on the sand when the weight came on his cramped legs. He swung one leg over the saddle and slid to the ground, holding on with one hand to steady himself. Yussuf pointed. Ben walked slowly forward, stiff, uncomfortable.

A tall figure stepped out of the shadow of the cliff. They stopped a few yards apart. They were very polite, exchanging greetings in the desert fashion.

Then Rasul stepped close and stared at his visitor. He was lean, hardened by months in the desert, his beard greyer than Ben remembered, his eyes sunk deeper under bushy brows. He looked as forbidding and unforgiving as his reputation.

He spoke slowly, precisely, in English. 'Mr Troy, I presume.' Then he laughed. It was an old, secret joke.

CHAPTER NINE

THE ADJUTANT shook Negley awake. 'Sir. Colonel Negley, sir.'
The colonel opened his eyes wide, then screwed them up
against the light from the bulb above his head. 'Yes. What is it?'
He propped himself up on an elbow.
'I thought I should call you, sir. I thought you'd want to know.'
'Come on, man. What is it I'd want to know?'
'It's about Doctor Shaw, sir.'
Negley sat up straight and swung his legs over the edge of
the bed. He had been using the camp bed in his office ever since
the emergency started. It seemed appropriate to active service.
'What happened? Where is she? Is she all right?' He was wide
awake, on his feet and pulling on his clothes.
'One of the patrols spotted her surgery truck, sir. It was burn-
ing. They landed and . . .'
'Is she all right? Is she . . .' He could not say it.
'She's alive, sir. In a bit of a mess. The chopper's bringing her
in now. I've called an ambulance.'
The colonel was dressed. He ran his fingers through his hair
and pressed them into his ears as if he wanted to hear no more.
'Did they catch them?'
'Who, sir?'
'The bastards who did it, you fool.'
'I don't understand, sir.'
'The Shotras, man. Bloody savages, the lot of them. Get a
company together. Two helicopters. I'll find them. I'll teach the
bastards a lesson they won't forget.'
'You mean, sir, that you think the Shotras attacked Doctor
Shaw? The patrol said nothing. I assumed it had been an
accident.'
'Why'd you assume that?'
'It seemed the obvious cause, sir. But . . . you may be right.'
'Of course I'm right. I never did trust that lot. Bad; bad
through and through. Get the men together, Captain.'
'Yes, sir.' He turned, then turned back. 'The chopper will be
here in five or ten minutes, sir. You might like to see how the
doctor is. And the patrol can give us the exact location.'
Negley nodded and walked out on to the parade ground and
across towards the landing pad. He lit a cigarette, puffed at it
once or twice, threw it down and stamped on it. I knew it. I
knew it would happen. I sensed it. I should have forbidden these
trips into the desert. Bloody savages. He lit another cigarette.

God, I hope she's all right. At least she's alive. But hurt. How badly? Shot, burned, bones broken, stabbed? God maybe raped. Please God, not that. But that's what they do. It's happened before. Last year. That woman walking on the coast. She was raped. By a Shotra, too. Bloody savages. His hands were shaking. He dropped the cigarette. He stamped it out, two, three, four times, sinking his boot into the sand. I'll make them pay. I'll hunt them down, every last one of them. I'll flog them, I'll flay them alive, I'll teach them. He was shaking all over as if burned up by fever. He could not rid his mind of the imagined rape.

The adjutant was beside him. 'The men are assembling, sir. The choppers will be ready in about ten minutes.'

The colonel nodded.

'Here's the ambulance, sir.'

It ran out and stopped close by. The ambulance men got out, opened the rear doors and readied a stretcher.

'Here they come,' said Negley, pointing. The helicopter was coming in low from the south east. It seemed to take an age. Come on, come on, hurry up. It was over the airfield, lowering all the time, over the pad, stopped, hovering, settling down on the concrete. Negley was up at the door before it was opened.

The lieutenant in charge of the patrol was first out. 'G'morning, sir.'

'How is she? Doctor Shaw?'

'She's just come round, sir. She was lucky. It was a nasty accident.'

'Accident?'

'Yes, sir. Didn't you hear? Her truck turned over. Went on fire. It's a complete write-off.'

'Oh. I thought . . . I thought maybe she'd been attacked. The Shotras, you know.'

'No, sir. Nothing like that. She'd been with them. She must have been on her way back. They told us she'd been there. Problem birth, something like that. They were very pleased. They're not a bad lot really. A bit smelly but quite decent. They just like to be left alone.'

'I see.' The colonel was stuck for words. 'But she's not badly hurt?'

'Well, I'm not a doctor, sir. She's been knocked about a bit, of course. But I think she'll be all right. Here's the stretcher now.'

The colonel stepped back. He was suddenly conscious of his emotional reaction to the news. He watched the men transferring her from stretcher to stretcher and carrying her to the ambulance. Only her head was visible. A stained wound dressing was bound round it. He stepped farther back. Doors slammed and the ambulance drove off.

'Captain. I'll be at the hospital if you need me.'

'Yes, sir. Don't worry sir. I'm sure she's not too badly hurt.'

Negley nodded and started walking towards his jeep.

'Sir. Will I dismiss the men?'

'The men?'

'The company you ordered, sir. To chase up the Shotras.'

'Yes, yes, stand them down. You were right. It was an accident.'

The colonel drove slowly to the hospital. He was very ashamed. He had to wait more than an hour before the surgeon saw him.

'Sorry to keep you waiting, John.'

'How is she?'

'Much better. Quite cheeky now. She's being rude about my stitching.'

'Oh.'

'She was quite lucky. Broken leg, bruised ribs, cut forehead, and burned hands. It could have been a lot worse.'

'It sounds bad enough.'

'That's nothing to Sue. She's as strong as a horse.'

'Yes, yes, I suppose she is. Well, thanks for letting me know. I'll be off now.' He turned away.

'Don't you want to see her?'

'No, I . . . I don't suppose she's fit to have visitors yet.'

'Maybe not but she knows you're here. She'll make my life hell if you don't go in.'

Negley nodded. 'If you're sure it's all right.'

'Come on. I'll show you the way.' He stopped at the door of her room. 'Not too long, John. And for goodness sake, cheer up.'

The colonel took a few deep breaths before knocking and opening the door. 'Hallo, Susan. Can I come in?'

'John. It's good to see you. I can't see you very well, in fact. I've lost my specs. Take a pew.'

He sat down beside the bed. There was an uncovered line of stitches on her brow and both her hands were swathed in bandages. 'You gave us quite a scare, Susan.'

'I gave myself quite a scare, too. It's my own fault. I shouldn't drive so fast.'

'No.' There was an awkward pause. 'Susan, I . . . I wanted to tell you something.'

'Good.'

'I'm . . . I'm going to retire when this trouble's over. I'm thinking of going to Australia or maybe South Africa, somewhere like that.'

'Good for you, John.'

'Em . . . I don't know how to say this but I wondered, I wondered if you might come with me.'

'You could say, "Let's get married."'

'Yes, yes, I suppose I could.'

'Well?'

He swallowed and dried his palms on his shirt. 'Susan, let's get married.'

'That's a jolly good idea, John. Let's do that.'

He put his head down, his lips on her plump left arm. There were tears in his eyes.

She smiled and stretched over her other bandaged hand and patted him gently on the back.

Kassim was not amused.

He had thought nothing of it when Troy did not turn up for last evening's conference. He knew he had gone down to South Base. Banner and Troy were good friends. They would be catching up on each other's news. But when Ben did not appear as usual after breakfast, Kassim started asking around.

No, Mr Troy wasn't at South Base. He had been yesterday. He'd left sometime in the afternoon. No, he did not say where he was going. Presumably back to Qashran City.

No, Mr Troy was not at the Residency. He'd gone to South Base yesterday morning and had not returned. No, he had left no message.

No, Mr Troy was not at the club last night. Mr Troy very seldom visited the club. Certainly not last night.

Kassim toyed with the idea of an accident. He rejected it. Then he wondered about abduction. That was more likely. If the plan had been to upset the British enough to get troops into Qashran, they might have kidnapped Troy Sahib. But the troops were already in. He rejected that idea and faced the suspicion growing in his mind. Yes, that was the answer. He had gone out into the desert to meet Rasul. The young sheikh was very angry. He did not doubt that Troy had his reasons for going. He did not seriously doubt that these reasons were genuine, even far sighted. He did not doubt that he would come back safely. The Bedu did not stab their guests in the back, not even with good cause. Kassim was livid at Troy taking such a step without so much as a by-your-leave. As if he, Troy, was running Qashran. It was an attitude Kassim had worked hard to change. He was angry to discover he had failed.

He phoned the barracks.

'I'm sorry, Your Highness, Colonel Negley's not here. Can I pass him a message?'

'That depends where he is. Is he in the city or out in the desert?'

'He's down at the hospital, sir.'

'What's the matter with him?'

'Nothing, sir. It's Doctor Shaw. She had an accident this morning.'

'An accident? I've heard nothing about this. Was it bad?'

'Bad enough, Your Highness. Her truck crashed out in the desert. She was lucky. I'm sure she'll be fine in a few days.'

'I hope so. Just tell the colonel to come and see me when he's free.' He put down the phone and scribbled a note to send Susan some flowers. Then he called Kirk and asked him to come at once.

Kassim was at the window when the major arrived. 'The city seems very quiet, Major. Congratulations.'

'Thank you, sir.'

'I've got a little job for you.'

'Yes, sir.'

'I want you to put some of your men on the helicopter patrols along the southern border. This area here, just north of the singing sands.' He pointed it out on a wall map. 'Colonel Negley will co-operate.'

'May I ask why you want my men there, Your Highness?'

'This job is, how can I put it, yes, diplomatic. It's better that my own troops are not involved.' He took a few steps across the room, then came back to face Kirk. 'Mr Troy is down there somewhere in the sands having a pow-wow with my Uncle Rasul.'

'I say. Isn't that dangerous?'

'Not for Mr Troy, Major. I'm not quite sure how it might turn out for me.'

Kirk looked puzzled.

'He'll come back through this area today, tomorrow, the next day. Maybe during the night. He'll almost surely be on a camel and he'll be wearing Bedu clothes. So you check every Bedu you see down there.'

'That's understood, sir. And when we find him?'

Kassim flashed a grim smile. 'When you find him, Major, you bring him back here. Under close arrest.

It was not only the water that was reviving Troy. That certainly was a joy, to be steeping in hot water, feeling his tired muscles relax, cleaning away the sand of the night's journey which had seeped into every crevice of his body. It was unusual enough, unheard of, to be offered a bath in the desert. The Bedu had more respect for water than to wash in it. But it was the other circumstances that excited Ben. The warmth of his welcome by Rasul. And the fantastic surroundings he found himself in.

A few yards away the Empty Quarter baked under the cruel sun. Here, in this vast cavern inside the basalt mountain, it was cool, the air damp, the whole place echoing the sounds of running water. Not the dripping water of caves anywhere but the roar and splash and gurgle of a torrent. Not seen, just heard, from far under the floor of the cave. At first it had just been startling, so unlikely that he shook himself to make sure he was awake, not still held in the dreamlike fatigue of the night. Then as he took it all in, surprise turned to wonder. The bath in which he lay was gouged out of the solid rock, raised high above the floor like an altar in a temple. The walls were smooth, shaped by man, decorated by man with much carving, telling tales so old as only to be hinted at in legends. There was no doubt in Ben's mind that he was in some ancient temple of some very ancient city. Outside, deep under the sand, there must be relics of that ancient city, buildings, tools, pottery, carving. Here was the site of one of the great lost cities of Arabia. Before the time of the desert, when the climate was kind and the land was fertile. Troy's father would gladly have given his right arm to be in that place.

Ben was intrigued, almost overcome, but it was the running water that fascinated him most. Here was the secret which let Rasul keep an army where no army could be kept. Even that was insignificant. What mattered was that here, maybe, was the first proof that under the desert lay a vast reservoir of water which could transform Arabia more quickly and more radically than all its reserves of oil. Just as in the Sahara where the oil men had found a limitless underground lake. Maybe destined like that Saharan lake to lie untapped while the politicians squabbled about who owned the water. It was like trying to decide who owned the air men breathed. Ben shook himself to try and cast off the spell the cave had put on him. Smells of cooking drifted in from outside. There was more immediate work to be done. It was a long time since he had faced the kind of gargantuan feast the old sheikh was preparing in his honour. That was part of the price of his journey.

He put on the fresh clothes laid ready for him and followed Yussuf out into the suffocating heat of the sand valley. In the great tent, all Rasul's men were assembled eyeing the array of food with ill-concealed relish. The sheikh put Troy at his right hand and thanked Allah for this meeting of old friends and for the food. The eating began. For a few minutes there was only the sound of hungry jaws.

Rasul tore off a choice piece of camel meat and offered it to Ben. He took it and nibbled.

The old man wolfed down several mouthfuls, the juices

spilling out of his mouth and down over his beard. 'What is wrong, Troy Sahib? Is the meat not to your taste?'

'It is delicious. It is just that the singing sands charm the ear but dull the appetite.'

Rasul thought about that then slapped Troy on the back. 'You have become a poet. How is that? You were never a poet before. Why has my absence put silver on your tongue? Is my nephew, Kassim, such an inspiration to you?'

'Kassim is not a poet, Your Highness. But he is a good sheikh. He does well by his people.'

'You have courage to speak like this. He spurns the faith. He is not Wahhabi.'

'He treats with the world beyond Qashran. There are many faiths. He was not brought up in the land of his birth.'

'That is true. Now I understand. I have lived in these lands of puny faith.' He ate for a minute or two. 'And why have you come this long journey?'

'I came to meet an old friend, to make my peace, maybe to make a greater peace.'

'That is good. That I understand. I, too, am here to make a greater peace. My peace with Allah, The Compassionate, The Merciful, King of the Last Judgement.'

Ben said nothing. He finished the meat and rolled some rice into a ball in his fingers.

'Why do you look at me so, Troy Sahib? Are you surprised that the teeth of an old man can still chew the meat of the camel?'

'No. I have learned much of the strength of Rasul's teeth these last few days.'

The sheikh grinned. 'Yes, you have indeed become a poet.'

'The sheikh's teeth have spilled much blood and given much pain. When will his belly be full?'

'Soon. You can tell me how soon.' He leaned closer. 'When will Mr Banner put out the fire at his oil well?'

'Maybe tomorrow. Maybe the next day. Maybe not until the next moon.'

'The day after tomorrow. That will be very good.' The old man stared out of the far end of the tent at the sweep of golden sand.

'It is said in the city that when the Great Djinn descends into the ground from whence it came, then Rasul and The Honoured Ones will rise up from the singing sands and sweep the infidels from Qashran.'

Rasul nodded. 'It is good that this is said.'

'But it is not true, old friend. You are not old beyond the age of reason. You know my people have their soldiers in Qashran.

You know that black camels and rifles will not defeat machine guns and armoured cars and aeroplanes.'

'It is a very Christian view that you must win battles to be victorious.'

Ben stretched out and plucked off a handful of meat. He was suddenly hungry. He chewed slowly and looked round the munching, grabbing, babbling company.

'Are you looking for remembered faces?' asked Rasul.

'It is said in the city that Sheikh Rasul has friends who are not Bedu and not Wahhabi.'

'One friend, other than you, my friend. He is not here. You will meet him later. I am displeased with him.'

'Why are you displeased? He did well at Qashran One. He has done well in the city.'

'It is nothing. It will pass by the time the sun sets. You are right. He has done well.' Rasul belched and tore off some more meat. 'Troy Sahib, we will plan my last battle together.'

'When you ride up out of the singing sands, Your Highness, we will be enemies again.'

'Of course. But I am offering you victory. I only wish to ensure that that victory is swift and complete.'

'Never can there have been such a council of war.'

'That is good, my friend. It is always good to be first. Now listen.' He pulled aside a rug and scratched in the sand. He showed Troy where he planned to cross the border, where he planned to make his camp. He marked the spot where the battle should take place. He reminded him of the customs of Bedu warfare. He wanted everything to be exactly right.

Ben watched and listened carefully. It was an elaborately planned mass suicide. It was what he had begun to suspect before he set out on his journey. He had come to stop it.

'Is this why you came back from exile? Is this all that the great Sheikh Rasul's war has been for?'

'Troy Sahib, I am an old man. I was not happy in that foreign land of mountains and water and snow. I came back to die in my own land. I came back to die as all my family have died. This land is changing. The whole desert is changing. There may never be another great Wahhabi Sheikh. Death comes to all of us, sooner or later. Surely it is better to die with honour than to live with shame.'

'Is it not possible that honour can be shameful?'

Rasul smiled. 'It is a joy to talk with you. You have lost none of that sharp wit. I remember many of our good times together.'

'I am not playing games with words. If you wish to die, that is your affair.' He held out his hand to the company. 'Do all these

men also have to die to satisfy your selfish whim? And what about
the legend of The Honoured Ones? They can come to no harm
in battle on the sacred black camels of Qashran. Have you told
them that the legend is not true? Have you told them that they
are going to die the day after tomorrow?'

The old man's face darkened but he forced a smile. 'You will
not anger me, Troy Sahib. I know what you are trying to do. It
is what you have to do. It is what you had to do when you took
my people and my land from me. It is all part of what you told
me the great Lord Curzon said: "Your independence will continue to be upheld and the influence of the British Government
will remain supreme." It is a very good joke. If I had put off my
return for another year or two there would have been no infidel
soldiers for me to fight against. Not British infidels. Maybe
American infidels. Or Russian infidels.'

'It is you who play with words, Rasul. Your lifetime is a long
time in politics. Things change.'

'Well spoken. Everything changes.' He waved his hand round
the tent. 'What of those who do not want change? Must they
have change forced upon them? Look at these men you are afraid
for, Troy Sahib. Look at them. None of them is young, they are
all in middle life, or old like me. They are Bedu. They do not
want change. They don't want to dig holes in the sand or screw
nuts on bolts. They don't want to go to school like small children.
They do not want to work in factories or offices. Speak not to
them of death. They are already dead. They have been here for
months, waiting, waiting willingly, without their women. They
will follow where I lead them. They are proud to be The
Honoured Ones. The legend is not false. It does not speak of
death. What real harm can come to a Wahhabi when he knows
he is assured a place in Paradise?'

Ben did not try to answer. 'You will not give up this folly?'

Rasul shook his head and smiled.

'Then it is agreed,' said Troy. 'I will do as you ask. I will bring
my people's soldiers when the time comes.'

The old man nodded. 'That is good. Give me your hand, Troy
Sahib. And look me in the eyes.' They stared at each other for a
long time. Then Rasul smiled. 'It is good. I know you will bring
the soldiers. I trust you. I know you will keep your word and I
also know you will try to cheat me. But this time I must win. All
the moves are mine.'

'So it seems.'

The sheikh clapped his hands. 'Now we will drink coffee
together. Then you must rest. Tonight you must go back to
Qashran and make ready for my last battle.'

The coffee tasted bitter in Ben's mouth. Rasul was right. All the moves were his. He was going to get his glorious death at the hands of the infidel soldiers. Major Kirk would be delighted. The old man was right too in thinking Troy would try to cheat him of his place in Paradise. Ben saw no hope of succeeding. It was an impossible task. The impossible takes just a little longer. This time a little longer would be too late.

Yussuf woke him late in the afternoon. He had slept far better than he had thought likely. He had refused the sheikh's offer of his own tent, preferring the coolness of the cave. He had expected only to rest. He had too much to think about to sleep. But he had slept. He woke refreshed but cold. He shivered and hurried to reach the warmth of the sunlit gorge.

That first flash of heat at the narrow entrance did nothing to warm him. The view chilled him to the marrow. He recognized it. The Bedu were drawn up along the three sides of a square, facing inwards. Rasul stood alone at the midpoint of the fourth side. In the middle of the square the great scimitar stood upright in the sand, its blade gleaming and its jewelled hilt flashing in the sunlight. The scene was set for an execution.

Troy could not believe his eyes. He was walking out across the sand, Yussuf following. Yes, Yussuf's following. He has to be there. He's Rasul's executioner. Ben's stomach was in a cold tight knot. I was wrong about Rasul. I was wrong right from the beginning. All that talk this morning was just play acting. He's become a savage, a killer for the sake of killing. He's not even a Bedu any more. Just a wild, crazed animal. And I made him that. I betrayed him once. He's not going to trust me another time. Maybe he's right. This will make sure that he gets his battle with Q Force. He didn't need me to arrange it. He needed my head to bait the trap.

He stopped in front of the sheikh. The old man's face was stern, unfriendly. Ben held his gaze. He could feel his wildly beating heart. He tried desperately not to think of death on his knees in the sand. He forced away the well remembered scenes. He had never enjoyed executions. He had never thought to look out at that expectant square from the centre. It was odd. He found himself thinking of Helen and the boys, now men. That was unexpected. The pictures faded and gave way to Rasul's dark eyes and cruel mouth.

The picture changed. Rasul was grinning, then laughing, rocking back and forward where he stood, convulsed with mirth, gasping to catch his breath. Troy gaped.

The old man stretched out his hands and supported himself

on Ben's shoulders. 'Troy Sahib, Troy Sahib.' He could barely
speak through his laughter. 'Troy Sahib, what have I done that
you have so little faith in me?' He leaned his head on Troy's
shoulder and gasped for breath. 'You thought this was for you.
You thought . . . you thought I would kill you when you were
my guest.'

The whole canyon echoed with the laughter of all the Bedu.
It was very funny.

Ben's heart was still racing madly. He closed his eyes and
strained to keep his voice steady. 'I am a great fool. I had forgotten
how much Your Highness enjoyed a joke.'

'You are not angry? I did not frighten you too much?'

Ben shook his head.

'Good. Then stand here beside me and see how Rasul punishes
a coward.'

Ben had not seen the man being marched out. He was tall, well
built, his hair cropped close to his head. He was stripped to the
waist, his hands tied behind his back. He wore khaki uniform
slacks and half-boots. His guards stopped him in front of the
sheikh.

'Troy Sahib, this is the friend you asked me about this morning.
His name is Hamid Babrah. He is an Arab but he is not a Bedu.
He does not understand. He wanted me to kill you. He said it
would make your people angry.' He turned to his prisoner. 'Look
now at the friend you would have had me murder.'

Babrah stared at Troy. He had hated the British for a very
long time. He spat in Ben's face.

Rasul's camel stick smashed his jaw and dropped him on the
sand. The guards picked him up and dragged him out to the
centre of the square. Yussuf walked behind them.

Ben spoke. 'Rasul, you must not kill this man on my account.'

'He is not dying because of his ignorance. He is dying for his
cowardice.' The sheikh stepped forward and held up his hands.
'Hear me. Hear me.' The crowd was silent. 'This wretch was
offered great honour. He was invited to ride as one of us, The
Honoured Ones of Qashran. He refused that honour. He who
was so brave when the enemy was far away, he did not want to
risk his neck with us when we rise up out of the singing sands
and sweep the infidel soldiers from our land. He is branded as
a coward. He has no right to live.'

Babrah was on his knees in the sand, his body thrust forward
to expose his neck. Yussuf held the great sword in both hands.
Troy shut his eyes. He thought he heard the swish of the blade.
He did hear the roar of the Bedu. He opened his eyes.

Rasul took his arm and turned him away. 'Now you must go,

old friend.' The camels were waiting, saddled, couched. 'You will remember our bargain.'

'Have no fear. The soldiers will be there.'

One of the men handed Rasul a saddle bag. 'Take this back as a gift for Colonel Negley. It is all Babrah's papers. The colonel will be able to find much of interest in them.' Yussuf was there, holding Babrah's head by an ear. Rasul opened another bag and the head was dropped in. 'Take this as a gift for my nephew, Kassim. Together they prove that I was unwilling to use help other than Bedu help. Maybe they will convince them that what you tell them is true, that all I want is to die with honour in my own land.'

It was a silent parting. Everything was said in the strength of their grip and the look in their eyes. They had known each other very well for half a lifetime.

Troy did not look back down into the sand valley when the camels reached the crest and he could see again the dark smear of the fire at Qashran One above the horizon. He felt sick. It was not the food gorged that morning on an empty stomach, it was not the fright of waking to walk out into that threatening square, it was not the revulsion at the grisly trophy dangling from his saddle. It was the knowledge that Rasul's joke had backfired. Ben now knew for sure how to keep his word and still betray his old friend.

CHAPTER TEN

THE HELICOPTER spotted him before he was a mile inside the border. For the last few hours of his journey through the dunes Ben had watched the flares dropping as the patrols searched. He had expected that. He would have been disappointed not to see them. He was very tired. He looked forward to exchanging his perch on top of his camel for the noisy rapture of one of the planes.

It was morning twilight when Yussuf stopped just short of the border. A plane whirled by not more than a mile away. The light was uncertain, strong enough to make the flares useless, not strong enough to reveal the travellers. The plane passed, Yussuf pointed out the route for the last quarter mile up on to the hard sand of the plateau. For Ben the journey was almost over. The Negro faced a gruelling return in the stifling heat of the day. He was barely polite in parting. He did not have his master's faith in the Englishman.

Up on the hard sand Troy prayed for the helicopter to return. It was not just the fatigue. Time was the enemy. There was a lot to do. But he did know that now he would be in time. Ahead the flaming pillar of Qashran One reassured him. Banner had not yet tamed the well.

The helicopter was back, dropping towards him, inspecting him, circling, ready to land. A metallic voice from a hailer was telling him to halt. He hauled the camel to a stop, pulled off his headdress and waved. The plane hovered. The camel struggled against the reins, terrified at the roaring monster in the sky. Ben let it turn away and walk a few paces. It calmed enough to let him slide to the ground. He unhooked the saddle bags and tied up the reins. The beast accepted its freedom and loped off across the sand with a peculiar grace for something so ugly.

The aircraft was down, its rotors still whirling, throwing up a cloud of fine dust. Ben walked slowly towards it, grimacing at the pain in his legs and back. He was surprised to see Kirk running crouched through the dust cloud.

'Good morning, Major,' he shouted above the din of the engine.

'Mr Troy, I have orders to place you under arrest.'

'Thank God for that,' bawled Ben.

'Sir?'

'I said "Thank God for that." I couldn't have taken much more on that camel. Let's get on board.' He walked to the plane and slung in his saddle bags. Two soldiers heaved him inside.

Kirk clambered in and slammed the door. The noise was still there but much less. Troy found himself a space and sat down on the floor. Kirk stood over him, hanging on to the roof like a rush hour commuter on the London Tube. Ben gazed up at him and smiled. All you need is a bowler hat, *The Times*, and a brolly instead of that popgun.

The major had mixed feelings. 'I'm sorry about this, sir, but the sheikh insisted.'

'Don't worry. I'm glad of the lift. If you're using the radio tell the sheikh I want a hot bath, some fresh clothes and a pot of coffee.'

'I think I should warn you, Mr Troy. The sheikh is very angry.'

'I expected that. He'll simmer down. I've got good news for him. Good news for you too, Major.'

'Really, sir.'

Ben nodded. 'You're going to fight a battle, Major.' Kirk was alert, like a pointer with a scent. 'Not your kind of battle. A Bedu battle.'

'I only know one kind of battle, sir. That's the kind one wins.'

Ben grinned. 'That's a very Christian attitude.'

'Pardon, sir?'

'Nothing. Forget it. It was just something someone said to me recently.' Ben dropped his chin on to his chest and pretended to doze. It could be fun baiting Kirk but it never lasted. The man was too predictable. Ben watched the major's legs disappear from view as he moved up the plane to talk to Qashran City on the radio. Good. Now I can concentrate on what needs doing.

Troy's head was clear, his wits sharp, the fatigue of the night dispelled. First he would check with Carl Banner. The dousing of Qashran One dictated the whole timetable. There's a thought. What if Carl fails to put out the fire? It could burn for weeks, months. Carl said that himself. While it burns, Rasul will stay down there beyond the sands. Now Babrah's dead and all his secrets are in that saddle bag, the trouble in the city could be finished. And if the troubles were over, there would be no need for Q Force. Whitehall would not leave Kirk here a minute longer than necessary. So the fire could burn, the sabotage and the killing stop, the troops leave, and I'd have failed to keep my promise. Worse than that, the old sheikh won't stay marooned in his secret base for ever. He'll quickly find a new reason to cross the sands. Without Q Force the result could be in doubt. Rasul might then achieve the glorious death he longs for. He might even win. Ben shook his head. That mustn't happen. Carl must succeed.

He pushed away these doubts and thought again about his plan. He had thought about it on and off through the long night. It could go wrong. There were so many factors. But if it succeeded it would destroy a host of legends. It might even make Whitehall change its mind. More important, it might guarantee peace through the whole of Trucial Oman for a long time to come.

He felt no guilt about betraying his old friend. The revulsion at what he had to do had faded with each passing minute since he had looked out from the top of that sand valley and fought off the sickness knotting his stomach. For Troy the choice had been between a people's need for a new life in an ancient land and one man's craving for glory and salvation. There was really no choice.

The major's legs were back in view. 'Mr. Troy.'

Ben looked up.

'We're landing in five minutes, sir.'

Ben nodded. Good. Let's get on with the dirty business.

There was bad news for Kirk at the airport. In the two hours before dawn there had been a fresh rash of incidents. An explosion at the power station—no serious damage; an explosion and a fire at the new *suk* where Q Force had its headquarters—several casualties, none fatal; half a dozen fire bombs at widely scattered points through the city; and some sniping. The major was grim faced in the car to the Corporation building. He had thought he had mopped up all the trouble. He now knew his show of force had only sent the saboteurs to ground, to rethink and replan.

Kassim was waiting in the conference room. Colonel Negley was with him. The sheikh took his time before speaking. He ignored Troy's greeting, just stood there looking at him, at the Bedu clothes, at the desert dust still coating his face like a thick layer of make-up. He shifted his eyes past his prisoner. 'Thank you, Major. Now maybe you should get together with the colonel. There's been more trouble in the city.'

'I've just heard, sir. I'll get on to it right away.'

'This might help,' said Ben, throwing one of the saddle bags on to the table.

They all looked at it, looked back at him.

Kassim's voice was hard. 'Don't tell me you're still on my side, Mr Troy. What is it? A gift from my dear uncle?'

'That's right. But not for you, Kassim. That's for the colonel.'

'Really.' The sheikh turned to Negley. 'You're in luck. Your first wedding present, Colonel. Do be careful. It's probably a booby trap.' He looked again at Troy. 'Surprised, Mr Troy? Of course, you won't have heard. You've been away. The colonel is getting married.'

Ben smiled. 'Congratulations, John. When did this happen?'

'Yesterday, just yesterday. Susan had an accident, you see.'

Ben failed to see the connection but he did not pursue it. 'I see. Well, congratulations to you both. When's the ceremony? Or have I missed that too?'

'No, no. There's no rush. We wondered if you would be the best man. It's going to be very quiet, just a few . . .'

'As you say, Colonel,' broke in Kassim, 'there's no rush about your matrimonial plans. There is some urgency about the new trouble in the city. Let's see what Rasul sent you.'

'Yes, of course, I'm sorry.' Negley opened the bag and tipped the contents on to the table.

The sheikh wanted the information quickly. 'What is it, Mr Troy?'

'I haven't seen it myself. It belonged to a gentleman called Hamid Babrah. He was Rasul's expert. He has quite a reputation for revolutions, guerilla warfare, sabotage, that kind of thing. He's been mentioned in intelligence reports for some years.'

'You say he *was* Rasul's expert. Was that a slip of the tongue?'

'No.'

'Where is he now? How did you get these papers?'

Negley and Kirk were leafing through the books.

Ben gave a twisted little smile. 'I got them from Rasul. As

to where Babrah is, you might say he's with us now, in a disembodied sort of way.'

'I'm in no mood for your jokes.'

'My apologies, Your Highness. By the way, your uncle sent
you a present too.'

Kassim said nothing.

Troy walked up to the table and emptied the second saddle
bag. Babrah's head bounced and rolled on the polished surface.
It came to rest on its left ear, the smashed jaw setting the mouth
in a lecherous grin. The smell of decay spread throughout the
room.

Kassim stepped back. He was suddenly very pale, a hand up
at his mouth, fighting to control the heaving in his stomach.
The two soldiers were stooped over the table, their eyes fixed
on the head, the papers and code books forgotten.

'This is, or rather was, Hamid Babrah,' said Ben. 'He displeased your uncle.'

The sheikh stared at the head and fought for control. 'Get
rid of it,' he said quietly. 'At once.'

Ben scooped the head into the saddle bag. 'Where will I put
it, Your Highness? Will I have it spiked on top of the palace
gates? Or have you gone off severed heads?'

'Get rid of it,' Kassim shouted.

Troy held the bag out. 'John, would you give this to that
policeman outside the door?'

Negley took the bag gingerly and carried it away.

The sheikh had control of himself again. His voice was cold
with anger. 'I hope you have a very good explanation, Mr Troy.
I am very close to the limit of my patience.'

'I'm sorry, Kassim, but all I did was deliver Rasul's present.
It had a purpose. It's an earnest of his good faith. He wanted
you to know that what I have to tell you is true.'

'That, for instance, I'm related to a savage who enjoys cutting
people's heads off.'

'No, not that. Babrah lost his head for two reasons. First,
Rasul did not need him any more. More important, Babrah
refused a place among The Honoured Ones when they come
back into Qashran.'

'So they are coming back.'

'Oh yes. As soon as the fire is out at Qashran One. The rumour
was not so much a rumour as an announcement.'

Kassim thought for a few moments. 'So Babrah was killed for
not wanting to be killed.'

'That's one way of putting it.'

'It's the only way. You said yourself that The Honoured Ones would be massacred in a battle with Q Force.' He eyed Troy warily. 'Or has your journey changed your mind on that?'

'Excuse me, Your Highness.' It was Negley.

'What is it?'

'These papers, sir. They're very important.'

'Are they? I'd forgotten about them. What's so important about them?'

'Well, sir, they're code books and supply lists and operational orders. They'll tell us a great deal when we've studied them. But this is the vital thing. It lists all Babrah's contacts here in the city.'

The sheikh turned back to Ben. 'Well, Mr Troy, your journey seems to have been profitable. I wonder what the price of it was. There was a price, I suppose. You didn't get all this for nothing.'

Ben smiled slowly but Negley spoke again before he could say anything. 'It's fantastic, Your Highness. Quite unbelievable.'

'What is it now, Colonel?' Kassim was getting annoyed again.

'According to this the key man here in the city is Sallal.'

'Sallal? Should I know the name?'

'Doctor Sallal, sir. The dentist.'

Kassim's eyes widened. 'Good heavens. Are you sure? He stopped one of my teeth last week.'

'Maybe you should have it checked,' suggested Ben. 'He could have popped a time bomb in it.' His flippancy came from his surprise. Sallal.

Kassim ignored him. 'Right, gentlemen. To business. I want everyone on this list picked up. You'll help with Q Force, of course, Major. I suggest you both make your plans for one time, say early afternoon, and make all the arrests within minutes of that time. That should cut down any chance of not catching the lot.'

'Good thinking, sir.'

'Thank you, Major.' The sarcasm was strong. 'I won't keep you, gentlemen. The best of luck. Keep me in touch with developments.'

When they had gone, he walked round the huge table and came up to Ben. 'I apologize, Troy Sahib.'

'What for? You've done nothing wrong. You reacted exactly as I expected.'

'That's bad. I shouldn't be so predictable. Why didn't you tell me where you were going?'

'You'd have forbidden it.'

'That's true. I'd have had no choice. What about the answers to these unanswered questions?'

Ben shook his head. 'Not now. Now I want a bath and some fresh clothes.'

'Of course. Upstairs to the penthouse. You know your way around. There are clothes there. I had your man bring some round.'

'Good. I wondered if you planned to sling me in jail in these things.'

'You should know me better than that, Troy Sahib. I always give my condemned prisoners one last request.'

Ben grinned. 'One more, please. And it's very important. Can you get a message to Carl Banner at South Base? Tell him I'm back and that he's not to do anything about snuffing that fire till he hears from me.'

Kassim nodded. 'So he knew where you were all the time. And you seem to know something about that fire that I don't know.'

'He hopes to have it out by tomorrow.'

'That's good. That's great. That's well within my time limit. I'm going to look a fool. I've been peppering Inoco in New York with cables demanding an expert. They've been trying very hard. They think they might be able to find one for next week.' He picked up a phone. 'You go and sluice the sand off. I'll send your message down to Banner.'

Ben had a shower first, then lay and steeped in a tub of very hot water. His tired body relaxed but his brain relaxed too, his memory playing tricks with him as he struggled to resist the threatening flood of fatigue. He was not in that white tub in the penthouse of a skyscraper in Qashran City; he was stretched out in front of an ancient altar of black stone in one of the long forgotten cities of Arabia. The round globe set in the roof was not a light; it was the glaring sun beating down on the endless sands of the Empty Quarter. The water soothing and supporting and moving his body was not water; it was the lurching back of a camel. The green tiles glistening with the condensing steam were not green tiles; they were the lush fields of England in spring. The music on the radio in the next room was not man-made music; it was the melancholy dirge of the singing sands. That face in the door was not the face of Kassim's valet; it was Rasul's face, then Babrah's, then there was no face because there was no head, just a headless trunk spouting blood across the sand. That brought him to. The face at the door was Kassim's valet. Troy's clothes were laid out next door and would he like toast with his coffee? He nodded and pulled himself up out of the bath. He went back into the shower and shivered himself awake under needles of cold water at high pressure.

His long-delayed breakfast was set on the patio. The shades

cut out the glare of the sun and an intricate arrangement of baffles trapped and directed the warm turbulent air at the top of the skyscraper. Ben did not feel hungry. He drank two cups of coffee then found a sudden appetite and ate all the toast. The sheikh arrived as he was pouring a third cup.

'Have you left any for me? I see there's a spare cup.'

Ben poured. 'It's the biggest and best pot of coffee I've ever seen.'

'Thank you.' He stirred in sugar. 'Was it a long journey? Has he got a real base down there?'

'It was long. It seemed longer. I'm out of practice on camels. He's certainly got a base. I still can't really believe it. There's water down there that sounds like a young brother of Niagara.' He told Kassim of the sand valley and the basalt mountain, of the cave and the water and the carving.

The sheikh listened carefully. 'It's a pity it's in Saudi territory. But as you say, it may be proof of a much greater store. Could you find this place again?'

'I might. But I couldn't find my way through the sands.'

'We could jump over them. A helicopter.'

'It's across the border, Kassim. Do you want to start a war?'

'We could be quick. Just long enough to get some water samples and rock chippings. Some survey data. It might give us a lead on where to look inside Qashran. This could be very important.'

Ben drained his cup and refilled it. 'You're worse than me, Kassim. Let's not think about the war you may start. We still have to finish the one we've already got.'

'That's true. But water on that scale, that's worth taking a few risks for.' He was excited. 'I'm glad you went, Troy Sahib.'

'Thank you.'

'Now tell me the answers you didn't give me downstairs.'

'What were the questions?'

'The first one was about cost. What did it cost you to get Babrah's papers?' His mouth tightened at the memory of that other Babrah relic but he said nothing.

'It cost me nothing,' Ben told him. 'But I suppose I got them because I gave Rasul a promise.'

'And the promise?'

'To arrange a battle with Q Force.'

'That leads on to the other question. Have you changed your mind about such a battle resulting in a massacre?'

'No.'

'So you promised to arrange a battle which will destroy Rasul and The Honoured Ones.'

'I promised to have Q Force at the appointed place at the appointed hour. I made no promise about the result.'

Kassim lay back in his chair and thought for a while. 'That's a Troyism if ever I heard one. Would you care to explain it?'

Ben drank his coffee and pushed the cup aside. 'I'll tell you how I see it. I've suspected it was this way right from the beginning. Now I'm sure.' He leaned forward in his chair. 'Rasul came back here to die. He's not sick except maybe sick in the mind as all old men are sick in the mind. He wants a sort of immortality. The only way he knows to get that is to die in battle defending the Wahhabi faith. Meeting Babrah started him off. Babrah had the expertise to get him back here, to supply him, to train his men, to organize sabotage here in the city. Babrah planned the whole thing with the idea of forcing you to ask for British troops. His strategy then would have been to keep them here for a long time, feeding them incidents which they would have to clean up, and in the cleaning up building themselves the kind of reputation that goes with cleaning up in the world today. Q Force and Britain would be discredited. You would be discredited because you would be what's known as an imperialist puppet or a capitalist stooge. Then, when they were ready, and it might have taken years, they would be ready for a real revolution. Having The Honoured Ones down in that desert base was shrewd. Babrah had Rasul's name behind him, he had a trained force that could be used to raid up into the desert, hit and run, wells, oases, herds. And he had the legend of The Honoured Ones. All good revolutionary stuff. But having Rasul caused problems. The old fox made a lot of the decisions. Study the pattern of his vengeance. South Base and particularly Qashran One. These he hated. But Banner was never attacked. Shops, offices, the old bazaar; most of these places had some connection with people who were here when he was exiled. But the only people who were attacked were Wahhabis who had deserted him. I wasn't attacked, you weren't attacked, Negley wasn't attacked. Old Sheikh Hithlan and the others, they were cut down in cold blood. The liquor store—that was an obvious choice for Rasul. Where he and Babrah fell out was when Q Force arrived. They had both planned for that but they had different reasons. Rasul wanted the British here not because they had deposed him but because they were convenient infidels and he saw his salvation in death in battle against the infidels. Babrah lost his head and you got his papers as an earnest of Rasul's good faith. The British were here, he had a promise of his last battle, everything else could now stop.'

Kassim shook his head. 'I suppose it's right but it's incredible.

For the first time in my life I'm sorry for the old chap. But he's got your promise. He trusts you. So I'll stand by you. You arrange with Major Kirk for the great Sheikh Rasul to have his death wish.'

'No.'

The sheikh took time to take that in. 'I see, yet I don't see. That "No" takes us back to your Troyism. You made no promise about the result of the battle. How can there be any doubt about the result?'

'Q Force will not fire a shot. Admiral Baston's planes will not loose off a single rocket. We will take Rasul alive.'

'You're mad, Ben. The sun's got at you. It's impossible.'

'You know what they say about the impossible out here.'

'Touché. How can you do it?'

'I'd rather not say. It might go wrong. I want you to trust me.'

'I trust you. Now tell me why. I don't see the point. Of course you cheat the old man of his glorious death. But you cheat me too. Once he's dead I can forget him and get back to running this country.'

'That's wishful thinking, Kassim. If Rasul dies with his men and his black camels under the Q Force guns, he creates a legend that will haunt this country for years to come. It will be used by every trouble maker from here to the Red Sea, the Indian Ocean and the Mediterranean. They won't be just revolutions, they'll be Holy Wars.'

'I see that. But won't the legends still grow if you take him alive and I lock him up for the rest of his life?'

'Not if we do it the right way.'

'And that is?'

'We take him and bring him back to his city. We take him into the square in front of his palace and put him in the stocks.'

'But these stocks aren't for criminals. They're only for restraining the crazy ones.'

'That's right. Not The Honoured Ones. The Crazy Ones. Moslems are kind to the crazy ones. They won't pelt him with rubbish or taunt him. They'll be sorry for him because he's lost his mind. They'll tell their children of his madness. And The Honoured Ones will have no honour left because we will round up every one of the sacred black camels of Qashran and we'll slaughter them and cook their flesh and have a great feast. The Honoured Ones will only have honour as a remembered taste in the bellies of the Bedu.'

Kassim got up from his chair and paced the patio. 'It's diabolical.' He came back and stood over Troy. 'Why? He is your friend. You were his guest just yesterday. Why?'

'The Rasul I knew and loved is already dead. This Rasul is just a selfish old man blinded by the imagined delights of Paradise. I won't give him his salvation at the price he asks.'

Kassim nodded slowly. 'I suppose you're right. I'll leave you to make your plans with Kirk and the admiral. I'll tell them that you're in charge. Will that do?'

'Thank you, Your Highness.'

'I don't want to sound ungrateful, Troy Sahib. I'm not. I know it's not going to be easy for you. But I rather hope you fail.'

CHAPTER ELEVEN

EVERYTHING WAS READY at Qashran One. Banner had only been waiting for daylight. Now the light was good, the sun well up in the east, striking in on his back. He did not feel its warmth. His bulldozer was stopped, its heat shield raised, a hundred yards from the blazing well. Here it was all heat and stench and gushing salt water hosing in from the dozers parked on either side. All the men were very expert now at keeping wet and keeping each other wet. They had had a lot of practice in the past ten days. This was the day they had been working towards. This was the day Carl Banner was going to try and snuff out the fire with one mighty puff from a quarter ton of high explosive.

They had done a dummy run yesterday with a drum of sand exactly the same weight as the charge. They had had their problems but that was what dummy runs were for. Today there had to be no problems or some of them might not come out alive.

Banner checked round. The two test rigs were spudded into the sand north and south of the wellhead, two hundred yards between them. The carrier wire ran through blocks at each derrick head down on to the winch drums. The wire's length lay on the sand between the rigs, passing close to the fiery gusher. When tightened it would rise up and be stretched right through the column of fire. That had to be left to the last moment. Even that wire would not last long in that flame. The men were manning the winches on the rigs, hosed down by crawlers and bulldozers on both sides Everyone was hooked up by radio, Banner, the hose carriers, the rigs, and the stand-by party at the end of the water pipeline.

Carl held the microphone over his mouth. 'Are you all ready? Check in now.' He listened as all the crews reported. That was good. That worked well. Their number first then their report. 1—2—3 and so on through. 'Right, Number Ten. Let's have that bomb.'

It came out slowly from the pipeline base. It looked innocent enough sitting on the front of a crawler crane. Just a big oil drum. But inside, wrapped in a thick layer of asbestos, was six hundred pounds of gelignite, detonators in, wires connected and coiled up. It was very carefully waterproofed. It had been keeping cool in one of Banner's caravans brought forward just for that reason. Now the hoses from the escorting vehicles played water over it all the way. It seemed to take a long time. It was watched all the way.

When it was only yards from the north rig Banner spoke again. 'Numbers One and Two. Set up the wire. And get it bang on these markers.'

'Number One, got it.'

'Number Two, here we go.'

Carl watched through the long slit cut in his shield. There it was, up off the sand, jerking and snaking as the tension came on it. He bit his lip. It looked too tight. But that was something they had found yesterday. It had to be that tight to allow for the sag with the weight of the charge. They had marked the wire after the dummy run so that the winchmen knew exactly when to stop winding in.

'Number Two. I'm on my marker.'

'Number One. Me too.'

'No, I'm two.'

'Shut it,' barked Banner. 'I'll crucify the next joker. Go ahead, Fourteen.'

Number Fourteen was the crane. It had the bomb in the air, a man on top of it holding the pulley block with its drag wire fixed. The crane's jib rose and the bomb rose with it up to the overhead wire. Water hosed over the bomb and the man all the way.

'Number Two. Give them plenty of slack on that drag wire.'

'OK, boss.' The drag wire ran along the ground from the southern rig. Its far end was shackled to the pulley block dangling the bomb from the overhead wire. When the time came, the south rig would winch in the drag wire and the bomb on its pulley would run along the overhead wire into the seat of the fire.

'Fourteen here. We're hooked on. I'm backing out.'

The crane crawled backwards leaving the bomb hanging in position, the drag wire trailing down and away across the sand.

'Number One, boss. I've got the cable end. Just checking you're on Safe.'

'Wait.' Banner checked the exploder and locked the plunger in the up position. 'Banner here. I'm safe. Go ahead.'

There was a long pause. 'Number One. You're hooked up, boss.'

'Now hear this all points. We're going now. Wind it up, Number Two. And listen in.'

'Number Two. Hauling now.'

Banner watched, shaking his head to clear the gushing water from his eyes. There it was. The drag wire was tightening. Come on, you sonofabitch, move. The wire was full tight. The pulley jerked and the bomb swung on its bridle. It was moving. It had a hundred yards to go. If the overhead wire held. If the pulley didn't jam. If the bomb didn't blow with the heat. There was no water to cool it now. Move, move. But not too fast. You'll jump the pulley.

'Easy, Number Two. Easy.'

'Easy, boss.'

Fifty yards. The wire was starting to sag as the weight came in towards the middle of the span. That would help. The pulley would run on the sloping wire. That's it, Number Two. That's it. Just pick up the slack now. Banner reached down and unlocked the exploder. His right hand gripped the handle. Thirty yards. He shook off the water and guessed at the distance. Fifteen yards. Ten yards. He tightened his fist. Five. Four. Three. Two. One. He rammed down the plunger as the bomb disappeared into the fire.

The explosion was dulled by his earphones. But he felt the blast as it shook the dozer. He felt it as a hot hard gust on his face through the sight slit in the shield. He saw the shattered span wire snaking across the sky. For a moment he saw nothing above his well. The giant candle was snuffed.

There was no time for cheering or congratulation. Where he had seen nothing there was now a huge black pillar of oil. 'Keep it wet. D'you hear me? Keep it wet.' This was the time of danger. That column of oil would soon start raining down over the whole site. One spark, one piece of hot wreckage could flash and relight the candle. 'Keep these hoses on the gear. Forget the men. The heat's off now.' The heat was off. After ten long scorching days and nights the only heat was the heat of the sun. It was nothing. Just pleasantly warm. The black rain was falling. Black, gritty, thin with its high benzine content, splashing and spreading over everything, spotting the sand, smearing the vehicles, drenching and staining the men. Its pungent smell came like perfume in place of the acrid stench when it was burning. 'All right, Number Ten. Send in these canopies now.'

The canopies were a Banner invention. Qashran One was going to be a classic in firefighting. The canopies were long wooden ramps built on angled frames, fifteen feet high at one end running down to only a couple of feet at the other. They had been made in eight separate units. When they were in position round the wellhead they would provide complete cover for the men underneath. The escaping oil would roar unchecked up through the open space where the high ends of the ramps formed a circle round the gusher. The falling mist of crude would strike the ramps and run off like rain off a roof. The trench digging machines would cut channels in the sand out from the well to drain away the deflected oil. Underneath the ramps the crews could work on the wellhead in the dry.

Carl watched the ramps being dragged out towards the well. He tapped his driver on the shoulder and signalled him forward. The heat was off but the noise was still there. Different but still there. Not now the great roar of the fire; just the rushing gushing of the uncontrolled oil and the smaller sounds as it dropped and splashed and oozed and gurgled. The bulldozer crept ahead, its escort trailing it, maintaining the deluge of water but not now directly on to the crew. 'Number Ten. Pass a message to Mr Troy. Tell him the fire's out.'

'OK, boss.'

Maybe you should tell him to say some prayers, thought Carl. One spark, one mistake will flash this gusher and bring back that cloud.

He looked up into the sky above the mountain high tree of Qashran crude. The black smoke cloud was still there hanging over the site but nothing was feeding it now. As he watched, Carl could see the edges of the cloud being teased out into streamers by the air currents up there. That's right. Pull it to bits. Break it up. Blow it away. That'll please Ben Troy. That's the bit he's interested in. Sending that smoke signal down to his old pal in the desert telling him to come out and play at being killed. Different men, different motives. All I want to do is plug this gusher.

He was off the dozer, supervising the placing of the canopies. He was under the canopies having a long look at the wellhead. There was barely an inch of pipe sticking up through the concrete cellar block, belching out the precious oil. The pressure behind that jet was a ton on every square inch. That was going to be tricky when it came to passing the casing-hanger then the Cameron valve through the jet. But that problem was a long way off. First he had to expose enough pipe to fit a new wellhead to.

Banner had made his plans. Pneumatic drills were ready to start breaking up that concrete block. Not the whole block. Just enough to expose the right length of pipe. There were non-spark chisels for the drills, soft metal but safe. Even so they would be drenched with water all the time. Pumps were ready to suck away the gathering water. In half an hour the area round the well was littered with machines and equipment. Piping ran across the sand in a well-ordered chaos. The noise of the drills added to the noise of the well to complete the bedlam. The black rain fell all around. It took two hours to chisel away enough concrete and strip the casing from the steel well pipe. The rubble was piled up. Carl wanted that loose fill when he came to pour the new cement. He wanted a quick job.

It was time for the casing-hanger, the flanged collar which grips the well pipe and makes a base for the huge Cameron valve. The crane came up with the hanger suspended. Guy ropes were fixed and run out in all directions. They would hold and direct the collar as it passed through the jet. The crane crawled forward. The hanger cut into the edge of the gusher, bucked under the pressure and sprayed oil all round. Tighten these guy ropes. Keep watching. Don't duck the spray. It's only oil. Hold it. Steady it. Better. Lower away. Slowly, slowly. Danger here when the collar comes over the pipe. Steel on steel. One mistake, one spark, and it's all over. Keep these hoses going. That's it. Easy does it. Watch it. Haul No. 4 guy. Better. Lower away. Lower right away. Unhook. The hanger was in place. Tighten it now. Easy again. Slowly does it. That's it. Good and tight. Fine. The collar was in place and set up tight.

Banner breathed again and wiped at the oil on his face. Next stage. Wooden shuttering round the cellar block to hold more concrete. Dump in the rubble to fill the space. Concrete now. The mixing truck backed up, its drum turning and churning the mix. Fix that shute. Take it easy. No sparks. That's it. OK, run it in. The concrete poured down the shute. Men leaned over the shuttering, paddling it round, helping it seep down into every space. Stop now. More paddling. The level sank inside the shuttering. More concrete. Slowly. Stop again. Paddle that down. That's it. Finish. Banner nodded and grinned and clapped the nearest men on the back. Take the truck away. Replace the canopies close round the well to let the concrete harden off undiluted by the falling rain of crude. Not finished yet. The trickiest bit was still to come when the concrete set and was ready to take the big valve.

But time now for a well-earned rest and a cold, cold, clean tasting beer. Maybe three. Carl pointed back to the forward base and jumped on to his bulldozer.

There was a long clear view from the airport control tower right across the desert plateau. Troy was up there with the navy lieutenant who had come ashore as liaison officer between Q Force and the Gulf Squadron.

'It still looks just the same to me,' said Ben lowering the field glasses. He was watching the dark cloud above the horizon in the south west. 'I don't understand. It's almost an hour since that message saying the fire was out. Something must have gone wrong.'

'May I look, sir?'

Ben handed over the glasses.

'It's thinning, sir. Definitely. It's less dense than when I last looked. More spread out.'

'Are you sure?'

'Yes, sir. It would take quite a time, you know. There may not be much upper air wind down there.'

'How about that?' Ben asked the met. man.

'That's possible. I can't be sure, of course. We've had no proper reports since South Base was destroyed.'

'No, you wouldn't. I believe they've been quite busy down there.' Ben was not pleased with the met. man. It was not the man's fault. He tried to predict the weather; he did not control it. 'But you are sure about that *shamal*?'

'As sure as I can be, Mr Troy. It's the right season and all the reports from the north suggest it's coming.'

Ben grunted. The *shamal* was the wind from the north west, sweeping down from the mountains of Iran and across the Gulf. In Qashran City it was a strong cool breeze. Out in the desert it sucked and whirled the sand and dust into choking clouds. It could ruin everything. It could stop Rasul coming. It could blank out the desert. It could blow for weeks, even months.

'It could be the squally type, of course, Mr Troy. One big blow, a day, half a day perhaps, then finish. We'll just have to wait and see.'

'I suppose we will. Come on, Lieutenant. Let's go and see Major Kirk.'

It had not been a useless visit. They had warned air traffic control that the Phantoms would be flying off. The tower was already accustomed to Baston's planes. This time they would all be up, all at once. That was no problem as long as the airport tower had warning. And, as the lieutenant said, it was just as well to know in advance about the wind.

Ben started up the car. 'We'll go and see the major, Lieutenant. If we move off about two-thirty that should get the whole force into position by sunset. We'll use the pipeline road south then cut off into the desert.'

'That suits me, sir. I can't really get accustomed to it, this knowing where a battle's going to be and when, more or less. I thought that only happened in history books.'

Ben grinned. 'The Bedu are very old fashioned.' He liked the lieutenant. He almost always liked navy men. 'After we see the major, I'll give you a curry lunch. You should fill up when you can. You may not eat too well for a few days. Then I'll tell you about Bedu battles.'

Admiral Baston was talking about battles. He was briefing the Phantom crews on board the carrier.

'I'm talking to you now because there won't be time when you get your call. It may come anytime. Most likely tomorrow morning, could be later, even the next day. But you're on stand-by as of now.' He smoothed his beard and looked round the men. 'You've heard the broad tactical plan. Don't forget it. And don't forget that once you're over the desert you'll be controlled from the ground. It's a family affair. My brother-in-law's in charge. And I mean in charge. You do what you're told when you're told.' He took another tug at his beard. 'Communication is the key. You know the channels, keep them open. You know the code names, use them. I'm Neptune,' he glared round, 'and the first man who makes a joke out of that will regret it.' There were smiles all round. 'Mr Troy is White Chief. Who is it that's leading?'

A lieutenant commander stood up. 'I'm Red Leader, sir.'

'You're what?' roared Baston.

'I'm Red Leader, sir.' He sounded uncertain.

'You're bloody well nothing of the kind. There're no bloody Reds in my squadron.' He rounded on the air commander. 'What's got into you, man? Change that to Blue Leader.' He swung back to the pilot. 'Have you got that? You're a blue blooded Blue Leader.'

'Yes, sir.' He sat down. It was said around the fleet that the admiral was so anti-Red he was trying to get all the ships' port running lights changed from red to purple.

'Where was I? Yes, I remember, communications. Very important. So make no mistakes.' He stepped down from the platform and walked among his men. 'Now I'm speaking off the record because Vice-Admirals are not supposed to say this kind of thing.' He stopped. 'You're going to do what you're going to do, to prove to a bunch of politicians and some desk-bound sailors that carriers have a place in a modern fleet. You'd better do a good job, gentlemen. If you don't, you can look forward to flying from door to door round some housing scheme selling vacuum cleaners or encyclopedias.'

The girls were having coffee at the Club. The girls had coffee at the Club every day. None of the girls was under thirty.

'Did you hear about Doctor Sallal?'

'Yes, he's been arrested. Is it true he's the one who's been throwing all these bombs?'

'Not him himself. He was the ringleader.'

'I just can't believe it. He lives next door to us.'

'Didn't I hear that his car was bombed?'

'Yes, that's what I mean. Why should he set fire to his own car? It was a gorgeous car.'

'He did it for the insurance. Jack told me. He was insured with Jack.'

'I don't believe that. Surely he'd do it to stop being suspected.'

'Maybe it was a mistake.'

'Anyway I'm glad they've caught him. I still can't get over it. But it does prove I was right all along.'

'What does that mean?'

'I never really trusted him. Too smooth, too foreign. He was a good dentist, of course. But you know what I mean. I'd never let him give me gas.'

'Oh.'

'I never thought of that.'

'I prefer gas. I just hate injections.' They all looked at her. Emma had not really been one of the group since she confided that her husband had never seen her with all her clothes off. It was not the kind of thing one admitted.

'Anyway, it's all over. I wonder what they'll do to him?'

'My Tom says they should horsewhip him.'

'That's a kinky idea.'

'Beryl, really.'

Beryl was supposed to be fast.

'Well I think they should hang him. I can't stand all this violence.'

'I agree. It's the children I worry about. You just felt it wasn't safe to let them out of your sight.'

'My kids are furious. They loved it. Young Timmy said it was just like TV but real.'

Polite laughter. Sonia was odd about children. She called them little monsters and second class citizens. She meant it too.

'Anyway, some people have done well out of the troubles. Did you hear that Susan Shaw got her man at last?'

'What's that got to do with the emergency?'

'She had an accident. As I hear it the colonel was caught off guard. You know, sympathy.'

'But it was an accident. It had nothing to do with the troubles.'

'What I want to know is why you think she's done well. The colonel's not my idea of a catch.'

'Beggars can't be choosers, can they.'

'I think you're all jealous of her.'

A chorus of denial.

'Yes, you are. I am too. Not because of John Negley. Because she's got a career.'

'What does that mean? I've got a career. My husband and children are my career.'

'I agree. And it's jolly hard work.'

'That's the point. It's work. It's hard labour.'

'But there's a sense of achievement. Running a home, that's what a woman's job is.'

'Rubbish. Nannies and maids do it far better. Look at the Royal Family.'

'That's different.'

'Anyway, you're one to talk about not liking work. You, the most successful hostess in Qashran. You work hard at that, dear.'

'That's not work, darling. That's fun.'

Kassim was thinking about fun. He was confessing to his diary. 'Day 11. Marvellous news this morning. Banner has put out the fire at Qashran One. He still has to cap the well but I'm sure that's a mere formality. I've just looked out of the window. There's only a faint smear left in the sky where that black cloud has been hanging for a week and a half. Banner has done an excellent job. I was right to push him.

'The last act has now begun. Q Force left the city this afternoon to meet Uncle Rasul in the desert. I sometimes wonder if he will really come. The wind is getting up. It's quite choppy out at sea. That means sand storms in the desert. Maybe Rasul will lose his way. Maybe he and The Honoured Ones will just disappear under the sand. Wishful thinking. I just want to be rid of him and get back to making this country grow. Troy Sahib must be worried about the wind. But he'll have his battle. I feel that. Although I hope he fails, because the consequences of success will be distasteful to me, I'm sure he'll win. He's the winning type.

'With the end in sight, I've suddenly realized that I have not even talked to a woman since it all began. I don't feel inclined to invite back any of those who flew off at the first sign of trouble after the *suk* party. No, on second thoughts, that's too exclusive a view. Maybe Denise. Better still, Lady Jean. Now there's a woman. It's an odd thing how fascinating I still find the English aristocracy after being at school with their brothers. But they do have this marvellously cool, haughty, keep-your-distance air about them. Yet you know, once you've seen them on horseback chasing after the hounds at a fox hunt, that they must be tremendously good in bed.

'My enthusiasm is getting the better of me. I can hear Ben Troy's advice. Re-establish confidence. Let the Bedu take you to their hearts. Remind them that you are their only sheikh. Good, unpalatable advice. So I'll get into the Rolls and be driven in broad daylight down to the palace like a prize stallion going to stud.

'I hope Allah appreciates how conscientiously I try to fulfil my destiny.'

It was his third inspection of the new concrete round the well-head. It would have to do. The quickset cement was dry and hard to the touch. Banner was worried about it standing up to the five ton weight of the valve. He had given it as long as he dared if he was to cap the well before sunset. It could wait till morning but that meant losing countless barrels of oil. It also meant another night and the danger of a flash fire. And the men were near the limit. It would have to do. Leave the wooden shuttering in place and shore it up all round. That should make quite sure.

He spoke into his radio. 'Let's go. It's exactly as planned. Bring some shoring timber too.'

'We're on our way, boss.'

He squatted under the canopy, his ears dinning with the roaring of the escaping crude. The view was short. Oil ran and dripped off the edge of the canopy. Beyond that, blown dust and sand obscured everything. Even his jeep, only twenty yards away, was only a vague outline. The cloud was blowing in from the north. The sand here would not have stirred in a hurricane. The rain of oil had turned it into a black quagmire. The blowing dust stuck to everything. There was nothing that was not soaked in oil. Carl wiped at his face to clear the dust building into a thick layer. That was another reason for speed. If this was the *shamal* it could blow for long enough.

He turned his face off the wind and spoke into the radio. 'Hear this all points. Take it easy as you close in. I want no accidents. We're still sitting on a bomb.'

A shape in the cloud, another. The crews were arriving. Check everything. There must be no mistakes. Shoring first. Use it all. Take no chances. Now drag away the canopies. We'll need room, lots of room. So we'll get drenched in crude. So what? It'll wash off some of this bloody sand. Shoring fixed. Good. Now for the valve.

The crane crept forward. Stop. Fix these guy ropes. Run them out all round the well. Everyone in position? Good. Heave up the valve. The huge Cameron valve rose on the end of the crane's wire, the jib throbbing under the weight. Hold it. That's enough. Come ahead now. Slowly. Very slowly. Stop. The valve was only inches from the edge of the gusher. Adjust these guy ropes. More. Further round. That's it. Hold it. Now take the strain and be ready to heave. Watch for the flood of oil when that valve gets into the gusher. Come on, crane; come forward, fast for just two, three feet. The crane jerked ahead, the valve swung into the jet. There was oil everywhere, a sea of oil, forcing itself into eyes and ears and noses and mouths. Haul these guys. Hold it. Hold it. The wave subsided. The gusher was roaring up again, up through the wide open gate of the valve. The Cameron was held dead centre above the well, its huge girth encircling the jet.

Carl spat oil from his mouth and clawed his burning eyes clear. Lower away. Lower away easy. Ready that hinge bolt. Easy. Easy. That's it. Hold it. Hinge bolt now. The long bolt slid into place. Lower away again. Very easy. Slowly, slowly. Down on to the casing-hanger collar. Stop. Bolts in. Quickly. Lower away, the crane. Unshackle. Back up that crane. Quickly now but not too quickly. Flange bolts in all round. Tighten them. All in. Good. All tight. Fine. The valve was in place.

Banner felt no pain in his eyes now; no discomfort, drenched in oil and caked in sand. I've tamed you, you wild well. D'you feel that squeeze on your throat? That's me, choking you, shutting you up, not killing you, saving your life. The valve was closing. Half shut and the full-throated roar of the gusher became a scream. Three-quarters shut, a shriek. Almost closed, an eerie plaintive whine. A whisper. Shut tight. The silence was uncanny.

The well was capped. The Great Djinn was dead.

CHAPTER TWELVE

THE WIND BLEW HARD right through the night, stirring up vast clouds of dust and rolling them south across the desert plateau. The dust cocooned Q Force, driving, drifting, sifting over and into vehicles and tents, layering men and guns and equipment. There was no protection against it. It penetrated everywhere.

Farther south, over the singing sands, there was not only the dust rolling down in front of the wind but also the soft, loose, dune sand which was stirred and flurried and driven, mingling with the dust, blanketing the dunes. shutting off all sight. All night the helicopter gun buses had flown patrols, looking down from above the dust clouds, dropping flares, trying to see through the darkness and the murk. Nothing was seen.

The dawn grew slowly, held back from the ground by the choking pall of dust. Then the wind dropped. For a minute, two minutes, there was no sound. Then a sharp puff of wind, a flurry, then silence again.

Troy had been up for an hour. He had slept badly, waking often to cough and spit and wipe his face clean, wondering each time if there had been a touch on his shoulder, if his old friend and enemy had slipped through the storm to settle their score with a quick dagger thrust. Now he stood outside the tent, listening for the wind.

Kirk joined him. 'Is that it finished, sir?' His voice was hoarse from his parched throat.

'It might be. There's no way of knowing. Sometimes it's like this for a few minutes, an hour even, then it starts blowing again.'

'I wonder what's going on out there?'

'Don't worry, Major. Rasul won't disappoint you. He'll be here, sometime.'

'I don't mind admitting that I don't like it, Mr Troy. Everything's wrong about this operation. We're breaking almost every rule in the book. I just hope you know what you're doing. Trusting the enemy's something I've never learned.'

'But you haven't fought a Bedu battle before, have you?'

'No, and if this is a sample, I won't volunteer for another.'

'There may never be another, Major. Doesn't that excite you? You may be the last British force commander in history to fight a pitched battle with the Bedu.'

'I don't know that I'd want my name connected with this battle, Mr Troy.'

'But you believe in winning battles. You told me so. You're going to win this one. I guarantee that.'

'That's what I mean. I'll win it because the enemy wants to lose it. That's what you said last night. That's not my kind of battle.'

'I also said last night, Major, that your kind of battle is the kind your political masters commit you to. I'm your political master here. The way you win it will be my way, not the enemy's. That makes a difference to him wanting to lose it.'

'I don't want to seem rude, sir, but that all sounds just like words to me.'

'Quite right, Major. That's what politics are. Words. But they disguise ideas and ambitions.' Ben was already bored with Kirk. 'Look. The light's growing. The dust's settling. Maybe the wind really has died.'

In half an hour the dust had all dropped, the light was strong, sunrise near. Q Force was about its military business. Jeeps and armoured cars and trucks were revving their engines, shaking off the dust of the storm. Drivers were poking into engines, cleaning and checking; weapons were being cleaned and oiled and rattled to check their movements; men were shaving, food was cooking, water boiling. It was clear now all the way to the edge of the dunes, almost ten miles. Over to the south west, eight miles away, lay the wreck of South Base. Nothing showed in that direction. Qashran One had been tamed. The sky and the horizon were clear. Ben smiled to himself. He had driven over there last evening through the growing storm to congratulate Carl on capping the well. The American had been sprawled in the cool of his caravan, very drunk. Of course he denied that. He was not drunk, just comfortably stoned. Ben did not argue. Banner had earned his leisure. He might have a big head this morning but at least his big battle was won. Troy knew his was very near.

He took the mug of tea gratefully and sipped it. He looked round the battlefield. Q Force was strung out in a long shallow crescent. Fox holes had been dug but the whole force was highly mobile. The armoured cars and other vehicles were drawn up behind the positions all the way along. If Rasul did have a change of heart and tried to come round one or other of the flanks, the line could quickly be changed. It was sensible to take precautions. But Ben knew they would not be necessary. The old sheikh would find Q Force and charge right at the centre of the line. The fire power levelled in that sector would be murderous. Farther back and out on the flanks, four of Kassim's helicopter gun buses were standing by. Their job was to complete the ring after Rasul arrived. They would drop in behind him to cut off any chance of retreat into the safety of the singing sands. The troops did not yet know that they were going to fight this battle without firing a shot. Troy had not divulged his plan. Not even to Kirk. The major's opposition was based on the static plan of battle. It offended his military instinct. He was also put out by Troy's certainty of victory, a victory predicted not because of the superiority of his force and his military skill but because Troy had a bee in his bonnet that the enemy wanted to be beaten. Kirk could not believe that. He believed Troy to be intoxicated with his knowledge of the Bedu. He believed that Troy had been duped by the old sheikh. The major had deployed his force with that idea in mind.

The loudspeaker spoke in the wireless truck. 'Gunbus One to White Chief. Gunbus One to White Chief.'

'Come in, Gunbus One.'

Ben could see the chopper down near the border.

'Gunbus One to White Chief. I've got them in sight. They're coming out of the dunes now.'

Ben walked round the truck and held out his hand for the

mike. 'White Chief to Gunbus One. Keep out of range. Keep
well away. Just watch and report.'

The chopper acknowledged and signed off.

Ben spoke to the Navy liaison officer. 'You'd better call
Neptune, Lieutenant. Give him a stand-by. It will probably be
two hours yet but he should be ready.'

Kirk was beside him with his glasses trained. 'Why should
it be two hours, Mr Troy? How can you know that? That
distance is barely ten miles.'

Ben was searching too. There was something there on the
edge of the plateau. 'You won't believe this, Major, but these
characters are human. To get where they are, they must have
ridden all yesterday afternoon, half the night, bedded down in
the worst of the storm, and started out again this morning
before dawn. They'll want to clean up, have something to eat
and drink, say their prayers, and after that there's still the
proper ritual to be observed. These men aren't just any old
Bedu. These are The Honoured Ones. Their mounts are the
sacred black camels of Qashran. They've got a tradition to
live up to. That's why I know, Major.'

'If all that's true, why aren't we attacking them now? They
won't be ready for us. This is the right time.'

'No, it's not. There are rules, Major. I thought I'd told you.
We don't attack them. They attack us. And they attack us when
they're ready. We wait.'

Kirk muttered and swept the glasses round the horizon.

Gunbus One reported the progress of the Bedu army across
the plateau. Two miles inside the border, four miles, six miles,
seven miles.

Troy watched. They should be stopping now. God, I hope
I've judged this right.

Eight miles inside the border. Two miles from the centre of
the Q Force line. Gunbus spoke. 'They seem to be stopping.
Yes, they're dismounting.'

Ben thanked Gunbus One and ordered it back to join the
other helicopters, to refuel, load its troops and wait.

Kirk was grudging in acknowledging the accuracy of Troy's
predictions. 'I just can't understand it, sir. I've never seen anything like this.'

'I told you Bedu battles were different, Major. We've probably got an hour. Maybe your men would like to brew up. I
could do with some more tea.' It was going to be a long hot
wait. The sun was high and climbing into a clear sky. 'Lieutenant, give Neptune a one hour stand-by, please.'

The liaison officer came back in a few minutes. 'I think the admiral's getting a bit grumpy, sir. The mike must be connected down to the bridge. He's giving everyone rather a bad time.'

Ben smiled. Yes, he'll be doing that. Rodney's not the patient type, especially with what he thinks is at stake. He certainly swallowed my suggestion that this mission might tilt the balance in Whitehall. Well, that's diplomacy. I never did say which way it would tilt it.

The tea came. Ben stood and drank it with Kirk in the shade of the wireless truck. The Bedu were in clear view. Smoke was spiralling up from the dung fires. He tried not to think about Rasul. So far everything had gone according to plan. He watched and waited. He had to decide when to give Kirk his orders. He wanted to leave it as long as possible. The fires were being put out. Now there would be prayers. Time to act.

He walked round and asked the operator for the Neptune channel. 'White Chief to Neptune. White Chief to Neptune. Do you read me, Neptune?'

'Neptune to White Chief. We read you loud and clear.'

'White Chief to Neptune. Request immediate fly off.'

'High bloody time too,' roared the speaker. 'Fly off, Commander.' Then the startled voice of the signals officer. 'Neptune to White Chief. Flying off now.'

Eight minutes, the admiral had said. Eight minutes to put twelve Phantoms in the air. Less if they keep their fingers out. Say ten minutes. Another ten minutes down here. Twenty minutes altogether. Ben checked Rasul's camp through the glasses. That should be just about right. They're just starting prayers now. After that, they'll mount up and form the battle line. Then listen to Rasul bellowing his battle cries across the sand. Time to talk to Kirk.

The major got his word in first. 'I must say sir, I don't see the need to call in air cover. If that's the enemy out there, all the enemy, Q Force can handle this with very little trouble.'

'Yes, Major, I'm sure you could if it was an ordinary battle. Put out these aircraft markers, please. Then I'll tell you what I want you to do.'

Kirk gave the orders and the soldiers ran out ahead of the positions laying the black arrow markers for the planes, pointing ahead at the Bedu.

Troy went to the wireless truck again. 'White Chief to Gunbus Leader. Take off now. Fly wide, east and west of Q Force, down to the border. You have your positions. Report back when you reach them.'

He went back to Kirk, standing at his scout car. 'Now, Major, your orders. On no account will any member of your force fire a shot without a direct order from me.'

'I beg your pardon, sir?'

'Not one single shot, Major Kirk. Not unless I order it.'

'I protest, Mr Troy. I can't accept that order. My men must be able at least to defend themselves.'

'I did say "Not unless I order it." If it's necessary, I'll order it, Major. I hope it won't be necessary. The admiral's Phantoms are going to do this job for me.'

'I'm sorry, sir. I think it's mad. Absolutely mad. Using an air strike against a few hundred Arabs on camels. I'm sorry, sir. I disagree with the whole plan of this mission. I'll say so in my report.'

'That's your right, Major. I hope I can say in my report that you obeyed my orders to the letter.'

'I know my duty, sir. I'll obey the orders, under protest, and until I judge that my men are in danger.'

'That should do very well.' He turned away as he heard the speaker in the wireless truck.

'Blue Leader to White Chief. We have your markers in sight. Splitting into three fours now. Have you a starting time?'

'White Chief to Blue Leader. Starting in less than ten minutes. What is your time to target?'

'Blue Leader to White Chief. Give us one minute.'

Ben searched the sky. They were north and high, maybe fifteen thousand feet and ten miles off. Only one minute from up there. It seemed impossible. He did not try the sum. He saw the vapour trails split as the sections broke away to take their positions.

'Gunbus Leader to White Chief. In position now.'

'White Chief to Gunbus Leader. Wait. Your orders are on no account to open fire. Repeat. Do not open fire.'

Gunbus Leader was surprised but not as vehement as Kirk. 'If you say so, sir.'

Praying was over. The Honoured Ones were mounting up. The beasts stirred the fresh dust which hung like patches of mist above the ground, the camels hidden, the mounted men supported magically.

'The flags, Major.'

'Yes, sir.' The two poles were raised and quickly guyed. The flags were broken out. They hung limp in the still air, then opened wearily as a puff of wind caught them. The Union Jack and the red, green and silver of Kassim's flag.

Ben nodded as he trained his glasses. Very well judged, Mr Troy. The huge two poled banner of old Qashran was there, bright green with the silver scimitar shining in the centre like a beacon. Ben imagined he could hear his old friend bellowing across the sand. 'I am Rasul, the chosen one, prince of Qashran, lord of the desert, friend of the great spirits, servant of Allah . . .' There was a lot more. Maybe about a minute more.

Ben took the microphone in his hand. He hesitated. He could still stop it. 'White Chief to Blue Leader. Attack, attack, attack.'

Rasul walked his big camel out in front of The Honoured Ones. The roar of their answer to his battle cry still rang in his ears. He stopped his beast and stared ahead at the line of vehicles. His eyes fastened on the flags in the centre. You are there, Troy Sahib. I know you are there, under your flag. I was right to trust you. You are a true friend. You have brought the soldiers. Praise be to Allah at whose feet I will soon sit as an honoured servant in the eternal gardens of Paradise.

The eyes that could still track the falcon were quick to pick out the diving planes. Aeroplanes. What is this? Troy Sahib said nothing of aeroplanes. What does it matter. To die with honour is to die with honour. It makes no difference what weapon cuts you down. The scream of the planes reached out and shrilled in his ears. We will not die standing still like criminals awaiting execution. He unsheathed the great scimitar and held it high above his head. When it dropped The Honoured Ones would charge the soldiers' line. The sound of the planes made him screw up his face. He could see them clearly now. Four of them. He lowered the sword and put his stick to the camel.

The sonic bang seemed to explode inside his head. His eyes shut and he saw lights and colours and shapes. The echoes seemed to run through every muscle of his body. He pulled on the camel's reins as it reared and swerved. The sword dropped from his hand. All round him he could hear the sounds of confusion as beasts reared and struggled and screamed and men roared and shouted and struggled to stay mounted. Hot blasts of burned kerosene rushed down as the planes zoomed overhead. Then more of these terrible bangs. And more. Rasul's camel was frantic. It swung from side to side, bucked, reared, desperately trying to escape the hold on its mouth and the terror from above. Yussuf saw his master in danger. He threw himself off his mount and ran to Rasul. He jumped for the reins, knowing his great weight could pull the beast down. The camel reared again and swerved. The reins whipped round Yussuf's throat and pulled tight. His fingers clawed to free them. The beast's head jerked and jerked and jerked again as it fought to free itself. Yussuf's neck snapped at the third jerk. The camel sagged to its knees then over on to its side. Rasul sprawled off into the dust.

Ben watched the writhing dust cloud, shaking his head to clear away the stunning noise. Camels were breaking from the cloud. Some riderless, some dragging their masters through the dust, others still with riders mounted, but bucking like mad things to break free. The Phantoms did one more pass, west to east, east to west, north to south. The Honoured Ones were routed. Camels were racing across the desert. Men were chasing them. Standing about. Walking. Lying down. Limping. There would be no fight in them now. The Bedu were realists. They knew when they were beaten. They would give up meekly to the soldiers. No shots would be fired.

Ben gave his orders to Kirk. His units on the flanks would join up with the troops lifted in by helicopter. The ring would be closed. The men would be taken. Their fate would be cruel. Kassim would not punish them. He would let them live as free men with the shame of their defeat by the magic thunder from the skies. The camels were to be left alone. Negley's men would round them up.

Kirk accepted and passed the orders. He made no comment.

Ben watched through the glasses, looking for Rasul. Maybe he's broken a leg. Maybe he's pinned under a camel. Maybe he's dead. That would be ironic. No, he's not dead. That's him out there in front, alone. He's standing up. What will he do? Should I go down there alone?

Rasul stood and looked down at Yussuf's body. Now you have the freedom I offered you but you refused. He stared round at the settling dust and the running beasts and the defeated men. He limped a few yards and picked up the great sword. He turned and glared at the distant flags. So you had a move, Troy Sahib. You think you've won. You think you've kept your promise and cheated me of death with honour. He limped back and unwound the reins from his slave's neck. He prodded the camel to its feet. He checked its legs. They were all sound. He pulled it down and clambered into the saddle. The camel stood up as he tightened the reins. Now, Troy Sahib.

Ben saw him mount and start to canter.

'What the devil's he doing, sir?' asked Kirk. 'He looks as if he's going to charge straight up here. He is.'

Troy nodded. The camel was already at full gallop, raising a trail of dry dust behind it. It was a long run at that speed and after a fall. Ben wondered what Rasul would do. Will he charge at me, try and cut me down, try and make some soldier fire a fatal shot? Or will he charge and stop, and dismount, and surrender? His mouth was dry. He felt sick.

It was too long a run. Three hundred yards from Kirk's command car, a foreleg snapped and the camel dived into the dust.

The old sheikh was catapulted over its head. He lay for several minutes, letting his head clear, listening to the bellowing of the injured beast. He sat up. He stood up. He picked up the sword and limped back and slashed the camel's throat. He watched it jerking its life away into the sand. The blood ran on the blade of the sword. He faced the hanging flags of Britain and Kassim's Qashran and walked painfully towards them.

Ben unlooped his field glasses and handed them to Kirk. He started walking.

'Mr Troy. Where are you going? What are you doing?'

He stopped. 'I'm going to meet an old friend, Major.'

He walked slowly, watching Rasul's limping figure all the way. He was not pleased with his victory. He was sweating yet he felt cold and sick. The battle would become part of the history of the desert. He did not know how he could look Rasul in the eye. But he had to try.

They stopped only a yard apart. They looked straight at each other. They both saw pride and wretchedness, pain and pleasure. They said nothing.

Then Rasul lifted the sword two-handled high above his head. Ben watched the blade, stained with the camel's blood, the metal gleaming in the sunlight. He felt he deserved death by that sword. He looked into his old friend's face. He knew the truth then. Rasul would not cleave him open with the sword. He would lower it and hand it to him and become his prisoner.

The swish of the bullet and the sound of the shot were almost as one sound in his ear. The sheikh's head snapped back and he was suddenly sprawled on the ground. The dust puffed and drifted and settled. The hole was above Rasul's left eye. It was a big hole. There was very little blood.

Ben dropped to his knees. He stared helplessly at the spread-eagled body. He heard the snarl of the scout car speeding across the desert. He heard it sliding to a stop. He heard the sound of running feet.

'Are you all right, sir? Mr Troy, are you all right? You're not hit, sir?'

Ben shook his head. 'No, I'm not hit, Major.'

'Thank goodness for that. When you went down I was really worried. It was a very narrow angle. Tricky shot.'

Ben looked up at him. He was still holding the Mannlicher in his hand. Ben turned away and pulled the sheikh's legs together and carefully arranged his robe. He straightened the cords of the headdress round the old man's forehead, his fingers almost touching the bullethole. 'My old friend, Sheikh Rasul, would want me to thank you, Major. He would want me to thank you for making him a legend. For transporting him safely to Paradise. For giving him a place of honour in Bedu history. Who knows, maybe for making him the inspiration for a great new Holy War.' He pulled the wide flung arms down on to the sheikh's chest. He reached out and took the sword and laid it on top of the corpse. He pressed the old fingers round the hilt. 'You're a fool, Major.' He looked up. 'You're a bloody fool,' he shouted. He saw Kirk's face as a distorted image through his tears. It was round and red and gaping. Ben's voice was shrill with anger and grief. 'You're a stupid, bloody, military fool,' he screamed.